JILL WILLIAMSON
TO DARKNESS FLED

BLOOD OF KINGS BOOK 2

MARCHER
LORD
PRESS

To Darkness Fled by Jill Williamson
Published by Marcher Lord Press
8345 Pepperridge Drive
Colorado Springs, CO 80920
www.marcherlordpress.com

This is a work of fiction. Names, characters, places, and incidents are products of the author's imagination or are used fictitiously. Any similarity to actual people, organizations, and/or events is purely coincidental.

Cover Designer: Kirk DouPonce, Dog-Eared Design, www.dogeareddesign.com
Cover Photo By: Kirk DouPonce
Creative Team: Jeff Gerke, Dawn Shelton

Library of Congress Cataloging-in-Publication Data
An application to register this book for cataloging has been filed with the Library of Congress.
International Standard Book Number: 978-0-9825987-0-2

To my little knight, Luke McKinley
And my little princess, Kaitlyn Noel.
Momma loves you.

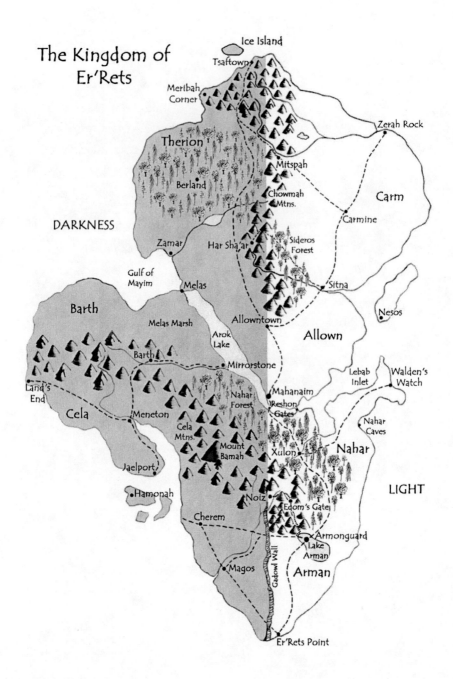

The Kingdom of
Er'Rets

Ice Island

Tsaftown

Meribah
Corner

DARKNESS

Therion

Berland

Zamar

Gulf of
Mayim

Melas

Barth

Melas Marsh

Barth

Land's
End

Cela

Meneton

Cela
Mtns.

Mount
Bamah

Jaelport

Hamonah

Cherem

Magos

Zerah Rock

Mitspah

Chowmah
Mtns.

Carm

Carmine

Har Sha'ar

Sideros
Forest

Sitna

Nesos

Arok
Lake

Allowntown

Allown

Mirrorstone

Mahanaim

Lebab
Inlet

Walden's
Watch

Nahar
Forest

Reshon
Gates

Nahar
Caves

Xulon

Nahar

LIGHT

Noiz

Edom's Gate

Armonguard

Lake
Arman

Gadowl Wall

Arman

Er'Rets Point

Advance Praise for *To Darkness Fled*

"Williamson pens an action-packed, imaginative second installment in the *Blood of Kings* trilogy. All the familiar epic elements and emotions are freshly rendered, with Vrell and Achan especially memorable as they grow during their journey. The pace gallops along, leaving readers hungry for the concluding book."

Publisher's Weekly

Praise for *By Darkness Hid*

"This thoroughly entertaining and smart tale will appeal to fans of Donita K. Paul and J.R.R. Tolkien. Highly recommended for CF and fantasy collections."

Library Journal

"Kings, politics, orphans (called strays), knights, squires, bloodvoicing (mind reading), darkness, and light. This book is packed full of everything you could possibly ask for."

USA Today Faith & Reason Book Club Blog

"Wonderfully written with a superb plot, this book is a sure-fire hit with almost any reader. An adventure tale with a touch of romance and enough intrigue to keep the pages turning practically by themselves."

Voice of Youth Advocates

"It is rare to come across a book in the fantasy genre that has such an organic feel....Once in awhile there comes along an author who takes classic fantasy plot contrivances and breathes new life into them."

Church Libraries, Fall 2009

"*By Darkness Hid* is the kind of fantasy that should be on Christian bookstore shelves everywhere. Fascinating and complete. If you like fantasy novels at all, you owe it to yourself to get hold of this one. I can't wait to explore it further. Highly recommended."

Christian Fiction Review

"I highly recommend it to fans of fantasy, and even to someone who is unfamiliar with fantasy and needs a good place to start."

Title Trakk.com

"I love a good fantasy, and *By Darkness Hid* more than fills the bill. With an unpredictable plot, twists of supernatural ability, and finely crafted tension between the forces of good and evil, Jill Williamson's book had me captivated. I jumped into the skin of the heroine and enjoyed her journey as if it were my own."

Donita K. Paul, author of the *Dragon Keeper Chronicles*

"Jill Williamson is a major arrival. She presents characters full of mystery and leaves room for plenty of further exploration. *By Darkness Hid* is a fast-paced addition to the world of swords and sorcery, using a backdrop of political and spiritual intrigue to heighten the tension. When readers begin lining up for the sequel, you'll find me at the front of the line."

Eric Wilson, author of *Field of Blood* and *Haunt of Jackals*

What readers are saying about *By Darkness Hid*

"I love the fantasy genre, and your novel was an enthralling masterpiece."

Eric Soo, 13

"*By Darkness Hid* had me arguing with my mom as I wanted to stay up all night to read it. Now anytime I think about knights, Jill's book comes to mind. I enjoyed reading it so much, and I cannot wait to read the next one!"

Keegan Pearson, age 13

"No! That can't be it! You'd better make a sequel. I was so into it. I loved it all! I didn't think you could just end it right there. Please write more! This was a great read."

Querida, age 16

PART I

A DARK
JOURNEY

I

What do you mean she's gone?

Vrell Sparrow smiled at Esek Nathak's sharp tone. She'd been hoping to intrude upon this moment. She twisted the false prince's silk sleeve in her hands and held her breath, thankful she'd kept the scrap of fabric. Personal items made it easier to look in on someone's mind like this, as did her tar-black surroundings.

Though she floated with four men in a small wooden boat gliding west across Arok Lake—and Darkness—she nevertheless looked through Esek's eyes. The former heir to Er'Rets reclined on a cushioned chaise lounge in his solar in the Mahanaim stronghold. The blazing fire from Esek's hearth warmed Vrell's . . . _Esek's_ right side. Her hands trembled with the fury coursing through his body. She forced herself to ignore it, knowing it was Esek's anger and not her own.

It galled Vrell that she had to share this man's mind. The man she had once thought to be Prince Gidon Hadar. The man who had demanded to marry her, putting so much pressure on her mother that Vrell had gone into hiding disguised as a stray boy. A disguise she still wore six months later.

Esek rose from the chaise lounge and circled his steward like a prowling dog. *How can this be, Chora? Did you not tell me yourself Sir Kenton posted three guards at her door?*

Chora, a short, dark-haired man in brown robes, seemed to shrink whenever Esek addressed him. *His b-best men, Your Highness. He swears no man left his post. But the chamber is empty. She must have escaped another way.*

Yet Lord Levy assures me that is impossible.

F-forgive me, my king, Chora croaked out. *The lady must be a mage. First taking on the appearance of a boy, now v-vanishing altogether.*

Esek threw back his head and groaned. *I am surrounded by fools. She's no mage, you nitwit. Both my prisoners have gone missing in the same hour, and only I can see the truth: the stray helped her. He means to steal my life—my crown and my bride. Find them!*

Of course, Your Majesty. Right away. Chora scurried to the door but paused.

Esek fell back on his chaise lounge and crossed his ankles. He snatched a handful of grapes from a tray. *Why are you still here?*

The steward turned, trembling. *F-Forgive me, Your Highness. It's only . . . the guards have s-searched the stronghold already. Th-There's no sign of them. I d-don't—*

The door burst open. Sir Kenton, the Shield, personal body-guard to Esek, strode into the chamber. A chill draft swept in behind him, followed by a group of New Kingsguard soldiers dragging two of their own—bound and gagged—between them.

What's this? Esek sat up, swinging his feet to the floor.

Sir Kenton shook his curtain of black hair at the guards, who yanked the prisoners to their feet. *These are two of the men who escorted the stray to the dungeons. They were found in the privy on the north wing, bound to one another.*

Esek stood and strode to the prisoners. He waved a finger at the gag on the taller man. Sir Kenton withdrew a dagger from his belt and cut through the cloth.

Well? Esek said. *What have you to say? Report.*

It was Trizo Akbar, Your Highness. The prisoner took a deep breath, as if winded. *He's turned traitor. Maybe always has been. Sir Rigil and his squire too. Trizo led the prisoner away while Sir Rigil and his squire bound us and stuffed us into the privy.*

Esek's temperature rose. *How is it a mere stray has garnered every competent servant in Er'Rets? Has not the Council voted me king? Take these fools to the dungeons, Sir Kenton. The rest of you, find the stray, find the boy called Vrell Sparrow, find Sir Rigil and his rosy squire, and bring them to me. Now!*

The chamber fell out of focus. Vrell's head tingled, her body tipped forward. She gasped, and musty, rotten-smelling air filled her lungs. She gritted her teeth and concentrated, putting a hand on the bow of the boat for support. Using her bloodvoicing gift for long periods of time always weakened her. If she could only stay connected long enough to learn Esek's plan. She concentrated on his face and pressed the wrinkled silk sleeve to her cheek.

The chamber came back into view. A door slammed. Esek and Chora were alone.

Issue a decree. Any traitor will stand before me to be judged. Then a bounty. Five golds for information on the Mârad, Sir Rigil, or his squire's whereabouts. Twenty golds for the man who brings me Achan Cham alive. Ten if it's only his head. Fifty golds for Vrell Sparrow, unharmed.

F-fifty, Your Majesty?

Have you written it down?

Yes, Your Majesty. Chora lowered his voice. *But why not disclose that the boy is really Lady Averella Amal?*

Because it would work to the stray's advantage. Should the people discover Averella travels with him, they might think the duchess supports his claim to my throne. No. Let them keep their secrets. The money will be enough to bring them both to me. The sooner the better. I am loath to marry Lady Mandzee Hamartano. Now that woman is a mage. Do you recall how she—

A sharp pain shot through Vrell's ear. She moaned and forced her eyes open. Blackness surrounded her, like the deepest, darkest cave. She no longer sat on the wooden bench of the boat but found herself scrunched in the bow, head bent awkwardly to one side, sleeve still clutched in her hand. Mosquitoes buzzed nearby. The boat rocked softly on the lake's surface.

A voice came from the darkness above. "Sparrow?"

Vrell jumped at the volume of Achan's voice. Noises always seemed louder after bloodvoicing, like her head had been wrapped in bandages that fell away all at once.

A hand patted Vrell's knee, then waist.

She jerked upright, not wanting anyone to feel her undergarment. The fake belly acted like a corset, padded with shorn wool rather than lined with whalebone. It gave her slender feminine shape that of a pudgy boy. "Do not touch me!"

"Whoa. It's just me, Achan."

She groped for the wooden bench and pulled herself back onto it. This was the longest she'd gone yet before blacking out. Perhaps she only needed practice to strengthen her ability.

"You fall asleep or something?" Achan mumbled, as if trying not to open his mouth when he spoke. The cuts on his cheeks must've been hurting him.

She strained to see him, but her eyes could not penetrate the surrounding blackness. She was blind here, dependent on movement, sound, and smell. The boat rocked gently beneath her. She could hear the Old Kingsguard knights—Sir Gavin, Sir Caleb, and Inko—murmuring in the back of the boat, Sir Gavin's paddle dipping in and out of the water. And the smell . . . as if they were sitting on a dung hill.

"It is difficult not to in this light," Vrell said.

Achan chuckled. "Well, if you're that tired, stay there." He paused, and his next words came out in a mumbled rush. "I'd hate to have to dive in and rescue you twice in the same day. 'Sides, I doubt I'd find you in this . . . *light*."

A sudden chill seized Vrell at the memory of nearly drowning that morning. She shoved Esek's sleeve into her satchel. "I am fine now."

"If you say so. You're the healer." Achan's boots *thunked* on the bottom of the boat, lurching it as he moved away. When he spoke again his voice was quiet. "Sparrow's just tired. So, Inko, finish your story about Barthos' temple."

Inko's raspy, jilted accent lifted out of the abyssal surroundings. "It wasn't being until King Trevyn was first visiting the village that any Kinsman was ever stepping inside the shrine."

"It's really a pyramid?"

"Yes. It's being made of stone, being hollow inside all the way to the top."

"How's it stand without the support of floors?" Achan asked.

"A structure like that would be quite stable," Sir Caleb answered, his voice low and polished. "With the large base and the way all four walls push against one another, not even the wind would sway it. It'd be much stronger than any keep."

"It was being designed to look like it was rising out of the ground to be honoring Barthos," Inko said.

As the Old Kingsguard soldier continued his tale of Barthos, the false god of the soil, Vrell pondered what she had witnessed through Esek's eyes. Her worst fears were confirmed. Esek now knew the truth: Vrell was really Lady Averella Amal, heir to Carm Duchy. What now? Should she continue to play the role of Vrell Sparrow when the man she hid from knew of her disguise? It seemed pointless.

What would her companions do if they discovered the truth? They would likely come to her aid—Achan especially. He would see it as a betrayal, though, and that would hurt him. He had been through so much already. So many lies . . .

Mother would know what to do. But Mother had not answered Vrell's bloodvoicing calls. Lord Nathak's men had done something to her. Vrell fought the tears stinging her eyes and prayed Sir Rigil and Bran were riding to her mother's rescue this moment.

Dear Bran. His service to Sir Rigil had made him a hunted traitor. *Please, Arman, do not let him be captured.*

Vrell shook her thoughts back to the present. For now she should at least inform Sir Gavin about the bounties Esek had ordered. As the head of Achan's personal guard, the knight should know what they were facing.

She scratched a mosquito bite on her cheek and stared into the starless void above. She must not despair. Arman, the one God, could see their path even if she could not.

"Bet Jaira hated that."

Achan sounded so amused that Vrell tried to focus on the men's conversation.

"Yes." Inko's low, raspy voice drew Vrell in. "But to be refusing her father publicly would have been bigger a disgrace. So she was allowing the Barthians to cover in mud her skin."

Achan's deep laugh made Vrell smile. "Oh, I wish I could've seen—"

Something scraped the left side of the boat. Vrell jerked her fists up to her chin, shaking at the horror of this dark place. It reminded her of the underground river from Xulon after their lamp had shattered. Did reekats live in Arok Lake? How would Peripaso, her pruny old friend who lived underground, fare in such a place?

"What's that?" Achan asked.

"Branches." Sir Gavin's paddle glubbed beneath the surface, thrusting the boat onward. "Dead, by the feel of them."

"Already we're being close to shore? Not the south shore, I am hoping?"

A long sniff answered Inko's worrisome question. Sir Gavin's odd habit of using his nose to calm himself. "Aye, Inko. The south shore."

"Is everything dead here?" Achan asked.

"Oh, no," Sir Caleb said. "You'd think so, without the sun, but life is . . . stubborn."

"Please be explaining, Gavin." Inko's voice sounded more stressed than usual. "Did you mean to be bringing us to the south side on purpose? Esek's men will already be following. We must be—"

The boat scratched to a halt in the twiggy branches. Vrell gripped the bow to keep from falling off her bench.

A heavy sigh. "And now we're being stuck."

Sir Gavin's paddle clunked on the side of the boat. "We must get off the water. Only I can't be certain how close the shore is with all this dead shrubbery. I need to seek out a bird, but . . ."

"What do you sense?" Sir Caleb asked.

"Our pursuers are close. Come over the side with me, Caleb. We must tow the boat out of sight. Now."

Out of sight? Vrell almost laughed. Who but Arman could see in this cursed place? She whipped around, scanning her surroundings for any trace of light and saw none. She reached out for an open mind, but everyone in their boat—even Achan—was guarding himself well.

Leather scraped against the left side of the boat, and someone grunted. Water glubbed and the boat rocked. Vrell swallowed, gripped the boat's edge, and prayed for Arman's protection. The boat tugged forward, ripping past the twiggy branches. The knights were pulling them along. Was the water shallow enough to wade, or were they swimming?

"Keep quiet, now," Sir Gavin whispered as the boat slid to a stop. "We're being hunted."

2

As if this day hadn't been intense enough already.

Achan crouched lower in the boat, staring over the wooden edge into the endless black. Inko, who sat behind him, made no sound. Vrell Sparrow's ragged breath puffed and hitched, but Achan couldn't see the boy. Water gurgled around the craft, slapping the sides in a slow cadence. The darkness made it impossible for Achan to know whether the waves were natural, caused by Sir Gavin and Sir Caleb's movement, or something else.

Mosquitoes buzzed in his ear. A sharp itch hinted at an attack on his temple, but he didn't flinch. He sucked in a deep breath of stale air and blinked. Had that been a light? He squinted at what he thought was an alcove of trees and blinked again.

The flames of four torches swept into view, casting a golden glow on a small barge. Over a dozen men stood in the feeble light. Achan sucked in a breath, recognizing one short, weasely New Kingsguard knight. Khai Mageia served Esek but also worked for Macoun Hadar, a twisted old man who sought to exploit Achan's and Sparrow's bloodvoicing talents.

Achan wanted to bloodvoice Sir Gavin, tell him about Khai, but his ability lacked control. If he tried to communicate, he'd likely give their presence away to those on the barge. For now—and for everyone's safety—he would only receive messages, not send any.

Sir Gavin must have sensed his apprehension because he bloodvoiced Achan. *Stay still, Your Highness, and keep silent.*

Your Highness. Achan bristled at the formality. This very day his life had changed forever. Sir Gavin, the famous Great Whitewolf himself, had taken Achan before the Council of Seven and proved he was the real Prince Gidon Hadar, rightful heir to the throne of Er'Rets.

The realization still nauseated him.

He closed his eyes and breathed a prayer to Arman, asking for protection. He didn't know why he bothered. Arman, the moody Father God, did as he pleased when he pleased.

The barge passed a jousting field away. The dull torchlight made his eyes water and tinted the black cloaks of the New Kingsguardsmen sickly green.

Esek's men. Sent to bring him back.

No one in Achan's boat moved until long after the torches had faded from sight and the darkness had settled over them again like a heavy blanket.

Sir Gavin's voice came from below. "A hand, Achan?"

Achan braced himself and reached over the side until Sir Gavin's calloused hand slid into his. He pulled the old knight up, rocking the boat and sloshing the water beneath it.

Sir Gavin sat, water dripping onto wood from his clothes. "Where are you, Caleb?"

"Here." Sir Caleb's voice came from the stern.

Achan moved that way and helped Sir Caleb aboard.

"I'm getting too old for this, Gavin," Sir Caleb said. "I've got leeches on me. I feel them sucking."

Achan wrinkled his nose. "Can you get them off?" Ah. It hurt to speak. His cheeks throbbed despite Sparrow's salve and awkward bandage. How he hated Esek Nathak.

"The ones I feel, yes," Sir Caleb said. "The ones I can't, however . . . well, they'll let go when they're done."

Achan shivered at the idea of leeches, which reminded him of something. "I saw Khai on the barge," Achan said over the pain. "Do you think he's here working for Esek or Macoun?"

"Both, likely." Sir Gavin's paddle dipped into the water and the boat lurched against more twiggy branches. "He's a Kingsguard soldier, so he'll go where he's sent. But he's also Macoun's man. If Macoun can't have you, he'll still want Vrell back. Bah!" The paddle clattered to the floor of the boat. "This won't do."

"He's a horrible man," Sparrow said.

Achan tried to talk without moving his jaw. "Macoun?"

"Oh, him as well, but I meant Khai. He tried to kill me."

Achan wanted to hear this tale, but Sir Gavin spoke. "We need to make camp. Caleb and I will tow the boat in as far as we can, then we'll leave the boat and wade the rest of the way."

"But still we are being on the wrong side of the lake," Inko said. .

"And we'll all get leeches." Sparrow squawked, as if his voice was finally changing.

Achan smirked. Maybe the boy would finally grow into his boots. "What? The herbalist has no use for leeches?"

Sparrow's voice fell. "Bloodletting is *not* one of my skills."

"We must be crossing the lake first." Inko's worry never ceased. "Tsaftown is being north."

"Is it really? North, you say?" Sir Caleb's tone brought a hush over the boat. "You think Gavin has forgotten where he grew up?"

"Of course that's not what I'm—"

"Then have a little faith, Inko," Sir Caleb said. "King Axel didn't make Gavin commander for his handsome face."

The silence lingered. Achan propped his elbows on his knees and set his forehead in his palms. He'd known Inko and Sir Caleb for two days. They never agreed. Inko risked nothing, trusted no one, and questioned everything. Sir Caleb, on the other hand, was game for pretty much anything. How in all Er'Rets had these men served together year after year?

His left cheek twinged. He fought the urge to scratch under the bandage Sparrow had wrapped around his head and chin. He must look like a man with a toothache. The memory of Esek drawing Ôwr's sharp edge across his cheeks filled his mind's eye, and he gritted his teeth.

"Did you really grow up in Tsaftown?" Sparrow asked.

"Aye."

Perhaps Sir Gavin knew Lady Tara? Achan pushed the useless thought away. Sir Gavin had never been one to open up, as Sparrow would soon discover. Achan shivered. The Evenwall had left his clothing damp. What would they do come night? How would they even know when night arrived?

At least he had one change of clothes. The shirt and doublet Gren had made him were in Sir Caleb's pack. No point changing now if they were going to wade. He clenched his teeth through another shiver and hugged himself.

"I feel as though my blood is freezing." Sparrow echoed Achan's thoughts. Had the boy read his mind? Achan still couldn't tell when someone was in his head. He really wanted to learn that trick.

"Wait until we reach Ice Island," Sir Caleb said. "It's so cold your beard will frost."

Achan laughed, and the wounds on his cheeks throbbed. "Hear that, Sparrow? You best get started on that beard or you'll have nothing to warm that chubby face."

"And your beard is so much better?"

Achan tried to sound wise despite the awkward lull his wounds gave his voice. "I've never tried for a beard, but I'm sure I could grow one if these men would stop shaving me. You, however, haven't even the fuzz of a peach on your chin."

"We'll stop shaving you now," Sir Caleb said. "We'll all need beards for Tsaftown, for warmth and disguise."

Inko exhaled a deep breath. "Gavin, be assuring me you're having more of a plan than to be traipsing across Darkness."

"We head for Mirrorstone. We need supplies."

"Mirrorstone?" Achan spun toward Sir Gavin's voice, his movement rocking the boat. "Is not Lord Eli loyal to Prince Gidon?" He cleared his throat. "I mean, Prince Esek?" He'd never get used to it. The man he'd always known to be Prince Gidon Hadar was actually Esek Nathak. And he—Achan—was the prince: Prince Gidon. So strange.

"Don't call him 'prince,'" Sir Caleb said. "He's a fake and usurper who doesn't deserve the respect."

"Regardless," Inko said, "Mirrorstone is lying on the south side of the lake. We need to be crossing Arok Lake, to be going north. The longer we're lingering, the more time we're allowing those Kingsguard soldiers to be—"

"Can we discuss this later?" Sir Caleb said. "I'd really like to get these leeches off me."

Sir Gavin sighed. "Back into the water then, Caleb. The rest of you might as well ride 'til we get a bit closer."

The boat rocked, leather scraped over wood, branches cracked, water splashed. Then the boat jerked forward. Sparrow fell backward off his bench into Achan's lap and squeaked like a mouse. Achan laughed and groped for the boy's arm to help pull him up, but Sparrow swatted him and scrambled away.

Achan ignored the boy's antics. "How do they even know where they're going?" He paused at the throb in his cheeks. "I can see as well as any of them, and I see nothing."

"But Sir Gavin is not using only his eyes. He can be smelling the trail like a wolf," Inko said. "Though I'm fearing he should be crossing the lake now."

Achan had never trusted his life to a man's sense of smell. He'd always assumed Sir Gavin's Great Whitewolf title came from his mismatched eyes and long white hair. But maybe the man had a wolf's sense of smell too. Regardless, Achan would rather be with Sir Gavin than anyone else. Except maybe Prince Oren, his uncle. All his life Achan had been a stray: a slave without any family to claim him. Lower even than a slave. Now that he found he had an uncle and cousins, Achan wanted to know them. He fingered his uncle's signet ring on his left middle finger.

A crown, however, Achan did not want.

The knights towed the boat inland. Branches scraped the sides and scratched Achan's arms if he wasn't careful to stay seated in the center. After hundreds of broken branches and dozens of mosquito bites, the boat grated to a stop.

"You all climb out now." Sir Gavin's voice came from Achan's left. "'Tis quite swampy, so keep your feet moving."

"This is insanity," Sparrow said, seized with a bout of his bossy nature. "How can you even know where you are going? You could be wading in a circle."

"Gavin is the best guide in Er'Rets," Sir Caleb said. "Plus, I've tied a rope to Gavin, and each of us will hold on. That should keep us together. If you don't like it, you and Inko may take your chances in the boat. But, Your Majesty, you don't get a choice. Come down next. Put your sword over your shoulder to keep it dry. And take care, the lake bed is quite mucky."

Achan unbuckled his belt, wrapped the leather band over his head and one arm, and fastened it so his sword—Eagan's Elk—hung down from his front right shoulder. He swung one leg over the side, the boat tipped, and he fell sideways into frigid water. In his panic, he took in a mouthful of putrid, slimy water before his boots sank into the sludge.

"You all right, Your Majesty?" Sir Caleb asked.

Achan spat, clearing the bitter taste from his mouth. "Aye." He patted Eagan's Elk to make sure it hadn't fallen off his shoulder. So much for keeping it dry. The water rose to his chest. An icy chill clapped onto his body. His muscles ached from endless shivering. Were leeches already biting his flesh?

A cold hand gripped Achan's shoulder and something stiff pressed against his chest. "Take the rope," Sir Caleb said into Achan's right ear. "There should be a knot."

Achan felt the coarse rope until his fingers found the knot. He clutched it in his right hand and tried to remain calm, though the blackness made it difficult. This must be what a blind man experienced daily.

"Inko? Vrell? Made up your mind?" Sir Caleb asked.

"Of course we'll be going with you." Though Inko's tone proclaimed displeasure.

"How deep is it?" Sparrow asked.

"Too deep," Achan said. "Even if Sparrow managed to tiptoe in this muck, only the top of his head would break the surface. I'll carry him on my back."

"Your Majesty, everyone is knowing that's no job for you," Inko said.

Achan reached out until his hand hit the side of the boat, then turned his back to it and almost lost a boot in the sludge. "Get on, Sparrow, before I change my mind. And if I'm holding you up, you get the rope."

After a long, ungraceful moment in which Achan nearly dropped Sparrow in the lake, the boy sat on Achan's back, clinging to his throat. He took the rope from Achan's hand.

Achan hiked Sparrow up his back again and held him under his knees. "Don't choke me."

Inko climbed out, and the companions left the boat behind. They waded along, tethered by Sir Caleb's rope, trusting nothing but Sir Gavin's nose to lead them. Achan hoped Sir Gavin's nose wouldn't start running from the cold. At least Achan had Sparrow's hot breath to warm his neck.

He trudged on, each step a battle between the muck gripping his boots and the branches snagging his clothes, as if walking in a lightless void weren't awkward enough. Sparrow had better hold on, because he made no guarantees that he could keep this up for long. Slowly, the water level dropped away. When it lapped around Achan's thighs, he set Sparrow on his feet.

Achan waded, rope tugging him along, body lurching through the sludge under his boots. Sound, smell, the cold . . . it all seemed to magnify without light. The water gurgled and splashed from the party's movement. But there were other sounds—a hiss, a rattle, a pecking—from overhead. The land smelled sour, like turned pudding.

"There's a cluster of trees here," Sir Gavin called from the front of the line. "Careful not to hurt yourselves."

The water sloshed around Achan's boots now. He held a hand out in front to feel for the trees. Pulled along by Sir Gavin's tether, Achan's hand smacked against slimy bark, and his body slid between several tree trunks, feet stumbling over the gnarled roots. He didn't want to know what made the trees slimy, especially considering the putrid smell.

Finally they stepped onto dry ground. Achan took his belt and sword off his neck and hooked it around his waist where it belonged. A chill snaked over him. His wet clothes clung to his body; his toes squished in his boots.

"I'm going to light a small torch," Sir Gavin sniffed in a strong breath, "just 'til we find a place to camp. I won't burn it long. Any light is a beacon to every living thing."

Achan bumped into Sir Caleb's back. Sparrow ran into his. Apparently they were stopping. Achan focused on the sounds of Sir Gavin digging through his pack, but pecking distracted him. Could it be a woodpecker? Some kind of cricket?

A torch hissed into a green flame. Achan's eyes widened at the brightness. Spots flooded his vision until he blinked them away. In the green glow, Sir Gavin's wrinkled face resembled a dried pear. His hair and frizzy braided beard looked like freshly shorn wool that needed washing. And his eyes—one blue, one brown—shone like emerald and bronze. Achan scanned the charcoal surroundings. Spindly trees rose around them, a forest of gnarled branches that appeared burned, like the dead side of the memorial tree in Allowntown.

"How is it your torch is dry?" Sparrow asked.

"It's not," Sir Gavin said. "I've a few torchlights made from sulfur and lime. Bought them from a Jaelportian vendor at the market in Mahanaim. They burn even when doused in water. Different colors too." He pointed left. "In the forest will be best."

The knight moved away, and the rope pulled the group along single file. Achan followed Sir Caleb, eyes fixed on the allown tree painted on the shield draped over Sir Caleb's back.

Sir Gavin and Sir Caleb were the only two who carried shields. Achan's sword, Eagan's Elk, was long enough to be wielded two-handed, like the longsword Inko carried. Inko also had a bow. Sparrow had a dinky little arming sword. More like a long dagger.

An occasional black shadow scurried up the twisted trunks. What kind of creatures lived in such a place? Achan used to believe nothing could live here until, at the recent tournament, he'd met people who'd come from cities in Darkness.

A prickle on his torso reminded him of Sir Caleb's leeches. Heat flashed over him. He pressed his fingers to his side and felt a hard lump beneath his clothing. His limbs twitched. Heart stampeding, he released the rope and pulled up his jerkin and shirt. The rope slid past his thigh. Sparrow knocked into his back and yelped.

Achan scratched off the slug-like attachment and flung it away. Squirming, he drew his fingers across his stomach and found another hard lump.

Pig snout.

"What are you doing?" Sparrow asked.

"Leeches. There are leeches all over me." Achan plucked the second one off and found another on his chest. "Ahh!"

Sparrow cried out. Achan turned to find the boy patting his legs through his trousers. His eyes widened in the green light as they met Achan's chest.

"You see another?" Achan asked.

Sparrow pointed a shaking finger at Achan's armpit. Achan lifted his arm, but a hand on his back stopped him.

"Leave them for now, Achan," Sir Caleb said, his voice commanding. "Don't pull them off like a madman, lest they leave their teeth in you."

Achan froze, hands above his head, and took a deep breath. His clothing shifted, then dropped back into place. He swallowed and faced Sir Caleb. "Leave them?"

"They'll do no harm. We'll get them off when we stop, if any are still there."

Sir Gavin's moustache arched into a frown. "Just a few more moments, I promise you."

Achan nodded, still panicked at the idea of the creatures sucking his blood, even more alarmed that those he'd removed might have left their teeth in his skin.

"They do not leave teeth in you." Sparrow's shaky voice came soft behind him. "But if you pull them too fast, they tend to retch. The excess saliva under your skin leaves a rash or swells—" Sparrow squealed and plowed into Achan's back again.

A creature fluttered past Achan's ear, brushing his hair with its wing. Achan ducked, pulse racing. A moth the size of a pigeon flapped wildly in the green glow.

"That is disgusting." Sparrow's voice cracked. "I hate this place. I hate it!"

Achan had to agree. He gripped the rope and straightened, keeping his eyes on the overgrown insect. The rope inched forward. So did Achan. They approached a grove of trees. The crooked branches above twisted together, forming a tunnel and forcing the moth to fly above the briary canopy.

Good riddance.

The trees grew thick and tangled, like a gnarled cage. Achan squinted at the smooth clay beneath his feet. They seemed to be on a game trail. As long as no one was hunting them now . . .

Sir Gavin ducked under low branches and crept on, tugging the rope along. Achan squeezed between slippery branches. His hair snagged on stiff twigs, ripping out wisps and leaving drips of slime running down his forehead. He wiped the gunk away with his free hand and found it sticky, like pitch.

Sir Gavin stopped suddenly and drove the torchlight into the ground. They were in a clearing the size of two small cottages. The ground was carpeted in soppy, grey moss. The tree branches were tight overhead, almost like a thatched roof.

Sir Gavin shrugged off his pack and shield, catching them before they hit the ground. "I sense humans to the west, which is in the direction of Mirrorstone. We must get there as soon as possible, but it's still a two-day journey on foot."

He propped his pack and shield in the branches of a tree on the perimeter. "We've only four bedrolls, so we'll take turns on watch using our ears, noses, and minds." He pointed behind Sparrow. "Privy is on that end, dinner and sleep is down here by me. Put your packs in the trees to let them dry. Be quick about it. The sooner this torch is out, the better."

Achan had no pack, only Eagan's Elk. His change of clothes was in Sir Caleb's pack. "Do you think the water damaged my sword?"

"Not in that short time," Sir Caleb said. "When did you last oil the blade?"

Achan's mouth hung open a moment, his vision flicking to Sir Gavin. "I've never done so."

Sir Caleb stared at Sir Gavin's back. "Were you not taught?"

Achan swallowed. "I—"

Sir Gavin sighed and answered while rummaging through his pack. "There was no time, Caleb. Nathak banished me the day I gave Achan the blade. Besides, you know I'm no teacher. I've done the best I could. But now that he has you, I freely relinquish the honor of his weapons training."

Achan was thankful for Sir Gavin's instruction. But could Sir Caleb teach him more? Teach him better?

Sir Caleb glared long and hard at Sir Gavin, as if the crime of not oiling a blade deserved years in Ice Island. Finally he turned to Achan. "I have oil in my pack, Your Highness. For now, remove the blade from the scabbard to give both time to dry. A wet scabbard can rust steel."

Achan lifted the hem of his shirt to dry Eagan's Elk. A black mark on his side caught his eye and it all came rushing back. "Can we get these leeches off now?"

"Yes." Sir Caleb unfastened his jerkin and shrugged it off. "Best take off all your clothes to make sure we don't miss any."

Achan set Eagan's Elk in a nearby tree and stripped down to his undershorts. He stacked his clothing carefully on the branch to avoid having it touch too much slime.

At least a dozen leeches spotted Sir Caleb's pale and wiry torso. "And that's why you don't rip them off. See how much you're bleeding?"

Achan looked down. Tiny streams of blood ran down his chest like water after a bath.

"Slide your fingernails under to wedge them off."

Achan mirrored Sir Caleb, plucking the parasites away.

"Be tossing them aside after." Inko draped his cape in a tree, his grey skin and pockmarked face like a potato full of eyes. "I'm not wanting them crawling on me in my sleep."

The men paired up to check each other's backs, Achan with Sir Caleb and Inko with Sir Gavin. Then they checked their own undershorts.

"I'm clean." Achan pitched the last leech into the trees.

A voice in the woods cried out.

Achan froze. "What was that?"

Sir Caleb wrenched his sword from the branches and advanced on the trees, weapon raised. "In the name of Câan, come out. We mean you no harm."

3

Vrell clapped her hand over her mouth to stifle another sob and wiped tears from her cheeks.

"Come out, now, or I'll come in after you," Sir Caleb said.

Vrell yanked up her trousers and tied her belt with shaking fingers. "It is only me." Her voice betrayed her, coming out soft, like a kitten's mew, expressing her true emotions. She inched toward the flickering light, thankful her entire body hadn't been underwater.

All four men stood in their undershorts staring at her, eyes wide. Trickles of blood were smeared across Achan's chest. The white bandage she had tied around his head had been knocked askew. She cast her gaze to the ground and casually drew her fingers along her thigh where a tickle spasmed. Could she have missed a leech? She had checked herself thoroughly but had hardly been able to see what she was doing.

Sir Caleb still held his sword ready. "What in flames were you doing in there, boy?"

Vrell stared at the sleek blade. "I . . . I had to . . ."

Achan's lips curved into a lopsided grin that faltered as quickly as it came. "Didn't realize you were gone." He winced, evidence that his cheeks still pained him. "Did my leech hit you?"

"Nearly." Vrell meandered to the edge of the clearing where Sir Gavin had promised food. She turned her back to the tree holding Sir Gavin's pack and folded her arms, still trembling at the memory of leeches attached to her legs. Achan spoke to Sir Caleb, his scarred back facing her. Pity doused her bad attitude. At least no one had ever whipped her.

Achan walked to Vrell's tree. He peeled his shirt off a branch as if thick cobwebs held it there.

"Wait." Vrell dug out a scrap of linen from her satchel and handed it to Achan. "Use this to stop the bleeding. You should let me rinse those wounds out as well."

"I'm fine." He wadded the linen in one hand and wiped the trails of blood away. He pushed the hair from his eyes as he worked. A thick strand stuck to his forehead, held there by a trail of slime. "Get your leeches off?"

Vrell stared at the moss beneath her feet. "I-I think so."

"Strip down and I'll check."

Vrell's eyes swelled. "I-I am fine. I am not . . . feeling well." She backed into the thicket of prickly trees, keeping an eye on Achan. A sharp branch dug into her shoulder. She bit her lip to keep from crying out. The trees were so close together it was difficult to get through.

Achan's gaze followed her. "What are you doing?"

She slid behind a thick trunk and held her breath, praying someone would distract Achan from his quest to be helpful.

But Achan called again, "Sparrow?"

"Leave him." Sir Caleb's low and commanding voice soothed Vrell's nerves. "He'll ask for help if he needs it."

"But how can he stand it?" Achan asked. "I didn't want the little beasts on my skin any longer than they had been."

"Worry about yourself. Get your sword and sit. Then I'll show you how to oil your blade and rub down your scabbard."

Vrell sank against the tree, stopping herself before she sat on the moist ground. She squatted, wrapping her arms around her knees. Now seemed a good time to try and contact Mother again, but she hated the idea of blacking out on this sodden ground. That would not matter if Mother did not answer.

Vrell concentrated on her mother's face and sent a knock.

She waited, listening, but heard only the men shuffling in the clearing, the crackling of the torch, the occasional click and hiss from above. She took a deep breath—gagged at the bitter smell of the forest—and knocked again.

"Vrell?" Sir Gavin called out. "Come back, lad. I've got to put out the torch."

Vrell forced tears away and stood. She paused to let a bout of dizziness fade from standing too fast and crept back to the clearing. Four bedrolls had been laid out around the torch. A moth the size of Vrell's hand fluttered around the flame. Achan, Inko, and Sir Caleb had each claimed a bed. Sir Gavin's pack sat on the last bedroll. The knight crouched beside the torch. Where would Vrell sleep? Surely they would not expect her to share one of those skinny little flaps of leather?

"Get yourself some meat, Vrell, and sit." Sir Gavin motioned to the bedroll with his pack.

An open burlap sack protruded from the top of Sir Gavin's pack. Vrell knelt on Sir Gavin's bedroll and took the top chunk of dried meat from the sack.

"Couldn't you be waiting until we're offering our thanks?" Inko's gaze locked on Achan, who had eaten half his meat.

Achan shot a questioning glance at Vrell. She pressed her hands together in a position of prayer. His head tipped back and he pursed his lips.

Vrell knew little of what Achan believed about Arman, but she knew he didn't follow the Way like she and the knights did. Likely, Achan held beliefs similar to the rest of Er'Rets' general populace, who believed in a host of gods for any and every superstition. The remnant who knew the truth—who followed the Way, believing in Arman, the Father God, as the one and only god—was a small group indeed.

"But why thank Arman for food?" Achan asked.

Vrell coughed and clapped a hand over her mouth. How rude to question Arman—or one's elders—in such a way.

But Achan charged on, clearly unfazed by his impropriety, chewing while he spoke. "I mean, if you thank him for food, why not thank him for everything? Clothes, companions, being alive, leeches . . . I don't see what good it does, why it matters."

A long silence passed, then the knights all spoke at once, as if eager to provide their future king with answers.

Sir Gavin tugged his beard braid. "It matters to Arman."

"Because it's showing thankfulness, respect," Inko said. "Without Arman's provisions, we wouldn't be having life."

"I thank him for all those things," Sir Caleb said.

Achan blew out a winded laugh. "Even leeches?"

"Leeches have their place in the world."

"Well, someone had better thank him for the meat, then, 'cause I'm starving."

Vrell hid a smile. How could Achan go from rudeness to acquiescence in a heartbeat and make it all harmless fun? She would never dare such boldness. And Achan had behaved that way as a stray. His nature had shocked her at first, but if she had been forced to serve Esek, she might have lost her patience quickly too.

Inko claimed the prayer. "Arman, we're thanking you for our lives, for safely delivering us from Esek's men, and for having given us this meat. Be helping us to be finding a way across the lake. In the name of your son, Câan, may it be so."

"So be it." Vrell lifted the greasy meat to her teeth and tore off an oily chunk. Her mouth watered at the smoky flavor. She stole a glance at Achan, and found his brow furrowed again. What was he thinking now? She dared not peek into his head. He would not be happy to find her there.

She studied the men around the torchlight. The dull green flame cast a pea soup fog over everyone, bringing out the worst in the Old Kingsguard knights. The flame glittered in Inko's pale eyes. With his grey, pockmarked skin and white hedge of hair, he looked dead. The green glow deepened Sir Gavin's wrinkles and greyed his white hair and braided beard. Even Sir Caleb, the youngest of the knights, in his mid-fifties, looked to have aged without the sun.

Only Achan's appearance benefited. Darkness shadowed his boyish features, straightened his posture, and broadened his shoulders. The torch cast a bronze glow over his brown skin and made his greasy black hair look silky. How could she have spent weeks healing his wounds and missed how much he resembled the Hadar family? But who would have thought a stray anything other than what he appeared to be? Vrell hoped the men would assume the same about her.

Sir Gavin jerked the torch from the ground and carried it to his bedroll. "Time to douse the lights. Everyone settled?"

No one complained, so Sir Gavin smothered the flame under the corner of the leather. Vrell edged back. The sudden darkness sent a prickle up her spine. She blinked, trying to see the men where she knew they were.

Sounds magnified in the dark. Fluttering. Clicking overhead. Steps across spongy ground. Sir Gavin, likely. Vrell hugged her knees to her chest. Would he sit with her?

Achan's voice rose above the subtle noises. "How long will we stay at Mirrorstone?"

"As little as possible without being rude." Sir Gavin's voice came from Vrell's left, where Sir Caleb's bedroll had been.

Good. She pressed her hands on the grimy leather and stretched out her legs. "And from there?"

"We look for a way to cross to the north shore. We'll fare best at Melas, rather than trying another boat."

"How far is that?" Achan asked.

"Another three days on foot. Two, if we can get horses."

Joyful heart! Horses would be merciful. Vrell still felt slimy from that water. She abhorred the stench of this place. She lifted her satchel off her neck and shoulder and opened it, looking for something pleasant to smell. Did herbs grow fresh in Darkness? Where would she find supplies for her healing kit if they didn't?

"You think Lord Eli will give us aid?" Achan asked.

"He has nothing to gain by refusing us," Sir Gavin said. "Either he'll arrest us and turn us over to Esek, or he'll help us. He won't send us away."

Vrell sniffed a small bundle from her bag. Mentha. Mmm. The mossy ground squished on her right. "Then we're risking everything to be going to him."

"We have no choice, Inko," Sir Caleb nearly yelled. "Surely you can see that much?"

"We should've been doubling back to Allowntown."

Sir Gavin sniffed in a long breath, as if to calm himself. "Esek will have men posted all along the Evenwall. We stand our best chance in Darkness."

Vrell inhaled another fresh breath of mentha. "How will we know we're not walking into a trap at Mirrorstone?" She still had not told anyone about the bounties Esek had offered for her and Achan's capture. She hated keeping secrets and not having a plan. If only she could speak with her mother.

"We won't," Sir Gavin said. "But I'll know his intentions as soon as I lay eyes on him."

"Can you teach me that?" Achan's mumble brought his injured cheeks to Vrell's mind. "I've always sensed emotions. Lord Nathak's tonic never doused my intuition. But I want to learn more. Sparrow showed me a few tricks, and—"

"I know little." Vrell's heart lifted at the idea of learning bloodvoicing from good men, not her maniacal old master, Macoun Hadar. "I should like to learn more, as well." Like how she could watch longer without blacking out and how to peek into gifted minds without being seen. Achan's mind.

"Think of your body as a fortress and yourself as its guard." Sir Caleb's voice drifted from Vrell's left. "Your duty is twofold. You must guard the fortress, allowing entry only to those you permit. Then, when you invite someone in, you must also guard the treasure, which is your mind. If you do this correctly, your guest may see only what you offer."

Vrell could do this already. She had a different way of accomplishing the same feat. She thought of her mind as a house and created a foyer in her mind where she let people in but kept them separated from her different rooms of thought.

"How do you do everything at once?" Achan asked. "When my mind is open, so many come at me. I can't keep them out, and I'm tired of shielding all the time."

"You can and you must, Your Highness." Sir Caleb sounded nobler when giving orders. "No one can guard your mind for you. Either you learn to do this, or you'll have to stay guarded always, never experiencing the fullness of your gift."

Vrell wished she could help Achan practice, but the knights had ordered him to keep his mind closed, for Achan's untrained bloodvoice rang like a beacon to anyone with the ability. Surely Esek had bloodvoicers monitoring for Achan's presence. Plus, unguarded, Achan's mind released a pressure that brought Vrell to her knees. She didn't miss the pain, but she did miss his sarcastic companionship.

A screech split the night. Vrell hugged her arms close. A mosquito buzzed nearby. She disliked the dark. "Sir Gavin?" She lifted her head. "We have been in Darkness for many hours, and I entered the Evenwall the day Achan fought the Poroo. I feel fine, except for these accursed mosquitoes. So why do people say Darkness drives one insane?"

"That's the subtlety of it, Vrell. If your mind is focused or distracted, 'tis easy to ignore the seduction of Darkness. When you were alone in the Evenwall, you had a task to perform. Now we're conversing steadily. This keeps our minds from wandering. But as we journey through this place, we must stay together and we must have conversation. No one will keep watch alone. See that no one is silent too long.

Darkness has a way of sneaking up and blinding you to your own conscience."

"What about when we sleep?" Achan asked.

"Bad dreams may come, but you won't lose your mind. Caleb and I will take first watch. Fear not and rest."

Vrell lay down on the greasy leather and curled into a ball, bringing her knees to her chest. Her body sank slowly into the wet lichen. She concentrated on Mother's face and knocked.

Still no answer.

4

Achan untied the bandage from his face. He lay on his back, ankles crossed, feet sticking off the end of the bedroll that was too short for his six-foot frame. He stared into the blackness above and traced his fingertips over the scabs forming on his cheeks where Esek had cut him. Would he bear these marks forever? If so, he would grow a beard, a thick one.

Had his father worn a beard?

Achan broke the stillness with a question, careful to move his cheeks as little as possible. "What happened to my father?"

A prolonged silence followed. He was thankful for these knights who'd made it their life goal to find him, yet so many questions plagued his mind. Did these men see taking care of him as penance for failing to protect their former king?

He tried again. "Were any of you there when he died?"

"Aye," Sir Gavin finally said. "But not when he died."

Achan propped himself up on one elbow. "What happened?"

"One of our own betrayed us. A young knight named Kenton Garesh."

"The Shield?" Sir Kenton, also known as The Shield, served as Esek's personal bodyguard. The human fortress had crushed Achan on more than one occasion. Most recently, just prior to Esek slicing open Achan's cheeks.

"Aye, he drugged our stew and we slept through the dawn. The king had a schedule to keep. He was headed to Carmine to consult with Duke Amal—this was before the duke passed on. Kenton urged King Axel to go on without us, to take the secondary guards, half of which were loyal to Kenton."

The pecking noise grew loud overhead, but Sir Gavin spoke over it. "I woke in time to hear my king bloodvoice for aid. But when I reached for him, he closed his mind, a sign he was hiding something. To this day I don't know why he kept me from seeing what happened. When I couldn't connect with King Axel, I called to Dara, for your mother was gifted also. But all I heard before she perished was the word—"

"Stray," Achan said.

It was common knowledge a stray had murdered the king and queen—Achan's parents. As a result, strays were branded, forced into lives of isolation and hard labor. Achan bore the S mark of a stray on his shoulder. Lord Nathak, the disfigured and menacing Lord of Sitna, had been his owner and had branded him in order to hide his true identity all these years, substituting his son, Esek, in Achan's place.

Achan knew what came next as well. "Darkness arrived almost immediately. Arman cursed the land."

"Nay, Achan," Sir Gavin said. "That's a myth. The world's way of assigning blame to what they don't understand. The evil in men's hearts brought Darkness to Er'Rets. It had been growing on the western horizon for years, threatening Barth and Land's End. The murder of our faithful king extinguished the only light left in the west. Darkness stretched across Er'Rets to the place King Axel died. You see, Arman gives the king the task of teaching the people what's good and pure and noble. Without a king, no man existed to spread the truth to the people, to shine the light. Until now."

The words spoken to Achan's soul when he had stood before the Council of Seven that morning boomed in his memory. *For I have appointed* you *as king over this nation. There is no one like you among all the people.*

Arman had spoken to him, singled him out as king. These knights claimed Arman was the only god, that all others were false. Sparrow also went in for that view. Achan wasn't convinced, yet he couldn't deny Arman's existence. No human voice sounded like Arman's—had the effect Arman's did. But did that mean every other god was false? Inko had prayed in Câan's name, Câan the warrior son of Arman. Didn't that mean there were two gods? How could they say there was only one?

It was all too confusing to grasp.

Liquid suddenly coated his heel. He bent his knees and pulled his feet away from the soggy ground and onto the end of the bedroll. He let his mind float to the past again. "But why kill my father? Sir Kenton seems to have gained nothing."

"These men were usurpers, Your Highness," Sir Caleb said. "They supported the one who wanted to overthrow the throne and take it for himself."

Achan could only imagine one man deceitful enough to lead such a cause. "Lord Nathak?"

"We're not knowing his name," Inko said. "But it is being someone beyond Nathak, we are believing."

Achan stared through the inky blackness in the direction of Inko's voice. "How can you suspect a man of trying to take the throne and not know who he is?"

"We sensed his bloodvoice," Sir Gavin said. "'Tis still strong today, but he shields well."

Who could be so powerful? "Then why'd he wait all these years for Esek to come of age? Why not take the throne by force after he'd killed the king?"

"Perhaps he didn't have as much power then as he would have us believe," Sir Caleb said. "Or he knew he couldn't defeat King Axel's army, so he designed this deceit with Esek to give him time to plot his takeover."

"So Lord Nathak and Esek work for him?"

"We don't know," Sir Gavin said, "but it's clear Nathak was involved. When you were lost, I sought your mind and found you right away. But you were so young. Not yet three years old. You couldn't articulate your whereabouts. You weren't in pain. You weren't afraid. But I couldn't guess your location. And then your presence vanished."

Sir Gavin paused as the mysterious beast screeched. "Two months passed before Nathak supposedly found you wandering in the fields south of Sitna. According to him, you wore King Axel's signet ring on a chain around your neck. He said he took you to his home and later journeyed to Mahanaim to give you to the Council of Seven. Of course, 'twasn't you at all. When I finally saw you—or Esek—he looked like you, though I could no longer sense your bloodvoice. I feared Nathak had done dark magic to you. Years passed before it occurred to me you might not be *you* at all."

Achan twisted Prince Oren's ring around his finger. He'd been alone, an abducted babe whose parents had been slaughtered.

Lord Nathak had given Achan to Poril, his cook, to raise. Poril had named him Achan Cham. *Achan,* which meant "trouble" in the ancient tongue, and *Cham,* a fire-breathing bear. All strays were given animal surnames to proclaim their lowly status.

Had Achan cried for his father in those first few days with Poril? Or had he simply forgotten the man and replaced him with the cook? Had he missed his mother? Achan's earliest memories were of Lord Nathak and Poril, who had beaten him at the slightest breeze. Achan shuddered as truth and understanding met in his heart.

"The young *prince* had, according to Nathak, taken such a liking to him during their time together," Sir Caleb said, "that the Council asked Nathak to raise the boy. They gave him a fief for his *loyalty.* He not only earned the title of Lord with the prince as his ward, but he expanded Sitna Manor and added guards and slaves. Over the years, he lobbied for a place on the Council, without success."

"Aye," Sir Gavin said. "The man is resourceful. Sitna was originally a poor trading and farming village. Nathak developed it over the years, mostly by stealing land and resources from Carmine. He proposed to Nitsa the very day her husband died. To my knowledge he's continued to ask for her hand again and again over the years. She's always refused."

Duchess Amal's constant rejection of Lord Nathak had been a favorite topic of gossip among the serving women in

Sitna. It startled Achan how Sir Gavin referred to the duchess by her first name, Nitsa. Could they be friends?

"The duchess is smart enough to be knowing Nathak is only wanting her seat on the council," Inko said.

"And her power," Sir Caleb added. "And her land. I'd wager that's Esek's goal in seeking to marry Lady Averella. Carm Duchy has traditionally controlled everything north of Mahanaim. If Nitsa never remarries, whoever marries Lady Averella is her heir."

Achan slapped away another mosquito. "Bran Rennan."

"Who?"

"Sir Rigil's squire. He and Lady Averella are to be wed. Sir Rigil told me."

Sir Caleb clicked his tongue. "That young squire with the red face? Who is his father?"

"How should I know? He's from Carmine."

"Then his father is no one of importance," Sir Caleb said.

"And why should *that* matter?" Sparrow's bossy voice spiked above the others.

Achan had thought the boy asleep. He shivered. His pants were still damp. He hoped it wouldn't get too cold tonight. The moisture from the ground seemed to rise into the rank air.

Sir Gavin rebuked Sparrow's concern. "Nitsa can't let her heir marry the first young buck she lays her eyes on."

Sparrow huffed. "Well, maybe the duchess wishes her daughter would marry for love."

A brief silence settled over the group, then deep laughter burst out from Sir Caleb. Achan didn't find it humorous. He had lost Gren to an arranged marriage.

"Don't be too skeptical." Sir Gavin's voice cut through the chuckles. "I don't doubt Nitsa capable of such mercy."

Pecking trilled above from two places. Achan pushed the surrounding fear from his mind, wanting to get back to the subject. "So you think Lord Nathak and Esek were plotting for Carmine, each trying to marry their way into controlling it?"

"So it would seem," Sir Gavin said. "But Nitsa is smarter than Nathak. Unfortunately, the rest of Er'Rets bought into his treason. After King Axel's death, we gave testimony before the Council. Kenton and his men had set up two of my men, my generals, claiming they were the assassins or had at least been involved with the stray who did kill them. I fought all I could for them, but no one would hear me. The evidence pointed to them and they were convicted."

"Your friends on Ice Island." Sparrow's raspy voice always sounded like he had a cold.

Achan considered the purpose of their journey into Darkness. "And we're going to free them?"

"That and more. There are over two hundred and forty Old Kingsguard soldiers on Ice Island. All my men, all falsely imprisoned over the years, most for being a stray at the time of King Axel's murder. They will be the start of your army, Achan. And we need an army if we're to turn this kingdom back into Arman's hands before it's too late."

"Before Esek becomes king," Sparrow said.

Two hundred and forty men didn't sound like much of an army to Achan, but it was better than just these three knights, he supposed.

Sir Gavin snorted. "Esek is the least of our concerns. The more Er'Rets turns from Arman and worships the false gods of fables, the more people kill and murder and hate and serve themselves, the more Darkness will consume this land. It grew at King Axel's death and it grows still. When I stood in the western watchtower in the Mahanaim stronghold five months ago, the Evenwall reached the sixth buttress. Yesterday, the mist had drifted within feet of the tower itself, five buttresses closer. 'Tis moving two hands' breadths a month."

Darkness was growing? Achan felt the blood draining from his face. "Can it be stopped?"

"Only one man can push back Darkness, Achan. Arman called him to this divine purpose. Darkness has spread these past years because the truth was hidden from Arman's chosen. But I knew he lived. For if he had truly died, Prince Oren—being next in line for king—would have begun to hear Arman's voice. But Arman did not speak to Prince Oren. He spoke to you."

Sir Gavin's words knotted Achan's stomach. "So it's be king and everything is great, or don't be king and the world is consumed by Darkness forever? Nice choice."

"Darkness will continue to grow no matter what you decide. Only when the Light grows stronger than the Dark will Darkness retreat. You must rally the people. Remind them who created them and why. Take them back to truth. Others are ready and willing to step in as king, should you refuse. Esek. Lord Nathak. Though they will not push back Darkness. The choice falls to you. Will you lead us?"

A silence descended upon the camp the darkness seemed to magnify. Achan didn't respond. He couldn't. The idea was so farfetched. First, that there might be only one god, and second, that this God had chosen Achan to push back Darkness, the magnificent curse of Er'Rets. Him. Achan. Barely a man himself.

He spoke in a whisper. "Why didn't Lord Nathak kill me when he had the chance?"

"I know not, lad," Sir Gavin said. "I can only guess he was afraid to, knowing who you truly are."

Achan recalled odd encounters with Lord Nathak: times when he'd sensed fear, how Lord Nathak had ordered the guards and Esek to go easy, to not kill him. "He's afraid of me."

"Perhaps he feared *the gods* would smite him if he destroyed you," Sir Caleb said, a lilt to his voice.

"That is what I'd be fearing if I was being him," Inko said.

Achan didn't doubt that.

"He had to," Sir Caleb said soberly. "If the true heir died, the gift would pass to Prince Oren, revealing Esek as a fake. His plan would work only while Achan still lived."

"Perhaps," Sir Gavin said. "Or perhaps he served a darker master who wanted you alive for some evil purpose." His comment brought a moment of silence over the camp.

Achan's mind reeled. Who might this mysterious blood-voicer be? Someone strong. Stronger and viler than Nathak. Could it be Macoun Hadar, the old wizard who had tried to use Sparrow? Or someone worse than him? Achan wriggled around, pulling off his doublet. He settled back onto the bed-roll and draped the heavy leather over his head, hoping it would keep the mosquitoes off his face.

He lay still, breathing deeply, telling himself the stench wasn't so bad. A vision grew in his mind. He was flying, riding a giant moth over the treetops. The moth arched into a sudden dive. Achan squeezed with his knees and grabbed for the saddle horn. No saddle! Only tufts of coarse hair. He grappled, lost his balance, and fell.

He sat up, pulse drumming in his head. His doublet slid into his lap. Had that been Darkness pulling at his mind? It had seemed so real.

Achan lay down and tried to focus his thoughts, not wanting that to happen again. Sir Gavin and Sir Caleb whispered to his left. If only Achan could use his supposed great power he could see into Lord Nathak's and Sir Kenton's minds and learn the truth of the past. He could find out who this mysterious chief bloodvoicer was who sought to divide Er'Rets.

Currently, all he could do with his bloodvoice was shield his mind. He wanted to practice, but not what Sir Caleb had suggested, letting one person into his mind at a time. He wanted to practice reaching into the minds of others. He had done it by accident several times. But only when someone else had initiated conversation. So how did one initiate? And if Achan went wandering into someone else's mind, who would guard his?

He tuned in to the sounds of the forest. The pecking, the occasional hiss, a rattling, the buzzing of hundreds of mosquitoes. Achan closed his eyes and pictured himself standing guard over his mind. If he couldn't leave his guard post, perhaps he could at least open the door and peek out. He imagined himself doing just that. He opened a steel door in his mind but stood on the threshold, should anyone try to enter.

The results were instant. Hundreds of voices spoke, many in foreign tongues. He could hear Sir Gavin and Sir Caleb, and when he tuned in on their conversation, their voices magnified. He shifted his concentration to Inko, who dwelled over how they'd manage to go north. Achan smiled. The knights did not seem to sense him.

A small thought distracted him from the knights. Hunger. A bird. It glided through the dark sky, over the shadowed outlines of trees, scanning the ground for its master, for it had news and wanted its reward. What news? Who was its master?

These thoughts faded when Achan realized something else: even in the Darkness this bird could see! Incredible.

A sniffle perked Achan's senses. He focused on the sorrowful sound. Crying. Alone. Muffled. Not wanting to be heard. Was someone hurt? In danger? Lost?

I cannot do this anymore. The voice belonged to Sparrow. *I do not know why you have allowed this to go on. The task is too difficult. I want to go home. I miss my family. Please, Arman, help me get home.*

Achan withdrew and rolled over, peering through the dark in Sparrow's direction, ashamed for intruding on the boy's mind. But Sparrow's words confused him. Sparrow was a stray. Strays were orphans. What family could he possibly miss? And why had he come along if he hadn't wanted to? Had someone forced him? Achan's stomach began to boil, slowly at first, then violently. He pulled his fingers into fists and squeezed.

If that little fox was still working for Macoun Hadar . . .

5

Achan awoke choking. Someone was dragging him by the neck of his tunic, off his bedroll and onto the moist ground. The wet soil seeped into his britches. He gasped for air. Sparrow. Macoun Hadar had sent the lad to kill him. The traitor! Achan grasped the spongy moss, searching for his sword.

Pig snout! He'd left it drying in the tree.

His fingers found the hand on his tunic. He pried—

"Your Highness!" Sir Caleb released Achan's shirt and clamped a hand on his shoulder. "Get your sword. Quick."

Achan paused to catch his breath, surveying where he'd last seen Sparrow. The boy pressed against a shadowy tree trunk, his already pale face ghostly in the dim light.

Heart pounding, Achan watched the knights scramble about, packing up gear. "What's wrong?"

"Do as I ask," Sir Caleb said. "Quickly please."

Achan clambered to his feet and the tree that held Eagan's Elk and its scabbard. He pulled the belt around his waist then froze.

He could see, albeit dimly, yet no torch burned in their camp. He whipped around. Three balls of flame danced on the dark horizon, obscured by gnarled trees, drawing nearer as if someone were carrying them up the game trail.

Achan latched his belt around his waist. "Who is it?"

"Ebens." Inko strapped on his sword, leaving his bow in the tree.

Achan rubbed the sleep from his eyes. "What are—"

"Giants," Sparrow said.

Giants. The word winded him. In the past few months, so much myth had been confirmed reality: the existence of Ôwr, the Kingsword, bloodvoices. And now giants.

Maybe Arman was the one God after all.

The knights stowed the packs in the branches and stood, swords drawn, facing the game trail. Surely they weren't going to fight. Achan considered himself brave enough but saw no reason to take on one giant, let alone three. "Uh . . . shouldn't we leave? Escape or something?"

"No point with Ebens on our tail, and we can't have them telling others they've seen us." A vein pulsed in Sir Gavin's forehead. "Besides, there are only three."

Achan focused on the line of torches, which now seemed but a breath away. "But . . . three giants."

"Correct." Sir Caleb threaded his arm through his shield. "Mercenaries. Sent to kill you."

Fitting. People had been trying to kill Achan for the past few weeks. Now that his true identity had been revealed, he'd best get used to it. But how had they found their camp?

And just how *giant* were giants, anyway?

"They'll likely try to burn us out." Sir Caleb lifted his sword to the edge of his shield. "Watch for fire and be ready."

Achan drew Eagan's Elk. Sparrow gripped his little sword, fingers interlaced as if to pray, and held it straight out in front, as if he were stretching to see how far he could reach.

Achan sidestepped to the boy. "Ever held a sword?"

Sparrow's wide eyes darted to Achan's. He took a breath as if to argue, then deflated and shook his head.

Great. "Best stay back, then."

"Look sharp!"

Achan crouched at Sir Gavin's warning. A single flame fell through the air, partially obscured by the twisted branches. It landed in the canopy above and smoldered.

"What now?" They'd lost their chance to flee undetected.

"Hold your position," Sir Gavin said.

Sir Caleb glanced at the smoking branches. "I doubt the trees will burn. They're too damp."

A reason to thank Arman for the slime. Then two more burning arrows struck the canopy, producing thick, putrid smoke that coiled around them. Achan tugged his tunic over his nose, but the smoke clouded his vision, diminishing the glow from the giant's torches. His eyes watered.

"Be staying low." Inko gripped his longsword with both hands. "It's not being so smoky near the ground."

Smoke furled around Achan until he couldn't see. He coughed, the rank fumes invading his senses. He sank to his haunches and found clear air near the ground. Three sets of boots stood before him, lit by a pale yellow glow from ahead.

Sir Gavin's voice burst in Achan's mind. *Stay back, lad.*

Madness! How could they fight giants blindly?

Wood splintered. A tree, trunk and all, slapped into the soppy soil to Achan's left. He gripped Eagan's Elk tighter and peered under the golden, swarming haze. Sparrow cowered behind a stump to his right, the knights stood straight ahead, and—Achan squinted and leaned forward—something moved beyond the knights. Side to side. Swinging.

The knights held their position. Squishing footsteps set Achan's arm hair dancing. He hopped backward, lost his balance, and put a hand on the moist ground to steady himself. More steps squished from the direction of the swinging . . .

Club.

Two sets of thick, pale legs stepped into view, bare and tattooed but not much bigger than a man's. Where was the third giant? Surely the giants couldn't see through the smoke. The knights crouched. Achan inched back a step. A sharp branch poked into his thigh. He stifled a cry just as a high-pitched battle song rose above it.

"Lee-lee-lee-lee-lee-lee-lee-lee-lee-lee!"

Mother! Sparrow's voice surged in Achan's mind. *Where have you been? Are you well? We are being attacked by giants!*

Achan spun around, looking for the boy. He no longer hid behind the stump.

A woman's voice, kind and oddly familiar answered. *Where are you, dearest? Are giants in the Council chambers?*

What in blazes? Sparrow had told Achan his parents were dead. So who was he calling Mother?

A guttural scream tore Achan away from Sparrow's curious exchange. The pale legs charged. The knights answered with a war cry. All three struck low, from back guard, slicing their swords through the giants' legs like scythes harvesting wheat. Achan cringed as horrifying screams ripped through the air.

The giants fell like the trees, their pale, hulking bodies slamming into the soggy moss.

That was it? If these three could defeat giants so easily, perhaps two hundred and forty more like them really would be a formidable army.

The giants' torches lay spluttering but for one distant flame. Achan strained to see under the smoke. Past the fallen giants, across the clearing, a white-haired, cornstalk of a man squatted, all limbs. Pelts covered little of his body. His milky white skin glowed as if his blood was made of moonbeams. He held a spear in one hand, a torch in the other. He stabbed the torch into the moss and withdrew an axe from a sheath on his leg.

It wasn't over.

Sir Gavin! I see the third one.

Aye, lad. We're watching him.

The giant tipped back his head and yelled another trilling battle cry. "Lee-lee-lee-lee-lee-lee-lee-lee-lee-lee!" He sprang off the ground, taking long leaps into the clearing, the wet moss squishing with each step of his fearless charge.

A grunt and the clash of metal made Achan jump. He stared into the haze backlit by the distant torch. The silhouettes of four men fought, three against one much taller. The foggy shape of Sir Gavin's long hair and beard flew about. The lanky shadow parried each blow with the crook of his axe and kicked out a long leg that sent Inko's figure flying.

Sir Caleb yelled, drawing Achan's gaze to the shadow whose hair sprung atop his head like a tuft of grass. The giant met Sir Caleb's blows with his spear.

The knights attacked ruthlessly. Achan couldn't help but admire the giant's speed. For being so tall, Achan imagined he'd move slower.

The giant's spear suddenly cracked under Sir Caleb's blow. Seconds later the giant howled. He crumpled to reveal the shadow of Inko, cylindrical hair shaped like a wooden drum.

"Who sent you?" Sir Gavin yelled.

The raspy breathing of a dying eben was the only answer. Achan inched over the lichen until the men came into view. Sir Gavin crouched on the giant's right, blade held to the pale throat. Sir Caleb and Inko stood panting on the giant's left side.

Sir Gavin pressed a knee on the giant's chest. "Who?"

The giant's ragged breath seemed to consume all his effort, but he blinked slowly and turned his dark eyes to Achan, his voice a raspy growl. "Tee saplaway sen katla sar."

The intensity in that gaze shook Achan's knees. The man had a black insignia inked onto his forehead, three lines, each thicker than the first.

"I *know* why you've come," Sir Gavin said. "I want to know who sent you."

"Faluk san."

Suddenly, all was still.

"Achan?" Sir Gavin stood. "Answer me, lad."

"I'm here." Sir Gavin turned around and Achan asked, "Lord Falkson? Is that who he means?"

"Falkson is Lord of Barth. You've seen him at Council."

Achan remembered the stoic, grey-skinned man. "He is working for Esek?"

"So it would seem."

Achan motioned to the other giants, trying not to look at their severed legs, though his eyes kept focusing there. "Was that your idea?"

Sir Gavin's white hair and beard still blended in with the smoky haze. "Strategy worked well, if you ask me."

"Too well." Sir Caleb's voice came from the smoke cloud on Achan's other side. "It was a slaughter and ignoble."

Sir Gavin puffed a short breath out his nose. "And attempting to burn us alive is good form?"

Sir Caleb didn't answer. His body came into view as he stepped closer. "Boy, where is your sword?"

Achan wheeled around to meet Sparrow's pale face.

"Uh . . ." Sparrow turned to look back through the smoke. Sir Caleb gripped the boy's arm and walked where Sparrow had glanced, their steps squishing into the soil as they vanished in the haze. Achan could hear Sir Caleb's lecture.

"Never drop your weapon. I don't care how scared you are. Never leave yourself unguarded or treat your blade with such disrespect."

Inko cleaned his sword in the turf and sheathed it. "I am not understanding how they are finding us. Perhaps it is not only our wolf who is being using his nose?"

Achan thought of the bird whose eyes he'd seen through. It had been bringing word to its master. Had the bird been a spy for the giants? He scanned the smoldering canopy overhead but could see nothing else. He decided to keep the thought to himself for now.

The knights piled the three Eben bodies atop one another and set their clothes aflame.

"We need to move. Get your things." Sir Gavin lifted the torch the giant had left burning in the ground and held it high. Orange light spilled over the smoky clearing. Caleb and Inko grabbed the other torches. The orange flames lit their faces in a more normal light than the green sulfur one from before.

With nothing to carry, Achan stayed put, awed and slightly horrified at the Great Whitewolf. Sparrow sidled over, small knapsack slung across his pudgy chest so it settled over his left hip. Face ashen, bleary eyes wide, he stared at the slain giants.

"You all right?" Achan asked.

Sparrow nodded and said in a watery voice, "Your speech has improved. How do your cheeks feel?"

"Better."

"You should not have taken off your bandages yet."

Achan stiffened, not wanting a lecture from a baby who still cried to his mother. A mother he wasn't supposed to have.

Sir Caleb handed the rope to Achan. "Hold on to this in case we need to put out the torches."

Achan looped the end through his belt and handed it to Sparrow. Sir Gavin led them down the game trail into clear air.

"Sparrow? Who were you talking to when the giants attacked?" Achan kept his voice low but didn't care who heard. If Sparrow was a traitor, the sooner they discovered it, the better. He glanced over his shoulder. "You said your parents were dead."

The boy's eyes bulged. "You read my thoughts?"

"Didn't mean to. They floated into my head."

"Well, stop it. You do not belong in my head."

"But you were talking to your mother. Your *dead* mother?"

Sparrow scratched his ear. "S-sometimes I still t-talk to her, even though she passed on. Especially when, um . . . when I am scared."

"Touching, Sparrow. My heart weeps for your tragic loss. Yet I can't help but wonder how a dead woman can *answer*. For I heard her myself, and I know I've heard her before. She's very much alive. And a woman so gifted in bloodvoicing must be known to someone. Save me the trouble of asking around and tell me the truth."

Sparrow said nothing.

Achan pushed back a stiff branch until it snapped. He wanted to turn and pounce on Sparrow, wrestle the truth from him. He'd been deceived for so long, he wasn't about to allow anyone to deceive him again. Besides, the boy avoided conflict like Achan avoided a bath. It wouldn't take much to scare the truth from him.

No. Achan would wait and consult Sir Gavin. If Sparrow was up to trouble, Sir Gavin would know what to do.

They hiked a brisk pace for hours. The torches helped. But it was maddening to travel so far without seeing the sun or moon. Achan's feet screamed as much as his mind. What time of day might it be in Sitna? What might Gren be doing?

His chest tightened. Gren, his childhood friend back in Sitna, had suffered an arranged marriage to Riga Hoff, the lazy son of a merchant. A month had not yet passed since their wedding. Not much could have changed, unless . . . Achan squeezed his hands into fists. If Riga harmed Gren in any way, he'd forever regret it.

Another pretty face drifted into his mind: Lady Tara Livna of Tsaftown. Unless something went wrong, he'd see Lady Tara soon enough. How much Tara looked like the goddess Cetheria. A crown of ivory braids. Eyes bluer than forget-me-nots. Achan smiled, recalling her beauty and spunk.

He looked into her eyes as if she stood before him. The gemlike sparkle of her gaze drenched him in awe. Her skin was gold leaf. She held a spear, which she drew back and lobbed at his chest. It pierced his flesh, jolting his heart. He stared at it, gasping, dumfounded to find himself still standing. He grabbed the shaft with two hands and pulled. It wouldn't budge.

Lady Tara giggled, her voice like a musical brook. She sauntered toward him and ran her fingertips along the spear. *"Shall I free you?"*

Pain shot through Achan's shoulder. He blinked. Darkness surrounded him, lit by the faint orange glow of firelight. Where was he? Had that been a dream?

The rope at Achan's waist tugged, pulling him tighter against a hard surface. He reached out and found a fat, sticky tree. He was in Darkness with the knights, running from Esek.

Sir Gavin called out from the circle of torchlight, "All right back there?"

"Are you hurt, Achan?" Sparrow's voice. Behind him.

"Uh . . ." Achan stepped around the protruding tree. "There's a tree here, Sparrow. Watch yourself."

"Just a tree, Sir Gavin," Sparrow yelled and the rope tugged Achan along again.

Sir Gavin Whitewolf.

Achan perked up. Sir Gavin was knocking, wanting to bloodvoice. Achan concentrated on opening the door like he'd done last night, allowing only Sir Gavin inside.

Would he know if he succeeded? He wanted to tell Sir Gavin about Cetheria—no, that had been Lady Tara, hadn't it?

Achan, Sir Gavin said. *Don't answer, simply listen. 'Tis vital you learn to bloodvoice straight away. I've no doubt you'll succeed. Our connection now is perfect. You've opened your mind only to me. I can sense your shields. Now you must learn to speak without dropping your shields. Duplicate yourself, like Caleb's guard explanation, leaving a man to guard your mind. Let the other speak. Cough if you understand.*

Cough? Why the secrecy? Did Sir Gavin suspect someone? Sparrow perhaps? Achan considered the little fox on his heels and coughed.

Good. Now do as I described.

Achan took a deep breath. He imagined himself standing sentry before the door to his mind, Eagan's Elk raised, ready to defend. He pictured himself stepping to the side. Instead of the guard Achan moving, another Achan stepped out of the first. The two stood side by side in his mind, looking at one another.

Go on, then, the first Achan said to the second. *I've got this.*

Achan smiled. He always had been a quick learner.

Twice before, Achan had passed through one mind and into another. Sparrow called it jumping. Achan had jumped through Sparrow to see Macoun Hadar speak with Lord Nathak. Then, when the Council of Seven had gone to deliberate as to who would be king, Achan jumped through Sir Gavin to watch the debate through Prince Oren's eyes.

Both times Sparrow and Sir Gavin had been watching already. Achan had merely touched them, used their energy, cheated really, like peeking over their shoulder to use what they had already accomplished.

This time he'd need to use his own strength. He hoped he wouldn't faint as Sparrow often did. Concentrating on Sir Gavin, the second Achan ventured out.

Achan now walked at the front of the line, staring out through Sir Gavin's eyes into the black void beyond, arm holding a burning torch above his head, dodging the occasional slimy, black branch. Sir Gavin's pack and shield hung heavy over his aching shoulders. The rope at his waist jerked, forcing him to stop.

"Gavin!" Sir Caleb shouted from behind.

Wait. Hadn't Sir Caleb been ahead of him?

"Aye?" Sir Gavin wheeled around, looking back to Sir Caleb, who stood over a body.

Achan's body.

"Achan's fallen. Fainted or something."

Achan wheezed, the sour smell of the forest overwhelming. He lay on the wet soil. His elbow stung. His hip too. He rolled onto his knees. Sparrow, Inko, and Sir Caleb stood over him, faces shadowed in the flickering torchlight.

Sir Gavin cut between Inko and Sparrow, torch wavering in his hand. "What happened?"

Achan rubbed his elbow. "I reached out, but forgot I was walking."

Sir Gavin burst into deep laughter. "No, Achan. That's not how to message. You were watching. Never watch and walk at the same time. Forgive me. Save yourself more bruises, and we'll try again once we've stopped."

No one asked any questions, thankfully. Achan had never fainted—not without the aid of a wound or tonic, anyway. It seemed weak. He hoped Sir Gavin could explain what he'd done wrong so it would never happen again.

Another thought shifted to the forefront of his mind. "Sir Gavin, I also saw Cetheria. She stabbed me, but I didn't die."

"Saw her where?" The knight reached out his hand.

Achan gripped his wrist and pulled himself up. His elbow throbbed. He must have scraped it when he fell. "Last time, when we stopped. Before I hit the tree. She stabbed me in the chest."

"Already it is happening, Gavin. I have been feeling my mind to be wandering also. We should be turning back, going to Light as fast as our legs can be carrying us."

"We are not going back, Inko. Achan, I want you to open your mind, like you did before, shields up, open to me. Then I want you to include everyone here. Do it now."

Achan repeated the process of duplicating himself to guard his mind. He looked from face to face and felt a connection tug in his mind.

Good, Sir Gavin said. *Now, we keep moving. Caleb, give us a little talk about Lord Falkson and Barth, so we all know who we are dealing with. Ask questions to see that no one is drifting.*

Well, the people of Barth worship Barthos, god of the earth . . .

With that, Sir Gavin turned and pulled them onward through the twisting black trees.

They made camp in a rocky area. Sir Gavin and Achan took first watch.

Achan settled onto a jagged boulder beside Sir Gavin. He looked up to the sky and noticed, for the first time, a variation in the blackness. A twisted stripe that was darker that the rest. A tree branch, perhaps? "How do you know the way?"

"I've always had a keen sense of smell." Sir Gavin put out the torch. Darkness sank over Achan like a shroud he couldn't lift. The knight chuckled softly. "Aw, that's not the full truth of it. I use my bloodvoice to share the senses of nearby beasts."

Achan recalled seeing through the bird's eyes. "You can do that?"

"I recall you did it once."

Achan tensed. "I did?" Had Sir Gavin known he'd been experimenting last night?

"When you killed your first deer."

"Ah." Achan shivered at the memory of sharing the doe's mind, tasting the bitterness of the tree bark it had been eating. It hadn't been a fair way to hunt. "Is that how you got your name?" Sir Gavin's stray surname was Lukos, after the big wolves that lived in the Chowmah Mountains.

"Sort of. I grew up in Tsaftown. We used sleds pulled by dogs to travel over snow. My lead dog was a wolf whose mother I'd killed when she attacked a friend. The pup hung around and I trained her. Chion. My white wolf. She was a good dog. Taught me much."

Achan thought of Dilly and Peg, the goats he'd tended in Sitna. He missed their companionship. "Where is she now?"

"Died years ago. I never replaced her."

Achan sensed a heavy grief that matched Sir Gavin's tone. He shifted his weight on the unforgiving rock. "How does sharing the animals' senses help you?"

"They are my eyes, nose, and ears here. I'm able to peek from one mind to another, using what I need to guide us. We follow an old road that once stretched from the south shore of the second Reshon Gate all the way to Mirrorstone. There the road divides: north across the sandbars to Melas and Allown Duchy or west across the rocky plains into Barth."

"So we're in Barth Duchy now?"

"We're in Nahar Duchy, in part of Nahar Forest. The volcanic rock of Barth Duchy reaches into the forest a bit. You can't see, but south of where we stand, the Cela Mountains separate us from Cela Duchy, where Jaelport and Meneton lie."

"What other cities are in Barth Duchy?" Achan asked.

"Only Barth. Barthians keep to themselves as much as Magos or Cherem, though they have a treaty with Jaelport."

Achan would never sign a treaty with the Hamartano family, for he didn't trust them to keep it. Not that he had accepted his role in this king business. But trust would have to be earned before he made a treaty with anyone.

Sparrow flitted to the front of his thoughts. "Sir Gavin." Achan lowered his voice to a whisper. "I don't trust Sparrow."

"Vrell? Why ever not?"

"Trivial things, really, that add up to something amiss. Last night as I bedded down I overheard him crying, saying he 'couldn't do this anymore' and wanted to go home. Then, when the giants attacked, I overheard him bloodvoice his mother— and she bloodvoiced back. When I confronted him, he lied. And I know that woman spoke to me when I first found my bloodvoice."

"Most strange. But if Vrell can bloodvoice, 'tis logical one of his parents can."

"But he's a *stray*. He swears his parents are dead."

Sir Gavin inhaled a long breath through his nose, perhaps joined to a wild animal's mind as it hunted. "I'll talk to him."

PART 2

ENEMIES

6

Vrell stumbled over rocky soil. "Sir Gavin? Achan?" Where had they gone? She stretched out her hands, afraid of walking into a sharp branch. The darkness pressed against her skin, her very eyes. "Hello?"

"Here, my lady."

The familiar hiss of Khai Mageia's voice chased a chill up Vrell's arms. How had he found her? She stopped, turned, scanning the darkness for any hint of light.

A heavy hand grabbed her shoulder, and Khai's voice growled in her ear, "Surprise!"

Vrell sucked in a breath that reached to her toes. Her eyes flashed opened to reveal Sir Caleb's shaggy head bent over her.

"Wh-what? Is it Khai?"

"No. It's time to rise, Vrell. We must get moving."

Joyful heart! It was only another dream. Heart still pounding, Vrell rolled up her bed and set it and her satchel on the edge of camp. Keeping the torchlight in view, she crept away to her own private privy as the knights packed up.

Darkness sickened her. How many more twisted visions would stress her heart? Everything was dead, useless for food or medicinal purposes. And how long could she keep her secret without being caught? Achan already suspected her of lying. If she was not careful, he would suspect her of treason, as well. His animosity burned into her mind like standing too near a blazing fire. She hoped he would let his suspicions go. Though he would not make a very wise king if he did.

But maybe Achan had already acted on his suspicions. Yesterday, when he fell, it was clear Sir Gavin had been training him in bloodvoicing. Excluding Vrell. Did Sir Gavin distrust her? Did he want to keep her from learning the technique he had been teaching Achan?

She could see the logic, no matter how vexing. Had she been in Sir Gavin's boots, she would do the same. Who was she to them? A stray healer who had recently left the service of their enemy. Not exactly a person to trust. The tops of her ears tickled. She pressed her hands over them as her mother's knock came again.

Lady Nitsa Amal.

A tear rolled down Vrell's cheek. She held the curtain in place around her mind, keeping Mother blocked out. Oh, how she wanted to tell Mother everything. But Achan had overheard them last night. Uncertain whether it had been Vrell's error or Achan's strength, she could not risk it again.

She relieved herself as quickly as possible, holding her breath and trembling, keeping her vision locked onto the torch glow back at camp. She finished and started back, squeezing between two pitchy branches.

Why not confess? Certainly they would understand. Achan respected Bran and would likely be honored to watch over his friend's betrothed. But so many had lied to Achan, tricked him, used him. She could not bear Achan thinking ill of her, even for a moment.

Yet he thought ill of her now. An explanation might clear everything up.

No. She wiped the tear away. Achan suspected Vrell Sparrow, the nearly fifteen-year-old stray boy who did not exist. He knew nothing of Lady Averella Amal, the seventeen-year-old woman in hiding, and it would stay that way. If Lady Averella ever met Achan, it would be under vastly different circumstances.

Her ears tickled again. *Lady Nitsa Amal.*

A twig snapped behind Vrell. She whirled around. How she hated this horrible place! The idea of creatures she could not see lurking . . .

Crack.

Vrell froze, straining to hear further noise. Something *was* out there.

Not caring what branches scratched her, she ran back to the rocky clearing. Sir Gavin hoisted Inko's pack up over the Barthian's shoulders. Achan stood gaping at Sir Caleb, who was showing off with his sword and shield.

Vrell considered mentioning the sound, but a sudden green spark flew over her head and stopped above the clearing, swelling into a glowing orb.

Achan drew his sword and held it before his face.

"Circle up!" Sir Gavin backed into the clearing, eyes fixed on the trees.

The urgency in the old knight's voice trilled Vrell's heart. More ebens? Or could this be another illusion Darkness conjured to snare her?

Sir Caleb pulled Achan between him and Sir Gavin and lifted his blade toward the forest. Inko shrugged off his pack and bow. A second and third orb shot out from the trees. The three knights turned their backs to Achan, blocking him in.

"Boy!" Inko waved Vrell forward as two more sparks flew above her head. She scurried toward the men. Inko pulled her inside with Achan.

The orbs formed a wide circle overhead, hovering and lighting the rocky clearing with a green glow.

"What is it?" Achan asked.

Inko drew his sword. "Sakin Magos."

But Sir Gavin's translation meant more to Vrell. "Black knights."

She sucked in a sharp breath. Her father had spoken of such mages when she was little. In fact, it was rumored at court that Sir Nongo—

A knight clad in black armor stalked out from the forest and stopped under one of the eerie orbs. Another knight advanced, identical to the first. Vrell clutched Achan's arm and twisted around to see five knights circling them, each standing under an orb.

Achan squeezed between Inko and Sir Caleb and raised Eagan's Elk. "Best draw your sword, Sparrow. This is no time to let fear win."

Vrell's hand flitted around her waist until it landed on the hilt of her sword. She had owned the weapon for only two days and had no idea how to use it. Still, the pointed piece of metal was better than nothing.

"Be wary of their appearance." Sir Gavin rocked from foot to foot. "They can be both illusion and solid."

Impressive illusion. The green light cast a sinister glow over the black armor. It had the dreamlike quality of some of Vrell's nightmares, but none of those had lasted this long before switching streams. This had to be a real attack.

"We are coming only for the marked one," one of the knights said in a thick accent. Barthian? "We are having no quarrel with any other."

"If you take our prince, you start a quarrel," Sir Caleb said. "So we might as well save ourselves time in chasing you down and fight now."

The black knight drew his sword. "Then be letting us fight."

An oily voice from Vrell's left yelled, "Phaino takmak!"

A gowzal's cry split the night. A green speck flew from one of the orbs and swelled, taking the shape of the flying rat bird and soaring toward Sir Gavin.

"Ignore it!" Sir Gavin shouted.

The black knights advanced. Five against three, they were evenly matched only if she and Achan fought. Achan had already made his choice—he could certainly hold his own. But Vrell did not know what to do.

The glowing gowzal soared into the cluster of Old Kingsguards, through Sir Gavin and through Vrell's torso. She yelled but felt nothing. An illusion?

Swords clashed around her. Sir Caleb screamed a battle cry. Inko grunted. The black knights drew back slowly, pulling the Old Kingsguardsmen away, exposing Vrell. Before her, Inko fought a black knight whose helmet covered half his face, allowing his short, coiled, black beard to hang free. To her right, Sir

Gavin fought a man with a similar beard. Sir Caleb, sword in one hand, shield in the other, fought two more bearded black knights. Her eyes widened as Sir Caleb swung his shield and stabbed his blade. He pushed his opponents back, but his movement left a wide gap in Vrell's sanctuary.

The fifth knight stalked between Sir Gavin's opponent and one of Sir Caleb's, as if invisible to all but Vrell. Dressed differently from the others, he wore black plate armor and a full helmet. The flat-topped, black cylinder had a scalloped crown and ribbed metal wings over each ear. Dark eyes glared through a slotted visor. A gowzal's head was stain-engraved in silver onto his breastplate.

Vrell clutched Achan's sleeve with a shaky hand. He pushed her behind him, eyes locked on the menacing knight, hilt gripped with both hands, rocking slightly from one foot to the other. Vrell squatted, holding her breath and cringing as blades clashed around her.

The black knight darted in at Achan with a small jab, which Achan deflected easily. The knight inched back. Achan stepped toward him.

The knight slowly drew Achan away. Bit by bit, the pair turned, until Achan faced Vrell. Only then did the black knight press forward.

"Don't let him drive you into the trees!" Sir Caleb yelled.

Achan swung his blade as if each stroke meant life or death, growling like a cougar. He stifled a cut from high guard with the flat of his blade, which brought him close to the knight, their weapons locked above their heads.

Achan yelled and kneed the knight in his engraved breast-plate. The knight stumbled back a step. Achan seized that moment to ram his shoulder into his opponent.

They tumbled to the ground, rolling about as if wrestling. The black knight's armor grated against the rocks.

Achan came to the top and tore off one of the knight's gauntlets. The knight punched Achan's cheek with his other, still armored, hand. Achan screamed and bashed the empty gauntlet against the knight's helmet. The knight struck Achan in the face again, and Achan fell back.

A sick thud and a grunt drew Vrell away from Achan. Inko staggered back, gripping his head in one hand, his sword arm drooping. Plum-sized rocks flew up and whacked him like raindrops from below. Inko's head lolled back, and he slumped to the ground.

Inko's attacker turned to stare at Vrell, then raised his sword. She stifled a scream and crawled backward. Three stones hovered behind her attacker's head. The black knight's coiled beard shifted, revealing a set of grimy, sneering teeth.

Memories of her father training his guard flitted through her mind. *Never be caught on your knees,* he had told the young trainees time and again. Vrell stood and lifted her weapon in trembling hands.

The black knight advanced, laughing, and flicked one finger forward.

One of the stones soared toward Vrell as if thrown. She lifted her sword to block but missed. The rock struck her shoulder.

The other two rocks zinged forward. Vrell ducked, but the rocks changed course and pelted her ear and temple. Gritting her teeth at the pain, she squeezed her sword and charged. The black knight stepped aside, causing Vrell to stumble. She spun around only to be hit in the forearm by another rock.

The knight swung at Vrell's neck. Vrell lifted her sword to block. The weapons met with a clang, sparing her death but knocking her sword away. It clattered to the rocks and left her fingers throbbing.

Oh, she wished Jax mi Katt, her giant friend, had given her even one lesson.

The black knight pursed his lips and blew. A ribbon of green light spewed from his mouth and flowed toward Vrell. She backpedaled, looking for her sword. It had landed several paces away, behind Sir Gavin and his opponent.

The light curled around her waist as if to hook her. She froze, waiting to see if it had done anything, but the ribbon of light continued to snake round her like coiling twine. Another rock shot toward Vrell. She lifted her hands to block her face, and the stone clipped her knuckles. She cried out.

"The light is only being an illusion, boy. Don't be giving in to it." Inko struggled to a sitting position.

Vrell broke through the green strands and sprinted toward her sword, but the black knight cut off her path. Just as another rock rose between them, one clunked off the back of the knight's helmet.

"Hey!" Achan pitched a rock. "You only fight little boys or what?" His first attacker writhed on the ground behind him, the visor of his helmet dented into his eyes.

Blood and dirt covered one side of Achan's face, and his tangled hair hung loose. He raised his sword like he wasn't the least bit winded.

Vrell released a shaky sigh as the knight approached Achan. She marveled at Achan's confidence. At sixteen—nearly two years her junior—Achan considered himself the man and Vrell the scrawny boy.

Sir Gavin and Sir Caleb were still fighting, but now Sir Gavin fought two opponents and Sir Caleb fought one. Sir Caleb plunged his sword into the torso of his attacker, and the black knight vanished in a puff of green smoke. Only an ebony gowzal remained once the smoke cleared. It squawked and flew over Sir Caleb's head. Sir Caleb crouched, watching the bird, waiting with his blade beside the edge of his shield. The black knight reappeared behind him, and Sir Caleb spun around in time to block the knight's blade with his shield.

What magic was this?

Inko struggled to his feet and inched toward his sword on the ground a few paces away. Vrell scrambled after her own weapon and ran to the edge of the clearing in time to see Achan cut through the black knight who had been throwing rocks. He disappeared into a green mist and, with the cry of a gowzal, reappeared at the opposite edge of the forest.

Vrell no longer cared if she was discovered. *Mother! There is a battle. Black knights. What can I do?*

Stay back, dearest. A battle is no place for you. Can you hide?

Is there a way I can help? As soon as one is defeated, he turns to smoke and appears elsewhere. How can that be? Are they men or magic?

It is difficult to say with black knights. There may only be one. Some have the ability to duplicate themselves.

But surely only in illusion?

Yes, unless they have called on dark spirits to aid them. Then they can give their illusions physical form. Black knights use the darkest magic. Can you guess the leader? Does one appear stronger than the others?

Vrell peered around the tree. *I cannot tell good sword fighting from the bad. I—wait. Four of the knights look identical.*

They all have the same beard. The fifth looks different, and he is on the ground, crawling toward the trees. Achan felled him.

The others are likely apparitions from a mage. Do you see another person, maybe standing a safe distance away?

Vrell scanned the tree line. A pale, raised hand and a set of eyes glinted in the green glow, back where she had made her privy. A sixth man, barely discernable in a long, hooded cape.

An unarmed man stands in the trees.

Does he see you? Move to a safe place, quickly!

Vrell darted back behind the pitchy tree truck.

I am going to step through your mind, Averella. I need you to focus on the unarmed man.

I understand. Fear prickled up Vrell's arms. Mother wanted to jump through her. Vrell had tried it before and failed. But Mother's strength far exceeded her own. What could Mother hope to accomplish by entering this mage's mind? *Master Hadar taught me of this technique.*

Very well. Prepare yourself, my love.

Vrell stepped around the tree and stared at the hooded man. She closed her eyes and pictured him. *I am ready.*

Sounds invaded. Swords clashed in the clearing. Men yelled and grunted. Boots skidded over rocks. But just as she had before, on the day Achan had jumped through her, she saw nothing, felt no different. Did this mean it was working? Vrell wanted to pray, but breaking concentration might ruin Mother's plan.

So she sensed a prayer, knowing in the back of her mind Arman was with her, holding her up, protecting her. Peace flooded her body, easing the sting of her bruises, silencing the sounds of battle. A song rose within, not from any instrument or voice she had ever known. A joyful song of hope swept around her, lifted her in its arms like pollen in the wind. She wanted to laugh, safe, free, and floating out of her body and up above the clearing.

"Vrell?" A hand pressed down on her shoulder, igniting sharp pain from a bruise there.

Her eyes flashed open. She lay under a large charcoal tree lit with faint yellow torchlight. The moist ground cushioned her rear and legs. Gnarly tree roots bit into back and shoulders.

A shadow loomed above, breathing heavily. She could not see his face. "Are you well? We almost lost you to the Veil."

Sir Gavin.

"Yes." A sharp root poked into Vrell's lower back, but she did not feel seriously injured.

"Who are you?" Sir Gavin asked.

"My memory is fine, sir. I am Vrell Sparrow, and we are in Darkness."

"Aye, but who are you really?"

Her breath snagged. "I . . . what?"

"Together you and I stormed the mage. We couldn't find his body. He must have had more men in the woods. Where'd you learn such a trick? I had been trying to battle his mind as I fought his apparition with my sword, but it wasn't until I had help that I could put an end to his mischief. Did Macoun teach you to storm?"

Vrell's heart lurched. Storm?

A torch flamed to life back in the clearing. Sir Caleb held it above Inko, who still lay on the ground.

Sir Gavin reached a hand down to Vrell. She gripped his calloused palm, and he pulled her to standing.

"Make no mistake," Sir Gavin said, "we'll talk more of this."

Vrell pushed past Sir Gavin and found her satchel at the edge of the clearing. She carried the bag to Inko's side, dug out her safflower salve, and tried to help him sit.

He shook his head. "Be seeing to the others, boy. I'm being fine."

She approached Sir Caleb, who had a gash over his left eye. He held his torch toward the forest. "See to the prince."

Of course. Vrell turned and found Achan propped against a tree on the edge of the clearing. She scurried to his side and knelt gingerly on the sharp rocks. "Are you hurt?"

His lips parted, baring a wide, toothy grin in his blood and dirt-covered face. "How'd you like yer firs' battle?"

"What makes you think it was my first?"

"Lucky guess?" Achan chuckled, then closed his eyes and moaned. The cut on his left cheek had been torn open.

"If it hurts, stop talking." With shaking hands, she opened her water jug and wetted a fresh cloth. She wanted to know what Mother had done, but forced the worry away for now. She dabbed the dirt and blood from around Achan's wound and grimaced at the sight of the swollen skin. She hoped it would not get infected. "For your information, Jax, Khai, and I met eben resistance on the journey from Walden's Watch."

Achan flinched at her touch. "And yeh hid 'hind a tree?"

Why did he always want to play? She acquiesced, only because his cheek looked incredibly painful. "*In* the tree, actually. Now be serious, Your Highness. Where else are you hurt?"

Achan groaned. "Sp'rrow. If yeh call me that one more time, I'll see that *yer* hurt."

"Just answer the question, stubborn boy."

Achan met her eyes and coughed out a laugh. "Me? I'm notta—"

"Look." Vrell nodded to Sir Caleb. "They are injured but will not hear of being treated until you are, so stop wasting time and let me help you so I may help them."

Achan lifted his right hand in front of his face. His dark, wet knuckles glistened in the distant torchlight. "M' hand *does* 'ting a bit."

"Sir Caleb," Vrell called. "The light, please?"

7

They journeyed over rocky terrain for hours listening to Sir Caleb talk on the sword and shield's strengths over the longsword alone. Achan's feet ached. Sharp pebbles poked into the soles of his boots. Sir Gavin wanted to get to Mirrorstone as quickly as possible. Achan didn't like the fact that more black knights might be shadowing them but could think of no better plan.

The terrain flattened. Sir Gavin stopped in a field carpeted in short, twiggy grass and urged they make camp in the open where no one could sneak up on them so easily. Did that even matter? In Achan's opinion, Darkness provided endless cover for anyone wanting to set up an ambush.

They laid out the bedrolls around a small, blue torchlight. Achan settled onto the stiff leather and nibbled a piece of dry meat. "I still don't understand what happened." He pictured

Eagan's Elk slicing through the black knight and the man vanishing into green smoke. "The first man I fought was flesh and blood. But the one who picked on Sparrow disappeared as I finished him."

"Deception," Sir Caleb said. "Black knights don't fight fair. Illusion is their biggest strength. And those who call on black spirits can give their apparitions physical form."

Black spirits? A chill raked Achan's arms. "I fought a demon?"

"Nay." Sir Gavin groaned as he sat on his bedroll. "The one with the helm was real. The rest of us were fighting the mage's enchantments. Black knights claim to be warrior mages. They believe sorcery combined with swordsmanship makes them stronger. They're under their own illusion. The power they wield isn't theirs."

Sir Gavin pulled his pack onto his lap and opened the flap. "The spirits aren't in control either. Both creatures, demon and man, are bound by each other's limitations. A man who falls victim to their spell is crippled by fear and rendered an easy target. That's why I stressed you understand the illusion. A very real illusion, but not as terrible as the black knights would have you think."

Sir Caleb squeezed Achan's shoulder, bushy eyebrows raised. "What I want to know is how you aren't dead, Your Highness. I thought you trained him, Gavin."

"I did, but . . . Achan uses what's at his disposal."

Heat spread over Achan at the idea of Sir Caleb's disapproval. "I thought I fought well."

"As did I," Sparrow said.

Sir Caleb winced. "Aye, you're brave, but you need proper training and practice."

"I competed in Prince Gid—Esek's tournament."

"Did you?" Sir Caleb's lips curled in a half smile. "What events?"

"The short sword and shield, though I'd never—"

"You were risking him to be playing games?" Inko's accusatory tone rang sharp. "What if he was being killed?"

"He should've been, judging by what I saw today," Sir Caleb said.

"He needed experience if he was to survive without me." Sir Gavin winked his brown eye at Achan. "Arman protected him."

"But you were *risking* him," Inko said. "Our future king."

"He's alive, is he not?"

Inko turned his disapproving glare to Achan. "It often is being said, Your Highness, that some training is being better than no training. But I must be cautioning you, sometimes no training is better than having bad training."

"Bah!" Sir Gavin slapped his palm to his thigh. "I trained him well enough!"

Sir Caleb folded his arms across his chest. "He fights like a drunk in a tavern brawl."

Achan blinked from Sir Gavin to Sir Caleb. A drunk?

"Aye, he's always been a bit of a brawler. I like that about him. Reminds me of his great uncle Preston." Sir Gavin sniffed in a long breath and released it slowly. "Forgive me, Achan. I've likely done a shabby job of teaching you to fight proper."

How was this criticism fair? Achan had defeated two of the five black knights. Sparrow had cowered like a girl. If Sir Caleb wanted to point out flaws, he should start with the boy. "What did I do that was so wrong?"

"Not wrong, Your Highness." Sir Caleb's brows furrowed as if he were searching for the right words. "You have courage and stamina, and you're strong and quite intimidating for a man your age. But you're full of risk. You leave too much to chance. Plus you've no respect for your weapon."

Achan shrugged. "What's a weapon but a tool to be used how its wielder deems necessary?"

"Well said, lad." Sir Gavin grinned, his thin, wolfish smile looking more like a grimace.

"Could I learn, as well?" Sparrow asked.

Sir Caleb nodded. "You can, boy. I must say, I thought you a coward until you turned veil warrior with Gavin and defeated the mage."

Achan frowned. Sparrow did what? "What's that mean, veil warrior?"

"It is meaning, Your Highness, that Vrell hasn't been being honest with us," Inko said. "He can do more with his mind than he has been letting on."

"No, I-I do not understand how . . ." Sparrow let his words die out, looking as though he had forgotten how to speak.

Sir Caleb gripped the back of his neck and pulled him into a one-armed hug. "Never mind your modesty, boy. Now, hand me your sword and we'll teach you to use it. Give those black knights something to fear on all accounts."

Despite wanting to string Sparrow up a moment ago, Achan's mind knotted at this line of conversation. The Veil was the world between Er'Rets and eternity in Shamayim or the Lowerworld. Not to be confused with the Evenwall, which separated Light from Darkness. How did bloodvoices work with the Veil?

Sparrow drew his sword from the ring on his belt and handed it, blade first, to Sir Caleb.

Achan rolled his eyes.

Sir Caleb frowned and twirled his finger. "Turn it around. Never hand over a weapon blade first."

"Sorry." Sparrow turned the blade and poked himself in the nose with the tip. He jumped, eyes wide.

Achan chuckled silently, fighting to keep his cheeks from curling, but the image of Sparrow's shocked face as he stuck himself with his own blade amused him to no end. Veil warrior or not, Sparrow was a bungler.

Sir Caleb took the weapon and examined it, then passed it to Achan, hilt first, with a sideways glance at Sparrow. "What do you make of Vrell's purchase, Your Highness?"

Achan gripped the thick, wooden handle, squeezing and releasing. He stood, backed away from the torchlight, and swung. The sword felt lighter than Eagan's Elk, which made sense for a short arming sword, but the handle weighed too much. It felt like he was wielding a pitchfork by the prongs.

He knelt before the torch, batted a moth aside, and scrutinized the blade. The cutting edges were crude, dirty with tool marks, gouges, and nicks. He held the sword flat in front of him, horizontal to the ground, and bent the end like he'd seen knights do to check the temper of the blade. It barely flexed.

He shot Sparrow a fleeting look. "How much did you pay for this?"

"Twenty pieces of silver."

Achan choked back a laugh. "Twenty!"

"Where does a stray come by twenty pieces of silver?" Sir Caleb asked.

Sparrow glanced from face to face. "My master in Walden's Watch gave it to me when I left."

Achan snorted. "You must be the luckiest stray I've ever met to have such a master."

"Lord Orthrop was more my warden than master. I apprenticed at the local apothecary."

Sir Caleb frowned. "The lord of the manor housed you *and* allowed you to apprentice? A stray?"

Sparrow's eyes cast down. "Lord Orthrop is a kind man."

"I'll say." Achan held up the sword. "Well, it's not worth five in my opinion. They didn't even bother to sharpen or polish it. It's unfinished, Sparrow. But that's not the worst of it." He peeked at Sir Caleb, confidence waning.

"Go on," the knight said.

"Well . . . it's got no flexibility. It'll probably break under a real blow. Plus, the balance is off. The hilt is heavy. The blade should be longer for the weight of this hilt, I think."

"But I'm short," Sparrow said.

"That doesn't matter." Achan paused. The knights watched him. Heat smoldered in the pit of his stomach. What did he truly know about swords? "Well, maybe it does."

"No. You're doing fine," Sir Caleb said. "Go on."

"Well, you'll build arm muscle using any sword, so the size of it based on your height isn't the issue. It's the reach, I think. If you're fighting an opponent with a longer sword, they'll be able to strike you, but you won't be able to reach them. Plus if they have a shield, which most do . . ." He stood and pointed to Sir Caleb's shield propped against his pack. "Sir Caleb?"

The knight handed Achan the shield. Achan tossed it to Sparrow who nearly fell over trying to catch it. The boy examined the shield and looped his arm through the straps.

Achan drew Eagan's Elk and handed it to Sparrow grip first. "Take my sword."

Sparrow accepted the weapon. "It is lighter than I expected."

"Aye. And you're much smaller than me. Take a swing."

"Easy." Sir Gavin's lecturing tone rang out.

Like the boy could actually do any damage. "Don't try and kill me, just reach out."

Sparrow did, slowly. Achan gripped the end of the blade between his thumb and fingers and jerked it toward his chest.

"There. See? You can reach me with a decent blade, despite your size. Look here." Achan gripped Sparrow's sword in his right hand. He was naturally left-handed, but Sir Gavin had taught him to fight with both. He reached out with Sparrow's blade. Even with his long arms, the tip remained a hand's breadth from the lad's chest. Sparrow's eyes bulged.

Achan dropped the cheap sword in the grass. "Switch with me."

Sparrow passed over the sword and shield and retrieved his sword from the ground. Achan gripped the shield in front of him, slightly to his left, and held the flat of Eagan's Elk against the shield's edge.

Sparrow gaped.

"Well?" Achan asked.

"I see my disadvantage immediately. Not only do you stand over a foot taller and are much stronger, but the shield covers most your body. Where am I supposed to strike?"

"My legs and head," Achan said.

To Achan's surprise, Sparrow darted left and lunged for his foot, but his blade struck the dirt.

Achan whacked Sparrow's head with the flat of his blade, the way Sir Gavin had done to him time and again.

Sparrow yelped and stumbled, clutching his head.

The knights laughed.

Achan fought back a smile. "You just lost your head. Keep your chin up. Look with your eyes so you can see as much as possible at all times and not leave yourself wide open. Oh, and you aren't digging a pit. Yours is a cutting blade. A dull one. But your grip is all wrong, as is your swing. Don't swing like you're afraid you'll miss. Put your heart into it. Passion increases a man's strength."

Achan shrugged his arm out of Sir Caleb's shield and let it fall on the ground. "But none of that matters if your blade can't even reach me. And if your opponent slips his grip to the pommel, he can get another four inches on you."

Inko chuckled. "It seems our prince is to be knowing a mite more than you were to be thinking, Caleb."

"Aye, he knows some, but there are strategies for fighting against a longsword with a shorter blade or dagger. You and I will work on that, Vrell, and see if we can outwit our prince." Sir Caleb raised a bushy blond eyebrow at Achan. "And I don't care how much you know, Your Highness. If you keep throwing swords and shields in the dirt, they won't be useful for long. Bring your blade here and I'll teach you to clean it. Vrell, you can learn too."

Achan knelt beside Sparrow at Sir Caleb's bedroll. "Honestly, you wouldn't stand a chance with that sword, even if you knew what you were doing. If we meet further opposition, I suggest you find a tree to hide behind. You'd cause more trouble in battle with us trying to keep you alive."

Sparrow's bottom lip trembled.

Pig snout, the boy was going to cry.

"There's no shame in it, Sparrow," Achan said quickly. "We need you as much as you need us. If not for you, who would patch us up when we're half dead?"

Sparrow folded his arms, but his lips curved up a bit.

"Now, Your Highness, that's not fair." Sir Caleb pulled his pack onto his lap. "If not for Vrell, we might not have survived those black knights, isn't that right, Gavin?"

"Aye. What concerns me is how they're finding us."

"Are you keeping your mind shielded, Your Majesty?" Sir Caleb asked.

"That shouldn't matter, Caleb," Sir Gavin said. "I sensed no ability to bloodvoice from the ebens or black knights. They found us by other means."

"Both attacks came in the morning. Ebens are good trackers. And black knights may have used gowzals. They can speak to them, you know, use them as messengers."

Achan recalled seeing through the bird's eyes. Guilt festered in his stomach. "I opened my mind after Sir Caleb's lesson that first night."

Every set of eyes focused on him.

"I know I shielded myself well. None of you sensed me. I . . . saw through a bird. It had information for its master. Made no sense to me at the time. Thought it might be Darkness messing with—"

"A gowzal, then," Sir Caleb said. "We must keep watch for the beast birds. The black knights are using them to track us."

Vrell opened her eyes to a black void. A hand nudged her side and she bolted upright.

"Vrell," Sir Gavin's whisper floated down from the darkness, "'tis our watch."

Vrell blinked her stinging eyes. Her back ached from sleeping on the ground. Oh, how she longed for a steamy, rose-leaf bath and her feather bed. "I am awake."

A blue torchlight whizzed to life, illuminating Sir Gavin's whiskered face. "Join me over here a moment, if you will." He walked away, his body blocking most of the blue light.

Vrell heaved to her feet and trudged after the faint glow, each step waking her further and bringing more and more of her circumstances to mind.

Sir Gavin stopped far enough away that she could no longer see the camp. Her heart thudded. She didn't like being so far from the others, but the light felt safer than the lack of it.

The Great Whitewolf stared down, the torchlight sinking into the surface of his skin, sharpening every wrinkle into deep gouges of shadow. "Who are you really?"

The question hung in the dark surrounding them. Arman, help her. Vrell pursed her lips and dropped her focus to her feet, though the torch did not cast enough light for her to see them. Tears pricked her eyes. She blinked them back. She had to keep control.

"I need the truth, lad." Sir Gavin softened his tone. "How is it you know such advanced bloodvoicing battle methods? I can't imagine Macoun taught it to you, fool though he is."

Battle method? She'd been dreading Sir Gavin's promise of a confrontation. Sir Caleb's veil warrior praise had only added to her apprehension. What had Mother done?

"You *will* answer me. I have no qualms about binding you and leaving you for dead. So tell me, do you mean us ill will?"

Tears flooded Vrell's vision despite her efforts to hold them back. "I cannot . . ." She lifted her fingers to cover her trembling lower lip. "Please don't . . ." A sob burst past her defenses.

"Aw, don't cry, now. I've no desire to see you hurt, but I've a responsibility to see Achan take the throne. I must know if anyone stands in my way. Are you Esek's spy? Macoun's?"

Vrell jerked her chin up, eyes wide. "No. N-nothing like that, sir, I promise you. I am on your side. I follow Arman too. And I-I want Achan to be king more than anything."

"Then tell me what you hide."

Vrell fought to stifle her tears. "I . . . do not think I can."

"You will."

Vrell glanced in the direction of the camp, her breathing ragged. "Will you tell . . . the others?"

"Not unless I have reason."

Vrell licked her cracked lips and met Sir Gavin's mismatched eyes. She wanted to contact Mother, ask what to do, but she couldn't very well go glassy-eyed in front of Sir Gavin. Her gaze darted from his blue eye to his brown one.

Enough misery. Exposing the truth must be Arman's will.

Vrell's voice came in a near whisper. "I am Lady Averella Amal of Carmine."

Sir Gavin's bushy white eyebrows sank over his eyes.

Before he could reply, she hurried on. "Prince Gidon—beg your pardon . . ." Vrell swallowed and took a deep breath. "*Esek* petitioned Mother for my hand last winter. She refused, but he would not accept her answer. His pressure grew so intense that Mother deemed it best I go into hiding. Only Lady Coraline Orthrop of Walden's Watch knew the truth of me. But while she was away, Jax and Khai arrived to escort me to Mahanaim. Macoun Hadar had sensed my bloodvoice ability and wanted me as his apprentice. I had no choice but to go.

"Lord Orthrop and the knights believed I was a stray boy with no rights. If I had revealed myself . . . well, I feared they would force me to marry the prince—Esek, I mean. And I could not marry him. He did not care for me. He only wants control of Carm. He is a horrible person. I pity the girl who becomes his wife. And I will die before I meet such a fate."

An ache seized Vrell's stomach. She gulped and wiped tears from her cheeks. How terrifying to admit the truth after so long, yet so freeing. She had only intended to pause, then explain how she had come into Macoun's service and eventually met up with Achan, but now that she had stopped, the tears would not. She hugged herself and let them come, gasping and sniffing to keep her nose from watering.

"Eben's breath." Sir Gavin drew her into an awkward, stiff-armed embrace. Vrell cried harder, her body shaking with sobs. Sir Gavin slapped her back. "Poor child. Why didn't you confide in me? I could've left you in Prince Oren's care."

Vrell clutched her sides and wailed. Staying with Prince Oren had been her greatest hope. She choked and coughed, trying to stop the tears long enough to answer. Her words came in slurred bursts. "I did not know . . . who to trust. I had planned to tell . . . Sir Rigil, but . . . when I found Achan and Sir Caleb . . . in the secret passage . . . Sir Rigil had gone." Vrell sucked in a breath. "Achan's cheeks were bleeding. He needed aid. I thought I could serve my king a bit longer."

Sir Gavin nodded, as if putting the pieces together. "You were going to reveal yourself to the Council on your mother's behalf so Achan would have his votes. Did she ask you to?"

"No, sir. She did not wish it. Not with Esek there."

"She was wise not to risk you." Sir Gavin groaned and rubbed his hands over his face. "My dear lady, you're a brave soul. To think I let Achan strike you this night. I'm ashamed of myself."

Vrell welcomed the excuse to smile. "Well, I must learn to fight, sir. It has been horrible all this time not being able to protect myself. I felt so weak and vulnerable. So useless."

"Aye. And you've joined a perilous journey, my lady. Did your mother teach you to storm? What you did with the black knight?"

"I know nothing of what my mother did. I blacked out. I called out to her for help and she jumped through me. Then . . . I saw nothing."

Sir Gavin spoke to himself, "Aye. Nitsa helped him once. I had forgotten."

Vrell straightened. "Helped who?"

"Eag—forgive me. 'Tis not my tale to share but something to ask your mother." Sir Gavin sniffed and stroked his beard braid. "What is your wish, my lady? How can an Old Kingsguard knight be of service?"

"My only wish is to go home. But Macoun Hadar and Khai Mageia know who I am. They told Esek. Now Esek has placed a bounty on both our heads. Mine and Achan's."

Sir Gavin tipped back his head, eyes narrowing. "Perhaps that's why so many small parties hunt us. They're after the reward." He gripped Vrell's shoulder. "We'll get you home, brave lady. Unfortunately it will not be soon. You're certain you don't want the others to know? It'll be easier on you."

Vrell drew her bottom lip between her teeth. "I never meant to deceive Achan. I had hoped to slip away without him finding out who I really am. Is that wrong of me?"

Sir Gavin stroked his moustache over the curve of his top lip. "I cannot say. Either way, 'tis probably best you stay dressed as a boy. It isn't proper for Achan to travel with a woman, no more than for you to travel with four men." He sniffed in a long breath. "We'll keep your identity between us. It won't ease your burden, though I'll try to help where I can."

Vrell shook her tears away and lifted her chin. "Please, do not interfere with my training. I never want to be unprepared in battle again. If I am going to survive, I must learn."

"I've never met a braver lady." Sir Gavin's eyes widened. "Eben's breath! No wonder you didn't want help with your leeches. Oh, my lady. I thank you, deeply, on behalf of our king for your service these past weeks. You saved his life after the Poroo battle, cared for him in the dungeons, called me to his aid, and sacrificed your own safety for his benefit. You should be commended." He shuffled his feet, threw up his hands, and sighed. "I'm sorry I cannot offer more than words."

Vrell hugged Sir Gavin, his prickly beard tickling her face. "It is a great comfort to finally have a confidant. Your kindness means so much, Sir Gavin. I can never repay you for it."

"I'd never accept it if you tried. 'Tis my duty as a knight to see you safely home, my lady. That I promise to do."

"Sir Gavin, please. I do not understand what Mother did. And Sir Caleb is bragging me up as a veil warrior. All I remember was concentrating. I heard a song and all my pain vanished. I felt as if I had floated in the air. And then nothing."

"When I found you, you were cold. I fear we almost lost your mind to the Veil. Though I appreciate your mother's assistance, you must not help her again 'til you learn properly. The Veil is a dangerous place for one untrained to navigate it. We'll tell the men you helped me by accident, that you didn't know what you were doing. 'Tis mostly true."

"How can one enter the Veil whilst they are still living?" Vrell had always understood that a man who entered the Veil was on the brink of death.

"It is done using bloodvoicing. A gifted man may leave his body and enter the Veil, or he may cast another man—gifted or not—into the Veil, which is the essence of storming. A man's soul was not created for Er'Rets, you see. It was created for Shamayim and longs for the peace and joy of that eternal home. Trust me, Vrell. You do not want to tempt your soul to the Veil before Arman pulls it there."

Vrell shivered. Without realizing it, she had gone into the Veil before, when Macoun had asked her to seek out Esek and Achan drew her into his mind. "So my mother sent the mage to the Veil? Is he still there?"

"I cannot say. People can be brought back, but only by those who know how."

"And do you know how, Sir Gavin?"

"I do, but I'm too old to risk it. 'Tis not a wise task for a man so close to Arman's final call."

8

Achan woke with a stiff back. He sat up and scanned the camp, Eagan's Elk poking into the grass behind him. The knights were packing up. "Where's Sparrow?"

Sir Caleb combed his fingers through his wild mane and yawned. "Watering the nearest tree, I imagine."

Achan pushed himself to one knee and rolled up his leather bed. His stiff legs and back ached, and his belt had cut a groove into his waist overnight that had left the area without blood flow. He scratched his waistline and heaved to his feet.

"From now on, Your Highness, do not wear your belt and sword when you sleep." Sir Caleb's owlish eyes glimmered in the torchlight. "It's wise to keep it close by, but how could you draw if you're sleeping on it?"

Achan grunted in response. No doubt Eagan's Elk was to blame for the majority of his stiffness as he'd slept on his back to keep the hilt reachable.

He crossed the dead grass to where Sir Gavin knelt, attaching his bedroll to his pack. Achan crouched beside the knight. "So? Did you speak to Sparrow?"

Sir Gavin cinched the leather cords on the bedroll. "I did."

"And?"

"'Tis none of your concern."

Achan's eagerness faded. "He's not hiding anything?"

Sir Gavin drew the pack over his shoulders and groaned as he heaved it on and stood in one motion. Achan stood with him and received his piercing gaze. "What Vrell hides is his own business and no threat to you. Leave him be about it."

Leave him be? "Yes, sir."

Sir Gavin clapped Achan's shoulder, his calloused hand scratching Achan's leather doublet. "Please, lad. You must not call me sir. You're my prince. I say 'yes, sir' to you."

Achan nodded, though frustration seared through his veins. Sir Gavin wanted him to be prince but kept secrets. Sparrow *was* hiding something, threat or not. Achan had met the boy first. Were they not friends? Didn't Sparrow trust him?

Sparrow bounded into the light and looped his satchel over his head and arm. They each took their place along Sir Caleb's rope and set off in the dark. Achan traipsed along, more comfortable blindly trusting Sir Gavin to lead on this third day of the journey. Truly? Had three days passed already? They'd slept before the giants attacked, then in the rocky clearing where the black knights had appeared, then last night in the field. That made this day four. Without the sun to rise and fall, it all seemed like one long night.

Their boots scraped over crusty grass. To keep their minds from wandering, Sir Caleb told a story of how Allowntown had come to be.

"Were my parents staying in Allowntown when they were killed?" Achan asked after some time.

"Nay, they were just arriving from Mahanaim. When your father traveled, he reveled well into the morning with his men and his minstrels. Your mother, not wanting to expose you to such behavior at your young age, had come along."

"She sounds like a prudent woman and a loving mother," Sparrow said.

Achan grinned at the thought of his father wanting to include him in the merrymaking at age three and his mother's desire to tuck him into bed.

"I'd never seen a prouder papa than King Axel," Sir Caleb said. "You lived on his shoulders if you weren't in your mother's arms. I'm surprised you learned to walk."

Achan's grin sobered, knowing this story didn't end well. "So they were killed when they reached Allowntown?"

"As Sir Gavin said the other night, when we awoke, the king and queen had already left. We had barely started out from Mahanaim when your father cried out."

"No one in Allowntown saw what happened?"

"Nay. If you recall, the fortress is small. Normally, when the king and queen traveled, a messenger would ride ahead to announce their arrival. This would have given the staff in Allowntown a chance to welcome the king properly. My brother, Lord Agros, said no messenger came that day."

"What was Sir Kenton's story?" Achan asked.

The crunching of dead grass pulled Achan's attention to the web of trees on his left. Could Sir Gavin sense every beast in the area? Or only those he shadowed? He could have sworn he'd heard a horse neigh.

"According to Sir Kenton and every guardsman and servant questioned, the king dismissed his men when they arrived, and he, you, and your mother went for a walk in the orchard. No one would have questioned this as your mother had a fondness for trees. She had her own gardens at Armonguard. They're still there. You shall see them someday."

"Who found them?" Achan tensed at the image of a family walk turned to slaughter.

"A farmer. He'd been out—"

Torches fizzed to life on all sides, bobbing in the darkness. Achan drew his sword. Men in armor appeared all around them. These weren't black knights, however. Nearly two dozen soldiers encircled them, each gripping a sword and a two-tone shield bearing the face of a reekat. Behind them, men on horseback stood sentry before three long carts filled with rock.

"By whose command do you tread upon this land?" a man said.

Achan couldn't tell where his voice came from.

"We serve no man," Sir Gavin said. "We seek an audience with Sir Septon Eli, Lord of Mirrorstone."

"And you are?"

"Sir Gavin Whitewolf, commander of the Old Kingsguard. We come in peace."

"Then you shall be received in such." A tall, husky man stepped through the row of soldiers and approached Sir Gavin. His face was shaded in a thick grey beard. "I am Belen. I would be happy to escort you to Mirrorstone."

Stay in the shadows, Achan, Sir Gavin bloodvoiced.

Gladly. Achan dreaded their arrival in Mirrorstone, fearing Sir Gavin intended to parade him about to rally supporters.

All his life he'd had but one goal: freedom. To be able to build his own cottage, cook his own meals, and, maybe someday, have a wife and family. He'd never dreamed of being king. And despite any notions of what he thought a prince or king's life might be like, the past few days had shown the truth. A king was not a free man in the slightest.

Belen led them across a wide dirt road to the wagons filled with rock. He tapped the side of one that was hitched to two horses. "Your men can ride in this. Come with me, Sir Gavin, and I'll see you are given a horse."

Sir Caleb nudged Achan toward the wagon. "You heard him. Into the wagon, men."

Achan slipped up on the wagon bed, legs dangling off, but Sir Caleb made him move farther in. He scooted back and leaned against a smooth boulder. Sir Caleb and Inko sat on either side. Sparrow sat in front of him.

Like shields.

"How is your head, Inko?"

Sparrow's voice sent a jolt of tension through Achan. The secret keeper excelled at pretending nothing was amiss.

"It's being a big lump. I'm thinking Arman was blessing me that it was being the third rock that was being thrown. Any other I might not have been waking up from."

Achan closed his eyes, wishing the act could forever silence Inko's irrational superstitions over lucky numbers and who knew what else.

"It's a relief to be headed for a stronghold," Sir Caleb said. "Pray it's a friendly one."

The wagon jerked forward, wheels crunching over dirt, rocks shifting against the wooden wagon and each other. Soldiers rode by on horseback, eyeing them curiously in the glow of the torches they held. Lulled by rolling motion of the wagon and the sound of creaking wood, Achan soon nodded off.

"How lovely."

Achan opened his eyes at Sparrow's voice. Hundreds of torches illuminated the size and shape of a tall, narrow castle. Flames burned bright, reflecting warm, flickering light in the surrounding moat of dark water. Mirrorstone. Lord Eli had it good. It was an impressive place for a man no more than twenty years of age.

They passed under a marble gatehouse intricately carved with foliage, faces, and animals. The soldiers peeled away from the wagon and crossed a deserted courtyard toward an archway topped with a double row of torches. The wagon stopped before a grand marble porch with pillars as wide as three men.

"Stay back and keep your head down," Sir Caleb said.

They piled out of the wagon. A guard led them inside through a pillared vestibule and into a luxurious great hall. A raised, white marble dais stretched across the far end of the room. Red linen draped over a head table set with golden plates and goblets. Three bronze candelabras, dripping with glass prisms, hung above the table, each holding dozens of white candles. The prisms cast sparkling light over the floor and walls. Guards stood beside each fluted pilaster, edging the room.

Achan kept his eyes down, wincing slightly. After so many days of gloomy shadow, the light seemed wrong somehow. Too bright.

Sir Gavin and a young man were seated at the high table looking like a grandsire with his grandson. Achan recognized the young man's pale, freckled face and shock of orange hair immediately. Sir Septon Eli himself. A man barely older than Achan. His parents had also died tragically, though Achan couldn't recall how. He did remember Esek monopolizing the young lord's wife on the trip to Mahanaim.

Achan stayed behind Sir Caleb and kept his head down as they crossed the wide room.

"I'm collecting rock to build a wall around my land," Lord Eli said to Sir Gavin. "The Poroo and ebens have been merciless of late. It appears they want to start a war with one another, yet Mirrorstone lies in between. It thrills me to no end they want to kill each other, but I want no part of it."

"You think a wall will keep them out?" Sir Gavin asked.

"It works for Har Sha'ar."

"Har Sha'ar is a mountain fortress. You're on the coast."

"A tall enough wall will keep them out. The kwon too."

"Kwon certainly," Sir Gavin sniffed, "but Poroo climb."

"Oh, I'm well aware. I was there when the Poroo attacked Prince Esek's procession. Horrible creatures. Can't be reasoned with. Can't be bought."

Sir Caleb stopped and cleared his throat.

Lord Eli's gaze jerked to the floor and he waved them forward. "You must desire to freshen up before dinner, but I wanted to greet you first."

Odd. Achan did not claim to be an expert at decorum, but Sir Gavin had taught him a guest's comfort always took priority. Either Lord Eli was clueless, extremely self-absorbed, or suspicious of his guests.

Sir Gavin pushed back his chair and stood. "These are my fellow Kingsguards, Sir Caleb Agros and Inko son of Mopti."

"Ah, a Barthian, are you?" Lord Eli smiled down on Inko. "Well, I won't hold it against you." He snapped his fingers and one of the servants pulled out a chair for Inko.

Achan instantly disliked Lord Eli's arrogant, Esek-like demeanor.

"And Agros is a noble title, is it not?"

Sir Caleb bowed. "My brother is Lord of Allowntown."

"And are you heir to the lordship?"

"By no means. My brother has three healthy sons."

"A shame for you and a joy for him, I'm sure." Lord Eli snapped again and a servant pulled out another chair.

Sir Caleb hesitated, then took his seat beside Inko.

Achan remained standing beside Sparrow, eyes cast to the floor. He could feel Lord Eli's gaze.

"And these are?"

"Our servants." Achan looked up at the sound of Sir Gavin's voice.

"Delightful." Lord Eli left his chair and descended the platform. "I should like to meet them as well."

This was the longest of tales. No man as pretentious as Lord Eli would even look at another man's servants, let alone desire a personal introduction.

"What's this? Your servant is injured." Lord Eli stepped so close Achan could count the freckles on the man's face. His breath warmed Achan's cheek. "Why I . . . can it be?" He spun to face the high table, eyes wide. "Commander, do not play me false. I have seen this young man before on the journey from Sitna. King Esek issued a royal proclamation to apprehend this man."

King Esek? Sir Caleb stood and drew his sword. Achan drew his as well, and pointed it at Lord Eli's chest. Lord Eli's guards charged from the perimeter, weapons ready. Sir Caleb slid over the top of the high table and jumped to the floor, raising his blade to Lord Eli's back.

"No, no! You misunderstand!" Lord Eli cowered, cheeks flushing so his head resembled a peach. "King Esek made me a fool, keeping my wife from me on the journey from Sitna. Please, stay, Your Highness. Build your campaign. My seer advised me that counsel would come from outside Mirrorstone, and here you are. I am your servant. I will stand with you as you take what is rightfully yours. Please, accept Mirrorstone's full support. My staff and guards are at your disposal." Lord Eli nodded to his guards and the men lowered their weapons.

Achan glanced at Sir Caleb, who sheathed his sword, "Perhaps instead of games, a little hospitality would melt His Highness' resolve."

"Of course, of course. Right away." Lord Eli raised his arm, as if to snap. "But first you must visit the temple shrine and make an offering."

Sir Gavin walked to the end of the dais. "That won't be necessary."

"It is unwise to ignore Avenis. The more attention you bestow on the god of beauty, the more blessings he returns." Lord Eli's piercing gaze bounced from face to face, eyebrows sinking. "No? Very well." He snapped his fingers at a servant who stood along the wall. "Prepare a bath in our best room for His Royal Highness. Prepare the adjoining rooms for his staff. And inform our other guests that dinner will be delayed."

The servant bowed and darted away.

Lord Eli turned to Achan. "You will join us for dinner?"

Sir Gavin descended the dais steps. "What other guests?"

"The future queen, her mother, and her sister."

"You house the Hamartano women?" Sir Caleb asked.

Lord Eli blanched. "They were traveling through on their way to Jaelport. How could I refuse such beauty? Avenis would not be pleased."

"The *future queen* is whatever woman weds Gidon Hadar," Sir Caleb said, gesturing to Achan. "Esek may marry whom he pleases, but she will not be queen."

"Quite so," Lord Eli said. "Yet it is my understanding that the best match for the king of Er'Rets is a daughter of Lord Hamartano. My seer has said as much. None are prettier than Jaelportian women, though do not tell my wife I said so." He chuckled. "Should not the king have the most beautiful wife?"

"Jaelport *is* a powerful force," Sir Caleb said. "But the Hamartano family cannot be trusted. Lord Hamartano voted against the true prince and has always acted in his wife's best interests. Perhaps it's best we skip dinner tonight."

"But he has *two* daughters," Lord Eli said. "Lady Mandzee has been promised to King Esek, but Lady Jaira is promised to no one. Personally, I feel Lady Jaira is the handsomer of the two. Why not come to the temple and see who Avenis would favor for the prince's bride?"

"Never," Achan said.

The men looked to Achan.

"Even if I wished to marry, which I don't, I'd never marry *Lady Scorn*. I'll not even jest of it. Beauty is as much an inward attribute as it is physical, Lord Eli. And I've never met a more hideous beast of a woman than Jaira Hamartano."

Lord Eli placed a hand over his heart, his wide eyes and freckled face giving him the appearance of a scared child. "Surely we are not speaking of the same creature?"

Your Highness, Sir Caleb said to Achan's mind, *do keep your charitable opinion of Lady Jaira to yourself. You do your reputation no service to speak so callously of anyone in company beyond our own.*

Sir Gavin stopped at Achan's side. "We're not yet marrying you to anyone, but we must remain open to all options." His voice boomed in Achan's head. *Play along, lad, and see where this leads. Tell him we'll dine with him.*

Achan gritted his teeth but lightened his tone. "Forgive me, Lord Eli. It is only the fatigue of the road speaking, I fear. We'd be pleased to dine with you."

Lord Eli's face brightened. "Excellent. And I insist you allow my tailor to service you with new clothing for the occasion. We must look our best or Avenis will be displeased."

Sir Gavin jerked his head in a bow. "You're most kind."

Achan wasn't convinced.

Achan's chamber was a mini great hall paneled in dark wood. The room stretched lengthwise with narrow doors for servants on each end. White crown molding edged the ceiling and lined pocket niches along the walls that held nude gilded statues. A turquoise rug covered the center of the intricately painted gold and black wooden floor.

A colossal bedstead, centered on the wall opposite the entrance, dominated the room. It had a turquoise and gold silk canopy that tied back against four fluted wooden pillars. The carved headboard ran up the wall and held a marble bust of Avenis. At least a dozen square and round pillows of black, turquoise, or gold lay piled on the mattress itself.

To the left of the bed, a fire burned in a marble hearth as high as Achan's head. Two massive candelabra hung from the ceiling, holding thin white candles. Fancy furnishings stood about the room: wooden chairs painted white with gold leaf flowers, half pillars holding ornate vases, paintings of half-dressed people framed in gold leaf, and ornate bronze wall sconces every three paces.

"*Delightful* host." Sir Caleb removed his shield and set it against the wall. He shrugged off his pack and fell onto one of the white chairs. It creaked under his weight. "I've never witnessed such a display of arrogance and ignorance in the same man."

"I have." Achan crossed the wool rug, thinking of Esek. Riga Hoff held both traits as well. Achan paused at the bed and stroked the silk bedspread.

"'Tis no matter," Sir Gavin said. "If we mean to promote Achan as king, he'll need to be seen, and often. We must form a plan for his presentation."

"But not until we have an army to protect him," Sir Caleb said. "As is, we're elk in a barren field. I don't trust Septon Eli. And I certainly don't trust Jaelport."

"Nor I, but we've little choice but to play along for now."

Achan sank onto the edge of the feather mattress. "Do I get to sleep in this bed?"

"Lord Eli does present a good point," Sir Caleb said. "Esek has obviously aligned with Jaelport. We should find a bride for the prince, as well."

Warmth tingled up the back of Achan's neck. "What?"

Sparrow nudged Achan's foot with his boot. "Lady Jaira *would* bring a powerful ally in Jaelport."

Achan snapped out of the daze Sir Caleb's comment had evoked. "That's not funny."

"If Hamartano would truly be marrying one daughter to Esek and the other to Achan," Inko said, "he's not really being our ally. By his pledging one daughter to each man, he's securing himself a queen. That's being his only agenda."

Sir Caleb snorted. "Don't assume Lord Hamartano has an agenda. He simply does his wife's will."

"And no woman I ever met would be more capable of assassination than Lady Jaira," Achan said. "I'd be dead in a week. She's hated me from first glance."

Sparrow nudged his foot again. "Only when she believed you were a lowly stray. Give the lady a chance to redeem herself now that she knows your true birthright."

Achan spoke through clenched teeth. "Enough jesting."

Sparrow shrugged. "I am only pointing out that Lady Jaira is known to fancy high-born, wealthy men."

Achan's tone lightened. "Well, I'm not wealthy. Am I, Sir Gavin?"

Sir Gavin stroked his beard braid. "Achan, don't worry—"

"I am sure we could raise enough to turn Lady Jaira's regal head," Sparrow said.

Achan stood up so he could tower over the boy. "Then why don't you marry her?"

Sparrow propped his fists on his hips. "We both know how she feels about strays, Your Highness."

"Hush, lads!" Sir Gavin said.

"And don't even joke about an alliance with Jaelport, Vrell." Sir Caleb's bushy eyebrows pinched. "You cannot trust them. Ever."

Achan fell back onto the cushy bed. "I don't want to marry anyone. I just want to lie low for a while."

"People swore fealty to you at Council," Sir Caleb said. "The people want you as their king. You cannot hide. And you *should* choose a bride soon. Align with a powerful ally. If Esek is sworn in as king and takes up residence in Armonguard, the people will likely protest, possibly revolt. We need to gather supporters who'll rally the people in our favor when the timing is right. We need organization. A bride is a necessary step."

"But not the first one and nothing we must decide tonight." Sir Gavin fell onto one of the white chairs and groaned. "Put it out of your mind for now."

"But I . . . why should I . . ." Achan stammered. "You're really going to force me to marry?"

"Every king must have a queen, Your Highness." Sir Caleb pulled his cloak off over his head, causing his short blond hair to frizz out. "Er'Rets has been without a king for too long. Even now, if Esek or even you were to take the throne, many won't follow. They've been following their own agendas for so long, they don't want a king. We must convince them they need one."

"Most Kinsmen, true Kinsmen, will follow you. But the Kinsman population alone won't give us enough allies to take the throne. The majority—Poroo, Otherling, Giants, Chuma, Wildermen, Cela—will follow the coin. We have little funds. A bride can rectify that."

Achan's stomach churned. "I won't marry someone for money, nor will I bribe people to follow me. Esek will always offer more, and when my back is turned, someone will stick a knife in it."

"Aye," Sir Gavin said. "Know then that you'll always have far more enemies than allies until this is over."

Achan stared into the blazing flames in the hearth. "That I'm used to."

A knock at the door stilled the conversation. Inko let in two servants, carrying a wooden tub between them. Three more followed with steaming kettles of water. The servants set the tub in front of the hearth and began filling it.

A sixth man entered holding dark blue folded fabric and bowed. He handed the fabric to Sparrow. "A robe for after His Highness' bath." He stepped toward Achan. "And I'm to measure His Royal Highness for his new ensemble."

"For the sake of the gods," Achan murmured.

Sir Caleb waved him forward. "Nothing too garish, now."

The tailor measured Achan's waist, chest, arms, and legs, then bowed and departed. The other servants left as well.

Sir Gavin turned to Sir Caleb. "I'll stay behind with Achan if you and Inko would like to visit the steams. He'll be ready to dress by the time you're finished, then I can go down."

"I can dress myself," Achan said.

Inko lifted his pack. "Vrell can be coming along. Vrell?"

Sparrow's eyes widened and he shifted from Achan's side to Sir Gavin's chair.

Sir Gavin put a hand on the boy's shoulder. "I need Vrell's help. He'll have to go later."

9

Vrell sat cross-legged on her bed in the servant's quarters adjoining Achan's chambers, perusing the sparse contents of her satchel. Esek's sleeve was the only fabric left. Perhaps Lord Eli would replenish her stores. She would hate to have to use Esek's sleeve as a bandage. She also hoped to bathe. Her skin felt like a tree in Darkness.

The tiny room was only big enough for two beds separated by a narrow fireplace. A sliver of mirrorglass hung above the fireplace. She carried her toothcloth and toothpick there and began to pick her teeth, savoring the opportunity to clean them without an audience. Her solitude inspired her to blood-voice Mother. She explained where she was and all that had transpired.

I am glad you confided in Sir Gavin, Mother said. *You can trust his wisdom.*

Sir Gavin said you stormed the mage. He explained the concept, but what did you do exactly?

Storming is a complicated process. You must not attempt to do it on your own. Sir Gavin told me how it weakened you. I was foolish to risk you without knowing how you would fare. When you are home, I will teach you all you want to know about your gift. For now, do nothing to endanger yourself. Promise me?

Yes, Mother. Vrell's gums itched. She traded her toothpick for the toothcloth and pressed it against her bleeding gums. *What happened the day of the Council meeting? Why did we lose contact?*

One of Lord Nathak's shadows had been working in our kitchens. He tainted my meal with âleh. It had been so long since I had tasted it, I didn't realize what happened until it was too late. I instantly requested karpos fruit but there was none to be found. My guards investigated and discovered that a servant was seen leaving the castle with a basket of karpos. It seems Lord Nathak's shadow stole them all.

Vrell rubbed her toothcloth over her bottom teeth. *Did you find out who he was?*

A new man, naturally. Went by the name of Jamon. Captain Loam believes the name is false and he was one of Esek Nathak's old squires.

Really? Which one? For Vrell had met many over recent years, though most did not stay squires for long. Esek tended to injure them.

Captain Loam did not recall. Only that he'd seen the man at tournament.

The door to Vrell's room swung in. Vrell closed her mind and hid her teeth-cleaning tools behind her back.

Sir Gavin entered, looking clean and tidy. His long white hair slicked back on top, partly tied back. The rest hung straight to his waist, as did his beard braid, now smooth and tight. He set a stack of clothing on Vrell's bed. "Achan went with Caleb to fit the clothes Lord Eli ordered. The tailor sent this for you. Should you like a bath, Achan's water is still warm. Sorry I can't get fresh, but I'll stand guard. Also . . ." He tapped a small leather bundle atop the folded clothing. "I asked Lord Eli if he had a gift I could take my niece in Melas."

Vrell looked from Sir Gavin's blue eye to his brown. "I did not know you had a niece."

"I don't." The old knight winked his brown eye. "Enjoy your bath, my lady."

Vrell opened the bundle and found a mirror, comb, and bar of rose-scented soap. She squealed and hugged Sir Gavin around the middle. "Thank you, good sir! I shall be quick."

Vrell turned every nude statue in Achan's room to face the wall, and, despite the used water, savored the bath. She couldn't tell her leech wounds from mosquito bites at this point. For all she'd been through in the past few days, she was remarkably unscathed. She tugged the snarls from her hair with her new comb. Mold speckled the belly of her padded disguise. She needed to air it out, fill it with fresh wool. How would she ever have the opportunity?

Reluctantly, she put the undergarment back on and dressed in the royal blue tunic and black trousers Sir Gavin had brought. She cracked open the door to the hallway.

Sir Gavin turned to the door. "Feel better?"

"Much." Vrell exited and closed the door behind her.

Sir Gavin offered his arm. "Time for dinner."

Vrell slid her fingers around Sir Gavin's forearm and allowed him to lead her down the hall. What freedom to be herself, however brief. She straightened her back and held her head high. Footsteps on the stairs caused her to release Sir Gavin's arm. A servant flowed off the landing and strode the opposite direction, holding a kettle of water.

Vrell flushed. How could she have been so careless?

"My apologies," Sir Gavin said in a low voice. "Probably not the best idea."

Vrell pushed the near miss away with a smile as they made their way downstairs. "How long will we remain here?"

"Just tonight. Lord Eli invited us for longer, but I'll not tarry. Not here."

Vrell agreed. She did not trust Lord Eli either.

Sir Gavin stopped on the landing halfway down where the staircase furled out into the pillared foyer like a river into the sea. Hearty smells drifted on the air. Vrell's stomach growled, then tightened when she saw Achan.

He stood with Lord Eli at the entrance to the great hall, looking every bit like a rich, exotic prince. He wore a black leather doublet over a royal blue tunic embroidered with silver thread. The sleeves dangled past his fingertips. Silver buckles cinched black trousers below his knees where they met shiny black boots. His black hair slicked back into a braided tail, held in place by a sparkling jewel. No bandage covered his scruffy cheeks, but his facial hair had been trimmed into the start of a beard that would eventually hide his scars.

But nothing could hide his sour expression. Such chagrin could be due to the fact he had been dressed like Esek, yet Vrell bet Lady Jaira Hamartano's presence was the likely cause. She stood with her mother, sister, and Lord Eli's wife at the bottom of the stairs.

Vrell paused beside Sir Gavin and frowned. Jaira's blue dress suspiciously matched Achan's ensemble. The gown clung to her every curve as if painted onto her skin. It had a wide, revealing neckline with little cap sleeves that dripped black beads down her slender arms. She wore black satin gloves to her elbows. The slender skirt fanned out from her knees like the tail of a fish. A silver chain draped around her narrow waist with a matching blue reticule attached.

Jaira's dozens of fine black braids were piled atop her head like an ebony crown, baring her long neck and shoulders. Shiny obsidian teardrops dangled from her ears. A third larger stone hung from a thin cord around her neck and plunged toward her low neckline. Her olive skin looked bronze under the flickering candelabras and sparkled as if she had bathed in mineral dust. Paint reddened her cheeks, outlined her eyes in black, and dusted each eyelid blue.

Vrell had never seen such repulsive beauty. She could hardly bear to see Jaira standing with Achan in such a way. Lord Eli had plotted these matching ensembles, she had no doubt. Vrell took a deep breath and tried to create a neutral expression, but a sudden thought stole her breath. *She* had been dressed to match Achan as well.

As his squire.

She turned her gaze upon the vestibule. Lord Eli left Achan to go to his wife, Lady Katiolakan. They wore matching ensembles of gold and green. He led his wife to Achan. Lady Mandzee and her mother walked behind them, themselves clothed beautifully. Appropriately. Mandzee wore violet and her mother wore peach. Neither was dressed as bait. Did these people think Achan a womanizing fool like Esek? Did they hope he might fall for Jaira's display?

Switch places with me, Sparrow? You be prince and I'll be squire.

Vrell jumped. Achan had just bloodvoiced her. Without knocking. Her shields were up, and still she sensed the open connection between them. How was he doing that? It had to be his power. She could not accomplish such a feat.

Sir Gavin inhaled through his nose. "Something smells sour," he said with a lilt to his voice. "What do you think of the colors blue and black tonight?"

Vrell wrinkled her nose. "They look like a bruise."

Sir Gavin laughed. "That they do, my lady. I quite agree."

Why didn't Sparrow answer? Perhaps Achan hadn't messaged correctly. He did forget to knock first, and he hadn't concentrated hard. Yet he'd managed to keep his connection open to Sir Caleb most the afternoon as Sir Caleb had groomed him. He had thought the same process might work for Sparrow. Apparently not.

Achan would have done anything to stand on the staircase with Sir Gavin and Sparrow. He hadn't moved since the women had entered. He wished everyone would pass him by. He made eye contact with Jaira when Lord Eli had brought the ladies over, but he didn't dare look in her direction again. Never had he seen a woman dressed so brazenly. He cursed his eyes for wanting to look back.

Sir Caleb, Sir Gavin, and Inko had been given matching white tunics with leather vests and brown trousers. Inko and Sir Caleb hadn't shaved. Getting started on their beards for Tsaftown, Achan supposed. He couldn't wait to be there.

Lord Eli led his wife before Achan and bowed low. "Your Highness, may I present my wife, Lady Katiolakan?" He held out his wife's hand as if passing her over for Achan to catch. She was pretty and plump with grey skin and sleek black hair. Achan lifted his hand instinctively, then lowered it. What did they expect him to do?

Take her hand and kiss it, Your Majesty, Sir Caleb said. *Have you never seen such a greeting?*

Kiss it?

You're the future king of Er'Rets and must act with dignity and respect in formal gatherings.

Hoping his expression was dignified, Achan reached out. His arm seemed to belong to someone else. He took Lady Katiolakan's dainty, gold-gloved hand and stared at it.

Try to look as if you know what you're doing, Your Highness, Sir Caleb said. *Say something witty and kind, then softly kiss her hand and let go. You're not marrying her. It's not meant to be heartfelt.*

Achan forced yet another smile from his lips. The act caused his freshly wounded cheek to throb. "It's an honor, my lady." He pressed his lips to the gold silk glove then released it.

Pig snout, he wanted to leave.

Lady Katiolikan rewarded his actions with a screeching giggle that took Achan back to the miserable days spent walking in Esek's procession. "The joy is being mine, Your Highness. I am being appalled to be discovering this treachery in Sitna. My heart is going out to all you have been suffering. The gods will be demanding retribution, I am being certain."

How should a prince respond to such? "Aye, it was an outrage, my lady."

Good. But next time say "yes" not "aye." You sound like a soldier.

Achan clenched his teeth. *Why is this evening necessary?*
Because we need supplies if we're to make it to Tsaftown.

Tsaftown. Yes. Achan would focus on Tsaftown. He'd
play this role for a chance to see Lady Tara again. A lady with
charm. And obvious virtue.

Lord Eli gestured toward the other women. "May I also pres-
ent to Your Highness my special guests from Jaelport. Queen
Torrezia Hamartano and her daughters, Princess Mandzee and
Princess Jaira."

Achan couldn't help his bulging eyes. *Princess of what?*

*Cela Duchy. Yes, I know the Hamartano women are vile
creatures, but you must not sink to their standards. Dignity and
respect, if you will.*

The ladies each curtsied. Thankfully, none offered her
hand. Achan bowed with rigid formality without making eye
contact. "I'm honored."

Jaira surged forward and fell to her knees, seizing the legs
of Achan's trousers. "My lord prince, I beg your forgiveness for
my serpent tongue. The words I spoke when last we met were
those of a spoiled child. I promise you, I have grown in wisdom
and grace since then, and I pray you do not hold my behavior
in Sitna against me."

Achan blinked at the pile of black braids pinned to the top
of Jaira's head. It seemed an eternity before he could fathom
how to respond, and when he did, he barely managed a whisper. "Not at all, my lady. Think on it no more, and enjoy your
evening. I've heard Lord Eli is a tremendous host. Please, rise
and tell me if the rumor is true."

Sir Caleb's voice invaded his mind again. *Well said, Your
Highness. You're your father's son after all.*

His insides coiled, but he offered his hand. He was slightly humbled at how she'd humiliated herself, but he still didn't trust her a hair. Now, if she were to treat Sparrow kindly with no witnesses present, he might believe her claim of having grown.

Jaira slipped her black-gloved hand in his. It felt oily. She smelled strongly of a spice he couldn't recognize, as if she'd bathed in the scent. He tried to pull her up, but her skirt had tangled under her knees. She gathered the layers of blue fabric in one hand and tugged. With a yelp she went down again. Achan caught her waist and lifted her to her feet. She stood in his arms, looking up into his eyes, cheeks flushed maroon.

She did that on purpose, you know.

Achan released Jaira and glanced over her head to meet Sparrow's eyes. The boy stood at the foot of the stairs, arms crossed, leaning against a fluted pillar. The smirk on his round face said it all.

You can hear me, Achan said. *Why didn't you answer before?*

She is such the actress. What performance will she give next? Perhaps the tale of the princess *who wins the heart of the young prince.*

Funny. I'd like to see you play my role. Sir Caleb put oil *in my hair. This isn't exactly fun.*

Oh, yes. It does look dreadful to have beautiful women literally throwing themselves at your feet. How ever do you manage?

Jaira pressed a hand over the black stone on her chest. "Thank you, Your Highness. The things a woman must wear to be beautiful. I'm afraid they can be a hindrance."

And now she fishes for compliments. Well? Go on then. You must oblige. It is only polite.

You're such a boil, Sparrow. Achan forced a smile. "They're more than worth the trouble, my lady, I assure you." He met Sparrow's eyes one last time. *Happy?*

Quite.

"We shall feast in my personal dining room," Lord Eli said. "It is more intimate than the great hall." He offered one arm to his wife, his other to *Queen* Hamartano, and led them through a set of painted doors as high as the vaulted ceiling. "Bring your men, Sir Gavin. Dinner is served."

Achan steeled himself and offered his arm to Mandzee, because she was older and Sir Gavin had taught him that was proper. Mandzee smiled and accepted his arm. Achan offered Jaira his other arm. She blinked her dark eyes slowly, then slid her fingers around his bicep.

He swallowed his angst and followed Lord Eli through a set of glass double doors into a narrow room, hoping he didn't trip on the gowns trailing alongside his boots.

Talking with Sparrow had lightened his mood a great deal.

A long table draped with white linen was set for twelve—five on each side and one on each end—with gold goblets, matching trenchers, bouquets of silk irises, and purple linen napkins. Two large candelabras hung from the ceiling. A painting of Lord Eli and Lady Katiolakan covered the right wall. Another set of double doors divided the left wall. A life-sized statue of Lord Eli stood behind the head of the table.

Lord Eli helped his wife sit at the end of the table and settled *Queen* Hamartano to her right. He moved to the head of the table and stood behind the chair, his own statue looming behind him like a shadow.

"My servants have set nameplates at the table," Lord Eli said. "Please take a moment to find your seat."

Achan released the ladies' arms. "Princess Mandzee Hamartano" was painted in purple ink on the small, white marble scroll to Lady Katiolakan's left. Next came Sir Gavin's name, Sir Caleb's, then Jaira's.

"Your Highness." Jaira stood before her nameplate. "Look, you're here beside me."

Heat coursed through Achan at the sound of her voice addressing him in such a way. Sir Caleb's hand on his back prodded him down the left side of the table. "Prince Gidon Hadar" painted in purple script marked his place to the right of Lord Eli and the left of *Princess* Jaira. Of course he'd be seated beside the host. Where else?

Sparrow stood dead center on the opposite side of the table. Good. At least Achan could make private jokes with his friend. He might not survive this evening without them.

Achan pulled out his chair and sat, ignoring Sir Caleb's glare, not caring whether decorum dictated he should wait until the women sat or pull out their chairs and fawn over them with flowery compliments. They could seat themselves.

A thin woman with sallow skin took the seat across from him. She wore a blood-red velvet robe over a black gown that bunched around her neck and up to her chin. Her gaunt face paled next to such vivid colors. Her cheeks caved in like she was sucking a lemon and her bloodshot eyes bulged in deep sockets ringed with dark circles.

A priest of Avenis with a stiff, ivory teardrop hat took the seat beside her. He wore an ivory robe with thick, rolled cuffs. At least ten gold chains in various girths and lengths hung around his fat neck. One long brown eyebrow stretched across his wide, flat forehead like a caterpillar. His eyes were small and fixed on Achan.

It had been days of dried meat and figs, and prison gruel for weeks before that, except for Sparrow's apples. His stomach growled at the idea of fresh, hot food.

Sir Caleb helped seat Jaira to Achan's left. Her spicy smell snaked up his nose, making his eyes water. She scooted closer to the table and her arm touched his. He froze a moment, then casually leaned away, reaching for his nameplate with his right hand. He pretended to examine it a moment, then put it back, careful to shift his weight so he no longer touched Jaira.

A tall and muscular, olive-skinned eunuch with a shaved head entered the room carrying a lidded basket. His eyes were outlined in black, similar to Jaira's. A maroon skirt fell to his sandaled feet, held in place by leather straps that crisscrossed over his bare chest and supported a sword at his waist as well. Achan recalled Jaelport employed eunuchs like slaves. This man must work for the Hamartano family. A shield, perhaps?

The eunuch stopped between Sir Caleb and Jaira and held the basket aloft.

"*Finally*, Larkos," Jaira said to the eunuch. She lifted the lid, and her tiny, hairless dog scuttled out of the basket and curled in a ball on her lap, tail wagging. Charcoal skin stretched over the dog's bony frame. Its huge ears reminded Achan of a bat.

Larkos backed against the double doors behind Jaira. The priest still stared at Achan from across the table, unfazed by the eunuch and bat-dog. Achan met Sparrow's curious gaze. *Having fun?*

Your discomfort is quite entertaining, yes.

Happy to help.

Do you like your seat?

Oh, I dream of torturous moments like these. Do you think it would be rude if I asked Lord Eli to open the doors to get a bit of a draft? If I don't get some fresh air, I may black out from the smell of the princess.

I do not think they have fresh air in Darkness.

Can't you smell her?

It is *a bit strong.*

What is it?

My guess would be a tropical lotion. Do you like the flakes of gold?

Gold? On her skin?

She sparkles for you.

Seems a waste of gold.

A piercing giggle rang out from Lady Katiolakan at the end of the table. Sparrow winced. *Jaelportians have always been brazenly flamboyant.*

Achan raised an eyebrow. *Well, you've got the brazen part right. She may as well be naked. I've never been so uncomfortable in all my—*

"Your Highness," Lord Eli gestured toward the snowball of a priest, "may I present my chief priest, Pontiff Latmus. And this is my advisor, Seer Rheala." Lord Eli laid a hand on the gaunt woman's shoulder.

Achan nodded once for both.

Pontiff Latmus spoke in a low, hoarse voice. "I would be honored, my prince, to show you Avenis' temple after dinner. I am sure the mighty Avenis understands your perilous journey, but to avoid him any longer is a risk you cannot afford, in my estimation."

Jaira set her gloved hand on Achan's arm. "Oh, yes, you must. It's the most beautiful temple I've seen. And Pontiff Latmus has displayed the offerings so you can see everything."

The doors to the dining room swung inward, and a long line of servants entered carrying heaping trays. A rich, meaty smell diluted Jaira's aroma.

"We shall try to make time," Sir Caleb said. Then silently to Achan, *Do not eat until Lord Eli bids you start. Most hosts serve their guest of honor first. I know not what to expect from Lord Eli.*

A servant leaned past Lord Eli and set a tray between Achan's and Seer Rheala's trenchers. It held a roasted bird sitting in a pile of garlic cloves and apricots. Another servant placed a tureen of dark gravy sprinkled with saffron beside it. There were also bowls of flaky whitefish with wedges of lime; pickled beets; tiny, red potatoes; a basket of dark, long loaves of bread; and a tureen of soupy corn.

Lord Eli reached forward and ripped a leg off the bird. He dunked it in the tureen of gravy and dropped it on Achan's trencher. "Do you play dice, Your Highness?"

"Some." But only with Gren or Noam. Most people had refused since it was considered bad luck to consort with strays.

"Do you eat fish, Your Highness?"

"I do." Achan could finish the whole platter himself.

"All our food is imported from Allowntown and Mahanaim." Lord Eli cut a large portion of the fish and slid it onto Achan's trencher. "It is tradition, you know, for the host to serve his most honored guest. For you, Your Highness, I will do the slave's job." He piled two scoops of potatoes next to the fish, then ripped an end off a loaf of bread and set that on top of Achan's pile of food. Lord Eli snapped his fingers, and a servant poured wine into Achan's goblet.

"Your sacrifice is noted." Achan glanced at Sir Caleb. *That's about what I might expect.*

Seer Rheala and Pontiff Latmus began to fill their plates. Lord Eli filled his own. Achan took a deep breath and let the meaty smell soak into him. Should he eat? He doubted Lord Eli's crowd prayed to Arman. Might they thank Avenis?

But Lord Eli simply started eating, so Achan followed suit.

He bit into the leg first, for he had never been given such a large serving—never tasted warm meat. It was juicy and rich, the gravy salty. An unintentional moan escaped. He lowered his eyes, hoping no one heard. He put down the leg and popped one of the little potatoes into his mouth next. His teeth pierced the skin and the warm center mashed in his mouth. The flavor was bland after the fowl. He pinched off a bite of fish. It tasted tart and peppery. He shoved another bite into his mouth and savored the flavor on his tongue.

His first meal as royalty. He circled his plate, alternating between all the different foods.

A small squeak, like a mouse, turned his head. Jaira stared at him, tiny jeweled knife in her dainty fingers. She smiled with all the warmth of a jackal.

A quick glance around the table and Achan saw everyone—except him—was eating with tiny knives and dainty utensils. Even Sparrow. Achan frowned.

"Seer Rheala, tell the prince what your stones said of his visit."

The seer's voice croaked lower than the pontiff's. "I have seen an alliance in the south under a single leader. And I have seen riches, prosperity, and beauty for Mirrorstone."

"Do you see Light?" Achan asked.

Silence fell over the table. Every face turned at him.

"We must not put our hope in the fables of a man who can push back Darkness," Pontiff Latmus said. "We must be practical and heed the warnings of the gods. Seer Rheala has predicted much prosperity. You can choose to be a part of that, or you can choose to go your own way."

"You speak wisely, Pontiff," Lord Eli said. "Seer Rheala, tell our young prince what you see in the north."

"Death."

Achan cringed, not buying a word this woman was peddling.

"I am glad you've come to Mirrorstone, Your Highness," Lord Eli said. "King Esek is overbearing and ignorant of the ways of the gods. Stay with us, and we will raise an army to march against King Esek, take Armonguard, and unite Nahar, Cela, and Arman duchies."

If Lord Eli wanted to convince Achan of his support, why continue to call Esek king?

"And what of Barth?" Inko asked. "Would they be supporting this campaign?"

Lord Eli waved his hand. "Barth supports itself."

"Do you get on well with Lord Falkson?" Sir Caleb asked.

Lord Eli's face tinged pink. "He and I have had our quarrels, as have many neighboring strongholds, but they no longer concern me. Seer Rheala predicted a mutual alliance with Barth long before Kati and I were wed. Ever since, Barth and Mirrorstone have gotten on fine."

Achan bit into his apricot and found the fruit warm, sweet, and juicy.

"Your Highness, have you fought much with the short-sword and shield since you defeated my brother?" Jaira asked.

Achan nearly choked on his fruit. He stiffened, searching for the perfect response. "Only the sword, my lady. I had the pleasure of a second encounter with your brother and some of his companions."

Jaira fed a chunk of meat to her dog. "And did you defeat him a second time?"

"Not as easily. He's a . . . *cunning* opponent." Who'd almost killed him.

"Was he responsible for the wounds on your face?"

Achan's cheeks warmed. "No, my lady."

Jaira smiled in such a way that Achan shivered. Her hatred poured into his senses like hot water in a bath. Still, she sat smiling, crafting friendly, almost flirtatious, comments. Why? Perhaps her mother had put her up to it. Regardless, he wouldn't be able to stomach this game much longer.

He glanced at Sparrow. *I think I'm going to be ill.*

Sparrow gave him a dopey smile. *But you look lovely together.*

You do realize we'll be practicing swords again soon, and when we do, you'll pay for your delight at my expense.

Sparrow snickered out loud, garnering a raised eyebrow from the pontiff.

Achan supposed this was fun for the boy. The lad had seen him beaten to humiliation, imprisoned in a dungeon, had nursed his wounds, and now Achan was the Crown Prince. It was the most outlandish tale. Had the situation been reversed, Achan would've enjoyed poking fun at Sparrow.

The servants filed in again. One whisked away Achan's trencher and replaced it with a silver bowl of berries floating in fluffy cream.

"Is that the Hadar signet ring you wear, Your Highness?"

Achan glanced at the gold ring on his left middle finger. The letters OAH were engraved in the imprint of a castle. "It is Prince Oren's."

"I imagine King Esek has your father's ring, then?"

Did he? And why did Lord Eli insist on calling Esek king? "I imagine he does."

"Pity." Lord Eli scooped cream onto his finger and licked it off. "Have you ever played one hundred, Your Highness?"

"I haven't."

"It is the simplest of dice games." Lord Eli raised his voice. "I have hidden a surprise in the dessert that will dictate your companions for the evening. Chew carefully."

Achan took a bite of berries; the sweetness distracted him from his surroundings entirely. He'd never tasted anything so wonderful. It was even better than Poril's ginger cake. He inhaled the dish until his teeth bit down on something hard and cold. He spit a plain gold ring into his fingers.

Lady Katiolakan shrieked and clapped her hands from the end of the table. "How wonderful this is being."

Lord Eli beamed. "Ah! His Highness found the gold band. How fitting. The gods are playing matchmaker, I suspect."

Achan turned to see Jaira licking the cream off an identical gold ring. He frowned at Sparrow.

The boy shrugged. *You are being positioned. First the matching ensembles, now matching rings. Do you like your intended?*

Achan's lips parted. How could he have missed the coordinating colors of their clothes? *Well, you match us as well, Sparrow. What say we trade? I'll be squire.*

Oh no, I shall not interfere with your special time with the princess.

Jaira's dog lapped the remaining cream from Achan's bowl. Achan stifled a growl. *Is there any poison on the table?*

For you or the dog?

Both.

10

The sitting room, like the dining room, was long and narrow. A fire crackled in an ornate marble fireplace that filled the back wall, heating the room to a sweltering state. Two small, square tables, each seating four, sat in the middle of the room. Fat candles burned in bronze sconces along the walls. A narrow door, likely for servants, was wedged beside the fireplace and the far corner.

Sparrow stood with Sir Caleb by the entrance. Mandzee and her mother sat at the table closer to the door with the pontiff and Seer Rheala. Sir Gavin and Inko never came in. It appeared they wouldn't be playing.

Lord Eli waved Achan and Jaira to sit with him and his wife at the table by the fireplace.

Achan tensed and glanced at Sir Caleb. *Must I?*

Sparrow looked away, fighting a smile.

Sir Caleb raised his brows. *The longer you stand gaping, the ruder you become. Whether Jaira is the love of your heart or Gâzar's spawn, Lord Eli is host and you have drawn matching tokens. Now, offer your arm before you garner the name Graceless Gidon.*

Esek has given the name Gidon enough shame. I doubt I could make things worse.

Take. Her. Arm. Go, Sir Caleb said. *Be charming and witty. Play games. Enjoy yourself, if you can. And if you cannot, pretend, for the sake of your father.*

You aren't playing?

Our time would be better spent gathering supplies.

Achan set his jaw. *But I want to help.*

You are helping, Your Highness. You make our host happy by letting him entertain you. When the host is happy, he shares horses and supplies. Be a charming fellow, now.

Achan stared at the sconce behind Jaira as he spoke, unable to stomach eye contact. "If you're willing, my lady?"

Jaira accepted his arm, nose in the air. "It would be my pleasure."

Sure it would. Achan steered her to the table beside the fire. Her hatred flowed into him, adding to his foul mood. Her spicy smell turned his overfull stomach.

Sir Caleb, if she hates me so much, why does she pretend?

It's likely her mother's wish. Play along. We'll be halfway to Melas before she's eaten her breakfast tomorrow. Should you need us, call. Vrell will be our eyes.

Achan stifled a groan and sat down opposite Jaira.

Larkos, Jaira's eunuch, stood against the wall, two paces to Jaira's right. Achan shot a quick peek at Sparrow, the boy who could barely hold a sword. So, if anything should go amiss, it was the scrawny boy against the muscle-bound eunuch. This didn't ease Achan's discomfort. He'd left Eagan's Elk in his chamber.

Lord Eli slapped a set of ivory dice on the table. "We each roll once, then pass the dice. The first team to reach exactly one hundred wins. You go first, Your Highness."

Achan rolled the dice. A six and a four. "Ten."

"Well done." Lord Eli nodded to his wife, who had parchment and quill. She scratched out ten hash marks.

The game went on. Achan and Jaira quickly made it to a score of ninety-seven, but they were unable to roll a three. Lord Eli and his wife took what felt like an eternity to reach eighty-eight. Then Lady Katiolakan rolled two sixes.

She giggled and threw up her hands. "What shocking a surprise that was being."

Lord Eli squeezed Achan's shoulder. "So close, Your Highness. I thought you'd beaten us for sure. Shall we play again?"

Achan shrugged. "If you like."

And so they played.

Queen Hamartano and Mandzee soon excused themselves for the evening, taking Jaira's bat-dog with them. The pontiff and Seer Rheala watched a few of Lord Eli and Achan's games, then they too retired. Achan hoped this was a sign he'd soon be excused to that massive featherbed he couldn't wait to try.

But Lord Eli ordered more wine and drank through two bottles himself. Achan slowly sipped one goblet. He'd never been permitted wine before but had seen what it could do to a man. Achan wasn't about to risk his sanity with this company, even for the pleasant tingle the drink left between his ears.

Lord Eli's behavior only solidified Achan's discretion. Before long, the young lord could barely keep his dice on the table when he rolled. When one struck Jaira's ear, Lady Katiolakan stood.

"I am begging your forgiveness, Princess. My husband has been having too much wine. I am fearing only his bed will be the cure. Please, be staying and enjoying yourselves as long as you are liking. I am bidding you all good sleep." She gripped Lord Eli's arm. "Septon, my love, it is being time to go."

Achan stood and helped Lord Eli to his feet.

He jerked away. "I can stand myself." He stumbled through the dining room doors.

"I am thanking you, Your Highness." Lady Katiolakan curtsied. "I am praying we will be seeing you at breakfast tomorrow, and then, perhaps, to the temple?"

"Perhaps." Achan didn't want to make any promises. "Good night, my lady."

She curtsied and scurried into the dining room. Her voice carried. "My lord! Oh, Septon, you are being hungry? But we are being finished with dinner, my lord. Let us be going upstairs and be finding your slippers and pipe."

Achan stood awkwardly and listened to the sounds of their hosts' footsteps receding. Relieved, he turned to Jaira, ready to make his excuse to depart.

Jaira laid her gloved hand on Achan's forearm. "You should visit Jaelport, Your Highness. You have never smelled anything like Market Street. The spices alone intoxicate the senses." Her eyes widened. "I can show you. Look."

She removed a small purple pouch from the reticule at her waist. She opened it, her lips curved in a coy smile, and she beckoned with one finger for Achan to lean closer. "You *must* smell this. I promise you, it will not disappoint."

Sparrow stood by the door, looking half dead. Achan could indulge Jaira a moment longer. He bent over the pouch and inhaled. A sweetness he couldn't place filled his nostrils. Much more pleasant than what drenched Jaira's skin. It filled his head with an indescribable joy. He breathed in more and shuddered. Enchanting. Again he took a deep breath, wanting nothing more than to live in the pouch, to roll in the scent.

He leaned back and blinked. Jaira hazed before him like a vapor. His head spun, rolled on his neck like a ball on a needle. He felt so light, so happy. His heart beat wildly as everything came into focus again. His breath caught in his throat.

Princess Jaira.

He'd never seen a more beautiful creature.

Her dark eyes widened, her full lips turned down. "Are you all right, Your Highness?"

He grabbed her hand, lifted it to his lips, and kissed it.

He was in Shamayim. Heaven.

Vrell rubbed her eyes. She thought she had seen Achan kiss Jaira's hand. There! He had done it again. She focused on his mind, hoping his guard was down.

Jaira's amplified giggle made Vrell cringe. "Your Highness. Do you really think so?"

"Princess, what must I do to win your heart? Name me any task." Achan's tone was low and husky, burning Vrell's cheeks. "All I have I lay at your feet."

Vrell gasped. She called out using Achan's connection. *Achan!*

He shook his head as if trying to upset a fly that had landed on his ear.

Achan! She has done something to you.

Achan fortified his mind quicker than Vrell thought possible for his skill, leaving her pushing against a cold wall.

His rapidly developing skills scared her.

Jaira whispered in Achan's ear. He stood and offered his arm. Jaira accepted, and they followed the eunuch through the servants' door, beaming like a pair of newlyweds.

Vrell crossed the room and called for help. *Sir Gavin? They have done something to Achan.*

Sir Gavin's voice yelled in her mind. *Is he injured?*

It seems not. But he is professing his love to Lady Jaira. Come quickly. They have gone.

Don't lose sight of them, Vrell.

Vrell slipped through the door and followed the eunuch, Achan, and Jaira down a cool, narrow corridor. Since Achan had closed his mind, Vrell could no longer hear them.

Jaira steered Achan up a circling staircase. Vrell followed a half level behind, stopping when they stopped, walking when they walked. Jaira's ongoing giggle fueled her anger. Vrell wanted five minutes alone with Jaira and a sword. She was certain she had learned enough to do the job right.

Seeing Jaira's blue train drag around the door jamb, Vrell waited a moment, then peeked down a wide hallway. Halfway down, the eunuch disappeared through a door, but Achan and Jaira stopped. Achan pressed Jaira's face to his chest like a cherished child. His fingers dug into her braids and pulled some loose. He lifted two handfuls to his nose and inhaled.

"Be my bride," he said. "If you'll wait, I'll build us a cottage in the mountains, hidden deep in the trees by a river or creek, a rocky one that sounds as beautiful as it looks."

"But you are to be king. We must live in the palace at Armonguard."

"I'll live wherever you live, for I cannot imagine ever departing from your presence, even for a moment."

Oh dear. Vrell rolled her eyes. Jaira had cast some spell to muddle Achan's mind so he would pledge to marry her, just as Sir Caleb had feared. Esek would marry Mandzee and Achan would marry Jaira, assuring a Hamartano queen on the throne no matter which man won Armonguard.

Sir Gavin? Are you close?

We're in the game room. Which way? What's happening?

Take the servant's exit and follow the tower stairs up three levels. They are here in the hallway. Sir Gavin, Achan proposed. I think she has befuddled him.

Watch them.

Jaira led Achan through a door. Vrell raced down the hall and burst into an antechamber. Larkos, the eunuch, stood like a shield before a set of double doors, painted in black and gold swirls. Two fat candles on thick stands stood beside the door.

Larkos' bronze muscles bulged under the leather straps that held up his skirt. "I'm sorry." His voice came silky and low. "You must have the wrong room."

"I have come for my prince. Let me pass."

Larkos tilted his chin and the candlelight gleamed off his bald head. "What prince?"

Vrell tried to push past him.

He grabbed her arm. "The temple is occupied at this time. The pontiff does not wish to be disturbed."

"Release me!"

Larkos held Vrell against the wall and stared deep into her eyes. Thick black paint outlined his eyes. His lips moved as if he were chewing. He crunched down and blew hot sweet breath in her face. Flakes of wet powder stung her eyes. Her nose burned. She coughed and blinked. Larkos held her until their eyes met again, then he released her and crouched to grab the beam that would slide across the door to lock it.

Vrell drew her sword. Larkos turned in a crouch, and she bashed the pommel against his head. He fell to his backside and reached out to grab her weapon. She struck him again, and he fell onto his side.

He gasped. "You're a woman! Without the antiserum, that's the only way to stand against the anabas dust."

Vrell swelled with a combination of fear and anger and slammed the pommel of her sword against his temple once more. Larkos slumped to the floor, this time unconscious.

She pushed through the double doors and stepped into the temple of Avenis. It was a vast, square room with a vaulted ceiling, dark but for the hundreds of candles in all shapes and sizes flickering on the floor along a narrow, wooden aisle that ran all the way to the statue at the far end of the room. Avenis, crafted from bronze and draped in a purple velvet robe, stood almost as tall as the ceiling. His handsome face cast a flirtatious smirk in Vrell's direction. A wooden altar ran out from Avenis' right and left, covered in gold cups, coins, wilted flowers, and jewels. Achan stood alone before the altar on the right.

"Achan!" Vrell started down the aisle, her boots tapping on the wooden floor.

Achan's blue eyes met Vrell's. "What are *you* doing here?"

"I have come to save your hide, Your Highness."

His brows knit. "You've come to steal her from me."

The very idea. "I do not want her, and neither do you. Think, Achan. You hate Jaira."

Achan's pupils doubled in size. "You lie. You want her for yourself."

A door on the far left wall opened, spilling a brief stripe of light over the dark floor. Vrell backed into the shadows.

Jaira entered with the pontiff. "You must agree this is what Avenis wants for Mirrorstone and for all Er'Rets."

"I see the benefits, Princess, yes. But I should like to consult Lord Eli, Seer Rheala, and the queen, of course."

"My mother said she has spoken to you already."

The pontiff sighed, his pudgy face flushed. "Yes . . . she did, but—"

"Marry us, then. Now."

Jaira and the pontiff reached Achan. Jaira left the pontiff's side and took Achan's hand in hers.

Achan released a ragged breath and fell to one knee. "You've seized my heart, fair lady. I beg you let me serve you. Give me a task. Nothing is too great."

Oh, for pity's sake. Vrell tried to knock and found Achan's mind open. What in all Er'Rets? *Achan!*

He jumped back to his feet, hand on where his hilt would be if he were wearing his sword. "Leave us in peace. We don't want you here."

Come out of here, Achan. This is a bad place.

"You are jealous!"

Jaira whirled, eyes wide. "What is it, my love? Do you hear someone?"

"Sparrow wants to take you from me." He pushed Jaira behind him. "Go away, Sparrow. I don't want to hurt you."

Vrell stepped into the light. "Achan, be serious. Come away at once."

"Frell, isn't it?" Jaira asked, stepping out from behind Achan. "How did you get in here?"

"The door was open," Vrell said.

"I don't like the way you disrespect the prince," Jaira said.

"Well, I do not like how you have stupefied him. It is my duty to protect him, and you have crossed the wrong squire."

Jaira giggled, throwing her head back so that the beads on the ends of her loose braids clacked together. "Your little squire is quite loyal, Your Highness, isn't he?"

Achan's lips twisted in a frown. "He's annoying, as usual."

Jaira sauntered down the aisle. "But he's such a brave young man." Her fingers slipped into the reticule on her belt.

Vrell backed toward the door. "Do not come near me. I saw what that dust did to him."

Jaira merely smiled. "Achan, would you hold him for me?"

"As you command, Princess."

Vrell clicked her tongue in disgust. "Achan, you fool! She has misted you. Do not do this. Pontiff, do you see the lady has bewitched my lord, the prince? She uses magic."

The pontiff shook his head. "Princess Jaira, this is most irregular. I beg you allow me to consult with Lord Eli."

Achan strode over to where Vrell stood and gripped her in a bear hug. Her feet lifted off the floor and her face pressed against his neck. He smelled like honeysuckle soap.

"The other way," Jaira said, "so I can see his face."

Achan dropped Vrell, spun her around, and gripped her from behind. Jaira lifted her hand.

Vrell squirmed, hoping the eunuch spoke truth and the powder would have no effect. Still, she lowered her head and bit Achan's arm through his thick brocade sleeve. He groaned but did not release her.

Jaira blew silvery powder in Vrell's face.

Vrell held her breath as long as she could, but when she could hold it no longer, she gasped. It smelled different from the eunuch's dust. Like spices and baking and flowers all at once. She smiled.

Jaira met Vrell's eyes and her red lips twisted in a smirk. "Release him."

Achan's grip vanished. The room spun. Vrell slumped to her knees, wishing to smell Jaira's powder again.

Jaira's voice came from above. "Now kill him. For me."

Achan's boots clomped away from Vrell. Praise Arman. Achan had refused.

"My lady!" the pontiff said. "I must protest. This is the temple of Avenis, and murder is disrespectful to the true nature of beauty. Don't touch that, Your Highness!"

Steel scraped against steel then more boot steps clomped, nearing. A sharp point pressed against Vrell's throat. "Must I kill him? Can't I knock him out?"

Vrell tensed at the prick against her neck. Achan must have taken a weapon from the offerings.

"Do you not love me?" Jaira asked.

"More than my own breath."

"Why, then, do you question me?"

Vrell drew in a long breath and refocused. Achan stood over her, facing Jaira. He clutched a long machete in one hand and had taken Jaira's face in his other.

"Forgive my foolishness. You're more beautiful than the stars." Then he kissed her.

Fire shot through Vrell. She leapt up and yanked Achan's braid.

His head snapped back and he spun around. "You little fox!"

"Kill him now!" Jaira screamed.

The pontiff scurried back to the side door, glancing over his shoulder every few steps.

Achan lifted the machete.

A tremble seized Vrell. She inched back. *Sir Gavin!*

"I told you. You can't have her!" Achan swung the machete.

We're in the third floor corridor. Where are you?

The temple!

The blade passed so close that Vrell felt wind on her nose. She backed up two steps. Achan pressed forward. Vrell pulled out her own sword, sad as it was against the machete.

Achan swung a powerful attack that knocked Vrell's sword from her hands. It clanged on the flagstones. He swung again. Vrell jumped against the wall, knocking over several candles. The machete struck the gilded plaster, splintering a jagged gash in the smooth surface. Achan growled when the blade would not come out from the wall. He let go and gripped Vrell's throat in one hand instead. He squeezed. A flame licked at the toe of Vrell's boot.

The door burst open. Sir Gavin, Sir Caleb, and Inko thundered inside. All three men drew their swords. Jaira screamed.

Achan released Vrell, wrenched his machete from the wall, and backpedaled in front of Jaira. "No!" he cried. "She's mine, I tell you. She's pledged her love to me. If you're not here to support our marriage, be gone or I'll kill you all."

Sir Gavin scanned the room, brow furrowed in disbelief. "Enough foolishness, Achan. Lower the blade."

"To be making an alliance with Jaelport is being most unwise, Your Majesty," Inko said.

"This is no alliance," Sir Caleb said. "This is Jaelportian mage magic. I can smell it."

Achan yelled and swung the machete at Sir Caleb. The knight blocked the attack and drew Achan away from Jaira. Sir Gavin snaked around Achan's back and thumped him on the head with the pommel of his sword. Achan crumpled to the floor, writhing.

"Get him out!" Jaira screamed. "I knew he held a grudge against me. I knew it!"

Sir Gavin wheeled around, scanning the temple. "Who?"

"This man! The prince!" She pointed a thin, black-gloved finger at Achan, whom Sir Caleb and Inko were trying to pick up. "He attacked me as I was trying to leave an offering."

"Do not be absurd," Vrell said. "The pontiff and I saw the truth."

Jaira's dark eyes flashed. "All night the prince begged for a moment alone, claiming he loved me. I refused. And when I finally withdrew for the evening, he followed me here. Before I could finish my prayers, he barged in and tried to attack me, in the temple of all places. I shall be surprised if Avenis does not strike him down."

Vrell stormed up to stand before Jaira. "You are a mage. You used a love powder on him. The same powder you blew in my face. The pontiff witnessed this as well."

"Ridiculous." Jaira arrested Vrell with a cold stare. "You clearly have not suffered any powder."

Vrell poked a finger against the silky bodice of Jaira's gown. "I know what you did and why. Give up this foolish quest. He will never marry you. You are beneath him in every way. He hates deceit and control and lies. All that the Hamartanos hold dear."

"Vrell." Sir Gavin drew her name out in warning.

"You think tricking him to marry you will make you queen? It only exposes your deceitful nature for all to see. We are not fooled. You seek to marry the prince while your sister seeks to marry Esek. Know this, there will never be a Hamartano queen. I will kill you first."

Jaira gasped and huffed. "How dare you threaten me, stray? Larkos! Where is Larkos?"

"Larkos has been detained," Vrell said. "And you will meet the same fate if you touch Achan again."

"Vrell!"

Sir Gavin stood in the doorframe. Sir Caleb and Inko held Achan's limp body between them, one of his arms over each of their shoulders.

Sir Gavin beckoned her with his hand. "Let's go, lad."

Vrell shot one more glare at Jaira. "Stay away from Achan, or you will regret it." She spun away from Jaira and followed Sir Gavin out the door.

II
_____

Achan woke, pulse pounding in his temples. He blinked until his bleary eyes focused.

His body lay sunken in a featherbed, tucked under warm furs. Where was he? He pushed up onto his elbows, struggling to sit, but pain rushed through his head and his stomach heaved. He collapsed back onto the mattress and breathed deeply, looking up through the open canopy at the flickering firelight dancing across the dark ceiling. When the nausea passed, he reached a leaden arm up and drew the curtain aside. Orange coals smoldered in the hearth beside his bed, sprinkling shadows over the carved birds and vegetation that ensconced the marble hearth.

This was his chamber at Mirrorstone. But he didn't remember coming in. There had been wine at dinner, and later, when they were playing one hundred. One glass couldn't have bested him, could it?

Achan reached out to Sparrow's mind for answers, but his head hurt too much to focus. He lifted a hand to caress his temple, but it was lost in his ridiculously long quilted sleeve. He rolled both sleeves to his elbows and traced the raw scar on his left cheek. A spicy scent lingered on his fingers. Jaira. Why did his hands reek of her? He'd barely touched her.

An image of him holding Jaira's face flitted though his mind's eye.

He sat upright and ripped back the curtains on the other side of the bed.

Sparrow slept on the floor, slouched against the wall beside his bed, one knee pulled up to his chest, an arm draped across it.

"Sparrow!"

The boy twitched, and his arm fell to the floor. He blinked wildly and clutched his pathetic sword. "Is she here?"

"Who?"

"Jaira." Sparrow jumped up and hurried to the bedside. He laid his sword on the bed and set his palm to Achan's forehead. "Oh, Your Highness. Are you well?"

"I feel ill. Fuddled, I think. I've never been fuddled, so I can't be certain. Was there wine with dinner?"

"There is always wine with dinner, but you are not drunk. You were poisoned."

Achan's heart thudded. "I was?"

Sparrow stepped back. "If you remember nothing of last night, perhaps that is best."

"No, tell me." Achan leaned closer to examine a long purple bruise on the boy's neck. "What happened to you?"

"You professed your undying affection for Princess Jaira."

Achan grinned. "Very funny."

"She is a mage. All the Hamartano women are, I suspect. She asked you to smell a powder that robbed your mind and turned you into a sentimental fool. For her."

The look on Sparrow's face sobered Achan quickly. Horror seeped up his spine, bolstered by the lingering scent of Jaira and the memory of the embrace. "Wh-what did I do?"

Sparrow wrinkled his nose. "You proposed. And when I tried to stop you, you attacked me."

Achan rubbed his throat in the place where Sparrow's throat was bruised. "I did?"

"You were right, Your Highness. Passion does increase a man's strength."

The door to Achan's room inched open. Sir Caleb poked his shaggy head inside. "Good. You're up." He threw the door wide and he, Sir Gavin, and Inko lumbered in, carrying their packs as if they were ready to leave that instant. They dropped them inside the chamber and surrounded Achan's bed.

Achan glanced briefly at the knights, then back at the bruises on Sparrow's throat. "Sparrow, I . . . I'm sorry."

Sir Gavin raised a bushy eyebrow. "Vrell has told you, then? What went on last night?"

Achan scratched behind his ear. "I don't understand—"

"There's no need to relive it," Sir Caleb said. "Get dressed. We'll leave as soon as you're ready. Lord Eli doesn't know what to believe. *Queen* Hamartano made her accusations before I could. The pontiff's story doesn't match Vrell's, so he's lying for whatever reason. We'd planned to go anyway. Leaving in secret might make you look guilty, but lingering to prove our case will only give more opportunity for attacks against you, and I'm not trained to fight Jaelportian mages. Are you well?"

"Uh . . . my head. It . . . hurts. But I'll love—" Achan pressed a hand to his neck as if a dry throat had caused that slip of the tongue. "I'll live."

Inko poured a mug of water from a tray on the sideboard. Achan took it and drank.

Sir Caleb pulled one of the wooden chairs over from the wall and sat beside the bed. "Never smell anything from the hand of a Jaelportian woman, Your Highness."

Achan groaned. "Now you tell me."

"Lord Eli was having a hand in this all, I'm being certain," Inko said.

"It simply proves my point," Sir Caleb said. "Achan should marry soon."

Achan fell back and pulled the pelt over his head. He didn't want to hear this again.

"Please." Sir Gavin sniffed long and hard. "Never in all my years of service have I seen anything like this. 'Tis nothing to fear will happen again once we're away."

Achan hoped not. That a simple powder could make him declare love for Jaira Hamartano . . . He shuddered.

Sir Caleb's chair creaked. "But if he's wed, there will be nothing to worry about."

"What is it you fear, Caleb?" Sir Gavin asked. "Once we leave, there will be no more danger of love dusts."

"I fear he falls for the wrong woman's charm. A beautiful woman can be convincing without love dust. If he's properly married, there's no fear of—"

"Many a king still finds beautiful women falling at his feet. His being married won't keep that temptation from him."

"It should," Sparrow said in his bossy tone.

Achan wanted to agree, but his feelings for Gren hadn't kept Lady Tara from his mind.

"But if Jaelport wanted to steal his heir, a child with his gift could be trained against him," Sir Caleb said.

Child? Achan pulled down the pelt and opened his mouth to comment, but could think of nothing to interject into such a statement. His head still hurt, and the conversation didn't help.

Sir Gavin tugged at his beard braid. "If they could steal an heir now, they can steal an heir when he's wed. What will be, will be, Caleb. Why worry over it?"

Sir Caleb scoffed as if it were obvious. "Because his first-born must be legitimate, of course. So no other child could make a claim."

"But should his firstborn be killed, the second could still make a claim, even if he were born out of wedlock."

Achan pushed himself to sitting. "Stop killing off children I don't have! This is madness." He threw off the pelt. He still wore his clothes from last night, but his boots had been removed. He wanted his own clothes, what Gren had made him, not this pompous garb. Besides, it reeked of Jaira.

He slid from the bed, the wood floor cool under his bare feet. He spied Sir Gavin's pack against the far wall and walked toward it, wincing at his throbbing head.

"Your Highness," Sir Caleb said, "as we've mentioned, a king is a target for much trickery and deceit. We second guess possibilities as our way of protecting you."

Achan threw up his hands. "But I wouldn't . . . I could never . . . Why would you all assume I'd betray my wife?"

"We cannot be knowing what you might be doing until you've done it," Inko said.

Accusation stabbed his heart. "None of you have faith in me to do what's right?"

"Truly we're knowing little about you, Your Highness. It'll be taking time to—"

"Aw, 'tis more we don't trust others not to take advantage of you," Sir Gavin said. "Look what Jaira nearly accomplished."

"Don't blame yourself, Your Highness," Sir Caleb said. "There's a reason women rule in Jaelport. Magic is not taught to men there unless they become eunuchs. Remember, Queen Hamartano, not her husband, rules Jaelport."

Achan continued across the room, pitying Lord Hamartano.

"Shouldn't have left him unguarded," Sir Gavin said.

"We didn't," Sir Caleb said. "Vrell was to bloodvoice any threat, and he did his duty."

"His duty?" Sir Gavin's voice rose in pitch. "One lad? To guard our prince? Vrell is untrained, unprepared for such responsibility."

"Since when do you care about a soldier's skill level?" Sir Caleb asked.

Sir Gavin gestured to Vrell. "The lad nearly died trying to protect his future king."

Achan recalled the ugly bruise on Sparrow's neck. He didn't feel worthy to have people willing to die for his stupidity. He opened Sir Gavin's pack and dug for his clothes.

Sir Caleb set a hand on Sparrow's shoulder. "Vrell took out Larkos on his own, which was very well done, boy. He's a hero who'll someday make an excellent Kingsguard knight."

Achan glanced across the room to Sparrow. "You bested Larkos?"

The boy's cheeks flushed. "I caught him slightly unaware."

"So let us at least consider the prince's options for matrimony," Sir Caleb said.

Achan groaned and went back to searching for his clothes.

"The first question is being, an ally or an enemy?" Inko said. "A marriage that will be strengthening current alliances or one that will be forging new peace?"

"Ally, of course," Sir Caleb said. "Er'Rets isn't strong enough to worry about making peace with known enemies. You see what people are willing to do to gain control."

"Then who is supporting our cause that we're trusting?" Inko asked.

"I can only guess," Sir Caleb said, "but Xulon, Berland, Carmine, Zerah Rock. Probably Mitspah, as well, and Tsaftown. Armonguard, of course."

Achan found the shirt and jerkin Gren had made him. He lifted them to his nose and found them stinking of mildew. Sir Gavin's pack must have gotten wet when they waded to shore. He switched the fancy blue shirt for Gren's brown one anyway.

"Does not Duchess Amal have a daughter?" Sir Caleb asked.

"Several, I'm thinking."

"Now Carm," Sir Caleb said. "She'd be our wisest ally. The North would rally behind a queen from Carm or even Therion."

"Wasn't Esek planning the same?" Inko asked. "Wasn't he trying to wed Averella Amal?"

Achan slipped his jerkin on. "Bran's lady? Didn't Macoun Hadar capture her?"

"Aye." Sir Gavin's eyes shifted. "But she escaped."

"Good." Achan had been feeling responsible for the lady when the trade hadn't happened. He started lacing his jerkin.

"Gavin, you know the duchess," Sir Caleb said. "Do you think she'd speak with us about a betrothal?"

Sparrow squeaked.

Betrothal? "Wait." Achan dropped the laces. "I've never met Lady Averella. You can't expect me to marry a stranger. Besides, she's Bran's girl."

Sir Caleb directed his eyes to Achan. "Kings do it all the time."

"Well, not me."

"This matter could be changing the course of who would be ruling Er'Rets," Inko said.

Achan scowled. "I'll not steal a friend's love or use any woman as barter in a war."

"Why ever not?" Sir Caleb asked.

"I . . ." Achan ran a hand through his hair. "Why can't I find my own bride?"

"We haven't time for you to comb the countryside in search of love," Sir Caleb said. "Do you know any noblewomen who are heirs to a duchy and come with a large army? Is there another you'd prefer?"

Achan wanted to scream. He didn't want to be king or marry some woman he didn't know. His head spun. He remembered sitting with Esek at his coming-of-age celebration observing the eligible maids of Er'Rets. Esek had found none of them desirable, but Achan had disagreed on one account.

He hesitated. "She must be of noble birth?"

"Aye," Sir Gavin said.

Lady Tara. He could think of no one else. He said in a small voice, "What of Lady Tara of Tsaftown?"

"Tsaftown is at the end of Er'Rets. No one much cares who they support," Sir Caleb said.

"But I've met Lady Tara. I *like* her. She was kind to me when she thought me a stray. Plus, she's beautiful."

"Ah. Forgive me, Your Highness," Sir Caleb said. "I thought we were attempting to save all Er'Rets from Darkness and peril, but Arman forbid our prince marry someone plain."

"That's unfair. I shouldn't *have to* marry anyone."

"That's the way of kings."

"Well, it's also the way of kings to . . . to change things," Achan sputtered. "To– to– to make new laws."

"Don't be ridiculous, boy," Sir Caleb said.

"Well . . . am I king?"

Everyone went silent.

Achan sucked in a sharp breath, horrified he'd used Esek's pompous catchphrase. "I-I'm sorry."

"Have no fear, Your Highness." Sir Gavin set a hand on Achan's shoulder and squeezed. "You'll not have to decide this day. It'll be a month before we free our men and many more until we reach Armonguard. You have until then."

Leather saddlebags creaked, hooves clomped, and tails swished at mosquitoes as the horses carried them through the dark void. North, supposedly. Sir Caleb had tethered the animals with his rope, so there was no need to steer. Still, it felt awkward to sit atop a horse again, especially in Darkness, but Achan liked Scout. The sleek black horse had a gentle disposition. Achan sensed he was eager to leave Mirrorstone.

Achan had ridden only once before, under Sir Gavin's instruction. He tried to figure how much time had passed, but the weeks blurred together. He'd left Sitna in early summer.

The battle had taken him out for days, then he'd sat in prison for another week or so. They'd been in Darkness five days now. So maybe a month had passed since he'd left Sitna?

It felt like years.

Whether Lord Eli had known of Lady Jaira's treason was unclear, but he'd been more than generous providing horses, food, and supplies for the journey.

The horses soon entered the marshlands. Their footsteps reminded Achan of the sound Gren's feet made when stomping wool in the fulling water. Gren was the only woman he loved enough to marry, and she'd married Riga. He closed his eyes and focused on her face.

Suddenly it was as if he were elsewhere. The dank smell of urine filled his nostrils, making him feel like he was standing beside Gren as she stomped in her tub. But the smell was stronger than fulling water alone. Cold dampness pressed in on Achan. He shivered.

Riga's voice filled Achan's mind. *You're full of dung, knight. I don't believe it.*

Truth is truth. Doesn't matter whether you believe it, a familiar male voice said.

I believe it, Gren said.

Grenny, don't be daft. That goat boy is no king.

Why else would we be here, Riga? You think Lord Nathak would jail us for talking to this knight? Now that's daft.

How was this possible? He'd only thought of Gren and—

"Achan!" Sir Gavin's voice pulled him away from the prison cell. "Stay with us, now. We don't want your mind wandering off."

"I'm here." But Achan's pulse throbbed. What had he seen? Could it have been real? Could Gren really be in prison—and because of him? Esek had done this. Achan had forgotten Esek's threat to hurt Gren and her family if Achan left his service. But what could Achan do? He was so far away.

Arman, help her.

A sharp ping needled Achan's temple. *Sir Gavin.*

Achan lowered his defenses to allow Sir Gavin inside. He was getting better at this.

'Tis a long journey, lad. And now that we're riding horses, we can practice without fear of walking into a tree. We must perfect your ability to bloodvoice. Vrell's going to practice with us. I'll invite him into our counsel now.

Achan's body rocked in the saddle. He closed his eyes, opened them, closed them again. No difference. Amazing how horses could see in the dark. If they neared a cliff, would Scout stop or plummet over the side? Achan sensed himself falling—

A soft prick to his temple. *Vrell Sparrow.*

Achan shook away from his wandering thoughts, embarrassed he'd lost control so quickly. He opened to Sparrow, and the boy's mind floated into Achan's head.

Achan could hear nothing from Sparrow. *How do you guard your thoughts so well? I've never once been inside your head. I mean, I can speak to you, but not see through your eyes.*

You are strong in some ways, but so am I. Arman has given us both what we need to serve our purpose in this life. At least you're shielding well. It no longer hurts to talk to you.

Was he shielding well? A rush of hope filled him. Maybe he'd get the hang of this after all. *Where's Sir Gavin?*

He told me to wait with you. It's strange, these knights knock differently than how I learned. I was taught to give the name of the person I wanted to speak to, but these knights give their own name.

Does it matter?

I suppose not. I usually sense the person as well anyway. Do you?

Never really thought about it. A bird screeched in the distance. Scout snorted and Achan patted his neck. "It's okay, boy."

Sparrow went on. *Do you think someone could give a false name?*

Why would anyone want to?

To get into your mind, fool you, storm or attack in some way.

Achan frowned. He supposed that could happen. *Do you think there's a way to force someone to lower their defenses? I mean, bloodvoicing is a powerful gift. I should think forcing secrets from my enemy would come in handy during a battle.*

It might. But bloodvoicing is good for other uses in war. Jax told me your father used to send orders to his generals in battles. Imagine the benefit of a coordinated attack controlled that well. That is why most Kingsguard knights have the ability in some measure. They are recruited because of it.

The giant knew my father?

No. Jax was a soldier, but he heard your father give orders.

Why didn't you mention this before?

It did not occur to me. We have been traveling a great deal.

Achan's temple prickled.

Prince Oren Hadar.

He straightened and fingered his uncle's ring. He saw a flash of the man on his knees, black hair slicked back over his head, blue eyes penetrating into Achan's as he offered his sword on both palms. The memory of his words brought chills.

"I swear fealty and service to the crown of Er'Rets, to ever give wise counsel, to uphold the laws and customs of our land, to serve where I might, according to my knowledge and ability. Thus swear I, Prince Oren Hadar, to you, my king."

Achan could sense his uncle, even recognize his voice.

Another prick came. *Sir Gavin Lukos.*

Achan lowered his guard to allow both men into his mind.

We'll postpone our lessons for the moment, Sir Gavin said. *Prince Oren, I've asked Master Vrell Sparrow to join us so he might learn ways to help Achan practice.*

Excellent, Prince Oren said. *Master Sparrow, Sir Gavin has informed me of your service to my nephew these past few weeks. All Er'Rets is in your debt.*

Thank you, Your Highness, Sparrow said.

How are you faring on your journey? Are you well?

I am, Your Highness.

Excellent. Nephew, you must learn to communicate without being overheard. I have much to speak with you about but not until you are ready. How do you feel about our link now?

Fine, Achan said.

And after your encounter with the Hamartano mage?

Heat crept up the back of Achan's neck. Did Sir Gavin have to share that blunder with his uncle? *I'm glad to know what she's capable of. I'll not be so foolish again.*

Well said. What is your agenda, Sir Gavin?

We head for Melas. I have a friend there who'll give us shelter and replenish our supplies before we head into Therion.

Good. Achan, I am glad to hear you are well and safe. You must be a student now so that later you can be a king. My prayers go with you on your journey north. Arman protect you.

And as quickly as he'd come, Prince Oren's presence faded away. Achan stared into the black void, the scraping of hooves over rocky soil grating loudly in his ears. Would he ever get to see his uncle on a regular basis?

Very well, Sir Gavin said. *For our first lesson, Achan, I'd like you to shield yourself against Vrell. You'll both stay connected to me. Vrell, you'll try to force your way into Achan's thoughts. Achan, you'll speak with me and try to keep Vrell out. Are you ready?*

Yes, Sparrow said.

Aye. Achan fortified his mind. He patted Scout a moment before more pinpricks needled his temples.

Sir Gavin Lukos.

Achan opened to the knight.

Talk to me about something only you know, lad. Anything will do.

Achan's mind spun. *Um . . . the longer bread raises, the rounder the loaf. Dough raises best in a warm place. Under a cloth and near the fireplace is where Poril always—*

Hold. You started out fine but distracted yourself from guarding your thoughts. Vrell heard half of what you said. Try again. A different topic.

Achan gripped his reins and concentrated on closing off his mind again. A different topic? His knowledge didn't range far. *Oh, I know. It's said goats will eat almost anything, but they're actually quite particular. Their stalls and troughs have to be spotless before they'll eat. Mold in their feed can make them sick. I almost lost Dilly one winter due to mold. Alfalfa is . . .*

Achan paused. His temple itched, almost like a knock, but no voice announced an intention to enter. Was that Sparrow trying to sneak in or someone else?

Achan duplicated himself, leaving one man to guard the door. The other stepped outside and pounced on the mysterious intruder.

A scream spilled out around Achan, but he concentrated, not willing to fail this test. He groped for the person, trying to discover this trespasser's identity, but the person blew away like a gust of wind.

12

"Inko, a light!" Sir Gavin yelled.

Achan's walls collapsed. He whirled around on Scout. "What's wrong?"

Boots splashed through water. A torch whizzed to life from the horse in front of Achan, throwing an amber glow over Sir Gavin's moving form below.

"Vrell's fallen off his horse." Sir Gavin crouched out of sight. "Achan, close your mind. You're spilling all over."

Achan drew up his shields and blinked rapidly, trying to see. He swung his leg over Scout and slid to the ground. His feet splashed into at least a foot of water.

Sir Gavin heaved to his feet, holding Sparrow's limp and dripping form. "He's breathing." Sir Gavin sighed. "Achan, what did you do?"

He did something? "I . . . I doubled myself, then attacked."

"I'll be ransomed." Sir Caleb's voice drifted down from his horse. "You taught him to storm?"

"I most certainly did not. Where'd you learn such a maneuver, lad?"

Maneuver? "I—nowhere. Seemed like the right thing to do."

"And you saw nothing of it, Gavin?"

"Nay. He blocked me. Must have duplicated himself first."

"Did I . . . Is he hurt?"

Sparrow wheezed in a long breath, coughed, sputtered.

"Are you all right?" Sir Gavin bounced the boy in his arms. "Can you stand?"

Sparrow coughed. Nodded.

What had Achan done? He could only stare as Sir Gavin lowered the boy to his feet. He didn't understand any of this. How could simple mind games wound someone? Was this what Vrell had done to the black knight mage?

"What happened, boy?" Sir Caleb asked.

"I am uncertain." Sparrow's voice croaked, eyes fixed on Achan's. "Achan did something strange. I felt . . . pushed from my body. I have a weakness, though. When I bloodvoice too long, I black out."

"It's Arman's blessing you did. A true storm can trap the strongest man in the Veil." Sir Gavin frowned at Achan. "It's not something to be played with."

Achan gulped. "I just wanted to see who was there."

"'Twas Vrell, Achan! We were having a lesson. Do you think it would be anyone else?"

"To be fair," Sir Caleb said, "it was wise to be suspicious of what you sensed. Just don't experiment with your power until you've learned. You could kill someone."

Sir Gavin tugged his beard. "Sir Caleb, surely you can teach this better than I."

"We made a bargain. I'd take over his weapons training if you trained his mind. Gavin, you're the strongest of us all."

"But I'm no teacher! What if Vrell had stormed Achan? What if we'd lost him?"

"You're knowing better than to be giving fear a listening ear," Inko said. "You should be thanking Arman for this warning and be having no more lessons until you can be giving the prince a proper understanding of the art."

Sir Gavin sniffed long and hard. "That's wise, Inko. But he and Prince Oren must be able to speak securely. So we must continue to practice sustaining a private connection. From now on I'll lecture in your mind, lad."

"If we each do our part," Sir Caleb said, "we might manage to train you properly."

"We need to keep moving." Sir Gavin gripped Vrell's elbow. "It's still hours to the sandbar. Come, Vrell. Let me help you onto your horse."

"Thank you, good sir."

Achan cocked his head as Sir Gavin boosted Sparrow into the saddle. The boy must be crazy to be so calm. It was the second time in two days Achan had attacked him. "Sorry, Sparrow. I didn't mean to—"

Sparrow turned his pale, round face down to Achan. "Do not think on it. I should have warned you how bloodvoicing weakens me. What I do not understand is when we first began

I sensed your mind like an icy wall. Macoun Hadar's mind was the same. Always a cold presence."

"I felt that in him too," Achan said as Sir Gavin slogged past to his horse.

Sparrow glanced at Achan, eyes wide. "But with you, the coldness faded. And then I could not sense you at all."

Sir Gavin mounted his horse, water drizzling off the heels of his boots. "The chill you sense is weakness. Achan's still learning. He starts out weak but gets stronger. With Macoun, the coldness is lack of control in his old age. That's why he seeks out strong, young apprentices. He cannot shadow people if they sense they're being shadowed."

"So when Achan learns fully, even those with the gift will not be able to sense him?" Sparrow asked.

"Aye. He'll be able to enter any mind in Er'Rets undetected."

Silence hung on Achan's shoulders like a chain coat. Water sloshed as a horse shifted its feet. A mosquito buzzed down by his elbow.

"Why give such a tool to a man?" Sparrow asked.

"Only to one man at a time," Sir Gavin said. "The man Arman ordains king."

The unattainable expectation gnawed at Achan. He reached up to Scout's saddle horn. "How do you know this?"

Sir Gavin looked down on Achan. "It was that way for your father. And it's written in the Book of Life."

Achan heaved himself back onto Scout. He'd never heard of such a book.

"Where is the book now?" Sparrow asked.

Sir Gavin sighed. "Only Prince Oren knows. Lord Nathak didn't find it a worthy enough treasure when he took Ôwr and the crown jewels from the palace at Armonguard."

Sparrow huffed, as if he had been a Kingsguard knight with Sir Gavin all these years and took this personally. "They discard the one treasure that matters."

Achan might as well be listening to one of Minstrel Harp's long tales. Could this truly be his life? Destined to be the most powerful bloodvoicer? Arman had not spoken to him since he stood before the Council of Seven.

What if he'd imagined it?

As they rode through Darkness, Vrell tried to picture Bran's face. She could see his sandy brown hair, brown eyes, and sunburned skin individually but could not put it all together.

Had it been so long?

Once she got home, her first task would be to plan her wedding. She envisioned herself in a blue gown standing with Bran before the priest and all their friends and family.

Yet in her vision Bran scowled down. *I revoke my proposal, my lady.*

A winepress squeezed Vrell's heart. *But . . . why?*

You are thin and homely and look like a boy. I wanted to be Lord of Carm, but that is not reason enough to settle for one such as you.

Vrell tensed, throat burning. *But you said I was beautiful. You called me a dove.*

That was long ago. I've had time to think. I mean, you've been dressed a boy for months and no one has ever doubted that is what you are. I'm to be a knight. How could I marry someone like that?

But you love me. You told Achan about me.

Only to brag. If you were here, maybe I could be persuaded, but you cannot expect me to wait forever. There are many truly pretty girls in Er'Rets.

Please, Bran, this is so unlike you. I do not . . .

Vrell gripped her reins and snapped back to her physical location. Another trick of Darkness? It had been a long while since she had spoken to another. "Sir Gavin, can we talk aloud? My thoughts are beginning to wander."

"Of course. Caleb?"

Sir Caleb filled the miles with tales of the kings of old. Hours later, they made camp on what Sir Gavin claimed was a sandbar that ran for miles along Arok Lake. The air was cool and damp this close to the water. After a meal of smoked fish and flatbread, Achan and Vrell practiced swordplay around a red torchlight stabbed into the sand. Sir Gavin kept watch with his nose and mind.

The red glow cast eerie shadows over Achan's face. It was difficult to see his sword when he swung it above his head.

"I like having my own weapon, even if it is a poor thing." Vrell held her sword the way Achan held his. "I felt so vulnerable without one."

"A man does tend to walk taller with a sword at his side." Achan swung at her legs and she managed to parry his blow. "I did when I first wore Eagan's Elk."

Vrell hid her smile. Achan walked taller every time he wore—she lowered her sword. "Did you say *Eagan Elk*?"

The red flame sparkled in Achan's eyes. "*Eagan's* Elk. Aye. That's my sword's name."

Vrell's mind spun. "Really?"

Achan grinned, lopsided. "What? Don't you like it?"

"Oh, no. It is a fine name." Only Vrell had heard the name Eagan Elk from her mother. It was a person's name. An odd name for a sword.

Achan tapped his blade against Vrell's. "Why don't you name yours?"

Vrell frowned at her little sword, feeling foolish to have paid so much for a weapon Achan found so inferior. Though she had only paid for half. Jax had paid the balance. Had the giant known the weapon was so flawed? "I would not know how to name a sword."

"Why not a name to fit the bearer? You're small and witty. How about Little Kwon or Firefox?" Achan broke out into a wide grin. "What about Gebfly?"

Vrell clicked her tongue. "Are you calling me a locust?"

"They *are* pests."

"Are you calling me a pest?"

Achan shrugged. "If the boot fits."

Vrell raised her weapon to middle guard and spread her feet in the sand, ready to fight. "I like Firefox, thank you."

Achan's hearty laugh made her crack a smile. "Very well. But I suggest you get it sharpened when next we stop, or *Dullfox* might be a more appropriate title."

Vrell gritted her teeth and swung. Achan dodged and Vrell lunged past. He slid an arm around her neck and brought his blade to her throat. "Hmm. Maybe *Slowfox*."

She jammed her elbow into Achan's ribs.

He released her, chuckling. "Ticklefox?"

She lifted her weapon again. "Arrogance does not suit you, Your Highness."

He raised his eyebrows. "Nor does the title *Your Highness*." He swung at her waist.

Stubborn man. Vrell lifted to parry, but his blade whacked her hip. She stumbled sideways, kicking up sand, thankful for the cushion of her disguise. It would not stop Achan's blade for long. "Maybe we should not drill without armor."

"We don't have any armor, and you want to learn to protect yourself. Besides, I'm not even swinging hard."

He went easy on her for a while. It bolstered her courage to hear Firefox hit his blade, but the exercise tired her quickly. Thankfully, he stopped often to explain things.

"If you parry with the edge, you dull your blade further. Parry with the flat . . . Don't try to defend from back guard. It leaves you vulnerable . . . Back up, Sparrow. No one in his right mind would begin with swords crossed . . . You swing too slow. Try for a combination of strong, quick thrusts. Your goal is to weaken my guard, to break it so you can strike."

Finally Vrell could take no more. She fell onto her rear in the sand, gasping for air, limbs aching. "I am pathetic." She took a short breath. "None of this will make a bit of difference." Another breath. "I am simply not strong enough."

Achan sat beside her and leaned back on his elbows, panting. "Remind me your age."

"I will be fifteen years this fall." Eighteen, actually, but who would believe her to be a seventeen-year-old man?

Achan took a deep breath. "So you're small for your age. Sir Caleb said he'd teach you some tricks. I'm no expert. You recall how Sir Kenton nearly killed me?"

She pulled her knees to her chest and wrapped her arms around them. "Achan, you are incredibly brave. You struck down at least ten Poroo."

"So? Poroo are terrible warriors. That's why they attack from the trees."

"Still, I would have run from the battles you faced. Sir Kenton has been a knight many years—and he betrayed your father. You have been sword-fighting how long? Three months? I could not have done all you have. I would never have tried."

Achan stared into the red flame, lips pursed, eyebrows furrowed. Always so hard on himself. Blaming himself.

Despite Vrell's best efforts, the cut on Achan's cheek had healed in a long, red slash. And his other cheek looked even worse after the fight with the black knights.

Achan dug a hole in the sand with the heel of his boot. "We each have our skills, I suppose. Just know, Sparrow, you're as much a hero with your bag of weeds as any of us are with a sword."

Vrell lifted her sword. "Fire*weed*?"

Achan chuckled. "I think *Weed* says it best."

Vrell and Achan put away their weapons and crawled into their bedrolls. Sir Gavin put out the torchlight, and Vrell replayed Achan's words again and again in her mind.

He thought she was a hero.

13

Achan held his shield over his head to protect it from the rocks the Poroo pitched from the treetops. The melon-sized stones clunked against the wood with such force that his forearm continually bashed against the top of his head.

A Poroo warrior charged from the side, spear held high. Achan lowered his shield in time to deflect the spear, but a rock struck his unprotected head and he crumpled. The Poroo poured out of the trees upon him, massing, swarming.

A screech woke Achan. He pressed his hands against moist sand and pushed himself to a sitting position, relieved the Poroo had only been in a nightmare. He patted the sand. Where was his bedroll? He blinked into the surrounding void, straining to see any sign of movement.

"Sir Gavin?"

The darkness returned only silence.

"Who's on watch? Inko? Sparrow?"

Achan's voice seemed so loud. Could he still be dreaming? He raised his voice. "Hello? Sir Caleb?" The sound sent a throb through his skull. Wincing, he lifted a hand and found a tender lump on the back of his head.

His stomach lurched. Had someone attacked while he'd been sleeping? Poroo?

He got to his knees and reached out to his right, then left, patting the moist ground, hoping to get his bearings, hoping he'd simply rolled off the bedroll in his sleep. Wet sand wedged under his fingernails. No bedroll.

Nothing but sand.

His heart pounded faster. "Sir Gavin?"

A piercing squawk answered from Achan's left. He cringed, eyes darting around the dark, searching for any change in the inky-black hue. One of the demon birds was close. He quickly fortified his mind, then reached out.

Sir Gavin?

His temple twitched, but no name accompanied the knock. He took care not to attack in case this was a test.

Sir Caleb?

Achan sought out Inko's mind next. Why did no one answer? Had they been taken? Killed?

Sparrow?

Whoever was trying to penetrate his mind increased their efforts. Achan's temples throbbed more than the welt on the back of his head. The pressure increased tenfold, brutal, forceful. Achan clutched his face and bent forward until his forehead met the grainy sand. He screamed.

An oily voice magnified in his mind. *Get up.*

Unable to disagree with the voice, Achan gritted his teeth and stood. In his head, he multiplied himself ten times and surrounded the fortress of his mind, forcing the oily voice, and its control, out. The pain subsided. He called for Sir Gavin again, then Sir Caleb, then Sparrow.

No one answered.

A green light shot into the air and hovered above his head, illuminating the sandy terrain in an eerie glow.

Achan released a long breath laced with a moan.

Black knights.

He squatted, groped for his sword. Pig snout! Where was it?

Four men slid into the green glow, dressed in black armor with hard black masks. The one on the end held his hand aloft, pointing at the green orb above Achan's head. Achan studied them, pausing on the third knight in the line. Lofty bean pole posture and graceful stride brought a familiar fury.

Silvo Hamartano?

The third knight lifted his hand and a green ball of light shot out from his palm, up above his head, lighting more of the sandbar and the greasy black hair at the top of his mask.

It *was* Silvo.

Achan punched one fist into his other hand. The bezel and crest on Prince Oren's ring pressed inside his palm. He rubbed his thumb over his engraving, sought his uncle's face, and called out. *Prince Oren?*

His uncle's voice shot into him with a staggering force. *Achan? What is it?*

I'm surrounded by black knights. They're going to attack me. I'm alone. I don't know where Sir Gavin and the others are.

Relax and let me see.

Achan breathed deeply. He couldn't feel when his uncle looked out from his eyes.

We shall fight them together. Sir Gavin told me you can storm.

Two more balls of green light shot skyward.

Um . . . I've only done it once. Accidentally.

Keep your sword ready. They will attack physically while the leader attacks your mind. Do you know where the leader is?

My sword is gone. I have no weapon.

Stay calm, Nephew. Look for the leader.

Achan scanned the dark sandbar. The four black knights had encircled him ten paces away. *I only see the four, but I think the leader spoke to me. Does that mean he's close?*

It may or may not. Perhaps he is one of the four apparitions.

Uncle, I don't think these are apparitions. One is Silvo Hamartano, I'm certain. Achan kept his eyes on the thin figure.

Then it will be easier to defeat them. I will take the two to your left. You take the other two. One at a time, seek out a mind and storm.

Easy for Prince Oren to give the order, but these men weren't trying to enter Achan's mind. They simply stood there, appearing weaponless, conjuring green orbs. How did one storm? He'd only managed before because he'd sensed Sparrow trying to get into his mind.

Achan concentrated on the knight he thought to be Silvo Hamartano. A familiar, lofty voice chanted words he couldn't understand.

Râbab rebabah râbah yârad. Rûwach âphâr mayim êsh, machmâd pârar.

Achan blinked. A dark line obscured part of his vision. He stared at a dazed pale man wearing a doeskin jerkin.

Wait. That was his body. Pig snout! He'd entered Silvo's mind, the black mask obscuring his vision. Why couldn't he stay in his own boots? Had he concentrated too hard?

Silvo's breath hissed, creating warm moisture between his face and the wooden mask. He continued to chant, oblivious Achan had entered his mind. *Râbab rebabah râbah yârad.*

The black knight on Silvo's right crumpled to the ground.

"Zinder? Zinder!" The wooden mask muffled the panic in Silvo's voice. "Marken? Zinder has fallen!"

Prince Oren had defeated one man.

"*Râbab yârad!*" a voice yelled from Silvo's left.

"Fine!" Silvo continued to chant the words in his mind. *Râbab yârad. Râbab yârad. Râbab yârad. Râbab yârad.*

A shadow stretched out in front of Silvo. He glanced back to see four figures—identical to him—closing in. To Silvo's left, another four approached the black knight there. The three remaining apprentices were acting as wielders, calling forth apparitions of themselves.

"Yes," Silvo whispered, looking back to Achan's dumfounded, empty body. "Fight these, *stray*."

Achan popped back into his own mind. He staggered, surprised to find his muscles weakened. The twelve apparitions glided past their wielders, advancing toward him. He couldn't stand here and be killed. He sprinted toward the fallen man.

"No!" Silvo yelled.

"Concentrate," another knight said.

Achan slid to his knees beside the body. He patted the man's waist, found a sword, and wrenched it from its scabbard. He spun around barely in time to meet a fierce cut from a black blade. He backpedaled and took stock of his opponents. They moved toward him slowly, as if they had overeaten and were too full to move faster. Behind them, the three wielders stood like statues, arms outstretched as if worshipping the green orbs.

A man's voice cried out and one of the wielders crumpled. Four apparitions vanished.

Achan calmed, glad Prince Oren—a capable warrior— fought with him. Eight apparitions now. Better. Still, it might be best to flee. Slow as they moved, he could likely escape.

He sprinted into the dark void, praying the sand remained level and dry. Two clouds of glowing green smoke whirled before him and solidified into two black knights. Achan skidded to a stop, head twisting as he tried to keep all eight apparitions in sight. He lifted the sword to the closest one, hoping he could stall it long enough to drive off the second.

The apparition swung. Achan parried, but the opposing blade sailed through his sword and body. He screamed, startled, and barely remembered to turn and meet the second apparition's blade. This one struck, rattling Achan's arms.

Why were some solid and some not?

Nephew? Prince Oren called.

The other apparitions had reached Achan now. He parried another blow and ducked, wishing there were rocks to throw. *I'm here.*

What happened?

Uh . . . I failed. Again.

How do you mean? Speak clearly, boy. This is no time for sarcasm.

I don't know how to storm. I ended up in Silvo's head. I can't understand the difference between watching and messaging and storming. A sword clipped his shoulder. He growled, rammed the offending knight with his other shoulder, and went down, tumbling on the wet sand.

Get back on your feet, boy. You're too easy a target on the ground.

Too late. The apparitions swarmed, kicking and nipping his flesh with their black blades.

Achan cradled his head, squeezing every muscle and groaning against the lacerations and strikes biting his flesh.

Call on Arman, Prince Oren said. *Only he can help you now.*

Arman? A boot struck lower back. He choked on a scream as the shocking pain flared his old arrow wound. What could he say to Arman? *I'm a fool who cannot use the gift you gave me? Please defeat these evil apparitions?*

A kick to the side of Achan's head ended his need to figure it out.

Achan jerked awake underwater. He sucked in a sharp breath, and tepid water filled his nose and throat. He gagged and tried to hold his breath but there was little in him. Thankfully, someone pulled his hair, yanking his head above the water line.

He coughed and sputtered and opened his stinging eyes. Dark, firelight, before a stream. But the rotten smell left no doubt: he was still in Darkness.

He knelt on sharp, rocky soil before a wooden tub, wearing only his linen undershorts. Water dripped down his face and neck and made winding streaks down his chest. His wrists were shackled behind his back, the metal cool on his skin. He groaned through another cleansing cough. A familiar trace of bitterness coated his tongue. Âleh?

He called out to test his fears. *Prince Oren?*

Whoever held his hair released it. Achan swayed, head throbbing, chest burning. He sat on his heels and turned. Two black knights stood behind him. Their wooden masks were flat with two straight slits, one long one for the eyes and a smaller one for the mouth. Achan craned his neck the other way. A campfire burned a few paces back. Beyond that, four horses were tethered beside a cart with a mule hooked to the front. Two bodies lay on their backs in the cart. The moisture on the spindly, black trees glowed in the distance, outlining a forest.

But only two black knights. Prince Oren had done well disabling his targets. But how would Achan get away? If they had silenced his bloodvoice . . .

Achan sniffed. "Where's your leader?" His voice sounded weak.

"He is advising us from afar," a man said. Not Silvo. His accent sounded like Inko's.

"What do you want with me?" Achan gasped in another long breath. "Where are my companions?"

"Lord Falkson wishes to sacrifice you to Barthos in a ceremony to honor our god and master." Silvo. The slender olive-skinned Jaelportian removed his mask and glared down on Achan, his eyes as oily and black as his hair.

Achan's mind reeled. "Lord Falkson is your master?"

"All of Barth will attend the ceremony. The slaying of Arman's king will be a day celebrated for centuries to come."

Slaying? Achan stalled, seeking a way to escape. "Come now, Silvo. You don't believe I'm anyone's king, do you?"

"Unfortunately, I do. You've changed jobs more than my sisters change gowns. First a stray, then a squire, then a servant, then a soldier. It should have taken much longer to work your way up the political ladder, but at least this way I'll see you killed faster."

If Achan could get to a horse . . . No boots and almost no clothes, but at least he'd be free. "Was Jaira also trying to kill me?"

"I no longer care what my sister does. I have aligned my future with Barth. Men have power in Barth, you see. Women rule in Jaelport. They always have. A Jaelportian man must leave Cela Duchy to find true freedom. This I have done."

"How's that work, exactly? Do women blow powder in your face every time you disagree?"

Silvo snorted. "You have no idea what my mother and sisters are capable of. I will never go back. My brother and I prefer to serve a more powerful and just master."

"Brother?"

Silvo's eyes narrowed. "What did you do to him?"

"Who?"

"My brother, Sir Marken, you fool."

"I didn't do anything."

"You hurt him. And Zinder. What did you do?"

Achan opened his mouth but didn't speak. He didn't know enough about storming to explain Prince Oren's actions.

Silvo grabbed Achan's head and pushed him toward the water. Achan twisted so his shoulder struck the top of the wooden tub. Silvo had better leverage and forced Achan down. Achan's arm scraped over the tub's rough edge. He managed a deep breath before his head plunged beneath the water again.

Blood rushed to Achan's head. His face burned with pressure. He held his breath as long as he could, then jerked up, hoping Silvo would think him choking and pull him out. He sucked in a mouthful of water by accident. He tried to swallow, but the liquid ran up his nose instead. It burned and caused him to gasp in more water. He tried to lift his head, but two sets of hands held him under. He shook and fought, all the while gulping water.

The hands released him. He pulled his head up and gasped, but air didn't enter his lungs. He coughed and slumped onto his side. His stomach heaved, and a mixture of water and bile streamed past his lips.

Silvo kicked him in the back. "That's disgusting, stray."

Achan panted and wheezed, ignoring the smarting pain from Silvo's boot. Between breaths, he managed, "I'm . . . not a . . . stray."

Silvo clutched Achan's hair. He lifted him up and dropped him on his knees. "What did you do to our men?"

Achan shifted his knee off a sharp rock. "*I* didn't do anything." He coughed up more water and spit it at Silvo's feet.

Silvo punched him. Fire shot through Achan's left cheek. He fell back and caught his weight on his right elbow, barely managing to stay off the ground.

"Did that hurt?" Silvo leaned over and dragged his fingernail over the wound on Achan's left cheek, ripping away the scab. "I like your new marks."

Achan grunted against the pain and slumped back to escape the pressure of Silvo's finger, falling on his bound hands. He tuned his open wound to the ground where Silvo couldn't reach. Silvo straddled him, grabbed his chin.

"Enough," a muffled voice said.

Silvo released him and stood. The second black knight removed his mask. His grey hair puffed out like a mushroom. Achan's brows furrowed. He recognized Sir Nongo as the towering black knight who'd attacked him—who'd nearly killed him—on the journey to Mahanaim.

"Are all of you mages?" Achan asked.

"Sakin Magos are being more than mages," Sir Nongo said. "We are being strong in our bodies *and* our minds. We are being invincible warriors."

Invincible? "When the four of you attacked me—alone, unarmed, and unaware—didn't two of you go down like redpines?"

Silvo kicked Achan's thigh.

Sir Nongo pushed Silvo back. "We are not having time for this." His pale grey skin and grey hair made him look like a living corpse. "We have been silencing your mind games. You might have been succeeding once, but you will not be again."

Achan ran his tongue over the roof of his mouth. The lingering bitterness was more than the rancid aftertaste of bile. They had given him the âleh tonic. A chill seized him. Not even Prince Oren could help him until its effects wore off.

Call on Arman, his uncle had said.

But Achan knew so little of Arman. Cetheria, the goddess of protection, had been the goddess he'd served all his life, though she had done nothing for him. In fact, the one time he'd entered her temple, he'd heard another voice—Arman's voice—claiming that Cetheria was a false god.

Well, if Arman could talk to Achan, why couldn't Achan talk to Arman? It seemed a bit bold to address any god outside his temple, though circumstances were dire. Perhaps if he—

"We must be moving," Sir Nongo said. "Silvo, be switching his cuffs to the front and hooking him to the cart."

Silvo kick-rolled Achan to his stomach, giving him a mouthful of moist sand. Achan spit the grittiness from his mouth. His right cuff came free and another sharp kick propelled Achan onto his back. Silvo drew his hands together in the front, but before he could hook the cuffs, Achan kneed him in the chin and used both feet to kick Silvo back. Silvo staggered.

Achan jumped to his feet and slugged Silvo's nose. Silvo grunted, shot a dark glare Achan's way, and lunged.

Achan darted aside and swung the iron cuffs into the back of Silvo's greasy head as the young lord stumbled past. Achan spun toward the horses and met Sir Nongo's black blade, pointed at his chest.

He froze and lifted his hands, sucking in long gasps of air. The metal cuff dragged his right wrist downward. His left knuckles throbbed from Silvo's nose.

"Silvo," Sir Nongo said. "Be putting out the fire. I will deal with the stray."

Silvo growled from behind Achan. He teetered past Sir Nongo, a trail of blood running down his neck from his oily hair. His nose didn't seem affected by Achan's fist.

Sir Nongo waved his blade, directing Achan to the back of the cart. "Soon you will be meeting Gâzar." The knight snagged the lose cuff, threaded it through a slat on the back of the cart, and secured it to Achan's free wrist.

Achan forced a brave response. "Arman will ransom me."

Sir Nongo stared down on Achan from heavy-lidded eyes. "Only Barthos is having power in Barth." He walked to a white and black horse and mounted it.

Achan studied the bodies in the cart but couldn't see well enough to recognize them. Silvo's brother, perhaps? Stormed? Trapped in the Veil?

To his left, Silvo kicked dirt over the campfire, bringing a deeper darkness, drawing Achan's eyes back to Sir Nongo, who now held a lit torch aloft. He rode ahead of the mule-drawn cart, pulling the other three horses on a tether behind him.

Silvo climbed up to the wagon seat and steered the mule after Sir Nongo. The wagon wheels grated over the sharp rocks, tugging Achan's wrists forward, then the rest of him.

Achan stumbled along in the dark, his bare feet pained on the sharp rocks. His heart quaked in his chest. He called out again, to see if the âleh had worn off.

Sir Gavin! Sir Caleb! Prince Oren! Inko! Sparrow!

No answers came.

Achan did not want to be sacrificed. He tipped his head back, as if to look up to Shamayim.

Arman!

14

Vrell's horse carried her north. Though her surroundings were black and Darkness called to her fears, she knew her horse was tethered behind Scout, who was directly behind Sir Gavin. She focused on Sir Caleb's voice as he lectured on the long-time feud between Magos and Cherem. Vrell had a pretty good grasp of history, but when Sir Caleb mentioned the Sar's custom of sacrificing his female children, she had to interject.

"The Sar kills all female children?"

"Only his own," Sir Caleb said. "Women are property in Cherem. A man may take two wives: an ishaw and a beten. A beten bears him children. An ishaw is poisoned so she may never bear children and serves as her husband's slave. Should a man's beten be unable to bear children, or should she bear only females, the man may banish her and choose another."

"That is despicable!" Vrell said.

"Esper was an ishaw. I met her in Armonguard when her husband was looking to buy a bow for sport."

"Who is Esper?"

"My wife."

Vrell sucked in a sharp breath. "I did not know you were married, Sir Caleb."

"You didn't ask."

Vrell paused to consider this. "Where is Esper now?"

"In Armonguard with Tyra. Tyra is Inko's wife."

Inko's wife? How sad to have your husband gone so long. Vrell wanted to hear how Esper came to be Sir Caleb's wife and not the Cherem man's ishaw. Then about Tyra and Inko.

"Achan, what do you think of Cherem's ways?" Sir Gavin asked.

Vrell waited, imagining Achan would be as horrified as she, but he did not answer.

"Achan?"

No answer.

"Light!" Sir Gavin called from the front of the line.

Vrell's horse stopped. Orange torchlight fizzed behind Vrell, illuminating Achan's slumped form on Scout. He must be sleeping. She hoped his mind hadn't drifted too far.

Ahead of Achan, Sir Gavin loosed the rope tethering the horses and reined his horse about. He rode alongside Scout, reached out, and grabbed Achan by the scruff of the neck. "Achan? Speak to me, lad."

Vrell could see Achan's left eye, open and glassy in the torch light. Her breath hitched. He seemed stunned or—dare she think it?—dead.

Sir Gavin gripped Achan's face in both hands. "Come out of this man, black spirit! In the name of Câan, the Son God of Arman."

Achan arched his back as if snow had gone down his shirt. A horrible screech flew from his lips, a sound Vrell knew he could never make.

Her pulse raced and she prayed. *Arman, please protect Achan from this affliction. Protect him from Darkness.*

Achan's body began to dissolve, slowly shrinking in the saddle like a mound of watery black mud. Vrell screamed. The mud took shape, slowly forming a large bird with a rat's face.

A gowzal.

The bird flapped its long, webbed wings, beating its foul stench over Vrell in bursts of air. Achan's horse reared. Sir Gavin gripped the animal's reins as the gowzal flew away.

Vrell's horse danced about and snorted. She held the reins tightly. "It is okay, boy."

"Eben's breath!" Sir Caleb said from the back of the line. "Where is the prince?"

Sir Gavin scanned the dark land. "They must have taken him while we slept."

"But we were being on watch, Gavin," Inko said. "How could we have been missing such a thing?"

Sir Gavin sniffed. "'Tis my fault for not speaking to him this morning. I should've been more cautious."

"It's not been more than a few hours," Sir Caleb said, "but they could be anywhere."

"I've called to him with no success." Sir Gavin blew out a breath in a whistle. "Will you all try?"

Vrell sought Achan's face, the scars on his cheeks, his wide grin. "He does not answer."

"Nor me," Inko said.

"None of you can hear me either?" Sir Gavin asked.

Inko's voice had a sharp pitch. "You now are calling out?"

"Aye."

Sir Caleb steered his horse beside Sir Gavin's. "The water this morning *did* have the slightest taste of mint."

Sir Gavin nodded once, almost bowing in shame. "We've been breached in more ways than one."

Vrell cast about for understanding. "Mint is bad?"

"It's strong enough to mask the bitterness of the âleh flower. Someone has silenced us." Sir Caleb's horse stomped its feet and the knight patted the horse's neck. "Whoa, girl."

Vrell ran her tongue over the roof of her mouth. A hint of mint lingered, but nothing resembling the bitterness of âleh. When could this have happened? How long until it wore off?

"Inko. Do you have any dried karpos?" Sir Gavin asked.

Inko reached for his saddlebag. "I'd be foolish to not be having it."

"Good. We must seek out the wielder before he escapes. No spirit can manifest without the help of a man. Someone must have followed us to keep up Achan's illusion."

Sir Caleb handed the torch to Inko, who was still digging in his saddlebag. Vrell met Sir Gavin's stricken expression and dared not speak.

Stones clicked in the distance, like footsteps.

Sir Caleb spurred his horse and galloped away. Sir Gavin rode after him.

"It's looking like they have been finding him."

Vrell stared into the darkness where the knights had ridden, listening to the horses' hooves receding. "Achan?"

"The wielder." Inko sniffed a leather pouch. "After all Gavin has been going through to be finding him, to be losing him to a mage and a gowzal is most distressing. May Arman be having mercy on our numerous imperfections."

Vrell prayed Arman would protect Achan, wherever he was. She hoped Inko had enough karpos for all of them. Jax had taught her it was the only thing that could counteract âleh.

Moments later Sir Caleb returned, holding a thrashing body across his lap. Sir Gavin rode up behind him and dismounted. He grabbed the figure by the back of the shirt and dragged him to the ground.

A pale-skinned boy, no more than thirteen, kicked and swung his skinny arms about. "Let go!"

Sir Gavin pushed the boy's face to the ground and pressed one knee into his back. "Where is he?"

"I know not who you mean." His voice cracked, caught between boy and man. "I'm bound for Melas to see my sister."

"Then where is your pack?"

"I have no pack, sir."

In one motion, Sir Gavin flipped the boy over in the watery sand. "I don't want to hurt you, lad. Don't tempt me."

Sir Caleb dismounted and took the torch from Inko. Light spilled over the boy, revealing pale, freckled skin and bright orange hair.

Vrell gasped. "I know him."

Sir Gavin's mustache curled down. "Well?"

"He is Locto Eli," Vrell said. "Lord Eli's little brother and squire."

"Are you?" Sir Gavin clamped a hand around the boy's chin. "Locto, we left your brother back in Mirrorstone. He didn't mention having a sister in Melas."

The boy hissed, the sound forming strange words. "*Gowzal, yârad. Pârar no ôyeb.*"

Sir Gavin clenched the boy's tunic at the base of his throat. "Don't try your witchcraft on me, lad."

"*Gowzal, yârad. Pârar no ôyeb! Gowzal, yârad—*"

"*Sh'ma Er'Rets, Arman hu elohim, Arman hu echâd.*" Sir Gavin's voice started low and grew to a yell.

Warmth bathed Vrell as if a summer breeze was blowing through Darkness. Locto's eyes went wide. His body trembled. Had he felt the warmth too? Arman's presence?

"That's the *true* old language," Sir Gavin said. "What you speak has been perverted far from what Arman originally spoke to the kings of Er'Rets. You worship a false god and call on black spirits. To what end? To be used, that's what. As a tool of Gâzar."

"That's not true," Locto squeaked.

"You worship demons, boy. You let them toy with you. You, a creature created to serve Arman. You defile yourself."

Locto shook his head. "Barthos is *not* a demon. He's a powerful god. I've seen him. I've seen his miracles."

"You've seen what Gâzar wanted you to see. What your feeble mind couldn't discern was false. If you've seen the One God and are not the chosen king or a dead man, then you've not truly seen the One God. Get up."

Locto struggled to sit, his face flushing. "Take that back! I follow Barthos, not Gâzar."

Sir Gavin picked the boy up by the back of his shirt and stood him on his feet. "We'll take you home and introduce you to our One God, Arman Echâd. Then you'll see a real miracle when Arman destroys your idol in front of you."

• • •

Every muscle in Achan's body screamed. His tongue stuck to the roof of his mouth. His lips had cracked, and no amount of licking brought comfort. He sat on a smooth rock—wrists still chained in front—and massaged his swollen foot, cut from the rocks he'd stumbled over for hours . . . days? A long time. His stomach pressed against his ribs, aching in its empty state. They'd given him only âleh tonic to drink and crusty bread.

Twice they'd stopped to sleep, so Achan figured two days had passed. He still couldn't bloodvoice. Arman had not restored it, despite Achan's pleas for a miracle. Perhaps Arman couldn't hear him through the âleh tonic, either.

His mind drifted like a twig in a fast current, dwelling on all he'd experienced in the past months. For what? To die in Darkness, sacrificed to a false god? And how exactly did that work? Would the Barthians kill him? Would they wait for their god to show up? And if Barthos didn't come, would they take matters into their own hands?

His thoughts rippled. Was his mind drifting out of reality?

Movement caught his eye and he glanced up. A crowd had formed around the rock he sat on. Scores of men and women with grey skin and hair. Every set of dark eyes fixed on his.

He stood, heart seizing in his chest. "What's this?" Where had these people come from? He shook his head to clear it.

The crowd parted. Silvo and Sir Nongo approached. Silvo grabbed Achan's arms, spun him around, and kicked out his knees, pushing Achan over the rock on his stomach.

Sir Nongo drew his black sword. "For Barthos!" He raised the blade above Achan's neck—

The image shifted. Now Achan hung from a tree, his cuffs looped over a branch.

A man in a blood-splattered apron stood before him, sharpening a long knife on a whetstone. "I've skinned my share of animals, but ain't never skinned a man. S'pose it works the same." He lifted the knife to Achan's waist—

Again a shift. Achan was now strapped to a wooden altar, looking up at a golden statue of Barthos, a creature with the body of a man and the head of a rabid wolf.

The temple was sweltering, filled with burning braziers and hundreds of people chanting, "Barthos. Barthos. Barthos."

A black knight wearing a wooden mask stood at the foot of the statue. He grabbed Achan's hair in his fist and held a dagger to his throat. "*Râbab yârad.*"

Nausea welled in Achan's gut. "Don't. Please. Arman!"

The chanting vanished abruptly. Achan again sat on his rock by the wagon. The campfire crackled to his left. Silvo and Sir Nongo sat beside it. A horse neighed. All else was silent, except for Achan's heavy breathing.

Darkness. Playing on his fears.

Maybe he could sing one of Minstrel Harp's songs. Achan sang aloud, for it seemed the only way to focus.

"Hail the piper, fiddle, fife,
    The night is young and full of life.
The Corner teems with ale and song.
    And we shall dance the whole night long."

"Quiet!" Sir Nongo scowled in Achan's direction.

Achan went straight into the next verse.

"Hear the pretty maiden sing,
  Hair and ribbons all flowing.
She can take my heart away,
  By her side I long to stay."

A stone struck Achan's knee. He jumped.
"Shut up, stray," Silvo yelled.
Achan lowered his voice.

"Never love a knight, he cares only for his sword.
  Never love a sailor, he spends all his life aboard.
Never love a merchant, he's too busy counting wares.
  Never love a prince, for himself, only, he cares.

"Never love a bard, for he'll put you in a song.
  And if he doesn't you will know—

"—ow!"

A rock the size of Achan's fist struck his foot. Surely the black knights thought him mad by now. He wished he were with Gren at the Corner. He could almost smell her, the mix of orange blossom and the subtle bitterness from the fulling water she used to clean wool. Was she still imprisoned?

Tired of singing, Achan returned to nagging Arman. *Why do you torture me? You say all other gods are false. You tell me I'm your chosen king. Then you play games with my life. Does this amuse you?*

Heat flashed through Achan's body as if he'd stepped into a bathhouse. He tensed, recognizing the heat as the signal that Arman was about to speak.

Trust in Me and I will direct your path.

The heat swelled and subsided in the length of one long breath. When nothing else came, he laughed bitterly. "That's it? Trust in You? How am I supposed to do that while lunatics drag me behind a cart? Sit and wait, I suppose. Well, I was already doing that, so thanks for finally speaking up, but You're not much help."

"Do you always talk to yourself?" Silvo's voice came from the campfire.

Achan shifted on his rock. "*He* started it."

"Who?"

"Arman. He keeps telling me things, like an old sage. He's so abstract I can't understand what He's saying half the time."

"You think the Father God talks to you?"

"No, I said He *told* me things. If He'd talk to me, a back and forth conversation, we might get somewhere. But no. He spouts cryptic proverbs. Whenever He feels like it, of course. I've been praying for two days and finally He speaks. But is it an answer? No. 'Trust in Me,' He says. *Trust.* For Cetheria's hand! I'm about to be killed and He says to trust Him."

"Darkness has rotted your mind, stray. Sacrificing you to Barthos will be a mercy to you. You're mad."

Achan sighed heavily and lifted the back of his wrist to rub his tired eyes. Another wave of heat racked his body. He wheezed at the overpowering sensation.

ACHAN. The voice sent burning tremors through his heart. *DO YOU KNOW CETHERIA?*

Saliva pooled in Achan's mouth. *N-no.*

HAS SHE SPOKEN TO YOU?

Achan swallowed, sweat dripping down his forehead. *No, sir. Never.*

YET YOU'VE LEFT SACRIFICE AND LOVE OFFERINGS FOR HER ALL THESE YEARS.

I thought that's what I was supposed to do. Sir.

AND NOW?

Achan sucked in a cool breath. *I haven't petitioned Cetheria since you told me not to.*

YET YOU SWEAR BY HER HAND.

Oh. Achan panted, the heat incredibly intense. *Well, that was just an expression.*

OF YOUR ANGER AT ME?

Achan winced. *I guess so. Sir.*

I HAVE CHOSEN YOU, BUT YOU HAVE NOT YET CHOSEN ME. YOU MUST TRUST ME FULLY. ONLY THEN WILL YOU BE MORE AT LIBERTY TO MAKE DEMANDS AND EXPECT IMMEDIATE ANSWERS. SO, TRUST IN ME, LITTLE KING, AND I SHALL DIRECT YOUR PATH.

A long stretch of silence followed. Achan dared not move. A chill brought goose bumps over his arms and he shivered. The heat had gone. It was over.

His chest heaved. Moisture filled his eyes. He closed them. *Arman, forgive me. I know not what I do. I've only ever wanted to be free, live my life as I saw fit, go where I wanted to, wear what I wanted to, love who I wanted to. I never aspired to king. I don't think I can do this.*

A wave of heat. *BUT I CAN.*

Achan gasped as the warm sensation faded. He opened his eyes. He sat atop his rock, temples itching.

Itching? Praise Arman, a knock! Achan slid off the rock and kissed the craggy ground. He jumped to his feet and raised the shackles above his head. "Praise Arman!"

A pebble struck his shoulder. "Be shutting it, stray!"

Achan lowered his hands. "Thank You! Thank You."

Sir Gavin Lukos.

Another small rock struck his back. "One more word about Arman and Sir Nongo says I can beat you," Silvo said.

Achan smiled and reached for Sir Gavin. *I've been captured. Silvo and Sir Nongo are black knights. They're going to sacrifice me to their false god.*

You're not injured?

No more than usual. My feet are sore and they took my clothes and boots. Arman spoke to me, Sir Gavin. He scolded me, then healed me. Bested the âleh.

Then we're truly on the right path. Achan could hear the smile in Sir Gavin's tone. *Look and listen for us. We're coming.*

Dozens of bonfires cast an orange glow over Barth. The city consisted of thousands of domed clay huts, coating the land like endless anthills. But the pyramid was the main feature of the city. Just as Inko had told him, the pyramid rose out of the center of the city. Its height stretched beyond the range of bonfire light, into the black sky. An arched portcullis bored through the center base of the pyramid like a mouthful of teeth, bright yellow light glowing from beyond.

The cart towed Achan past the first bonfire. The flames heated the left side of Achan's body, stung the cut on his cheek. The fire burned in a pool of shimmery liquid contained in a round stone brazier sitting inches off the ground, twice as wide as the cart pulling him.

People lined the road, staring with wide, white eyes, their grey skin covered in dark mud. Their half-naked dress and dirty skin made them almost invisible against the dark backdrop.

Olive-skinned men also peppered the crowd. Refugees from the plague of female mages in Jaelport, no doubt.

People chanted and jeered as Achan passed. The ground trembled with distant drumming. Ritual drums. The thrumming crescendoed as they neared the pyramid. A lonely wailing song rose above the rhythm.

A shiver snaked through Achan's stomach and coiled around his heart. This was like the daydream he'd had. One of the ways he might die. Surely Arman wouldn't let him die?

The cart stopped, and Achan stumbled into the end of it. Shouts in a language he didn't understand drifted back from the front of the procession. Clinking metal told him the portcullis was rising.

The cart dragged him over a moat of fire burning over shimmery liquid. The heat of the flames lapped at his heels and stung his cuts and blisters. Achan wished for some outer garments to shield his skin from the heat. He passed under the portcullis and into Barthos' sweltering temple.

It seemed the entire pyramid was hollow on the inside, as if it were a giant stone tent, its four sides converging at the top and covering an underground amphitheater. The stone grandstands were big enough to house a small army. Indeed, it seemed an army of barely clad spectators had already gathered for the show. More streamed down four aisles approaching the middle from the four corners of the compass. Narrow trenches of fire lined each path as if marking the way.

The main feature of the temple stood in the middle of the dirt floor below: a huge, elevated platform. Men walked around on top, several levels above the heads of the spectators on the bottom few rows of seats.

This must be where they planned to kill him.

Two massive beams rose from the floor on either side of the platform and leaned diagonally toward one another, their sharpened tips almost touching. A wooden scaffold reached almost to the tips, as if they regularly hung decorations from the spot—or perhaps took turns sliding down the giant spikes to the floor far below. Barthian fun.

What might such a contraption be used for?

Sir Nongo approached from the front of the cart and removed the chain holding Achan's shackles to the cart. He towed him toward the stairs and paused at the top. "We will be going down many steps."

"Where are we?" Achan asked.

"Barthos' temple."

Achan knew this already, but the answer brought a chill to his sweaty skin. Sir Nongo started down the stairs toward the bizarre platform. The chains on Achan's wrists tugged, pulling him along.

Vrell stood on a rocky cliff overlooking a distant, fiery glow that Sir Gavin claimed was the city of Barth. Achan was there somewhere, alone. But not for long. Soon Vrell would be the one left alone, as the knights were planning to go rescue Achan and leave her with the horses.

Sir Caleb held the only torch. It cast a golden glow over the trees. The knights stood with the horses, making plans to free Achan. Locto, the boy who had tricked them all with the illusion of Achan's body, sat bound on a boulder, whining incessantly. Vrell stood near a fat, slimy tree beside the path Sir Gavin had claimed led down to Barth. She studied the tree in the weak light. Its trunk had split, as if once struck by lightning. Had it been that way before Darkness had come?

After Locto had been discovered, they had all eaten Inko's dried karpos fruit and traveled back toward Mirrorstone. Their bloodvoices had returned, and Sir Gavin had discovered from Prince Oren that black knights had taken Achan. So they had changed their course to head for Barth. Then Achan had messaged. Now Sir Gavin believed Achan was to be sacrificed in Barthos' temple.

Fear for Achan overwhelmed Vrell. The knights were preparing to go into the pyramid-shaped temple and rescue him. Sir Gavin had insisted Vrell stay behind. He had even bloodvoiced her mother to ask permission to leave Vrell, and Mother had agreed! Mother was to talk with Vrell during their absence to make certain Darkness would not twist her mind.

To make matters worse, Vrell could not deny the familiar cramps in her abdomen. Her month-blood was coming.

Why was this happening now? She should be home, resting. The last time her month-blood had come she had been in Mahanaim, training with Macoun Hadar. It had been difficult to deal with, but not impossible. But now . . . it was unheard of for a woman to travel—to ride a horse!—at such a time.

Vrell wrung her hands as Locto's pleas echoed her own.

"Please don't leave me in Barth! Just let me go."

Sir Gavin picked up his shield. "We cannot allow a boy schooled in witchcraft to roam free."

"Then leave me in Melas. If Sir Nongo finds me . . . he'll kill me."

"I can do nothing about that, lad." Sir Gavin walked toward Vrell, his form a backlit shadow.

Locto took up his plea with Sir Caleb. "I beg you, change your mind!"

Sir Gavin took Vrell's elbow and turned so that half his face was lit and the other half shadowed. "Take these. It's a torchlight and firesteel."

Vrell's hand's trembled as she took the items from Sir Gavin. The idea of staying behind, alone in Darkness, perched on this cliff . . . "Please take me with you."

"I'm sorry, Vrell." Sir Gavin's visible eyebrow wrinkled. "Someone must stay with the horses, direct us back. We'll light a red torchlight when the time comes, so be looking for it. When you see it, light yours."

"But I want to help."

"Please don't fight me on this. We're walking into a perilous situation. We must leave Locto and bring Achan back. And we can't escape without a light to show us the way."

"But I am . . ." Vrell leaned closer and whispered . . . "frightened."

Sir Gavin set a heavy hand on her shoulder. "Then pray."

A distant squawk made Vrell jump. She inched closer to Sir Gavin. "What if gowzals come? I do not understand how they can do such . . . evil."

"'Tis not the birds themselves. Alone, they are merely animals. Mages call on black spirits to do their bidding. The spirits possess gowzals because the creatures are weak-minded."

"That is how the black knights work their illusions?"

"Aye. Black knights use the spirits as their tools. Little do they know it's truly the other way around." Sir Gavin slapped her back. "Look, no one knows you're here, Vrell. You've nothing to fear. Arman will protect you." He walked toward Sir Caleb, boots scraping over the rocky ground.

Vrell wanted to resist but she knew someone must stay with the horses. As much as it vexed her, she was the logical choice. She turned back to the split tree and made plans to wedge the torchlight in the crack later, when the red flame came into view.

She watched the three men drag Locto off into Darkness, toward a temple dedicated to evil, and she prayed Arman's protection over them all.

15

Sir Nongo led Achan under the platform at the center of the temple. Here, in the shadow of the platform and those log spikes, a pit had been dug. Sir Nongo seemed to be heading right for the gaping hole in the earth. Achan dug his heels into the dirt and clutched the knight's tunic, heart hammering, not wanting to fall.

Sir Nongo elbowed Achan's stomach. The sharp pain stole his breath. He folded against his knees, gasping, and Sir Nongo shoved him over the edge.

Achan's insides stretched as if they were trying to escape up his throat. He plummeted downward, falling a distance more than twice his height.

His back slapped onto soft dirt, batting the breath from his lungs again. He lay panting tiny hitches of cool air. All was dark but the square of fire glow outlining the bottom of the platform far above. Did Lord Falkson intend to sacrifice him like an animal? Would he simply slit his throat on the altar and let him bleed out? Would he set fire to him? A burnt offering for Barthos?

Achan stood, his legs shaky. There must be a way to climb out. He kicked his left toes into the dirt wall, reached his still-cuffed hands up, and drove his fingertips into the dirt as high as he could. He jumped with his right leg and pulled himself up, clinging to the side of the pit, arms trembling. He drew his right leg up and kicked in, but the force threw off his balance and he fell on his rear in the dirt, soil sprinkling on his head.

He jumped back up and screamed, pounded the dirt wall, bashed his shoulder into it, elbowed it, then sank to his knees and pressed the top of his head into the side of the pit, panting.

Arman had helped before. Achan could call on Him. He didn't know the fancy words priests spoke but gave it his best. "Oh, great Father God, Arman, creator of Er'Rets, maker of the sun, moon, and stars. Cast Your gaze upon Your servant. Help me, oh great God. Have mercy on my circumstance."

Arman did not answer.

Achan was tempted to yell, but perhaps Arman had every-thing under control. He tried another tactic. *Sir Gavin! They put me in a pit. What can I do?*

Long seconds passed before Sir Gavin answered. *We're coming, lad. Stay calm.*

Achan flipped to his rear and pressed his back against the cool dirt. He shivered, rocking back and forth to warm and calm himself. If only he could convince his mind to think casually about his situation, that all would work out . . .

"Great and powerful Arman, I am Your servant. My life is Yours. Extend it beyond this pit. You've called me to be king, so I trust You'll not let me die here."

The more Arman didn't answer, the hotter Achan's anger burned. "Arman!" He stood and yelled at the light above. "Tell me Your plan!"

"Why waste breath on a codger like Arman?" a hissing voice said from across the pit.

Achan jumped against the dirt wall, heart trampling. He blinked hard, straining to make out the person who belonged to that snake-like voice. He could see nothing. "Who's there?"

"It matters not what I'm called. It is what I come to offer that is of importance."

Achan could barely see the shadow of a man draped in a black cloak. "A ladder?"

The man hissed, a wedge of butter tossed in a hot pan. "I know what it's like to be cast aside. Do not settle for what they offer you, boy. I can teach you to use your power. We can make things right in Er'Rets—for strays, for peasants, for all."

Achan's mind whirled, trying to understand. "How did you get down here? And what do you know of my power, anyway?"

"You crave freedom. You should not be made to wait for men to fulfill their own agendas."

"And you can give me freedom? How? We are together in the same pit."

"I cannot only set you free, but I will show you how to obtain the deepest desires of your heart. To make Er'Rets a better place. To have what you want when you want it. You are the Crown Prince. These things should be yours already."

Achan huffed. "Darkness has spoiled your mind. Do you even know your name?"

"I am called Hadad."

The name, so similar to Prince Gidon *Hadar,* sent a shiver up Achan's spine. "So, what must I do to have this freedom, Hadad?"

"Renounce Arman. Leave the knights and come with me. Take my hand, and we will vanish from this place."

Achan's stomach coiled. He sensed deceit from this shadow. He shot back a witty comment to ease his discomfort. "You *do* have a ladder?"

"Reach out for me!" the man hissed.

Achan considered it. But this faceless shadow emitted a chill, just by his presence. Achan preferred Arman's warmth. Sure, Arman bossed him around and paid no attention to Achan's schedule, but if Arman spoke truth, if He was the only god, Achan couldn't afford to betray Him. And he didn't like the audacity of this Hadad trying to get him into more trouble.

"Thanks, but I'll take my chances with the black knights."

Wings rustled as if Achan had upset a flock of chickens. A bird cawed, high and shrill. Shadows swirled in the square of light above, a swarm of gowzals circling.

One dove and nipped Achan's chin. He batted it away, chains clanking. Another flew against his chest, knocking him into the wall. Teeth sank into Achan's nose.

He screamed, grabbed the creature's neck, and squeezed until it let go. He threw it to the ground, stomped on it.

Another bat-bird fluttered by his ear and bit his head, tugging bits of his hair and scalp. Achan grabbed the creature's leg and flung it across the pit. They swarmed him.

He cowered, covering his head with his arms. The beasts nipped at his back.

"Stop it! Arman, help me!"

The birds howled and fluttered away in a gust.

Hadad also seemed to have vanished. Was the man a black knight who had used gowzals to create an illusion of himself?

Achan slid into the corner to catch his breath. He dabbed his wounds with the back of his hand, waiting for his heartbeat to slow. The bites stung.

Suddenly, all his pain magnified. His chapped lips, cut feet, cuffed wrists, bruised torso, bleeding scalp and nose. He wanted relief. His memory drifted to his bath at Mirrorstone. He longed to soak his filthy, sore body. Even the cold shallows of the Sideros River delta would do.

He closed his eyes, recalling the last time he'd bathed there. The sky had been fierce blue dotted with white clouds, tufts of cotton floating in a field of forget-me-nots. Real birds—not beasts—had chirped their spring song.

He let his mind drift to Gren. Was she still imprisoned? He focused on her face.

Intense sorrow poured down his throat. Tears pooled in his eyes. Forsaken by the gods. Riga. A new home. Alone. People staring. Rumors. Throwing rocks.

"You're certain he's down there? I can't see a thing."

Achan snapped away from Gren's depression. That haughty voice belonged to the man who'd stolen his life. The former Prince Gidon Hadar: Esek Nathak.

Achan wiped his eyes and stood, looking up, veins throbbing. "Yet I can hear you, *Esek*. What brings you to Barth? Another throne to steal?"

Esek's callous laughter floated down. "You *have* got him, Sir Nongo, you devil. Well done. No one could imitate such insubordination."

"One cannot be insubordinate to a fake," Achan yelled, "or did Lord Nathak forget that little snag? I always thought people called you *Puppet Prince* because Lord Nathak pulled your strings. Now I see both father and son are playing a role. Guess what, Esek: the time is coming for the curtain to fall."

"You'd like to think that, stray, yet who's in the pit?" Esek's voice lowered. "Bring him up. Let's get this over with so I can get back to the land of the living."

A deep voice mumbled words Achan couldn't decipher.

"I do not care if it's not time. I want to see him die."

A rope flew down and whacked Achan in the head.

"Be taking the rope," Sir Nongo said.

"And be cut open before throngs of Barthians? Thank you, no." Achan sank into the corner of the pit.

There were a few more mumbles above, then silence. What might they devise to get him out? Voices rose again overhead. A ladder, black against the firelight, jutted over the edge and slowly descended.

Achan stayed put until the ladder pressed into the dirt. He crept toward it and crouched underneath the rungs. If he could get out on the other side of the pit, maybe he could run for it.

A shadow shifted above. The ladder trembled as someone climbed down. Achan waited until the man reached the bottom, then he slammed against the ladder, pushing until it tipped up and fell against the opposite wall.

A thud. A man grunted. Achan scaled the ladder as fast as he could with cuffed wrists, chains clanking against wooden rungs. A hand grabbed his ankle. Achan slipped down a rung but managed to hook his arms around the next rung with the insides of his elbows. He kicked his free foot, made contact a few times, and the man let go. Achan climbed a few more steps, but the ladder began to rise, being pulled from above.

Achan froze. Better to be caught out of the pit or to stay in the pit with an enemy? The pit had better odds. Plus, Sir Gavin was coming. He jumped off.

He landed on his right arm in the dirt. He scurried to his feet. Hands groped at his arm. Achan swatted like a girl, unable to see what he was fighting. His assailant managed to punch his chest. The force sent him stumbling into the wall. Dirt peppered his eyes. His assailant struck again, mostly missing, just grazing his ear. Achan dove to the right, blinking wildly to clear the dirt from his eyes.

"Sir Nongo! I need light!" Silvo's voice.

Firelight flamed above. The moment Silvo's lanky form came into view, Achan charged, bashing his shoulder against Silvo's waist. They fell to the ground. Achan straddled the bean sprout and beat his shackles down on his face.

A hand gripped Achan's braid from behind and struck his temple so hard, he went limp. His mind whirred. Voices murmured.

Get up, he told himself. But he had lost the ability to communicate with his body.

Sir Nongo's voice spoke over him. "He is being still now. Be lowering the rope."

• • •

Achan tasted dirt.

He shook himself awake and found himself still in the pit, but hanging from his wrists against the dirt wall. His feet dangled. Worse, he was slowly being hoisted upward. His face scraped against the soft soil. He twisted around and spat the dirt out. His body continued to rise until a hand seized his cuffs and dragged him over the side.

A bee buzzed in his ear. He blinked and shook his head, hoping to clear the sound. Then he realized it wasn't a bee. People were talking. A lot of people.

A male voice spoke in a foreign tongue from the platform directly above, silencing the crowd. Achan realized too late they'd freed his wrists when a thicker, cold metal cuff clamped around his left wrist. He sat up, wincing at his sore body, and pulled.

"Be watching him," Sir Nongo said.

It was dim under the platform, but Achan could see well enough from the firelight streaming from the temple trenches. Thick posts and diagonal support beams held up the platform. Beyond, the grandstands rose on all sides. He could see only the bottom few rows, but they were crammed full of the mud-covered Barthians, faces fixed on the speaker.

Sir Nongo stood four paces away, holding a black iron ring the size of his head. It was attached to a long chain that connected to the cuff on Achan's right wrist. The chain was stretched taut, pulling Achan's arm to the side like he was reaching. His left arm lifted away, connected to a chain and ring held by Silvo, whose cheek was puffy and smeared with blood.

Achan frowned, pulse thumping in his temples. What were they going to do? He twisted around. Khai Mageia stood behind him, looking down. Khai must have left his barge and tracked them inland. Had Esek followed on his own barge, or had Khai met him here?

A staircase on Khai's right rose to the platform. Some men were walking down it. But a squawk pulled Achan's gaze to the support beam in front of him. A gowzal stared at him with beady eyes. Its mouth hung open like a dog's, panting and revealing a row of fang-like teeth. Was Hadad here too, watching?

"Your back is a nightmare," Khai said. "You must have been a lousy stray."

"He was." Esek stepped before Achan, followed by Chora and Sir Kenton, the Shield, whose size, scowl, and pale skin reminded Achan of the Eben giant that had taken three knights to best.

Chora, Esek's valet, tittered, as if Esek's sarcasm were actually funny. Achan supposed a man who wore a wool cloak in this heat wasn't right in the head anyway.

Esek wore black trousers and a red silk shirt. The armpits were wet with sweat. A fancy gold crown pushed his black hair off his sweaty forehead. His short, thick beard coated his cheeks and chin.

Achan's stomach coiled. Ôwr gleamed at Esek's side. And with all the rings on the man's fingers, one of them had to be his father's. Achan glanced at his hand. A stab of panic shot through his chest. He no longer wore Prince Oren's signet ring.

"Give me back my ring!"

Esek raised a dark eyebrow. "You should have shaved his face, Sir Nongo, so we could see the marks on his cheeks. Further evidence of his failure in this world. He might as well meet Gâzar hiding nothing."

Achan didn't want to meet the ruler of the Lowerworld. He didn't want to die at all. He forced valiant words out his mouth. "You should know, Esek. I don't intend to die today."

"Irreverence!" Chora barked.

Sir Kenton bent over Achan and cuffed his ear. "You will address His Majesty formally or not at all."

Achan steeled himself, gritting his teeth. It would do him no good to fight back from his position. Silence was his best move.

Esek leaned against one of the vertical support posts, looking down his nose at Achan. "Your death is not for you to decide, stray. No, you'll not claim my life, my sword, my ring, my bride, as you might wish to do. I am certain you'll fit in fine in the Lowerworld. Do tell Gâzar hello for me."

Chora sniggered. "Well said, my king."

"You and Gâzar are close, are you?" Achan forgot he had decided not to speak.

"Enough of his cheek." Esek waved at Khai. "Get on with it!"

Khai pushed Achan to his knees, then prostrate on the ground. Bony hands held him down while his arms were brought behind his back and hooked together. The long chains attached to his cuffs dragged over his legs, heavy and cold.

Achan reached out for Esek's mind, desperate to try something. As usual, he found himself inside the man's head. Fine, he could make do.

"Release him," Achan said through Esek's voice.

"No!" Esek said of his own volition. "Sir Kenton?"

The Shield swung his curtain of black hair around so that he faced Esek, his protruding brow sinking low over his dark eyes. He cupped Esek's cheek.

Achan suddenly spun in a circle, as if his eyes were caught in a whirlpool. He flew up out of Esek's mind and hovered above the man's greasy head.

Sir Gavin! My mind is out of my body.

What?

I tried to attack Esek, but I think Sir Kenton stormed me.

Focus on your body, Achan. You must get back to it.

Achan's perspective floated up to the support beams of the platform. He concentrated on his body that lay flat on the ground, arms outstretched. He suddenly looked out from his own eyes. *It worked! Sir Gavin, where are you?*

Eben's breath, lad. Don't try that again. Stay in your own mind or we'll lose you for sure. We're inside the temple.

Praise Arman!

It took us longer than we thought to get here. We had to find a place to leave Locto, but he kept begging to stay with us. I had to knock him out and leave him in an empty tent. I paid the owner handsomely to arrange transportation for Locto back to Melas. But now that we're here, we're unsure how to free you. There are thousands of people here.

Pig snout. Achan sucked in a breath through his nose, willing himself to stay calm. The knights were here. All would soon be well. *Don't take too long.*

Sir Nongo and Silvo each seized an arm, lifted Achan to his feet, and towed him to the stairs, chains slapping the back of his calves with each step. Brightness and heat engulfed him as he left the underside of the platform. He lowered his head, blinking the scene into focus as they dragged him up the stairs.

When they stepped onto the platform, the audience burst into cheers. Achan shut his eyes, wincing at the ringing in his ears. His shin smacked a sharp edge. His eyes snapped open.

209

Sir Nongo and Silvo stood on the first rung of the ladder leading up to the gangway and spikes high above the platform.
Each had looped a ring over his shoulder that held Achan's
chains. They pulled his arms up.

Oh, no, no. Achan went limp, pulse throbbing. The black
knights dragged him up, rung by rung, to the top. He struggled, tugged, and pushed, but Sir Nongo and Silvo were stronger. The crowd cheered their every ascending step.

At the top, a wooden railing ran along both sides of the
gangway, like a narrow bridge. Three gowzals perched on the
rail. The knights pushed Achan along the trembling plank. The
sharpened tips of the giant support beams glistened before him
in the firelight. Would they impale him?

He leaned back, trying to stay put, but the knights inched
him along. When Achan reached the gowzals, he elbowed the
rail and the beast-birds squawked and fluttered away. The gang-
plank swayed from the force of Achan's movement.

The knights forced Achan to the end of the gangway
until his toes stuck off the end. He peeked down. His breath
hitched at the dizzying drop. It hadn't looked so high from
below.

Thousands of people filled the grandstands, focused on the
man on the platform below, who was talking in the strange
language. Achan recognized him now. It was Lord Falkson
from the Council meeting in Mahanaim. He was tall and grey-
skinned with a pudgy gut and short, grey hair like a shorn
sheep. He wore a flowing black tunic and trousers. A huge
gowzal perched on his shoulder.

Could Lord Falkson be Hadad, the man who'd visited
Achan in the pit? Had he transformed himself like a black
knight? Was he their leader?

In the air above Achan's head—a mere arm's-length away—the wooden spikes met, the tips not quite touching. Were they going to hang him? Push him off?

Achan curled his toes over the edge and pressed back. Sir Nongo let him back up to the center of the gangway, then kicked in the back of his knees. They slammed against the wooden platform. Sir Nongo pushed Achan to his stomach and pressed a knee into his back.

Silvo separated Achan's wrists from one another and stepped over his head to the end of the plank, chains clanking against the balusters and railing. Achan couldn't see what Silvo was doing. Overhead, metal scraped against wood. Achan's arms jerked away from his sides, up into the air.

The pressure left Achan's back. Rough hands grabbed his waist and lifted him to his feet. Here it came. Would they toss him out onto the crowd? Would the spikes fling him forward somehow?

"Not to be worrying too much about it, stray," Sir Nongo said. "All soon will be ending."

Achan's arms were loose at his sides, but he soon saw the problem. The metal rings at the end of each of his arm-chains had been looped over the tips of the spikes. Those rings had already slid down past the level of the gangway. If he fell, his weight would force the rings farther down the spikes, pulling his arms away from his body. If his arms managed to stay attached, he'd be left dangling over the center of platform.

What then? Would they stone him? The audience was too far below to do much damage. Shoot arrows? Maybe. But he could see no archers. Perhaps the sharpened beams would shift away from one another, tearing him in half.

On the platform below, Esek strode to Lord Falkson's side, flanked by Sir Kenton and Chora. The crowd erupted into cheers. Esek raised his hands above his head in a familiar arrogance. "Tonight we honor Barthos, god of the soil."

Lord Falkson translated to the audience, his voice deep and booming.

Achan gripped the rail with both hands, desperate for a way out. If he could somehow keep from falling...

"This man is a usurper." Esek pointed above his head. "He would have you turn your backs on Barthos. We must destroy him."

Lord Falkson translated and the people cheered. The gowzal on his shoulder screeched.

Sir Gavin! Where are you?

We're coming. Remember, Arman is stronger than Gâzar.

Right. Achan gripped the rail tighter and hooked his left foot around the last baluster.

Behind him, Silvo laughed. "It will do you no good, stray."

Lord Falkson clunked to his knees on the front corner of the platform and lifted his hands to the pointed ceiling, as if worshipping an idol. *"Rûwach âphâr mayim êsh, machmâd pârar. Gowzal, yârad. Pârar no ôyeb. Barthos pârach. Barthos yârad. Barthos lâqach. Barthos dâshên. Lâqach no minchâh. Lâqach no ôyeb."*

The garbled and phlegmy-sounding words hushed the crowd and weakened Achan's knees. He expected green orbs to shoot out from Lord Falkson's hands but none came.

"Thanks for the ring," Silvo whispered in Achan's ear, stretching his hand in front of Achan's face. Prince Oren's ring gleamed on Silvo's olive-skinned hand.

Achan loosened his grip on the railing and swung around to lunge for Silvo.

"Time to die." Silvo pushed him, dark eyes glinting, olive lips twisting in a smile.

Achan lost his balance. A flash of heat seized him as he fell sideways off the platform. A scream tore from his throat.

The rings caught him—nearly jerking his shoulders and wrists from their sockets. Achan's weight pulled the rings farther down the wooden spikes, drawing Achan's arms down and out inch by inch.

He writhed, kicking and gasping and shouting every curse in the king's language. The cuffs cut into the tops of his hands. His arms and wrists throbbed. He dangled above the platform like an animal in a snare.

He had to ease the strain on his arms. He thrashed back and forth, trying to grab the chain with his fingers to spare his hands from the cuffs. He grabbed for the opposite chain, but his sweaty fingers slipped over the metal. With each twist of his body, the rings slid down more, pulling his arms further apart.

Under his feet, Lord Falkson continued to chant his strange language, somehow raising a physical wind with his words. Several gowzals fluttered to perch closer to the man. *"Barthos pârach. Barthos yârad. Barthos lâqach. Barthos dâshên. Lâqach no minchâh. Lâqach no ôyeb."*

Liquid tickled through Achan's beard and dripped from his chin. Sweat? Tears? Blood? He didn't know. He only knew he was going to die. *Sir Gavin!*

He looked out at the field of faces, scanning for red Old Kingsguard cloaks. But of course they wouldn't wear them if trying to infiltrate this crowd.

Achan's temple prickled. *Vrell Sparrow.*

Achan opened to the boy, thankful his rescue had come.

Achan. Are you well? Sparrow asked. *What is happening?*

Achan swung and reached again to the left. How could Sparrow not see? *Where are you?*

Sir Gavin made me wait with the horses.

Achan's fingers slipped over the chain and the cuff wedged back into the top of his hand. He gritted his teeth. *Blazes, Sparrow. Wait with the horses, then, and keep out of my head.*

You sound weak. Are you hurt?

Achan grunted and swung right. *You could say that.*

What can I do?

Sit and wait like you were told! Achan closed his mind to the boy, enraged his rescue hadn't come after all. His lungs were on fire. He could barely breathe. Where was Sir Gavin?

Achan's temples pricked again.

Vrell Sparrow.

He managed to grip the chain above the cuff on his left hand, but his sweaty fingers slid down and he had to grip it again and again. He started to swing like a pendulum, side to side, until his left-hand grip was firm and secure. He ignored the searing pain from where the cuff cut into the skin of his right hand.

Sir Gavin! Where are you?

Straight out in front, lad. Do your best to hold tight.

Achan almost laughed. Holding tight wasn't the problem. He was holding quite tightly at the moment.

He squinted to locate Sir Gavin but failed. The wind picked up, tickling the hairs on Achan's legs and chilling his sweaty body. He swung toward the right spike. The chain drooped a bit. He jerked the chain, causing the large black ring to inch up the spike. In the same motion he crawled his fingers along the chain to keep it tight when he swung back. If he could climb off the top of this thing . . .

When he swung right again, he slid that ring up higher. It caught on a knot in the wood. His arms were crooked now, the right higher than the left.

He jerked the left chain up, twisting the excess around his hand to shorten it before he swung back. The higher he managed to raise the rings, the closer his arms were to the spikes—and the less he felt his arms would be ripped out.

He stopped, tried to catch his breath, but could hardly pull air into his lungs. His biceps burned. He wasn't strong enough for this. The chains coiled around his hands, cutting off the blood flow. They looked purple.

"*Barthos yârad. Barthos lâqach. Barthos dâshên.*"

Dirt joined the wind rising from the platform below. The blowing cloud twisted into a funnel. Gowzals flew into the gale and were swept away, darkening the cloudy haze to black.

The whirlwind lengthened. Lord Falkson's phlegmy chanting droned louder. A gowzal squawked. The crowd grew silent, many of them dropping to their knees.

A form coalesced in the swirling cone. The black wind funnel began to take the shape of a man, five times taller than normal—with a doglike head, long pointed ears, and a shaggy mane. His body consisted of black dirt particles spinning together under invisible skin.

Barthos, god of soil.

The people in the temple fell prostrate. On the platform below, Silvo, Nongo, the guards . . . even Esek fell to his face.

"Arman, Arman, Arman," Achan whispered between short breaths, staring at the *thing*. His arms shook, ached, burned. Please. He gasped. "Please."

Sir Gavin Lukos.

Achan's head throbbed from Sparrow's persistent knocks so much he barely heard Sir Gavin's knock over the boy's. Achan opened immediately. *Where are you? What do I do?*

Remember, lad, he's made of black spirits like the black knights use.

Wonderful. But what do I do?

Barthos is a creature of Gâzar, not a god. He has no authority over Arman's children. We cannot kill him with steel, but we can rebuke him.

Scold Barthos? That huge creature? *How?*

Tell him to leave.

Sir Gavin's voice yelled from the crowd on Achan's left. "Arman hu elohim, Arman hu echâd, Arman hu shlosha be-echâd. Hatzileni, beshem Câan, ben Arman."

Achan scanned the crowd in that direction but couldn't see him.

The creature too turned toward Sir Gavin's voice, revealing its lupine face. A kuon, the rabid black wolves that were said to be so prevalent in the Cela Mountains. That explained why Barth's crest displayed a kuon.

Achan whimpered, doubting this beast would listen to him. He sucked a short breath between his teeth. "Go away!"

Barthos' neck twisted. Eyes locked onto Achan's, he roared a guttural sound that curled Achan's toes.

The beast swung a clawed paw. Achan moved his legs aside in time. But the ring on the right spike slid loose, jerking Achan's right arm down.

Now he knew why he'd been strung here. He was to be plucked off his chains and devoured by this god of the under-world like a choice morsel.

Achan writhed back and forth, legs swinging, right arm jerking the chain back up the pole. His arms were killing him. His hands were numb. Pain stabbed his temple.

Vrell Sparrow.

Achan screamed. He was going to maim Sparrow if he survived this.

From the crowd behind him, Sir Caleb's voice shouted, "Arman hu elohim, Arman hu echâd, Arman hu shlosha be-echâd. Hatzileni, beshem Câan, ben Arman."

The kuon tipped his head back and howled like a hundred vultures circling their carrion. It fell to all fours and lumbered under Achan, shaking the platform and spikes with each step.

Inko's voice rose from somewhere on Achan's right. "Hatzileni, beshem Câan, ben Arman."

Barthos spun toward Inko and roared.

Clearly, Achan didn't know how to scold the beast properly. Anyway, what was this doing but whipping the creature into more anger? This wasn't the rescue he had in mind. He realized that if he wanted down, he'd have to do it himself.

The right ring had wedged between two knots close to the spike's point. That drew his legs closer to the right beam. Achan kicked out, trying to hook a leg around the right spike. He missed and fell back, his arms jerking taut.

He grunted and kicked up again. This time he was able to curl his right calf around the spike.

The pressure in his right arm eased immediately. He hung for a moment, took a deep breath, then pulled his other leg over until he managed to wrap it around too. He clutched the spike with both legs and his right arm. He tipped his head back, left arm still stretched to the left spike.

Barthos stalked through the crowd, knocking the spectators aside. Black dirt billowed under his transparent skin.

People screamed. Some sang a warbling song in their foreign tongues. The knights' voices chanted low and steady, their rhythm contradicting Lord Falkson's slurred tones.

Sparrow continued to knock, the little boil.

Achan struggled with his left hand, jerking the chain up the spike inch by inch until at last the ring slipped over the top of the spike and fell.

The weight jerked his left arm, and his body slid down the wood spike. Rough splinters pierced his torso, arm, and thighs. He squeezed, stopping himself from sliding further, and pulled his left arm up to the spike.

He alternated hugging the spike with his arms and twisting his hips then squeezing his legs around the spike and moving his arms. The chains and metal rings still hung from his wrists, but at least his arms were no longer being yanked out. In this way he slowly inched his body around the beam until he was on the outside of it, hunched upon the slope as if riding Scout up a steep hill.

He shimmied up awkwardly. When he reached the sharpened tip, he worked the right ring up, for it had wedged between the spike and his body. Once he pulled the ring off the spike, he looped it over his arm like a metal sleeve. He pulled the left chain up and threaded his left arm through it.

Now what?

He was free of the spikes, but he was so high up that a smoky haze from the torches on the platform blurred the floor beneath him. Achan caught sight of a red blur running down the stairs followed by two dark blurs. Not so cocky now that the beast had been distracted, huh, Esek?

He looked out into the grandstands. The knights had successfully diverted Barthos. He could see them now. They wore the clothing Lord Eli had given them—white tunics, leather vests, and brown trousers—and were standing halfway up the grandstands on his left. The beast raged through the crowd, circling Sir Caleb, but never getting too close. People in the crowd screamed and trampled each other to get out of Barthos' path.

The platform was empty but for Lord Falkson and the gowzals that perched on him as if he were a scarecrow. Achan scanned the crowd for Silvo and Sir Nongo. He spied the black knights with Khai pushing through the crowd toward Sir Caleb.

Sir Caleb, three of Esek's men are coming your way.

I see them, Your Highness. How did you manage to unhook yourself? Well done!

Achan didn't answer. His arms shook so hard they'd likely give way and he'd fall to his death. He slid down a bit. A fat sliver stabbed into his thigh like a rose thorn. He clenched his jaw and kept going. Halfway down, he paused to check the knights.

The crowd had scattered, leaving a wide circle where Sir Caleb and Sir Nongo now clashed swords. Silvo gestured toward the platform and yelled the phlegmy language at Barthos, whose head bobbed back and forth as if unsure what he wanted to do next. Achan could still hear Sir Gavin and Inko chanting. What they were saying?

Ignoring the splinters, Achan slid further down. Part of him wanted to just let go and drop to the platform, but he'd probably break a few bones, so he maintained his controlled slide.

Finally, the chains clattered to the platform. Achan twisted around the beam as if coming down off a low tree branch and dropped to his feet.

On guard, Your Highness! Sir Caleb yelled in Achan's mind.

A coarse paw struck Achan's back and sent him sprawling across the platform. He rolled to his side against the supports of the ladder and tried to stand, but he was tangled in the chains.

Barthos stood in the center of the platform, Silvo right behind it. The creature roared, baring a mouthful of sharp teeth.

Achan sat up and untangled the chains. He threaded them behind his back and slid the opposite ring up over each shoulder, hoping to keep them out of his way.

Join us in rebuking him, Achan! Sir Gavin said.

Achan shifted his weight from one foot to the other. *But I don't know what you're saying. Speak the common tongue so I can understand.*

It matters not what you say but that you believe Arman can deliver you.

Oh. *You're calling on Arman?*

'Tis the only way to destroy it.

Achan closed his eyes and licked his cracked lips. "O, powerful Arman, father of all Er'Rets. Have mercy on Your servants. Send this ugly beast back to where it came from."

Warmth spread through Achan.

Barthos screeched and swiped his paw. Achan backpedaled into the ladder supports to try to avoid Barthos' strike, but he could not. The massive paw descended to cut him in half.

But the only thing that passed through him was swirling wind. Merely a chilled breeze on his sweaty skin.

Barthos looked surprised. The creature's hind legs morphed into a whirling tunnel. The kuon's body spun out of form. No longer a dog-man but only a funnel of wind and dirt again.

Once the head vanished, the funnel scattered into hundreds of gowzals. The black birds soared over the audience squawking and biting. The crowd screamed and ran.

Achan headed for the stairs leading down off the platform, but Silvo cut him off.

Achan lowered his left arm and let the ring slide over his hand, gripping the chain when the ring hung inches from the ground. He swung it up over his head like a mace and ran toward Silvo, screaming.

Silvo's eyes widened. He fled down the steps. Achan stopped and flung the ring. It struck Silvo in the back of the head. The black knight's legs crumpled. He fell down the stairs and lay still at the bottom.

Achan looped both rings over his left shoulder. Master of the iron rings, he was. He scrambled down the steps, tugged Prince Oren's ring off Silvo's hand, and joined the throng.

"Stop him, Sir Kenton! He's getting away!"

Esek's order came from the crowd behind Achan. He ducked his head and squeezed between people, mud from their bodies rubbing onto his. A portly man plowed into Achan's side and knocked him to the floor. The mob stepped over him, on him. He crammed Prince Oren's ring on his finger even as his face was pressed into the dirt floor. The smell of soil filled his nostrils. Pain and fatigue engulfed him, vision swirling, blackening, his breath finally used up.

A voice whispered in his ear, sending an icy chill over his body. "Say the word! Call on me and I shall end this." Hadad.

Someone tripped over Achan, kicking him to his side. He curled into a ball, waiting for the people to pass. But he had to get up. Sir Kenton was coming.

"Say it, boy! Hadad. Call on my name."

"No." Achan mumbled a weak prayer to Arman. This was how the supposed future king was going to die, crushed in a stampede in a temple to a false god.

Strong hands seized his arms. Sir Kenton! He tried to pull away.

"I've got you, Your Highness." Sir Caleb's familiar voice calmed him. The knight draped a cloak around Achan's body and pulled him to standing. The crowd still pushed past, their muddy backs fleeing toward the exits. "Put on the hood," Caleb said.

"Sir Kenton." Achan swayed. The dull throbbing of scratches and bruises fatigued his nerves like a strong drought of Sparrow's tea.

"Inko and Gavin are dealing with him." Sir Caleb pulled up Achan's hood and put an arm around his waist. He helped Achan ascend the stairs.

"Sir Gavin?" Achan's mind was groggy. Had he been told where Sir Gavin was?

Sir Caleb didn't answer.

Inko joined them halfway up and supported Achan's left side. The three exited the pyramid, the knights all but carrying Achan away from the temple.

They darted around mud huts, weaving their way up the hill.

16

Sir Gavin Lukos.

Finally! Vrell opened her mind. It had been hours since Achan had shut her out.

Do you see our light? Sir Gavin asked.

Vrell stood. A cramp stabbed her lower back. At least Mother had advised her how to accommodate her month-blood. She had bided her time crafting compresses out of the linen Lord Eli's servants had given her for her healing kit. Hopefully no one would be seriously hurt until she could get more supplies.

She located the fiery glow of Barth below and scanned the blackness between the stronghold and her position. A prick of red light shone in the distance to her left, lower than where she stood but higher than the city. A ridge must lead to the valley.

I see it, sir.

Then fire the blue torchlight and ready the horses. We must ride.

It will be done. Vrell patted the ground beside her until her fingers found the firesteel and torchlight. It had been a while since Vrell had used a firesteel. She had one by the fireplace in her bedchamber back home but her servants usually lit the fire.

It took Vrell three tries to ignite the torch. The blue flame hissed to life and warmed her face. She stood to get her bearings, legs and back aching.

Must her whole body hurt during this time of the month?

The flame lit the tree and the path in an eerie blue glow. Vrell inched over the dark ground and wedged the end of the torchlight into the knot hole in the tree where it could be seen. She hoped no one else would come investigating the blue light until she and the knights were long departed.

Vrell crept to where the horses were tethered. Normally she would have taken off their saddles and bits and wiped them down, but she had not known how long the knights might be. She went from horse to horse, petting them to keep them calm. They had been waiting a long time and were eager to ride.

When she got to Achan's horse, she fingered the ivory pommel of his sword hanging off the saddlebag. How could she have missed it the morning he had been taken? Achan always wore his sword, had slept with it on until Sir Caleb had scolded him. If she had noticed it on his saddlebag sooner, she might have suspected something was amiss.

No reason to dwell. They were coming back and would soon be on their way. Vrell could no longer see the red light. Her stomach clenched. Sir Gavin had not said whether they had found Achan. What if they had failed?

Of course Achan would be with them. Sir Gavin would not have returned otherwise. The man had dedicated his life to Armonguard's rightful king.

Vrell checked the tether from one saddle to the last, then returned to her horse and patted his nose. Should she get on? How quickly did Sir Gavin plan to ride?

She inched back to the tree and stood in the blue glow, staring at the distant lights of Barth and the dark void between. Were the men close?

You're ready?

Vrell jumped, not expecting to hear Sir Gavin's voice without a knock. She must have been so excited she had forgotten to put up her shields. How careless.

Yes, Sir Gavin, she said. *Everything is set.*

She fortified her mind and carefully mounted her horse. There. Now she would be ready when they arrived and would not have to hurry. The blue torchlight had almost faded. She hoped they were—

A twig snapped. Fabric rustled. Vrell gripped her reins, and her horse shuffled his feet, ready to ride. Shadowed forms crested the hill and entered the clearing. She counted four and sighed. Good. Achan was with them. Where had they left poor Locto?

Sir Caleb and Inko peeled away from the light and went straight to their horses. Sir Gavin helped Achan mount his horse. He wore a black cloak—and, she couldn't help noticing—almost nothing but a black cloak. His feet and legs were bare and chain clanked as if he were bound and dangerous. He settled into the saddle and his hood slipped off, revealing a disheveled profile. Vrell's eyes prickled and she blinked away grateful tears. Where were his clothes? Why the chains? If he was injured, she should see to him right away.

Sir Gavin fetched the dim torchlight from the tree and mounted his horse.

Vrell could bear the silence no longer. "Does Achan—?"

Sir Gavin Lukos.

Vrell opened her mind.

Converse only in our minds until I say otherwise. I sense we're being followed already. He extinguished the light. The blackness encompassed them again.

How Vrell hated it.

They went slow and steady without a word. Every rocking motion of her horse sent jolts of pain through her tender body. The horses' hooves scraped over the rocky terrain, kicking pebbles aside. Every sound seemed louder now that they were trying to be quiet. Leather packs creaked. Mosquitoes buzzed, garnering the occasional hand slap against skin. And the horses breathed heavily, interrupted by an occasional snort.

Vrell ached to speak, to know what had happened, but no one knocked. The idea of being followed again left her feeling vulnerable and alone. She called out to her mother, told her the knights had returned with Achan and they were traveling again.

Finally, Vrell's ears tickled. She straightened, eager for news, but no name was given. The knocks continued until a terrible headache squeezed her skull. She wanted to yell at whoever it was to stop, but Sir Gavin had asked for silence. Besides, the knock might be Master Hadar or Khai seeking her. She kept her mind closed, gritting her teeth against the pain.

Achan's voice blurted into her mind, *Annoying, isn't it?*

She gasped, tears pooling in her eyes, remembering the way she had persistently sent knocks to Achan hours ago. *I—forgive me. I had not meant to annoy. I only wanted to know what was happening.*

Then why not look through my eyes?

She released a shuddering breath. *I-I forgot to try.* And she could not have risked blacking out.

Brilliant, Sparrow. Next time you forget, *just forget trying to contact me at all.*

Are you all right? When they brought you in I thought you were nearly unconscious. But you sound—

I'm fine.

So you say. Do you know what they did with Locto?

Sent him to Melas. Now leave me alone.

Why are you being so mean?

Look, I realize you had no idea what was going on, but when I said to wait, you should've listened. Not only did your endless knocking stab, I was already in a tight spot. The last thing I needed was more pain or distraction.

She wiped tears from her cheeks. *I am desperately sorry, Achan. I was scared. It was so dark and I did not know if you were safe. Please forgive me.*

Silence stretched on for a long agonizing moment. *Just don't do it again.*

Once Sir Gavin declared they had reached the old road north, they spurred the horses as fast as the beasts would go in the dark, which was not above a canter. Vrell cried most of the journey, both from pain and with grief for how she had angered Achan. She considered throwing herself from her horse, when it occurred to her that Darkness might be playing on her sorrow, not to mention how her month-blood always darkened her moods. She hummed praises to Arman and soon felt lighter.

They steered their horses across the wetlands of what Inko told her was Melas Marsh, sloshing water for hours. Sir Gavin had them stop on a small, dry knoll. He drove a torch into the ground and they made camp around it in silence. Either the men were exhausted or something truly horrible had taken place in Barth.

Vrell was thankful for her own bedroll. Lord Eli had provided that, at least, despite his trickery and betrayal. She laid it a few feet from the torch and sat cross-legged, watching the bugs flock to the light, waiting for someone to speak.

Clinking metal drew her attention to Achan. He carried a long length of chain looped over his arm that hung past his knees, jingling as he limped about. Why would no one talk of what had happened? How had they managed to free Achan?

Achan lay on his bedroll on the other side of the fire, chains scraping each time he shifted.

Sir Gavin handed out rations of bread and apples. He crouched at Vrell's feet and set her food on the end of the leather hide. "Would you mind looking at Achan's feet, Vrell? They might need care."

Before she could respond, Sir Gavin moved to Inko's bedroll. Achan looked to be sleeping now. She picked up her satchel and circled the torch by way of Sir Caleb. She could not suffer another verbal beating. If Achan was still cross, she would need reinforcements.

"Sir Caleb," Vrell said softly, "I am to check Achan's wounds. Would you mind holding the torch so I can see?"

"Of course." Sir Caleb jumped up and jerked the torch from the sand. Shadows danced as the only light for miles was moved. Vrell knelt at the foot of Achan's bedroll. Sir Caleb crouched beside her and held the torch low. Dirt caked footprints on the soles of Achan's bare feet. Vrell cringed at the blisters and streaks of dried blood that were nearly impossible to see against the dirt.

Sir Caleb laid his hand on Achan's bare shin. "Your Highness?"

Achan's breathing hitched, then fell back into a soft rhythm.

"Asleep already, poor lad. Can you imagine? A stray one day, a king the next. And in both lives, targets of wicked men's wrath."

Vrell's chest constricted. "No, I cannot."

"You think you can work on those feet a bit without waking him?"

"I shall do my best, sir." She hoped she had enough supplies.

Vrell used water from her jug and a strip of linen from her satchel to wipe Achan's feet as clean as she could without soaking them. Achan slept so soundly, he barely moved. She rubbed yarrow salve into the cuts and scrapes and used the rest of her linen to wrap his feet to keep out more dirt.

When she finished, she held the torch for Sir Caleb so he could pick the locks on Achan's shackles. Once those were removed, Vrell did what she could with her remaining supplies to nurse the lacerations on his hands and wrists.

She packed up her satchel, leaned over Achan, and whispered, "I'm so sorry."

• • •

The next morning—if a dark sky with no hope of light all day could be called morning—Sir Gavin made sure to greet each of them face to face, then they mounted and rode without a word.

Vrell's mind began to wander into a waking dream, scrambling reality with fear in a bizarre ongoing hallucination. If only she had brought along Achan's chains, she could punish herself by wearing them. How might they look with a wedding gown? Would Sir Gavin approve? Life would be blissful when she and Sir Gavin finally wed, but would their children have long white beards? Different colored eyes? And would Bran object? Would he challenge Sir Gavin?

She managed to break free from the chain of thoughts and center her mind on Arman, but each wild imagining left her shaken. Had Sir Caleb run out of lectures? Why did no one speak?

"No!"

Vrell jerked upright in her saddle. Her horse stopped and snorted. A horse ahead of hers whinnied and stomped, splashing the marshland water. A man grunted. Water splashed, followed by quick footsteps in the water. Who was running?

"Achan!" Sir Gavin cried out. "Stop!"

"Her child! He's dying!" Achan called from the darkness to Vrell's left. "I must go to her!"

"Who's dying?" Sir Caleb said from behind Vrell.

Leather slid against leather and boots splashed into the water at the front of the line.

A torchlight fizzed green behind Vrell, illuminating Sir Gavin's white hair, flying out behind him as he bounded through the marsh.

Sir Caleb dismounted and followed, taking the green light with him. "Light a torch so we can find our way back!"

Inko started to dig in his pack. Vrell clutched the reins and listened to Achan's screams in the distance. From the sounds of things, the men had caught him and he did not approve.

"What is he doing, do you think?" Vrell asked.

"Going mad, I'm guessing. It's being the way of Darkness to be calling to your fears."

Who did Achan think was dying? Vrell did not have to wonder long. Soon Sir Gavin and Sir Caleb dragged a sobbing, struggling Achan back to the horses.

"No!" Achan jerked against their hold, trying to get away. He plowed back and forth between them, causing all three men to stagger and slip in the ankle-deep water. "Let me go! Gren needs me. She's all alone. They killed him."

"Who did they kill?" Vrell asked.

Achan sobered and stopped struggling, eyes wide. He sniffled. "I must go. I must protect her from Esek. He intends to use her to get to me."

Vrell's face tingled as the blood drained away. She had thought Achan suffered from Darkness' hold, but this seemed all too real. "Who did Esek kill, Achan. Who?"

"Her baby!"

Baby? Vrell frowned. "Achan, Gren has only been married a short time. She could not have a child yet."

"He's dead, I say!" He glared up at Vrell. "You don't believe me? I don't care. I don't need any of you. I'll go alone. Let me go! I must go to Gren!"

Sir Gavin's voice swelled in Vrell's inner ear. *He's delusional, Vrell. Don't encourage this line of thought. Do you have something to help him sleep?*

I have hops tea. But I will need hot water to prepare it and time for it to take effect.

"We'll rest here a moment." Sir Gavin spread his feet as Achan tried to pull away. "Inko, please help Vrell heat a bit of water to make Achan a drink."

Achan grunted with his effort to break free. "I don't need a drink. I need to get to Sitna. Let go!"

But the knights did not. They stood in the marsh with Achan and tried to distract him from his worry of Gren's dead baby. Inko lit a torch and helped Vrell heat enough water to drink in a small tin cup. She had to wear one of Inko's thick leather gloves to keep the little cup from burning her hands as the torchlight heated the water.

"I've grown lax." Sir Gavin's face had darkened with his effort to hold Achan. "I shouldn't have ordered everyone to stay silent. Losing Achan should've made me more careful, not less. We must continue to communicate, focus our minds."

Vrell added the herbs and the smell cleansed her sinuses and relaxed her nerves. When it had steeped, she poured it into a cool mug and brought it to Achan.

He shook his head. "You're trying to give me âleh. You want to silence my bloodvoice so I can't see Gren. Get away!"

Achan swiped at Vrell and nearly upset the cup. Sir Caleb grabbed his arms, but Achan fought him. They fell and rolled in the water until Inko and Sir Gavin managed to drag Achan off of Sir Caleb. Achan elbowed Sir Gavin and sprinted off again.

It took all three men to restrain him and a very long time for Vrell to get him to swallow the tea. Then they had to wait for it to put him to sleep. He fought it until he went limp. Sir Gavin tethered Achan's horse beside his own, the knights hoisted Achan up, tied him to the horse, and they moved on.

Vrell prayed for Achan and for her own sanity. The horses' hooves soon found the dry ground of the sandbar again. Vrell spotted light to the north. A single flame winking on the black horizon. Sir Caleb bloodvoiced techniques for fighting with a short sword, and before they could stop for their second meal, the whole horizon seemed to glow as if a fire ravaged the land.

Melas.

PART 3

FRIENDS AND ALLIES

17

Vrell nibbled a piece of dried fish and passed her gaze between the orange glow in the distance and Achan, curled up on a bed-roll beside Sir Gavin. Achan had suffered so much. Would the people of Melas be kind? Depraved? Would they seek to exploit him? Kill him? Melas was the only place separating Southern Er'Rets from Northern Er'Rets this side of Mahanaim. It commanded the only way to cross the Strait of Arok.

Vrell could no longer stand the silence. "Will they let us enter through the gate?"

"My friend is expecting us." Sir Gavin took a swig from his water jug. "He'll meet us inside."

"Who is he?" Vrell asked.

"A former Kingsguard soldier turned priest."

Vrell hoped for a priest of the Way. It had been so long since she had heard Arman's word.

Though the lights of Melas seemed close, hours passed before they approached the narrow bridge that crossed the mouth of the inlet and led up to a solid cast iron gate. A massive stone wall stretched along the northern shore of Arok Lake and out of Vrell's eyesight. Torches blazed from the parapet, flames mirrored on the dark water. A fortress on a moonless night.

The hollow clunking of the horses hooves on the bridge rattled Vrell's nerves after hours of sandy terrain.

A voice called out from the gate: "Who comes this way?"

"Sir Gavin Lukos and company. We're here on business with Trajen Yorbride."

"Hold."

The horses stopped. Vrell's eyes adjusted to the torchlight on the curtain wall. Achan slumped over his horse. She hoped he would wake with no memory of his strange behavior.

"Stand back for the guard," the voice from the gatehouse said. "They will exit, count your party, then follow you inside. Then the gate will close again. Agreed?"

"Aye, we agree." Sir Gavin twisted around on his horse. "Steer your mounts to the right of the bridge to make way for the guards. Do what they say and don't argue."

Vrell guided her horse as close to the right railing as possible. Why so much security just to enter Melas? What would happen if Achan woke and had another fit? Would they arrest him? Kill him? Leave him outside the gate?

A boom shook the bridge. Vrell's horse jerked. Vrell patted the animal's neck as the clanking of chains echoed over the water. The gate slid left like a curtain, baring a sliver of orange light from within. When the gate was wide enough for one man on a horse to pass, the chains stopped rattling.

Hoofbeats clomped nearer as the guards approached, single file.

Three rode past Vrell. They wore long dark capes over dark armor. Vrell tensed, remembering the black knights. When the hoofbeats stopped, she glanced back. The guardsmen had circled their mounts and now faced the gate.

One of the guards called out. "There are five in the party. Move forward!"

Sir Gavin rode through the gap in the gate, pulling Achan's horse behind. Vrell clicked her tongue and her horse followed. Two guards stood on either side of the gate, swords drawn. Vrell avoided eye contact as she passed under the gatehouse. She murmured a prayer over her uneasiness.

Inside the gatehouse, the knights circled the horses and waited for Sir Caleb to pay the guard.

Beyond the gatehouse, flaming torches perched atop three-level high stone walls gave everything an orange and brown glow. Melas seemed made of mostly stone. Narrow cobbled streets split off from the gate like branches on a tree.

When Sir Caleb returned, Sir Gavin rode out from the gatehouse. Vrell followed the knights down a wide street. Lanterns hung from iron hooks high along both walls. Flickering candlelight and shadow danced over stone walls and board and batten doors. The clatter of hooves on the cobblestone drowned out the voices inside. Thick grime and cobwebs coated the occasional glass window. No point in cleaning glass if the sun never shone through, Vrell supposed.

Sir Gavin rode up to a double arch separated by a thick drum pillar. A slender, dark-haired man dressed in brown linen stood before the pillar and waved, a kind face in a dark land.

Sir Gavin dismounted. "'Tis good to see you, Trajen. We've had a time of it out there."

"Then let's put up your horses and get some food in your bellies." The man's voice was friendly and deep.

Sir Gavin passed his reins to Trajen and led Achan's horse under the right arch. Vrell followed into a stable. They left their horses and returned to the street. Sir Gavin walked with Trajen. Sir Caleb and Inko carried Achan between them. Vrell wished the men would lift Achan higher. She didn't like his feet dragging over the soiled street.

Trajen led them down several cobblestone alleys lit by hanging lanterns. Narrow, two-level stone homes lined the streets, some no more than a man's height wide. Sounds and voices reverberated between the stone walls. Vrell couldn't tell what noise came from where.

Trajen entered a small house with the number twenty-seven carved on the door. Unlike the neighbor's door—coated in broken cobwebs flecked with dead flies and moths—door twenty-seven was clean and dust-free.

Vrell entered into a tiny foyer facing a one-wall kitchen. A dog yipped incessantly. A baby cried.

"Ressa? I've found our visitors," Trajen said. "Could you come out, please?"

"A moment, Tray," a woman's voice called.

"Ressa will be able to look at his wounds," Trajen said, nodding to Achan.

"No trouble," Sir Caleb said. "We have a healer with us."

Vrell swelled at Sir Caleb's reassurance in her abilities.

A small, shaggy, black dog scurried from leg to leg, sniffing. Vrell took in the cramped space. A sideboard covered the entire left wall. Before her, a rough-hewn table and eight chairs took up the left side of the room. A linen curtain draped over a doorway behind the table. On the right side of the room, two deep couches faced each other. They had backs made of lashed sticks and straw-filled cushions. Between them on the far right wall, pillows in a variety of colors made a mound as high as the couches.

Behind the table, a hand drew the curtain aside and Ressa entered, holding a crying child on one hip. She was a tan-skinned woman, Vrell's height but much curvier. Her reddish-brown hair pulled back in a long braid. She smiled. "Hello."

The child tugged at the neck of Ressa's auburn tunic, pulling it off one shoulder. "Bite bite, Mima. Bite bite."

"Shh, Romal. Mima will feed you soon." She approached Trajen and tried to hand the child off, but he clung to her arm.

"Bite bite, Mima. Bite bite!"

Trajen peeled the child away, and Romal broke into a horrible wail. His face flushed crimson and his tongue curled in his mouth. Trajen bounced the child in his arms and offered his knuckle for sustenance. Romal pushed Trajen's hand away and craned his neck from side to side looking for his mother.

Ressa had moved to where Inko and Sir Caleb held Achan. "You have an injured man? What's happened to him?"

"I gave him hops tea," Vrell said.

Ressa's dark eyes didn't leave Achan. "Was he in pain?"

"We were having trouble controlling him." Sir Gavin shrugged off his pack. "He was hallucinating."

Ressa skirted the table and waved a lazy hand over her shoulder. "Bring him." She lifted the curtain aside.

Sir Caleb and Inko carried Achan through the narrow doorway. Vrell followed, not wanting that woman to steal her job. She ducked under the curtain into a narrow hall, stretching the length of the house. The curtain fell closed, dousing the light. Vrell ran her fingertips along the wall until a flash of candlelight revealed the silhouettes of the men ducking through a low doorway halfway back. Vrell hurried after them and stepped around another curtain.

The men settled Achan on a pallet on the floor in a room barely bigger than the straw mattress. A stool sat in the corner, topped with a water basin. A long shelf stretched over the bed and held a lone candle burning in a jar. The men left.

Ressa dropped to her knees beside Achan and set the back of her hand to his forehead. "He has no fever."

Vrell kneeled on Achan's left. "No. I bandaged his feet as best I could in the torchlight."

"My light is not much better. You're the healer?"

"Yes. I am Vrell Sparrow."

"Where'd you train, Vrell?"

Ressa's direct questions and her low, silky voice inspired Vrell to give an impressive answer. "Under the Maysens of Walden's Watch. Wayan is the apothecary. Mitt the midwife."

"So you have a wide variety of training."

"I do." Vrell searched for a more impressive feat. "I also learned some battle healing from Jax mi Katt."

Ressa's lips curved into a small smile. "A giant?"

"Yes. Jax's guidance enabled me to remove three arrows from the prince. He does manage to get hurt a lot."

Achan's dark eyelashes fell thick against the tops of his cheeks. Tiny cuts and smudges of dirt seasoned his skin. Dried blood caked the slice Esek had made on his left cheek. More blood pasted his greasy hair to his scalp in several places.

"*This* is the prince?" Ressa sat back on her heels and stared. "He's so young."

"Sixteen," Vrell said. "He is called Achan."

Ressa grabbed the candle and scooted to the foot of the pallet. She set the jar beside her and started to remove the bandages on Achan's right foot. "Why don't you unwrap his left foot and tell me what I'm looking at?"

Vrell crawled to the end of the bed and tugged at the bandage on Achan's other foot. "I'm not certain what happened. When I got to him, his feet were covered in dirt and quite cut up. He also had iron cuffs on his wrists."

"And you didn't ask?"

"Sir Gavin bid us not speak. By the time we made camp, Achan was asleep. Sir Caleb didn't want me to wake him."

"This happened last night?"

"Or the day before. It is difficult to measure time here."

Ressa lifted Achan's foot into her lap, examining it with narrowed eyes. She sniffed. "You put yarrow on it?"

"Yes, ma'am. It was all I had."

"You've done fine. They're shallow cuts and should heal quickly." She lowered Achan's foot. "His head wounds seem to be healing on their own. We'll let him sleep it off."

Vrell seized the moment to ask about supplies. "I would like to redress his feet, but I have used all my linen."

"I have some we can use. And I'll take you to the apothecary to restock your bag. When he wakes, I'll make him a nice hot bath so he can soak those feet a bit. Sound good?"

"Yes, ma'am."

She smiled at Vrell and her eyes sparkled in the torchlight. "Now let me see what I might have to feed all you men."

• • •

Vrell followed Ressa back to the main room and found the men at the table, deep in a heated discussion. Vrell sat on the bench beside Sir Caleb.

He smiled at her and turned back to the men. "But who sent the black knights?"

Sir Gavin spoke from the head of the table. "Esek or Lord Falkson."

"I'm not liking it, Gavin," Inko said. "We are being far too vulnerable on this journey. I'm being afraid we won't be making it all the way to Tsaftown."

Sir Caleb shot a disapproving glare Inko's way. "Your fear is proof you don't trust Arman."

"I am trusting Arman, but I am not thinking it is wisest to go this route with so few men."

"Then you don't trust Gavin."

"You are pulling words from my mouth that I am not saying. We need—"

Sir Gavin slapped his palm on the table. "The smaller the party, the easier to hide, blend in. We are safest small and in Darkness."

"But twice already the prince's life has been—"

"Shh." Ressa held a bowl under one arm and stirred its contents. "The prince will feel better if he wakes on his own. And I'd rather you not wake the children."

Children? Just how many children did they have?

Sir Gavin pushed back from the table. "We'll discuss this further when Achan wakes."

Trajen gave a verbal tour. Three chambers lined the back hallway. The knights would sleep in the first—one man on guard—Achan in the second, and the back chamber belonged to Trajen and Ressa and their children. Vrell would sleep on the couch in the front room.

Vrell sat at the table, watching Ressa dart about the home. Vrell liked her more by the minute. The woman created a feast for seven with black beans and rice, set water heating for Achan's bath, fed her babies—for she had twins!—answered Trajen's calls, and still looked like she had energy for more.

Achan stepped through the curtain, looking around with sleepy eyes. Vrell's heart raced. She hoped he had forgiven her.

Sir Gavin jumped up and made introductions. "Trajen Yorbride, meet King Axel's son. He goes by Achan."

Trajen bowed his head, took Achan by the shoulders, and kissed his forehead. "A great honor, Your Majesty."

Achan's posture stiffened. "Thank you."

Trajen motioned to Ressa on the pile of pillows holding a sleeping babe in each arm. "My wife, Ressa, and our children, Romal and Roma."

"You're welcome here, Your Majesty," Ressa whispered.

Achan nodded once and rubbed his cheek, staring at the lady of the house with a puzzled expression.

"Trajen, if you'll take Romal, I can make the prince a bowl," Ressa said.

"Never you mind, my love. You rest. I can serve the prince." Trajen dished a bowl of beans and rice and set it at the head of the table. "It's not much, but Arman does provide."

"Thank you." Achan claimed the stool, moving slowly. "It's not dried meat *or* porridge, so to me, it's a feast."

Sir Gavin sat beside Inko. "We must hear the story of what happened when you were taken from camp. If you're up to telling the tale. Prince Oren told Gavin some."

"To the point when you returned," Vrell added, not wanting any detail left out.

"Aye," Sir Gavin said. "Vrell and Ressa would like to know how you were injured and if you're injured elsewhere."

Achan set his bowl down. Vrell didn't like the looks of the rings edging his eyes. She hoped he would sleep again soon.

Achan stared at the table with glassy eyes. "I woke alone on the sandbar. I called out but no one answered. I still don't understand why I could only reach Prince Oren."

"Locto spiked our drinking water with âleh and mint," Sir Caleb said. "He knocked you out, dragged you away, and conjured the illusion while we slept."

"Explain that," Achan said. "This illusion actually looked like me?"

"Aye," Sir Gavin said. "Just as black knights are able to duplicate themselves, they duplicated you."

Achan nodded. "They surrounded me when I woke. Prince Oren stormed two, but I ended up inside Silvo Hamartano's head and left my body empty for attack."

Vrell's insides coiled. Silvo Hamartano was a black knight?

"Needless to say, I lost. I must learn to do this right before someone kills me." Achan glanced at Sir Gavin. "Please?"

"We'll work on it tonight if you're up for it." Sir Gavin sighed through his nose. "But I wish you'd stop experimenting. It's not safe for you or us. That's likely how Esek's men found us. Kenton or Khai could be tracking your bloodvoice."

Achan hung his head. He combed his fingers through his tangled hair and yanked them free. "I woke with my head in a water trough. They had taken my clothes."

Achan went on to name Sir Nongo as Silvo's accomplice, and how Arman had restored his bloodvoices. He'd been thrown in a pit, met some crazy man called Hadad, was attacked by gowzals, then strung up on some sort of spikes as an offering to Barthos. It mortified Vrell to discover Achan had been hung there when she had knocked repeatedly. He kindly skipped over her intrusion.

Eyelids heavy, Achan turned his gaze to Sir Gavin. "What do those words mean? The ones you all said to Barthos?"

"*Arman hu elohim, Arman hu echâd, Arman hu shlosha be-echâd. Hatzileni, beshem Câan, ben Arman.*" Sir Gavin's face, which always looked so weathered, now relaxed as if the mere act of speaking those words calmed him. "It's the old language for Arman is God, Arman is One, Arman is Three in One. Deliver me in the name of Câan."

"Ah." Achan yawned. "How is it you speak the old language?"

"I've learned it from the Book of Life. You'll learn it too."

Ressa left to pour Achan's bath in his room while the men continued to talk out front.

"Will we leave first thing?" Achan asked. "I'm eager to get to Tsaftown and see the sun again."

"Achan, the sun does not shine in Tsaftown," Sir Gavin said. "The city sits over five leagues west of the Evenwall."

Achan's dark eyebrows wrinkled. "I don't remember that."

"I taught you in a hurry, Your Highness. I apologize for the confusion. We won't see the sun again until Mitspah."

"And we'll go to Mitspah when?" Vrell asked.

"After we build our army in Tsaftown."

Vrell only wanted to know how close they were to Carmine. "So from here we go to Tsaftown, then to Carmine?"

"Nay." Sir Gavin's eyes focused on hers. "From here we pass through Berland, then on to Tsaftown. We'll go to Ice Island first. Once we free our army, we'll go to Carmine."

"How long will all of this take?" Vrell asked.

"I cannot say. Much could waylay us. If all goes smoothly, we could be in Carmine before the fall harvest."

Vrell sucked in a sharp breath at the long journey ahead. "Wh-what season it is now?"

"Early summer," Trajen said.

"And will we raise support here as well?" Vrell asked.

"Nay," Sir Gavin said. "Melas is a dangerous place. The sooner we reach friendly soil, the better. Duke Orson voted for Achan at Council. Berland will be a good place to rest."

"I agree it wouldn't be wise to linger in Melas," Trajen said. "But we have a remnant here that serve Arman. Could you not stay to meet our flock?"

Sir Gavin stroked his beard braid.

"I, for one, would like to stay, at least for Teshuwah," Sir Caleb said. "It's been many weeks since I rested and many more since I've had the opportunity to attend a temple service. It would do us all good. Besides, Achan has probably never experienced a service like ours."

"Strays weren't permitted to enter the temple in Sitna."

"They're welcome here," Trajen said. "Everyone who asks may eat at Arman's table."

The curtain rustled and Ressa appeared. "Your Highness? Your bath is ready."

Achan twisted on the stool and stood. He limped to where Ressa held the curtain aside.

"What say you, Gavin?" Trajen asked. "It's only two sleeps until Teshuwah."

Sir Gavin's gaze followed Achan. "What would our prince like to do?"

Achan stopped, keeping his back to the table. When he spoke, his words were a whisper. "Whatever you think best, Sir Gavin. As long as they don't call on Barthos." He ducked through the opening and his footsteps shuffled down the hall.

18

Sir Gavin's mustache lifted at the ends, indicating a smile, as he watched Achan go. "I think it's best we stay for Teshuwah."

Trajen clapped his hands. "Excellent. I'll be honored to introduce His Majesty to the temple of Arman."

Vrell smiled. It *would* be nice to stay here a bit longer. She bet Sir Gavin would see to it she got a bath. And she couldn't wait for the Teshuwah service. The last time Vrell worshipped Arman in the company of believers had been last winter in Carmine. She couldn't believe how much longer it would be until she were safely home. Fall harvest . . .

When Achan finished his bath, Ressa and Vrell went to his room to redress his wounds. Ressa removed several splinters from Achan's arms and legs while Vrell bandaged his feet. Achan sat patiently, hair shaggy around his face, still dripping from his bath. Vrell put ointment on the welts on his wrists and the bites on his nose, cheek, and a bad one in his scalp. She tried to put balm on his chapped lips, but he snatched the jar from her and did it himself.

When Ressa finished, she left Achan and Vrell alone. Trajen had given Achan new clothes and boots. Green looked nice against his dark skin and hair.

Achan stretched his arms above his head. "Pretty lady."

Vrell flushed, then flushed again when she caught his meaning. "Ressa?"

Achan tousled Vrell's hair and laughed. "Do you see any other women around?"

Vrell blinked, annoyed at her misunderstanding. "She's Trajen's wife."

"And he's a fortunate man to have such a wise, hardworking, and beautiful wife."

"I suppose." Vrell scooted back against the wall. "So that is why you sat so still and didn't fuss like you do for me."

Achan grinned, but Sir Gavin ducked into the room before he could answer.

"You're certain you're up for a lesson tonight? We could do this in the morning."

"No. I want to do it now. Please."

"Very well." Sir Gavin moved the basin off the stool and sat down. "Ahh. My weary bones are getting a mite too old for this kind of adventure." He rubbed his opposite shoulder. "So, whenever you try to message, you end up watching?"

Achan shook his head. "No matter what I try, I end up watching. I tried to storm Silvo, and I ended up in his head."

"I beg your pardon, Your Highness," Vrell said, "but you called on Prince Oren and did not watch through him."

"When he helped me fight the black knights. That's true."

"You understand the difference between the different skills?" Sir Gavin asked.

"Well," Achan wiped balm from his bottom lip, "watching is to look through another's eyes. Jumping is when I look through another gifted person to see through the mind they're watching. And I think storming is when I attack the mind attacking mine?"

"Let's put storming aside for now. The most important methods I want you to learn are messaging, sending and receiving conversation, and watching, seeing through another's mind and allowing another to see through your mind. And doing all this while your mind is shielded."

"If I may add something?" Vrell said. "You message people all the time. The problem is, you rarely remember to knock. You simply barge through our shields and we answer. We cannot do that. If a gifted man's shields are up, we must knock and he must let us in before we can speak. I think when you are *trying* to message, you trick yourself into thinking it is more difficult than it really is. You concentrate too hard and end up watching instead of simply messaging. I suspect you don't need the extra concentration."

Sir Gavin stroked his mustache. "Try it as Vrell suggests. Speak to only me. Will you help us, Vrell? Try to overhear our conversation. And, Achan, do *not* storm Vrell. Ignore him."

"Gladly."

Vrell sneered at him and concentrated. She found only a slight chill in the air.

Sir Gavin's voice broke the silence. "Well done. Now speak to Vrell and I'll try to break in. Don't storm me, either."

Achan's voice burst into her mind. *Can you believe all she does? I mean, I've never had beans and rice together. So simple.*

Likely inexpensive. I wonder what Poril would have said about such a dish?

Vrell stifled a groan, annoyed at Achan's captivation with Ressa. *Can you at least knock before barging your way into my mind, Your Highness? And what is so shocking about beans and rice?*

Not shocking. It was just . . . Do you think Lady Tara can cook?

Vrell rolled her eyes. *I doubt it.* Tara was more of an artist. *What does she have to do with anything?*

Sir Gavin clapped his hands once. "Well then? Did you succeed? I could hear nothing."

"We had a *delightful* conversation, didn't we, Sparrow?"

Vrell averted her eyes. "Riveting."

Sir Gavin tugged his beard braid. "I'd like you both to try watching someone you know isn't gifted. Choose someone safe who would never betray us, should you accidentally speak. And keep in mind, bloodvoicing is a gift from Arman, not a game. Should you intrude upon an intimate moment, please disconnect immediately. Go ahead and try, both of you."

Vrell had wanted to look in on Bran for ages, but it had seemed so invasive. She was thankful for permission to try. She closed her eyes and pictured his face. Unable to see the whole of it, she concentrated on each feature. Sunburned nose. Thick brown hair, tousled by the wind. Dark, brown eyes.

A room came into view from a low angle. Small and clean and quite sparse. A cottage, like the peasants' homes in Carmine. The sun shone through a curtainless window, casting a bright beam of light across a wooden floor. Chopping filled the room along with the smell of onions. A young woman stood at a table, her back facing where Bran sat on a squat, wooden stool. At first Vrell thought of Ressa, but this woman seemed taller, and her hair was russet and longer than Ressa's, bound in a single plait that dangled past her waist.

She wore a brown dress with a linen apron tied in back. The ivory ties cut into her waist and accentuated her hourglass form. Yet Bran stared at her bare ankles that peeked out between her long dress and black slipper shoes.

Vrell frowned.

I'm sorry my father's not here, the young woman said, keeping her back to Bran. *He could be out a while. He'll need to get used to the soil here. It's not that he won't be able to do as good as he did in Sitna. It'll just take time. He wove excellent fabrics for Lord Nathak and the prin— Well, he wove excellent fabrics.*

She turned and smiled at Bran. Her face was lovely: caramel, freckled skin with rosy cheeks; wide, brown eyes, watery from the onions, with dark lashes. Her thick chestnut hair pulled back from her face into the braid, but wispy tendrils had escaped and framed her rosy cheeks. No wonder Bran stared. Vrell wished she could elbow him.

You sure I can't get you some ale or tea or . . . or water? Her chest heaved with a deep breath. She fidgeted with the frayed top edge of her apron, then jerked her hand away as if realizing she might call attention to her neckline. She spun back to the table so quickly her skirt coiled around her legs and slowly unwound.

Bran's attention drifted back to her bare ankles. *A glass of water might be nice, madam, if it's no trouble.*

Madam? This pretty young girl was married? Praise Arman. Vrell relaxed a bit.

The young woman curtsied, *No trouble at all, sir,* and scurried from the room.

Bran straightened on the stool and chuckled softly.

The young woman returned in a moment holding a mug in two hands. She crossed the room, her eyes focused on the mug. She stumbled and some of the water slapped to the floor. Her eyes bulged and her whole face darkened.

Oh! I'm so sorry, sir. I didn't mean—

A clap of hands and Sir Gavin's, "Did you succeed?" zapped Vrell away from the mystery girl and her spilled water.

Vrell faced Sir Gavin, but her thoughts were back in Carmine. What was Bran doing at that peasant's cottage? He had wanted to speak to the girl's father? Why? Who were they?

"Well?" Sir Gavin asked.

Achan frowned and traced the red welt around his right wrist. "I've looked in on Gren before. I mean . . . I think I have. I didn't know if I was bloodvoicing or if Darkness was playing with my mind. Last night on the sandbar . . . I think I misunderstood. But Sir Gavin, something is amiss. Why would Gren have left Sitna and why would Bran Rennan be visiting her father?"

Vrell's eyes widened. Bran with *Gren*? Achan had looked in on Gren and saw Bran . . . Vrell's breath caught. *That* was Achan's Gren?

Sir Gavin grimaced and shifted on the stool. "Aw, I'm sorry, lad. Prince Oren bid me tell you when I found the right moment, only we have been running since I got the message. I planned to tell you—this night, actually, once we were alone."

The floor seemed to fall out from under Vrell. "Would you like me to leave?"

"No." Achan lifted his chin. "There's no need."

Sir Gavin nodded. "When you escaped from Mahanaim, Esek sent Lord Nathak back to Sitna to keep an eye on the Duchess of Carm and Gren's family. Leverage over the two things he wants most. Control of Carm and control of you."

Achan stood up as if he planned to run out the door and save Gren.

Sir Gavin clutched the hem of Achan's tunic. "Esek sent Khai into Darkness to track you. But Macoun Hadar had his own agenda. Since Khai also works for him and was already following you for Esek, Macoun sent Jax to Sitna to kidnap Gren before Lord Nathak got to her. Macoun, of course, is hoping to use Gren as leverage against you as well."

"Pig snout." Achan dropped back to the pallet.

Sir Gavin continued, "As you both know, Jax is a Mârad spy, loyal to Prince Oren and to us. Prince Oren asked Jax to move Gren's family to a safe place. Sir Rigil and his squire, Bran Rennan—" Sir Gavin peered at Vrell—"were already in Carmine since they had gone to aid the duchess. Jax met Sir Rigil and his men outside Sitna Manor.

"Bran, being the least intimidating of the group, was sent to initiate contact with Gren's family. But Gren's father rejected Bran's warning, so Bran went to speak with Riga. He didn't listen either. Sitna has been overrun with thieves since Lord Nathak left. The people trust no one for fear of being swindled. Sir Rigil made a second attempt to contact Gren's father but found the Fenny home deserted. When he knocked at the Hoff home, he was arrested."

Vrell's breath hitched. She hoped nothing had happened to Sir Rigil.

"When Sir Rigil didn't return, Bran managed to find out from the local peasants that both families had been arrested.

He and Jax broke into the Sitna dungeons and rescued all but Riga Hoff, who died trying to defend his wife."

Achan's eyes grew as wide as full moons. "Riga's dead?"

"Aye. I'm sorry, Achan."

"Trying to save Gren?"

"That's right. Sir Rigil said he took a sword for her, during the rescue attempt, I believe."

"*Riga* was her baby?" Achan's brow crinkled and he sank back on his elbows.

Vrell pulled her knees to her chest. The poor girl. To be married to a man she didn't love, then to see him killed . . .

"Yesterday on the sandbar," Achan's voice broke. He cleared his throat. "I heard Gren crying about her baby, thought she'd lost a child. It seemed so real, yet I thought Darkness had twisted my mind."

"Ah, yes. Well, Gren *is* expecting a child. Her mother informed Sir Rigil once they settled in Carmine, which happened a few days ago."

"Oh!" Vrell clapped a hand over her mouth. Sir Gavin could have delivered that bit of information at another time. Not heap it all on poor Achan at once. Did the man not see how weighed down Achan already was?

Sir Gavin focused on Vrell. "So, that's that. Vrell, were you successful with your attempt to watch?"

Vrell nodded but refused to elaborate. She wanted to respect Achan's moment of grief and not run over it as Sir Gavin appeared willing to do.

Achan only stared past Vrell's left ear with a dazed look.

• • •

Achan meandered out to the front room, limping on his bandaged feet. His muscles were tight and stiff. Sir Caleb and Inko sat at the table, playing a dice game.

"Want to join us, Your Highness?" Sir Caleb asked.

"No thanks." Dice reminded him of Lord Eli and Jaira.

He paced to the door, then doubled back and plopped in the middle of one of the sofas. He disliked this house. Too cramped. He wanted to be outside—not in Darkness but by the allown tree in Sitna, watching the clouds sail across the blue sky. His body throbbed. He inspected the welts on his wrists again, the most visible of his injuries besides his cheeks.

As he pondered how long it might take until his beard hid the scars on his cheeks, Ressa walked out from the hallway carrying one of the babies. Achan couldn't tell the boy from the girl. The child turned its wide, brown eyes on Achan and all he could see was Gren and her child, staring at him.

Ressa smiled. "Trajen and Romal are sleeping. They've taken the whole bed and left no place for Roma and me to go, didn't they, my precious?" She kissed the child's forehead and settled down in the pillows. She cradled the baby across her lap. "Do you mind if I feed her?"

Achan opened his mouth, then shook his head. He picked at a bit of skin on his wrist, wishing for a way to escape the confinement he felt. The baby's suckling filled the room. Achan stood and bolted down the hallway. But Sir Gavin and Sparrow were still talking in his room so he turned and strode out the front door.

Outside, the night—day?—was cool. He took in a deep breath and found the air thick with smoke, pitch, and dung. Wheels clattered over the cobblestone in the distance, bringing to mind his journey behind Silvo's cart. The street stretched out on both sides, narrow and hemmed in like a canyon. He counted ten doors across the street. Did that mean ten homes? Moths fluttered around the lanterns, their shadows darting over the stone walls below.

Gren hadn't looked to be with child. How long until that changed? Goats tended to carry for five months before they delivered. Were women the same?

Did she grieve for Riga? Achan couldn't imagine the same pot-bellied peasant who had bullied him, beat him, and stolen Gren away could have the guts—or the heart—to even try to defend someone else, much less take a sword for anyone.

But maybe he'd done it for his child.

This thought made Achan cringe all over again. The very idea that Riga had touched Gren, let alone . . . He shook the anger away. It didn't matter. Riga had been Gren's husband, had every right . . . but she hadn't wanted to marry him . . . and they'd been married only a little over a month. Achan didn't understand. Perhaps married people managed to bond somehow. If Gren had come to care for Riga . . . well . . . Achan hoped she wasn't suffering.

One thing brought comfort: he knew Bran to be honest and kind. When next he spoke with Prince Oren, Achan would request that Bran look after the Fennys for a while. He pushed aside Gren's nervous thoughts of Bran Rennan, the *handsome squire.* Bran was betrothed to Lady Averella, after all. Nothing to fear there.

The door to the house opened and Sir Caleb stepped outside. "Are you well, Your Highness?"

Achan folded his arms. "It's so small in there."

"It is that. Nice of them to put us up, though." The knight stood beside Achan. They were roughly the same height, but Sir

Caleb's blond hair frizzed out, making him seem taller. "Melas is well-known for its crime. It's best we stay inside."

Achan's shoulders sagged. "Fine." He pushed past Sir Caleb and into the house. Ressa was still feeding the baby so he went down the hall to his room. As soon as he entered Sir Gavin and Sparrow stopped talking, as if he'd interrupted some secret discussion.

"Do you need something, lad?"

"No." Achan slipped out again and walked toward the glowing curtain to the main room.

"Achan?"

Sparrow's voice made him jump. He turned to find the boy standing behind him, cat-like eyes peering up into his. "Are you well?"

"As well as one can be in Darkness, I suppose."

"Hearing news of Gren must have been . . . shocking."

Achan's muscles tightened. "Sparrow, if you think I—" He sighed. The boy could read him like a scroll. He smiled sadly. "Aye, I wish to help her. But Bran is there. That will have to be good enough."

"Bran is a good man," Sparrow said. "You trust him?"

"I sense he's as righteous as Prince Oren himself."

Sparrow beamed. "I think so too."

Achan shifted and the linen curtain to the main room clung to his back. He swiped it away and inched closer to Sparrow. "This cottage is so cramped. You'd think it wouldn't bother me so, my having slept under an ale cask all my life, but I . . . the dark is so oppressive. I never realized what a gift the sun was until it was gone."

"The sun brings light and life to the world."

"Aye."

"Sir Gavin is asking for you," Sparrow said.

"Oh. Right, then." Achan turned sideways to edge past Sparrow. He ducked into his room, relieved to have somewhere to go.

Sir Gavin still sat on the stool, elbows propped on his knobby knees. "Achan. Would you sit a moment?"

Achan settled on his pallet.

Sir Gavin slouched against the wall and stretched out his legs. "I've never been good with words, sentiments especially. I'm a soldier, you understand. I'm great with a sword, I excel with a battle plan, and I can track better than most hounds, but . . ." He tugged at his beard braid. "Vrell thinks I . . . Well, anyway, he's right. Achan, I've got the sensitivity of a bull in a pumpkin patch. I just don't know what I'm walking on, if you get me."

"Sir?"

"I'm trying to say I didn't handle telling you the news about Gren well. I should've . . . Well, 'twas a shock to you and I just kind of flattened everything like a stampede of . . . Anyway, sorry about that. I'm sorry about everything, really. All the way back to your parents' death. I've always felt responsible, you know. Your father would've agreed with me about the bull in the pumpkin patch too."

"How so?"

Sir Gavin winced. "Well, when we were a great deal younger, there was a young lady."

Achan grinned. A story like this just might lift his spirits.

"It's not that I never recognized women were beautiful—are beautiful. I do—I'm just called to a different life. I'm too busy to bother with romance. And when I've tried to woo, I've only ever managed to make ladies scowl." Sir Gavin sniffed a long breath as if pulling a memory out from the air. "Akami was your mother's attendant and best friend. She grew up with Dara in Nesos and—"

"My mother grew up in Nesos?"

"Aye. Your father had his eye on Lady Dara Pitney ever since he knew boys and girls were different. No one could doubt who he'd choose when the time came."

Achan tried to imagine what life might have been like had his parents lived. He would've been raised in Armonguard, traveled Er'Rets with his parents, attended court, and fought in tournaments. He would never have known Gren, true, but he may have always known Lady Tara.

"So what happened with . . . ?"

"Apparently, Akami fancied me." Sir Gavin shrugged. "So Dara put your father up to getting us together. But Axel told me, 'My wife desires you to escort her attendant, Akami, to the Hepta Festival. Wear something nice, Gavin, and bathe.'"

"When the Hepta Festival arrived, there were so many visitors, and rumors of Cheremites sneaking in to cause trouble, I knew my skills would be best used with the guard. So I sent one of my men to escort Akami to the festival."

Achan chuckled. "What did she do?"

"She married him."

"Your guardsman?"

"Eventually, aye, but not before your mother tongue-lashed me. I never would've agreed to be the girl's escort had I understood Dara's plans. Your father was never vague with me again. And the next time your mother set to matchmaking, Axel laid it out plain for me to reject entirely. Arman didn't make me for romance, my lad. I'm a warrior and to that cause I've dedicated my life."

Achan wished he could have witnessed Sir Gavin's moment of understanding.

"Know that I'm still as thick as ever with people, so if I seemed cruel before, it wasn't my intention." Sir Gavin shifted on the stool. "So, you know what I have to say now isn't meant to hurt, right? Though Gren's situation has changed . . . you and she could never . . ."

Achan met Sir Gavin's brown eye and forced his voice to remain even, though his stomach clenched. "Of course."

Sir Gavin slapped Achan's shoulder twice. "Good lad. Now, Prince Oren would like you to message him. I think you've got it down, so I'll see no one disturbs you."

Sir Gavin hoisted himself from the stool, groaning, and passed through the curtain. Achan stared at the rippling fabric until it stilled.

Why torture me, Arman? I wasn't good enough for Gren. Now she's not good enough for me. Why can't I do as I please? Esek would have.

But Esek hadn't been able to marry just anyone either.

I beg You protect her, then, if I cannot. Keep Bran at her side to make sure no one harms her or her family.

Lying down would be most comfortable for messaging. If he somehow left his body again, at least he wouldn't fall.

He pulled off his boots and lay back on the straw-filled mattress. He held up his right hand. Prince Oren's signet ring looked strange on his finger. In the same way wearing his bejeweled belt and sword had first made him feel small and insignificant, this ring dwarfed him even more. He stared at the crest of Armonguard, mesmerized. Armonguard should've been his home. He should've grown up in the castle as prince, the delight of every woman, the pride of every man.

The hope for the future kingdom.

Yet all had been lost. If Achan continued with these men, they'd do everything in their power to make him king. He hadn't wanted that, yet the idea grew more comfortable the more he learned of his parents. He wanted to be a good son. Would the people of Er'Rets accept him? Prince Oren had.

Achan closed his eyes and let his mind drift to the servant's chamber on the bottom floor in Mahanaim where he last saw Prince Oren. His uncle's kind words came back.

"We share the same blood, you and I."

Achan hung on to those words for a long moment, cherishing them. Then he called out. *Prince Oren?*

When it is only us, you must call me Uncle Oren or Uncle. I could feel you. I wondered what was taking you so long.

I was looking at your ring, Uncle. Achan smiled. He liked saying the word uncle.

Clunky old piece of gold, isn't it?

I think it's amazing. The history, especially.

I suppose it is. How do you fare? Your face? Has it healed any?

One side has scabbed over. The other broke open again. Silvo Hamartano.

Sir Gavin told me what happened in Barth. I'm proud of the way you handled yourself.

Thank you, sir.

When we last saw each other, I asked you whether or not Arman had spoken to you as king. We were interrupted and I never heard your answer. Tell me, have you heard His voice?

The mere mention of Arman's voice seemed to heat Achan's insides. *Aye. He's spoken to me several times.*

So it is true! His uncle's voice sounded anxious, excited. *What has He said?*

Uh . . . He appointed me . . . king . . . over the nation. Before that He said to listen to Sir Gavin. Recently He yelled at me for calling on Cetheria. Then He restored my bloodvoice and kept some gowzals from eating me alive. He banished Barthos. Though his uncle couldn't see him, Achan shrugged. *I like Him all right.*

Prince Oren chuckled. *Well, that is the best news I have heard since you were found. Now, tell me all you have been through since you left Mahanaim.*

Achan filled his uncle in on the journey thus far. The conversation lasted a long while because Prince Oren kept asking questions, inquiring as to a detail Achan had skipped over or to ask Achan's feelings. Achan liked Prince Oren's attention. The man cared about his well-being.

Sir Gavin expressed concern to me about this Hadad fellow. He did not want to burden you, but I think it wise for you to be on guard. When this man spoke, did you feel a knock? Any mental intrusion at all?

No. Achan's mind spun. *I did feel cold. Sir Gavin said a chill can be a sign of bloodvoice ability. Hadad wanted me to renounce Arman, to shake on it.*

Touch increases bloodvoice connection. Take care to keep your mind guarded, nephew. There are so many who might seek to harm you.

So many already had. A meaty smell drifted into the room. Achan's stomach growled. Ressa was cooking again.

You are hungry? Prince Oren asked.

Achan smiled. *A little.*

Then go and eat. We can talk again later.

Achan didn't want the conversation to end. *Uncle, do you know how Gren is doing?*

She is safe. I am grieved over what happened to her husband. I thought sending Jax and Sir Rigil would be enough to protect one family, but I fear Lord Nathak did not want to part with them.

Will she stay in Carmine, do you know?

For now. Perhaps you will be able to visit her when you arrive there. I understand Carmine is one of the places Sir Gavin plans to visit.

Aye. It'll be months before we're there, though. Could you have Bran or Sir Rigil keep watch over her? To make sure she's okay?

I will. But trust her to Arman, lad. He'll watch over her better than anyone.

But Gren does not follow Arman.

That does not change the fact that He watches over her. He loves all of His children, whether or not they know or believe. Good-bye, nephew. Go and eat.

Good-bye, Uncle.

19

When Achan entered the kitchen two days later, people filled the house. The table had been pushed lengthwise against the inner wall and people sat on it, dangling their legs over the edge. The chairs also lined the walls, occupied by men and women, chatting amicably. More people occupied the couches and floor. No one paid any attention to Achan.

He scanned the room. *Sparrow? Where are you?*

On the floor, other side of the table.

Achan squatted. Sparrow sat cross-legged behind the front table leg on the other end. *What are you doing over there?*

This is the best seat I could find.

Where am I supposed to sit?

Stay where you are. You can see from there.

Achan would much rather hide with Sparrow than stand in the doorway where someone might introduce him, possibly make him strip off his shirt and show his scarred back. He didn't relish another bout of humiliation. Besides, he'd spent most his life under the tables in the kitchens of Sitna Manor, scavenging crumbs from the floor. He crawled under the table and sat on the inside of the table leg by Sparrow. He stretched out his long legs, though he had to hunch to keep his head from hitting the tabletop. A man's legs dangled beside his face.

Sparrow peeked around the table leg. *How do your feet feel today?*

Better. I'm hungry. Achan pressed a hand to his stomach. *Did you eat?*

No. Sparrow nodded toward the sideboard crammed full with bowls draped in cloths. *Ressa cooked all morning. I think we are to eat after the service.*

Mmm. Achan studied the people in the room. Most were peasants or lower except for a well-dressed man beside Sir Gavin. The people chatted as if passing the time for a tournament to begin. A man and woman entered the front door, and Ressa greeted them with a smile. *There's so little room in this cottage, why do so many come here today? What exactly is this Teshuwah about? Do we parade to the temple?*

Teshuwah is our holy day. These people have come to worship Arman.

Here? This is a dwelling of people, not a god.

Arman has no temple besides His people.

Achan wrinkled his nose. The temple was people? That made no sense.

So many now filled the cottage that no surface remained bare. People stood along the walls, two deep in some places. Some men held children on their shoulders. The voices suddenly quieted, gazes drifting to the curtained doorway. Achan peeked out from under the table.

Trajen entered the room dressed in a white hooded cloak over a white tunic with the same brown trousers he always wore. He walked to the entrance of the house and faced the room. This position not only gave him space, it made him visible to everyone.

He lifted his arms high above his head. "And on the day called Teshuwah all who believe shall be gathered to one place, and the word of Arman will be spoken. Then we shall rise and pray. And when our prayers have been heard, we shall give praise and thanksgiving. Then we shall eat, for food brings nourishment to the body and celebration to the soul. We assemble on the Teshuwah because that's the day Arman wrought a change in the hearts of men. That's the day His Son, Câan, rose from the tomb to give us Light.

"For he was murdered by men, put in a dark tomb, and on the day of the Sun, which gives light and life, appeared to King Willham and his men and taught them all these things."

A chorus of agreement, "So be it" and "May it be so" burst forth from the crowd. From somewhere Achan couldn't see, one of the twins said, "Bite bite, Mima," and the crowd chuckled.

Trajen closed his eyes, inciting a hush in the room again. "In the beginning was Câan, and Câan was with Arman, and Câan was Arman. Câan was with Arman in the beginning. In him was life, and that life was the Light of men. The Light shone in the Darkness, but Darkness did not understand it."

A man above Achan grunted in agreement.

"And in those days Er'Rets had no king; everyone did as he saw fit. The people forsook Arman to serve other gods. So Arman gave Er'Rets a king; his name was Echâd Hadar.

He came as a witness to testify concerning that Light, so that through the Light all men might believe."

Trajen paused. "But the people did evil in the eyes of Arman and Darkness began to push away the Light."

A chill raked up Achan's arms at the ultimate evil that had brought Darkness upon the land: killing Arman's chosen, his father.

"But Arman so loved His people that He gave His Son, Câan, as a ransom for the transgressions of every man. He was buried in Noiz on the same day King Simal II breathed his last. Both men were buried that day. And to this day, the tomb of King Simal II remains sealed. But Câan's tomb did not remain sealed. Three days later, Arman opened Câan's tomb and raised Him from the dead to sit at His right hand, a testament to what He longs to do in the life of men."

Achan had heard this tale many times over the years from Minstrel Harp in the Corner back in Sitna. It was a neat story, though he'd never heard it quite like this.

"King Willham believed, and through the power of Câan, took hold of the Darkness and pushed it back. The battle ceased for a time. But many a king has come and gone since then. Some have obeyed the call of Arman. Some have answered the call of Darkness. For many did not recognize Câan as the source of all Light."

Câan was the source of all light? Might Achan need His help, then, if he was to push back Darkness? And wouldn't his calling on Câan offend Arman?

"Though many did not recognize Him—including His own Kinsman people—those who did receive Him, those who believed in His power, He gave the right to become children of

Arman—children not born of natural descent or a husband's will, but born of Arman."

"For we know that Arman is light; in Him there is no Darkness at all. If we claim to have fellowship with Him yet walk with Darkness, we lie and do not live by the truth. But if we walk with the Light as Arman is in the Light, we have fellowship with one another, and the Blood of Câan, Arman's Son, purifies us from all evil, even in this dark place."

People yelled out "Praise Arman" and "May it be so."

Trajen opened his eyes and scanned the room. "For this reason, I've not stopped petitioning for all of you that Arman will fill you with the knowledge of His will, so you may live a life worthy of Arman and may please Him in every way: bearing fruit in every good work, growing in the knowledge of Arman."

A chorus of agreement, "So be it," "May it be so," and "As it has been said," burst forth, only this time, the voices did not quiet. A woman's voice broke into an upbeat song. Almost every soul in the room quickly joined in, Sparrow included.

> Er'Rets was lost in the darkness within.
> The Light of the world is Câan!
> Like sunshine at noonday His glory shone in.
> The Light of the world is Câan!

> No darkness have we who in Arman abide.
> The Light of the world is Câan!
> We walk in the light when we follow our Guide.
> The Light of the world is Câan!

Ye dwellers in Darkness with tar-blinded eyes.
    The Light of the world is Câan!
Go, wash, at His bidding and light will arise.
    The Light of the world is Câan!

No need of sunlight in Shamayim we're told.
    The Light of the world is Câan!
For Câan is the Light in the city of gold.
    The Light of the world is Câan!

The song ended in a heavy silence. Then a man started to sing from the table above.

Come to the Light, 'tis shining for thee.
    Sweetly the Light has dawned upon me.
Once I was blind, but now I can see.
    For Câan has brought Light that is free.

The people sang this twice, then, on the third time through, a clear woman's voice began a measure behind, leading several other women in a round. When the refrain finally ended, Trajen sang a phrase—nearly a chant. Everyone joined in.

"Sh'ma Er'Rets, Arman hu elohim, Arman hu echâd, Arman hu shlosha be-echâd."

The words were the old language like what Sir Gavin and the knights had said in Barthos' temple. How strange that so many would know this language. And what were they saying about Arman?

When the singing ended, Trajen said, "Some of you may have noticed a few unfamiliar faces this day. We often welcome new followers into our fold, but today our guests have been walking with Arman for many years. We have heard of the deceit in Sitna and knew in our hearts it was true. Our promised king is not the evil man we thought him to be, but a man who, like Câan Himself, was made a servant for his people, scorned and beaten, until Arman pulled him into the Light where all could see the truth.

"We have with us this day Sir Gavin Lukos and his companions who are escorting the rightful heir to Er'Rets—the true Crown Prince, Gidon Hadar—north to safety. There they plan to raise support so the true king can return to Armonguard and proclaim *Arman hu elohim, Arman hu echâd, Arman hu shlosha be-echâd*, a truth so bright it will push back Darkness forever."

The crowd murmured. Achan shrank back against the wall under the table. He had expected an introduction, but who could live up to such words? He'd almost rather they strip him down and fawn over his birthmark.

Boot steps clunked across the floor. The voices hushed so suddenly, Achan couldn't help leaning forward to see what was happening. Just as he peeked out from under the table, a set of legs cast a shadow over his face. He glanced up to see Sir Gavin looking down into his eyes.

Achan's stomach rolled as he realized the crowd had been watching Sir Gavin.

"'Tis true," Sir Gavin said. "I found him once, and I'll not lose him again, wherever he may hide himself."

The crowd chuckled and Sir Gavin reached down with his calloused hand. Achan clasped his wrist and allowed the old knight to hoist him to his feet.

Sir Gavin clapped a hand on Achan's shoulder. "Here stands King Axel Hadar's *only* son. Here stands your future king. For in less than a year's time, this young man will sit on the throne in Armonguard and bring an end to the Darkness."

The people burst into cheering.

Less than a year? Achan tensed, yet couldn't fight his own smile, so contagious was the joy on the faces around him.

"A feast for our two kings!" Trajen yelled. "For this earthly king and our King who reigns in Shamayim!"

"Hear, hear!" a man said and the people cheered again.

Everyone moved at once. Those who'd been sitting on the table jumped down and put it back where it belonged. Ressa set one of the covered bowls on the table, and other women joined in to help. Sir Gavin guided Achan to the entrance. People clustered around, blocking his view of the food.

A portly man with a wisp of black hair took Achan's hand in both of his. "A pleasure and honor, Your Majesty."

"Thank you," Achan said.

Another man, stocky with a scarred face, pushed forward. "Say the word and I'll fight with you, my prince."

"We'd be honored to have your sword." Sir Gavin clasped the man's shoulder. "Trajen will keep you posted as to where our army will assemble. Likely Carmine."

Achan's stomach roiled again. They were truly going to build an army and fight against Esek? Good men like this, family men, might die for him? Before he could dwell on the matter, three more men pledged their swords for Achan's sake.

A pretty young red-haired girl curtsied before him. "My heart fills with hope to see your face, Your Highness. I can see you're brave and strong. With you leading our men I know we shall not be in Darkness much longer."

Achan felt taller at her words. He bowed, took her hand, and kissed it. "Thank you, my lady. Your words inspire me to crush any enemy who would stand in my way."

The young woman's face flushed. She tugged her hand free and stumbled back, her eyes locked with Achan's until she sank into the crowd.

Easy, Achan, Sir Caleb said. *This is not a noblewoman who requires such courtesy.*

Heat crept up Achan's neck. *Well, why should that matter? You told me I had to act with dignity and respect in formal gatherings.*

Aye, but you must consider your subjects' social class or you'll start a scandal with every young maid you meet. These women are not used to such flattery and may take your words as more than they were.

Achan met Sir Caleb's critical gaze. *But I meant what I said.*

The corners of Sir Caleb's mouth twitched, like he was fighting a smile. *I see I must teach you about women next.*

I know about women, thank you very much.

Sir Caleb laughed out loud. Achan scowled. The knight looked quite mad laughing alone on the other side of the room.

Trajen spoke in a loud voice, and Achan found the man standing at the head of the table now packed with steaming bowls of food. "We are one in heart and mind. We claim no possessions as our own, but share all we have. Darkness may surround us, but in our hearts, the Light is blinding. As we continue to testify to the love of Câan, truly there are none needy among us. For Arman provides our every need." Trajen met Achan's eyes and held out an arm, beckoning him forward. "Come, Your Highness, sit at our humble table and be filled."

Achan somehow managed to cross the room and sit on the stool at the head of the table. Thankfully, Trajen didn't ask him to offer thanks the food, but said the words himself.

"Arman, we thank You for Your many blessings, for this food, fellowship, and the hope that dines with us this day. Let us break bread with glad and sincere hearts, praising You in all things. So may Your will be, forever."

A chorus of "So be it" and "May it be so" erupted. The rest of Achan's party was ushered to the table. Sir Caleb sat to Achan's left, Sir Gavin to his right. Sparrow sat beside Inko on the other end.

Bowls of steaming flatbread filled the table along with seasoned brown rice, cuts of chicken, diced tomatoes, wedges of apples and peaches, peas, steamed carrots, shredded lamb, and stacks of toasted trenchers. The aroma watered his tongue, but no one touched the food. Every face watched him.

Ressa swept forward. She set a trencher in front of him, then arranged several pieces of flatbread on it, scooped rice, chicken, and tomatoes onto the flatbread, and rolled it up. She raised her eyebrows and smiled with a nod of her head. "Go ahead and eat, Your Majesty."

Achan lifted the rolled-up meal to his mouth and bit down on the rich and spicy mixture. He chewed, unhinged that everyone still stared. He smiled with his lips closed to hold in the food and said, "Mmm."

The crowd burst into cheers and applause. Achan kept himself busy chewing, eyes downcast. His approval of the meal seemed to be all everyone had been waiting for. People began filling their trenchers. Achan, happy to have the attention off him, glanced at Sparrow and found that the boy was the only person still staring. *What?*

You did well. That must have been terrifying.

Achan smiled. *You think I'm going to have to do that every time we eat with strangers?*

Yes. I am afraid this will soon be how you eat for the rest of your life.

Achan lowered his gaze to his plate. *The first tradition to go if I ever sit on any throne. There's no reason I should eat first, especially with everyone watching.*

It is meant to honor you.

I don't need to be honored. Though it was nice for Ressa to rescue me. If she hadn't I might still be staring at the food.

You only like her because she looks like . . .

Achan stared at Sparrow, who'd looked away. *Looks like who?* Ressa resembled Gren in so many ways, but how could Sparrow know that? Achan had told no one.

Not looks. She cooks like I suspect the king's chef might.

I don't see you pushing the food away. Achan tucked his last bite of flatbread roll into his mouth and reached for another. *You're right, though. Vile, evil woman! How dare she feed us so well?*

Then why not ask her to join our group? She can be your personal chef.

Achan scooped rice and lamb onto his second flatbread. *Why don't you eat, or better yet, talk to Inko. He hasn't had the pleasure of your chiding conversation as much as I have. Go on then, share your wit with him a while.*

You spoke to me, *not the other way—*

Achan blocked Sparrow out, rolled up his flatbread, and bit into it. He caught the boy's slight frown and grinned. Having stronger bloodvoicing skill than Sparrow was fun.

• • •

Vrell reclined on the pillows in the front room, holding Romal loosely so his feet touched the floor but he could bounce freely and not fall. The baby boy stared at her with wide, brown eyes. She made a face, puckering her lips and squinting. Romal giggled and bent his knees, his chubby cheeks dimpling.

What a sweet creature.

Ressa had handed the baby to Vrell so she could groom Achan. The two of them had been gone for a while. They were not alone, of course. Sir Gavin and the men were with Achan, discussing the plans to depart the city in the morning. Vrell felt excluded out in the front room. She had considered carrying Romal back there, but knew the little boy would cry the moment he saw his mother.

Muffled voices rose in the hall. The curtain shifted, and Achan held it open for Ressa.

Vrell rolled her eyes.

"Bite, bite, Mima!" Romal squirmed, reaching for his mother.

Ressa came straight over and swept him up. "Mima thinks it's time for Romal to nap."

"Bite, bite."

"Yes, you may have dinner first, my sweet."

Ressa left from the room without another word. Achan fell onto the pillows beside Vrell. His hair hung loose around his face, but the ends had been trimmed, as had his scruffy facial hair, to keep up his shadow of a beard.

"What?" Achan slapped Vrell lightly on the back of the head.

She flinched and shied back. "*You* smell like rose water."

He smirked. "It's not nearly so bad when a woman washes your hair." He put his hand on Vrell's ear and pushed her.

She tipped onto her side, grunted, and struggled to sit upright again. "Stop."

Achan's lips curved in a small smile. He snagged her arm, drew it behind her back, and grabbed her other wrist in the same hand. Then he flipped her over his lap and pushed her down to the floor. Her cheek slapped against the wood floor. Achan's knee pressed into her back and squeezed the air from her body in a rush.

"What are you doing?" She gasped in a quick breath. "Get off me!"

Achan leaned over, his wet hair tickled her ear. "You're a weakling, Sparrow. And you eat too much. What if you have to fight a warrior hand to hand, no weapons? It's my responsibility to make sure you know enough to live." He released her.

She took a deep breath and barely managed to stand before he darted forward and tucked her head under his arm. She flailed her hands about, slapping wherever she could, and managed to pull out a handful of his hair.

He laughed. "You fight like a girl. Come on, Sparrow. At least *try* to hurt me."

She drew back, but he had her chin locked tight in the crook of his elbow. "I do not . . ." she pulled back again, grunting with effort . . . "want . . ." another pant and tug . . . "to hurt you." She kicked at his leg, hoping to make him trip.

"Don't worry." He kicked her feet out from under her and released her head. "You can't."

She fell onto her side. Her elbow hit the floor at an awkward angle and stung.

He leaned over her again. "That's my point. Now, stand up and try again. A leg sweep has to come from behind my leg, not in front. You need to kick out the back of my knees and push me down at the same time."

Vrell scrambled to her feet and grabbed Achan around the waist, trying to hook her leg around his in the process, but like a solid tree, he did not budge. She reared back and charged again. He caught her shoulders, twisted aside, and swiped her feet out from under her again. Her back slapped against the floor, knocking her lungs useless. She sucked in, but no breath came. She closed her eyes and tried again, barely managing a hitch of air.

Achan sank to the floor and sighed. "Sleep in my room tonight, Sparrow."

Vrell's eyes flew open and she croaked, "Sleep where?"

Achan drew both hands over his head, sweeping his hair out of his face. "It's creepy back there alone. I miss the campfire and bedrolls. I don't know why everyone feels I must have my own bedchamber."

Vrell inhaled a long breath. Feeling had returned to her body again and it hurt. "You just want someone to beat on."

Achan nudged Vrell's shoulder with his bare foot. "I want someone to talk to. Please?" He cast a begging pout her way.

Vrell could not help but laugh. "You look as if you are a puppy who has been put outdoors. Ask Sir Gavin. If he does not disapprove, I suppose it would be all right."

"Why should Sir Gavin care?"

Vrell sighed, searching for a logical reason Achan might understand. "All this protocol is new to me too. When I met you, you were a soldier. Now you are a prince. I will not be accused of treating you poorly."

"Sparrow, you're so full of moss you're soft in the head. You're the only person who doesn't treat me like a prince every hour of the day. Imagine why I like you so much?"

Vrell's cheeks warmed. Oh, Shamayim. If her mother knew she planned to share a bedchamber with the prince, she would never hear the close of it.

Achan lay on his pallet and stared at the webs of light flickering on the ceiling from Sparrow's candle, glad they were leaving in the morning. Trajen and Ressa were kind, but Ressa's similarities to Gren haunted Achan. He wanted to get to Tsaftown and see Lady Tara, a girl he hoped could fill the cracks in his heart left by Gren.

Thankfully, Sparrow had agreed to sleep in the room. Achan couldn't stand another night alone with thoughts of Gren, memories of torture, and pondering his dead parents. If he wasn't careful, Darkness turned every thought sour, though he hadn't had any dark visions or nightmares here. Sir Caleb claimed Arman protected Trajen's household from such evil.

Light still danced on the ceiling. Achan propped himself up on his elbow. Sparrow sat cross-legged on his bedroll by the foot of Achan's pallet, a finger and rag in his mouth.

"What in blazes are you doing?"

Sparrow's round eyes focused on Achan. "I am cleaning my teeth."

Achan laughed. What an odd duck.

Sparrow shot him a lofty smirk. "You shall not be laughing when you have a toothache and nothing can be done but to have it pulled."

Achan sobered a moment thinking of Sir Gavin's thin and wolfish teeth. "So if I wipe cloth over my teeth I'll not get a toothache?"

"Not necessarily. But at least you will not have stink breath."

Achan frowned. "I don't have stink breath."

Sparrow raised his eyebrows and went back to rubbing.

Achan crawled out of his bed and over to Sparrow.

The boy shrank back, regarding him warily. "What?"

"I want to see what you're—" Achan leaned close and breathed in the boy's face.

Sparrow's eyes bulged and he sputtered. "Eww, Achan. How revolting. I thought Sir Caleb was teaching you manners."

Achan cackled and dove back to his pallet. "For everyone but you, Sparrow. For everyone but you."

20

Achan wanted to think they left for Berland bright and early, but who could guess the hour? Trajen took them to the stables for their horses and escorted them to the northern gate. Before they passed through, Sir Caleb tethered the horses in a line.

Trajen bid them farewell and the guards opened the gate. No horizon met them, only a black void. Achan didn't want to go into it again. How could Lady Tara live in Darkness and stay so agreeable?

He tried to focus on Lady Tara, but his thoughts kept drifting back to Gren. Ever since Sir Gavin's lesson, Achan continually checked on her, found her cooking, cleaning, even sleeping. It took a bit before Achan realized she'd been sleeping. He first feared he'd ingested âleh, but he remained focused and almost fell asleep himself. At least he now knew a way of getting to sleep when his mind refused to rest.

Sir Caleb Agros.

Achan opened to the knight. *Aye?*

We have a long journey. Inko has agreed to keep the others in their heads by discussing the Great War. While this is information you need, I feel there's a more pressing matter. Women.

Achan frowned. *Is this about what I said to that peasant girl?*

That and more. I managed to get word to her through Ressa that you are just learning the rules of courtesy and did not mean to flatter her so. But I can't keep doing that. I fear we must spend a great deal of time retraining you. I assume no man mentored you on your coming-of-age day?

Should someone have?

It's tradition. Under the circumstances of your upbringing, you've turned out much better than I could have hoped for. You carry yourself well, are brave, honorable, and loyal, all traits necessary for a good king. But I fear you came to these traits of your own will, therefore you'll always look at them through your own perspective. I must teach what no nobleman took the time to impart.

Achan steeled himself against whatever flaw concerned Sir Caleb, thankful the conversation would be silent between the two of them. *Say what you must then.*

When a boy becomes a page—with hopes of someday becoming a knight—he begins certain trainings. Aye, he learns to fight, but he also learns a code of conduct, for a knight is sworn to protect the weak and defenseless. Should a man accept this path, he must eat, sleep, and breathe loyalty, courage, and honor.

Exactly why Achan had craved knighthood.

Many knights ignore this and seek instead to exalt themselves through sport of tournament, philandering, exploits at war. But true knighthood isn't about exalting the knight. It's about the knight becoming a servant to his people. As king, you're to be the knight of all knights. Nobility is not a birthright. It's defined by one's actions. You've seen firsthand how Esek behaved in this position. You're nothing like him, yet it's easy for a man who suddenly gains fame and fortune to stumble. And the higher a man is exalted, the farther he has to fall. I seek only to help you navigate the righteous road ahead.

None of this surprised Achan. *Very well. What must I know?*

Now that you're a man, and a prince, you must not trust only your heart in matters of right and wrong. A man's heart is deceitful above all things. Your own heart will betray you if you don't guard it wisely.

That seemed a bit farfetched. But Sir Caleb hadn't known Achan very long. Maybe he feared Achan would start behaving like Esek. *How do I guard myself?*

My best advice is to wait on Arman in all matters.

What if He doesn't answer? He's a little spotty on the advice.

He always answers, my boy. Many times, the answer is simply no. But men complicate matters because they listen to their heart more than to Arman. Your ability to honor Arman and obey His will for your life and Er'Rets is what will set you apart as a good or bad king. Remember, His ways are not man's ways and are often confusing, especially when a man's heart is convinced something is right.

So how did I err in speaking with the peasant girl?

You played with her heart.

Did I? How?

Sir Caleb paused a long moment. *Arman has created men and women differently.*

And I thank Him for it.

There's more to it than outward appearance. Our hearts are different. Women are more attentive to words and feelings than men. Aye, there's always an exception, but this is a general rule. When you speak fondly to a young woman, even if you're only being polite, she may conclude you're interested in her romantically. So you must choose your words and actions carefully in order to honor—but not mislead—each woman you meet. You want to leave them better off from having encountered you, not worse.

How could I have left her worse? She seemed to like the compliment I paid her.

You are the Crown Prince. Women will love you for that alone. You must be kind and courteous without encouraging their hearts to attach. And you must never take advantage of their eagerness to please you. If you indulge them, they'll only become more attached. The more attached, the more devastated they'll be when you don't make them your queen.

Achan huffed a dry laugh. *I didn't think I got to choose my queen.*

Your Highness, please. Do not take this lightly. This charm you have is a power you must not abuse.

Achan sighed. *Then what would've been the proper way to respond to the young lady?*

Your words were a bit inflated but would have been acceptable had you not kissed her hand. Only kiss a hand offered, which no peasant should do. Hand kissing originated as a sign of fealty, man to man, as in the kissing of a signet ring. Nowadays a lady might offer her hand in greeting, but only if her social status is equal to yours. For you to take a woman's hand when it's not offered signifies personal interest on your part. Remember, the greater the capacity for pleasure, the greater the capacity for pain. For the sake of Er'Rets, you must not be naive to temptations that could tarnish your name, your calling, and your future family.

Achan closed his eyes. His body swayed from side to side from the horse's movement. *I do not relish my birthright. I'm terrified of ruling anyone, let alone all Er'Rets. I don't intend on doing anything rash and am thankful you're here to keep me from humiliating myself.*

Ah, but it's the very things a man never intends to do that sneak up and ensnare him. I'll do all I can to keep you safe, but I pray you won't forget Arman is with you always and is your foremost advisor.

Sir Caleb went on to describe more etiquette regarding women of different classes. Then he added, to Achan's chagrin, another lecture on what kind of woman Achan could marry, as if he had forgotten. This only set Achan's sights on Lady Tara more, despite Sir Caleb's claim she wasn't prominent enough.

"Sir Caleb," Sparrow's audible voice startled Achan, "when might we practice sword fighting again?"

"When next we stop," Sir Caleb said. "And as you are nearing fifteen, we should be working to promote you to Achan's squire. To be officially declared a squire, you must go on a hunt. Darkness is not ideal for game. We could make an exception, allow you to hunt a gowzal."

"But I do not know how to hunt a gowzal." Sparrow's small voice made Achan smile.

"I'll teach you," Sir Caleb said.

Achan twisted around in his saddle, despite not being able to see. "No one taught me. Sir Gavin dropped me off in the forest with a knife and told me to walk back." Not that Achan had hunted fairly. He'd used his bloodvoice on the doe.

"We cannot use your training as a guide," Sir Caleb said. "Sir Gavin was . . . out of his element."

"How will I hunt what I cannot see?" Sparrow asked.

Sir Caleb hummed. "Setting a snare might work best."

Achan closed his eyes, seizing the moment to look in on Gren now that Sparrow had distracted Sir Caleb from his lectures on propriety. He found her walking in a forest—a field. Her gaze traveled over deep, green vines, past a cluster of tiny grapes, and back along the vines. A vineyard. The sun shone high in the pale blue sky. Achan's heart beat faster at the sight of such beauty and warmth on his skin, Gren's skin.

Gren laughed and the sound seemed to grab Achan's heart and squeeze.

It must have died. Gren glanced at the young man walking beside her. Bran Rennan. Achan would recognize that sunburned face anywhere. Bran stood only slightly taller than Gren. He had sandy brown hair and a wide smile, which he flashed at Gren, seeming pleased to have made her laugh.

On the contrary, madam. My Averella is quite the experimentalist. She rarely fails altogether. The duchess harvested her hybrid vines last season and had a special bottle of wine made for our wedding day.

That's so romantic. How long has she been gone?

It's been nearly nine months since last I saw her. We took a walk here in the vineyard, then I left Zerah Rock with Sir Rigil. When I returned, her mother told me she'd gone into hiding.

And you don't know where?

Only that she's safe. Prince Oren has assured me of that much.

Gren ran her fingers through the leaves on the vines as they walked along. *I wonder if Achan's safe.*

We saw him off in Mahanaim.

Gren's heart leapt and she searched Bran's eyes for any sign of bad tidings. *How was he?*

Shocked, I fear. We swore fealty to him, Sir Rigil and I. Prince Oren did as well.

I wish I could've been there. Gren's chest tightened and her eyes stung. *I can't believe it's true. I mean, I can believe. I do. Achan's such a special person. I'm outraged at what they stole from him. You can't imagine the cruelty he suffered. Even as a stray he didn't deserve it, though he was a bit outspoken for a slave. That courage probably came from his royal blood.* Achan's smiling face popped into Gren's mind, which almost made Achan disconnect. How strange to think fondly of his own appearance. *The whole thing's a long tale. I keep waiting for the story to end, so life can go back to normal but . . .*

Gren clamped a hand over her mouth to stifle a sob. Tears squeezed past her eyelids, out of her control, and streamed down her cheeks. Achan wiped the tears off his own cheeks and tried to separate himself from her grief. Gren's chest heaved with sobs and she tried to suck in shallow breaths so she wouldn't look pathetic in front of this squire.

Bran gripped her elbow and pivoted to stand before her. *Madam, please. I—*

Stop calling me madam! Gren jerked away. *I'm no one's wife.*

Oh. I . . . Bran's throat bobbed. He opened his mouth, stammered, lowered his eyes. *I—Forgive me. Please . . . please don't cry, Mad—Miss . . . Hoff.*

Fire seared through Gren. She pushed Bran into the vines. One fell from the trellis onto his head. *I'm* not *a Hoff!* She stormed away, walking as fast as she could.

Achan squeezed his reins. How could Master Rennan misunderstand her feelings? And how could she have treated the handsome squire in such a fashion?

Achan blinked. Handsome squire? This connection grew more binding, confusing, awkward, but Achan held on.

Something wet and rank slapped against Gren's face, drawing Achan deep into her mind again. She screamed and shook her head. The moist mixture fell from her face and plopped to the ground. She hopped back to keep it from getting on her shoes.

Cow dung.

Achan's chest heaved with horror and fury. He breathed in and out with Gren through her mouth, trying not to smell it. Warbled sounds met her ears. Voices. Laughter. Yelling.

Master Rennan stood to Gren's left, before a narrow path shooting between two rows of vines.

I say, explain yourselves this instant!

Two boys, barely of age, stood well into the path, doubled over in laughter.

The taller of the two, skinny with black hair, straightened. *We made your trollop a pie, Rennan. Now she smells as low as she stoops.*

Master Rennan propped his hands on his hips. *Barbarism! You will show a lady respect.*

She's no lady, the boy said. *I heard she's the prince's mistress.*

The other boy guffawed. *And now she's yours.*

Master Rennan growled and took off down the path after the boys. Achan urged him on. The miscreants deserved every pounding Bran gave them.

Gren took a shaky breath, then let loose another long cry. She was a widow! Not a trollop or anyone's mistress. Rumor of her baby had spread. Most of Carmine believed she was Master Rennan's lover, that he had brought her here to provide for the baby, explain to Lady Averella, and beg forgiveness. This wretched falsehood made Gren despised, for the people of Carmine felt Master Rennan belonged with Lady Averella.

Sounds of a struggle rose out of the vineyard where Master Rennan had chased the boys. How unfair that he had to put up with Gren's problems. He was too kind for such an assignment.

A shadow shifted to Gren's right. A rawboned man crept through the vines, his legs and arms moving slowly, like the spider crabs she'd seen when Father had taken her to the sea.

Achan didn't like the gleam in the man's eyes. *Run, Grenny.*

Gren tilted her head and gasped. *Achan?*

Run!

Gren spun around to face a fourth man who'd been standing behind her. He was a boar, bulky and tall with arms like clubs.

He stared down through heavy-lidded eyes. *You'll come with Mak and me, little morsel.* He seemed to growl each word.

Queasiness flashed in Gren's stomach. *I will not!* She pivoted and stalked into the vines on her left, down the path Master Rennan had taken. One row to her right, she glimpsed Mak, the spider crab, creeping parallel through the vines.

Gren, please run, Achan said. *Find Bran.*

Gren started to jog. A hand snagged the ties of her apron and jerked her back. She twirled around and pushed the big man's bull-like chest, fire engulfing her limbs. *Let go of me.*

The man swung a fist. Gren screamed, ducked, and tore after Bran. Mak leaped in her path. She darted left, thrusting her body through the vines, and let her legs take over her swirl-ing mind. Achan urged her on, his own heart pounding with the horror of Gren's reality.

Gren sprinted, darting from path to path toward the hedge wall that grew around the perimeter of the vineyard. Exits cut through hedge wall every so often. She had to find one. A quick glance over her shoulder revealed no one. She slowed to a stop, gulping in deep breaths, and listened. Leaves rustled. Had the noise come from behind her or . . .

Cetheria, great goddess of protection, shield me from those scoundrels. I beg you keep me safe. Lead me to the exit.

No, Gren, Achan said. *Call on Arman.*

Arman?

Mak stepped out of the vines and stood, legs apart, hands on his hips.

Gren wheeled around and plowed into the big man's chest again. Achan fumed. How could a man so huge sneak up on anyone?

Gren edged back, but this time the big man lunged for-ward and grabbed her wrists. With all the power her lungs contained, she screamed. *Bran! Help. Two—*

The man struck her and she crumpled to the ground, head ringing, throbbing. Her vision blurred, cloudy and strange. She couldn't concentrate. She must get up, right? A vague urgency nagged at the back of her mind.

Aye, Gren. Get up! Achan heard her groan but could no longer see. Her body scraped over leaves and dirt, her shoulders ached. Vines, leaves, and twigs slapped at her feet.

She stinks! the big man said.

The boys threw cow dung at her, Chod. Mak's voice, nasal and high-pitched grated on Achan's nerves.

Next time I'll pay them less if they can't hit the right target.

Gren! Grendolyn Fenny, wake up. What could Achan do, trapped in her mind? He concentrated on Mak's jarring voice and suddenly found himself in the young man's mind as he leered at Gren's limp body. Achan wanted to kill this man for the thoughts in his head.

Chod dropped Gren's feet and smiled at Mak with rotting teeth.

Achan attacked through Mak. He punched Chod twice, only seeming to hurt Mak's hand. Fire shot through Achan's.

Chod stared at Mak, sluggish eyes sad. *What's that for?*

Achan ripped down a trellis and broke the narrow board over his knee. He lunged, poking Chod in the chest. Chod snagged it away. Achan charged, but Mak's size was no match for Chod, who knocked Mak flying with one punch.

Achan's mind floated into the air, drifting, detached from any other. He looked down on the scene from above. Gren, Chod, and Mak in the center of the vineyard. A dozen rows away, Bran searched.

Achan blinked and found himself inside Bran's head. The squire was filled with a fury and fear that matched Achan's. Aye, Achan much preferred Bran's thoughts.

Achan concentrated in Gren's direction. *She's that way.*

Thank You, Arman! Bran took off, sprinting, ducking under trellises, dodging low vines, cutting across paths.

A scream tore through the air, and Bran poured on the speed, heart beating as though it might erupt.

You passed them! Achan concentrated harder on the location. *Go back two rows and turn left.*

Bran obeyed and found Gren and Chod rolling on the ground. Gren clawed at the big man's bloodied face. He tried to hold her down, but Gren kneed him and wriggled free.

Bran drew his sword, steel scraping over wood. Chod froze.

Pulse thudding in his ears, Bran's hands trembled, making his blade quiver. *Get up!*

Chod stared, heavy eyes sizing up his opponent.

I could kill you or let you rot the rest of your days in the dungeon. Decide now!

Chod pulled one knee up and pushed himself to—

Icy water doused Achan's head. He jerked and gasped. He lay on cold ground on a dark night. Shadowed men stood above him. How had he gotten here? Was this Chod's reality? In the dungeon?

"Achan, for Lightness sake, lad, speak to us!"

Achan pushed himself to one elbow. "Sir Gavin?"

The sound of a long sniff and sigh met his ears. "Welcome back, lad."

Achan clutched the frosty grass beneath him and shivered. "Gren." Bran had arrived in time. He relaxed but his throat tightened, his eyes flooded. He blinked rapidly, not in the mood for his emotions to best him. "I looked in on Gren." He panted, sniffed away his agitation. "All is well now."

"Tell us," Sir Caleb said.

So Achan did.

Inko groaned. "This is going to be the end of him. You're all knowing that, right? If he's not being taught the proper way to use his gift, we'll be losing him."

"How?" Achan asked. "What did I do?"

"'Tis my fault," Sir Gavin said. "I told him to look in on a friend the other night, to teach him to watch. I forgot to explain he shouldn't do it often."

"What Sir Gavin means," Sir Caleb said, "is you should never watch without someone staying with your body, to check on you. The longer you watch, the more comfortable you can get. You can forget to come back or be lost to the Veil—"

"Or be killed," Sir Gavin said. "'Tis happened plenty of times. Man gets too fond of watching and someone stabs him while he's out of his body."

"And you mustn't control others with your mind," Sir Caleb said. "That's not an ethical use of your gift."

"It is a dark use of your power," Sparrow said. "Macoun Hadar wanted to teach me. Thankfully I left before he could."

Achan recoiled under the weight of so many rebukes. Hot frustration took over. "But I was saving her! You don't know. You weren't there. I couldn't let them . . . What was I supposed to do?"

"You must focus on your task, in your own body," Sir Caleb said.

"There's nothing to focus on! We're riding through Darkness for days on end."

"The lady is not your responsibility," Sir Caleb said. "You must leave her to Sir Rigil and Master Rennan."

Achan fought to bottle his anger. "Sir Rigil wasn't present. Bran was easily fooled by dung-wielding rascals who got paid for their diversion. No offense to Bran, but he failed today."

"And he'll learn from this experience and next time be more prudent," Sir Caleb said. "These things happen to us all. It's part of learning how to—"

"I'll not risk Gren to his inexperience." Achan stood and brushed the wetness from his britches. "He should learn *before* being entrusted with a lady's well-being, not during."

Another long sniff and sigh from Sir Gavin. "Let's keep going and we'll talk more of this tonight at camp."

Vrell kept a close eye on Achan. She worried for him. All he'd lost. And now his guilt over putting Gren in harm's way. She could think of nothing to do but pray.

They found the Zamar River and followed it north. Their horses carried them over the first patches of snow. Sir Caleb gave Achan and Vrell capes he'd acquired in Mirrorstone. Then he taught Vrell to make a snare out of twine, though they blessedly never stopped long enough to try it. He also gave more swordplay lessons and lectured Achan and Vrell on technique. Vrell's confidence grew the more she learned, but she dreaded every rustle or creak as an impending battle she would fail to survive.

The weather got colder and, thankfully, there were no more mosquitoes. Vrell woke one morning to find fresh snow covering her bedroll. They were still a day or two from Berland and were not supplied for such weather. When they stopped the next night, Sir Gavin allowed Sir Caleb to build a campfire. Sir Caleb tried to talk Vrell into going hunting with him along the river, to sneak up on a gowzal nest. Vrell did not want to kill anything with a knife. She went to Sir Gavin and begged his help. Sir Gavin urged Sir Caleb to take Inko instead.

But once they had gone, Sir Gavin lectured her. "If Vrell Sparrow doesn't wish to be Achan's squire, he should be honest with Caleb about it. There's no shame in being a healer. 'Tis a noble profession for a young man. Squiredom isn't for everyone. Caleb will understand."

"I'll find a way to tell him." Vrell cleared a spot in the snow beside the fire and put out her bedroll, loathing the impending confession. She stared into the orange flames. Sir Caleb might understand why Vrell Sparrow did not want to be a squire, but would Achan?

21

Achan trudged through the snow into the small clearing the knights had dug out. Sparrow sat cross-legged on his bedroll, pink fingers outstretched toward the flames.

Achan crouched beside the boy, numb from the cold. He drew his cloak tighter. Sir Gavin stood by the horses, rummaging through his saddlebag. Inko and Sir Caleb were hunting. The day's ride had been long and tedious. He had to do something active or he'd freeze. Or go insane.

He glanced at Sparrow. Time for another lesson. He pounced, knocking the boy off his bedroll. Their heads sank beneath the snow edging the clearing. Sparrow squirmed like a fish on the bank and beat his fists on Achan's chest. Achan rolled to his knees, flipped the boy over, and straddled his waist. Sparrow was a feather, despite his chubby gut.

"Get off!" Sparrow yelled. "The snow is freezing."

Achan swung his leg off the boy and fell into the snow on his back. "You should be more aware of who's around you."

Sparrow crawled to his bedroll. "I was aware you were warming your hands, but I did not expect you to attack."

Achan sat up and shook the snow from his hair. "If you don't take this seriously, I'll have to replace you as my squire."

"I have been practicing hard—" Sparrow paused. "Ah, well, now that you mention it, I am certain another would be better qualified for your squire."

"Exactly my point. I don't want someone else, but you're a weakling. There must be a way to help you grow some muscle. Maybe you should start carrying Sir Gavin's pack."

"You are supposed to be a king, not a jester."

"I wasn't jesting. Sir Gavin made me do exercises to strengthen my arms. You should too. Come here."

"But I am cold."

Achan stood. Snow fell over the tops of his boots and melted down his legs. "Come here, Sparrow. Now."

Sparrow sighed and stood. He trudged through the snow and stopped before Achan, slouching, eyes rolled in defeat.

It amused Achan how well Sparrow obeyed. "Try the leg sweep again. Knock me down."

"I cannot do the leg sweep." Sparrow's voice warbled. "You know that."

"You can, you're just afraid. The trick is to get close and push. Best if I don't see it coming."

"But you *do* see it coming, you are telling me to."

"Then try to get me off balance another way, use my weight against me. See that rock by the river?"

"No. I see a lump of snow."

"It's a rock covered in snow, Sparrow. Stop being difficult." Achan positioned himself in front of the rock. "If we were fighting, you could back me up to the rock and I'd trip. Maybe fall in the river. Both are to your advantage."

"Thank you for the riveting advice, but I am cold and do not want to learn at the moment. Do not forget I bested Larkos to save you from marrying Jaira. If the circumstances arose, I could do it again. But I do not respond to mock lessons."

Achan grabbed Sparrow's head in one hand and pulled it against his side. He pushed the boy's face down into the snow. "Mention Jaira again and you'll wish you hadn't."

Sparrow elbowed Achan in the abdomen, then twisted the skin on the back of his hand. Achan laughed and shoved Sparrow forward. The boy sprawled head-first into the snow. He rolled over, and Achan pounced, folding his arms over the boy's chest, pinning him again. "Watch where you swing those elbows, Sparrow. You almost crippled me."

Sparrow got one hand free and pulled Achan's braid. "I meant to," he said over a grunt.

"Oh ho?" Achan snagged Sparrow's hand and pushed it back in the snow. "If you're going to fight cheaply you best be prepared for the repercussions."

"I can take anything you throw at me."

"This said by the boy immobilized in the snow. That so?"

"Yes, *Your Whininess.*"

The contempt in Sparrow's voice deserved a lasting lesson. Achan considered something painful but not debilitating. He brought up his knee—

"Achan!" Sir Gavin called. "I need you, lad."

Achan pushed off Sparrow. "Well, Luckyfox, fate has intervened and saved you from a world of hurt."

"Now, Achan!" Sir Gavin's tone seemed almost angry.

Achan scooped two handfuls of snow over Sparrow's face and backpedaled toward the horses, laughing. Sparrow sat up and shook his head like a wet dog, snow sizzling into the fire.

Achan trudged to Sir Gavin. "You need me?"

Sir Gavin clutched a dead gowzal by the feet. "You must go easy on the lad."

"Sparrow? I was only playing with him."

"Aye, but . . . some are natural fighters. Others . . . less so."

"That's my point. Sparrow's about as far from a warrior as a maiden at a joust."

"Aye, and there's reason for that. He . . . well, he, uh . . . He has a . . . condition."

Achan's enthusiasm sobered. "What? Like a weak heart?"

"Something like that."

Achan looked back to Sparrow at the fire. No wonder the boy was so scrawny. "That's the secret he's keeping?"

"Uh, sort of."

"Why doesn't he say so?"

"'Tis Vrell's decision, Achan. Let it be."

"But he wants to learn to fight. He asked me."

"You can teach him. Just be . . . gentle." Sir Gavin stepped past Achan, toward the campfire.

"Gentle?" Gentleness and fighting were as much a match as darkness and light. What fellowship could they possibly have with one another?

• • •

Sir Gavin approached Vrell carrying a dead gowzal by the feet. "Cooking has never been my strong suit. Inko handed me this, and he and Caleb are still hunting. Can you help?"

Vrell's eyes widened. "I do not think I can stomach eating a black spirit, Sir Gavin." Plus, she knew nothing of cooking.

"The creature is merely a bird. The spirit leaves it when it dies. Eating it now is perfectly safe." He dropped the beast at her feet and whispered, "Thank you, my lady. You've saved an old man from a terrifying ordeal." He walked back to the horses.

Vrell scanned the camp for ears, heart pattering at the sound of "my lady" spoken aloud. Achan and Sir Gavin stood by the horses. The others were hunting. Still, Sir Gavin's gutsyness unhinged her. She stared at the bird, hesitant to even touch it. She removed her knife from her satchel and crouched before the dead thing. She pinched a feather and sawed it off.

There must be an easier way. People spoke of plucking birds. Vrell held the beast down, grabbed a feather, and jerked. The sound of the shaft ripping from flesh sickened her. Her body inflated with tension. Being female did not mean she knew how to cook. Was it not enough that she had the stomach to heal grievous wounds? For the first time ever, she regretted having confided in the Great *Tactless* Whitewolf.

She grabbed another feather, winced, and yanked it out. She gripped another.

"What are you doing?" Achan's voice came from behind.

She pulled, the feather vane slipped through her fingers, and her fist whacked Achan's leg. "Sorry. Sir Gavin asked me to cook this, this . . . thing for dinner."

"Do you know how?" His words were laced with laughter.

Vrell held up a feather. "How difficult can it be?"

His hand stretched over her head. "Give me the knife."

Vrell handed it over. Achan carried the bird to the large mound of snow at the water's edge. He knelt and swiped off the mound with his forearm, baring a large, flat boulder. Vrell's posture slumped. She had truly believed it to be only snow.

Achan laid the gowzal on its back. "Plucking will take too long, and there's more to it than ripping out random feathers. Besides, we've no need to be fancy, so I'll skin it."

Vrell recoiled. "Skin a bird?"

"Sure." Achan turned the gowzal on its side and straightened its head. He cut the neck again and again until he was able to pull it free. The sound of ripping tendons grated worse on Vrell's nerves than feathers ripping out.

"First the head, then the feet." Achan set down the knife and took one leg in two hands. He twisted the leg at the knee, pulled and twisted until it hung by threads, then used the knife to sever the remaining tendons.

Vrell tried not to look, wincing at every snap and crack of the beast's dead body. Achan's lips curved slightly, as if he were actually enjoying himself.

He twisted off the wings next, rotated the bird to its back, smoothed the feathers aside, and cut the belly open. He slid his fingers in and pushed back the skin, feathers and all. Vrell's stomach lurched. She closed her eyes and stifled a whimper.

"See?" Achan said. "Not too hard. It might not look pretty for a feast, but it'll taste fine. All we have left is to gut it."

Vrell did not learn how to gut the bird because her eyes were closed. She hummed a chorus to drown the sounds of tendons ripping and skin tearing. When she opened her eyes, Achan pushed a pile of feathers and bloody goo to the side. The beast did look to have nice chunks of meat on it.

Achan washed the meat in the river. "Go get your sack."

Vrell hurried away and returned with her satchel that bulged with supplies from Ressa's apothecary friend. Movement in the distance caught her eye. Sir Caleb and Inko returned carrying three more gowzals. She cringed, hoping the men would not insist she learn this horrible skill. She appreciated Mother's cook more than ever.

Achan laid the meat on the rock. He scanned the ground near the water's edge and picked up a sturdy branch. Using Vrell's knife, he stripped bark from the branch and growled. "Is there no green wood in Darkness? I'm surprised the whole land hasn't gone up in flames."

Sir Caleb arrived and set his birds beside the rock. "What are you two doing?"

"Achan is teaching me to skin the bird," Vrell said, as if the idea fascinated her. "He says plucking will take too long."

"He's right on that account."

Achan sharpened the stick like a spear and handed it to Vrell. He rinsed his hands in the river and pointed at her satchel. "What have you got in there? To cook with, I mean?"

Vrell's mind raced. What herbs were good for cooking? "Um . . . cloves?"

Achan wrinkled his nose. "Not for fowl. What else?"

"Fennel?"

"Okay. What else?"

"Yarrow?"

Sir Caleb chuckled.

Achan's shoulders slumped. "Let me see."

Vrell handed him the bag. He set it in his lap and drew each bundle out one at a time and smelled them. "Rosemary. Is there any garlic in here?"

"Yes. At the bottom."

He handed her the satchel, but kept her bunch of rosemary. "Can you find it?"

She dug until she found a bulb of garlic wrapped in leather where it could not overpower the rest of her herbs.

Achan slicked open the bird's breast and shoved the rosemary inside. He took the clove of garlic from Vrell's hand and smacked it against the rock to knock the skin loose. He tucked a clove in with the rosemary and handed the rest back. "Sir Caleb, do you have any twine?"

Sir Caleb burst into a hearty laugh. "I think so. I'll go look." He trudged toward the horses, laughing all the way.

Vrell put away the garlic. The smell of rosemary and garlic masked the stench of blood. "Where did you learn to do this?"

Achan cocked an eyebrow. "Your first clue is on my back. Forgetfulfox."

Vrell flushed, the image of Achan's scarred back fresh in her mind. "Right. Sorry."

"I didn't hate Poril, you know. Deep down, for most my youth, I thought of him as my father. I never understood why he . . . Well, he'd beat me for the lightest transgression and show no remorse. Did your master ever beat you?"

Vrell glanced down at her hands. "No."

Achan huffed. "Luckyfox."

Sir Caleb returned with twine. Achan tied the breast to the stick to keep the spices in. He carried the stick to the campfire.

Vrell trudged after him.

"Not bad, Your Highness." Sir Caleb nodded at Achan's meat, now propped over the fire. "Care to see how I do it?"

Achan shrugged. "What other way is there?"

"The hunter's way." Sir Caleb walked to the riverbank, Achan and Inko at his heels. Vrell followed, uninterested in seeing another bird gutted, yet what other way could there be?

Sir Caleb set a gowzal on the ground on its back and spread the wings to the side. He stepped on them, pressing his boots against the body, grabbed the legs, and pulled. At first nothing happened. Then something popped inside the bird.

Vrell jumped and started at the dead bird, wincing.

Sir Caleb continued to pull, eliciting more cracks and tearing from the carcass. Suddenly, the feet ripped away from the rest of the body. Vrell shrieked and jumped back. The innards were still attached to the legs.

"Whoa!" Achan's eyes were wide, like he'd never seen anything so amazing.

Vrell did not think she could take much more.

"This gets you right to the meat." Sir Caleb held up the feet, dripping with guts. "All the innards are right here. And, see? The breast is bare. Just pull it out and cook."

Achan leaned forward to look. Vrell stayed put.

"Then strip back the innards over the leg . . ." Sir Caleb demonstrated. "Snap them off at the knee . . . and you've got two drumsticks ready to go. Toss the rest."

Achan reached for one of the other gowzals half-covered by snow. "Can I try?"

Vrell walked back toward the fire. "I shall keep watch on the one cooking."

• • •

Dinner warmed Achan's insides, but Sir Gavin extinguished the campfire and the darkness and cold returned.

Achan didn't feel like sleeping. He wanted to talk. "Do we follow the river all the way to Berland, Sir Gavin?"

"Nay. We'll leave the river here and head north."

"And follow your nose?" Achan asked.

"For a while."

Achan decided to look in on Gren, just to confirm her safety. *Sparrow, I'm checking on Gren. Make sure no one stabs me.*

Achan, you should tell one of the knights. Mocking them is not—

Achan closed his mind and concentrated on Gren's face. He saw nothing. Weariness gripped his limbs. She was sleeping.

On a whim, he sought out her father instead.

A dark room came into focus lit by a candle on a bedside table. Master Fenny lay on his back, staring at the ceiling.

Don't say that, Master Fenny said. *There's always hope.*

It's false hope. Tears laced Gren's mother's voice. *No man will marry a widow. We shouldn't have given her to Riga. She didn't want to marry him. It was a poor choice.*

You blame me?

We should've let her marry Achan. She could be queen now.

Master Fenny snorted. *They wouldn't have let him marry a weaver's daughter.*

But don't you see? Had we given in, they would've wed already. She'd be queen by default. They wouldn't have taken his wife away.

We cannot live in the past, Frida. She married Riga and he's dead. We must look to the future. I for one will not give up hope. We have a new life here. Carmine has rich soil. And I've never met such kind people. You yourself said this morning how kind they are here.

I did. They are kind. To us. But to Gren . . .

We must put all our hopes in this young squire. He's been good to us, and I've seen him looking fondly at Grendolyn.

He's betrothed to the duchess' daughter. We cannot compete with nobility. If we're to find Gren another match, we must set our sights lower.

Master Fenny recalled his time in the fields with Master Rennan earlier that day. *I think the man fancies her.*

What does that matter? Prince Gidon fancied every girl in Sitna. Did that make him a good match for anyone?

Do not speak that name! I say, Achan should be named again. Really, for that boy to take on a name so tainted—

Achan pulled away, thoughts drifting. He wrinkled his nose. It felt stiff in the icy air.

Gren's parents wanted her to remarry. It would be best. Why hadn't Achan demanded Sir Gavin let him marry Gren? Shouldn't he have put up a fight? His heart didn't ache any less for what he and Gren had lost when she had married Riga.

Had Riga kept him silent? The baby? Achan didn't know.

Master Fenny suspected Bran had feelings for Gren. But Bran had spoken passionately to Gren about his betrothed, Lady Averella. Could the squire's feelings have changed in her absence? Master Fenny had likely read more into Bran's polite behavior. Besides, no man could help looking twice at Gren.

His eyes ached. Time to sleep. *Sparrow? I'm back and alive, so stop worrying. I'm going to sleep now.*

After a long pause, Sparrow said, *Good night, Your Highness.*

Achan felt he'd hardly slept when Sir Caleb shook him awake. They rode into a thick forest. The horses slowed to a lazy amble in the snow. The trees were so close together there seemed to be no room for the animals. Branches swiped at Achan's arms and face, knocking snow over his head and arms. He kept his wool cloak fastened tight, the hood up, but it wasn't enough to ward off the chill. His fingers were numb.

Before long Sparrow began to complain. "Are we unable to find the road?"

"There's no road to Berland." Sir Gavin's voice carried back. "This trail is narrow on purpose."

Achan breathed on his fingers, making them moist. "Then how does one travel to Berland?" Before they freeze?

"No outsider travels to Berland," Sir Gavin said. "They're brought there."

Sparrow's heavy sigh hissed from behind him. "But should Berlanders travel elsewhere, they must have a way home. Why can we not take their road?"

"This is their road. Berlanders train their horses for these narrow hunting trails. They don't want it widely known where their stronghold is located."

Achan shifted in his saddle, his bruised body aching and saddle sore. He guessed eleven days had passed since Mirrorstone. Three nights in Melas, and he'd walked two days to Barth, but the other six had been spent on horseback. What did Sir Gavin have in mind once they freed the men from Ice Island? A long stay in Tsaftown where Achan might court Lady Tara? The idea seized him with a thrill of excitement and fear.

They rode all day, ate lunch on horseback, and kept going. Therion Forest made noises similar to those in Nahar Forest. Pecking, the occasional flutter of wings, snapping branches. Just as Achan was beginning to crave his bedroll, a loud *click, click, click, click, click, click, click* sounded from the trees above.

Achan tipped his head back to the blackness above. The sound was right above him.

Wump wump wump.

"Something's up there." A clump of soft snow fell in his eyes. He lowered his head and wiped the moisture away.

"Probably an animal," Sparrow said.

"That's what I'm afraid of." Achan pulled his hood tight. "Do you know what kinds of animals live around here? Do you know what a cham is?"

Sparrow tsked. "A cham would not make such a sound."

"How do you know what sound a cham would make? Have you seen one?" Achan really wanted to see a cham, but not in Darkness, though a fire would be nice.

Click, click, click, click, click, click, click.

"I think a cham would roar," Sparrow said. "And if he did, we would see his fire."

Chee wa. Cheeee wa. Chee wa. Cheeee wa.

Achan looked again to the blackness above, shielding his eyes with his hand. "Then what do you suppose that one was?"

Sparrow didn't answer.

Picka picka picka picka picka picka picka.

Click, click, click, click, click, click, click.

Shweeeeeeeee.

Balls of yellow light illuminated the forest around them. "Black knights?" Achan reached to draw his sword and found his scabbard empty. His stomach clenched. Had it fallen?

"Not black knights." Sir Gavin said, calming his horse. "Don't fight them. All will be well."

Achan twisted on his saddle, feeling for Eagan's Elk, squinting for the glint of the blade in the pale light. The multitude of strange sounds seemed to magnify.

Shweeeeeeeee.

A furry beast fell from the treetops, hovering to Achan's right. Achan cried out. Metal scraped over wood on his left. He swiveled in his saddle. A fur-clad man held Eagan's Elk to his throat. These weren't beasts. They were men in fur clothing.

Achan lifted his hands above his head. The chilled air snaked in the gap of his cloak and up his torso.

"Where you go to?" the man holding Eagan's Elk asked.

"We travel to Berland to seek the hospitality of Duke Orson," Sir Gavin yelled. "We are friends of Prince Oren. The young man behind me carries his ring."

The creature glided over the back of Achan's horse, somehow hanging mid-air. He grabbed Achan's hand and inspected Prince Oren's ring, then drew Achan's hands behind his back. Achan tried to jerk free, but the man holding Eagan's Elk pulled a burlap sack over Achan's head. Achan stood in his stirrups and tried to throw himself from Scout's back. Strong hands gripped his shoulders while another rope was threaded under his arms, bound around his chest. Achan's muscles tensed. What had Sir Gavin meant by "Don't fight them"?

A hand slapped Achan's back, a voice yelled, "Hay oh!" and his body zipped into the air. He screamed as he flew, feet swinging out behind, ripping past branches. He sucked in a breath and burlap filled his mouth. He spit it out, desperately wanting to grab something. Before he could think what to do, his flight slowed. Hands caught his arms, pulled him forward.

His feet landed on a wood plank. The rope around his chest tugged away, and he was ushered along a platform that swayed under his trembling steps. In the distance, Sparrow screamed. Achan couldn't help but smile. The little fox was flying.

His captors led him along the wooden bridge for some time, surrounded by the bedlam of clicking and drumming. His breathing heated up the bag on his head, moistening his face. Soon, voices rose above the percussion, chanting in low tones.

"Hey ya hey! Hey ya ho! Hey ya ha! Hey no no!"

Achan's guides stopped. His wrists were freed. The sack slipped from his head and cold air engulfed his sweaty face.

A man's hairy, familiar face looked down, framed by fat, black, frizzy braids and curly sideburns. A small bone ring looped through the top of his left ear.

Shung Noatak, a man Achan had fought at Esek's coming-of-age tournament, grinned and slung a cape of furs around Achan's shoulders, blanketing him in warmth. He held out Eagan's Elk. "Little Cham. We have been expecting you."

22

Achan gripped the log railing and took in the scene. An entire village lived in the trees, built on branches and platforms. Wattle and daub huts perched at a myriad of levels, connected by rickety split-log staircases and narrow bridges.

Two levels down, a wide, round platform had been built into a clearing of tree trunks. A log banister edged the platform, forming an outdoor great hall. In the center, a low, circular stone hearth held a bonfire. People dressed in fur and leather danced around it. Smoke curled up from the flames, drifting out of the clearing in the treetops above. In the surrounding trees, blazing glass balls of colored light in red, blue, green, and yellow dangled from branches, railings, or lampstands that stood along the bridges.

Achan pointed at the nearest glass ball. "What is that?"

"Come. Shung will show you."

He led Achan along the bridge, down a short staircase, and across another gangway to a blue ball that hung from a lamp stand on a chain like a lantern. It had a round opening that let out heat and smoke from a blue torchlight burning inside.

"We call luminaria. Pleasant, no?"

"Aye. Very."

"Let go of me!" Sparrow's voice carried from the trees across the platform. "I can walk myself!"

Shung chuckled. "The small one did not like lift."

Achan scanned the staircases and bridges but did not see the boy. *Stop making so much noise, Sparrow. You'll call the chams.*

These fur men nearly killed me, yanking me into the trees like a bag of meat. And those, those . . . singers are making more noise than I am. "I said, I can walk myself!"

Shung started back down the stairs. "Another little cham?"

Achan followed. "Naw. That one's a fox."

"I heard that!" Sparrow called out.

"Little Cham has come to Berland. Shung is glad."

Achan looked into Shung's dark eyes, recalling their sword match at Esek's tournament months ago. Shung had won, technically. He'd also promised if Achan ever came to Berland, he'd take him hunting. "Are we going to hunt a cham?"

Shung grunted. "Not this night, Little Cham. Come. The celebration awaits."

Shung guided Achan down a maze of stairs and bridges to a wider staircase that led to the center platform. Three thrones were arranged on one arc of the perimeter, facing the bonfire. A young man sat in the throne on the far left. He was as hairy as Shung, but slimmer. His tunic and trousers were made of short brown fur. Red fox tails hung around his neck like edging on a robe. It also circled around the tops of his deerskin boots. He wore a necklace dripping with at least two dozen cham claws.

The center, and largest, throne was empty. A matronly woman sat in the throne on the far right. She wore a tunic of white fur with matching boots and dark leather trousers. A white fur hat tied under her chin. Long salt-and-pepper braids spilled down into her lap.

The dancers and drummers were still chanting. "Hey ya hey! Hey ya ho! Hey ya ha! Hey no no!"

The young man stood and held up his hands, palms out. The drums trilled, voices warbled, all sounds increased. Achan shrank into himself at the noise level. The young man clenched his hands into fists and the noise stopped. He stared at Achan and spoke in a commanding voice. "Prince Gidon Hadar, also called Achan the Cham of Sitna. We welcome you to Berland, we do. We welcome you, our future king."

The man went down on one knee.

Beside Achan, Shung went to one knee. All around him fur-clad men, women, and children knelt. Across the platform, one boy still stood, looking lost. Sparrow.

Achan didn't bother hiding the grin in his voice. *Still trembling after your flight?*

Sparrow jumped, eyes darting everywhere but Achan's direction. *Where are you?*

The young leader stood and approached Achan. They were about the same height, but this man was several years older. He wore straight spears of white bone through each ear that looked to have been stabbed through and forgotten.

"I am called Koyukuk Orson. I am heir to Berland and Therion Duchy, I am. My father, Duke Orson, has not yet

returned from Mahanaim where he attended Council."
Koyukuk gripped Achan's shoulder and steered him before the
matronly woman. "Please, meet my mother, Duchess Crysta."

Achan bowed. "I am honored, my lady."

The crowd cheered.

Koyukuk led Achan to a slender young woman standing
beside his throne. "Please, meet my betrothed, Kumna Attu."

The woman curtsied. She wore a creamy suede tunic and
trousers. White fur fluffed out of her neckline and cuffs. Dark
braids twisted in a pile atop her head. She had wide eyes and
full lips, yet a small loop of bone through the center of her nostrils gathered all Achan's attention.

"Kumna will be your first dance, she will," Koyukuk said.
"In this you will show me honor."

Dance? Achan had never danced a day in his life. Gren
had never been willing, afraid of getting in trouble. Achan tore
his eyes away from Kumna's nose ring and took in the pretty
woman. How fortunate for Koyukuk that all the women in
Berland didn't look like his foreboding sister, Lady Gali, who
had been among Esek's prospects to marry. Achan steeled himself. Did that mean Lady Gali was now among his prospects?
The woman was as broad as a Kingsguard soldier.

Achan bowed and said, "Thank you," because he could
think of nothing else to say to the gift of a dance.

Koyukuk led him to the center throne, cham claw necklace
clacking. "Our guest of honor will sit in my father's chair."

Achan froze. Koyukuk wanted him to sit on a throne?

"You honor us to do so," Koyukuk said.

Achan reached for Sir Caleb's mind but guessed what the
knight would say. He spit out a flowery response. "Thank you.
You honor me with your offer."

Koyukuk smiled and gestured for Achan to sit.

Achan stared at the wooden throne. Could he really do this? Play king? It still felt like a game.

Sometime tonight, Your Highness, Sir Caleb said.

And here I thought you'd deserted me, Achan said.

You were doing fine until now.

Emphasis on "were"?

Sit.

Achan turned, lowered his eyes, and sat.

The forest filled with cheers. The drumming and chanting commenced. "Hey ya hey! Hey ya ho! Hey ya ha! Hey no no!"

A cluster of men wearing painted, wooden masks skipped out in front of the throne and began to dance and sing.

We come from land of forest,
    Where kuon and cham roam free.
Sun fled far and took our stars,
    And night will always be.

The Darkness tries to catch us,
    And cause us all great fear.
No matter how it blinds us,
    Arman is always near.

"Hey ya hey! Hey ya ho! Hey ya ha! Hey no no!"

The dancers scurried away, and the crowd formed a circle around the platform from one edge of the thrones to the other. Kumna pulled Achan from the chair. Her hands were small and warm, and the white fur on her cuffs tickled the tops of his hands. Achan's fur cape slid off his shoulders and landed in a heap by the throne. Cold air crept up his tunic. He tensed as Kumna drew his trembling form into the open space.

Everyone watched.

Kumna lifted their hands above their heads, stepped close, and stomped with one foot. Her dark eyes met his and she drew back, released his hands, and danced around to his back. He tried to turn, but she set a hand on his shoulder. "Stay."

She shimmied to his right and stomped her right foot, shimmied to his left and stomped her left foot. She danced her way around him until they faced each other again.

Achan merely had to stand still? No trouble there. But the couples pairing off around them proved the dance more complex. Not only did Achan have to stomp when Kumna did, he had to shimmy the opposite way, and when they finished the sequence, had to take the lead while she stood still.

Achan stumbled through the routine several times. Would this "song" ever end? Koyukuk appeared with a sweet-faced girl with wide, sparkling eyes and fat braids.

Koyukuk placed the new girl's hand in Achan's. "Yumikak is Kumna's little sister, she is. Very beautiful, yes?"

Achan bowed and met the girl's mischievous eyes. "She is indeed."

Yumikak rewarded him with a wide smile and slid her other hand into his. She started moving immediately as if she'd invented the dance. By now, Achan knew enough to keep up.

The tips of Yumikak's braids whipped Achan when she spun—a move she must have added since no other dancers were spinning. She also stomped with style. A double stomp. A stomp in slow motion. A stomp where both feet danced a jig. Achan tried to keep up, curious what she might do next.

Though he sensed no change in the drumming, Yumikak began a new dance. She twirled and rocked back and forth, whipping him repeatedly with her braids. He didn't mind—it didn't hurt—but could think of nothing to do but stand and watch.

Having fun?

Sparrow! Achan's gaze swept the crowd. *Are you dancing? She looks a bit young for you.*

Does she? Achan smiled at Yumikak. *I think she's charming.*

Sparrow snorted. *Of course you do.*

Are you jealous? Sparrow didn't answer. *Admit it, Sparrow: you want to dance with Yumikak, don't you?*

I never dance with people whose names I cannot pronounce.

Achan gripped Yumikak's shoulders and yelled in her ear, "We must find my friend. He needs to dance but he's shy."

Yumikak's dark eyes widened. "Your friend? Some are over there, they are." She pointed to where Sir Gavin, Inko, and Sir Caleb were dancing with some older Berland women.

Achan laughed. "No, another boy. Short. Round face."

Yumikak grabbed Achan's hand and towed him through the mob of dancers to the perimeter. Sparrow sat on the bottom step of the main stairs. Yumikak abandoned Achan and dragged the wide-eyed Sparrow into a dance.

Achan sat on Sparrow's step and chuckled as Sparrow stood, blushing like a girl, flinching each time Yumikak's braids struck. Another young woman seized Achan's hand and pulled him back into the circle. Not long into the dance, Lady Gali interrupted, giving Achan the pleasure of dancing with a woman taller than him. More of a soldier than a lady, really. Her face was fierce, concentrating. Bone bangles circled her entire neck and she seemed . . . stretched.

The drumming slowed as did the chanting. Softer. Up down, high low. "Hey ya. Hey ya. Hey ya. Hey ya."

Lady Gali curtsied awkwardly and stalked away. Seconds later, Yumikak sidled up. She pulled Achan through the crowd, bobbing backwards in slow motion to the beat. Achan couldn't help but smile at her almost hypnotic movement. Feet from the bonfire, she put her hand against his chest to stop him, then pranced around him, trailing her fingers along his chest, his arm, his back, his other arm. When she faced him again, she flashed a coy smile, then strode away, leaving him standing before the blazing fire. His eyebrows sank as she approached Sparrow and pulled the boy over.

She performed the same little dance with Sparrow, strutting around him. Sparrow turned red as a beet. Achan folded his arms and smirked, hoping to make the boy more uncomfortable. *You stole my dancing partner.*

What is she doing?

I think she likes you.

But Yumikak danced her way back to Achan. She danced around him and sang in a soft, haunting voice.

View not my face, I am undone beside you
  The beating of my heart will not cease
  Whilst I am near you, whilst I am near you

Pity on my heart, from the day I first saw you
  Your pleasing face burns my memories
  Whenever we're apart, whenever we're apart

Though I am nothing to you, I love you, I do.
  How shall I make it known, that I love you?

Yumikak leaned in and touched her nose to his cheek. Then she slinked toward Sparrow and sang the song to him, looking at Achan the whole time.

What in all Er'Rets?

I think she's trying to make you jealous, Your Highness.

But Achan didn't get to discover whether Sparrow spoke true. Koyukuk tapped his shoulder and escorted him back to Duke Orson's throne. A servant stood beside the chair with a platter of steaming food. Achan's stomach growled.

Koyukuk patted the throne's arm. "You have danced well, you have, and now you must eat."

Achan sat and the servant handed him a small knife. Achan helped himself to the food. Cedar-smoked salmon with maple sugar and cranberry sauce, slices of seasoned mushrooms, flaky pies filled with rich gravy and minced cham.

Koyukuk sat as well. "I have a gift for you, I do. Shung!"

Across the mob, Shung danced and laughed with Lady Gali. The hairy man bowed to Lady Gali, then weaved his way to Koyukuk's throne. He bowed to Koyukuk then Achan.

"I understand you have only knights to watch over you," Koyukuk said. "You must have shield. Shung is excellent swordsman. He also speaks blood voice. My gift to you. Shung. You honor me to accept."

Shung banged his foot on the floor, then went to one knee before Achan. "No man will touch you in Shung's presence."

Shield? Achan stared at Shung's shaggy braided head and swallowed the bite of mushroom still in his mouth. He couldn't take a man as a gift.

"Shung is old friend, he is," Koyukuk said. "I wish he remain in Berland until my wedding. Sir Gavin tells me you will go to Mitspah after Tsaftown. Shung will meet you there. Does this please you?"

"You spoke to Sir Gavin about this?"

"Sir Gavin says Shung will be great help to you."

Achan must have misunderstood. Shung would be joining their army, not serving as a slave. Achan bowed his head. "Thank you. This honor pleases me."

Koyukuk jerked his head to Shung, who bowed and darted back to Lady Gali's side. He swept her into the dancing crowd. Achan continued to eat, watching Shung and Lady Gali, amused at how fond they seemed to be of one another.

The drumming switched to a new beat and the dancers scattered, forming the outer circle again and joining in the chant. "Hey ya hey! Hey ya ho! Hey ya ha! Hey no no!"

A young man who resembled Koyukuk approached Achan's chair. He clapped to the beat then started to sing.

My name is Kotlik Orson.
    I hunt the cham to eat.
They give us fur for clothing,
    And much delicious meat.

Our land is dark and dreary.
    Do not get lost out there.
If chams fail to roast your hide,
    Charmice will take their share.

A cheer rang out. Achan clapped as well. Another man entered the circle and sang. This went on through ten or more men and women. Then Yumikak skipped into the circle, braids bouncing.

My name is Yumikak.
    My homeland's very cold.
I should go to bed, I should,
    And do what I am told.

But here's a mighty king,
    A very handsome man.
I'll dance all night with him, I will,
    If Father says I can.

The crowd went wild. Achan's temperature rose with the volume. Yumikak curtsied, eyes sparkling brighter than the luminaria. He grinned and hoped Sir Caleb wouldn't think he'd encouraged her affection. She skipped to a grey-bearded man and pressed her nose against his cheek.

Koyukuk danced his way before the throne next, his cham claw necklace swinging and clicking.

They call you Achan Cham.
    You come from land afar.
You bear the mark of stray,
    But your name is Hadar.

Cham bears are fierce and mighty.
    They breathe chains of fire all day.
So will you bring back the sun,
    And set the sky ablaze.

The cheers broke out again, so loud Achan's ears rang. People flooded back into the center of the platform and began dancing. Achan continued to eat.

• • •

A hand on Achan's shoulder jolted him awake. Sir Caleb stood before the throne holding a white luminary ball attached to a wire handle like a lantern. Shung stood beside him. Beyond, the platform was deserted and silent. Achan couldn't guess how long he'd been asleep.

"Let's find you a bed, shall we, Your Highness?" Sir Caleb asked.

Achan stood. Shung wrapped Achan's new fur cape around his shoulders and led them through the labyrinth of staircases and bridges. They creaked and swayed under their feet.

Achan yawned. "I don't suppose chams climb trees?"

"Only cubs," Shung said. "Sorry we will not hunt cham. Perhaps in Mitspah?"

"How do you kill one?" Achan asked.

"Pierce with arrow behind front shoulder, straight to core."

Achan frowned. "Is there no other way to hunt one? I've never used a bow."

"Sword could be thrust same place, though man so close to cham would fare better cutting off head."

"Why?"

"Chams thrash about and breathe fire when pierced. Man too close will burn."

That would make hunting more difficult. "Shung, why do you speak so differently than Koyukuk?"

"Shung is Wilderman."

"Berland was built by your ancestors, Your Highness," Sir Caleb said. "Koyukuk's accent is a combination of original Wilderman and the king's tongue. But many Wilderman still live in the forests."

328

They climbed up a steep spiral staircase, crossed a rope bridge, and climbed five more steps to a hut built on the upper branches of three massive trees.

Shung pulled aside a heavy leather drape. Sir Caleb ducked inside and Achan followed. Sir Caleb's luminary lit up the round space. The mud did not cover the twigs as much on the inside walls. Strips of branches poked out of the walls like ribs. A wide, low pallet covered with furs hid most of the clapboard floor.

"Do you need help with your boots, Your Highness?" Sir Caleb asked.

Achan shot a quick glare at the knight. "I think I can manage."

"I apologize if the question sounded strange. You'll soon have a valet whose sole employment will be to help you dress."

Achan pulled off the fur cape and his wool one and tossed them on the bed. "I don't need a man to dress me."

"It's not a question of need, Your Highness."

"Well, I don't *want* a man to dress me, then." He sat on the low pallet and pulled his boot, but the tall, fitted leather clung to his sweaty leg. Sir Caleb had helped him every night since Melas, when Trajen had given him the boots.

Achan struggled with the boot. Sir Caleb handed the luminary to Shung and pulled the boot off, then the second. Achan gritted his teeth. If they insisted he wear fancy clothes, perhaps he would need help getting dressed. How pleasing his old orange stray's tunic looked now.

"Shung and I will stand guard. Sir Gavin will relieve me later, but Shung will be outside all night should you need anything."

Achan glanced at Shung. "Thank you."

Shung nodded. He handed the luminary back to Sir Caleb and slipped past the drape.

"Sleep well, Your Highness," Sir Caleb said. "I shall wait until you're tucked in and take the light out with me."

Achan nodded. He pulled his shirt over his head and tossed it on his capes. He shivered and crawled under the heavy furs. It would take a bit for the bed to warm.

Sir Caleb carried the luminary out the door and the leather curtain flopped back into place.

The dark room trembled. A bed in a tree was a sensation that would take time to get used to. He stared at the outline of light around the edges of the curtain. His eyes fell closed, and he forced them back open. He sensed excitement and fear that refused to let him sleep. Were people still celebrating?

He wished Sparrow were here. Achan hated having his own chambers.

Soft steps padded across wood. He tensed. Could animals get into these huts? The sound crept toward his pallet. He slipped backwards out of bed, onto the cold floor, heart racing, hand grasping for his sword. Where had he left it? A shadow darted past the light at the door, past the foot of his bed.

Achan sprang, quickly finding the intruder's neck with his hands. As Achan hit the floor, a girl's scream urged him to let go. He rose to his knees. The intruder ran away, room shaking.

The curtain whipped aside. Yellow light blinded Achan. He raised an arm up to block the luminary's glare.

Sir Caleb knelt beside him. "Did you fall? Are you hurt?"

"I, uh . . . had a guest." Achan nodded toward his pallet. The lump of fur blankets shifted.

Shung, short sword clutched in hand, approached the bed. "Who is there? Come out now." He pulled back the furs.

A small gasp and Yumikak's frizzy head poked out from the top of the furs.

"Blazes, Yumikak!" Achan said. "What were you thinking? I could've hurt you."

"I came to sing you to sleep, I did," she said in a meek voice.

Shung growled, his hairy eyebrows becoming one. "Did your father send you?"

Yumikak's eyes went wide. "Oh, no, Master Noatak. It was my idea, it was. Please do not tell my father."

"You shame us." Shung faced Achan and stomped one foot, shaking the hut. "Shung will take intruder to her father and return shortly."

Yumikak's head hung so low her chin touched her tunic. Shung steered her out the door by the scruff of her neck. The hut trembled. Sir Caleb helped Achan up. He climbed back into bed, hoping Yumikak wouldn't be in trouble for her actions. But why would she sneak into his room to sing to him?

"I see that in the future, it will be necessary to sweep your chambers before allowing you to bed," Sir Caleb said.

Achan rolled onto his side. "She wasn't trying to kill me."

"No, but had she been, she might have succeeded. It would also be wise to review the customs of each village before we arrive. It has been almost twenty years since I last visited Berland. I had forgotten."

"That women sing men to sleep? Or is that a special custom for visitors?"

Sir Caleb chuckled. "It's a special custom for a betrothed couple. It appears you have survived your second offer of marriage, Your Highness."

"Be moving over, boy!" Inko's bony elbow jammed into Vrell's side.

She gasped and fought the urge to elbow him back. "Where? To the floor?"

Inko did not answer, so Vrell rolled on her side and curled into a ball. How ridiculous! She couldn't believe Sir Gavin hadn't helped her make other arrangements when they were given this privy of a room. Granted, they were in a treetop. How big could the rooms be? But surely Achan had been given his own bed. Vrell would rather sleep on Achan's floor than cram into a bed with an old, crotchety—

You will tell me where they are.

Vrell gasped at the sound of Esek's voice in her mind. Sensing a connection with her mother, she closed her eyes and focused.

Mother stood behind the jade desk in her study. The sun streamed through the window and lit the colorful wall murals and niches. Beautiful sun.

Esek and Sir Kenton stood on the redwood floor before Mother's desk.

I do not know where she is, Mother said.

You are both gifted, Esek said. *You must communicate.*

When my daughter calls to me, we talk, but she has not done so in several days.

When did you last speak?

A week past.

And where was she?

Approaching Melas.

Esek's posture swelled. *I know they are coming here. He means to marry her and take my throne.*

Mother walked around her desk. *My daughter is engaged to Master Bran Rennan. I have told you this numerous times.*

Lady Averella is engaged to me. I shall have her with or without your permission.

Mother laughed. *I think not, young man.*

Sir Kenton slapped her. *Do not disrespect your king.*

Mother set her jaw and straightened before Sir Kenton, who towered over Mother's petite form. *This man is no one's king. He bought his Council votes. Lord Nathak sat as my proxy because he killed my manservant and forged my name. The true Council will never crown this impostor.*

The true Council, as you know it, is no more, Esek said.

Mother frowned and studied Esek's haughty face. *What do you mean?*

The Council has elected members to replace those charged with treason. Your membership on the Council has been revoked. You still rule Carm—until I wed your daughter and take it legally. Esek stepped up to the arched window overlooking the northern fields. *But since you refuse to aid your king, I will burn your vineyards.*

Mother's heart rate spiked. *That is madness! You want control of Carm because it is vast and powerful. Without its vineyards it is nothing.*

Then at least it will not stand in my way. Esek started for the door then paused. *If you give me Wren, I shall spare your eastern vineyard.*

Mother blinked. *Who is Wren?*

Esek spun around. *The stray's lover, fool woman! Give her to me and your eastern vineyard will go unburned.*

I have never met a woman named Wren.

Do not twist the truth, Duchess. I know she is here with Sir Rigil and that traitor giant. You have one hour to save your biggest crop. Send word to me before—Esek wheezed, his face purpling.

Your Highness? Are you well? Sir Kenton asked.

Esek fell to his knees, gripping his throat, eyes bulging. *Release . . . my . . .*

Sir Kenton crouched at Esek's side. With The Shield's back turned, Mother darted behind the changing screen to the left of her desk. Anillo beckoned Mother with an outstretched hand from the open secret doorway built into one of the niches. Vrell gasped, shocked to see Anillo alive after Mother had accused Lord Nathak of having killed him. As Mother slipped past, Vrell noticed a hideous fresh scar across Anillo's neck.

Never mind me, fool! Esek rasped. *Where did*—

Anillo shut the secret door on Esek's question. He and Mother swept soundlessly along the dark, cool passage, lit by the occasional arrow loop, and up the spiral staircase. Not until they had climbed five levels and exited into the gazebo-like top of the Ryson tower did Mother speak.

Are the troops ready, Anillo?

They are, my lady.

Attack, and show no mercy.

Yes, my lady. Anillo bowed and retreated down the stairs.

Mother leaned against the stone ledge. *You will relay all this to Sir Gavin, Averella?*

Yes, Mother.

Good. Now I am weak from having given you my strength and must rest. Be safe, my love.

Mother withdrew. Cold gripped Vrell's pores. The room spun. She slid off the edge of the bed onto the cold floor and faded into darkness.

23

Achan's jaw ached from relentless shivering. His cheeks and nose were numb. His shoulder snapped back a stiff branch, causing snow to dump over his head. Icy flakes fell through the neck of his fur cape and slid down his back. He squirmed so they'd melt faster and pulled the hood over his head.

They'd spent one night in Berland. Achan wanted to stay longer, but Sir Gavin received word from the Duchess of Carm that Esek had ridden north after a threatening visit. Sir Gavin wanted to get to Tsaftown as soon as possible. Achan doubted they stood a chance of beating Esek as slow as their horses moved through the snowy mountain pass.

Camping proved miserable. Sleeping on frozen ground, even with the furs and blankets Koyukuk had given them, was terribly uncomfortable. To keep their minds focused, Sir Caleb lectured on the reign of King Bole II.

But Achan couldn't keep his mind from spinning. Lady Tara. Yumikak's song. The gift of Shung's service. Riga's death. Gren's growing affection for Bran. Silvo pushing him off the platform in Barth. Jaira's spicy smell. His aching backside. Lady Tara.

His thoughts always circled back to Lady Tara. She alone had shown interest in Achan when he was nothing more than a stray squire. Surely the people of Er'Rets would accept a woman as beautiful and agreeable as she? He couldn't help but pray Arman would allow—

Achan's horse stopped and neighed. Achan nudged his flanks. "Come on, Scout. Got to keep moving or we'll freeze."

"Why did you stop?" Sparrow asked from behind.

Sir Gavin's voice came from the front of the line. "The trail is blocked. Avalanche."

Achan's chest tightened. This would surely delay their arrival in Tsaftown.

"Can we go around?" Sir Caleb asked.

"Nay. I'm afraid we'll have to take an alternate route."

"Meribah?" Sir Caleb asked.

"Aye." Sir Gavin sniffed in a long breath. "Arman knows I'd rather not trespass upon Lord Gershom's . . . hospitality, yet it's the quickest route. Hopefully we'll find the man in good spirits."

"Being in his right mind, you're meaning?" Inko said.

"Is he ill?" Achan asked.

"He's suffered more than his share of misfortune," Sir Caleb said.

"He's being four times a widower, Your Highness," Inko said, "but having been blessed with no heirs, male or female, last I was hearing, he's seeking a fifth bride."

"At his age?" Sparrow said.

"The man has not yet reached his seventieth year, Vrell," Sir Gavin said. "Marriage is uncommon at such an age but not unheard of."

Sparrow gasped. "Oh, Sir Gavin, do not take offense. I did not mean to suggest *you* could not marry. I only meant—"

Sir Gavin chuckled long and hard, and Inko and Sir Caleb joined him.

When the men's laughter finally dwindled, Sir Gavin said, "I made my choice long ago, Vrell. I pledged my life to Arman and the throne. I'm His servant. I seek no other love in my life."

Nice one, Sparrow, Achan said. *Insulting my Kingsguard commander . . . I wouldn't have expected such from you. You're normally so polite and well-mannered.*

Achan's connection with Sparrow vanished. The little fox had pushed him out. He chuckled and let his laugh carry on longer than necessary. "Okay, Sparrow, I can take a hint."

The long and windy road to Meribah Corner added two nights to the journey. The wind seemed made of needles, piercing through to Vrell's bones. She could no longer feel her toes, fingers, nose, or ears. She prayed they were not black with frostbite. When she first caught sight of the lights of the stronghold, she thought she was seeing things.

Sir Gavin cleared the matter. "Meribah Corner, yonder."

Conflicting emotions pulled Vrell in two directions. She longed for warmth, but she did not relish seeing Lord Gershom again. All the times she had been blessed with his company, he had been irritable, insulting, and nearly insane. Her mother's uncle was a wanton man who gadded about as if he were forty years younger. The jest of Er'Retian court claimed that a girl truly came of age when Old Lord Gershom first proposed his undying affection.

Vrell shivered, recalling the slurred offer of marriage he'd made her when she was but thirteen. The chill in her bones prolonged her shiver, leaving her bones aching. She prayed Arman would get them to the stronghold before she froze.

The final leg of the journey seemed the longest. Despite the icy surroundings, Vrell caught the scent of salt in the cold air. They had reached the northwestern edge of Er'Rets.

The scratchy trees fell away and distant torchlight lit up their destination. Perched on an incline at the top of a cliff, Meribah Corner slowly took shape. The torches along the curtain wall formed a diamond, the wider side facing forward. Where the two walls met in the front corner, a gatehouse stood, half buried in a heaping snow drift.

The horses kept up their slow pace, unable to move faster on the steep slope. Why did Lord Gershom's men not clear the trail so close to the gate?

The curtain wall stood three levels high. A thick layer of snow edged the top and icicles draped over the sides like icing spilling over the edge of a cake. The torches on the sentry wall cast faint light over their party. The men's beards were covered in frost.

Sir Gavin reined his horse before the doors. "Lo! 'Tis Sir Gavin Lukos come to seek an audience with Lord Gershom." His deep voice echoed in the deathly quiet. The following silence sent a chill over Vrell's arms. After a long moment, Sir Gavin called again. "Hello! Is anyone there?"

Achan's voice filled Vrell's mind. *Hello. Hello. Hello. Is anyone there? There? There?*

Vrell smiled. Always a boy first. It would be interesting to see this boy become king of Er'Rets.

"Surely they wouldn't leave their gatehouse unguarded," Sir Caleb said.

"It appears they have," Sir Gavin sniffed and released a breath that hid his face in a white cloud, "unless something has happened here."

"But the torches are being lit. And Poroo are not coming this far north."

Sir Gavin called out again, and again received no answer. "Have you a boarding hook, Caleb?"

"Aye." Sir Caleb dismounted and drew his pack off the side of his horse.

"What are you going to do?" Achan asked.

"I'm going over." Sir Caleb drew out a wad of leather and unrolled a coil of rope with a three-hooked rod attached to one end. He turned his gaze to the wall and pulled the rope through his hands, unwinding it from the tangle. "I suppose it would be best to go up here."

Sir Gavin dismounted and untethered their horses. He took the reins of Sir Caleb's horse and his horse and walked them downhill, away from the gatehouse. "Achan, bring your animal back a bit, will you?"

Achan nudged his mount back beside Sir Gavin's.

Sir Caleb dropped the hook and line at his feet and stretched his arms up over his head. "I'm nearly too old for this, you know, Gavin."

"Not as old as the rest of us."

"I'll go," Achan said, grinning. "I'll try, anyway. I've never used a . . . rope hook."

"A boarding hook," Sir Caleb said, "used to board ships from a smaller craft. And thank you, Your Highness, but a prince is never the first man to enter any stronghold."

Achan folded his arms. Vrell could guess the stubborn thoughts raging through his mind. She tried to send a sarcastic comment, but his shields were fortified more than ever.

Sir Caleb picked up his hook and line and backed up five paces, facing the doors. He gripped the hook by the shaft, raised it above his head, and backed up a few more paces in the knee-high snow. Then, in one motion, he lowered his arm and tossed the hook up toward the wall. The metal clanked against the frosty ledge and fell back, bringing shards of broken icicles with it. The hook thumped deep into the snowdrift along the curtain wall.

Vrell jumped, thankful the hook had not fallen on Sir Caleb's head.

"Sorry." Sir Caleb pulled the rope until the hook flipped out of the hole in the snow and slid toward him. "It's been a while."

He lobbed the hook skyward again. It landed in the snow on top of the wall, but when Sir Caleb tugged, the hook hadn't snagged and plopped back to the snow. He growled.

"Three is being a lucky number, Caleb," Inko said. "Try again."

Vrell pursed her lips at Inko's ridiculous superstitions.

Sir Caleb tossed the hook quickly. This time it sailed over the top. He jerked the rope, which cut a deep slice in the snow on the curtain wall and answered with a muffled clank.

"See," Inko said. "Three is being a good number."

Vrell rolled her eyes.

Sir Caleb waded through the snowdrift. The closer he got to the wall, the deeper the snow. When the snow reached his waist, he jumped and, hand over hand, pulled himself up. Once his feet cleared the snowdrift, he set them against the wall and walked up, his boots slipping every so often on the icy stone.

Vrell held her breath, praying he would not fall. He had almost reached the top when a soldier peeked over the crenellation. Men's muffled voices rose, steel struck stone, and Sir Caleb fell, straight down, as if jumping feet first into a lake. His arms flailed a moment before his entire body vanished into the deep snowdrift.

Vrell clapped a hand over her mouth. A soldier with a bow appeared beside the first and shot an arrow where Sir Caleb had fallen. The first threw Sir Caleb's hook down.

Sir Gavin lifted his shield over his head. "Retreat to the tree line! Take the horses!" He ran to the snowdrift and dug with his free hand.

Vrell urged her horse downhill as fast as she dared. She reached the forest first. Achan and Inko rode in behind her, each leading an extra mount. Achan dismounted.

Inko caught him by the hood of his fur cape. "Be holding here, Your Highness." Inko drew his bow and pulled an arrow from the quiver hanging from his saddlebag. He did not let loose his arrow, however, but waited.

The guards looked down on Sir Gavin.

Vrell prayed. *Arman, please let him be well, please, oh, please.*

Inko kept his bow ready. "We're coming in peace," he shouted. "We are Kingsguard knights who are seeking an audience with Lord Gershom."

"Lord Gershom isn't interested in your business," the guard yelled back.

Vrell's mouth gaped. Of all the rude and cruel things to say to visitors . . .

"He'll be seeing us if you'll only be asking," Inko called.

"Lord Gershom don't like Barthians," the guard yelled. "Neither do I."

"I'm being but one servant of the crown of Er'Rets and being the only Barthian in our party. We're coming to be seeking shelter in the name of the king."

"There is no king!"

Sir Gavin had managed to dig out Sir Caleb and helped the knight to his feet. He held the shield above their heads like a sunshade. Vrell continued to pray, asking that they would make it to the trees unscathed.

"If you'll be relaying our message to your lordship, I'm assuring you he'll be changing his mind. We're having with us Prince Oren's signet ring."

The guard answered with his bow. The first arrow stuck the edge of Sir Gavin's shield. The second brought a cry from Sir Caleb.

"Oh!" Vrell dismounted. She dug her satchel out of her saddlebag so she would be ready to assist Sir Caleb.

Inko let his arrow fly. It struck the bowman's shoulder and the man collapsed out of sight.

"Nice shot," Achan said.

Sir Gavin arrived with Sir Caleb. "Help me, Achan."

Achan and Sir Gavin lowered Sir Caleb into the snow behind a wide tree trunk. Vrell knelt beside him. "Where are you hurt, Sir Caleb?"

Sir Caleb groaned. "I'm fine, just sore."

"And the arrow?"

"Nicked my shin. I'll live."

Vrell examined Sir Caleb's wound. A small tear on his pant leg revealed the scrape beneath. It could wait.

"What of these gatemen?" Sir Caleb asked. "Why attack after a declaration of peace?"

"Maybe they thought you were lying since you tried to scale the wall," Achan said.

"But why not answer in the first place? Why hide?"

"We cannot continue without aid." Sir Gavin tugged on his beard. "We had enough supplies to make it to Tsaftown, but this detour will leave us lacking."

"We can hunt and melt snow," Sir Caleb said. "We can make it."

"That's wide of the point. Lord Gershom should be an ally. Refusing us is to side against us." Sir Gavin picked up his shield. "Stay here. I'll make one more attempt at diplomacy."

Inko and Achan helped Sir Caleb stand.

Sir Gavin walked toward the gatehouse, holding the shield out to protect himself. "Lo! I'm Sir Gavin Lukos, Kingsguard commander to the Crown Prince. We stand outside your gates in peace with a message from the prince for your lord. Will you grant us entry?"

Sir Gavin's voice echoed in the silence. Then a series of arrows bit into the snow around him. At least three plunked into his shield.

Sir Gavin backpedaled, mumbling to himself. He reached the safety of the trees, slid onto his backside, and pulled the arrows from his shield one by one.

"What will we do now, Sir Gavin?" Achan asked. "Shall we go on to Tsaftown?"

"No, Achan. I'm going to seek out a mind inside. One I can get a message to who might report to Lord Gershom. I don't doubt the old man told his guards to turn away all visitors, but I also know that man, if in his right mind, would answer to a call from the prince." Sir Gavin closed his eyes.

Achan turned his concerned expression to Vrell. His voice barged into her mind. *Some welcome for the prince, huh? Not nearly as nice as Berland, but at least you don't have to fly.*

Must you always jest when the situation is dire?

Jesting is better than worrying. At least I don't give myself a stomachache and a sour expression on a daily basis.

Sir Gavin's eyes opened. He handed the arrows to Inko. "We'll wait here a moment longer."

"You were successful?" Achan asked.

"Aye. I found someone I know."

Vrell swelled with joy. "Really? Who?"

Sir Gavin shot Sir Caleb a knowing look. "An old friend."

A man's voice called out, "Sir Gavin?"

Sir Gavin stood but remained behind the shield. "Aye?"

"Stand by for the gates to open," the man said. "I'll meet you below."

That was all? "What assurances do they give that they will not attack us once we enter? Why should we trust them now?"

"It was a misunderstanding, Vrell. Do not fear."

Easy for Sir Gavin to say. If he would share who he spoke with, it might ease Vrell's apprehension.

Blessed Achan asked that very question. "Who was that?"

Sir Gavin slid his shield strap over his arm and grabbed his horse's reins. "Carmack is a young man from Tsaftown. I should like to know why he's here."

The name Carmack was familiar, though Vrell could not recall why.

Wood cracked as if a branch had been ripped from a tree. The right gatehouse door drew in, leaving a drift of snow between them and the bailey. Vrell took up her horse's reins and followed the men. By the time they reached the gate, three soldiers were shoveling the snow where it had caved in on the doorway. Sir Caleb went to retrieve his boarding hook.

Once the path was clear, Sir Gavin led the way, followed by Sir Caleb, Achan, and Inko. Vrell entered last. Snow covered the ground inside the bailey. Deep trenches crisscrossed one another like a spider's web, leading from dozens of wooden dwellings on the left of the keep to the larger outbuildings on the right.

The keep stood in the center, a dark shadow dotted with golden light gleaming from within through arrow loops and cracks in shutters. Windows also lit up each tiny wooden cottage. The scene reminded Vrell of a winter night in Carmine. A man's hearty voice drew Vrell's attention away from her surroundings. She'd heard that voice before.

"As I breathe, it's the Whitewolf himself. What brings you to Meribah Corner?"

A bear of a man approached the gate. He stood a hand taller than Achan and twice as wide. He wore a short bushy beard covered in a layer of frost, making it impossible for Vrell to guess his age. Vrell's mind spun trying to remember where she had heard his voice.

Sir Gavin greeted the man in a brief, fierce hug. "Carmack, 'tis good to see you. I feared your guardsmen might leave us to freeze if they didn't slay us first."

"Not my guardsmen, I'm afraid. But I do apologize. Lord Gershom is not himself. We've not had visitors since . . . well, not since I arrived."

"And why are you here, my boy, if not a guardsman? Did Lord Livna send you away?"

"Aye, in a sense. All will be explained soon enough. Let's get your horses to the stables and you all inside to thaw your beards. I wish we had the manpower to put your animals up ourselves, but . . . well, we're doing what we can to keep Meribah Corner on its feet."

The men took off toward the stables at a brisk pace. Vrell didn't blame them. The idea of sitting by a warm fireplace quickened her step as well.

The stables were thick with the familiar smell of hay and dung. Vrell led her horse in only to pass Achan, Sir Gavin, and Carmack coming out.

Vrell hurried inside to see Sir Caleb taking the saddle off Achan's mount.

"Help us with the horses, won't you, Vrell?" Sir Caleb asked. "We'll let Gavin and the prince get warm."

Vrell swallowed, ignoring the ache in her chest, and unbuckled her saddle. The Crown Prince should be taken in to get warm. Vrell traveled as his squire—his servant—nothing more. Putting up the horses was a squire's duty. Still, that Sir Gavin left her behind when he knew—

No. She chose this. No one had forced her to keep her identity a secret. She lifted a brush from the wall and worked it over her horse's back. It wouldn't be long until they reached Carmine. Then she could be pampered again. She just needed to keep reminding herself to stick to her plan.

24

Achan followed Carmack and Sir Gavin along narrow trenches cut through waist-high snow. His toes were numb, though walking warmed him some. He couldn't wait to take his boots off by a fire. And sleep in a bed, a real mattress, not the icy ground or a trembling tree.

Carmack opened a door on the side of the keep. They filed into a narrow, stone corridor, lit by a lone torch. The chill lessened despite the thick layer of frost that coated the outer wall. Carmack passed the torch that had burned to a stub. The flame danced about, seeming to reach out and grab at Achan.

Carmack stopped at a door just past the torch. His brown eyes met Achan's and he bowed without breaking eye contact. "You may wait in here, Your Majesty." He pulled open the door and it scraped over the stone floor.

Achan entered into the back of a warm solar through the servant's door. Iron sconces hung on timber plank walls. They held fat white candles that gave off the faint scent of jasmine and left the room smelling like a woman was nearby. Achan smiled at the thought.

He stood behind a round table. Across the room, a large pair of antlers was mounted above a simple stone fireplace that glowed with warmth. A sofa with a high, carved back faced the hearth, flanked by two matching chairs with brown cushions. There were no elaborate tapestries, no silver trays with grapes and tarts, no marble pillars or busts.

Achan liked this room a great deal.

Carmack closed the door before Sir Gavin could enter. Achan reached for the door handle. *Sir Gavin!*

All is well, lad. Warm yourself. I shall join you shortly.

Achan pulled off his mittens, shrugged off his cape, and set them on the tabletop. His fingers were pink. The crackling fire drew him around the sofa. He knelt beside a wrought iron poker stand and held out his hands.

"You intend to warm yourself by my fire without an introduction?"

Achan jumped up and whirled around, knocking the poker stand to the hearth with a terrible clank. A woman in a red gown sat in the center of the high-backed sofa, looking small, almost royal, as if sitting on a throne. Achan paused in shock at her familiar white-blond curls and blue eyes.

Lady Tara? He lunged forward to greet her, then remembered the poker stand. He spun around and righted it, mind fogged. He hadn't expected to see Lady Tara until Tsaftown.

He popped back to his feet only to snag his scabbard on the poker stand. It clattered to the stone hearth again, rattling

Achan's nerves. He blew out a frustrated breath and righted it, stepping away more carefully this time.

"Lady Tara." He bowed, clueless what to say. "Wh-What . . . uh, what brings you to Meribah Corner?"

A slow smile spread across her face and she scooted to the edge of her seat. "Why, Master Cham. Meribah Corner is my home now, and I welcome you to it. Though I would ask the same of you. Why are you here?"

Her home? What about Tsaftown? Young nobles often lived in the household of a relative or friend to learn a trade— or perhaps Lord Gershom had taken her as a ward to earn a fief from her father. Achan's stomach twisted. His stay here might be his only opportunity to ask for her hand. How did a man ask such a thing of a woman he barely knew? And should he do it now, before Sir Gavin returned with the others and reminded him her rank wasn't high enough?

Lady Tara stood. Her gaze darted to the door he'd entered through, then to a larger door to the right of the table. "Do you travel with your prince, Master Cham? We had not received word that His Highness was coming or, I assure you, we would have prepared for his arrival. I hope he will not be too put out."

She didn't know of Lord Nathak's deceit? How could he explain such a thing? "No, my lady. I'm afraid . . . it turned out that . . . well . . ." Achan swallowed. "Haven't you heard?"

She laughed softly. "Only that your tongue is somewhat knotted, good sir. How can I ease your mind?"

Before Achan could answer, the servant's door opened. Carmack and Sir Gavin entered.

Sir Gavin strode before the sofa and bowed. "My lady. Thank you for permitting us to enter. We're in your debt."

Lady Tara curtsied. "As if Meribah Corner would refuse the Crown Prince. Please, think nothing of it, Sir Gavin. Lord Gershom is not himself of late. I pray you forgive his orders. Had he understood who sought entry . . . Well, I am glad you were able to message Carmack." She gestured to the chair on her left. "Please, Sir Gavin, won't you sit? Master Demry, could you inform Ghee we will have our dinner in the great hall?"

Carmack bowed. "Of course, my lady." He exited through the large door. Before it closed, Achan could see a vast great hall beyond.

"Master Cham?"

Achan met Lady Tara's tired eyes. They did not sparkle as they had when he first met her. With slouched posture and pale skin, Darkness clearly did not agree with her. "I'm sorry? Did you say something, my lady?"

"Won't you sit as well?" She motioned to the chair across from Sir Gavin.

"Yes, of course." Achan claimed the chair. He set his hands on his lap, shifted them to his sides, then back to his lap. What was the proper thing to do with one's hands? They trembled slightly. He squeezed them into fists and jerked his head up at the sound of his name.

Lady Tara stared, forehead wrinkled. "Did you hear me, Master Cham?"

"I'm sorry, my lady." He forced a smile. "I'm afraid my mind is preoccupied."

Her sculpted eyebrows sank. "Of course, you are concerned for your prince. Forgive me. He is welcome to this room, but we have an elegant receiving room opposite the great hall he would likely prefer. My staff is preparing it as we speak. He could relax there until dinner is served."

Achan leaned forward and set his elbows on his knees. "My lady, Prince Gidon is not with us. He . . ."

Pig snout. How did one explain such a mess? His face flushed and he hoped she couldn't see his discomfort.

Sir Gavin raised an eyebrow at Achan. *Allow me.*

Thank you. Achan studied a knot on the floorboards between his boots. How might Lady Tara respond?

"Lord Nathak has deceived us all, my lady. Prince Gidon, as you knew him, is and always has been false. He's Lord Nathak's son. Shortly after King Axel and his queen were killed, Lord Nathak found the real Gidon Hadar. Before giving the prince to the Council, he switched the boy with his own."

Achan peeked up. Lady Tara brought her fingers to her gaping mouth.

"Aye, he hid the true Crown Prince all these years in the kitchens of Sitna Manor. Lost to all. But Arman exposed the treason. The man you see before you is the real Gidon Hadar, the rightful heir to the throne of Er'Rets."

Lady Tara's wide eyes brimmed with tears, then drooped, as did her hands. She gripped the edge of the sofa, slid off and onto her knees, head bowed.

Achan jumped up and grasped her elbow, pulling her back to her feet. "Please, my lady. Kneeling is not necessary. I've not yet been crowned. In fact, the Council voted Esek king, so until we challenge . . ." He helped Lady Tara sit on the sofa. The scent of jasmine flooded his senses. As he reclaimed his chair, his eyes darted to the candles he thought had held the scent.

Lady Tara's forehead wrinkled. "Who is Esek?"

"Nathak's son," Sir Gavin said. "The one we'd always thought was Gidon. The Council wasn't willing to give up control, you see. Since Esek has always been their puppet, they voted in his favor, four to three."

"So Master Cham is not king?"

"Not by the Council's ruling, no. But he's Arman's anointed despite what any man claims. Berland, Nesos, and Armonguard stand with us. We head for Tsaftown to gain your father's support, then on to Carmine to assemble an army."

"We are at war, then?"

"Aye, my lady, on the brink."

She turned to Achan, face pale. "Prince Oren supports you?"

Achan nodded and held up his hand bearing the signet ring.

"Do you have the king's gift, then?"

Again Achan nodded. He sensed her overwhelming shock and reached out for her thoughts.

It is almost too much. That Gidon is false and this sweet creature . . . He's so young. Can he do what's necessary? To overthrow Darkness? If he has the king's gift . . . "Prince Gidon—I mean, Lord Nathak's son did not have the gift, you know. But my father said the prince had it as a . . . child." Lady Tara stared at Achan, sapphire eyes glazing. "What an answer to the prayers of your people, for we feared Arman had forsaken us with an evil king. I know you are a man worthy of such a calling."

Achan cast his gaze to the floor, overwhelmed by the pressure of such flattery. "You're too kind, my lady." But she'd thought him a sweet creature. That was a good sign, wasn't it?

"You will fight, then?"

"At some point we'll have to," Sir Gavin said. "We realize Lord Gershom may not want to take a political stand, but we'd like to ask for supplies to aid us on our journey to Tsaftown.

And might we spend a night or two to rest? As of now, we have no way to compensate Lord Gershom's hospitality, but should Achan win the throne—"

"I beg of you, do not fret over compensation. You are welcome to stay here without recompense." She stood and smoothed out her skirt. "I will have our best rooms readied for you and your men. I—how many are in your party?"

Sir Gavin stood as well, so Achan did too. "Five, my lady," Sir Gavin said. "The others are settling the horses."

"I'll see that Ghee prepares a feast in your honor."

Sir Gavin bowed. "I thank you for your courtesy, my lady."

"As do I," Achan said.

Lady Tara's lips curled into a small smile. "Would you like a tour of the ground floor?"

She had asked the question of Achan. She now knew his rank was higher than Sir Gavin's and followed protocol by addressing him first. Achan needed to act his part if he hoped to impress her enough to want to marry him. The mere idea sent a wave of heat through his body.

"That would be nice, thank you." Achan offered his arm to his—he hoped—future bride.

Vrell stood inside the front doors to the diamond-shaped great hall with Sir Caleb and Inko. A wooden staircase wrapped around the right half of the room until it reached a door on the second level. The rough-hewn head table arched in a quarter circle from the wide corner of the room. Four long, wooden tables fanned out from it like sunbeams.

Servants trailed in and out, setting the tables. It appeared Lord Gershom would dine with them after all. She prayed he would let them stay a day or two. She longed to sleep in a real bed. Hopefully, one she would not have to share with Inko.

Achan and Sir Gavin had been gone a while. Where had Carmack taken them? Sir Caleb and Inko stood on the outside of the banister, whispering. Vrell did not care to eavesdrop. Those two argued over the pettiest concerns.

A woman's familiar giggle straightened Vrell's posture. Three figures entered the great hall through a door on the far wall. Sir Gavin, Achan, and Lady Tara Livna, who clung to Achan's arm like lint to wool.

Vrell emitted a small squeak and sat on the bottom step. Every muscle in her body tensed. What was her cousin doing in Meribah Corner, of all places? She peered between the banister railing, up between Inko and Sir Caleb's bodies. The trio had not yet reached them.

Sir Caleb muttered, "Well, well. What *has* our young prince found?"

"Trouble," Inko said. "I'm insisting Lady Tara is not being a wise choice. It'll be gaining us nothing we're not already having."

"But should he choose her, it *is* his choice, despite what we say," Sir Caleb said.

Inko propped a hand on the doorframe. "I am doubting he is knowing that. This choice will be affecting so much. We should not be allowing him to be making it alone."

Sir Gavin stopped beside Inko. "My lady, allow me to introduce Sir Caleb Agros and Inko son of Mopti, two fellow Kingsguardsmen. It's been our sole purpose these past years to find the true prince and see his birthright restored."

Vrell watched between Inko and Sir Gavin's arms.

Tara wore a stunning red gown and her white-blond curls were pinned up under a golden net. She curtsied. "It is an honor to make your acquaintance. I hope you will enjoy your stay at Meribah Corner."

"I'm sure we will, my lady," Sir Caleb said.

"If you will excuse me a moment, I would like to check on dinner, then I shall return and see you to your rooms."

Achan released her arm and bowed. "Your kindness is beyond measure. We've not been so welcomed in all Er'Rets."

Except when Koyukuk threw a ball in his honor. Vrell rolled her eyes. Achan had royal blood, all right. He could spread on charm like icing when a pretty woman was around.

Tara beamed, her cheeks as pink as the inside of a watermelon. Oh, yes. Vrell was familiar with the way Achan's smile could fluster a girl.

But Tara's good breeding didn't allow emotions to affect her perfectly polite response. "It is my humble pleasure, Your Highness." She curtsied again, and walked back the way she'd come, looking back over her shoulder twice before exiting the great hall.

"My, my, Your Highness," Sir Caleb said. "I see why you favor her so."

Achan sucked in a deep breath, seeming taller somehow. "She'd make a charming queen, wouldn't she?" He beamed, evidently quite pleased with himself.

Vrell snorted. "If you desire only beauty and polite conversation."

Achan leaned between Inko and Sir Caleb and peeked over the banister. "That's all you see, Sparrow? I don't discount her virtue, for we all can see that clearly. But I see much more. She is kind, wise, well-spoken—more so than I'll ever be. I'd even go so far as to call her a diplomat for having accepted us here in spite of Lord Gershom's refusal." He glanced at Sir Gavin. "Doesn't that show her strength of character and wit?"

Sir Gavin inhaled deeply. "Aye, Achan. She's a stunning woman, I'll grant you that."

"Plus she was kind to me when she thought me no more than a servant. Where else could I find such nobility of character amongst nobility? All the rest are like Jaira."

"That is unfair," Vrell said. "How many eligible noblewomen have you met, Achan? Four at my count. I don't trust Mandzee, though she is not as calculating as Jaira. But Lady Gali's kindness equaled Tara's."

Achan paled slightly. Vrell knew he loathed the idea of marrying Lady Gali.

Sir Caleb jumped in. "Try to see the bigger picture, Your Majesty. We've traveled hundreds of miles and only passed over a *portion* of your kingdom. A king must reach as many of his people as he can—all of them, should be your goal. Taking Lady Tara as a bride will help little. Meaning her no disrespect, but she's no one to the majority of your subjects."

That stung. The way these men spoke of a woman's future . . . as if any woman would be thrilled with whatever offer came her way. Vrell dressed as a boy because she refused to fall victim to the false Prince Gidon's demands. But she sympathized with Achan's desire to choose his own wife, even if he had set his sights on the most perfect-looking woman Vrell knew.

Achan's scowl told Vrell he understood and didn't like it. "And you would have me marry who? Lady Gali?"

"No," Sir Caleb said. "Someone of greater title than Lady Tara or Lady Gali."

"And what if this person doesn't want me? Should we suffer an unhappy life together?"

"For the sake of your kingdom? Yes," Sir Caleb said. "You're misled indeed if you think being king is a warrant to do whatever you please. A good king sacrifices his needs for those of his kingdom. A good queen would do the same."

"You're wanting to be a good king, are you not?"

Achan's smoldering glare fixated on Inko. "I never said I wanted to be king at all. Maybe I'll sign treaties with everyone and marry Gren." He pivoted on his heel and stalked away.

"Arman be helping us," Inko said.

Vrell hung her head. She wanted to be angry at Achan. Why, she couldn't say. Jealousy over the way he doted on Tara, her own cousin? She hated to think herself so catty. She hadn't wanted to marry Esek enough to go into hiding dressed as a boy. What if Achan fled as Vrell had? What would Er'Rets do without him? Esek would rule unchallenged.

Achan faced a terrible burden indeed. Vrell would not wish it on anyone.

True to her word, Tara showed them to their rooms. Before Vrell could follow Inko into the chamber, Sir Gavin drew her aside.

"I'm to follow Lady Tara downstairs to discuss what supplies we need. Would you like to speak with her privately regarding your situation? You're family, are you not?"

"She is my cousin. Do you think I should remain here?"

"If that's your wish, but I'd have to settle it with your mother first. I promised to see you safely home. For now, shall I speak to Lady Tara on your behalf?"

What would Tara think of Vrell traipsing across Er'Rets with a pack of men? "Yes, thank you, Sir Gavin."

She followed Sir Gavin down to a small solar with a crackling fireplace. Vrell waited in the doorway while Sir Gavin requested supplies. He sat beside Tara on a high-backed sofa. Carmack stood at Tara's side, recording Sir Gavin's requests. With his furs removed, Vrell recalled where she knew him. He had been a high-ranking soldier on Lord Livna's guard, a man Tara and their other cousin, Lathia, had fawned over on Vrell's many visits to Tsaftown. How strange to see him acting as Tara's servant. Why was he here? And why was Tara here?

Vrell's stomach clenched, heavy with dread. What if the knights permitted Achan his wish to marry Tara? She *would* make a lovely queen. She was so beautiful . . . So perfect.

Sir Gavin leaned close to Tara and whispered. Carmack straightened, his dark eyes boring into the top of Sir Gavin's back, clearly concerned for his mistress. Vrell's heart pounded. She licked her lips, praying Tara would not make a scene.

Sir Gavin bid farewell to Tara and winked his brown eye at Vrell on his way out.

Tara kept her eyes downcast. "Leave us a moment, Master Demry? Stand guard outside?"

Carmack's scowl flashed between Vrell and Tara. "Of course, my lady." He bowed and marched out the door, casting his stormy expression down on Vrell as he passed.

"Close the door, *boy*," Tara said.

Vrell obeyed, flushing at Tara's playful tone.

"Now come closer where I can get a good look at you."

Vrell took a deep breath and moved before the sofa.

Tara's narrowed eyes darted over every inch of Vrell. "Averella? This cannot be true!"

Despite Vrell's smile, tears gushed from her eyes. "Oh, Tara."

Tara stood and seized Vrell in a tight embrace. "Dear one, sit and tell me your tale. I had heard from your mother you were on holiday." Tara held Vrell's hand, sat on the sofa, and drew Vrell beside her. "Aunt Nitsa confessed Prince Gidon still sought your hand. I could not blame you for your refusal. I hid in this room trembling when I believed he had come here today. But what of it now? For I discover the stray squire in my solar and not the evil prince. I can scarcely believe it. Certainly that traitor no longer seeks you?"

"Oh, but he does." Vrell told Tara of Esek's warrant for her arrest, both as Vrell Sparrow and as Lady Averella Amal. "I only want to get home. Can you assist me?"

Tara's expression tightened. "I wish I could, but I am all alone here, as you can see. We have little funds, and I do not trust my husband's men—"

Vrell's breath snagged. "Your husband?"

"Lord Gershom." Tara held out her left hand to show a thick silver and jade ring. "My father made the match three weeks past."

Vrell clapped a hand over her mouth, but it did not stop the tears.

"Oh, Averella. Do not cry on my account. It is not *so* bad. He is rarely lucid and when he is, he forgets what he is doing and often falls asleep."

Vrell managed to squeak out, "Is he ill?"

Tara nodded. "He had a fever last year that left him altered. It still comes and goes. Sometimes he is quite pleasant, sometimes he is a tyrant, but mostly he is queer or sleeping."

"But you . . . are you well?" Vrell couldn't imagine anything so horrible. Arman, why?

Tara's expression softened. "I confess, I never imagined I would be the lady caught in Old Lord Gershom's web. But Mother sent Carmack as my guard. He makes sure I am safe. Do not dwell on my marital woes," she squeezed Vrell's hand and whispered, "for our marriage has yet to be consummated. Thank Arman for that—and Carmack. He manages to steer me and my husband in opposite directions every chance he gets."

Vrell threw her arms around her cousin. "Tara, I am so sorry I was not here for you."

Tara squeezed Vrell tight. "You are, and always will be, forgiven. Let us talk no more of my depressing life. What of you?" She raised her sculpted brows and grinned. "Traveling with the lost prince? How thrilling it must be. He is the most handsome young man I've ever met, and sweet too, don't you think? The story will undoubtedly go down in history, and you are in the midst of it all."

The heaviness left Vrell's stomach. Tara could not marry Achan. Joyful heart!

Then she squeezed her eyes shut. Arman forgive her! That she should be pleased with Tara's misfortune . . . She could hardly think straight.

"Tara. Achan . . . he . . ." She opened her eyes. "He seeks to marry you."

Tara gasped. "Me?"

"He doesn't know you are already wed. None of us did. Weeks ago, the knights told him he had to marry. Jaira tried to get her hands on him in Mirrorstone—it was the most disgusting display. But Achan thought of you instantly. You so enamored him at Esek's coming-of-age banquet. Sir Gavin and the knights said you were not the best match, and he has been cross ever since. He can be quite stubborn, Tara. I do not doubt he will go behind their backs and try to speak with you. Have you told Sir Gavin you are Lord Gershom's wife?"

"I did not." Tara reached under the sofa and pulled out a wicker basket. She drew out a handkerchief, dabbed her eyes, and fell back in the sofa, her golden curls spilling over the brown cushion. "What bad timing my life has had! Who will they choose for him then? You? It must be you, for I can think of no one else but Glassea, and she is a Hadar already."

Vrell shook her head. "Achan thinks me a boy—his squire, Tara, and a poor one at that. I do not wish him to know who I am. Not like this."

"But you are Lady Averella Amal, heir to Carm! Surely they would consider you. The traitor did."

Vrell sighed. "They *have* mentioned my name."

Tara grasped Vrell's knee. "You mean . . . they don't know you are you? They talk about you as if you're not there?"

"Not often. Sir Gavin is the only one who knows who I am. The rest believe I am a boy."

Tara sucked in a sharp breath. "Even Achan, the prince? He thinks you're a boy?" Tara's eyes sparkled, intoxicated with the juiciness of this information. "So they still might choose you."

"No. Maybe. Tara, even if they did, I would refuse. I love Bran, as you well know."

"Bran." Tara rolled her eyes and waved her handkerchief. "*He* is not to be king."

Vrell drew in a sharp breath. "I have been hiding nearly a year to avoid what has happened to you. The title of king means nothing to me. Achan is like a brother. And besides, he loves you."

Tara threw up her hands. "He cannot possibly love me. We've only spoken a total of five minutes in our lives. No, he loves the idea of me, poor dear." She sniffled. "I am convinced, Averella, that true love is a myth. Still, I do hope you and Bran can make it work. And I pray whoever is chosen for Achan . . . well . . . that he will be happier than I." She reached out and stroked Vrell's hair. "Averella. You are disgusting. When did you last bathe?"

Vrell wrinkled her nose. "In Mirrorstone, and then the water was not fresh."

Tara clucked her tongue. "And how many days have passed since Mirrorstone?"

"Almost three weeks, I am afraid," Vrell whispered.

"Gracious! The men as well?"

"Oh, no. They have taken several baths, but . . . Oh, Tara. It has been such a trial. And men can be so revolting. They bathe together, often in a steam room or lake where I could not go. If not for bloodvoices, and Sir Gavin's help, I would have been discovered long ago."

Tara straightened. "You have the king's gift too? How could I not have known this?"

Vrell shrugged. "We only discovered it before I left for Walden's Watch."

"You went to Coraline?" Tara's eyes sparkled. "How did Shoal look?"

Vrell grinned. "Handsome as ever, and in love with a fisherman's daughter."

"Mercy. Let us speak no more of thwarted love." Tara dabbed her eyes again. "I may not be able to take you home, but I can help you bathe, at least. Go gather your things. I will have a bath drawn for you in this room. Tell Sir Gavin you are staying with me tonight, then come back here. If I have not returned, wait outside the door. I am going to fetch a few things from my room." She took Vrell's hand in hers and squeezed. "I will take care of you tonight, dearest."

25

Achan stood by the door of his bedchamber listening to Sir Gavin's heavy footsteps fade down the hall. He glanced at the tub, at the steam rising above the clear water. A bath would warm his very bones, but first . . .

He cracked open the door to an empty hallway and crept out, uncertain what he was looking for or how he'd know if he found it. He turned a corner and almost ran into Sparrow.

The boy frowned, his cat-like eyes scanning Achan. "I was told you were talking a bath."

"And?"

"Well . . . clearly you have not."

Achan narrowed his eyes. "Why do you care?"

"I simply . . . Well . . . I thought . . ."

Achan laughed. "Take my bath, Sparrow. Tell Sir Gavin I said so if he asks. Enjoy." He leaned close to Sparrow's ear. "I do believe they scented it with rose water." He waggled his eyebrows, stepped around the boy, and continued to the stairs.

"Achan."

He spun around.

"Please do not go to her."

Achan's muscles stiffened. "To who?"

"Lady Tara."

Achan gripped the boy's shoulder. "Are you reading my thoughts?"

Sparrow's eyes widened. "Of course not. I just know you. But you might save yourself the trouble and hear her thoughts first."

"I won't violate her mind." Again. "It isn't right."

Sparrow shook his head. "I only meant . . . Well . . . You do not have all the information."

"And you do?"

"I . . . I believe Lady Tara is married. She wears a ring on her finger."

Achan couldn't tolerate Sparrow's meddling today. "I wear a ring and I'm not married." Achan spun the boy around and shoved him toward his bedchamber. "Don't fret, Sparrow. Go, take my bath, enjoy it, smell like roses, and leave me be."

"But—"

"Now!" He winced at the level of his voice and added in a soft tone, "Please. I'll beat you if you insist." He grinned to make it clear he was only jesting, then walked to the stairs where he met a boy carrying a bolt of cloth.

"Boy? Can you tell me where I might find Lady Tara? I must speak with her."

"Aye, m' lord. I'll take you to her."

Achan followed the lad to a large wooden door on the third floor. The crest of Meribah Corner was carved into the wood with great care, the dagger fabulously ornate with jewels encrusted into the hilt. Odd that Lady Tara should have the best chamber in the house. Perhaps Lord Gershom slept in the garrison with his men as some captains did.

"Many thanks, boy."

The boy bowed and hurried back down the hall. Achan knocked on the door. After a long moment, the door swung in and a slender maid curtsied. "My lord?"

"I wish to speak with Lady Tara. Is she in?"

"One moment, my lord."

The maid shut the door in Achan's face. Hurried steps clumped inside the room followed by whispers and scurrying about. Again the door opened.

The maid said, "Lady Tara will see you now."

Achan stepped into a warm bedchamber. Tapestries hung over the timber walls, depicting the history of Meribah Corner. A dark wood sideboard ran along one wall, a large fireplace beside it. Two large windows, solid with tracery circles, filled another. A vast canopied bed with green and blue striped drapes trimmed in gold fringe dominated the third wall. Two white fur pelts covered the center of a red clay tile floor. A pair of man-sized slippers sat on a long footstool near the bedside. Achan frowned and found more signs of a man. Two swords hanging on the wall. A fur jerkin draped over a chair.

Yet there was also a standing embroidery frame and stool. Nearly complete, it depicted a large ship at sea.

"It's my brother's boat, the *Brierstar*." Lady Tara stood before the sideboard, wringing her hands.

Achan glanced at her fingers. Indeed, she wore a large gold ring. He swallowed. Sparrow couldn't be right, could he? There must be another explanation. Achan pushed aside his doubts and forged ahead with his plan.

He bowed low. "Lady Tara, I must speak with you." The maid who stood against the door watched him with narrowed eyes. "Alone, if that's permissible?"

The maid looked at the floor.

Lady Tara's cheeks darkened. "No, Your Highness. Forgive me, but that would be quite improper."

Of course. Achan's resolve shrank. He didn't know how to offer marriage properly. His heart galloped in his chest. He licked his chapped lips and took several short breaths.

"Are you well?" Lady Tara poured liquid into a mug and offered it with trembling hands. "Drink. The ale will settle your stomach. I hope Meribah Corner has not made you ill?"

Achan gulped the lukewarm ale and handed her the empty mug. "No, my lady. It's nerves alone that have upset me."

She set his mug on the sideboard, keeping her back to him. "Nerves, Your Highness?"

Achan didn't speak. He couldn't do this. Yet he clenched his fists, determined to try. He wouldn't marry a stranger. If he won Lady Tara's favor, surely Sir Gavin and the others wouldn't force him to go against his oath.

Lady Tara spun around. "You are a mystery. When first I met you, you were a squire. Later that evening, you donned a servant's uniform. The following days you were a Kingsguard knight. Now you are a prince. Tell me, what will you become next?"

One long step brought him within inches of her blue eyes. "Your husband, if you'll have me."

She clapped a hand over her mouth and closed her eyes.

The maid squeaked and ran out of the room.

Achan's heart raced. He should do something better, more dramatic. He knelt at Lady Tara's feet and grasped her free hand in both of his. She shook her head and tried to pull away but he held fast. "As heir to the throne I've been charged with choosing a bride. I would have none but you."

Tears snaked down her rosy cheeks. This wasn't going well. He reached up to dab her cheeks with his fingers.

She grasped his hand and squeezed. "Your Highness, I am desperately sorry, but—"

"Unhand her!" Boots stomped over the floor. Before Achan could turn, a strong hand gripped the neck of his doublet and dragged him back.

"Carmack, stop!" Lady Tara yelled.

Carmack flung Achan back through the embroidery frame. He skidded over the tile on a white pelt, rigid with shock.

Carmack rounded on him. He gripped his doublet with both fists, lifted him to his feet, and slammed him against the wall. "You have no right to be in here."

Achan shook his surprise away, trying not to look winded from the breath Carmack had knocked from his lungs. He sized up his opponent, trying to recall Sir Caleb's advice to Sparrow on attacking someone bigger than you.

"Carmack! Release him at once!" Lady Tara took a deep breath, her face a mask of fury, and laid her hand on Carmack's bulging bicep. "Please, Master Demry, there is no need. The prince simply came to inquire about my husband's well being."

Achan's shoulders slumped, though Carmack held him fast against the cool wall. Sparrow had been right, that little fox. How had he known?

Carmack glared at Achan. "He should not have come into your chambers."

"That may be true, but the girl was here until she fled just now. You will release him and wait outside. Now."

Carmack's eyebrows twitched. Clearly the man didn't relish leaving Achan alone with Lady Tara.

"Master Demry!"

Achan tensed at the volume of Lady Tara's voice.

Carmack released Achan but stared as though Achan were a pile of maggots in his soup. "Two minutes." He stormed past the maid, who stood trembling in the doorway.

Lady Tara ushered the maid out and closed the door. She released a shaky sigh and spoke over her tears. "I am already married, Your Highness, to Lord Gershom." She wrung a handkerchief in her dainty hands, baring the ring she wore.

Closer now, Achan could see the crest of Meribah Corner engraved into the gold. He swallowed his frustrated humiliation. He'd proposed to a married woman. They were in her chambers. Alone. Sir Caleb would berate him. One look at the lady's tear-streaked face and Achan couldn't help but whisper, "But you cannot possibly love Lord Gershom."

Lady Tara flushed. "This is not a world where one marries for love."

"It should be."

Lady Tara straightened, holding her chin high. "My father and my great aunt, Lady Merris, plotted this match. In exchange for my hand, Lord Gershom gave my father the northern cape of Therion Forest. His men can hunt there and bring their kills back along the coast by dogsled to the people. It is a good exchange for Tsaftown, they—"

"How could your father do this to you? His daughter?"

Lady Tara folded her arms. "My father has more concerns than my comfort. He has a village to feed and little to feed them. My marriage feeds Tsaftown indefinitely."

"There must have been another way."

Tara sniffled. "Had I but known I was favored in your eyes—who you truly were—I might have convinced my father to alter his plans." She scowled suddenly, wrinkling her slender nose. "Were you not taught that proposals of marriage are made to the father of a lady, not directly to her? A lady has no say in who she marries. This is terribly awkward and could have been avoided altogether. And why would you come to my chambers? I should not have let you in."

"Forgive me, Lady Tar—" He ran a hand over his hair and sighed. "Madame G-Gershom, please forgive me, for I'm still learning decorum. I'm afraid I've blundered terribly. I didn't know of your union, nor the best way to inquire about—"

A fist pounded on the door. "My lady?" At Carmack's dire tone, Achan wished for a second door through which to exit the room.

He could take no more. "Forgive me, madam. I was foolish." He strode past Lady Tara and pulled open the door. Carmack framed the doorway like a gate. Achan patted Carmack's shoulder as he slipped by. "Good man."

He fled down the stairs, praying Carmack wouldn't follow. Pausing on the second floor landing, he leaned against the wall and closed his eyes. Of all the stupid, foolhardy, sentimental . . .

• • •

Vrell followed Achan to the ground floor, wondering what inspired his stiff posture and stormy gait, but suspecting she knew. He jerked a torch from a ring on the wall and slipped out the front doors.

Vrell clomped through the dark foyer and pushed open the doors. The cold seized her, stealing her breath. She scanned the dark bailey and spotted Achan's torso midway down one of the trenches, moving so fast each step nearly put out his torch.

"Achan, wait!" Vrell ran—boots crunching over the snow, icy air burning her lungs—until she reached his heels. "Are you . . . Where are you going?"

He half-glanced over his shoulder. "You're not my nursemaid, Sparrow. Stop following me around." He waved his arm. "Lo! Where is the firewood kept?"

Vrell leaned around Achan. A man carrying a load of kindling jerked his head toward to the side. "Behind the stables, my lord."

Achan surged down the trench, past the stables, then tottered down a narrow channel sprinkled with bits of bark, his breath a thin, grey cloud above his head in the torchlight.

He slowed in an icy clearing before a shelter filled with chunks of firewood. The air smelled of bitter sawdust. Vrell wrinkled her nose. What kinds of trees had these been? The core looked like regular wood, but the outer bark was black.

Achan jammed his torch into a ring on the side of the structure, wrenched an axe from a wide stump, and grabbed a piece of firewood with his other hand.

"Ahh." The wood slipped from his grip and clunked onto the icy ground. Achan grimaced at the black slime smudging his fingers. He wiped it on his trousers and picked up the wood again. "Cursed Darkness." He set the wood on a fat stump, twirled the axe in his left hand, and circled, glaring at the wood as if it were Jaira Hamartano. He swung the axe above his head and brought it down. Crack! Two chunks flew in different directions. Vrell twitched and she backed up a few steps.

Achan grabbed another piece of wood and chopped it.

Vrell wanted to speak, but no words came. Her heart ached to see him so angry. She watched helplessly as he split log after log. She sent a knock to Sir Caleb. If Achan would not speak to her, maybe Sir Caleb could help. Besides, Tara expected Vrell to come have a bath, which Vrell longed for.

But she didn't want to leave Achan alone.

Eight logs later, a hand gripped her shoulder. Sir Caleb stood beside her now, watching Achan with furrowed brows.

"How long has he been doing this?"

"He has chopped eighteen logs, sir."

Sir Caleb sat on a second chopping stump under the eaves of the woodshed. "You've still not bathed or changed?"

Achan brought the axe down, cleaving a sliver off the wood chunk. He rotated the chunk, heaved the axe over his head, and this time, chopped it in two. "Does it look like it?"

Sir Caleb folded his arms. "I'm sure Lord Gershom will appreciate your efforts to stock his firebox, but we're expected at dinner soon. The household will be waiting for you."

"You know what the worst is?"

"Canker sores?" Sir Caleb asked.

Vrell smiled.

Achan let the axe swing to the ground, the head scraping over the snow and woodchips as he stood, panting. "I would have loved them well." He yanked another piece of wood from the shed. Two more fell to the ground. Achan set it on the stump and twirled the axe in his left hand, circling.

"Loved who, Your Majesty. Or am I to guess?"

"Gren. Tara. They deserve better." He brought down the axe and the wood split. One piece tumbled to Vrell's feet.

"Better than what?"

Vrell knew she should go now, but Achan's words had ensnared her.

He reached back and snagged one of the fallen wood chunks. "Than pigs. Lazy men who love only themselves."

"You would love them both?"

He swiped the back of his forearm over his forehead. "Yes—no. I don't know."

Sir Caleb sighed. "You're too young for this burden. If you'd been trained all your life, things would be different. But for now, Achan, let us take this kingship one day at a time."

"I'm trying. But it's not fair."

"What's not, Your Highness?"

"Everything. Why did my parents have to die? Why did Nathak do this to me? Why did Poril beat me? Why did Gren have to marry Riga? Riga! Of all the men in Sitna, why him? And now he's dead and she's alone with child. An outcast. And Tara's father has married her to an insane man almost four times her senior. Why?"

"Lady Tara has wed Lord Gershom?" Sir Caleb rubbed his short beard and sighed. "You ask questions I cannot answer, and even if I could, would it matter? It's the way of the world. What's done is done. The past cannot be changed."

Achan let the axe fall to the ground and buried his face in his hands. "I'm sorry."

"Whatever for?"

"I'm headstrong. Foolish. Know nothing of being a prince."

"You will learn."

"I don't listen very well."

"How so?"

"I asked Lady Tara to marry me."

Sir Caleb uttered an, "Ahh," as if discovering the answer to a riddle long pondered.

Achan straightened. "I know you think me foolish, but I thought . . . Well . . . I hoped . . ."

"That she would love you?"

Achan kicked the log at his feet and sent it rolling. "I was certain she might . . . given time. She seemed so agreeable. *I'm* agreeable."

"Achan, whomever you marry will grow to love you."

"How do you know? Look what happened to Gren. Look at Tara. Will *she* grow to love her husband?"

"Perhaps."

"How can you say that?"

"Because I've lived longer than you. I've seen things that would surprise you greatly." Sir Caleb set his elbows on his knees and clasped his hands. "Gavin and I, we had a friend like you. Passionate about everything. He fell in love with a woman whose father had other ideas."

"What happened?"

"In the end, she obeyed her father and married another. And I can tell you she did grow to love her husband. They raised several wonderful children."

"And your friend? What became of him?"

"Ah, well. I'll let him tell you himself. He's one of the prisoners we'll free from Ice Island."

"He's in Ice Island? That is your story of comfort?"

"Your Highness, I know this is difficult, but you and I are called to something bigger than ourselves. Er'Rets is depending on us to deliver them from Darkness. We're talking about the life and death of a world. Can you try to understand that?"

"Aye." Achan slammed the axe into the stump and left it there. His next words were so soft, Vrell almost couldn't hear them. "I just don't want to be alone anymore."

Sir Caleb stood and came to Achan's side. He put a hand on the scruff of his neck. "I know we're old men, but we're your friends. And you've got Arman."

"And Sparrow."

"Aye, you've got Sparrow as well."

At the mention of her name, Vrell snapped to her senses. She returned to the keep for a bath and Tara's side of this story.

The rest of the day passed in a blur. Sir Caleb didn't leave Achan's side, grooming him, encouraging him. Achan appreciated his efforts but found it patronizing.

Dinner's full course of awkward conversation didn't help matters. Carmack seated Achan to Lord Gershom's right. The man was a child's stick drawing—frail and withered—who reeked of body odor and rotting teeth. Lady Tara introduced him to Achan, but he didn't respond, simply stared straight ahead, a dab of drool at the corner of his mouth.

Then, halfway through dessert, he revived and yelled at the servants, accusing them of trying to kill him. He threw his cobbler at Lady Tara, knocked over the wine, and tried to choke Carmack.

The whole scene only depressed Achan further.

At breakfast the next morning, Achan sat at the arched high table with Sparrow, staring at his food, half asleep. Thoughts of his blunder the day before flitted through his mind like a dream. He shoved it away. His eyes drooped, then popped open in time to see Sparrow snag a slice of bacon off his trencher. The boy shoved the bacon into his mouth.

Achan scowled. "Thief."

Sparrow shrugged and grinned, cheeks bulging.

Achan elbowed him. Sparrow fell off the bench and crashed onto the floor.

Achan slid in front of Sparrow's trencher. He lifted the boy's honey bread and smiled. "Thanks for the seat."

As Achan bit into the bread, Sparrow scrambled to his feet and pounced. Achan laughed as he tumbled off the bench. Sparrow landed on top, and Achan shoved the remaining honey bread against Sparrow's cheek. Sparrow reached for the bread, but Achan flipped him onto his back before he could grab it. He pinned Sparrow's arms above his head with one hand. He peeled the honey bread from Sparrow's cheek and took a huge bite, over half the slice, and chewed slowly.

"Mmm. Thanks for sharing." He squished the remaining bread back on Sparrow's face and stood. As he stepped over the boy, Sparrow grabbed his boot, causing Achan to slip. His chin nearly whacked the tabletop, but he managed to get a hand on the bench and hop on one foot to catch his balance.

Sparrow let go and scurried back to Achan's place at the table. So Achan claimed Sparrow's spot. The boy fought to keep a straight face as he ate another slice of Achan's bacon as if nothing were amiss, bread still stuck to his cheek.

Achan reached over and peeled the honey bread away. He shoved the whole thing into his mouth.

"Really! Is this how the Crown Prince and his *squire* behave in a foreign stronghold?"

Achan's chewing slowed. His gaze flickered to Lady Tara, who stood beside Sparrow, her scowl fully devoted to the boy. Sparrow grinned sheepishly, face as pink as the bacon.

"Vrell!" Sir Gavin stood at the entrance of the great hall, waving Sparrow over.

Sparrow stood, bowed to Lady Tara, said, "Good morning, my lady," and scurried away.

Achan wanted to ignore Lady Tara but supposed that, after all his mistakes yesterday, a little decorum might go a long way. He stood and gave her a small bow. "Lady Tara."

She pressed her fingers to her lips, then pointed at his face. "You have some bread on your chin, Your Highness."

Achan rubbed his prickly chin and pulled away a sticky crumb of honey bread. "Thank you."

"Your Highness, I am grieved our last words were unpleasant. I wanted to encourage you. I see a day none too far in the future that finds you happily married. I trust Arman will give you a dear friend for a wife."

Achan stared at his plate, stiff with discomfort. What compelled her to discuss this further? "I've no female friends, save you and Gren who—" He stopped himself from whining like a child. If he didn't speak, perhaps she would leave.

Lady Tara smiled, as if she knew a secret he did not. "You only have to open your eyes to see she is with you always."

Achan huffed a laugh. Was Lady Tara poking fun at him or being philosophical? "I've never been good with poetry, my lady, but I thank you for your kind words."

She curtsied. "Good day, Your Majesty."

Achan fell back to the bench and stared at his cold food. He hadn't been hungry anyway. Inko stumbled to the table and sat on his other side, looking as if he hadn't slept a wink either.

"Are you awake, Inko?"

"Been sleeping too long, I guess. Sir Caleb is saying we're leaving today. I am wishing we could be staying longer. I am not looking forward to more cold."

After a lifetime in Barth, where the air made one sweat, Achan could imagine the cold would be an unwelcome change. "How long did you live in Barth?"

"My village was being pillaged when I was being five years aged. Since all my family was being killed, I was being taken to Meneton and sold as a slave. It is being warm there as well."

Achan blinked, suddenly filled with compassion for this cranky, paranoid old knight. He wanted to know more, but Inko shoveled food into his mouth as if he were starved, so Achan settled on polite conversation.

"At least you got to sleep in. You must be refreshed."

Inko snorted. "You would be thinking so, Your Highness, but you were not having to share a bed with young Vrell."

"What's the problem?"

"Always that boy is talking in his sleep, calling out to his mother, making his nightmares mine."

Achan frowned, but Inko wasn't finished venting his frustrations.

"The first night we were staying in Berland, he was falling out of bed. I was jumping up to see if he was being ill or drunk, then Sir Gavin was making me leave. I am still not understanding this. I was having to stand out in the cold air until Sir Gavin was allowing me to be coming back inside."

Achan made no sense of this. "Inko, should you witness other strange behavior regarding Sparrow, would you tell me?"

Inko smiled. "You are thinking he is being a traitor? I am not trusting his eyes, Your Highness. Green is being the color of jealousy. Not being a good trait for a servant to the king."

Achan only wanted to discover what Sir Gavin and Sparrow were hiding, not hang the boy for his green eyes. "I only wish to know anything odd."

"I will be shadowing the boy for you, Your Highness. Do not be worrying."

Achan wasn't worried and felt a little sore for siccing Inko on Sparrow. But he didn't doubt Inko could be a fox when he set his mind to it. Perhaps it would take a bigger fox to catch a smaller one. "Thanks, Inko."

For three days they rode through frigid Darkness. Achan no longer cared what happened next. His goal had always been to see Lady Tara. Now that he'd lost that objective, there was nothing to do but let the knights dictate his life. Still, he couldn't bring himself to accept his birthright. What was the point if he acted like a puppet? They may as well have Esek.

But if you want the girl, you should have her. You are king, not these knights. I would always let you have your way.

Achan tensed at the serpentine voice. Hadad? He fortified his mind, uncertain whether he had really let down his guard or if Darkness was taunting him.

Lights winked into view. A squat city glimmered to the right. To the left, torches illuminated another stronghold, some burning far above the others. Could that be a tower?

"We're on the Benjen cliffs." Sir Gavin's voice came from ahead. "Yonder lies Tsaftown."

Achan peered into the darkness, the icy air pricking his eyes. "Is that the stronghold to the left?"

"*That* is Ice Island. See the torches in the sky? They top the Pillar. 'Tis what we must penetrate to rescue our men."

Fabulous. This town, this mission . . . it no longer had any pull without the hope of Lady Tara. The doom of his station hung heavy on his shoulders. "How will we get there?"

"Sled dogs," Sir Gavin said.

"Sled *wolves*, is more like it," Sir Caleb said.

Apprehension gripped Achan. Soon he'd have to make a choice. He would *not* be a puppet. They'd come all this way to free his army. Fine. Achan would do his part, then he'd have to decide to take charge or refuse the call to be king.

26

Sir Gavin led them through the city gate without incident. Their horses carried them down roads slick with ice, around log cottages blanketed in snow. Torchlight shone through cracks on shuttered windows. Families were home and warm.

"It must be night," Sparrow said.

Frost glistened in Sir Gavin's beard. "Seems to be."

Sir Gavin stopped at an inn. The wide building stood three levels high. Two steps up from the street, a long, narrow porch stretched across the face of the building, its sloping shed roof covered in snow. Lanterns and icicles hung from the eaves. A wide oak door divided the porch with two long, frost-covered windows on either side. Music and voices spilled out from the building, but Achan could only see shapes of people through the frosty glass. Dozens of chimneys stuck out from the roof, pouring silver smoke into the black sky.

A painted sign hung above the door. *The Ivory Spit: Tavern and Inn.*

"Really, Gavin? This place?" Inko asked. "We should be going to Lytton Hall."

"Lytton Hall is being watched. Besides, Old Merrygog McLennan's got the tightest lips in Tsaftown."

Inko lowered his voice. "You are thinking it is being wise to be bringing Kurtz here after years being in the Prodotez?"

"Wise or not, 'tis our only option." Sir Gavin climbed the steps and went inside.

"What's the Prodotez?" Achan asked.

"The king's personal prison in Ice Island," Sir Caleb said. "The Fisherman's Quarter has ears. Hold your questions until we're inside."

Sir Gavin returned and tossed a key to Sparrow. "Third floor. Our rooms have a dagfish and a stag on the door. We'll take the back stairs to avoid the tavern."

They led their horses after Sir Gavin, down the side of the building to a stable where they unlatched their packs. "Inko and Vrell, put up the horses and meet us upstairs."

A rickety staircase zigzagged up the back of the inn. They climbed up two levels and entered a door on the third floor into a narrow hall. Three pairs of snowy boots clumped over the worn plank floor, leaving wet footprints on the wood. They passed doors on both sides, each with an image painted on the door, faded from age. A reekat, a charmouse, a cham . . .

Sir Gavin's key opened the door with a stag. The room stretched out, long and narrow, with a small fireplace at the end. No windows. Two pallets with straw mattresses and a table with two chairs lined the left wall, leaving only the width of a man to navigate down the right. A single door hung open on the right at the end of the room.

Sir Gavin ducked through the interior door and returned just as quickly. "Leads to our other room. Achan, you're not to leave without one of us knights. Vrell doesn't count."

Why would he even try?

Sir Gavin sniffed long and exhaled a sigh. "We'll wait for Inko, then go over our plan."

Vrell and Inko found the door with the dagfish. Raised voices carried through an open door in the back. Vrell walked past the fireplace, where a stack of kindling and logs sat ready to be used. She entered the other room and found it identical to hers. A crackling fire beside the adjoining door warmed her face. The men sat at two tables wedged together near the fireplace, pouring over a piece of parchment between them. It seemed they had taken the table and chairs from Vrell's room to make a larger one.

"It looks like Meribah Corner," Achan said.

"Aye, both were designed and built by Livnas." Sir Gavin met Vrell's gaze. "Good, you're here. Where is Inko?"

"Unpacking, I believe," she said.

"Well, call him in."

She rolled her eyes and went back to find Inko removing items from his pack. "Inko, Sir Gavin needs you in his room."

Inko heaved a dramatic sigh as if it were bad luck not to unpack his belongings straightaway and Sir Gavin's orders could doom them all.

Vrell ducked back into the room and stood behind Sir Caleb, where she could see the parchment clearly.

It appeared to be a sketch of Ice Island. A painting of the prison hung in Mother's study, which used to be Father's study. Father's brother served as warden of Ice Island. Vrell had always wondered why Mother had kept the horrible painting around. Who wanted to look on a prison all day?

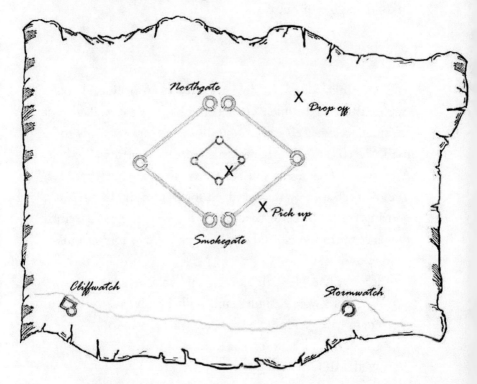

Inko ambled through the doorway and stood beside Sir Gavin. "What are you needing?"

"I need you to stand here and listen. Now, Verdot will meet us at Stormwatch tomorrow with the dogs and sleds."

Vrell's interest piqued. Her uncle was going to help them?

Sir Caleb huffed and leaned back in his chair. Though his hair was blond, his short beard had grown in red. "You always do this, Gavin. You tell no one your scheme until there is no time to change it. When did you plan this?"

"Over the past few weeks. Nitsa helped me arrange it."

"Figures." Sir Caleb slapped his palm on the table and stood. "This is really for her, then? Risking our future king for a childhood romance is—"

"You know full well that's not why we're here." Sir Gavin's bushy eyebrows scrunched together. "If you'd been sent to Ice Island, you'd hope someone would come for you."

Vrell watched the men, mouth gaping. How did this situation involve her mother?

Sir Caleb glared, his eyes so wild Vrell inched back. "None of our men would have gone to Ice Island if Verdot Amal wasn't a coward."

"That was years ago. Nitsa assures me the man is changed. Guilt can change a man."

"That may be, but *I* still do not trust him."

Achan voiced the very question that plagued Vrell. "What are you talking about?"

Sir Caleb shoved his chair. "You tell him, Gavin." He stomped into the other room.

Sir Gavin stroked his beard. "When your father died, I told you Kenton and his men had drugged us . . . I knew this because I had a witness. He saw Kenton and his men. He tried to rouse me, and managed, with a lot of water, to succeed."

"But is was too late."

"Aye. My point is, when it came time to testify before the Council of Seven, Verdot refused. Kenton had threatened him, bribed him, who knows, but Kenton and his men went free, their false story went unchallenged, and there you have it."

"Eagan, Kurtz, and the rest of our men in Ice Island these past thirteen years." Sir Caleb leaned against the adjoining doorframe.

Her uncle had let so many good men go to prison?

"What about the childhood romance?" Achan asked.

"Remember the friend I told you about, the man who lost his love to a higher-ranking man? Eagan's lady was Nitsa Amal."

"And she wants him rescued."

"I don't doubt it. Duke Amal has been dead for years."

Vrell swallowed, tears pricking her eyes, throat burning. She knew of Mother's heartbreak with Sir Eagan, but she never thought Mother still cared for the man. After all this time?

"Caleb." Sir Gavin leveled a glance at his friend. "Verdot is a good man who got scared. I trust him."

Sir Caleb huffed and disappeared back to Vrell's room.

"Wait." Achan frowned. "Eagan? Like my sword?"

"Aye, the sword is his, lad."

Now Achan looked as forlorn as Sir Caleb. "How can Verdot help us?"

"He is warden of Ice Island and brother to Pinot Amal, Nitsa's late husband." Sir Gavin glanced at Vrell. "He owes the duchess a favor and has agreed to help."

"Gavin, Verdot would be making us a party of six. Five or seven people would be giving us stronger favor."

Achan spoke over Inko's comment as if he did not hear it. "If he's warden, why can't he simply free the prisoners?"

"Because he cannot do it alone. Our men are spread out over thirteen levels. Tomorrow, he scheduled all the guards who openly oppose Esek's claim. They plan to free our men. Since he cannot get to the Prodotez, that's where we will go. Everything will happen at once, which will also create a diversion for our escape. These men are Kingsguard soldiers trained by me and Caleb. We need their help to win Armonguard. We cannot wait. Caleb?"

Sir Caleb's voice came from the other room. "I'll hear your plan. That's all I promise."

Sir Gavin set his weathered finger on Stormwatch. "We'll ready ourselves here and take sleds over the water, northeast of the stronghold." He pushed his finger over the paper and stopped at an X marked above the stronghold.

"Over the water?" Achan asked.

"The sea is being frozen solid for miles," Inko said.

Sir Gavin tapped the X by the words *Drop off*. "We'll leave Inko and Verdot here with the dogs. Achan, Sir Caleb, and I will enter through Northgate under the guise of bounty hunters delivering a criminal to the Prodotez. I'll go by the name Vindo Relz. Sir Caleb will be Wil Markson."

"What criminal?" Vrell prayed the answer was not what she feared. "Me?"

"No, Achan." Sir Gavin's mustache formed a straight line. "The only way we can get into the Prodotez unchallenged is to have a high priority prisoner. Verdot has already sent word to Mahanaim that Achan has been captured."

Achan straightened. "You're turning me in?"

"Under pretense only. No one has ever escaped Ice Island without inside help. We have to be . . . creative."

"You tell us this now?" Achan asked.

"I saw no reason to burden you with details until you required them."

Sir Caleb sighed from the doorway. "Now this also vexes me. Not even two hundred are worth the expense of my king."

Vrell couldn't blame Sir Caleb for his concern. How could Sir Gavin even consider using Achan as bait?

Sir Gavin leaned forward and propped his elbows on the table. "Caleb, Arman has called Achan. He will protect him."

Sir Caleb banged his fist on the wall and Vrell jumped. "Then why must we continually come to his rescue? Arman has trusted him to our care. Why knowingly endanger him?"

"I want to do it." Achan's voice turned every head. "I can do it, whatever it is. I can."

Sir Caleb glared into the fire and released a shaky sigh. The flames flickered in his eyes.

"The Prodotez is a dungeon in the Pillar, this tower here." Sir Gavin smoothed out the map and tapped the center diamond. "It's twelve levels high. The only way up is the north or south towers. The only way down is the east or west towers. There's no other entrance. We must go up and over."

"You're going to pretend you're taking me to the Prodotez in order to break out your Old Kingsguard companions?"

"Aye. I've no doubt we'll succeed in getting in. My concern is the trip back out."

"Will we go out the way we came in?" Achan asked.

"No. The guards will be taking our men out the main gate on dogsleds. But I feel that is too risky for us. So, Inko and Verdot will wait with the dogs outside the southeastern curtain wall. We'll free my generals and return to this point." He tapped an X on the Pillar. "Caleb will toss his boarding hook to Inko and we'll slide down."

Achan's eyes bulged. "To the ground?"

"Over the curtain wall, aye. Caleb, show them what you've worked out."

Sir Caleb stared at Achan, then walked to the closest bed. Chairs scraped the floor as the others followed. Five iron hooks lay on the bed. They were shaped like a letter J with a one-sided barb on the hook end and a fat eye-hole at the top. The hooks were two hands long. Each had a length of thick rope threaded through the eye with the ends tied together.

"You're fortunate Carmack gave me an extra." Sir Caleb picked up a hook and shook it at Sir Gavin. "I still think this plan is reckless. The prince should stay out of Ice Island at all costs." He ran a hand through his shaggy hair, making it stand on end. "After I throw the boarding hook and Inko and Verdot secure the end, we'll each tie one of these to our belts. We all need a thick rope belt. I have extras if anyone has need."

He looped the circle of rope onto his belt and cinched his belt under his armpits. "Might as well start it here. As soon as the hook takes your weight the belt will ride up anyway."

"What kind of hooks are these?" Achan picked up a hook and pretended to snag Vrell in the neck.

Vrell jumped back, caught her breath, and rolled her eyes.

"Dagfish hooks," Sir Caleb said.

Achan tossed the hook back on the bed. It clanked against another. "Must be a big fish."

"Most are twice your size." Sir Caleb lifted the hook above his head. "Once your belt is secure, hang your hook on the line and sail away. I've sanded and oiled the crook of each hook so they won't snag. If you stop, pull yourself along. It's such a steep descent, I doubt that will happen. Try to face the sentry wall, and, before you hit, catch yourself with your feet." He tapped the sole of his boot against the wall.

Vrell frowned at the hooks. "You are certain these will not fall off the rope?"

"Not holding a man's weight. They'll carry us to the sentry walk. Then we'll climb over and take the rope down to Inko."

"Won't there be guards on the sentry walk?" Achan asked.

"Aye. Inko will pick off any trouble-makers with his bow."

"I guess just taking over the mind of the gatekeeper and having him unlock every cell for us is out of the question, huh?" Achan asked.

"We can confuse their minds, but not control them," Sir Gavin said.

Vrell found this whole plan insane. "What will you do once you are all down?"

"Take the sleds back to Stormwatch. No guards there. The towers have been closed since Darkness came."

"And what about me?" Vrell asked. "What will I do?"

Sir Gavin sniffed in a long breath. "You'll wait here. Should we not return, inform Merrygog McLennan in the tavern. I've instructed him to send word to Lord Livna, who'll collect you here."

"But I want to help," Vrell said.

Inko clapped a hand on Vrell's shoulder and beamed. "Five is being a much stronger number, boy. If you are staying behind, you are doing your prince a service."

Vrell scowled at Inko. Sir Gavin's words gave her a more reasonable purpose for staying behind.

"Should we fail, Vrell, word must be given to the right people. Prince Oren, the Duchess of Carm."

"Yes, sir." But Vrell did not like it. What if they failed?

"Achan should be the one to stay behind," Sir Caleb said.

Vrell did not want to be the prisoner. "Can you pretend Sir Caleb is Achan? We cannot risk Achan getting lost."

"I *said* I'm going." Achan's eyes dared anyone to tell him no. "I'll be fine. No chains have managed to hold me yet."

Vrell huffed. "Not due to your own strength."

"Exactly. Someone will come for me."

"And how long will that take?" Sir Caleb asked. "The men we seek to rescue have been imprisoned thirteen years."

Achan stared Sir Caleb in the eye. "I'll be fine."

Vrell could not believe his recklessness. "Do you never worry about anything?"

"I worry about whether or not Sparrow will nag me."

"Enough!" Sir Gavin rolled up the map. "We must trust Arman to protect us. 'Tis His will Achan be king, and His will always triumphs."

Vrell did not doubt that, but faith did not always keep fear from circling.

27

Achan's eyes watered as the sled whooshed over the snow-covered sea. He marveled at how fast the sleds went. Faster than a horse, maybe. A much smoother ride, anyway.

He and Sir Caleb were tucked under pelts beside one another in the bed of the dogsled. Behind them, Sir Gavin stood on the runners and navigated the dogs after the other sled, driven by Verdot Amal. Inko rode in Verdot's sled.

Verdot Amal, a short, round man with white hair, had provided two sleds with dogs hitched in tandem and furs to burrow under on the ride. He had also brought two extra horses for his generals in the Prodotez. Verdot had spoken only to Sir Gavin, ignoring Inko and Sir Caleb as much as they ignored him.

The knights' differing opinions over involving Verdot Amal drenched Achan in doubt. Was he wrong to agree to this plan? What if he did get caught? They were about to enter the strongest prison in all Er'Rets—one that had not only marked Achan a wanted man, but also believed he'd been captured. They probably had a cell all ready to put him in. What if he had to live on Ice Island forever?

Before they'd left Stormwatch, Sir Caleb had clamped shackles onto Achan's wrists and ankles. Even though Achan wore the key on a string around his neck, and even though Sir Caleb put them on loose, the feel of iron on Achan's limbs reminded him of the other times he'd been captured, tortured, and nearly executed. He tried not to think about them.

Achan's ear twitched. He reached a mittened hand up to scratch, irons clinking, but could find no way into the layers of fur. "I think my furs have fleas."

"It's always a possibility," Sir Caleb said.

Achan groaned. He'd been joking. No matter how many times he had fleas over the years, he never got used to them. Maybe due to Gren. She always refused to be near him until they were gone.

Achan faced Sir Caleb, but the knight was looking at the torchlights of Ice Island. Achan's stomach roiled. The lights were so high up. How could they ever succeed?

He sensed Sir Caleb's fear and again agonized over the situation. He understood Sir Caleb's desire to keep him safe, but Achan couldn't sit around and mope over Lady Tara's marriage to Lord Gershom. This insane mission not only preoccupied his mind, it also affirmed him. He had made a choice.

His first royal command, perhaps?

He pulled his knees up. The dagfish hook in his trousers slid from his knee to his thigh. Sir Caleb had insisted they wear their hooks from the start to save time. This way they could fix their belts under their arms and fly.

But Achan didn't want to think about that. Nor the fact that he'd left Eagan's Elk back at the inn, the sword that would no longer belong to him after today. His only weapon was Inko's small, leather-wrapped knife hidden inside his boot.

When the sleds stopped, Inko climbed out and took Sir Gavin's place on their sled.

Sir Gavin helped Achan stand, torch burning strong in his hand. "You've got Inko's knife?"

Standing up made his feet sink into knee-deep snow and invited frigid air up his fur cape. Achan shivered. "Aye."

"Let's go, then."

Inko and Verdot drove the sleds away to their position east of the stronghold. Ice Island stood before them, black but for the torches outlining the massive watchtower and surrounding curtain wall, casting pockets of light onto grey stone. Achan trudged toward the imposing fortress between Sir Gavin and Sir Caleb, dragging his leg chains through the snow. With each step, snow fell over the tops of his boots and melted down to his ankles. The dagfish hook slid back and forth, scratching his kneecap every so often with its barbed hook.

"Keep your shields up to all but us." Sir Gavin's breath spewed from his nose like a cham bear. "The prisoners are given âleh, but there may be guards with the ability."

Achan repeated the instruction to himself. His cheeks stung from the cold, his nose and ears were numb. He should've put up his hood. Too late now.

They stopped before Northgate, twin towers that loomed five levels high, connected by a black iron portcullis. The curtain wall shot away from each tower. All was dark but for the randomly spaced torches along the parapet and the sporadic arrow loops glowing with light from each tower.

A nasal voice called through the gate. "Who are you and what do you want?"

"Markson Will and Vindo Relz with a prisoner for the Prodotez," Sir Gavin yelled.

"Prisoner's name?"

"Achan Cham. Also known as Gidon Hadar."

Achan's stomach swayed. How long might it take for Esek to get word he had arrived? Hopefully, Esek had gone south from Carmine and not north like the duchess suspected.

With a soft clank, an iron gate swung open from within the portcullis. Sweat broke out over Achan despite being half frozen. Two guards, all but their eyes clad in pelts, stepped outside, swords raised, and beckoned them enter. The knights tugged Achan forward and they entered the bailey of the prison.

Achan glanced at the guard on his right. Their eyes met and Achan sensed conflicting emotions. Hope and despair.

Sir Gavin and Sir Caleb pulled Achan along as if they knew exactly where they were going. His chains slid over a slippery stone ground. The snow in the bailey had been piled against the curtain walls in huge mounds. Achan tipped back his head to see the towering Pillar. Icy wind snaked down the neck of his tunic. He hunched down, sniffing his watery nose.

Every guard seemed to stare. Achan opened his mind and a vast array of emotions washed over him. Like the guard at Northgate, the guardsmen seemed conflicted by his presence. Some were a part of tonight's escape plan. Some were not.

Sir Gavin and Sir Caleb led Achan into the northern tower of the Pillar and started up the spiraling staircase, deserted and dark but for torches and a guard or two on the landing of each level. It was just as cold in the tower as it had been outside and smelled oddly like dirt. The stomping of three sets of boots and chain banging on the steps echoed in the stairwell.

Careful to shield his mind, Achan opened to the lone guard on level four.

The man's deer-like eyes never blinked. *He's the mirror image of the painting in Lytton Hall.*

Achan let go, curious about this painting.

The guard on the fifth level turned his back to Achan. *We can't keep him here. We mustn't.*

On level six, two guards stood together, necks twisting together like twin owls. Achan tried to peek at both minds but only managed to hear:

Ahh. This one's too young to be . . .

. . . live to see the day.

On seven, the guard's mind was closed. Achan glanced over his shoulder to get a better look at the dark-bearded man, but the continually curling staircase swept him away.

Achan's legs ached. He pulled against Sir Gavin's grip. *Can we stop a moment? This hook keeps scraping my knee.*

Sir Gavin slowed his pace. *Sorry. I'm a bit on edge. I expected to have to declare you to more than the men at the gate.*

Seems odd, Achan said.

Aye. Keep your eye out. And remember, Eagan and Kurtz will answer to Chion.

The name of Sir Gavin's old wolf dog had apparently been a password amongst the Old Kingsguardsmen.

The eighth floor guardsman leaned on his sword like a cane. *He won't last the month.*

The ninth floor guard sneered like an angry dog and had an equally comforting thought. *Prisoners'll chew him up.*

The guard on ten had closed his mind. He spat tobacco juice on the floor as they swept past.

The guard on eleven stared like a starved wolf. *Will King Esek give me the bounty if I kill him myself?*

The twelfth level hit Achan with a blast of icy wind that blew open his cape and knifed through his tunic. The roof. Sir Gavin barged past the guards standing there and moved along the northeastern wall toward the eastern tower.

Sir Caleb ducked his head against the wind. *Surprising no one's spoken to us yet.*

Aye. Sir Gavin sniffed a short breath. *'Tis a mite peculiar.*

They entered the eastern tower, Achan's chains rattling on the stone steps. This tower had no exits on any levels. No doors or arrow loops. It simply twisted down, an endless spiral lit by an occasional torch. A rank combination of mildew, urine, and torch smoke turned Achan's stomach. His head began to feel light. His mouth filled with saliva. *I'm getting dizzy.*

Almost there, Sir Gavin said.

They finally spilled out into a stone chamber that sat on the diagonal. Two narrow passages stretched out, left and right, from the stairwell's corner. A slack-faced guard with shaggy, salt-and-pepper hair reclined with his feet on a wooden table, carving lines into the table with a long knife. Behind him, a wall of stone slats each held a scroll and a key on a ring.

The guard let his feet fall to the floor and stabbed the knife into the table's surface. "What you got here?"

"New prisoner," Sir Gavin said.

The guard's gaze traveled up and down Achan. "Roiz!"

Pattering footsteps from the right corridor preceded a scrawny old man, hunched and balding. He wore a tattered brown cape. The man grinned, rotten teeth darkening his smile.

"Where they assign 'im to?" the big guard asked.

"Prodotez," Sir Gavin said.

The guard snorted. "Get that, Roiz?"

"Old as I may be, Beck, I ain't deaf." Roiz drew his hand along the stone slats, counting in a whisper. He pulled out a scroll and key, tossed it down on the table, then pointed up to a jar of ink. "Get my ink and quill for me?"

Beck glared at Roiz, as if standing wasn't part of his job. But he heaved himself off the chair and handed the ink and a thin, white feather down to Roiz.

Roiz unrolled the scroll and weighted down the top with the key ring. "Name?"

"Gidon Hadar," Sir Gavin said.

The old man wrinkled his nose. "You tryin' to be funny?"

"Certainly not." Sir Gavin's eyebrows met in one shaggy white line. "There's a bounty on this man's head. We've caught him. We want the credit and the gold and we'll be on our way."

Roiz dropped the quill and circled the table. He waved a hand. "You can let go o' him. He ain't goin' nowheres."

Sir Gavin and Sir Caleb released Achan's arms.

Roiz peered into Achan's eyes, pulled off his fur cape and mittens, and tossed them on the table. "These'll only get you hurt. Prisoners fight over clothin'. Gimme that knife, Beck."

Beck jerked the knife from the tabletop and flipped it around, handle out.

Roiz took it, waved the blade at Achan. "Turn 'round."

Achan obeyed, chains grating over the stone floor. What was Roiz going to do? The man's cold fingers slid across the back of Achan's neck, pushing his ponytail aside. Achan's fingers twitched. Every reflex wanted to move, to pull the knife from his boot. His gaze flicked to the stone-faced knights. They'd step in if he were in danger, wouldn't they?

Roiz clamped a wiry hand on Achan's shoulder. "Stay put. This won't hurt." Roiz's fingers gripped the back neck of Achan's shirt. The linen ripped in an instant.

Sir Caleb lunged forward a step. Roiz didn't notice. He dropped the knife to the table, his cold fingers folded back Achan's tunic, and Sir Caleb's posture relaxed.

"Well, I'll be the son o' Thalessa. You see this, Beck? It's just like they said."

Beck shrugged. "He's a stray. So what?"

Roiz scratched his balding head. "Prodotez, you say? We call that the Pit 'round here." He picked up the scroll and studied it. "Men who kill your pappy 'r' in the Pit, boy." He snorted. "Cetheria's got a dark sense o' justice, she has. After thirteen years, I bet these men'll like to have a word with you." He chuckled. "All right, then. Bring 'im along. This way."

Roiz lifted a torch from a ring beside the slats and started down the left corridor, brown cape flapping behind. Sir Gavin and Sir Caleb followed, leading Achan after him.

The dark and cold corridor seemed to stretch on forever. They passed narrow doors on both sides with iron grates at the bottom, staggered, so no two faced one another across the hall. Chains clanked inside each cell. Filthy fingers wiggled out the grates. Voices called out, but Achan couldn't make out words over the sound of his own chains dragging over the stone.

Roiz turned right down a short corridor and they stepped into a diamond-shaped atrium. They stood at one wide angle. To their left, in the narrow corner, two fur-clad guards looked their way. A diamond-shaped grate covered the center floor with a narrow stone path around it. Achan blinked and leaned forward. Dozens of sets of eyes stared back from below.

"Hold him right there." Roiz whistled, and the fur-clad guards approached from the end of the diamond.

The knights stopped. Achan looked up. He could see all the way to the roof, twelve levels above, and each floor in between. Torches, mounted between each narrow cell door, lit up the inner cavity of the Pillar. From the second level to the roof, iron grates covered the open ledges.

Roiz stomped on the floor grate. "Back, you vermin. Back, I say."

The fur-clad guards flanked Roiz, swords drawn. The old man crouched and inserted the key into the grate. He swung the door open until it clanged against the grate on the other side. The noise echoed to the ceiling.

Roiz waved a hand. "Bring 'im over."

Sir Gavin gripped Achan's elbow but didn't move.

Achan stared at the glinting eyes peering up from below. *That's the Prodotez?*

Looks to be, Sir Caleb said. *Gavin, we can't let them put the prince down there.*

Sir Gavin released Achan's elbow. *Achan, back against the wall.*

Achan inched backwards. His leg chains sounded so loud, scraping over the metal grate.

Sir Gavin crept forward, hand on his hilt. *Caleb, draw on my command. You take the shorter guard and Roiz, I'll take—*

"Hold," a lofty voice spoke from the corridor behind them.

Achan twisted around to find a sword pointed at his chest. His gaze traveled up the blade to Sir Kenton's pale face and curtain of long black hair. Behind Sir Kenton, Esek Nathak strode into the atrium, wrapped in a thick red wool cloak.

Pig snout!

Sir Gavin drew his sword.

"Really, Sir Gavin?" Esek shot Sir Gavin a scathing look. "Do you honestly think you stand a chance of escape?"

Esek's soldiers spilled into the center hold from every corridor, swords drawn, wearing the black capes of the New Kingsguard.

"Put it away, Sir Gavin," Esek strolled, one step at a time, posture straight, nose in the air, "and I *might* let the stray live."

A chill washed over Achan. *How'd they get here so fast?*

Verdot told them we were coming, Sir Caleb said.

Sir Gavin sheathed his sword. *You can't know that, Caleb.*

I can. Sir Caleb glared at Sir Gavin.

Any one of Verdot's guards could have passed on the information.

Esek locked eyes with Achan. "I see you are still trying to hide your scars with this pathetic excuse for a beard. I thank you for putting yourself into prison. Saved me a lot of trouble."

Achan clasped his hands, ducked under Sir Kenton's blade, and bashed him in the temple.

Sir Kenton staggered long enough for Achan to lunge past and tackle Esek, knocking them both to the stone floor. Achan landed on top. He gripped the chain on his shackles in both hands and pressed it over Esek's neck.

Esek's face flushed. Achan pushed harder, furious this coward had tried to hurt Gren. Esek croaked.

A hand grabbed Achan's hair and lifted. Achan flailed for a decent foothold. His attacker threw him backwards.

He tumbled over the grate and met the eyes of a prisoner below. He flipped over in time to take Sir Kenton's boot to the chest. The kick knocked the air from his lungs. Another kick rolled him to his side.

Sir Kenton grabbed the back of Achan's tunic and lifted. His cut tunic ripped further, and he fell back to the grate. Sir Kenton snagged the back of Achan's belt and swung him forward.

Achan flew—inches over the grate floor—then sailed head-first through the door of the pit.

The prisoners broke his fall. Several sets of hands caught him, set him on his feet in a dark, rank chamber. Someone tackled him, knocking him onto the cold, sticky stone floor that reeked of human waste.

Hands grabbed his foot and wrenched. Achan's skidded over the floor on his rear. He put his hands down to balance himself and bent his knee, trying to free his foot. But his boot slowly slipped down his leg, under the loose shackle, and popped off.

Achan fell onto his back. "Hey!"

He could barely see the shape of a man step into his boot, then lunge forward and grab Achan's other foot.

Achan sat up and kicked the man with his bare foot, but the man held fast until the second boot tugged free. The boot knife clumped to the dark floor.

Achan dove for it, unwrapped it, and held it out. He pushed to his feet and turned in a circle, his bare feet tacky on the cold stone floor.

"Back away, all of you!" he yelled.

Several prisoners laughed.

"Home at last?" Esek's voice carried down into the pit. The open door in the grate above framed his pompous face.

"If you fight me alone, without the aid of your overgrown shadow, I'll kill you," Achan said. "But you know that, don't you? Which is why you're unwilling to give me that chance."

"You're not worth my effort." Esek pulled his head back, and the grate door slammed shut.

Achan trembled and lowered his gaze to those around him. A shadow shifted to his left and Achan jerked his knife that way. "Stay back!"

"What's your name, boy?" a deep voice asked.

Sir Gavin? What's happening?

We're going to fight Esek's men. The guards are freeing prisoners and giving them weapons to join us. Find my men. They'll protect you.

Shouts broke out above. Swords clashed and a dozen guards trampled over the grate. Achan cringed at the sound it made in the pit. The footsteps receded until there was silence.

Achan inched forward, knife ready, until the faint grid of torchlight fell over a group of haggard, hairy men. Most had beards as long as Sir Gavin's, many of them grey or white, though Achan spotted some dark hair in the bunch.

He swallowed and released a shaky breath. "I've come for the friends of Chion."

A man cackled, the sound a cross between a gowzal call and a woodpecker. Achan waved his knife and backed up.

"I wouldn't do that," the nasal voice said.

Achan sidestepped toward the wall. He didn't want anyone sneaking up behind him. But as he reached it, his right foot fell into a trench. He caught himself with his right hand and found the wall as moist and sticky as the floor. He pulled his foot up and it scraped the sides, coated with cold wetness.

Snickers rang out.

"He found the pot!" a man yelled. The cackler. He broke out into another jarring fit of laughter. Achan cringed.

"Privy's along the perimeter, it is," another man said. "Two-foot wide trench. No one knows how deep it goes before it drains out, eh?"

"'Cept those we've thrown in," the cackler said.

Achan scraped his foot over the floor, not that it probably made much difference. He faced the crowd, shaken at the squalor these men endured. "What crime does a man commit to end up here?"

"Murdering children," the cackler said. "Give me that knife and I'll show you."

"Murdering men."

"Stealing from the king."

"Destroying a temple."

"Forcing women to love me."

The cackler chittered long and loud at this confession.

"Arson."

"Perjury to Lord Levy."

"Poisoning my customers."

"Looking too long at the queen." A bearded version of Sir Kenton stepped out of the crowd. His ratty, black hair hung like twigs around his face. He'd tucked his braided beard into his tunic. "You look like him, you know. And a bit like *her*."

The crowd murmured.

"Bazmark's right," another man said. "That other one was a fake."

"You King Axel's son?" the deep voice asked.

"So I've been told," Achan said.

"You got the mark of the stray?"

"Yeah."

"And the birthmark?" Bazmark asked.

"Yeah."

"Let's see it, eh?"

"We can't see anything down here," the nasal voice said.

"If he moves to the center we can."

"Come into the light."

"Let us see."

"Why?" Achan asked. "My father put you all here. You want to kill me because of it?"

"Levy put *me* in here," the deep voice said.

A raspy voice came from behind the crowd. "Most who were sentenced by your father have long since died, boy."

"How many are still here?" Achan asked. "Speak up."

The cackler hooted.

"Oh, shut up, fool," the nasal voice said.

"There are five left whom your father imprisoned," the raspy voice said, well-spoken, formal. "The other twenty-seven were sent by the Council. Some deservedly so, some not."

"Who're you to say who deserves this place, Elk?"

"My pointing fingers does not change the truth."

Achan searched the crowd for the man called Elk, suspecting he must be Sir Eagan, but could find no face to match the raspy voice. He needed to get these men on his side before they hurt him.

"Believe what you will, but Arman, the One God, has spoken to me, appointed me king in Er'Rets. I've come to free my comrades, and though I've come to the Prodotez for two in particular, I'll pardon each of you, give you a second chance to serve your king. Darkness is growing as the corrupt Council and Esek rule. I must amass an army, quickly. Hundreds of men are escaping tonight to join us. I would welcome your service. Or you may rot here. The choice is yours."

The cackler chittered, but he was the only one.

Achan continued his plea, clueless what else he could do. "You saw the false prince. Help me stand against him. If my father wronged any of you, if the Council did, I beg your forgiveness. I cannot offer you more than an apology and your freedom."

"What if we did wrong?"

"You're pardoned. I leave your judgment to Arman. Join me and fight. Just know, if you go back to your old ways, I'll not be so forgiving next time."

"'Tis too late for me. Arman would never forgive."

"I cannot speak for Arman, but it's never too late to be noble."

"We can't get out."

"There's always a way," Achan said.

"Show us the birthmark."

Achan squeezed the knife. "I'd rather not turn my back to you. You stole my boots."

"You ask us to trust you," the nasal voice said. "Trust us."

Vrell sat alone at the table, staring into the flames in the hearth. She paced the room a few times, then lay on her pallet. Cobwebs had gathered where the timber ceiling slats met the wall. A broad-bellied spider wrapped a fly in pale web. Vrell's thoughts flashed back to the day Achan had been struck with arrows and she had used spider's webs to pack his wounds.

Please, Arman, keep him safe.

No need to dwell. She forced her thoughts to Bran. It had been too long since they'd spoken. It wouldn't hurt to look on him, would it? If she passed out, at least she was in bed.

Closing her eyes, she focused on Bran Rennan.

It's not my fault! Bran stood outside a cottage. Vineyards filled the landscape behind him, green and lush. *What would you have me do? She must have protection. This is not the first attack. I'm ashamed to be a Carminian. The people have been merciless.*

Sir Rigil stood before a small garden in the cottage's yard, arms crossed, his demeanor calm yet reproachful. *Regardless, it is inappropriate for you to continue to be her protector.*

Could we move her elsewhere?

Her father does not want to relocate again. I fear I must move you.

Bran's posture slumped. He had served beside Sir Rigil since his eleventh year. He did not want to be dismissed before he became a knight. *Where will I go?*

The stronghold. The duchess desires more guards in the manor since Esek's last infiltration. I will tell Madam Hoff you have been reassigned and will watch her myself until I can find an old, married *replacement.*

Bran sighed, relief stretching through his veins. He would not lose his position with Sir Rigil. *Can I at least bid her farewell?*

That is unwise, Bran.

I'm her only friend. If I were to vanish without a word . . . it's cruel.

Very well, but I will accompany you.

Bran nodded and entered the cottage. Sir Rigil followed.

Gren? Bran called.

Sir Rigil glared at him.

She asked me to call her Gren, Bran whispered.

Gren entered the room from the bedroom doorway. The right side of her face was bruised, purple and grey. When she met Bran's eyes, her face lit up. *Hello.*

Bran's heart tightened. If only he could protect her. His failure boasted every time he looked on her beautiful face.

Vrell tensed. Beautiful face?

Madame Hoff, Sir Rigil said. *We must discuss an unfortunate matter. I apologize that you have become a target here in Carmine. I feel Master Rennan is part of the problem, since people seem to think there is something clandestine between you two.*

Gren's face flushed and she wrung her hands. *I assure you, sir, Bran has always treated me real nice.*

I do not doubt Master Rennan's character, or yours. I simply must do what I can to protect both your reputations. Ideally, it would be best if you did not go out for a while, but—

You intend to cage me? All I've done is lose my husband. How's this fair?

Please, you misunderstand me. I only suggest keeping to the cottage as an extra precaution, but if you do go out, you must have a female companion.

I only have my mother.

She will do perfectly.

But she has her own work.

Then I will speak to the duchess about finding you a companion.

Gren bowed her head. *Thank you, sir.*

Master Rennan will be taking a new post in the stronghold. I will take over his position here until we can find a suitable replacement.

Gren's brown eyes shot to Bran's, glistening. She straightened and held her head high. *Thank you for telling me about this change. I know Master Rennan has to think about his reputation and betrothal. I never meant to harm either.*

I thank you for your understanding, madam. Sir Rigil nodded at Bran, then walked to the door.

Bran crossed the room. *Gren, I'm sorry.*

She shook her head and a single tear dropped to her chin. *Don't apologize. I appreciate all you've done for me.*

Bran glanced back at Sir Rigil, then stepped closer and lowered his voice. *I'll miss talking to you, Gren. This isn't my idea, you know. I only want to do what's best, and Sir Rigil says—*

She pressed a finger to his lips. *I forgive you, Bran.*

He gripped her hand, held it to his cheek, then kissed her fingertips. *Thank you.*

Vrell's throat stung.

Sir Rigil cleared his throat.

Bran let go. *I'll see you around.*

Gren smiled. *I hope so.*

Sir Rigil opened the door and Bran exited.

I'll be outside, madam, should you need anything, Sir Rigil said. He closed the door behind him and slapped the back of Bran's head. *What was that?*

Bran shrank back. *I don't know.*

You don't know. Well, you'd better start thinking before you act.

You're always kissing maiden's hands. At least four or five a day.

I am not betrothed to the duchess' eldest daughter and heir.

Nor am I. Bran blew a gust of air out his nose. *The duchess never gave her blessing.*

The villagers believe it. Your attention to Miss Fenny fuels their hatred of her. They feel you betray Lady Averella in her absence.

I miss Averella terribly, but what if she never returns? What if Arman sent Gren to me because he knew I'd lost Averella? I've never been worthy of her, anyway. And Gren needs someone. She's all alone.

Sir Rigil set his jaw. *Lady Averella* is *coming back.*

Then why has she not sent word?

Jax tells me she is in Tsaftown, so it won't be long now.

She sends word to everyone but me. Either her messages aren't genuine and she is truly lost, or she cares too little to send word to me.

Regardless, you will remain faithful until her return. Then if you must, break your engagement in person, like a man. I will not employ a coward.

Vrell blinked away from Bran's mind, taking deep, calming breaths. In over eight months she had never sent word to Bran. Why had it not occurred to her? She focused on the spider in the web. Had Gren caught Bran in her web? Or could it be that Bran and Vrell had never truly loved one another as much as they had claimed?

And why did this realization not bother Vrell more?

28

Turning his back to these criminals could get Achan killed. Sir Gavin's men hadn't come forward. Who could he trust? He still held them all at knifepoint, rotating slowly.

TRUST ME. I WILL PROTECT YOU.

Achan gasped at the swell of heat that accompanied conversation with Arman. *It's been a while since I've heard from You.*

YOU HAVE BEEN TOO FOCUSED ON YOU TO HEAR ME.

Achan supposed he had been busy, but surely he couldn't have missed it if Arman had spoken. *A lot has been going on.*

TRUST ME. I WILL PROTECT YOU.

Okay . . . "This is hardly a shirt anymore anyway." He pulled out the cord from around his neck and unlocked the shackles on his wrists. He tossed them against the wall. They clattered down the privy trench. Silence reigned a long time before a soft clink echoed from below. "Blazes."

Achan unlocked the shackles on his ankles. He tugged his scrap of a shirt over his head and dropped it. Gripping the knife tightly, he stepped to the center of the pit and turned.

Bare feet shuffled over the sticky stone floor. Achan cringed inwardly as stale breath wafted over his neck and clammy fingers pawed at him. The crowd murmured.

"It's on the wrong side," the nasal voice said.

"Lord Nathak branded me over my birthmark in an effort to hide it."

"Lord Nathak's a snake."

"Won't argue with you there," Achan said.

The prisoners were silent a moment. Whispers rose to murmurs. Achan turned to see them hashing it out, grappling with the facts, deciding whether they agreed with one another.

Finally, a man in the back said, "I'll stand with you."

"And I."

"I will."

"Me too, eh?"

A chorus of affirmatives rose out of the darkness. Achan held back his smile, determined to look the part of a leader. He thrust the knife above his head. "For Arman!"

"Arman!" the crowd yelled.

Achan lowered the blade. "Now, who is my master thief? I have a knife and a lock to pick."

Bazmark, the big man who'd been imprisoned for looking too long at the queen, became the designated booster. He hoisted Brien, a sliver of a man, to stand on his shoulders and gripped the man's ankles. Brien made quick work of the lock. He silently flipped back the grate door and climbed out. The men cheered. Then several mobbed Bazmark, trying to climb up his body. He growled and threw one man to the floor.

"Quiet!" Achan said. "We must not call attention to ourselves or none of us will get free."

Brien's thin face peered down through the open grate. "I don't see no guards."

Bazmark waved Achan over.

It went against instinct to say it, but he forced himself. "I'll go last." He needed to look out for his people, after all.

Liquid dripped against stone. Every eye stared. Achan pushed a man toward Bazmark. "Go. Let's go."

"I can help too, I can." A broad-shouldered, blond man, who was as hairy as Shung, stepped forward.

"What's your name, man?" Achan asked.

"I'm called Kurtz, I am. I'm a friend of Chion, eh?" Kurtz grinned, his cheeks dimpling under his bushy beard.

Excellent. Hopefully Sir Gavin's other man would come forward soon. Kurtz started hoisting men alongside Bazmark. For over forty in the pit, they made quick time of it.

Achan checked in with Sir Gavin. *What's happening?*

Insurrection. Our men, along with most of the other prisoners and the guards who released them, are fighting Esek's men with us. We're on the roof. It may be awhile until we can get back down to you. How do you fare?

We're coming up but have no weapons. Am I leading these men to their deaths?

My Kingsguardsmen know how to fight with their fists.

Sir Gavin, these men are rail thin. Yours have been here thirteen years. Some others not as long, but I doubt many will have the strength.

Others?

I freed all the men from the Pit.

Eben's breath, lad. Be careful.

You as well.

Bazmark hoisted up Kurtz, which left only him and Achan in the pit. "I doubt you can lift me, Your Highness."

"Perhaps we can lower that other fellow down or . . ." Achan scanned the dark floor for his leg shackles, thankful he hadn't tossed them down the trench. He draped them around his neck and gasped as the cold chain fell against his skin.

Bazmark bent down, fingers interlaced. Achan stepped into his hands and jumped at the same time Bazmark lifted. He flew up through the air, barely managing to get his other foot on Bazmark's shoulder. He would have fallen back, but a hand from above grasped his and pulled him up. More hands grabbed his arms and torso and set him on his feet.

A man with a weathered face and deep, brown eyes set Achan's boots at his feet. "Forgive me, Your Majesty."

Achan set a hand on the back of the man's head. "You're forgiven. Now stand and help me lift Bazmark."

They lowered the chain to Bazmark and pulled him out. When all stood in the center hold, Achan slipped the grate door closed. The cackling man, tall and red-haired, loped along the cells, banging on the doors and laughing.

Achan groaned. "Someone stop him."

Bazmark took off after the cackler.

Achan peered up the tower and found the corridors empty. "Strange no guards stayed behind."

"There are usually only two in the center hold, Your Majesty," a raspy voice said from behind him. "And it appears they have gone elsewhere."

Achan turned to a dark-haired man with lazy, blue eyes. He might have been Achan's height if not for his hunched posture. His once-white shirt was so thin Achan could see his chest hair through the weave. A tattered black beard covered his round face. He had a hooked nose—once broken, perhaps?

"My fellow Kinsman," Achan said, "you are called?"

"The prisoners call me Elk. Kurtz and I are friends of Chion. The false prince spoke Gavin Lukos' name. Is he here?"

Elk. Of course. This must be Eagan Elk, the owner of the sword. "We came together and will hopefully leave together."

"You came to rescue us?"

"Sir Gavin says we cannot take Armonguard without you. All of you."

Elk lowered his eyes. "Thirteen years have passed, Your Highness. I am not the soldier I was."

Achan set a hand on Elk's shoulder. "Let us focus on escape for now."

Achan waved the men close. Bazmark hauled the red-haired cackler to Achan's side. The stench seemed worse now that cleaner air surrounded him. The prisoners stared. Their long beards made them appear wise and intimidating.

Arman, help me. He took a deep breath, unsure what to do. "We'll take the western tower." He glanced from face to face, unsure why he'd said this. Thankfully, no one questioned him.

The weathered man offered Achan his boots again.

Achan shook his head. "You need them more than I."

The man's eyes widened. "Thank you, Your Majesty."

Achan flushed, coming back to himself. How could he lead these men? These prisoners? Was he mad?

Brien handed Inko's knife back, handle first. This Achan accepted gratefully. "Thank you, Brien. We're going up, armed with only this." He held up his knife. "Stay together and pray."

Sir Gavin? I've found your men. We climb the western stairs. Can someone meet the other men and show them where to join our army?

I'll send someone. Look for a man whose fur cloak is reversed. You go meet Caleb on the roof. Grab a torch to signal Inko if you can.

Achan jogged to the western tower, dagfish hook scraping his knee. He took the stairs two at a time, but the prisoners didn't have his stamina. He slowed until they lessened the gap. Few torches burned in the tower and Achan missed steps repeatedly, whacking his toes. He'd thought the steps long when they'd come down, but the journey up seemed endless. Frigid air and frosty steps beneath his feet preceded the exit. He jerked the next torch out of its ring and slowed.

He held the torch back and peeked out onto the roof. Only a dozen men battled here and there, swords clanking, boots slipping over the icy roof. Achan scanned the mêlée. No sign of the knights. At least he didn't see Esek or Sir Kenton.

A guard with a frosted beard stepped into the stairwell. His fur cloak was turned suede side out.

"I'm Fin," the guard said. "You friends of Chion?"

"Aye." Achan spun around. "Here we must part. There's a battle taking place. I urge you all to be careful. Fin will lead you out. I need Elk and Kurtz with me." Achan turned to Fin.

The man stepped into the doorway. "If you get separated, the northern and southern towers will take you down. If you can find warmer clothes, our men are wearing their capes inside out as a sign of which side they are on. I urge you to do the same. We are running sleds out of Smokegate. Meet there for a ride. In two days time, meet at Lytton Hall. Let's go!"

Fin jogged across the icy roof. The prisoners shot after him, two by two. Achan patted several on the back as they went, saying, "Arman be with you." He winced as many had no shoes and thin clothes. He prayed they wouldn't freeze.

Shortly, only he, Elk, and Kurtz remained.

Achan took a deep breath. "Stay close." *Sir Caleb?*

Your Highness! Gavin tells me you're free. Where are you?

Just inside the stairwell on the western tower.

I'm behind you, close to where we will toss the boarding hook.

Achan crossed the doorway and peeked the other way in time to see Sir Caleb strike a soldier's leg. The soldier screamed and swung one last desperate swipe, but Sir Caleb finished the man with a stab to the chest. He shrugged off his pack.

"Come on." Achan darted out of the tower and over the icy roof. Every few steps, his feet stuck to the roof and ripped free, leaving his feet smarting. How daft to have given his boots away. He thrust the torch to Sir Caleb, dropped his knife, and fell beside the dead guard, clawing at the man's boots.

Sir Caleb waved the torch, sweeping it from side to side. "What happened to your—" He looked above Achan's head, eyes wide, and dropped the torch. "Well, I'll be ransomed."

"Hello, Caleb," Elk said.

The men embraced in a fierce hug. Achan shoved his right foot into the boot. It was too small, but better than the alternative. While Sir Caleb shook Kurtz's hand, Achan tugged on the other boot then tossed the dead man's fur cape to Elk.

Achan passed the guard's sword to Kurtz. "Keep watch, will you?" For now they had the entire southeastern wall to themselves, but it might not last.

Sir Caleb seized his pack and dumped a coil of rope onto the roof. "I'll toss the hook to Inko—see his light?"

Achan squinted out over the curtain wall. A single torch burned in the darkness. In the bailey below, a massive mêlée was underway. Achan's stomach tightened at the idea of going over the side of the tower while men were fighting underneath.

Sir Caleb arranged the coil of rope by his feet. "Achan, show the men how to attach their hooks."

Achan pulled the strap and hook out of his trousers and moved his belt up under his armpits, then imitated how he would set his hook on the line.

"Stand back now." Sir Caleb backed up, the boarding hook in his right hand. "Achan, hold the end, just in case?"

Achan snagged the end of the rope poking out from under the huge pile.

Sir Caleb skipped forward and pitched the boarding hook toward the distant torchlight. At first it appeared right on target. The rope in the pile beside Achan spun away as the hook sailed toward Inko, but the hook fell before it passed over the snowy white sentry wall. Halfway down, it clunked against the wall and bounced back into the snow.

Sir Caleb sighed. "Nothing to do but pull it quickly." He grabbed the line and started to bring it up.

The hook tugged through the snow, flew onto a patch of ice and slid and bounced about. It neared a group of fighting men. One of the guards unknowingly straddled the rope.

Move, Achan thought.

The man lunged forward with his sword just as the boarding hook slid past.

The hook lifted off the ground and up along the side of the tower. Achan blew out a steamy breath.

Sir Caleb gripped the boarding hook again. "How many tries did it take me at Meribah Corner, Your Highness?"

"Three."

Sir Caleb hummed. "Better get it in two or I'll never hear the end of the lucky number three from Inko."

Achan grinned. "Good plan."

This time Sir Caleb lobbed the hook much higher. The aim was off a bit—Inko would have to play fetch—but the hook sailed over the wall with several feet to spare.

"Nicely done, Sir Caleb."

"Thank you." Sir Caleb took the end from Achan, looped it around the nearest crenellation, and tied a complicated-looking knot. The rope bounced over the air like a wave.

"Do you think he's got it?" Achan asked.

"Aye, but thinking isn't good enough. He'll light the blue torch, then we'll know."

Achan stared at the yellow flame in the distance until it blurred. He blinked and it focused back to a small dot. Suddenly another flame appeared beside it, blue and bright. The yellow torch went out.

"Okay, Your Highness, that's our signal. You ready?"

"If I may." Elk held his dagfish hook in one fist. "Allow me to go first. If something were to happen, let it be to me."

Achan shrank with such an offer. "You're a brave man."

Elk smirked. "To be the first one to escape? Perhaps I'm only selfish, Your Majesty."

"You there, what're you doing?" A man strode toward them, his fur cape rising and falling with each step.

"Watching the action, we are," Kurtz said.

"Of all the lazy . . . hey!" The man drew his sword. "Prisoners escaping on the roof! Prisoners esca—"

Kurtz ran him through before the man could even raise his weapon. "Not a bad sword," he said, jerking it out. The guard slumped over onto his side. Kurtz swiped the blade on the guard's trousers. "Think I'll keep it, I will."

Elk set his hook over the line and straddled the parapet. His breath clouded in front of his round face. "This is a bit intimidating."

"Help me lift him over, Your Highness," Sir Caleb said.

Achan gripped Elk's right hand, Sir Caleb his left. Elk swung his other leg over the wall and they lowered him. When their arms stretched as far as possible, Elk's rope still had some slack.

"You're going to fall a bit." Sir Caleb grunted. "Just a few inches, but it will likely be a bit of a scare. Achan, let go first."

Achan released Elk's hand. Elk gripped the eye of the hook, his knuckles white. He took another deep breath then nodded at Sir Caleb.

Sir Caleb let go. Elk fell down and away, legs flailing. He seemed to be trying to stifle a scream as a loud groan slid away with him. A V notched into the cable where Elk's hook propelled down the line.

"I forgot to tell him to put out his feet," Sir Caleb said.

Achan winced as Elk slammed into the sentry wall. He struggled a moment, like a fish on a line, then managed to pull himself up. His body vanished as he fell over the parapet. A moment later he stood and lifted a hand.

"It's absolutely insane, it is," Kurtz said. "I love it."

Sir Caleb clapped Achan on the shoulder. "Okay, Your Highness. You're next."

Achan's gut clenched. He pulled his hook into his shaky hands and set it over the cable.

"Wait! Take these, eh?" Kurtz slapped a pair of leather gloves against Achan's arms. "A gift from my dead guard."

"Thanks." Achan slipped the gloves on, disturbed to find them still warm.

"Help me lift him over, Kurtz," Sir Caleb said.

Achan straddled the parapet, as Elk had done. Sir Caleb and Kurtz lowered him down. His forearms twitched, muscles tight. Short breaths puffed out of his mouth like steam from a soup pot. Sir Caleb let go first. Achan's hand flew to the eye of the hook. A shadow fell over Kurtz's back.

"Behind you," Achan yelled.

Kurtz glanced back and lost hold of Achan's hand.

Achan's insides seemed to fly up and out of his mouth. He fell, weightless, away from the Pillar, screaming louder than he ever had, not falling any longer, but shooting along on the cable. He strained to see how the men fared on the Pillar, then remembered he needed to turn around.

He swung his leg out and spun in a complete circle. Maybe he could slow himself down before trying to turn. He lifted his left hand to the cable but jerked it away at the smell of burning leather. Another attempt to swing himself around and—

SLAM.

His back struck the wall. Pain flashed over him, stealing his breath. He hung limp, unable to move, and focused on the fighting below. Amazing that no one had seen or heard him.

"Your Highness?" Elk called from above.

Hands gripped under Achan's arms and pulled. His too-tight boots scraped up the stone wall. His body slipped over the parapet. He lay on his back on the sentry walk, staring at the black sky, sucking in long breaths of icy air.

Elk leaned over him, his wispy beard tickling Achan's chin. "Are you well, Your Highness?"

Achan nodded and rolled onto his hands and knees. He sat back and pulled his hook off the cable, barely able to see where the other end of the rope attached to the parapet atop the Pillar. "That's very high."

Elk laughed. "I cannot believe I did it either. Climb down the rope to—wait. Here comes Kurtz. Help me steady this."

Achan gripped the cable, which was already quite taut. Kurtz hung like a dead man, and for a moment, Achan feared something horrible had happened with the shadow on the roof. The cable sank awfully low with Kurtz's weight. About halfway down, Kurtz kicked a leg out, trying to spin, no doubt.

Sir Gavin Lukos.

Achan opened the connection at once. *Where are you?*

Almost up the south tower, with Sir Kenton on my heels. Where are you?

Kurtz's weight slowed him to a stop before he hit the wall. Elk reached out to pull him the last few feet.

I'm on the outer sentry wall with Elk and Kurtz.

Praise Arman. You three return to Stormwatch. Get a start on us.

Achan and Elk helped pull Kurtz over the parapet. *Not until I see you on this wall.*

This is not a negotiation. You might be the prince, but you cannot argue when it comes to your safety. Go. We'll be right behind.

Achan closed his mind and stood. The rope jerked sideways and nearly tripped him.

Elk reached for it. "Help me!"

Achan and Kurtz grabbed the rope and held it steady. Sir Caleb soared backwards, his short, frizzy hair billowing out to reveal a bald spot.

Like Achan, Sir Caleb remained backward, though with three sets of hands extended to catch him, he didn't hit hard.

Sir Caleb panted, his face pink. "Achan, down you go. Kurtz, go back to Stormwatch with him and wait for us."

"Is Sir Gavin coming?" Achan asked.

"He said he was almost to the roof and to go."

"You should've waited for him," Achan said. "What if he needed help?"

"He said Sir Kenton and his men were chasing him. My waiting would only have slowed down our escape. Now when he gets to the cable, he simply needs to come."

"Time to go, eh?" Kurtz snaked one arm around Achan's waist and carried him to the outer edge where the rope dangled to the ground. Inko and Verdot stood holding the end.

"Will any of you be coming down finally?" Inko asked.

Achan lowered himself over the edge. He tried to walk down the wall, but his boots had no traction on the icy stone. So he went hand over hand for a moment, then slid the rest of the way, thankful for the leather gloves.

Inko caught him at the bottom and shoved him to the dog-sled. Kurtz hit the ground seconds later, then Elk. The two men hurried to the sled. Elk took the reins. "Sit, Your Highness. Kurtz, run with me."

Elk said, "Hike!" He and Kurtz ran and pushed the sled over the snow. The dogs took off.

Achan watched Ice Island as they slid into the darkness, barely able to glimpse the rope stretched between the Pillar and the outer wall before it faded from sight.

They arrived at Stormwatch and waited. Sir Gavin didn't answer Achan's knocks, so he called out to Inko instead.

I'm approaching Stormwatch now.

What about Sir Gavin?

He was hitting his head on the wall, but is breathing.

The second sled arrived. Sir Caleb, face drawn, jumped from the bed and pulled Sir Gavin limply to his feet.

Achan ran forward to help. He positioned himself under Sir Gavin's arm and supported the weight on his right side. "What happened?"

Sir Caleb started toward the horses. "He struck his head on the wall."

Inko untied Sir Gavin's horse. "Be helping us to be boosting Gavin up."

Achan panted under Sir Gavin's weight. The knight could not ride alone. "Inko, take Scout. I'll ride with Sir Gavin."

Achan handed Sir Gavin's arm off to Elk and mounted Sir Gavin's horse. Elk, Sir Caleb, and Verdot lifted Sir Gavin up. Achan grabbed him under the arms and pulled while Elk pushed Sir Gavin's leg over. Achan settled the knight onto the saddle in front of him and held him in his arms.

Sir Gavin? Don't leave us, now.

The men all mounted the horses. Achan itched to ride, to get Sir Gavin to a bed to rest, but Sir Caleb spoke. "Thank you, Verdot, for helping us."

Verdot nodded. "It does not repay my mistakes."

"Your mistakes are in the past."

"I do not deserve such mercy, Caleb."

"Neither did most the men in the Prodotez, eh? But the prince pardoned their crimes, he did," Kurtz said.

"And I pardon you as well," Achan said.

Verdot's face glowed crimson in the wavering torchlight. He bowed to Achan. "Best of blessings, Your Highness."

Achan nodded.

Sir Caleb looked to Elk. "To the *Ivory Spit.* Do you remember the way?"

"Like I remember my own name," Kurtz said.

Sir Caleb nodded. "We'll split up then. You two take the east gate, Inko and Achan come with me."

"I will be riding with Kurtz," Inko said. "Three and three are being more favored numbers than two and four."

"Fine." Sir Caleb nudged his horse toward the distant lights of Tsaftown. "Stable your horses, then come to the room with a stag on the door. Do *not* stop in the tavern, Kurtz."

"Wouldn't dream of it, eh?" Kurtz asked. "Not without a bath first."

29

The warmth of their room in *The Ivory Spit* hit Achan like a word from Arman. He and Sir Caleb laid Sir Gavin on the bed by the fireplace. Sir Gavin moaned but did not open his eyes.

Sparrow poked his head in through the adjoining door. "Praise Arman! I feared you were—what has happened?"

"I'm not certain," Sir Caleb said. "He hit his head, I know."

Sparrow's green eyes flitted over Sir Gavin and the boy darted back into his room.

Achan fell to his rear before the fire, pulled off the too-tight boots, and stretched his toes. He held his pink, stinging fingers toward the flames.

Sparrow scampered back into the room with his satchel.

"What do you see?" Sir Caleb asked.

"His leg is bleeding," Sparrow said. "Could you go to the tavern and see if they have any clean linen we could purchase?"

Sir Caleb shot back out the door.

Achan examined Sir Gavin's trousers. They were soaked from the snow, like everyone else's. How did Sparrow see—

"Help me get his clothing off," Sparrow said. "I shall need water too. There is a kettle on the hearth in the other room."

Achan jumped up, darted for the door, then jerked back to help Sparrow with Sir Gavin's clothes. Balls of snow and ice clinging to the fur tunic had started to melt, dripping water onto the bedspread. Achan draped the tunic over one of the chairs and came back to Sir Gavin's side. The man was lethargic, eyes partially open, mouth gaping.

"Sir Gavin," Sparrow said. "Sir Gavin, look at me."

The old man's eyes flicked to meet Sparrow's.

"Good. Can you speak? Tell me your full name."

"Theowin Gavin Leofrick," came, barely a whisper.

Sparrow frowned. "I think he is stunned."

Achan snorted. "What gave it away?"

"I mean, his mind is frozen with the shock of pain to his body. It happens sometimes, physically. It happened to you with the Poroo arrows."

Achan had little memory of that day. "Oh."

Sparrow dug in his satchel. "His boots, Achan, please?"

Achan tugged off Sir Gavin's boots, then his trousers, which streaked blood down the old man's leg. At first Achan couldn't see where the wound was, then he saw black seeping into the green blanket just above Sir Gavin's right knee.

Sparrow stood. "Help me turn him over."

Achan jumped around to the other side of the pallet, and he and Sparrow rolled Sir Gavin to his stomach. A dark hole bored into Sir Gavin's right thigh. Blood trickled down his inner leg and pooled in a new place on the bedspread.

"The water, Achan," Sparrow said. "There is a basin of cold beside my hearth. Add hot water from the kettle until it is warm to your fingers."

Achan ran to the other room and did as Sparrow asked. He heard the front door scrape over the floor in the next room and several sets of boots clump over the wooden floor.

"I'm glad you've booked rooms above *The Ivory Spit*, I am," Kurtz said. "I nearly died for lack of ale and female companionship in the Pit all those—"

"What is wrong with him?" Elk's voice.

"A barbed arrowhead is buried in his thigh." Sparrow's voice, eerily calm.

"Ouch, eh?"

"Do you have an arrowspoon?" Elk asked.

"I do not," Sparrow said.

Achan carried the basin to the floor beside Sparrow. The boy held Sir Gavin's wadded trousers against the wound.

Elk stood looking over Sparrow's shoulder. "What are you planning to do?"

"Stopper up the bleeding until Sir Caleb returns with linen."

Elk nodded.

Inko stood on the other side of Sir Gavin's bed, eyes wide as he took in the scene. "How is he being?"

"He has lost much blood." Sparrow glanced up at the faces watching him. "Is anyone else wounded?"

"A bit scraped up," Kurtz said. "We'll manage, eh?"

Elk peeled off his guard's fur cloak and slung it over an empty chair. "I was once a healer. Would you like assistance?"

"Have you ever removed a barbed arrowhead?"

Elk raised his dark eyebrows. "I have. Many times."

Sparrow sighed. "Praise be to Arman, then, for I have only ever removed bodkin arrows."

Elk tucked his beard into the neck of his shirt. "You are young to have accomplished such a feat." He took a small bowl off the mantle. He dipped it in Achan's basin of water and set it on the table, then plunged his hands in to wash them. "I shall need two small blades I can sterilize in the fire."

"I'm having some in my pack." Inko slipped past Achan and into the other room.

Sir Caleb burst through the door carrying a stack of white linens.

Elk took them from him. "All of you go into the other room to clean up. Allow us some room to work."

Achan cast one more concerned glance at Sir Gavin's leg and retreated with the others. Inko sat on the bed nearest the door. Sir Caleb sat on the edge of the other bed that Kurtz lay on. Achan squatted before the fireplace and held out his numb hands. He slapped at a twitch behind his ear and searched for the cursed mosquito. Wasn't it too cold for mosquitoes?

"Whoo!" Kurtz screamed.

Achan spun around on his toes, still squatting.

Elk appeared in the adjoining doorway. "Do you mind?"

Kurtz turned on his side, head propped on one hand. "We're free, Elk. Free, we are!"

"I realize that. Do try to keep it down." He closed the door with a soft clump.

Kurtz sat up. "Going off that tower . . . thought I was dead. But then I flew, eh?"

"I thought I was dead when you dropped me," Achan said. "Again when I hit the wall."

"I could not stop myself either," Sir Caleb said. "Perhaps the hooks did not need oil."

They talked more about the rescue. Kurtz's glowing rendition of Achan's time in the Pit so enhanced the story it sounded like something a minstrel might turn into a song.

Kurtz jerked his head to the door. "Who's the minnow, eh?"

"Vrell Sparrow joined us in Mahanaim," Sir Caleb said. "He's a bit of a healer."

Kurtz's brown eyes raked Achan up and down. "And you're the mirrorglass image of your old man, you are. Couldn't tell so much in the pit, but here . . ."

"Aye," Sir Caleb paused to look at Achan. "I thought the same when I first saw him."

Kurtz grinned and folded his arms across his broad chest. "I'm sure you've heard many tales of me, eh?"

Achan scratched behind his ear. "Nothing, actually."

Kurtz clapped a hairy hand over his chest. "Caleb, you wound me. How could you not tell him of the Chazir, eh?"

"I didn't want to give the lad nightmares."

"Bah." Kurtz stood. "I'm starved, I am. Let's go down to the tavern, eh?"

"No, Kurtz," Sir Caleb said. "There will be no tavern."

"But tavern food is hot, it is. And I can dance while I wait."

Achan scoffed. "I can't imagine any woman would look at you. You look like a scavenger."

Sir Kurtz clapped his hands. "The prince raises a good point, he does. We need water in here for a shave, eh?"

Sir Caleb walked to the door. "I'll have some food brought here. After we eat, we'll go to the bathhouse. No tavern."

Achan went to check on Sir Gavin while Sir Caleb was gone, but Sir Eagan and Sparrow looked to be in deep concentration, so he left them to their work.

Sir Caleb returned with two serving girls dressed in white blouses and red skirts. One carried a smoking pot, which she hung on an iron hook above the fire. The other held a stack of wooden bowls. "Where's your table?"

Inko took the bowls. "It's being in the next room. We'll be bringing it back before we are leaving."

"Try these." Sir Caleb handed a pair of brown leather boots to Achan. He turned to the girl at the door. "Might you bring up a bathing tub next?"

"Aye, but that'd be too much water to haul for all you men. Wouldn't you rather use the bathhouse?"

"We will. But we have a sick man who'll need a tub."

Achan pulled on the boots. They didn't fit as nicely as the pair Trajen had given him, but they would do. He wasn't picky.

The women left and Sir Caleb dished up a bowl of stew for each of the men and set out a stack of clean clothing for Achan. After everyone ate, Kurtz, Sir Caleb, and Inko left to go down to the bathhouse. Achan, not permitted to leave the room, was to bathe in the tub as soon as it arrived.

Achan found Eagan's Elk under Inko's bed and started to polish it as Sir Caleb had taught him. He may as well return it to its owner in pristine condition.

The women delivered the tub and filled it with hot water. Once they had gone, Achan stripped off his clothes and inspected the scrapes on his knee from the dagfish hook. No more than cat scratches, really, but they stung when he settled his bruised body into the warm water. Dozens of mosquito bites peppered his chest and arms and itched something fierce. He was scrubbing his neck with a brick of honeysuckle soap when Sparrow opened the adjoining door.

Sparrow's eyes popped wide and his cheeks flushed.

Achan asked, "How is Sir Gavin?" but Sparrow backed right out of the room. Odd duck.

Elk came through a moment later, face completely shaven. With his round face and dark hair, he looked no older than forty. "Everyone has gone?"

"To the bathhouse," Achan said. "How is Sir Gavin?"

"Sleeping. We were able to extract the arrowhead and have wrapped the wound. I am confident he will make a full . . ." Elk's gaze dropped to the floor beside the tub where Achan had shed his clothes. "Is that your sword?"

Achan scratched his shoulder. "I suspect it's yours. Sir Gavin gave it to me. It's called Eagan's Elk."

Elk pressed his lips in a straight line.

The door opened and Sir Caleb entered, followed by Kurtz and Inko. "I don't care. The answer is no."

"One hour, eh?" Kurtz had trimmed his scraggly beard short and combed his bushy hair into a tail. He looked twenty years younger, like a slender, blond version of Shung.

"No one goes out again tonight, Kurtz," Sir Caleb said. "Esek's men might be anywhere."

The men resituated themselves on the pallets. Elk still stood staring at Achan's sword.

"Eagan's Elk is yours, isn't it?" Achan asked. "Sir Gavin said it belonged to you."

"Achan," Sir Caleb said, "this is Sir Eagan Elk, former heir to the lordship of Zerah Rock."

Achan straightened in the tub. "But . . . isn't Elk a stray name? How could you have been heir to Zerah Rock? And why the dagfish? That's Tsaftown's crest."

Sir Eagan's brown knit. "A stray name?"

"Ten years ago, no such practice of naming strays existed," Sir Caleb said. "Back then an animal surname labeled one disowned by his family. Eagan's father—"

"My father did not approve of my serving the king as a soldier. He wanted me as Lord of Zerah Rock, nothing less. He did not understand. Rhomphaia originally belonged to one of Lord Livna's uncles. I squired for him in my youth."

"Rhomphaia." Achan stared at the ivory pommel, wishing he weren't in the tub so he could hand the blade over properly. His heart ached that he would have to give it up.

Sir Caleb jumped in with a change of subject. "Are you hungry, Eagan? We have stew."

Sir Eagan called through the cracked door, "Boy, come have dinner," then sat beside Kurtz on the bed nearest Achan.

Sparrow poked his head through the doorway, glanced over the room, and disappeared again.

Achan wished he'd bathed faster. How awkward to dress in front of so many spectators. He turned as he stood, facing the wall, water trickling into the tub. He stepped out, dried quickly, then pulled on his clean undershorts and trousers. He pulled his shirt over his head, and, finding nowhere to sit, slid down against the wall in the corner.

"What do we do next?" Achan asked.

"If Gavin is not up to it, I'll go to Lytton Hall tomorrow, first thing," Sir Caleb said. "He intended to officially ask for Tsaftown's support. It's my guess Lord Livna will throw a banquet in your honor tomorrow night. If I know Tsaftown, the celebration will last several days."

Kurtz rubbed his hands together. "Excellent."

Sparrow opened the door, peeked in, and entered fully. Sir Eagan dished the boy up a bowl of stew and handed it over.

Sparrow beamed. "Thank you, sir."

Kurtz pointed at Sparrow. "You and the minnow have the same face, Elk."

Sparrow paled and stared at Sir Eagan, who quirked an eyebrow at Kurtz. Sparrow and Sir Eagan stood awkwardly, glancing between one another.

Achan tipped his head to the side. Kurtz spoke truth. Sir Eagan and Sparrow both had round faces, thin lips, and fine, black hair. Easily mistaken for relatives.

"Do you know your father?" Achan asked Sparrow. Many strays knew the identity of one parent. Sparrow had bloodvoiced his mother, but if he didn't know his father's identity . . .

Sparrow swallowed and croaked out, "I do."

Sir Eagan chuckled. "I fathered no son, Kurtz, as you well know. And Rigil would be much older than this boy."

"I've met Sir Rigil," Achan said. "He's a fine knight."

Sir Eagan snorted. "Is he now? Last I saw him he was eleven and begging to be my page."

"I hear he excels at the joust," Achan said.

Sir Eagan snorted again. "That does not surprise me."

"He swore fealty to Achan," Sir Caleb said.

"Did he?" Sir Eagan slapped his arm, then scratched it.

"The mosquitoes got me bad, too," Achan said.

Sir Eagan laughed. "Fleas, Your Highness."

Blood seemed to slow in Achan's veins. "Fleas?" He glanced at Sir Caleb. "From the furs on the sled?"

Sir Caleb wrinkled his nose. "So it would seem."

"And from the squalor of the Pit, eh," Kurtz said. "Fleas have been our companions these past years."

Achan sighed and scratched a red bite on his arm. At least there were no women around to complain.

"What time do you suppose it is now, eh?" Kurtz asked.

"You're not going to the tavern, Kurtz," Sir Caleb said. "We cannot risk our king for a night of mead and dancing."

"But we've been in prison thirteen years, we have. We've earned a night out, eh, Eagan?"

"Leave me out of your escapades, Kurtz," Sir Eagan said. "I am enjoying the quiet."

"But it's just downstairs. And *The Ivory Spit*'s a classy tavern, it is. A tavern fit for a king." Kurtz winked at Achan. "What say you, Highness, eh? Fancy a mug of mead?"

"Absolutely not!" Inko said. "He's only being sixteen years of age and I—"

Kurtz puffed out his chest. "Sixteen's a man, it is."

"Being out gallivanting with you isn't being fit behavior for a king."

Kurtz swung his legs off the pallet. "What's wrong with my behavior, eh?"

"I'm remembering a time when you were being thrown out of *The Ivory Spit*."

"Once, when I first joined the Kingsguard." Kurtz shrugged it off as if it were nothing. "They didn't like me dancing on the tables."

Achan stifled a laugh.

Inko glared at Kurtz. "Be imagining that."

"Do you dance, Highness?" Kurtz asked.

Achan winced, recalling his awkwardness with Yumikak. "Not really, no."

"That settles it, it does. You can't introduce him at court if he can't dance. What will the maidens think, eh?"

"Achan is a quick study," Sir Caleb said. "And Tsaftown is hardly court."

"Livna is a noble lord, he is. Sounds like court to me."

"Enough, Kurtz," Sir Eagan said. "We stay indoors tonight. Let us hear no more of it."

"Bah!" Kurtz fell back onto the bed and tucked his arms behind his head.

"Vrell?" a voice whispered.

Vrell opened her eyes. A shadow crouched beside the bed she shared with Sir Gavin. In the pale glow from the coals in the fireplace, Sir Eagan's face glowed.

The man's familiarity unhinged her. And Kurtz's pointing out their similar looks prayed on her mind. Darkness had no doubt been the cause. She should have stayed in the other room where the conversation would have distracted her mind.

"What time is it?" She sat up and glanced at Sir Gavin, whose breathing rumbled a steady snore.

"It is late. Kurtz snuck out to the tavern and took the prince with him."

Vrell jumped out of bed. "What?"

"Shh." Sir Eagan set a finger to his lips. "I do not want to wake everyone. I hoped you could help me convince him to come back to bed without a scene."

"Achan is not a drinking man." Vrell knew that much. But what could he be thinking? These men had sacrificed so much for him. He would endanger that for a night in a tavern?

Vrell snuck out of the room with Sir Eagan and down the interior steps. Voices grew as they descended, then music and laughter. As they neared the first floor, light spilled into the stairwell, shadows bobbing inside it.

Vrell followed Sir Eagan into a stifling room crowded with at least three dozen people. Worn square tables lined each wall. Those in the center had been pushed haphazardly into one another to create a small dancing area. The walls were paneled timber, decorated with antlers, carvings of fish, and various hooks and sconces. Iron candelabras with three fat candles each hung from the ceiling. In the far corner, a band played an upbeat tune. The band consisted of three men dressed in blue tunics. One played a lute, one played a flute, and the third beat on a tabor drum.

Those dancing were not behaving with any decorum whatsoever. Each couple danced in their own fashion, separate from the rest, not in a line as Vrell was used to. This was not a proper place for a lady to spend time, nor a prince.

She tore her eyes away from the tawdry display. "Do you see them?"

Sir Eagan pointed to a table before a frosty window. Achan and Kurtz sat alone, a large pitcher between them. Achan wore a burgundy head scarf over his hair like some sort of marauder. Kurtz wore one in navy blue.

Sir Kurtz met Vrell's reprimanding stare and whispered in Achan's ear. Achan looked up, a big grin on his face, and waved Vrell over.

Foolish boy.

Sir Eagan and Vrell wove around the tables, past the lively dancers, and stopped before the table.

"Kurtz, I see you have decided to disobey Caleb," Sir Eagan said, "Not the best way to resume your service to the crown."

Kurtz waved a hand to the two empty chairs at their table. "Join us, eh?"

Vrell rolled her eyes. "Achan, we must—"

"No," Kurtz whispered. "I'm Hal Rackham, I am. Sailor aboard the *Mirfak*, just into port from Hamonah. And this here's one of our oarsmen, Pacey."

I'm an oarsman, Achan told Vrell. *That means I row.*

Oarsman. Really, Vrell scolded.

But Achan grinned so wide Vrell couldn't help but smile.

Sir Eagan drew in a groaning breath and claimed the seat beside Kurtz. "You will finish your drink and we will go."

"But we've already ordered more, we have," Kurtz said. "Pie and a dance."

Vrell sat next to Achan. "You ordered a dance?"

"Two ladies," Achan said in an amused tone.

Vrell cast a scathing glare at Kurtz.

Kurtz leaned across the table toward Vrell. "Barmaids, Minnow. Friendliest women in all Er'Rets, you wait and see. Told them we're celebrating Pacey's coming-of-age day."

Achan winked at Vrell.

"What are you hoping to accomplish on this outing?" Vrell asked. "A chance to get drunk, or something more?"

"Blazes, boy! I've been in prison for thirteen years, I have. The prime of my life lost! I deserve some fun. Besides, our future king should see the master at work, eh? I'll teach him a thing or two about attracting a female."

Vrell gritted her teeth. As if Achan needed help with that. "Sir Eagan, you deem this noble behavior?"

Sir Eagan's expression remained somber. "I do not."

"Bah!" Kurtz leaned back in his chair and sighed heavily. "Well, Pacey, it seems Mother and Father found us, eh? What mischief can we get into while they're watching?"

Vrell did not understand Kurtz's motivation. "You claim to follow Arman, Kurtz? Can He possibly be pleased with your deceiving Sir Caleb and endangering Ach—Pacey?"

"I'm not in danger," Achan said.

Kurtz leaned across the table, his sour breath wafting over Vrell's face. "Me and Arman, we got us an understandin', boy. I'm a work in progress, I am."

"Thirteen years in prison and your work in progress has progressed little," Sir Eagan said.

A barmaid stopped at the table and set two plates of a dark berry pie in front of Achan and Kurtz. She had long brown hair tied back in a long plait and a kind face. "There you are, boys."

"Thank you, Darri."

Vrell pursed her lips. Kurtz *would* already be on a first-name basis with the barmaid. Thankfully, the woman was old enough to be Achan's mother. Round in all the right places for Kurtz' attention, she wore a sleeveless corset top and a long red skirt.

Darri cast her brown eyes from Vrell to Sir Eagan. "And what can I get fer you two?"

Sir Eagan smiled. "Nothing, th—"

"Another round, eh?" Kurtz pushed the jug to the edge of the table.

"Will do. And I found some willing partners for you and your young lad, here." Darri raised her eyebrows at Achan, a coy smile curling her lips. "They'll be right out."

"Heh hay!" Kurtz sipped his mead. "Now the fun begins, eh?"

"Achan, please come back to the room where you will be safe," Vrell said.

Kurtz sighed. "I say we ditch the minnow, Pacey. He's already poor company, eh?"

Achan shoved a large bite of pie into his mouth and licked his fingers. He pushed the plate toward her with his other hand. "Want some?"

"I do not."

Darri approached the table again. In one hand she held a pitcher frothing over with amber liquid, in the other, two empty mugs. She plunked a mug before Sir Eagan and Vrell, filled them with mead, re-filled Kurtz's mug, and set the pitcher down in the center of the table.

A small consolation, Achan was so preoccupied with the pie, he hadn't seemed to have touched his mug.

Two women flanked Darri and she introduced them. "This here is my sister, Meldeen, and her daughter Beska."

Vrell's insides coiled. Meldeen was Darri's age, but Beska, a tall, slender woman with long, dirty blond hair, appeared to be in her early twenties. They were both dressed in corset-laced white tops and red sweeping skirts like Darri's.

"What's it yer wantin'?" Meldeen asked, a suspicious gleam in her eyes.

"Only a dance or two, lassie." Kurtz grabbed the scruff of Achan's neck. "Pacey here turned sixteen. Needs to learn to move his feet, eh?"

"And a handsome one he is," Meldeen said. "Best wishes to yeh on yer comin'-of-age, Master Pacey. May Thalassa bless yeh and bring yeh endless joy."

Achan grinned. "Thank you, ma'am."

Sir Kurtz stood and stepped past Sir Eagan's chair.

"Wait," Achan said, shoving the last bite of pie in his mouth and he stood and inched past Vrell's chair.

"Thirteen years," Kurtz whispered. "Pick up the pace, eh? I need to dance, I do."

Vrell disapproved of this. "Are you not married, ma'am?"

Meldeen scowled down on Vrell. "What's that yer business?"

Vrell glanced at Beska in accusation.

"Don't yeh worry, lad," Meldeen said. "We won't taint yer pa 'n' brother. An' if yer sweet, Beska might dance with yeh, too."

Vrell's cheeks blazed. As if she wanted to dance with . . .

Kurtz barreled between Meldeen and Beska, grabbed both their hands, and tugged them to the dance floor.

Achan chuckled and kicked Vrell's boot. "You're sure you don't want to come?"

"What good could come of this, Ach—" She pursed her lips, not wanting to speak Achan's name aloud. She whispered, "Do you serve Arman or your flesh?"

Achan blinked, his smile fading. "It's just a dance, Sparrow. Have you never wanted to be just one of the men?" He placed his hands on the table and leaned down to speak in her ear. "I'm not a fool. My life is changing before I've had much chance to live it. I only want to relax for a few hours. Be nobody. Won't you come dance with us?"

Vrell shook her head. "Thank you, but I shall watch from here with Sir Eagan. Someone must act as your conscience if things go sour."

Achan's cheeks darkened. "I don't need a nursemaid."

"You do not need a *barmaid*, either," Vrell said.

"Fine." Achan shrugged. "Miss all the fun if you like." He strode to where Sir Kurtz and the women were dancing.

Sir Eagan wrinkled his nose. "That went well."

Vrell glared at Sir Eagan. "You had little to say."

"We shall give them their dance, then end it."

Vrell folded her arms and glowered at the dancing mob. Kurtz and Meldeen held hands and skipped from side to side, a harmless enough dance, though they plowed through others without bothering to apologize or tame their steps.

Beska and Achan, however . . . that woman led with brazen confidence. She held his hands above her head and twirled before him, drew closer and stomped her feet to the beat. Achan's cheeks reddened three times during the first song alone. That and his novice dance skills made him even more charming. Vrell sighed. If given the chance, he would dazzle every eligible noblewoman in Er'Rets.

To her dismay, the song slowed. Beska wrapped her arms around Achan's neck and pressed against him in ways no noblewoman would deem proper.

She caught Sir Eagan's stare from across the table. Why did he watch her instead of Achan and Kurtz? Did he find her familiar too? How? He had been on Ice Island since Vrell was four. She wanted to ask Mother about him. After all, it was due to their thwarted love that Mother had agreed to consider allowing Vrell and Bran to marry despite his lesser noble status.

But Vrell did not understand Sir Caleb's comments about Mother wanting Sir Eagan freed. Did Mother plan to rekindle her old relationship? That should not bother Vrell.

But the color of Sir Eagan's hair did. Black as a raven. A plain, common color to be sure, but her mother's hair was auburn and her sisters were all blonde like her father. He used to tease that Vrell was a child of the gods. The direful facts of Mother and Sir Eagan's past, and Mother's forced marriage to Duke Amal, haunted her.

But such a thing could not be true! Mother had always been incorruptibly dutiful.

Yet Vrell had assumed the same about Achan, and there he stood cavorting with a woman who could very well be a strumpet. She glanced back across the room. Beska slid her hand up the back of Achan's neck and kissed him.

Vrell stood up so fast her chair fell back. "Do you see this, Sir Eagan? Why does the band play only slow songs? If I give them a coin, might they pick up the tempo? Do you have any?"

Sir Eagan's mouth twisted into a crooked grin. "I have no money. Do not fret, Vrell. One kiss will not shatter his virtue."

Vrell pursed her lips and took a deep, Sir Gavin-like breath through her nose. "Sir Caleb might disagree."

Sir Eagan chuckled. "No doubt he would."

Vrell righted her chair and fell into it, glaring at Achan, who now, to her delight, held Beska at arm's length.

Oh, much better.

I'm doing my best, Sparrow. Why don't you come try?

Achan's voice in her mind made her jump. *She frightens me.*

Achan twirled Beska under his arm. *Did you see her kiss me?*

Vrell rolled her eyes. *How could I have missed it? She is probably after your coin purse. She has been feeling for it since she met you.*

Achan laughed in his head. *Well, I haven't got a coin purse, so it's her loss and my gain.*

Taking advantage of a woman is never a gain to her, even if she is too dim or drunk to see it.

I didn't take advantage, and Beska isn't drunk.

The song ended. Achan bowed his head to Beska and thanked her for the dance, earning a look of surprise. Apparently the girl was not used to being treated kindly. Achan returned to the table and took a long drink from his mug.

He wrinkled his nose. "An odd concoction. Bitter and sweet at the same time." He set the mug down and leaned back in his chair, folding his arms over his chest like a sullen child. "Sparrow, I can't read you. Sometimes you're more naive than a babe, other times, you're an old man passing out proverbs of wisdom. Why must you spoil my fun? These knights are going to marry me to a stranger. It's refreshing to be looked at as a man with no crown. Beska kissed me for me, not for my title."

"A great sacrifice, I am certain."

"What do you think, Sir Eagan?" Achan asked.

"That you dance well, Your Highness, but I do not think such behavior noble."

"Esek would," Vrell said.

This earned her a nasty glare from Achan, and she instantly regretted her words. She wanted Achan back upstairs where he belonged, but she did not want him cross with her.

But then Achan sighed. "Aye. You've nailed it, Sparrow. I don't want to be Esek. Not even a bit. Ever." He stood and pushed in his chair. "Think we can tear Sir Kurtz away?"

Sir Eagan smiled at Vrell. "Well, there are three of us and one of him. I think we stand an excellent chance."

Vrell woke and found Sir Gavin in good spirits, though pained and limping terribly. No one seemed aware of Achan and Kurtz's late-night visit to the tavern.

Sir Gavin insisted on going to Lord Livna himself. He rebraided his beard, tied off the end with a bit of twine, then he and Sir Caleb left while the rest of the men slept.

A short while later, a serving woman knocked on the door. She hung a pot of porridge over the fireplace in exchange for the dirty stew pot.

The men got up and ate. Vrell told them Sir Gavin wanted them packed and ready when he returned. It did not take long.

Kurtz tried to sneak out to the tavern again, which prompted an argument between him and Inko as to why he could not.

"But, Inko. The number five is favored over the number six." Kurtz's determined brow looked sincere, but Vrell knew better. "If I go out, the prince will be safer."

Inko's dark eyes shifted. Was he actually pondering this nonsense?

Kurtz inched toward the door. "Not letting me go could curse us all, eh?"

Achan's lips pursed as if trying to hold in his laughter.

"Do not think I'll be falling for your mocking me." Inko pulled a chair from the table and set it in front of the door. He sat down and quirked an eyebrow at Kurtz.

"Bah!" Kurtz fell onto his bed. "I always said this bunch were duller than a blind dowager, Highness. I urge you to appoint yourself a Kingsguard with a bit more spirit, eh?"

Achan laughed. "I didn't know I'd get to appoint anyone."

Kurtz didn't answer. He stared into space, a look of awe relaxing his scowl.

"As king, you will be needing to be appointing your staff eventually," Inko said.

"I'll be stormed!" Kurtz bounded from the bed. "It's back!"

"What?" Vrell asked.

"Elk bloodvoiced me. It's been so long, I forgot to even try, I did. The âleh must have worn off, eh?"

"You must be bloodvoicing the prince next," Inko said. "I am betting you will be surprised at his strength."

The men practiced bloodvoicing. Vrell, content to watch and not wanting to weaken herself before the ride to Lytton Hall, did not participate.

When Sir Gavin and Sir Caleb returned, Sir Caleb said, "We will leave right away. Lord Livna has agreed to host us."

"We are ready," Vrell said. "I would like to check Sir Gavin's leg first."

Sir Gavin fell into a chair at the table, groaned, and brushed the frost off his beard. "You can check it later. Lytton Hall is but a short ride."

Vrell scowled but had no intention of arguing with Sir Gavin.

Achan held out his sword to Sir Eagan. "I return your sword with gratitude. It has served me well."

Sir Eagan blanched. "Oh, no, Your Highness. I do not have the strength to wield it. Please, use it well."

"But it's yours."

"And what of Ôwr?"

Achan frowned. "Esek has it."

Sir Eagan reached over his shoulder to scratch his back. "Then you must use Rhomphaia until you get Ôwr back."

Achan nodded. "Thank you." He strapped the jeweled belt around his waist. He seemed to stand taller whenever he wore it. "I had forgotten Ôwr should be mine."

"Oh, yes," Sir Eagan said. "Ôwr belongs to the anointed king of Er'Rets." He nudged Achan, approached the table where Sir Gavin sat, and winked at Vrell. "Gavin, you gave the prince my sword?"

Sir Gavin's mustache twitched, curling down at the ends. "You weren't using it."

"Because I was rotting away in an icy prison. What was wrong with *your* sword?"

"Nothing." Sir Gavin patted the weapon on his belt. "Which is why I didn't see reason to give it away."

"And you told him the sword was called *Eagan's Elk*?"

Sir Gavin shrugged. "He asked its name and I couldn't remember. I figured, if all went well, at least your name might be honored, defeating many in the hands of the king."

Sir Eagan cocked one eyebrow at Achan. "That good with a sword, is he?"

Achan shook his head. "No, sir. I'm not."

"But he is," Vrell said. "He killed a dozen Poroo protecting Esek."

Achan groaned. "Sparrow, I told you, Poroo are hardly swordsmen."

"That's like killing a dozen women, eh?" Kurtz yelled from the other room.

Vrell scowled. She could hear Kurtz cackling in the other room. As if women were incapable of protecting themselves. Well . . . most were quite helpless, actually. But not her.

Sir Eagan sobered. "That I might be known for having killed a dozen female Poroo . . ." He bowed deeply to Achan. "You do me great honor, Your Majesty." He bowed to Sir Gavin. "And you, Gavin. Now that I have been given a second chance at life, I shall try to live up to my heroic reputation."

How could Sir Eagan dare mock Achan's bravery? But she glanced at Achan and found him shaking with silent laughter.

PART 4

TRAITORS

30

Lord Livna, a sturdy, red-faced man with white hair and a trim beard, met Achan and his party at the entrance to Lytton Hall and threw an arm around Achan's shoulders.

"You're welcome here, my boy. Very welcome. Glorious news to hear that arrogant vulgarian is not our king. And what a stir out at Ice Island! Never been such an escape in the history of the prison. Over a dozen have come looking to join your cause. Aw, but you must be tired. I declare we shall have the finest celebration tonight. The finest. Keep in mind, now, I've got three nieces who'd each make a handsome queen. Quite so. I'm sure these old schemers have advised you to choose a lady of greater title. You just keep your eyes open and see if one of my nieces doesn't steal your heart, you hear?"

Achan opened his mouth to respond, but Lord Livna said, "Wish I could have offered you Tara, but she recently wed Lord Gershom."

Mention of Lady Tara rekindled Achan's frustration. "I had the pleasure of meeting Lord Gershom this past week."

Lord Livna's blue eyes peered into Achan's, concerned, fearful. "Was she well, do you think?"

Achan grit his teeth. He wanted to say, "As well as a young lady wed to a grandsire could be," but held his tongue. If the man had doubts over his daughter's marriage, he should have entertained them before the ceremony, not after.

Sir Caleb rescued him. "She was very well, my lord. And Master Demry was there, making sure she remains safe."

Lord Livna nodded. "So far out and with her husband's age, I felt better knowing a fighting man was looking after her." His eyes went wide, focused over Achan's shoulder. "Well, quiver my timbers, Eagan? Is that you, my boy?"

"It is, my lord."

Lord Livna greeted Sir Eagan with a hearty embrace. "Eric still claims you swindled him out of Rhomphaia. Where is it now?"

Sir Eagan gestured to Achan. "The prince wears it until he can reclaim Ôwr."

"Aw," Lord Livna beamed, "a more worthy owner I could not supply. Come, let me show you to your room."

Lytton Hall looked to be the dwelling of a champion hunter. The walls were built of logs and sea stone. Antlers and hides were mounted on every wall. Much of the furniture had antler arms or legs. Lord Livna whisked them up a wooden staircase to the fourth floor and a short, wide hallway. Three narrow doors on the right and a set of double doors on the left.

"This whole floor is yours. The double doors lead to the prince's room. He should have a hot bath waiting. You men can decide between you how to use these other rooms, and Eagan can show you to the steams."

Kurtz grabbed Sparrow's chin. "What say you, Pacey? A shave for the minnow? We'll help him grow a beard yet."

Achan grinned. "Perfect."

Sparrow jerked his chin away. "I am *not* shaving."

"But the first one helps the whiskers grow, eh?" Kurtz reached for Sparrow again, but he ducked behind Sir Gavin.

"Leave Vrell be," Sir Gavin said. "He must check my leg. Lord Livna, might it be possible to have a tub brought to my room as well? I wouldn't ask, but my leg is injured."

"Should you like, Gavin, I'll have one brought up."

The men parted ways. Sir Caleb accompanied Achan into his chambers. The room had a simple oak bed covered in gold blankets and a hewn sideboard. A plank changing screen hid a hearth and a deep, wooden bathtub.

Achan bathed, scrubbing the flea bites on his legs and arms until his skin stung. The scratchy sponge eased the itch.

Sir Caleb had set out the outfit Lord Eli had made in Mirrorstone. Achan put on the blue tunic, black doublet, and black trousers, grumbling over the ridiculously long embroidered sleeves and the silver garters on the trousers.

Though he loathed to admit it, he said, "I need help, Sir Caleb." He came out from behind the changing screen to find Sir Caleb asleep on the bed. Achan fiddled with the ties at the neck of the tunic and the garters, but couldn't manage to work Sir Caleb's magic, especially with such long sleeves in his way.

The door to his room cracked open, revealing Inko's face. He slipped inside and closed the door. "I am coming from having been watching the sparrow."

Achan knotted his left garter. "Go on, then."

"Sir Gavin was taking the boy into his bedchamber. They were being in there a moment then Sir Gavin was coming right back out and was standing."

Achan looked up from his absurd garters. "Doing what?"

"He was just standing like a guard." Inko withdrew a handkerchief from his pocket and mopped his brow. "Your Highness, you might be asking Lord Livna to be moving you to the third or fifth floors. Four is not the most favored num—"

Achan held up a hand. "Why do you suppose Sir Gavin stood outside the door?"

"I am not being able to guess, but when the door was opening again, the *bird* was flying out with wet hair."

Wet hair? Achan patted the man's shoulder. "Thank you, Inko. You're an amazing shadow informer. Keep it up."

Inko pointed at Achan's knees. "Are you wanting help to be tying those for you?"

Achan sighed and released the silver ties. "Please."

Inko crouched down, untied Achan's knot, and started over, looping the long strips of fabric into a tight bow. "So what are you thinking Vrell was doing?"

Achan scratched his temple. "Bathing, I suppose."

Inko stood and started in on the ties on Achan's shirt. "But why not be going to the steams like the rest of us?"

Achan didn't know. "Perhaps Sir Gavin wanted him dressed to match me?" But an hour later, that proved false. Achan sat on the edge of his bed while the rest of his party stood in his chamber, Sparrow wearing a black tunic with a grey linen vest.

Achan voiced his concerns aloud. "Why doesn't Sparrow wear his blue satin?"

"Because Vrell would rather be a healer than a squire." Sir Caleb said. "In a week or so, you'll have Shung as your Shield. You won't need a squire until we go to war. By then, I'm sure we'll find you another. Perhaps in Carmine."

Achan's stomach felt like it had been kicked. He frowned at Sparrow. "You don't want to be my squire?"

Sparrow's cheeks flushed. "I am excellent with herbs and healing, but Arman has not called me to such violence."

"But you just need—"

"We *need* men called to both," Sir Caleb said. "I'm glad you know your heart, Vrell."

Sparrow smiled until he met Achan's eyes. Then he focused on his hands in his lap.

How could this be? Sparrow was deserting him?

"Don't feel obligated to dance tonight, Your Highness," Sir Caleb said. "We're here to recruit men, not inappropriate love interests, of which there will be plenty."

"I disagree," Sir Eagan said. "He must dance with every lady, for most have fathers who'll be pleased to see him pay their daughters mind and will support him because of it."

Sir Caleb sighed. "I suppose. But take care not to pay more attention to any one girl, Your Highness."

Achan's stomach flipped. No pressure there. "Wouldn't it be safer to skip the formality of a banquet and keep moving? I mean, since Esek is nearby, won't he come looking here?"

"We have voiced the same concern," Sir Gavin said. "But Lord Livna refuses to hear us. Tomorrow we'll meet with him and the captain of his guard to discuss when the army will assemble and depart for Carmine."

A tingling haze clouded Achan's mind as if this were all a dream. He could scarcely imagine that in two days' time, he'd lead a host of soldiers south with the intent of starting a war.

That evening, the guard stopped them before they could enter the great hall. "Wait to be announced."

To Achan's utter horror, a trumpet sounded and a herald cried out at the top of his lungs, "Make way for Prince Gidon Hadar and his royal Kingsguardsmen!"

The guard nodded and stepped aside.

Applause burst forth, bringing a chill over Achan's arms. "Gee, I wonder where that Achan fellow might be? No one will ever find him with *that* introduction."

Keep the sarcasm in your head, Your Highness, Sir Caleb said.

Achan took a deep breath and entered. The great hall stretched out before him, long and narrow built of rough hewn logs. A three-tier chandelier made of deer antlers and lit with dozens of stubby white candles hung in the center of the hammer beam roof. Flags bearing Tsaftown's gold and black crest hung from every other beam.

Achan stood on the center of a narrow platform that stretched the width of the hall. A half-dozen steps descended from it. A golden runner covered the floor under his boots, spilled down the center of the stairs, and ran all the way to the dais platform. A black and gold checkered cloth covered the high table that was only half occupied. A dagfish carved from wood was mounted in the center of the wall behind the high table. Antlers were mounted on either side of the dagfish.

Tables stretching the length of the hall were packed with food and people dressed in expensive, courtly attire, who all stood staring. The applause died down.

Sir Caleb's finger in Achan's back sent him walking forward, dream-like, down the stairs and up the center aisle. He briefly opened his mind and sensed overwhelming excitement and support. He also sensed a hint of deceit. He stopped where the golden rug split around the length of the dais and ran up a small stairs at each end of the platform.

An unpleasant feeling grew in the pit of Achan's stomach. He scanned the hall, seeking for the source of the deceit. *Be ready*, Achan said to Sir Gavin. *I sense some trickery.*

From Lord Livna?

Achan bowed to Lord Livna, who stood behind his seat at the high table, and concentrated on the man's thoughts.

My, he looks like his father. Praise Arman, we'll be spared. Spared!

No, Achan said to Sir Gavin. *Despite having sacrificed his daughter to a lunatic, Lord Livna is true.*

Keep your grudge to yourself, Your Highness, Sir Caleb said. *We need this man. His people are housing your army right now.*

Lord Livna spoke. "I, and all of Tsaftown, wish to extend our support to you, my prince, in all matters you may require. It is our fervent wish for you to occupy your father's throne without delay. I pledge my soldiers to aid you in this effort. I welcome you and swear to serve you in any way I can."

Achan bowed and quickly thought up a flowery reply. "You honor me with your loyalty to my father's throne."

"Come, sit beside me and be blessed."

Achan ascended the platform and sat beside Lord Livna, with Sir Gavin to his left, then Sir Caleb, Sir Eagan, and Inko.

To Lord Livna's right sat his wife, Lady Revada; his son, Sir Eric; Sir Eric's wife, Lady Viola; and Captain Demry.

A line formed along the wall and up the right side of the dais. A valet stood at Achan's elbow and announced each person or group as they approached. Sir Caleb offered the occasional, private commentary.

Lord Livna and Lady Revada gave Achan a gilded helm and breastplate, etched and embossed with chams and vines.

"One can never have enough armor," Lord Livna said.

Especially armor that once belonged to Moul Rog the Great, Sir Caleb said. *His bust is in Mahanaim's hall of greats.*

Sir Eric Livna and his wife, Lady Viola, presented Achan with a long hooded hauberk of fine chain. "And my service. I'll ride with you when you depart."

"Captain Roxburg Demry; his wife, Madam Demry; and their daughter, Meneya."

Achan found Captain Demry's muscular build and dark eyes familiar. "I'm honored to pledge my Fighting Fifteen."

Who are excellent fighting men, Sir Caleb added, *but have the tendency to drink themselves into hibernation. We met Captain Demry's little brother, Carmack, in Tsaftown, who used to be among the Fifteen. Apparently, he's been replaced.*

Achan took in the strapping dark-haired man, recalled Carmack's grip on his throat, and was thankful the Demrys couldn't bloodvoice. What might Carmack have told his brother of Achan's blunder with Lady Tara?

"And this dagger." Meneya held out a black leather sheath with a carved ivory handle that resembled a leaping cham.

"My brother is a smith," Madam Demry said. "We thought this would fit you."

Achan gripped the handle and pulled the gleaming blade from the sheath. It was two hands long with a single raised rib that stretched along the double-edged blade to a sharp point.

His own knife, not on loan like Eagan's Elk. "Thank you."

The valet's voice sent the Demrys on their way. "Lady Merris, mother to Lord Livna."

And mother to Lord Gershom, the instigator of Lady Tara's unfortunate union.

The old woman cracked a wrinkled smile and curtsied. "I have several unwed granddaughters who would make suitable queens. I give you my blessing for any of them."

Can I tell her I'd chosen the one granddaughter she's forsaken?

Best to hold your tongue, Your Highness.

So Achan forced a smile. "I'm honored, Madam."

"Captain Freddel Wenk, his wife, Lady Wenk, his son Derby, and his daughters Julianna and Moriah." Captain Wenk offered his service, then hurried his daughters along as if he feared Achan might ruin them as Esek was known to do.

Achan received gifts of horses, food, ale, clothing, tents, and armor for his men.

"Master Webb Ricks and his son Matthias."

The man bowed. "I'm the local netmaker. My eldest son'll replace me someday. I've two other sons, five daughters, and little Matthias, here. He's a good boy, but took a bad frost to his hands. He can use 'em fine, just not for tying knots. I can barely feed my family, let alone pay for Matthias to apprentice in another trade. I'd like to give him to you, Your Highness."

Nine children. The dirty-faced tot was no more than seven. He had a thatch of blond hair over big brown eyes. Achan swallowed hard. "Y-You're giving me your son?"

Master Ricks plowed on, as if his very life hinged on Achan taking his son. "He's a bright lad, honest to a fault and quick. He'd make a good page or valet. Learns fast, he does."

Sir Caleb turned to Achan. *What do you say, Your Majesty?*

I cannot take this man's son. I'll not keep slaves.

He doesn't offer you a slave but an employee. He sacrifices his son to give the boy a bright future in the king's household.

Little Matthias blinked, his eyes wide and fearful.

You think we should take him with us?

Only if you'll be willing to let the lad learn to dress you.

Achan set his jaw. *Perhaps he can become my advisor when I demote you to jester.*

Perhaps. "Deliver the boy to Carmine within the month and we'll give him a position in His Majesty's household."

Master Ricks' eyes filled with tears. "Oh, thank you, Your Highness, thank you kindly!"

Achan watched the small boy walk away with Master Ricks as the valet announced, "Master Polk Mafellen."

A tanned man with cropped blond hair and round brown eyes knelt before Achan, reminding him of a baby chick. "I squired for the false prince 'til he fired me for winning a match with swords. I'm a strong swordsman, I can't help it, so you're getting a good man in me, Your Highness."

Achan could relate to Esek's cruelty, but Polk's pride ruffled him. "I thank you, Polk, and welcome your service."

Two familiar faces from Ice Island—Master Matar Bazmark and Master Brien Gebfly—pledged Achan their service.

Then Lord Livna's voice pulled his attention away. "The servants will take the personal gifts to your chambers, Your Highness. Let's have some dancing!"

Vrell watched from the end of the lowest table, with a critical eye, thankful this was formal, proper dancing, not that brazen groping Kurtz had forced her to witness in the tavern. Kurtz stood across the room, hovering over poor Julianna Wenk. He was supposed to be watching the entrance with Vrell, not sniffing around for a dance partner. He should take care. Julianna's father did not take kindly to men who spoke to his daughters without his permission.

Achan had danced with the highest ranking, married ladies first, who gave him opportunity to learn the steps before he had to dance with Grandmother Merris, a conniving old woman whom Vrell had never been fond of, despite their blood relationship. Now, the young women formed a line to bask in their moment of attention from the Crown Prince. Vrell recognized many of the commoners: Meneya, Julianna and Moriah, Christola, and Bettly.

But now Achan danced with Lady Lathia, Uncle Chantry's youngest girl of seventeen. Vrell trusted Cousin Lathia with Achan as much as she had trusted Beska, the serving wench.

Vrell forced her gaze away from Cousin Lathia to where her aunt and uncle danced. She had never been close to her uncle. Lord Livna was a man's man with little time for female relatives, Tara's unfortunate union a prime example. But Vrell adored Aunt Revada. She longed to confide the truth to her, and to ask about Tara's wedding, to get it from her aunt how such a thing had come to pass. Aunt Revada could not have given up Tara easily, Vrell knew that much.

She sighed. How strange to be in Lytton Hall and not be dancing, for there was little else to do in this place. She had visited countless times throughout her childhood, Tara and Lathia dragging her around by the arm to point out which new soldier they thought was most handsome.

Those days were gone to the Veil now.

For Achan, the dancing proved more difficult than in Berland. Everyone moved together in coordinated steps, exposing every slow and disoriented move Achan made. He walked about, pranced in circles, and at one point, had to grab the waist of his partner, lift her up, turn, and set her down on his other side.

He stumbled about with several forgiving ladies. Lady Revada. Lady Viola. Both safely married. Then came the unmarried girls, who showered him with flattery and smiles. He favored the shorter ones, for towering over them made him feel older, and the fact that he could lift them like feathers made him feel strong. Achan kept his eyes peeled for Sir Caleb, hoping he didn't accidentally cross the fine line between being cordial and giving false hope.

Finally the food came. Achan took his seat. The servants filed onto the dais holding jugs of drink and platters of rich-smelling food. Achan's stomach growled. He ate heartily, chatting with Lord Livna.

A young serving boy refilled Achan's plate when he ate all his fish and fricassés, then took his goblet away to refresh it.

Achan scanned the hall. He couldn't see Sparrow, but found the boy's mind easily. *Are you certain you don't want that job? Clearing my dishes.*

Quite.

Achan didn't want to admit how much it bothered him that Sparrow had deserted him. *But it's mostly standing around.*

Today. But tomorrow I might have to fight a battle to the death with daggers. I am sorry, Your Highness, but it is not for me.

Sir Eagan crouched behind Sir Caleb's chair. "It does not look good for the prince's servant to be sneaking gulps of wine when he is supposed to be filling his cup."

Achan looked over Sir Eagan's shoulder to see his serving boy crouched in the corner of the dais, gulping from his goblet.

Achan rolled his eyes. What in flames was the lad thinking? Achan would have been flogged for such a thing.

"Unbelievable!" Sir Caleb said. "Send him away, Eagan. I'll serve the prince myself."

"Patience, Caleb. I'll talk to him." Sir Eagan walked away.

Sir Caleb sighed. "Carmine, Your Majesty. I am certain we can find you a worthy page and squire in—"

Lady Revada cried out, "Oh! The boy! Help him!"

Lord Livna's wife gaped at a spot behind Achan with a panicked expression. He whipped his head around to see his serving boy lying on the floor, eyes glazed, Sir Eagan crouching at his side.

Achan dove from his chair and seized the boy's arm. "Boy! What's wrong?"

The boy's eyes flickered to Achan's.

Sir Eagan asked a white-haired serving man. "Was it the wine?"

Achan stared up at the servant, who nodded, clearly horrified at the implication in Achan's expression.

"I-I . . . only poured . . . th-this." He held out a large clay jug.

Sir Eagan snatched it and smelled the opening. Frowning, he sniffed again and set it on the floor. He shot the servant a dark look. "Don't touch that." He scrambled on his hands and knees along the dais, just above the steps, and grabbed the goblet that had rolled against the wall.

Achan lifted the boy's head into his lap. *Sparrow! My serving boy has fallen. What can I do? He's not moving.*

Has he a heartbeat?

Achan lowered his cheek to the boy's lips. *He's breathing.*

What did he eat? Sparrow asked.

He drank my wine. Help him.

The boy's body trembled, then shook violently. With the exception of the people staring on the dais, chatter filled the rest of the hall, the other guests oblivious to what was happening on the floor behind the head table.

Achan clutched the boy's shaking head. *Sparrow!*

At last, Sparrow slid between two guests and knelt at Achan's side. He set a hand to the boy's pallid face and leaned forward to look in his eyes.

Sir Eagan, now standing at Achan's side, handed him the goblet. "Look."

Achan accepted the cup. A soggy clump of olive green leaves clung to the bottom curve, leaking a froth of watery white slime, like wet sugar. Achan's breathing slowed. Poison?

Sir Eagan's voice drifted down, confirming Achan's fears. "A pellet containing poison. Someone must have put it in—"

"Cranberry verbarium!" A man shouted from afar.

"The pass code!" Lord Livna pulled out his chair. "An attack, my prince! You must escape."

Achan looked up, dazed, still clutching the cup. Escape?

Sir Eric fell to his knees and pushed back the edge of the gold carpet. He lifted a trapdoor, slid the wood cover onto the floor under Achan's chair, and jumped down into the hole.

He motioned Achan to follow. "You must hurry. Our guard has been compromised. This will lead you out."

Achan pushed the boy's rigid body toward Sir Eric, who pulled the boy down, feet first. Achan went next. Then Sparrow, Sir Gavin, Sir Caleb, Inko, and Sir Eagan.

The trapdoor closed, extinguishing all light but what filtered through the lattice wall of the dais. Achan crouched in the cavity under the platform, squeezing the goblet.

Someone had tried to kill him.

Chairs shifted above. Murmurs hummed beyond the lattice wall. A party oblivious to the attempted murder.

"Your Highness?" Sir Eric squatted in the back corner, his face shadowed. "The door out is here, come."

"But the boy." Achan knelt beside him, slapped his cheek lightly, whispered, "Boy, come back to us."

"Where's Kurtz?" Sir Gavin asked.

"He was sitting near the entrance with me," Sparrow said.

"He is still there," Sir Eagan said. "He tells me a squadron of New Kingsguard soldiers approaches the door."

Esek!

Achan dropped the cup and crawled before the holes in the lattice. He peered out into the great hall. Sir Eric knelt at Achan's side. Silence had fallen on the great hall. A pattering of distant boot steps on hard wood the only sound.

A crowd of men in black cloaks spilled onto the entry platform. A flash of red and a figure pushed to the front. Esek Nathak, wearing a red wool doublet, clumped down the steps and strode up the aisle, his black, knee-high boots seemingly filled with lead. Sir Kenton followed behind.

"Lord Livna. I have no time for niceties. Where are you keeping the stray?"

Footsteps clicked over the dais above, down the steps on the right, and Lord Livna passed before the lattice and met Esek halfway down the aisle.

Lord Livna blocked Achan's view of Esek and Sir Kenton. "You enter my home, uninvited, kill my guards, and interrupt a private gathering. Do not make demands of me."

Esek's voice sneered. "Am I king, old man? I answer to no one. Tell me what you have done with Achan Cham and his ancient knights, and I might let you live."

"You are king of nothing. Best take your pompous self out of here before you and your men end up in my dungeon."

A scrape of steel on wood, a flash of light, and a blade's point protruded from Lord Livna's back.

Women screamed. Men bolted to their feet. Guards along the wall drew their swords, only to have Esek's Kingsguards draw against them. No one struck. No one seemed to know what to do next.

Beside Achan, Sir Eric let out a small groan.

Esek jerked Ôwr free and Lord Livna slumped to the floor. Esek held the sword out to his side, the white steel blade streaked red. "Who is next in line to rule this shabby manor?"

A chair scraped back on the dais above. "My son, Sir Eric, is next in line," Lady Livna said in a commanding voice.

"And where is he?"

Sir Eric's arm trembled against Achan's, but Achan couldn't tear his eyes away from Ôwr's bloody blade. Esek still held it out to the side, a gruesome reminder of his power.

Lady Livna's answer brought Achan back to reality. "He is escorting our guests to Berland, Your Majesty."

Berland? She was attempting to throw Esek off his trail. Achan didn't deserve such devotion.

"Berland," Esek said. "Why there?"

Lady Livna's voice rang smooth and calm in spite of her husband's body, lying between her and Esek. "I do not know, but I overheard my husband and son talking of Lord Orson's invitation to host a celebration. It is my understanding that men intend to duel for rank in . . . Gidon Hadar's army."

Esek shifted his posture from one foot to the other, his face tinged pink. "There is no Gidon Hadar! The stray deceives you." He waved Ôwr's blood-streaked blade at the crowd. "Consider well what an alliance with such a man will get you." He kicked Lord Livna's body and spun around. "Chora!"

From the mob of Esek's guards on the entry platform, a voice called, "Let me pass. The king needs me."

Esek's men parted. Chora, Esek's valet, scurried down the steps, brown robes billowing. He swept beside Esek and took the bloody sword. As Chora wiped Ôwr clean with a handkerchief, Esek and Sir Kenton whispered to one another in the center of the great hall. Esek scanned the crowd. Did he think Achan would simply be cowering behind some woman?

Not that hiding under the dais was any braver. Achan wanted to go out and fight Esek, but he didn't dare make things worse for the Livna family. He would wait for Sir Eric's lead.

Esek strode from the room, Chora and Sir Kenton trailing behind. When he passed through the doorway, Sir Eric moved away from the lattice and croaked, "This way."

They crawled through a hole in the back wall. Achan paused to help Sparrow with the boy's body. Sir Eric pushed open a second door; a sliver of yellow light lit his face as he crawled out. Achan wriggled on his side, pulling the serving boy's body to the second door with Sparrow and Sir Eagan's help. Sir Eric reached through the door, grabbed the limp boy under the arms, and pulled him through.

Achan emerged from the bottom cupboard of a sideboard and onto a wool rug behind the desk in Lord Livna's study. He looked up to the shelves crammed with scrolls and books that filled two walls, the cold fireplace in the corner. He stood to see Sir Eric across the room, sliding a board into slats to bar the door. The boy lay on the floor in front of the desk, eyes open, lips parted. Achan closed his eyes and stepped back against the cold hearth so the desk obscured the still body.

The boy had saved his life. Died in his place.

The sideboard door slammed and Achan jumped. Sparrow climbed out, followed by Sir Eagan, Sir Gavin, Sir Caleb, and finally Inko.

"Any word from Kurtz?" Sir Gavin asked.

"He's says Esek and his men are mounting up in the bailey," Sir Eagan said. "He'll shadow, see where they go."

Achan caught sight of himself in a mirrorglass above the hearth. A closer look proved it wasn't a mirrorglass but a painting of a man in a gilded frame. The man, possibly in his thirties, had a walnut complexion, a square jaw, and stared back with sapphire eyes. Glossy, black, shoulder-length hair hung in neat ringlets beside his short black beard. A golden crown studded with rubies and emeralds sat on his head.

Achan recalled the Ice Island guard's mention of the painting in Lytton Hall. This was King Axel, Achan's father. He stood staring, unable to look away. An odd ache stabbed through the pressure already pushing on his stomach.

A hand on his shoulder sucked the pain and pressure away. He looked over to Sir Eagan's raised brows. "Every manor in Er'Rets was given such a painting after his coronation."

Little doubt as to why Sitna Manor had never displayed their painting where anyone could see it. "He looks older than I expected."

"Few kings are crowned as young as you. He was thirty-five at his coronation. Fifty-eight when you were born."

"So old?"

Sir Eagan smirked. "Even in Ice Island, I heard songs of King Axel's long-awaited son."

Achan tore himself away from his father's confident expression. He had not thought to connect the rhymes of bards to his own past. Perhaps Sir Caleb should teach him of his father's reign next.

Sir Eric slid down against the barred door. "We should stay until . . . Mother will come . . ." He put his head in his hands and his body shook with silent sobs.

Sir Eagan crouched beside the serving boy and sniffed. "Devil's porridge." He closed the boy's eyes and sat back on his haunches.

"What's that?" Achan asked.

"Hemlock." Sparrow looked over Sir Eagan's shoulder, tears pooling in his eyes. "It is very potent."

Achan squeezed his hands into fists and paced back a step, wishing he could draw Eagan's Elk and hack away at Lord Livna's desk. A glance at Sir Eric stilled him and he voiced his original question aloud. "How could this have happened? Whoever put the poison in likely got away."

"It couldn't have been the chief servant, Your Highness." Sir Eric's voice cracked but grew stronger. "Arne has been with my family for years. It doesn't make sense."

"The jug did not smell of hemlock," Sir Eagan said. "But there was a pellet in the prince's goblet. How much of your wine did you drink, Your Highness?"

Achan's jaw dropped. "Uh, I . . . Half a . . . not quite half. Then the food came."

"It had not dissolved enough to affect you, but by the time the boy took it to refill . . ." Sir Eagan heaved to his feet. "Someone dropped it in your goblet. Maybe during the gifts?"

"It should've been me," Achan said. "Someone was trying to kill me. The boy was a fool to drink from my cup."

"My guards did not permit just anyone into the great hall tonight," Sir Eric said. "Until . . ."

"But who could be vouching for all the servants?" Inko asked.

"My wife could, I expect. At least the servants who were stationed on the dais." Sir Eric frowned. "I'll question them all. Haddie too. She's our cook. My real concern is that this man might join your army. Continue to travel with you. Try again."

Achan lay awake that night overwhelmed by the evening's festivities. He wanted to help, to at least speak to Lady Livna—to offer his condolences. But the knights had locked him away in his chamber. If he was to be king, shouldn't he be able to make some decisions? Shouldn't he be able to tell the knights what to do? At least make suggestions?

Being cooped up in his chamber left him no viable task but to shadow the minds of the knights who weren't guarding the outside of his door. Sir Gavin and Sir Caleb met with Captain Demry to talk circles around the poisoning. Sir Eagan met with Sir Eric and Lady Livna, as he apparently spent much of his youth living here and was as grieved over Lord Livna's death as they were. Sparrow lay in bed, weeping over who knew what.

Achan had never considered how much people would sacrifice for their king. Treasures, merchandise, service, their own children.

All for a man locked in his chamber with no power whatsoever.

31

The next morning, the knights, Sir Eric, and Captain Demry came to Achan's chambers. Achan sat against the headboard on his bed, legs outstretched, ankles crossed. He wanted to take part in this discussion, to add something significant, but what would he say? He didn't know what they should do next.

Kurtz had returned from shadowing Esek's men and gave his report. "Esek and his soldiers—around ninety—exited the Tsaftown gates and rode for Berland."

"Roxburg, and as many men as I can spare, will join you on your journey," Sir Eric said. "I must stay to console my mother and rule Tsaftown until my brother returns from sea. Then I will join you."

Achan piped up before anyone else could. "We thank your mother for her diversion. How does she fare?"

"She is in seclusion. I will pass on your concern," Sir Eric said, as if he couldn't be bothered with any more emotion. "I know you plan to visit Carmine next, but it is unwise to set out until scouts check the way. Since you should not linger here, either, I suggest taking the hunting trail over the mountain to Mitspah. Send scouts on the dark and light roads to report what they see. By that time, if any of Esek's men block the road to Carmine, you could ask Duchess Amal to send aid."

"The pass will slow us down greatly," Sir Gavin said.

"Why not be sending scouts into Light now?" Inko asked. "If it's being safe, that direction is being quickest. The duchess could still be sending aid if we were to be needing it."

Sir Eric shook his head. "Lingering keeps your men open to attack. What's left of the Ice Island guard is searching for prisoners and traitors. The refugees are being housed all over the city. All are at risk until we can get you on your way."

People were in danger, hiding Achan's army in their homes. How many others had lost their lives for Achan's sake? Lord Livna. The serving boy. Achan's stomach lurched, queasy. He clenched his fists, willing away the soft emotions. They would do him no good.

Months ago Achan would have given anything to change his station. But king? He'd never dreamed of such a calling. It was too much. He missed his old life. Sleeping under the ale casks. Milking the goats. Chatting with Noam at the Corner. Sitting with Gren under the allown tree by the river.

Gren would know how to comfort him. But these men? Not one tear shed for that serving boy. Though he knew he shouldn't, Achan looked in on Gren.

—*trying to put it through the strainer and into the jar, but it spilled. It took me hours to clean up.* Gren stood looking at a table covered with jars of pickled apples. She reached behind her back and worked at the knot on her apron.

Smells good, though, Bran said.

Gren's heart raced. *You're just being kind.*

No, I love pickled apples, especially over lamb chops.

Gren fought the knot a second more, then stomped her foot. She turned her back to Bran, her skirt twirling around her legs. *Help me untie this? My fingers are all prunes, and the knot is too tight.* Bran's fingers tugged at the ties. *I'm glad you came to visit.*

Bran didn't answer right away. *I'm glad you're liking the kitchens. It's safer in here, I think, with all the women.* The apron loosened. Bran's hands fell away. *There you are.*

Thank you. She folded the apron and peered into the kitchen. Jespa, the cook, engrossed in trimming the pastry off the edges of a pie, paid them no mind.

Bran watched Gren with a crooked smile.

Her stomach zinged to her heart. *What?*

Nothing. He looked toward the stairwell. *I should go. I need to get back to my post.*

Gren blinked repeatedly, not wanting to cry. This had been the first time Master Rennan had come to visit in days. What could she do to make him stay longer? She brushed her finger against the side of his hand. He snagged her hand in his and released it just as quickly, but at least his eyes were locked with hers again. She inched closer, gazing into his brown eyes, willing him to care. He leaned forward, ever so slowly.

Achan jumped through Gren into Bran's mind and found himself aching to kiss Gren. *No,* he said to Bran, alarmed at the course this friendship had taken. *Don't you dare.*

Bran's chest swelled with a deep breath and he stepped back. *I'll try and come again tomorrow. Good-bye.* He took two steps back, then darted up the servants' stairs.

Achan concentrated on Gren and returned to her head.

Good-bye, she mumbled, sticking out her bottom lip. Surely Master Rennan cared more than he let on. She went back to her jars of pickled apples, started adding lids, but by the time she got to the third jar, she was crying.

Achan withdrew, but kept his eyes closed, struggling over what he'd seen. Clearly, Gren and Bran fancied each other. A pang of loneliness dug into his gut like a chisel. Any hope he harbored at reconciling with Gren was hopeless now. He pictured himself sitting on a throne, haggard, staring at his wife, a woman who despised him, who'd never wanted to marry him. Their children hid behind her skirt, afraid of the man Mother despised.

He coughed, choking on the rush of saliva in his throat. Darkness had a way of attacking whenever he pitied himself. He took a deep breath and steeled himself. He had lost Gren long ago. No need to relive it.

Still, he worried. Bran shouldn't spend time with Gren when he was betrothed to another. Sir Caleb had spoken true. Gren's heart had attached to Bran because Bran hadn't guarded his actions toward her. It wasn't fair to either lady.

Achan hoped they got to Carmine soon. He'd like to have a word with Bran Rennan.

Betrayal fresh on his mind, an idea seized him. If a traitor existed amongst his newly formed army, he needed to find the man before anyone else lost their life. He could do this for himself, for his men, and for all Er'Rets. And he wouldn't stop until he succeeded.

• • •

Yet another myth come reality, Achan sat atop a massive white festrier, looking over the tops of every head around him. His new army—over three hundred, Sir Caleb had said—gathered in the courtyard outside Lytton Hall, preparing to depart.

The icy air smelled of pitch and dung. Lamp stands threw light and shadows over the mob of men and horses. The din of voices kept Achan on edge. Three hundred had not sounded like a large army, but now that he saw them he felt small perched above this crowd.

Scout, loaded down with gear, had been tethered behind Achan's new warhorse, Dove, a gift from Sir Eric. Whether or not Scout was bothered by his demotion to pack horse, guilt kept Achan talking to the animal. *It would have been rude to say no, Scout. I can't imagine riding this beast all the time. You and I will still ride.*

Dove heaved a sigh beneath Achan, as if he perceived the kinship between Achan and Scout and was exasperated by it. The movement rocked Achan in the saddle. He gripped the saddlehorn with his gloved hand and tried not to think about how it would feel if the animal took off running. The width of the beast's back stretched Achan's legs wider than he was used to. He felt like a child, boots dangling a league above the snowy ground. He hoped he'd be able to control the beast.

"Don't let his size fool you." Sir Eric patted Dove's neck. "He's as gentle as his name. A gift from Lord Dromos after Father took him on a fishing expedition."

Sir Eric's generosity and endurance amazed Achan. Sorrow sagged the man's expression and posture, bled into Achan's senses, yet Sir Eric plunged ahead with wisdom and energy.

"Are you certain you can spare so many men? What if Esek should return?"

"Only sixty-five of my soldiers have joined you. The rest of these men are from Ice Island, be they former Kingsguards, former prison guards, or former prisoners. Does that concern you?"

"Not at all." Except that one of them was probably a traitor. Achan studied the motley recruits.

Captain Demry's men wore fur capes over gold and black armor and carried round shields emblazoned with dagfish, like the one Achan had used in the tournament last spring. The other men wore fur capes over peasant clothes. No one would suspect Brien Gebfly—the thief who'd used Achan's knife to spring the lock in the Pit—had been a prisoner. Even his scraggly beard blended in well.

"Thank you for dressing the men, I suspect that was you?"

Sir Eric nodded. "Most pardons come with clothing. You know, to the men who've accepted your offer, you've given them more than freedom. You've given them a purpose to live for. That makes a man stand tall. They respect you already. I see why Arman chose you to lead Er'Rets."

Achan flushed at the compliment. He'd come for the Kingsguard prisoners to form his army, but he hadn't freed the other prisoners with any forethought. It had all happened so quickly. And the prisoners could just as easily have killed him for his boots and knife than decide to sign on.

Polk stopped beside Dove and glanced up with his round, brown eyes. "I'm a good horseman, Your Highness. Should you need help caring for that animal, my father was a breeder."

The words were kind enough, but Achan sensed dishonesty in Polk, as if he were making the whole thing up to impress him. "Thank you, Polk. I shall keep that in mind."

The cavalry set off south toward Mitspah by way of Sir Eric's suggested hunting trail, though the men hadn't been told their destination in case a bloodvoice traitor was among them.

Achan blinked to keep his eyelashes from freezing, though he may as well keep his eyes closed for all he could see, despite the half dozen torches spaced along the line. Sir Gavin led the procession with Sir Eagan and Captain Demry. Each horse was tethered to the one before it. Achan, Dove, and Scout were in the middle of the procession with Sir Caleb and Kurtz before him and Inko and Sparrow on their mounts behind him.

The wind howled and pressed against Achan's back, reaching through his furs and skin to shake his bones. He knew not how long they journeyed before the procession stopped and dozens more torches flamed to life.

The soldiers cleared away a spot in the snow and erected Achan's tent first, a brown, double-pole pavilion made from yaks' wool. Achan tried to help, but the men wouldn't allow it.

Achan presented his concerns to Sir Caleb in his mind, where no one would overhear. *I'm very capable of helping. I don't want to be treated like Esek.*

But you're not simply one of the men, either, Your Highness. You're their future king, crowned or not. They want to serve you. They need to. It's their way of serving Arman.

I'm not a god.

No, but you're His emissary, His flesh on earth, so to speak. When you show the men approval, they'll soar, and when you scold them, they'll feel Arman's judgment. This is why you cannot act like a mere man. You must hold yourself to a higher standard. You must sacrifice your own wants and comforts to fill this role.

And since my comfort is to work, I must sacrifice that by sitting on my backside?

Exactly. And if you praise your men for their efforts they'll never tire of serving you.

Achan sighed and rubbed his gloved fingers against his temple. *There must be something I can do?*

Practice your reading and writing?

Achan groaned. In Tsaftown, Sir Caleb had given him ink, parchment, and a copy of a history text with the intent of furthering Achan's reading skills and teaching him to write.

Achan removed the saddlebag from Dove and carried it into his tent, thanking the men who'd erected it as he entered. Unfortunately, Polk had been one of them.

"I've set up tents before, Your Highness, all by myself. None were more complex that the fake prince's pavilion."

Achan forced a smile and entered his tent. The air inside smelled like a wet dog. A small campfire burned in an iron brazier directly under a hole in the center of the roof between the two peaks, filling the center room with light. Above his head, spokes fanned out from each pole like two, oversized wagon wheels on their sides. On the right, two brown, linen curtains hung from spokes, sectioning off a private room.

Sir Caleb followed him in. "Not a bad home, is it? This end room is for you. Us knights will sleep out here. Go in and relax. Kurtz and Bazmark are standing guard outside your walls, so you needn't fear anyone slipping under the edge."

Achan ducked between the curtains. Straw mats had been layered over a bed of frozen moss and twigs, Achan's bedroll arranged on top. An oil lamp atop a chunk of firewood at the foot of his bed cast dancing light over the walls and spokes.

Achan pulled off his gloves and sat on his bed. He removed the parchment and quill from his saddlebag. Even with the slight warmth from the fire, his fingers were too cold to pinch the quill. The ink was probably frozen too. He set the writing tools aside and leafed through the book.

The letters jumbled together. His mind drifted. One of his men had betrayed him. Could there be others? Working together? Or perhaps each with their own agenda? Maybe Achan could use bloodvoicing to monitor each man's thoughts and discover who'd tried to poison him.

But what about gifted men? They would guess their destination soon enough and could communicate the information to Esek—or someone else. Hadad, maybe? The person—was it a demon? a shadow mage?—who had visited him in the pit in Barth, what was his agenda? He had wanted Achan to join him, but to what end? Would Achan's death get Hadad the same goal, whatever that might be?

Supposedly, Achan was stronger than any other bloodvoicer, yet he didn't yet know how to push past a man's shields and enter his mind. What, then, was the best way to discover who could bloodvoice without having to probe every mind in camp?

Achan reached out to Sir Gavin. *Is there a way I can tell which of our men can bloodvoice without having to look into each mind?*

Sir Gavin took a moment to reply. *It's difficult. We talked about a novice giving off a chill. A skilled bloodvoicer can focus in on that cold, but it takes practice, and you'd be leaving your body, which I'd rather you not try until we've had a chance to teach you more. Sir Eagan would be the best man for the task. I never did much reconnaissance.*

Achan's first instinct was to beg Sir Gavin to help him anyway, wanting assistance from someone he knew well, but speaking with Sir Eagan would help him get to know the man.

Sir Eagan, could you come to my tent when you have a moment? Please?

Achan scratched the back of his neck. The fleas were still with him. The stinky wool tent wouldn't help matters, apparently, neither would the cold.

A gust of icy air rustled the pages of the book. "Yes, Your Majesty?" Sir Eagan stood between the curtains.

Achan stopped scratching. "Come in and sit down."

Sir Eagan stepped out of view and returned with a tied bedroll. He dropped it beside the curtain and used it as a chair. His blue eyes pierced Achan's shield of comfort.

"Sir Gavin tells me you're the man to ask for help," Achan said. "I'd like to determine which of the new men possess the ability to bloodvoice. Sir Gavin says you can teach me how to leave my mind and focus in on those with the gift."

"You are wise to want to know who has the ability, but what you ask is a difficult task."

"Can you teach me?"

Sir Eagan pressed his lips together. "I can, but there is an easier way. A combination of logic and bookkeeping."

"Not a new bloodvoicing method?"

"Nothing so complicated, no, Your Highness. Simply look into every mind to see if you can. A gifted man would likely be trained to keep his mind closed. If you cannot see into a mind, you know that one is gifted."

"There's never a case where an ungifted man may be able to guard his mind?"

Sir Eagan shook his head. "It is impossible. You could keep a list of the men and note your discoveries by each name. Then you will learn who is gifted and who is not."

Achan knew all this already. "There are over three hundred. Is there a faster way? I am trying to find the traitor."

Sir Eagan frowned. "You believe he can bloodvoice?"

Achan took a deep, chilled, breath. "Esek did not look or sound as if he expected me dead, and his timing cannot be ignored. So there might be more than one traitor. Perhaps one man who seeks the reward for my death, operating apart from Esek, and another with the ability to bloodvoice Sir Kenton and keep Esek informed of our plans. I wish to determine who is capable of bloodvoicing so that I can monitor their thoughts."

"Sound deductions, Your Highness. The simplest way might be to ask the gifted men to come forward. Their good faith should set them apart from those who do not confess the gift. But the ability to bloodvoice is not enough to prove a man guilty. A traitor may have had other means of communicating with Esek. You need evidence and reason before accusing any man, for your accused could claim to have been daydreaming.

"I suggest you share your discoveries with Gavin or Caleb or myself so that we can verify your findings. Should you go pointing the finger without proof, you will quickly become an object of ridicule. That would be tragic."

Achan's shoulders slumped. Consumed by anger and fear—and his quest to be useful—he might have done just that. His stomach knotted. He didn't know how to be king. He'd be a laughingstock within a month.

A sudden calm wrapped him like a cloak cast upon him from above. He gasped at the contrast to how he'd just been feeling.

Sir Eagan smiled knowingly. "A little trick I learned, Your Highness. I hope you do not mind. I have always been sensitive to the emotions of those around me. Imagine walking by a hungry man and not offering him food. I feel cruel if I do not help."

"You calmed me? With your bloodvoice? Can you teach me?"

"I shall think on it. I am not entirely certain how I do it."

"Thank you, Sir Eagan." Achan reached for the ink, determined to start right away on part one of his plan: a roster of all his men. He'd have to get his ink thawed.

"My pleasure, Your Majesty." Sir Eagan stood and picked up his bedroll. "And I shall teach you how to leave your body once we are back in Light. It is much safer there."

Another thought drifted into Achan's mind. "Sir Eagan? Do you think it would be good if . . ." His face warmed. "I think I'd like to make some . . . appointments?"

Sir Eagan's lips curved in a small smile. "Yes, Your Majesty. But you might wait a few more days and get to know the men better. Time may inspire several assignments that have not yet occurred to you."

"Of course. You're very wise, Sir Eagan."

"Only because I have made many mistakes."

Achan's stomach clenched again. "I don't want to make mistakes."

"No man sets out to make mistakes. It is when he listens to his desires over what is true and right that he fails. Humility is a most difficult trait to develop. I am pleased to see you have a great deal of it already. For you shall be tempted more than any other."

Sir Eagan sighed, glanced at his hands. "Your Majesty, I am not a bold man, nor am I good with sentiments, but . . ." He lowered himself to his knees, his blue eyes intense. "I swear to you . . ." He paused to breathe, his eyes glistening. "As I served your father, I shall serve you with equal devotion.

"I swore over his dead body that I would avenge him. Kenton might have put me away for thirteen years, but he did not kill me. And only death could keep me from my vow. It is my life's purpose to serve you, to teach you all your father would have taught you. For there is no one to blame for his death but me." He squeezed his eyes shut. A tear leaked down his cheek. He forced himself to look at Achan again. "I alone am responsible. I was his Shield. I failed him. And you. I shall not fail again."

Sir Eagan helped compile Achan's roster by patrolling the camp. There were three hundred fifty-one men in their group. Sixty-five with Captain Demry, fifty-two ex-guards from Ice Island, two hundred eleven escaped Old Kingsguards, and only eighteen from the Prodotez. Sir Eagan indicated with small dots which men had confessed bloodvoice ability. There were eight on the list, not including Sir Gavin, Sir Caleb, Inko, Sparrow, and Achan. Fifteen confessed bloodvoicers in all.

That night, Achan scratched off another list of names. Sir Eagan had inspired him to practice wisdom before action. Achan dipped the quill into the ink—which had thawed at the edge of the fire—and set it to the parchment. He intended to add every possible suspect, including those he knew couldn't possibly be against him. Sir Eric Livna, for example. He also wrote down Lady Viola, Lady Revada, and Lady Merris.

Verdot Amal also concerned Achan, even though Sir Caleb had forgiven him. Someone had alerted Esek that they'd been heading to the prison. Merrygog McLennan could have had a man track them. Any of the missing prisoners from the Prodotez could have followed them as well. Achan racked his brain to remember as many as possible. This only frustrated him. It was impossible for this list to be thorough.

He couldn't stand to think that one of his companions might be deceiving him, but he'd lived long enough to know that even close friends sometimes had secrets they were unwilling to share.

Like Sparrow.

The boy's secret festered in light of recent events. Achan shook Sparrow from his thoughts and concentrated on his list.

It took time, but eventually he felt satisfied with it. The next task proved harder. Shadowing these men was the only way he might discover the traitor. He informed Sir Eagan of his plans—so he could check on Achan and make sure no one stabbed his body while his mind was elsewhere—then began the tedious quest of watching through the eyes of each name on his list, starting with Verdot Amal.

Vrell shivered. Her tent was so small and drafty. She had gotten used to the extra warmth her fake belly provided. She held it in her lap and reached inside to remove another handful of moldy wool. The pile at her feet filled her tent with a musty smell, reminding her of hemlock, which reminded her of the serving boy, which reminded her of her uncle.

Tears filled her eyes. She hadn't known Lord Livna well, but he had always been kind to her. She could still see his bulging eyes after Esek had—Stop. Mother had counseled Vrell on the long day's ride, made her promise not to relive the horrible scene.

Darkness was preying on her mind again. She focused on something more pleasant. Achan had changed since Tsaftown. Maybe it had been the trumpets, or the gifts, or the death of the serving boy and her uncle. But he walked around taller, brow furrowed, finally taking his birthright seriously.

She recalled Achan's expression when Sir Caleb had said she would not serve as his squire. She had not meant to hurt his feelings. She shivered at the timing of her choice. Any other day it would have been Vrell standing behind Achan, fetching his wine. What if she had somehow tasted his wine?

She spilled out a fresh batch of tears over the circumstances as she finished empting her fake belly of the old, moldy wool. She grabbed a handful of the fresh fleece Sir Gavin had bought her in Tsaftown. She prayed it would make a difference in the smell.

Thankfully she would be home soon. Very soon.

Achan had been so preoccupied with his new army he had not seemed to notice that Vrell was missing from his tent. It was for the best. The busier he was, the easier she could sneak away in Carmine, unnoticed. The day might come when Achan would ask Sir Gavin, "Whatever became of Vrell Sparrow?" And Sir Gavin would say, "The lad wasn't cut out for war. Left us in Carmine to seek out an occupation as healer."

And that would be the end of it.

She was glad, really. It was Arman's will. Yet her heart ached, and her mind dwelled on mythical situations. A ball in Armonguard. Would Achan recognize her if she attended? Would he kiss her hand?

She shook the petty daydream aside. She would never have to attend a ball in Armonguard. She would be a married woman. Right?

Why pretend? Bran clearly no longer cared for her in such a way, and if she were honest, the same was true for her. Had time changed matters? Or had they simply fooled themselves into believing they were meant to be?

Maybe Tara was right. Maybe love really did not exist. Maybe it was purely a decision a person made, a business arrangement, a matter of who was available or had the largest inheritance? Vrell's heart told her otherwise, but as Sir Caleb said, "The heart is deceitful above all things."

Vrell certainly did not trust hers.

Achan lurched awake, parchment clutched in hand. He'd been looking in on Merrygog McLennan, hoping the old man would implicate himself, but apparently, the man had fallen asleep and taken Achan with him. A faint orange light glowed through the brown linen curtain separating Achan's bed from the knights. All must be sleeping here, too.

Achan found shadowing harder work than he'd imagined. After hours, Sir Eric and Lady Viola were the only names he'd crossed from his list. He had shadowed the minds of Lady Livna, Lady Merris, Arne, and Verdot Amal and discovered nothing, which meant he would have to continue shadowing their minds until he proved them innocent. Or guilty.

This could take a long time.

He yawned and took one last look at the list, with the intention of blowing out his lamp right after. He tapped his finger on the name that continued to haunt him.

Vrell Sparrow.

Achan had taken Sir Gavin at his word for weeks, accepting Sir Gavin's explanation despite his curiosity.

Until now.

A tiny voice inside disagreed. He should continue to trust Sir Gavin. But as the future king he had a job to do, however unpleasant, and would not be mocked behind his back because he'd been too naïve to verify every possibility.

Sparrow's name *was* on the list. To complete his inquiry, he had to check at some point. His new resolve to do this job well demanded it. Kindness was his only objection, and he couldn't afford to give away kindness anymore. Not when the serving boy's life could have been spared. Not when more lives were at stake until the traitor was found.

Come to think of it, Sparrow had abandoned his post as Achan's squire just before that banquet.

Achan sat up on his bedroll and put his face in his hands.

He pictured Sparrow's chubby face, sensed the shield around his mind, and pushed. As usual, Sparrow's mind was shrouded in armor he couldn't penetrate. Yet if he were the strongest bloodvoicer, there should be a way. He just needed to figure out how.

32

The snowy hunting trail wound through the mountains, slowed the horses, and deepened Achan's frustration. He could walk faster than this. He hadn't realized they crossed the Astrape River until Inko and Kurtz stopped to count the group and make sure no one had fallen through the ice. Their second night out from Tsaftown, they camped along the bank of the River Betsar, though Achan could hear or see no sign of a river, even when a bonfire was lit.

It should have been a three-day journey to Mitspah, but on day four, they still hadn't arrived, though there was less snow and the River Betsar was now flowing freely within its icy banks. That night they ate fresh fish.

Sir Caleb kept Achan's mind busy with a discussion of Mitspah. *It's a mining town. They bring in much income from wealthy travelers who come to see Paz Falls and Temple Arman.*

Temple Arman? I thought Arman's temple was His followers.

True, but two temples to Arman exist in Er'Rets. One is in Armonguard, the other in Mitspah.

How interesting to see how this temple differed from Cetheria's temple in Sitna and Avenis' temple in Mirrorstone.

Achan peered up the line, then realized, despite the few torches men carried, he could see his surroundings. His heart quickened. He blinked at the sky. Though he could see no moon or stars, something lit the woods as if he were standing outside at night under a full moon.

He called up to Sir Gavin at the front of the line. *I can see.*

Aye, we're entering the Evenwall near Mitspah, though the trail will take us to the valley first. Then we'll come back up along the king's road.

Why must we go around?

'Tis far too dangerous to ford the river here. It is very rocky near the top of the falls. Therefore we'll continue down to the valley and cross there.

How much longer?

Two more days, I expect.

Achan groaned. Why, when they were so close, did their final destination seem so far?

As they descended the mountain trail, shapes in the landscape appeared like shadows at dusk. Achan fidgeted at the idea of sunlight. Leafy trees took shadowed form around him. His furs glistened as the mist of the Evenwall clung to the fibers. The men began to talk about the coming day until a restless energy took hold of the entire group.

Well, Sparrow, we entered Darkness and lived to tell the tale.

No answer came. Achan suddenly realized he hadn't spoken to the boy since the day Lord Livna had died. Too many days ago to count. Maybe Sparrow was upset. He tried again. *Or maybe we haven't all lived. Are you still breathing, Sparrow?*

I am. Do you need my assistance, Your Majesty?

Achan stiffened at Sparrow's lofty tone. *Thank you, no.* Not wanting to deal with the boy's attitude, Achan pushed him out.

The light grew brighter, the air clearer, then, as if a fog had lifted, Dove carried Achan beyond the chill of the Evenwall and into a warm breeze. His breath snagged at the view. They'd left the forest and were descending a trail that wound its way down the lush countryside.

A green valley spread to where it met the sky on the horizon, a bright, cloudless blue. Tufts of trees and the occasional cottage dotted the peaceful landscape. The dirt road under the horses' hooves was the color of Poril's ginger cake. The grasses alongside were as tall as Dove's knees and seasoned with yellow, lavender, and white blossoms. A mix of sweet and acrid fragrances filled the air.

His army had gone silent, wonder spread across each face. Ages had likely passed since many had seen such beauty.

The blessed sun beat down as they descended the mountains. Achan shrugged off his cloak and doublet. The warm breeze snaked up one sleeve to his armpit and he sighed at the comfort of creation.

When the river came into view again, the men broke the single-file formation, galloping their mounts to the water. Some dismounted and ran for the shallows, stripping off their clothing as they went. Others jumped in fully dressed. Achan grinned. The men had lost their senses. He could hardly blame them.

When Achan reached the river, he slid off Dove's back, stripped off his tunic, and knelt at the water's edge. The wide and shallow river had little current near the bank. The men laughed and splashed one another. Their horses drank.

Achan's reflection rippled in the water below him. Scruffy. How long had it been since the day he'd tried to shave?

He thrust his hands through his reflection until his palms lay flat on the sandy riverbed. He lowered his face to the water, as if to kiss it, then eased beneath the surface, nose first, then chin, cheeks, and ears. He pulled back and slurped the cool, refreshing water.

"It is never wise to duck your head under completely, Your Majesty," Sir Eagan said from behind him. "If I had wanted to kill you, it would have been all too easy."

Achan sat back on his haunches and wiped his mouth with the back of his hand.

Sir Eagan seemed taller in the sun. He pointed along the riverbank. "Regard your men. Many have overindulged in—"

"Can you blame them?"

Sir Eagan's round cheeks balled up in a way that made Achan feel as though he had lived this moment before. "Hardly, but if you study their behavior, you can learn who might make the best soldiers. Take Bazmark, for instance. He scoops the water into his hand, keeping his head up so he can see not only who is before him, but any reflection that might come up behind him. He was a Kingsguard soldier, you know."

"I didn't." But he could bloodvoice, so it made sense, since gifted men were recruited. "He said he'd gone to prison for looking too long at the queen."

"Your mother was a beautiful woman. No man could avoid at least glancing at her when she passed, and your father would never imprison a man for that. Bazmark took it too far. Became obsessed."

"Did he shadow her?"

"With his mind. I am sure Sir Gavin has explained how inappropriate it is to use your gift to observe people's private moments." Sir Eagan raised a dark eyebrow.

"I see." Achan glanced back at Bazmark, frowning.

"Do not judge him for his past, for you have pardoned him. But do not forget his weakness, for once a man falls, it is often easy for him to fall again."

"You were saying I should study the men? You think it's time I make appointments?"

"Not yet, Your Majesty. Things will likely play out like this: Each lord who is loyal to you, if he has not already, will appoint his own captain to lead his soldiers. Those captains will take their orders from whomever you put over the army. Those from Tsaftown will follow Roxburg Demry until Sir Eric arrives. You might recommend that Roxburg promote Bazmark to a sergeant or lieutenant. Think about it."

"Okay."

"For now, Your Majesty, if you would like to swim, I shall see your back is covered."

"Thanks." Achan tugged off his boots and waded into the cool water. He couldn't remember the last time he swam for pleasure. The shallows were not deep enough to tread, so he floated on his back, staring at the bright blue sky. So beautiful.

Thank You, Arman.

• • •

Vrell steered her mount along behind Inko's, but her gaze wandered the landscape, each new sight stealing her breath. They were back in Light, home nearer than ever. And she had stopped twice to cut plants to replenish her kit. Once for clover and once for wild ginger.

She watched Achan from a distance, admiring how he had changed and how he had remained the same over the journey through Darkness. He looked no different than when she first met him. Tall and strong. But his confidence had grown some, though she bet he still doubted his ability to lead these men. Vrell could only imagine how he must feel. As if anyone should tell the Great Whitewolf what to do. But still, how exciting! Er'Rets would have a king. Arman's chosen.

Behind her, some men laughed. She tensed. Could they be laughing at *her*? Now that Darkness no longer aided her disguise, she felt awkward and exposed. She kept telling herself she had been fine before. Neither Lord Orthrop, Macoun, Carlani, Khai, or even Lord Levy had recognized her. But she could not help her apprehension. For one woman to travel with three hundred men . . . beyond inappropriate. Scandalous!

And that there might be a betrayer among them. The thought chilled her arms. If Esek had sent the spy, he would be looking for her as well as Achan. She should flee for Carmine now. At top speed, it would take a day and a half. She would only have to camp once. No reason to think she would not make it. She missed Mother so.

She would be vulnerable, though. If anyone untrustworthy happened upon her, she could not defend herself. She needed the protection of these men. It would not be much longer. Another week, perhaps? There was no reason for Achan and the army to linger in Mitspah. Maybe only be two or three days. She smiled. She could be home before the week's end.

And when they stopped tonight, she would pick some rue and make a juice for Achan to help with his fleas.

Achan and the soldiers followed the road until it split: north to Mitspah, south to Carmine. They headed north and soon passed one stone cottage after another, each with its own farm. Children ran alongside the horses waving and laughing, though their parents kept their distance. Some called their children back, casting suspicious glances at the soldiers.

The procession passed the last stretch of flatlands and started up a steep trail surrounded by thick trees and ferns. The trees and trail created a gap in the distance where a snow-capped mountain loomed, half-covered by Evenwall mist. Achan's stomach roiled at the sight. Hopefully Mitspah was far enough east that they would not have to enter Darkness again.

"I hear the falls," a soldier said.

Sure enough, the sound of water gushing over rock met Achan's ears. Each corner they rounded, Achan expected to see the falls—they sounded so close—yet the army zigzagged up the trail and didn't seem to get any closer.

The trail straightened but rose so steeply they dismounted and pulled their horses along. Achan led Dove over the crest of the hill and stopped. The road continued rolling over smaller hills, but he could see the Mitspah stronghold clearly.

"Nice, isn't it?" a breathless man said. "My great, great grandfather on my mother's side helped build it."

Achan swung around to see Polk gripping the reins of his horse, so drowned in sweat he looked like a wet animal.

Achan quickly led Dove down the hill a few paces, then remounted. Dove followed the other horses, and Achan was able to take in the magnificent stronghold.

Looming over a grassy bailey, the castle keep was built into a mountain cliff, the Paz Falls spilling over the turrets, down the sides, and pooling into a moat as if the stronghold were a fountain. The cliff morphed with multicolored stone masonry. Moss and ivy clung to every surface.

Two large turrets of different heights stretched up on the left and right of the castle. There were two watchtowers, as well, at the center front and back. The front, a squat, circular inner gatehouse sat over the moat. The back, and highest point of Mitspah stronghold, protruded out of the mountain. It had a carved stone roof that curled so the river spilled off both sides into two waterfalls, each spilling to one of the turrets. The turret stone roofs had been carved in spirals that sent the water circling down until it spilled off the outside of each turret to the moat in a fantastic cascade.

The water collected at the base of the castle keep, forming a moat that was a tranquil pool on the left side of the castle. The current sailed from that pool, under the inner gatehouse's drawbridge, and along the left side of the keep until it passed through an iron grate in the stone curtain wall.

The wall stood three levels high topped with another three levels of spiked black iron fence. It arched out from the cliff in a wide half circle, encasing the vast, grassy bailey.

Soaked orange and silver checkered banners sagged from the top of each tower. Achan smiled at the cham bears emblazoned on each standard. He'd never seen a real one, and now with a war brewing, and his planning to journey south, he wondered if he ever would.

Far ahead, at the front of the line, Sir Gavin led the men under the portcullis and into the outer bailey, like a long line of garland. Would Mitspah have room for them all?

Once inside the bailey, Sir Caleb reined his horse around. "Your Highness, you and Vrell meet Sir Gavin at the inner gatehouse. Inko and Kurtz, come with me."

Sir Caleb rode off where the soldiers were milling in a group. "We will camp in the bailey," he yelled. "Pitch your tents along the curtain wall on the right. Their stables aren't large enough for all our horses, so tether your animals along the moat. Some guards are coming to set up a makeshift pen."

All around, men dismounted and unsaddled their horses. The clinking of iron chain turned Achan's head back to the inner gatehouse. The portcullis was rising.

Achan nudged Dove across the grassy bailey to the inner gatehouse where Sir Gavin and Sir Eagan had stopped their horses on the drawbridge.

Sir Gavin waved his hand overhead. "Achan, Vrell, you'll accompany us inside."

The quaint inner courtyard had more flowers than the temple gardens in Sitna. Ivy and moss wrapped around stone arches that led who knew where. Water seemed to drizzle over every inch of the castle walls, and mist filled the air—not foggy, like the Evenwall, but wet, like a spray of rain. The keep stood at the end of the courtyard. The entrance, two large board and batten doors, looked unnatural against all the nature.

"Little Cham!" a low voice called out from behind Achan.

Shung Noatak ducked under an archway in the courtyard.

Achan dismounted, smiling broadly. "Hello, Shung! When did you arrive?"

Shung tackled Achan in a bear hug. "Three days past."

Achan patted Shung's back. The Charmice tails on Shung's jerkin tickled his hand. "How was Koyukuk's wedding?"

"Fine celebration. You honor him to ask."

Sir Gavin dismounted. "Delighted to see you, Shung."

"You need Shung's sword?"

Sir Gavin chuckled. "That we do, Shung. That we do."

A man in a long brown cape stepped through the double doors. He had stringy brown hair, a close-cropped beard, broad shoulders, and the gate of a soldier. His robe puffed as he descended the steps, and Achan glimpsed a sword at his side. Achan rested his hand on the grip of Eagan's Elk.

Two men in orange tunics scurried behind the man in brown. One looked to be in his forties, the other, just a boy.

Strays.

The man in brown stopped by Sir Gavin's horse. "I'm Atul, Lord Yarden's steward. Our men'll put up yer horses 'n' bring yer things inside. Lord Yarden awaits yeh there."

Sir Gavin walked up to Atul. "Where is Winze?"

"Winze fell ill two weeks back. Lord Yarden granted him a leave 'n' the country 'til he recovers."

The stray man approached Dove and unhooked the saddle-bag. When he got it free, he set it on the grass, then stepped toward Sir Eagan's horse.

The stray boy—about Sparrow's age, rail thin with choppy brown hair and freckled cheeks—patted Dove's nose.

"This one looks just like Dove, don't he?" The boy twisted around to the elder stray, but the man kept his head down and lugged Sir Eagan's saddlebag over to Sir Gavin's.

"Cole!" Atul slapped the boy's ear. "Shut yer yap and do yer job!"

Cole cowered and lifted both arms in front of his face.

Achan lunged between Atul and Cole. "It's all right." He gripped the back of Cole's neck and drew him into a one-armed hug, all the while staring Atul down. "This *is* Dove. A gift from Sir Eric Livna."

Atul's thick eyebrows scrunched into one bushy stripe over his eyes. "Sir Eric give away his father's horse? Why'd he do that? Somethin' happen?"

Achan swallowed and searched for Sir Gavin.

The knight was halfway to the door of the stronghold. "Come along, Your Majesty. We'll convey our message and intent to Lord Yarden."

"O' course yeh will." Atul sidestepped Achan, then hurried ahead and opened the door before Sir Gavin reached it.

Achan inspected Cole's ear and found it red and swollen. "Are you all right?"

"Cole!" The older stray had taken the reins to Sir Gavin and Eagan's mounts and was leading them across the courtyard. "See to the other horses."

"Yes, sir." Cole stepped away from Achan.

"Your Highness?" Sir Eagan stood in the open doorway at the top of the steps.

Achan needed to go inside. Lord Yarden would be waiting, though he hated to leave Cole. Long before Achan had known his true identity, he had considered fleeing to Mitspah to escape his own cruel fate. Had he come here, he and Cole might have been subject to the same masters.

Achan reluctantly headed for the entrance to the Mitspah stronghold. A shadow flanked his on the grass and he turned to see Shung one step behind him. Achan smiled and fell into step beside his new Shield.

They passed into a narrow hallway with a low ceiling he could easily touch without fully extending his arm. The castle smelled strongly of mildew and dogs. Atul led them over a wet stone floor covered in soggy rushes to the end of the hall and up a spiral stairwell that Achan guessed to be the rear tower.

On the second floor, they walked down a hall and passed a half dozen open doors to a great hall on the right. At the end of the hall, Atul opened a door on the left and they entered a warm receiving room, blanketed in damp tapestries.

A thin man with a face like a possum slouched on a throne-like chair opposite the door. He had fine grey hair, a large nose, and beady black eyes. Twin dogs—as big as colts—flanked the chair with better posture than their master. They were beige, with short fur and black faces.

Achan reached out to the one on the left. *Hey, boy.* The dog's eyes shifted to Achan's, his jaw dropped, he licked his mouth, and shifted.

Atul closed the door. "Your Highness, this here's Lord Yarden, Lord of Mitspah."

Lord Yarden nodded, slowly. His version of a bow? "I am relieved to see you well. We hear rumors, but facts come to me so late. Only two weeks have passed since word of this treachery with Lord Nathak reached me. I feared the worst."

Achan didn't want to do the talking, but it was time he started speaking for himself. "I'm well, Lord Yarden, though we do come bearing great sorrow."

"Go on," Lord Yarden said.

"While we were at Lytton Hall, Esek Nathak, the traitor prince, murdered Lord Livna."

Lord Yarden jumped to his feet. "What? How?"

"Stabbed during the dinner celebration."

"In front of witnesses? This is outrageous!" Lord Yarden said. "My poor, dear sister. What happened? Did they duel?"

Trust you to not to mince words, Your Highness, Sir Caleb said.

Achan had merely wanted to speak. He hadn't bothered to think of what he should say. *I'm not as flowery as you, Sir Caleb.*

Clearly, just don't forget compassion.

Achan chastened himself and went to his knees before Lord Yarden's throne. "The fault is mine entirely. Esek sought to kill me, but Lord Livna would not give me up. A servant boy was also lost that night—to poison intended for me."

Lord Yarden set a hand on Achan's shoulder. "Do not kneel before me, Your Highness, please. Esek is a traitor."

Achan looked up. "Still, I feel quite responsible."

"A concern you must push aside, Your Majesty. Had you been staying here, I would not have forsaken you either. Blame no one but that murderous fool who thinks he's king."

Achan stood, and Lord Yarden eased back into his chair, eyes downcast.

"Would you be willing to join us as we stand against him?" Sir Gavin asked. "He hunts us now. We do not wish to put your people in harm's way."

"I'd fight that cur even if no one else was! My son will want to fight as well. We are not many, but we'll stand with you." He turned to Atul. "Prepare rooms for the prince and his men, Atul, and arrange a feast."

"Right away, m' lord." Atul jerked his head in a quick nod and strode from the room.

JILL WILLIAMSON

• • •

Vrell sat at the back of the great hall with Kurtz, as she had in Tsaftown, assigned to entrance duty. Achan and the knights had been seated at the high table, though Achan, Shung, and Sir Caleb were standing, appearing to argue with Lord Yarden.

Cole, the young stray who'd taken care of their horses, stood against the wall, face pale. Since all three minds in her party were shielded, she looked through the boy's mind to listen in and found him filled with excitement, hope, and . . . dread?

The prince's nostrils flared. "I appreciate your gift, Lord Yarden, but no more innocents will die from my cup. Perhaps I could make use of Cole as a stableboy, as I have no one to help me with my horses."

Yes. Hope surged through Cole. He could do that, for sure. He could take care of Dove. He dared not hope this could be true. That he could serve the prince—a kind one too.

Lord Yarden looked down his huge nose at Cole and shrugged. "I care not what you do with the stray. I just don't want to see you poisoned, especially under my roof. I've done what I could to prevent it. You just take note of that."

"Shung will drink and eat for the little cham." The Shield banged a fist to his chest. He seemed almost eager to take some poison as if to prove he were strong enough to withstand it.

Cole wished he were as brave, but he'd heard rumors that a boy had died in Tsaftown, drinking from his Majesty's cup.

The prince glared at Shung. "I will not allow it."

Vrell shook her head and withdrew. Men. Achan stood no chance of negating Shung. When that's man's mind was made up . . . look out. At least people would think twice before

512

challenging Achan with Shung at his side. Vrell smiled. Achan now had his own Shield, and, apparently, a horse boy.

To Vrell's relief, she did not have to make small talk with Kurtz. He poured all his attention on the blonde woman seated to his right, even feeding the lady food off the tip of his knife. Vrell tried to distract herself, but his overt declarations were hard to ignore.

"Arman give you health and joy, beautiful lady. He favors me tonight with your company, He does."

The lady batted her eyes and twirled her finger around a lock of her golden hair. "I apologize for the absence of my husband. He is a sailor aboard the Brierstar."

"He's a fool to leave you, he is." Kurtz leaned so close he may as well kiss the woman. "*I* would never. For if I turned my back on such a pretty face as yours, surely I'd die, I would."

The woman's cheeks flushed. "You flatter me, my lord."

"I love you, I do. Have mercy on my bleeding heart, eh?"

Vrell bit into her roll to hold her tongue.

The lady giggled. "Do not forget, good knight, I am married. Please do not ask anything of me that would soil the honor of myself or my lord husband."

Sir Kurtz lowered his voice. "Nothing would keep me from serving you all my life."

Vrell rolled her eyes. Dinner had long since ended, but Lord Yarden's wife liked to tell stories. Vrell had eaten in this hall before. All were forced to endure Lady Rubel until her husband ended it or she got so full she needed to lie down.

Unfortunately, Lord Yarden never seemed to tire of hearing the same tale time and again. Perhaps it was Lady Rubel's low, silky voice or the fact that her curvy figure drew even Vrell's attention. The woman had Chuma heritage; that could not be argued. Her black hair hung lustrous against her olive skin. She rambled on and on about how they had ordered cranberry wine but the spicy clove wine had come instead.

Vrell had never cared for clove wine. Wine should be sweet, not spicy. But no servant had bothered to bring water to her end of the table, so she had forced herself to drink the pungent liquid to wash down the dry fish. The best platters of everything always went to the high table. It would not be long until she had that pleasure again.

Vrell stared at a hound and a small terrier, watching them duck in and out from under the table opposite hers, sniffing and nibbling along the floor. The person sitting across the hall, opposite Vrell, had not moved in a long while. She blinked out of her trance and focused her eyes to the further distance.

It was Polk, and he was staring at her.

She straightened and gave him a half smile and a roll of the eyes. He must be equally bored by the tale of wine flavors. But instead of smiling in return, Polk lifted up the knife from his empty trencher and began to twirl it in his fingers.

Vrell had no more patience for men and their strange ways. Achan did not need her assistance. She slipped out the closest door, doubting anyone had noticed. She walked carefully over the wet floor and started up the stairwell. Sir Gavin had seen to it she had her own chamber on the fourth floor, and she looked forward to a bath.

A noise below prickled the hair on her arms. Lady Rubel must have finished her story. Vrell passed the third floor landing and started up the next flight.

"Vrell."

She spun around, hand clamped over her heart.

Polk dashed around the third floor landing and up to where she stood. He grinned, his tanned face wrinkling. "Pretty boring dinner, huh? They should have let me tell a story. I tell the best stories. No one ever gets bored."

What was Polk doing? Only the Old Kingsguard knights, Achan, Vrell, and Shung were being housed in the keep. Maybe Polk wanted to see Temple Arman at the—

Polk gripped Vrell's tunic in his fist and slammed her against the outer wall of the tower stairs. Pain poured through her head, freezing her breath. Polk lifted his other hand to her face and traced her cheek and jaw with the back of his fingers.

Vrell flushed, heart pounding. "What are you doing?"

Polk's face contorted into a gloating sneer. "I know the secret of your blush, fair Vrell."

Another wave of heat gripped her. "M-My blush?"

"You do, you know. Far more than any *boy* would."

33

Polk lifted her right hand. "Am I making you uncomfortable? I have that effect on ladies." He pressed her hand to his lips.

Vrell punched his cheek and gasped at the pain it caused her knuckles. She tried to duck under his arm, but he grabbed her arms and slammed her against the wall again. Voices and laughter filled the stairwell from below.

Polk dragged her up to the fourth floor. Vrell squatted, trying to twist out of his grip and dart under him.

His knees bent with hers. "Oh, no you don't."

She elbowed his thigh, stomped on his foot, and slipped on wet rushes. He caught her by her throat.

She reached out for Sir Gavin. *Vrell Sparrow.* Tears flooded her eyes, blurring Polk's stoic expression. She sucked in a diluted breath and sent a knock to Achan.

When no connection opened, she whimpered like a puppy. Why did no one answer?

She blinked to clear her blurry eyes and focus on Polk's face. Tears rolled down her cheeks. "Wha—"

Polk clamped his hand over Sparrow's mouth, the other hand continued to squeeze her neck. "They can't hear you, can they, blossom? Surprised? Cloves have the same affect on âleh as mint does. Bet you didn't know that."

Sparrow pushed against Polk's chest with her free hand. She kicked him, kneed him, scratched his face.

Polk tugged her body, dragging her head along the stone wall, his strength far exceeding hers. "None of that, now. There's a price on your head I intend to collect. I've earned it."

Everything became clear. Polk was Esek's former squire. Had he been the one in the kitchens in Carmine? Who had drugged Mother? Had he poisoned Achan's goblet in Tsaftown? Switched the wines tonight so the âleh would not be detected? How could she have been so careless? Being close to home was no reason to let down her guard.

He kicked in the door to her room and hauled her inside. The door swung closed, blanketing the room in darkness. Polk towed Vrell across the small space. After a few steps, her eyes adjusted to the pale, grey twilight from the window, revealing the general shapes of the bed and sideboard. Firefox hung on the bedpost. Polk dragged her toward the sideboard. Her mind grappled to recall where she'd left her knife. He pushed her to the floor and a heavy weight crushed her back.

Vrell screamed. "Help me! The traitor—" A thick strip of leather tugged into her mouth. Polk cinched it back against her molars, so tightly the top edge knifed up under her cheekbones. She held her breath against the pain and reached out with her right hand. She opened one of the bottom cupboards of her sideboard. Her fingers grabbed for the first thing they could reach: a stone basin. She pulled it toward her. It fell off the ledge of the sideboard with a loud clunk.

"Good idea, blossom." The pressure on her back shifted as Polk leaned over and pulled her hands behind her back. He tied them with something thick and itchy. Hemp, maybe? He quickly dug out the items from the bottom shelves of the sideboard. Linens flopped around her face and dishes clanked and rolled across the wooden floor.

He picked her up and shoved her in the bottom cupboard, face first, folding her feet up behind her. Her nose pressed against the unfinished oak. The cupboard doors clicked shut, blackening her vision. Something scraped the wood above.

"That ought to hold you." His voice was muffled now. "Be a good blossom and wait right there while I kill the prince. My clove wine was wasted on him tonight, for I never saw him take a sip."

Sobs rattled her frame. She gasped in short breaths, calming herself enough to send another knock to Sir Gavin.

Âleh didn't last forever.

Achan and Shung made their way up the stairs. The long dinner had exhausted him. He didn't feel up to searching for the traitor tonight. All his hours of watching had uncovered nothing sinister and left him feeling like a traitor himself, betraying his men's private thoughts.

The patter of footsteps above slowed Achan's steps. Shung pushed Achan behind him. Who was in such a hurry? A shadow preceded the answer.

Polk. Red-faced and out of breath. The man slowed, his eyes blinked wide, flashed to Shung, and he bowed, panting slightly. "Your Majesty, good evening."

Achan nodded his greeting, overcome by a sudden burst of excitement he sensed in Polk. "What brings you to this part of the castle, Polk?"

"Temple Arman is as I've always heard, Your Majesty. Glorious. I'm not even tired from the long hike."

Of course he wasn't. "I've not yet found the time to see it. Where is your belt, Polk?" For the man's tunic hung loose.

Polk patted his stomach. "Oh, well, you know, dinner was so good, I couldn't stop eating. My belt made things worse. I've had better feasts, though. Nothing like Poril's cooking, I'm sure you know."

Achan grimaced at the mention of his former master. "Sparrow might have something to settle your stomach."

"An excellent suggestion, Your Majesty," Polk said. "I pray you sleep well."

Achan nodded once more to the soldier. "You as well."

Polk's footsteps resumed their hurried speed, descending from where Achan stood. Achan met Shung's dark eyes and opened a connection.

Stand here with me a moment, Shung, I want to look in on Polk.

Shung will wait.

Achan concentrated on Polk and immediately looked out through his eyes. Polk circled round and round the stairwell and stepped off on the second floor. He walked down the corridor and entered the great hall. There were still a dozen or more people sitting at the tables. Lord Yarden stood behind his chair on the dais talking to Atul. Polk fell into a chair at the end of the table closest to the door and bit into a roll.

Polk watched Atul until the man glanced his way. A slight nod of acknowledgement from Atul, and Polk looked away and took another bite. His thoughts were curiously blank.

Achan left him there.

"See anything?" Shung asked.

"I don't think so." Achan headed up the stairs and to his chamber, filling Shung in on what Polk had done.

Shung entered Achan's chamber first and held the door open. "Strange he was full but ate more."

Achan walked inside and sat at his desk. "Yeah." The chair was upholstered in blue velvet, but the cushioning did not relieve his tailbone. After hours in the saddle days on end and a long, tedious dinner on a hard bench, he'd rather stand.

He scanned the list again. Some names he suspected more than others. He'd shadowed them all more than once. Who deserved another peek? Polk's name jumped out from the list.

Something was off with Polk. Why, Achan couldn't say. The fellow simply needled him, but so did Inko. Perhaps some people had a gift for being obnoxious.

Lady Rubel and her stories, for example.

But Polk was lying about being full, that much was certain. And why lie about that? Achan shook himself back to the task at hand. Polk. Then he'd try Verdot Amal again.

Polk no longer sat in the great hall. He crept along one of the castle corridors. The soft swish of his pant legs and the squish of his boots over soggy rushes increased his heartbeat. What was Polk still doing in the keep? He should have gone back to the tents by now.

A faint thought surfaced in Polk's mind. Soon all would be finished and he could get back to the good life. A single torch lit the hall. Polk lifted it from the ring and carried it with him.

Achan jumped up and opened his door, losing his connection with Polk. The hall on his floor was empty. Polk must be on another level.

"What is it, Little Cham?"

"Nothing, Shung. Sorry." Achan returned to his chair and found Polk again.

Polk stopped at a door. He looked both ways before pushing it open and slipping inside. All was dark but for Polk's torch. He walked across the room and stubbed his toe on something that rattled across the floor. Polk cursed and hopped on one foot. He squatted and the torch lit the floor of a chamber that looked to have been ransacked. Polk righted a heavy jug and slid the torch inside. He carried the jug to a sideboard and set it down.

His gaze fell onto a wooden spoon wedged between the handles on the lower cupboard doors. Polk's pulse increased. He slipped the spoon free. *I've come back, little bird.*

Polk opened the doors. Achan's heartbeat thudded in time with Polk's. Had the man trapped someone in a sideboard? Why? Achan should try to find Polk, yet if he started walking, he'd lose contact. He could watch or he could walk. Not both. Not yet.

He withdrew. *Sir Gavin, Polk is up to some mischief on one of the floors. Can you go see?*

A moment passed before a sleepy voice said, *Aye, right away. Polk, you say? How do you—*

Achan cut off the knight and focused back on Polk, who had pulled a body out from the sideboard. A great foreboding coiled in the pit of Achan's stomach.

Someone screamed.

Sparrow? Achan stood so fast he nearly knocked over his table. He would know that raspy screech anywhere.

What in all Er'Rets?

Polk pulled at something around Sparrow's throat. A belt. He wedged it back into Sparrow's mouth. Sparrow's eyes grew wide. He kicked Polk's chest with his feet, repeatedly, stamping on the man's torso.

Polk threw himself onto Sparrow, squeezed the boy's throat with one hand. *None of that, blossom. I've been waiting for some time to confront you. It's made me a bit . . . impatient.*

Sparrow grew limp, stopped fighting. Had he blacked out? Polk dragged him by the feet, out of the pile of rubble.

Now, I've done real good work and I don't mind rewarding myself for all the trouble it's taken. Like I said before, I've earned it.

Polk slid his hand away and pressed his mouth over Sparrow's with a crushing force that revived the boy. Sparrow turned his head, then bashed it against Polk's forehead. Polk returned his hand to Sparrow's throat and held him down. The boy's small frame was no match for Polk's strength.

What in flames was that rat playing at? Achan pulled back, trembling. *Sparrow! I'm coming.* He blinked away from Polk. "Shung! Polk is attacking Sparrow!" Achan tore out the door, sprinted down the hall, down the spiral staircase, glancing into empty hallways before remembering Polk had entered a room. Had it been Sparrow's?

Sparrow? What room is yours? Where does he have you?

Sparrow didn't answer.

Sir Gavin! Where are you?

In the courtyard. I saw nothing in the halls, so I came out—

Sparrow's quarters, where are they?

On the fourth floor. Achan, what's wrong?

Polk is attacking Sparrow. Achan sprinted back to the stair-well and took the steps three at a time. He ran down to the fourth floor. Unsure of which door to try, he skidded to a stop over the wet stone. *Sparrow! Where are you?*

When the boy still didn't answer, Achan found Polk's mind again and looked out through the deviant's eyes. Polk had pinned Sparrow to the floor, straddling the boy's body and arms. His thrill brought a scream to Achan's lips. He had no time to search every room. What could he do?

Polk! Stop, Achan commanded.

Polk froze, scanned the room, then reached back and pulled his boot knife. He held the small blade against Sparrow's cheek. *Not a word, you hear? Or I'll slice you from top to bottom. No one skins an animal like I do.*

He cut open Sparrow's tunic, baring a strange undershirt that blossomed bits of wool where the knife had cut.

Polk laughed. *Let's see how you look without your fake fat, shall we?* He slid the knife under the neckline of the disguise and started to cut.

Achan concentrated. He was Polk. His hands were Polk's hands. He was cutting.

He stopped cutting. He pulled the knife back.

Polk yelled, dropped the knife.

Achan forced Polk to stand, to walk to the door and open it.

A man stood at the other end of the hall, by the stairs. The Crown Prince. How had he—?

For the first time ever, Achan moved his own body without leaving Polk's mind. He walked slowly, boots slapping over the wet rushes. He reached Polk, released his mind.

Polk wheezed and cowered against the wall, staring, eyes wild. "What did you do to me? Are you a mage?"

Achan punched Polk in the face. Once. Twice. He pulled back to punch him again, but Polk, already unconscious, slid slowly to the floor. Achan took a long, calming breath, shook his throbbing hand, and pushed open Sparrow's door.

The torch in the jug had burned beneath the lip and lit the room with a dull glow. A narrow bed, the sideboard, a stool. The floor was littered in dishes and linens.

Where had Sparrow gone?

A shattered breath pulled Achan's gaze back to the sideboard. He spotted the boy wedged between the sideboard and bed, sitting in that small Sparrow way, knees against his chest. Achan approached him, stepped on something soft and looked down.

He moved his boot to reveal a wad of shorn wool. He squatted and picked it up, sniffed it. Mildew.

He held it up. "Sparrow, wh-what *is* this?"

Sparrow watched him with wide, bleary eyes.

Achan's heart was still pounding in his chest. "Are you hurt?" He held out a hand to help the boy up.

Sparrow's bottom lip protruded, trembled. He sniffled and released the most high-pitched moan Achan had ever heard, as if trying not to cry and failing miserably.

"Little Cham?" Shung stepped into the room, sword drawn.

Uncertain what to do, Achan waved a hand. "Sparrow, come out of there."

But Sparrow only cried harder.

"It's okay." Achan reached for him, grabbed his shoulders.

Sparrow tensed, shook his head. His hair, completely loose from its thong, fell over his eyes. "Please do not touch me."

"I'm not going to hurt you." Achan grabbed Sparrow's upper arms and pulled.

"No!" Sparrow tucked his chin against his knees, pushing his shoulders against the wall so Achan failed to lift him.

"Shung, help me."

Shung and Achan each grabbed an arm and hoisted Sparrow—kicking and screaming—out of the crack. They set him on his feet before the bed. The boy stood trembling, slouched, chin down. A leather belt hung around his neck. Polk's belt. His arms were bound behind him and his tunic hung open to reveal the padded undergarment, sliced down the belly and sprouting wisps of shorn wool.

Boot steps slapped stone in the corridor, growing nearer.

Achan could only stare at the fake belly Sparrow wore, his mind filled with questions but completely choked.

Sir Gavin ran inside and slid to a stop.

Achan finally managed to utter, "I don't understand."

"Shung does." Shung's bushy eyebrows cocked like two caterpillars. "The little fox is a vixen."

34

Achan's breath caught. Sparrow was a *her*? "I thought Polk . . ."

Sparrow's bottom lip protruded again. "He put me in the sideboard then went to kill you." Her voice cracked, morphing back into that keening whine.

"No, now . . . don't do that. Don't cry." A girl. A woman. All this time? "Blazes! Why?"

"Achan." Sir Gavin crossed to Sparrow's side. "We saw no reason to tell you."

"You knew. *This* is the big secret. Why Sparrow sneaks off in the woods, bathes in your room, cleans his teeth. *Her* teeth." Achan linked his fingers and set his hands on his head. What was he supposed to do with this information?

"Shung, bring Polk in and close the door." Sir Gavin loosed the belt from Sparrow's throat, removed his boot knife and cut the bonds on her wrists. She immediately hugged herself and burrowed her face against Sir Gavin's chest, weeping. The old knight wrapped an arm around her and patted her ear. "There now, child. He didn't hurt you, did he?"

"Me?" Achan's veins smoldered. *Sir Gavin, I don't understand what this is all about.*

Sir Gavin cocked an eyebrow at the door. *Polk, Achan. I'm asking her if Polk violated her.*

A chill turned the heat in Achan's veins to ice.

Shung dragged Polk into the room by his ankles and kicked the door shut.

"My mouth," Sparrow said. "The belt."

Sir Gavin took hold of Sparrow's ears and tipped her head back, eyes fixed on her face. "Aye, I see you'll have some bruises there. Anything else?"

"Throat."

As Sir Gavin examined Sparrow's neck, Achan stewed, wedged between overwhelming sympathy for this petrified creature and consuming disgust for her blubbering.

This was why the little fox had been acting so odd. Ever blushing. Sitting so small. The portly stomach and gangly limbs. Achan had discovered Vrell Sparrow's secret at last. That's why *he'd* been such an odd duck.

But what of it? Why go so far to conceal her gender? He supposed it *was* a horrible world for a stray woman. He had been treated badly, but the stories he knew of young stray girls—pretty ones, especially . . .

It made some sense, he supposed. The Kingsguards had come to take her to Master Hadar. A boy would have been safer traveling with men, especially a man like Khai Mageia.

Sparrow's voice pulled him from his mental tirade. "Achan saved me."

He studied Sparrow's face. Knowing now that he looked on a girl—an awkward thought as she wore trousers and that ridiculous fake belly—he could see Sparrow was a pretty little thing. Round face with porcelain skin and those ever-blushing cheeks, wide eyes, a small mouth that always seemed to be frowning slightly, likely due to all the worrisome thoughts under that mess of black hair.

Again, Sparrow spoke, pulling Achan out from the fog in his mind. "Polk said he was going to kill you. He poisoned your goblet in Tsaftown and slipped us all âleh tonight in the clove wine. Someone should sweep your room for poison."

Achan blinked. Poison? But before he could formulate a reply, Sir Gavin spoke.

"A blessing that I abhor clove wine, then. But the rest of our men are likely silenced too. I'll go tell Caleb and Eagan to search Achan's chambers right away. Achan, you find Kurtz and Inko and ask them to take Polk to the dungeon. I'd like Shung to stay outside Vrell's room until we get this sorted out." Sir Gavin patted Sparrow's ear once more and stepped toward the door.

"Wait just a moment, Sir Gavin." Achan wasn't done with this. "I don't know why you deceived me. But tomorrow, *Miss Sparrow* will get herself a dress and come clean to everyone."

Sparrow's cheeks darkened. "You think you can tell me what to do because you are the Crown Prince?"

His gaze flitted from her eyes to the red welts across her cheeks. "No. Because I saved your hide."

Sparrow turned her head away, jaw set.

Sir Gavin shook his head. "That's unwise, Achan. We must keep Vrell's secret a while longer. Shung, I ask the same of you. 'Tis improper for an unmarried woman to travel alone with one man, let alone hundreds. Let's see her safely to Carmine—where she can start a new life. You tell everyone she's a woman, you bring her a whole host of trouble."

Achan shrugged. "I'll tell the men she's to be left alone."

"Ah, then it looks like you're claiming her as your own and that isn't proper. It'd also ruin both your reputations if it came out you'd been traveling together all this time."

Again Achan was making decisions without considering the repercussions. He should consult Sir Eagan on this matter. "But I don't feel comfortable with this." He gestured to that strange belly. "I'm afraid I'll be the one to bungle it."

Sparrow's green eyes met his. She straightened. "If you don't mind my asking, Your Highness, how did you find out?"

"Uh . . . I've been seeking the traitor. Shadowing people. I suspected Polk had sour motives." Achan scratched the back of his neck. "I'm truly glad you weren't the traitor, Sparrow."

A shaky breath blew past her lips. "How could you even consider that?

"In my experience, a man who—someone who lies once, lies about other things. What was I supposed to think?"

Sparrow's glare could freeze the waterfall overhead. Achan didn't care. Let her stew about this for a while.

"Achan, allow Vrell to play her role a bit longer," Sir Gavin said. "She'll stay away from you so you won't have to worry about a slip of the tongue."

Achan squeezed his hand into a fist. Sparrow was his friend. He didn't want her to stay away from him, and he didn't want her to go off and start a new life. He couldn't say that, though.

Sir Caleb would have his hide for misleading a woman's heart. Still . . .

"She will not stay away. She'll come back to our chambers where she should've been all along. I realize you were trying to help, Sir Gavin, but by putting her out of our presence, you endangered her life. She'll take Sir Eagan and Kurtz's room. They can bunk with me or you."

"Do not blame Sir Gavin." Sparrow's raspy voice caught. "He is the only one who has looked out for me."

Achan clenched his teeth. "If you would have told me, I'd have done the same."

"Do you have *any* idea how hard this has been?" Sparrow asked. "For eight months I have been alone. I have kept my secret without a soul discovering it. Even Macoun Hadar could not pry it from me. But you . . ." She scowled at him as if he were some beast of Barth.

"I had a job to do," Achan said. "I'm sorry if your life has been hard, *Miss Sparrow*, but—"

"Oh, do not start with the sad tales of Achan Cham, the prince raised as a stray."

"—but I had thought we were friends."

"What happened to you was rotten, but it is all better now. You have nice clothes, handfuls of servants."

"And since I couldn't go back to Sitna, you became my *only* friend."

"People love you wherever you go. Women fall at your feet—"

"So forgive me if I'm a little upset that my *friend* not only lied to me—"

"—you are handsome and clever. You do not need me, or anyone else, to hold your hand."

"—but I can no longer spend time with my *friend* because it's improper."

"If you cannot comprehend why I refuse to marry a pig and be forced to bear him children, then you—"

"As a woman, you talk a lot. So forgive me, *Miss Sparrow*, but I liked you better a lad."

"—have a lot to—"

"Enough!" Sir Gavin stepped in between them. "These walls aren't thick enough to guard this conversation. If you two cannot speak peaceably, don't speak at all."

Sparrow folded her arms, turned her head, her nose tilted up, her eyes downcast.

Achan frowned. Sparrow's cheeks were pink from yelling. "You think I'm handsome?"

Sparrow rolled her eyes. "When you shave your face, comb your hair, and wear clean clothing. You do not think all these women throw themselves at you only because you are the prince?"

Actually, that's exactly what he'd thought. Either way, why should she care what other women— He propped a hand on his hip and laughed. "Oh, I see. All this time, all the strange things you've said on my behalf. Jaira, Ressa, Yumikak, Lady Tara, Beska. You were jealous."

Sparrow shot him a withering look. "I see being prince has brought on a new level of arrogance."

"You deny it?"

"Absolutely."

"Ha." Achan grinned and scratched behind his ear. "No, no, it all makes perfect sense."

Blood flushed to Sparrow's round face. She stepped up to Achan, eyes narrowed. "You. Are an arrogant pig."

Sir Gavin seized Achan's upper arm and pulled him back a step. "I can see the only way to end this madness is to drag one of you out. Achan, let's go see about your chamber."

Achan allowed Sir Gavin to tow him to the door, watching Sparrow closely, smirking as her anger melted.

She sent one more wide-eyed plea. "You will not tell?"

He bowed low and dramatically, fighting to conceal his smile. "Your gender is safe with me, *Miss* Sparrow."

She strode up to Achan, stopping inches from him. She gripped his bicep in one hand and pressed her finger over his lips with the other. He straightened, tense, and exhaled as if her finger were a switch that controlled his breathing. He could only stare into her green eyes, befuddled.

Her finger trailed down his chin, tapped his chest once, then she grabbed his shirt and elbow, and pushed. He fell back. Her leg hooked perfectly behind his knee, sweeping his foot out from under him.

His body twisted as it fell. He hit the floor on his left side, cracking his elbow against the wood. A tremor shot up his arm.

Sparrow looked down, her lips pursed in a thin smile. "Do not call me *miss*."

Sir Eagan and Sir Caleb discovered several poisons in Achan's chambers. A tray of tarts, a bottle of wine, the water pitcher, even his bed sheets had been dusted in a powder ground from a deadly coral Sir Eagan called rôsh. Lord Yarden insisted Achan move across the hall into new chambers, just to be safe.

This room was identical to his previous one, except that it looked out over the eastern side of the stronghold rather than the western side. Sparrow had moved into the servants' quarters on the northern end of Achan's room with Sir Gavin. Sir Caleb, Sir Eagan, Inko, and Kurtz were using the larger servants' quarters on the southern end. Shung would sleep on a pallet in Achan's room.

Now they occupied a small meeting room on the second floor. Everyone but Achan sat crowded around a rectangular table, going over—yet again—the evening's events, with the exception of Sparrow's secret, of course.

Achan stood at the window, glaring at the torchlights on the curtain wall. He couldn't sit at the table, for he couldn't stop staring at Sparrow. And now the discussion had somehow turned into a lecture, one he felt he did not deserve. "But if controlling a man's mind is the only way to save someone, why is it wrong?"

"Because it's immoral," Sir Eagan said. "Arman didn't give you the gift to force a man's free will."

Achan spun to face Sir Eagan. "Yet it's okay to physically harm him? Bind him, lock him up. Even torture is allowed, but not controlling his mind? Making him stop hurting someone? Why would Arman give me the ability if He didn't want me to use it?"

Sir Gavin sighed out his nose. "Everything is permissible, but not everything is beneficial. Achan, I'll not tell you how to use your gifts, but I will always hold you accountable."

"Gifted men have gotten accustomed to this kind of control so that they do it without even realizing they are manipulating others," Sir Eagan said. "You might think, in exasperation, that your valet go jump off a cliff for advising you to wear fancy clothes, only to find that he has done just that, subconsciously unable to disobey your command. Few men have such bloodvoicing power, but it is plain that you do. Controlling others will not make you a better man."

"We worry for you, Your Highness," Sir Caleb said, "that you'll become addicted to this control without realizing it."

"He needs proper training by someone powerful enough and young enough to keep up with him," Sir Gavin said.

Achan lowered himself onto the wooden bench, which creaked under his weight.

My, what have we been eating, Your Highness? Sparrow asked, instantly drawing his eyes to her face.

Achan closed his mind, startled he'd forgotten to keep his defenses up.

"Sorry," Sparrow said from across the table.

She wore her fake belly again and the effect confused Achan's thoughts. She so looked like a boy—yet he knew better now. *You startled me. I hadn't realized I'd left myself unprotected again. How do you remember to guard so well?*

Sparrow shrugged, cheeks darkening so her complexion looked like marbled opal and rose. Achan forced his eyes and mind away from Sparrow's appearance. How was he to deal with her teasing now that he knew she was a woman?

"Why cannot you be teaching him, Eagan?"

"I am quite rusty, Inko. I suggest Duchess Amal."

"A logical suggestion," Sir Gavin said. "I'll ask her when we arrive. We'll leave in two days."

Achan's attention flitted back to the men. Who was asking who what?

"And what shall we do with Polk?" Sir Caleb asked.

"He cannot bloodvoice," Sir Eagan said. "It stands to reason he has a partner who can."

"Why? If he's Esek's man, or even a greedy man seeking a fat reward, he could be working alone, eh?" Kurtz asked.

Sir Gavin sighed and stroked his beard braid. "Achan and I will question him."

Achan followed Sir Gavin to the dungeons, which smelled worse than any Achan had even seen. The moisture must add more mildew than usual. The guard led them into Polk's cell. Achan stood inside the doorway and folded his arms.

Sir Gavin approached the wall where Polk sat chained and nudged his leg with the toe of his boot. "Get up."

"I'm trying to sleep."

Achan had no desire to play this game. He'd been a prisoner himself several times and knew every prisoner justified their behavior somehow. Polk would be no different.

He sighed. "Going into his mind will be much faster."

"You only think so because you have never tried," Sir Gavin said. "What you don't understand is that truth cannot be taken from any man's mind. He must give it freely. If he is able to concentrate on other things, you can only read those thoughts, not the ones you want. There is no way to force his mind to remember something you have never experienced. He must allow it."

"Will you keep it down?" Polk said. "I thought I had my own cell."

Achan wanted to shove his fist through Polk's head. "Why do you help Esek? He was horrible to you."

"How'd you know?"

"Because I served as his squire longer than anyone should have to."

"I only left him four months ago. How long could you have served?"

Achan scratched his arm. "A few weeks. And that was too long. He's a madman."

Polk lowered his head and mumbled, "You wouldn't understand."

"Hmm. Let me guess. He has your mother, brother, sister, or lover locked away. If you don't do exactly what he asks . . ."

Polk met Achan's eyes.

"Esek is lying," Achan said. "He'll keep using you as long as you let him. And then he'll kill your loved one anyway."

Polk shook his head. "I have to try."

Achan supposed he'd have said the same. "Just tell me if there are any more of Esek's minions in my army."

Polk met Achan's gaze. "There's one, but I don't know who he is. He can do that mind thing, though, like you."

Achan straightened. His list would finally come in useful. "Thank you, Polk. That narrows it down quite a bit."

Achan spent the next three days watching the eight bloodvoicers, barely leaving his room. He'd nearly failed Sparrow, just as Bran had almost failed Gren. It would not happen again. He stared at Polk's name on the list circled in bleeding black ink. Why could he discover nothing of the second traitor? Had Polk sent him on a bootless errand?

When Achan entered the Great Hall for lunch, followed by Kurtz, his temporary shield while Shung was in the bathhouse, he overheard a servant tell another that the prince was ill and not to get too close.

Perhaps he *had* spent too much time in his chambers.

So many stared at him in the great hall he took his chicken leg outside, not bothering to take Kurtz away from his new, red-haired lady friend.

Kingsguards and servants roamed the bailey. Achan sighed, in the mood for brainless banter. If he found any of the knights, they'd only make him think about being a king. Except for Shung, who was taking a well-deserved break. Achan strolled across the south side of the bailey lawn and bit into his chicken leg, scanning the men for a familiar face. He spotted Sparrow, sitting alone by the moat, boots on the grass, bare feet in the water, staring up at the waterfall that spilled over the southern tower.

He snuck up behind her and steeled himself. Mindless banter? Or another fight? "You know the privies empty into the moat, don't you?"

Sparrow didn't move a muscle. "Not in this castle. The privies empty into an underground stream that merges with the Betsar a ways down."

Achan fell onto his backside next to Sparrow and bit into his chicken leg. The wind blew a strand of her hair across her cheek. Her green eyes were fixed on the waterfall, reflecting the shifting water in miniature. Achan swallowed, heart pounding like Berland drummers. What in all Er'Rets was wrong with him? "I—I've missed you." Missed her? That didn't come out right. What happened to his plan for mindless banter?

Her eyes widened. "Missed *me*? Whatever for?"

He forced himself to look away and managed to gather his senses again. "Oh, I don't know. Everyone is so serious all the time. At least you jest."

"There has been little to jest about of late."

"Aye. For the longest time, I truly believed an older, wiser man would step in and be king and I'd be able to go off and build my cabin in the woods. Then suddenly—and I can hardly remember when—I just accepted it."

"That is good."

Her praise made his heart beat faster. "You think so?" He glanced back and her eyes threw off his composure again. He looked at the ground and scratched the back of his neck. Blasted fleas. "I must admit—though don't tell anyone or I'll have to beat you—I'm quite nervous."

"A natural feeling, I am sure."

Perhaps. "But what if I mess up? What if I fail?"

"I am certain you will mess up, but you cannot fail."

He wanted to defend himself. He intended to make no mistakes. "How can you be so sure?"

"Because Arman does not fail."

"Right. I keep forgetting."

"It takes time."

"What? Becoming a good king?"

"That too, but I mean, getting to know Arman."

Hmm. "Ever been to Carmine?"

"Sure I—" She choked on her words. "I mean . . . yes. I have. Before Walden's Watch. It is a lovely place."

He bumped his arm against hers. "Do you have any concerns for me? Any premonitions of young married women I might accidentally propose to?"

She laughed and her voice, that throaty sound . . . how convenient for her to have such a voice. It had aided her disguise well. Lady Tara couldn't have pretended to be a boy even for five minutes.

"No," Sparrow said, "but the Carmine vineyards are the prettiest land in all Er'Rets. On a summer day like this, when the sky is so clear and blue and it meets the endless green vineyards on the edge of the horizon as far as you can see in all directions . . ." She sighed, head tipped back to stare at the sky. "It's the most peaceful, breathtaking view."

Achan stifled a smile. Sitting with Sparrow like this, as much as she talked, Achan couldn't believe it had never occurred to him that she was a girl.

He remembered the drumstick in his hand and bit into it, the meat now turning cold. "So. You don't want to marry a guy like Lady Tara's husband, and I *want* to marry a woman like Lady Tara. Why can't we figure this whole thing out?"

She faced him, eyebrows pinched together. "What would Sir Caleb say if he saw you talking with half a chicken leg in your mouth?"

How like a woman to be so critical. At least the mystery of Sparrow's moodiness had been resolved. He ripped off another chunk of meat with his teeth and forced himself to burp.

Sparrow turned away. "Charming."

"I'm serious, though. Do you think we'll end up miserable despite all our protests?"

Sparrow stirred her feet in the water. "I think you will probably war until you are forty. Then you shall finally move into Armonguard and take a bride of twelve."

"Take a bride . . . Sparrow, I tried to find a bride my age. I failed." He took the last of the meat off the chicken leg and spoke over a full mouth. "Perhaps I'll wed thrice *my* elder."

Sparrow giggled. "And what good would it do you to have no heir?"

"Who says I won't have an heir?"

Her cheeks pinked, and she straightened, prim and proper. "Old women cannot bear children, Your Highness. Their seeds have all dried up."

Achan frowned. "Really?"

Sparrow shook her head and poked out her bottom lip. "Such a fool is to be our king?"

"Watch your tongue, *Master Sparrow*, or I shall have to best you. You know I can."

She rolled her eyes. They were silent for a while. The sun cast a golden glow atop Sparrow's black hair. It had grown since Achan had met her, now long enough to tie back in a tail, the way Achan wore his. Was it soft like Gren's hair?

Her voice jolted him away from his drifting. "Did you love her dearly? Lady Tara?"

"Love her?" Achan shrugged and tossed the chicken bone into the moat. "I don't know. No. I loved the idea of her. When first I met her, she treated me kindly in spite of my station. It was like a test of character that she passed so well. I knew she was worthy through and through. And she could ride a horse like a man. And, of course, she is not painful to look upon. I could think of no better combination." He sighed. "I knew I'd never marry—who would have me?"

"Another stray?"

"Ah, well, I'm sure you know most are taken as mistresses. No, Sparrow. Marriage wasn't for me, and I didn't mind so much. I had Gren and Noam, two excellent friends." He paused, picturing Gren's warming smile. "Now Gren I loved."

"Might Sir Gavin allow . . . ?"

"He's already told me no."

"I am sorry."

"Though I must say I'm surprised how short a time it's taken me to give up that fight. Perhaps it's because of Riga. Or the baby. Or both. Plus, I fear Gren is smitten with Bran Rennan. I cannot decide how I feel about *that*. Part of me is vexed. Bran's duty was to protect Gren, not woo her. Yet, no one knows the pull Grendolyn Fenny has on a man better than I. So I suppose I cannot blame Bran for being what he is."

Sparrow snorted. "Too foolhardy to realize a woman is flaunting herself before him?"

Achan straightened. "Gren doesn't *flaunt*."

Sparrow turned her angry eyes on him. "A beautiful woman hardly has to. Am I to pity all you men who can barely hold onto your hearts every time a pretty girl enters the room?"

"Our hearts? That's woman's talk, Sparrow. It's harder than you would think."

She scoffed. "And now you see why I would rather play a man. A man is not disdained for admiring more than one woman. A man is not expected to fight off unwelcome advances at every turn. And no one thinks poorly of a man who is not wed before he is twenty. As Vrell Sparrow, I am safe from men."

"Save Polk." She didn't answer, so Achan went on. "I'd agree what you suggest is true of *most* men. But not all are free to love who they choose." Achan scratched the back of his neck. "We're two of a kind, Sparrow, you and I. Both masquerading as something we're not. You're not a man, and I'm not a king."

Her nose wrinkled in a disdainful scowl. "And you never will be with such an attitude. I can prove I am not a man, but you *are* to be king despite your whining sarcasm. If you do not start believing it, you shall be a bad king, a weak king, and someone will kill you in your sleep." She cocked an eyebrow. "A stray mistress perhaps?"

Achan couldn't resist teasing her back. "You're volunteering to be my mistress?"

Sparrow glanced away, rosy cheeks darkening. "You may dream, Your Majesty."

Achan scratched a flea bite on his arm. "Actually, I cannot. Ever since I've started shadowing my army, I haven't slept well. Plus, Sir Caleb has forbidden I ever consider a mistress. You know me. Until his advice, I had been planning to take hundreds."

"I do not find your jesting humorous."

My, she had an arrogant way about her. "I thank you, Sparrow, for your insight and scruples. You've chastised me well and good, but you forget your place. I have six men to advise my every breath. I don't need lectures from you too." He stared at a leaf sailing past in the moat's current. "I should warn you, if you want to play the boy, I'm afraid you must get tousled like one. It's all part of the deception, after all."

He grabbed her shoulders and pushed. Sparrow squealed and splashed into the moat. Achan started to laugh, but his leg jerked forward and his backside slid right off the bank. The cold water shocked him as he sank beneath the surface. His boots found the bottom and he popped to his feet and gasped.

Water splashed over his back from behind. He spun around in time for Sparrow to splash him again. The breeze wrapped around him, making him shiver. He spit out a mouthful of water and dove toward her. After losing her twice, he managed to tuck her head inside his elbow and drag them both beneath the current.

A few sharp finger-jabs to his ribs, and Achan released her head. He stood, shivering in the breeze. Where had she gone? Movement snagged his gaze to the waterfall. A dark shape shifted behind the spray. Achan dove under the water and opened his eyes, thankful the privies didn't drain into the moat.

All he could see was froth from the waterfall. He swam around the falls until a pair of brown trousers came into view. He glided to her legs and popped up before her.

Sparrow squealed and backed against the stone wall, water dripping down her face, off her jaw. They stood in a pocket the waterfall created with the castle. The cascading wall of water behind Achan stroked Sparrow's face in moving bits of shadow and light. Her chest heaved with the heavy breaths fogging slightly from her lips.

She splashed him again but he didn't move. It was as if he had never seen Vrell Sparrow before. Everything about her in this moment seized him, sent his heart banging a tribal rhythm again. The shape of her face, the lock of ebony hair plastered to her cheek, her piercing green eyes.

"Hey, Sparrow." He set his hands on her shoulders and leaned down until his forehead settled against hers. Her eyes were so close, so deep, shifting back and forth to focus on his. Droplets of water trailed down the bridge of her nose, ran under her eyes and down her cheeks.

Achan pushed all rational thought aside, tilted his head. But her hand on his chest caused him to pull back. She ducked down, sinking beneath the water. The dark shape of her body shot away like an arrow.

Pig snout. He'd missed his chance.

He walked under the falls, letting the water beat down on his head and back for a moment before wading into stiller waters. No sign of the little vixen. Moments later he saw her climb onto the bank, shove her feet into her boots, and walk away, headed toward the inner gatehouse.

Achan slogged to the shore and hoisted himself out. He jogged up behind her, soggy boots squishing over the lawn, and was just about to pounce, when Sparrow spun around, her sword pointed at his chest. A stream of water drizzled off the cheap crossguard.

"Please don't strike me." Achan cowered behind his hands in mock fear. Water trickled down his arms. He peeked between his fingers. "Uh, did you ever learn to use that thing?"

She thrust the blade forward and poked him in the stomach.

"Ow!" Achan stepped back and rubbed his gut. "Put that away before you hurt someone." He waved at a group of soldiers who had started coming their way. The men stopped, but continued to watch them. He lowered his voice. "Or before you get arrested for attacking the Crown Prince."

"I am merely practicing, Your Highness. How else will I learn?" Sparrow pursed her lips and thrust Firefox at him again. This time he darted aside and grabbed her wrist. He pressed his thumb between the fine bones, gently at first, then harder. My, Sparrow was a stubborn little thing.

She grimaced—trying to be tough?—but finally yelped and opened her hand. Her sword clunked to the ground.

Achan grabbed it and tucked it under his arm. "I might have to keep this until you learn some manners. I mean, pulling a sword on your future king? Honestly!"

Her nose wrinkled as she scowled. "You do not even want to be king!"

"Now, that's not the point, Miss Sparrow, and I've—"

Sparrow shoved him and whispered, "Do not call me that! Someone might hear."

He chuckled. "Very well. That's not the point, *Lady* Sparrow."

She heaved a sigh. "I suppose you think you are clever?"

Achan grinned. "I do, actually."

She folded her arms, lips turned down, pouting. "You would never treat Lady Tara the way you treat me."

"Don't be silly. Lady Tara is a noblewoman. You're just . . . well . . ." He shrugged. "One of the men."

Her wet face flamed. She bounced toward him and punched him in the eye.

"Ahh!" Pain stabbed his eye. She'd punctured his eyeball. "Blazes, Sparrow!" He palmed his left eye and cried, "Ahh!" again. He squinted through his right eye. "What did you do that for?"

She shrugged. "Jest bein' one o' th' men, Yer Highnuss. We men like t' brawl, yeh know." She spun on her heel and marched away.

He yelled after her retreating form, "Next time you'll get one in return and don't think you won't!" He squatted beside the moat and scooped up cold water to put on his stinging eye.

Blazes!

He released his eye and tried to open it, but it was already swollen shut. He couldn't see. Those tiny little fists . . . They fit right into his eye where a man's fist couldn't possibly reach.

"Y'all right, Yer Hignuss?"

Achan spun around to see Brien, his scraggly thief from Ice Island, shadowed by three others. Heat flooded into Achan's face. Caught being bested by a woman.

"You want I should teach that healer lad a lesson?" Brien asked.

Achan relaxed and reminded himself that no one knew Sparrow was a woman. "No. Thank you, Brien. The lad is finally growing into his boots. Been trying to toughen him up for a while now."

Brien and the soldiers chuckled and wandered off. Achan stewed beside the moat until his violent shivering forced him inside. He stormed through the dank keep and up to his room, adding his own small river to the damp floors.

Everyone was already there.

One look from Sir Gavin and the old knight rushed forward. "What happened? Did you fall in the moat too?"

Achan studied Sparrow out of the corner of his eyes. She stood by the window, hugging her shivering arms. He unlaced his doublet and pried it off, doing his best to act nonchalant. "Sparrow bested me. For the first *and last* time, mind you." He peeled his tunic over his head, wadded it into a ball, and pitched it at Sparrow. It whacked her in the face and she squeaked. "Well done, Sparrow."

"Yes, well done, minnow!" Kurtz said.

"Gracious, don't kill him, Vrell." Sir Gavin's mustache curled. "We can't show up in Armonguard with a black and blue prince. Go easy next time."

Laughter rang out.

Achan shot Sir Gavin a bland look. "Fear not for my well being. It is I who'll no longer be going easy on Sparrow." He spun around the room, trying to locate his pack with one working eye. He fixated on Sparrow's pale face and cast her a challenging, one-eyed stare.

She grinned, a smile that vitalized her whole face despite her tangled, wet hair and dirty cheeks. Achan's stomach zinged.

"I assure you, Your Majesty," she said, "I do not need you to go easy on me. I can take anything you toss my way."

35

For an hour that afternoon, the knights and Achan discussed the future. The plans for leaving the next day, what would happen in Carmine, and of course, more discussion over Achan's future bride. The knights talked, actually. Achan simply sat, overwhelmed, stewing and daydreaming—even dozing at one point. Thankfully, Sir Gavin dismissed him early. Achan entered into his chamber to see Sparrow standing at the window that overlooked the courtyard below.

Her eyes widened. "Forgive me. My new room does not have a window. I thought you were meeting with the knights, so . . ."

Achan closed his eyes and peeked through Sir Gavin.

He is too young to marry, Sir Eagan said. *Why not focus on a long betrothal? Give him time to get used to the idea a bit more.*

What's to get used to? He can figure it out, he can. If he needs help, he's got me, eh?

Thank you, Kurtz, for your offer, but that is not what concerns me.

Achan pulled away from the discussion and sighed. "Aye, they're still . . . talking. Sir Gavin excused me. The conversation had begun to annoy." He didn't want to explain the ongoing debate over who he should marry. For here stood Sparrow and he could no longer see her as anything but a pretty young woman in trousers. A breeze from the window blew a wisp of ebony hair across her alabaster cheek.

She smiled and brushed the strand away.

What folly. Why was he such a fool where women were concerned? Why did he continually choose the wrong ones? Why couldn't he simply accept his position with grace and marry whomever the knights ordained would be best?

He recalled what Poril had always said of his stubborn spirit. *Ah, yer a fool, yeh are, boy. Had to smart off. Had to fight back.*

Achan had never liked being ordered around.

"Are you well, Your Highness?"

Sparrow moved to the center of the room. Her wide green eyes were fixed on him, her slender eyebrows pinched together.

"As well as anyone in my position would be, I suppose," he mumbled.

She walked toward him, toward the door. She was leaving? Achan reached out and grabbed her elbow. He let his grip slide down her arm and caught her hand. A tingle danced up his arm. "Where are you going?"

"I— " Her cheeks tinged pink. "I-I should not be . . ."

Achan pulled her close and reached up with his free hand to tug out the thong in her hair. With both hands, he combed her silky hair around her sweet face.

Her lips parted, her breath a tremor on his neck. He held her warm cheeks in his hands and drew his thumb over her lips, marveling at the softness of her skin.

What could she be thinking? He didn't dare look inside, for fear it would ruin this moment.

He tilted his face down and closed his eyes. She inhaled a sharp breath and tensed beneath his hands. His lips pressed against hers. They were soft and sweet like honey. Warmth shuddered through him as her breath mingled with his, entered his mouth and seized his soul.

She grabbed two fistfuls of his tunic and tugged him closer, deepening the kiss. Her hands snaked up the back of his neck, into his hair, and held tight.

A door clicked shut. Sparrow turned to stone in his arms. Achan broke away and found no one there. He frowned, uncertain if the noise had come from the door to his room or Sir Caleb's. He turned back barely in time to see Sparrow's hand flying toward him. It struck his cheek with the force of a cham bear. He staggered sideways to keep his balance.

He set his hand to his cheek and found the skin hot. "What was that for?"

She blushed, her eyes liquid with tears. "I would think it would be obvious."

He sucked in a deep breath but could think of no *obvious* answer. "First my eye, now this? For not wanting to kill, you're a violent woman, Sparrow."

She propped her hands on her hips. "*Never* kiss a girl without asking first."

"Why not?" He massaged his smarting cheek.

"Well . . . because . . . it is rude. She might not want you to."

"How am I supposed to know that? I've never kissed anyone at my own instigation."

Sparrow raised her eyebrows. "You kissed Jaira."

Curse Jaira Hamartano to the Lowerworld forever. "That doesn't count."

"Beska?"

"*She* kissed *me*." Looking back, something occurred to him. Sparrow *had* been jealous.

Her voice wavered. "Not even Gren?"

Achan shook his head slightly, feeling odd to be speaking of Gren. Why did girls have to talk so much? He met her eyes and grinned. "*May I* kiss you, then?"

She shrank back. "Absolutely not!"

He stiffened, as if she'd slapped him again. "Is this because I spared Polk? I'm sorry, Sparrow. Prison is fairer than death. Esek had been threatening his family."

Her scowl faded. "You have a kind heart. It is not a thing to apologize for."

"Why, then?"

Her brows pinched. "Because I am *not* a wanton woman. I explained that fully out—"

"It was only a kiss. Don't get your britches in a bind."

She pursed her lips and huffed through her nose. "My britches are *not* in a bind. I do not expect you to understand having been raised by . . . Well, I am simply not the kind of girl who kisses a man she does not intend to marry."

Marry? Could he marry Sparrow? It was laughable. He could imagine Sir Caleb's response to the idea. "Well, what if—"

She held up a finger. "Do not say things you are not permitted to say."

He straightened to his full height. "I can say what I want."

"Then do not waste your breath saying things we shall both regret."

"*I* won't regret it."

"This is utterly inappropriate. You should never have entered a room with a woman alone. Have you no propriety?"

"Me? This is *my* room, Sparrow. And you're the woman running around in trousers. I'm no expert at propriety, but I'd say you were in violation first."

"*I* was simply looking out your window, as my room does not have one. I will leave. Good day, Your Highness."

"Sparrow, wait."

But she stormed past like a winter wind and jerked the door shut behind her.

Pig snout. Achan fell back on his bed and stared at the low timber ceiling. It had been going so well there for a moment. Hadn't she kissed him back? A moment of abandon—bah! No doubting it. He was a miserable failure at romance.

The door to Sir Caleb's room scraped open. Achan twisted his head to see Kurtz closing the door behind him, a handful of clothing under his arm.

Achan sat up, heart thumping wildly. Had Kurtz entered back when Achan heard the click? Back when . . . ?

Kurtz crept to Achan's door, eyes shifting slightly as he reached for the handle.

Achan jumped to his feet. "Kurtz!"

The knight paused, facing the door.

"Kurtz . . . uh . . . please sit a moment." Achan swallowed, for his mouth had gone quite dry. "It, um . . . what you saw . . . it wasn't what it looked like. I can explain. Sparrow's not—"

Kurtz pulled open the door and spoke to the floor. "Your business is your own, it is." He swept out the door as fast as Sparrow had.

Achan groaned and fell back onto his bed.

Pig snout!

Vrell fled down the stairs, trying unsuccessfully to stopper her tears. Her boot caught and she stumbled down the last four steps. She caught herself on the door jamb at the foot of the stairwell and held tight, gripping the stone as if doing so might remove the last few minutes of her life.

How could she have been so foolish! She had convinced herself that she had misunderstood Achan's behavior at the waterfall. How wrong she had been! Had she encouraged him? But they had been playing games since they had entered Darkness. She turned her back to the curve of the tower and sank, weeping to the floor. Silent wails shook her.

Approaching footsteps in the hallway broke her tirade. She gasped in short breaths, calming herself, hoping the person would pass right up the stairs without seeing her. She smoothed her hair back behind her head, twisting it into a tail, though she no longer had a thong to fasten it.

A brown rope swept through the door jamb, followed by Atul's weathered face. As if he knew she was there already, he immediately looked down. "Master Sparrow, just the person I was lookin' fer."

"Me, Atul?" She sniffled and lifted her chin. "How can I assist you?"

He held a hand out. "Need approval on 'n alteration. Fer the prince's wardrobe."

"But that is something to ask Sir Caleb. He supervises the prince's wardrobe." She tucked her hair into the neck of her tunic and accepted his hand. A chill combed her spine when he pulled her to her feet.

"Sir Caleb's 'n a meetin'. 'Tis a simple matter. But my seamstress don't wanna proceed without a go-ahead o' some kind. Won't yeh take a look?"

"Of course." Vrell followed Atul to a room on the first level, attempting to keep the memory of Achan's kiss from kindling more tears. Atul held open the door.

Vrell walked inside. The long and narrow room was lined with shelves that were loaded with folded fabric. A small candle burned in an iron sconce mounted beside the door, muting the many colors of fabric to dull, earthy tones.

There were no seamstresses here.

The door clicked shut. Vrell spun around. Atul grabbed her and clamped a moist cloth over her mouth. The familiar, bark-like scent called forth panic from every nerve in Vrell's body. This was the same substance Macoun Hadar had given her outside the Council meeting. She seized Atul's robes and pushed him, hooking his leg at the same time. His dark eyes flew wide as he thudded to the stone floor.

Vrell leaped over him, but Atul grabbed her ankle and she tripped. Her hands scraped down the bottom half of the door. She winced at the stinging splinters in her palms and tried to push herself up despite the pain. A fog settled over her mind, blunting her movements. She tried to focus, to call out to Achan, but even her mind had been crippled by the soporific.

She could hear Atul moving, feel him pulling her across the moist floor by her boots, then all went dark.

Vrell moaned, stretched her stiff back. Her head throbbed. She tried to stretch her arms, but they did not move. She pulled harder, opened her eyes to discern the problem.

A thick knot of hemp bound her wrists in front. A swell of nausea gripped her at the memory of Atul the traitor. She lifted her head and looked around. She was in a single-pole, circular pavilion. A small fire blazed in a bronze brazier in the center of the room, lighting the extravagant tapestries on the walls. The smoke trailed out a hole in the roof into a dark sky.

It must be night.

She lay on a burgundy silk blanket that covered a pallet of goose down. A table, two chairs, and three massive trunks sat to the right of the bed. A changing screen hid the left side of the tent from view. An elaborate red and blue gown hung over the side of the screen. Could this be a woman's tent?

She needed to bloodvoice Achan, to tell him Atul was a traitor and had taken her. But what if it were a trap to lure him here? Perhaps she should at least discover where she was before contacting him.

Men's voices grew outside the tent, drawing near.

"It will take me three days to prepare more. Why didn't you tell me you were out?" The familiar, raspy voice brought a shiver over Vrell. Khai Mageia.

"I never had none to be out of." This bad grammar belonged to Atul. "Polk was s'posed to give me some, but Sir Gavin took all Polk's gear. What could I of done?"

"You could've asked me to make you more days ago."

"Enough. This matters not. If she calls to the stray, he'll come for her."

Esek Nathak's snide, condescending voice brought tears to Vrell's eyes. Caught, after all this time, by the very man she had been hiding from. Arman, why?

"Send scouts to watch for him, Sir Kenton—but not you. You ride with me."

"Yes, Your Majesty." Footsteps faded out of earshot.

A gust of cold air swept into the tent. "*Still* she sleeps? I have no time for this. You said it wouldn't last long, Mageia."

Strong hands grabbed Vrell's waist and rolled her over. Khai Mageia's dark eyes stared through his flop of greasy brown hair. His wild mustache twitched, baring yellowed teeth in a malicious smile. "She's awake, Your Majesty."

Esek Nathak peeked over Khai's shoulder, sending a chill up Vrell's spine that coated her palms in sweat. She tensed at how much Esek resembled Achan. Blue eyes, tanned skin, and dark hair . . . They could be brothers.

Esek's nose wrinkled in a disdainful grimace. "She smells like rot. Are you certain this is Lady Averella?"

"Positive," Khai said.

Esek grunted. "I'll have to have that coverlet aired. Stand her up so I can get a good look."

Khai pulled Vrell off the bed. She wanted to struggle, but her head pounded so much she found it difficult to focus. The next thing she knew, she stood before the bed facing Esek, Khai, and Atul.

Esek wore a long, red, wool cape buckled at his throat with a ruby and gold cabochon the size of her fist, black trousers, and black boots. A thin gold crown sank into his oily black hair that had been slicked back into a braided tail. His beard had thickened since she last saw him and made his jaw and chin look like it was trimmed in black rabbit fur.

Esek's blue eyes met hers. "Really, my dear, am I so revolting you would sink to this level just to avoid me?"

"Just kill me," Vrell said, though she did not want him to.

He slid his bejeweled fingers over his short, black beard. "But you are to be my bride. I marry you to keep tabs on the north. *And* I'm quite fond of grapes."

Vrell tried to spit at Esek, but her saliva dribbled down her chin. Her face flamed. How did men always spit so far?

"Ug!" Esek shrank back. "The things I do for this land. I recall having seen you quite fetching, my lady. Do tell me you have not forgotten how to wear a dress?"

"I will die before I marry you."

"Yes, well, I cannot allow that. But you are welcome to death anytime after the wedding."

"You honestly think Carm would fight for you if you took me without my or my mother's consent?"

"I care not. Frankly, I've no time to chat, my dear. I am at war with Mitspah. My men are weakening the stronghold as we speak. Get yourself presentable and you may bid me farewell." He turned and strode from the pavilion.

Vrell seethed. "I care not whether you leave!" She focused her gaze on Khai and Atul. "What do you want?"

"You're to wear this." Atul skirted the bed and walked to the changing screen. "I took it from Lady Rubel's closet."

Vrell snorted a laugh. "If you think for a moment that Lady Rubel's gown will fit me, you are blind."

Atul draped the gown over the bed. The beaded bodice and skirt sparkled in the firelight. Khai stepped forward and drew a dagger from a leg sheath. Vrell drew back.

"I'm to cut your bindings, my lady."

"Oh." No sense arguing there. Vrell held out her wrists.

Khai sawed through the hemp. "The tent is surrounded. Do not bother trying to escape. I will return in five minutes, my lady. If you are not dressed, I will do it myself."

Vrell felt ridiculous in such a gown. It was as fine as many of her own, but the fit mocked her insufficiencies. As promised, Khai returned and escorted her from the tent.

Esek's camp was in a clearing beside a dirt road. Torch posts held lanterns and torches, filling the air with the smell of pitch. New Kingsguard soldiers scurried around, armor jangling beneath their black capes. There appeared to be at least fifty armed men here, though it was difficult to count with so many tents. Horses whinnied and snorted. Khai led her past a tent where men were laughing around a game of dice.

The smell of horses reached her before she saw Esek in the gloom. He stood with Sir Kenton and Chora beside his ebony courser. In the torchlight she could see that the animal was draped in red banners embroidered with the crest of Armonguard.

She scowled. Armonguard's crest should appear on a purple background, not red. She reached out for Achan and sent a knock. No answer.

"Ah, a vast improvement." Esek twirled his finger in the air. "Turn around. Let's see."

The audacity of this man, barking orders as if she were his property. She folded her arms and stared him down.

A sharp point pricked her back. Stale breath blew hot in her ear. "Obey your king, my lady."

Vrell darted around to see Khai holding his dagger out.

He waved it forward. "All the way, my lady."

She blew out a bitter breath and twirled. The beaded skirt funneled, sucking a chilled draft up her trouser-clad legs.

"Better. Though something doesn't quite fit." Esek reached out for the bodice of the gown.

Vrell slapped his hand away.

He chuckled. "Atul tells me the stray is unaware of who you are." He raised a dark eyebrow. "Oh, yes, my lady, you and I are of the same mold, I see. Why do you fight it?"

Vrell sent another knock to Achan. His lack of response ignited a fear in her mind. Did he lie bleeding on the grassy lawn of the Mitspah bailey, a sword protruding from his heart? She gasped as the familiar fear settled into her veins, inspiring one disturbing image after another.

This was not night. This was Darkness! How far from the castle was she?

She sent a knock to Sir Gavin.

Sir Gavin's voice came and went in a breath. *A moment, Vrell. Mitspah is under attack.*

She groaned inside and sent a knock to Achan again.

Esek held up his arms. Chora buckled a belt and sword around his waist. Ôwr. Achan's rightful sword. "This moment my Kingsguards are weakening the stray's so-called army. Can you believe he wasted all this time freeing a legion of withered grandsires?"

Esek laughed. "Now I will ride, find the stray, and cut him down once and for all. Once he is dead, I return for our wedding. But you are disappointed, my lady. Yes, I too would prefer something more elegant and formal, but since your mother refuses to cooperate, I shall take what I can get."

Esek tapped his cheek with his black-gloved finger. A row of rings glimmered over the leather. "A little kiss? For luck?"

Khai's dagger found Vrell's waist again. Her stomach coiled as she inched toward Esek's inclined head. She grabbed his face and bit down, sinking her teeth into his hairy cheek.

The familiar pressure of Achan's mind pressed in. *Yes, Miss Sparrow? You seem quite determined to get my attention this afternoon. Have you reconsidered hearing me out?*

Esek growled, the sound increasing to a full-on yell. His leather glove squeezed Vrell's neck, pushing her away.

Vrell released her bite. *Achan! Are you hurt? Esek has taken me captive to his camp in Darkness. He said his men have attacked—* she screamed, but Esek's strong fingers silenced her, cutting off her air. He held her at arm's length, still squeezing. He bashed his other hand against her cheek. Her legs crumpled under her, and Esek, now holding her up by her neck, lowered her to her knees.

Her released his grip some, leaned down, and tenderly kissed her cheek. "Oh, yes. You and I will have a splendid wedding night." He pushed her down, stomped on her face, and all went black.

36

Vrell Sparrow.

Achan opened his eyes to the low, timber ceiling. Sunlight beamed through the slats on the shutters, painting stripes of light across his wall. It must be late afternoon. He sat up, vision hazy, left eye still tender. He scratched his leg and sighed.

He'd been trying to watch the eight bloodvoicers again. He must have fallen asleep.

His head ached. Could bloodvoicing leave such an aftereffect? He reached for his list. Of the eight, Achan had solid feelings about Bazmark, Joab, and Nevon. He should cross those three men off and focus on the remaining five.

Another throb stabbed his temple. He clutched the scroll and lay back on his bed. Ahh. Maybe he should see if Sparrow had any tea for headaches.

Wait. Sparrow loathed him because he'd kissed her. Of all the foolhardy things. He could barely stand to relive the wondrous and horrifying moment.

And how much had Kurtz overheard? If he still thought Sparrow a lad . . . This might be awkward. Achan knew he would be the one to bungle Sparrow's secret, but this . . .

Sir Gavin had rebuked him for having tussled with Sparrow earlier. Said it was inappropriate and that Achan might have hurt her. Well, Sir Gavin would likely tar and feather him when Kurtz told him what he'd seen. Sir Caleb more so.

It wasn't entirely fair, the way they'd harped. He was the one with the black eye. And Sparrow had been the one to draw her sword in the bailey, though Achan had probably set things off by pushing her into the moat.

A shallow moat at that. More of a wading pool, really. There were no beasts in there. Maybe minnows. Like Sparrow. He smiled at Kurtz's nickname. What would the love-crazy knight do when he knew Sparrow was female? The idea of Kurtz admiring Sparrow filled Achan's chest with heat. Sparrow had been right about men. Kurtz a prime example. And now Achan had proved her right as well. After all she'd done to hide from men, how could he have let himself take advantage? What if she never forgave him?

Vrell Sparrow.

Oh. Apparently Sparrow was the reason for Achan's pounding skull. She never had gotten the hint how painful this kind of persistence was.

Achan rubbed his temple and opened his mind. *Yes, Miss Sparrow? You seem quite determined to get my attention this afternoon. Have you reconsidered hearing me out?*

Achan! Are you hurt? Esek is holding me at his camp in Darkness. He said his men have attacked—Sparrow's ragged scream filled his mind.

Achan swung his legs off the bed. *Sparrow?*

But the connection had vanished. He reached out, looked through her mind and found darkness. Surely she couldn't have fallen asleep in mid-sentence.

Had someone killed her?

A man's scream brought him back from the dark place. He jumped off his bed and ran to the window. The bailey smoldered with grey smoke. Achan could barely make out the shapes of men fighting. His men against black-cloaked New Kingsguard knights.

Sir Gavin! Why didn't you tell me we were under attack?

Shung told me you were sleeping. I felt it best to leave you. Stay in your chambers, Your Highness. We will deal with this rabble.

Unbelievable. If Achan's men heard he had slept through a battle, they might lose any thread of respect he had fought to earn. He ran into Sir Caleb's room and found the trunk containing his new armor. He had no way of securing the breastplate by himself, but he could manage the chain coat. He lifted the heavy chain out of the trunk.

Cole! Ready Dove and Shung's horse to ride.

Your Majesty? Cole sounded confused. *Where are you?*

In my chambers. Achan carried the chain coat back to his chamber and spread it out on his bed. Cole likely thought he was going mad. *Do not fear, Cole. I am speaking to you with bloodvoices. I will meet you at the stables in a moment.*

Uh, okay, Your Majesty.

Achan scrunched up the chain and ducked his head through the neck opening. His hair snagged and the chain hung heavy around his neck. He struggled and finally managed to get it on. It hung heavy over his clothing. He should probably put on another shirt, but there was no time. He seized Eagan's Elk and the knife from the Roxburg family. He threaded the knife's sheath onto the belt and buckled it around his waist.

Achan prayed Sparrow hadn't been hurt. He pulled open the door to find Shung standing outside. "Let's go, Shung. We've a battle to join."

Achan and Shung exited into the castle courtyard. The air was thick with smoke. Cole stood outside the stables between their horses. Achan started toward him.

"Your Highness!" Sir Eagan's head peeked over the top of the inner gatehouse, looking down. "Come up and take a look."

"I've no time for that. Atul has taken Sparrow captive. He's holding her at Esek's camp. Shung and I must ride."

Sir Eagan raised an eyebrow. "Her?"

"Please. She's not answering my bloodvoice calls."

"That is wide of the point, Your Majesty. We cannot open the gate just yet. Come up to the tower and you will understand."

Achan blew out an angry breath. Every second he lingered, Sparrow could be dying. He stormed to the gatehouse, Shung at his heels, and up the narrow, spiral stone staircase to the tower roof above the inner portcullis.

Sir Eagan stood with Sir Gavin looking over the crenellations. From here, Achan could see the entire bailey. Three tents along the southeastern curtain wall were on fire. The outer gate was shut. The forest outside the curtain wall blazed. But the wooden structures within the stone stronghold had not caught fire. Too moist, perhaps. The smoke had faded, leaving only a few pockets coiling up into the sky, burning the shaft of arrows they flew in on.

Dozens of men lay on the ground, some motionless, some writhing, some with arrows protruding from their bodies.

"It is over?" Achan asked.

"Not yet," Sir Gavin said. "We've pushed them down the road and they have retreated somewhat. Yet their cavalry has yet to come. Once our men are ready, we'll take the battle to them."

Achan watched his army readying their horses. "What happened?"

"When we left Tsaftown, we sent scouts ahead. Those who went to Carmine tell Gavin they've seen no sign of Esek's men. Those to Berland have not reported. Without their eyes, we could not know how close Esek's men were."

"Take my hand, Your Highness," Sir Eagan said. "I will show you."

"I don't understand."

"Open your mind and you will."

Achan held out his hand and opened a connection with the knight. He felt Sir Eagan's fingers grip his palm. Images flooded his mind's eye.

Sir Eagan explained what Achan was seeing. "I was returning from Temple Arman, paused at the northern tower, and saw men climbing onto the sentry walk. While I notified Gavin, they took out the guards at the outer gatehouse."

Achan saw the scene unfold, felt Sir Eagan's racing heart and sense of urgency.

"I befuddled a few with bloodvoicing, but many of them had shielded their minds. Gifted."

In the recitation of the event in his mind, Achan saw the New Kingsguard knights lower their weapons and look up to the sky in a daze.

"By the time Gavin made it out here, our men had already taken arms against the intruders. We took back the gatehouse before they managed to raise the portcullis."

Achan watched his men sprint across the lawn and enter the gatehouse. He recognized Bazmark at the front of the pack.

"Archers shot fire arrows over the wall. I moved down here with Gavin and searched the minds of the attackers to see what I could learn. A squadron—likely the ninety-plus men Kurtz saw leaving Tsaftown—came upon us unaware from the north. From Darkness."

Sir Eagan released Achan's hand.

Achan shivered as Sir Eagan's memories faded. "How did you do that? Give me your memories?"

"You saw my thoughts, but I chose which to show you."

"I too have looked into the minds of these men," Sir Gavin said. "From what I can tell, Esek is not with them. They answer to a Captain Keuper."

"I know him," Sir Eagan said. "He trained under Sir Kenton. Arrogant fellow."

"He's a fool," Sir Gavin said. "Why does Kenton not point out that shooting fire at Mitspah is a bootless errand?"

"Is Sir Kenton out there?" Achan asked.

"Not that we can sense," Sir Eagan said. "Nor is Lord Nathak. A shame, really. Many good men fight for Esek. I sensed their discord with this mission."

"Why do they fight for him if they are conflicted?"

"It is their job. It feeds their families. A man must think twice before leaving his only source of income and trailing after a rogue king."

"That's me? A rogue king."

"We have no coin to pay soldiers. For a man to leave his job and join you, he would have to believe the cause was worth the sacrifice his family would be making. Esek sabotages himself, though. He asks his men to die for his personal agenda. Killing you. I am surprised Sir Kenton allows this."

"Indeed. Something is amiss. Kenton, at least, would know better than to shoot fire at Mitspah stronghold."

Achan concentrated on Sparrow's face. Blackness. Hysteria gripped him. Arman, please don't let her be dead. He could tarry no longer. He darted between the men and grabbed each of their wrists, opened a connection, and remembered Sparrow's message, her scream, and how she went silent.

He opened his eyes to see Sir Gavin pale. "She called out to me. Eben's breath: I told her to wait."

"What are your orders, Your Majesty?" Sir Eagan asked.

Achan glanced at Shung. "We must take the road north, into Darkness. She's at Esek's camp."

Sir Gavin frowned. "Achan, we cannot allow you to go."

"I am not asking permission, Sir Gavin. Arman will protect me. I will take Shung."

"And me," Sir Eagan said. "I will go with you."

"Thank you," Achan said.

"Gavin, we will ride out with the men, ride through as they attack."

Sir Gavin sighed. "I'll inform Caleb. He won't be pleased."

• • •

"You could have put on your helmet, Your Majesty." Sir Caleb looked like a sullen child standing at Dove's side.

"Do not worry, Sir Caleb. I am wearing my chain armor. And my Shield and my father's Shield are with me."

"That's one more Shield than Esek has," Sir Eagan said.

Achan grinned. "See? All will be well, you shall see."

Sir Caleb's nostrils flared. He nodded, walked to the gate, and mounted his steed. Kurtz sat atop his horse beside Sir Caleb, looking fierce in armor.

Sir Caleb heaved his sword into the air and bellowed, "For King Axel and his queen!"

In response, the men raised their swords and echoed Sir Caleb's cry. "King Axel and his queen!"

The portcullis rose. Achan's heart raced, expecting to see a mêlée already in place or arrows flying his way. But the road was deserted. The army rode out behind Sir Caleb and Kurtz, and turned south along the road.

Then Achan saw them. In the distance, Esek's men, on horseback, riding toward them. Two in the lead fell from their mounts. Achan glanced back to see archers on the sentry wall of Mitspah letting their arrows fly to hold back the enemy.

Kurtz roared, raised his sword, and his horse galloped into the lead. Dove raced along in the cavalry. Achan reached out for Sparrow again and received no answer. His muscles clenched at the thought of losing her. How could he feel so strongly, having only known she was a woman a few days? He knew only that his life would not be the same without her quirky comments, her easy banter, even watching her clean her teeth.

The realization struck him like a gauntlet to the gut. She was the one for him. No matter what, he had to bring Vrell Sparrow back. He saw it as clearly as if it had been there all the time. He had to make her his, despite what Sir Caleb or any of the other knights had to say.

Sir Caleb, Kurtz, and Bazmark led the fray. They peeled aside one by one to engage the enemy. Achan, Shung, and Sir Eagan rode straight through.

A familiar voice cut through the clatter of hooves and swords. "There he goes, Sir Kenton! The white horse! The big one!"

Esek would give chase. Achan spurred Dove on. *Faster, boy. We must go faster.*

Twilight had fallen and the trees filtered most of the remaining light. Dove did not slow until a mist coated Achan's arm. The horse flattened his ears, his apprehension prickling Achan's arms.

Achan agreed with Dove. He loathed the idea of entering Darkness again. *I know, boy, but we must go back in. Sparrow is there.*

Dove slowed to a trot, tossing his head in protest. Achan urged him on, patting his mane.

Yellow light flamed behind him. Sir Eagan now held a torch in one hand.

Achan nodded, holding Dove back so Sir Eagan could lead. "Make haste, if you can. I'm sure Esek is not far behind."

Sir Eagan spurred his mount through the mist, torch fire streaming. Achan and Shung followed.

They found Esek's camp just past the Evenwall, a couple dozen tents erected in a clearing beside the road lit by torches mounted on wooden stakes. Sir Eagan rode into the camp and dismounted where two horses were tethered by a squat tree. Achan and Shung dismounted as well.

They weaved between two tents and stopped before a large, round pavilion that glowed with firelight from within. Judging by the drab tents surrounding it, this extravagant one had to belong to Esek.

Two armed New Kingsguardsmen stood at the entrance, swords drawn. Achan recognized both immediately. Atul and Khai. Achan drew Eagan's Elk.

An itch to Achan's temple preceded a knock. *Eagan.*

Achan opened his mind. *What's your plan?*

Shung and I will lure these guards aside. Achan will go in and free Vrell. Keep your minds open to each other.

Shung nodded. Apparently Sir Eagan had forged a connection with him as well.

Achan hung back while Sir Eagan and Shung approached the guards.

"Atul, you dog," Sir Eagan said. "The punishment for treason is death, you know."

"I serve my king faithfully."

"Ah, but Esek is no one's king. He is just a poor sap like you. So who is the bigger fool? The insane man who thinks he is king or the man who follows him?"

"It ain't crazy to follow the Council's anointed."

"Again, if the Council is filled with deranged men, I have to disagree. We have come for Sparrow. We believe you took her. Mind if we take a look in that fancy tent?"

"We do mind, actually," Khai said.

"A shame. For we shall have to kill you then." Sir Eagan's battle cry ripped through the quiet.

Steel clashed, feet scuffled over the moist dirt. Sir Eagan instantly drove Atul away from the entrance. Achan kept back, waiting for Shung to get Khai out of the way.

But why wait?

Achan charged and chopped Eagan's Elk at Khai's back. It grated against the chain he wore underneath his cape. Khai spun, swinging his gargantuan sword Achan's way. Achan ducked. The sword slashed into the canvas wall of the tent. Khai grunted and pulled it out, but Shung knocked him out with a crack to the back of his head.

Well done, Shung! Achan sheathed his sword and ran inside. Incense filled his lungs. A brazier crackled in the center of the round room. A small form lay curled on a bed on the other side of the brazier. Achan raced to the bedside. It was indeed Sparrow. She was wearing a red and blue dress. The deep colors against her fair skin made her look like a goddess, though her face was swollen in two places: below her left eye and on the left side of her forehead.

He scooped her onto his lap and tucked her head under his chin, stroking her soft hair, inhaling her rosewater scent. She felt so small in his arms. Warm. That was good, right? Warm meant alive.

"Sparrow." He shook her gently. "Wake up." He heaved to his feet, holding her against his chest. Her long skirt draped over his left hand and down to his knees, the beads on the skirt rattling against his chain armor as he carried her to the door.

Shung stood in the doorway, holding the curtain open. Achan turned sideways to duck past, shielding Sparrow's head with his own. He paused outside to adjust his grip, and Sir Eagan's posture sent a shock of cold through him.

The man stood, crouched, sword ready, facing two men who were dismounting.

Esek Nathak and his Shield, Sir Kenton.

Esek cried out. "Atul! This is *not* finishing him!"

Sparrow moaned, shifted in his arms, opened her eyes.

Praise Arman! "Oh, Sparrow. I feared the worst. If anything had—"

She squirmed in his grip. "Achan, we must hurry. Put me down."

"It's too late to run, Sparrow." He set her on her feet, keeping one protective arm around her shoulders, holding her against his side. "Look."

Her face seemed to pale further in the surrounding torchlight. He took her hand and squeezed.

Dove is just beyond those tents. Achan nodded toward the tents behind Esek and Sir Kenton. *Get to him and ride as fast as you can back to Mitspah.*

She shook her head. *We go together, please.*

If we all run, Esek gives chase. If it's just you . . . He looked down on her face. *It's me he wants. Let me fight him, distract him while you get away.*

I will not leave you.

Achan paused to knit this information together in his brain. She *did* care for him.

Sparrow. I have two Shields and Esek only has one. I will be safe. When the fighting starts, you run for Dove? Do you understand?

She nodded, tears streaming down her flushed cheeks.

"Here we are again, stray." Esek sighed. "This does grow old. I abhor all this traveling. Why won't you simply die?"

"Arman will not let me die." Achan took in his surroundings. Sir Eagan stood before Esek and Sir Kenton. Shung stood on Achan's left, Sparrow on his right, clutching his hand. Atul lay gasping by the tent opposite Esek's.

Achan scanned the area. *Were did Khai go? His sword is gone. I thought he was unconscious.*

Shung did not see.

He ran off, Sir Eagan said. *Must not have hit him hard enough, Shung.*

Esek snorted. "Arman, indeed. Sir Kenton, finish the gnat. I am tired of his charmed existence."

Achan pushed Sparrow behind him and drew his sword.

But Sir Kenton hadn't moved. "I'll tire him for you, toy with him if you like, Your Majesty, but I won't kill him."

Esek's eyes widened. "Explain yourself, Sir Kenton."

"I'm your Shield, true, but I serve Lord Nathak. He's my master and he ordered me not to let this man be killed."

Esek's posture swelled. "Have you always informed Lord Nathak of my plans?"

Sir Kenton bowed his head. "I have."

"Of all the insolent—" Esek thrust an arm in Achan's direction. "He is the only one who stands in my way. If he is dead, the throne is mine!"

Sir Kenton shook his head. "Do you honestly think your father would have let him live without good reason?"

Esek narrowed his eyes. "Do not refer to *that man* as my father."

Go, Sparrow, while they argue. Now!

She released his hand, and he heard her soft footsteps retreat around the back of the tent.

Sir Eagan's order came next. *Shung, you take Esek, I'll take Kenton. Your Majesty, stay back.*

Sir Eagan and Shung attacked. Achan stood, furious at being coddled yet again. Sparrow's raspy scream stifled his anger. *Khai!*

Achan ran around the tent, the way Sparrow had gone.

Of all the men to catch her! Khai?

His strong hand gripped Vrell's arm. A sharp point pricked the back of her neck. "Silence, my lady."

The clash of swords sounded from the other side of the pavilion. The men were fighting, but Vrell had failed to escape.

Khai's stale breath blew hot in her ear. "You and I will wait right here while the king kills your pathetic hero."

But Achan raced around the curve of the pavilion, sword in hand. He stopped a few paces away. "Let her go."

"Or perhaps *I* will kill your pathetic hero." Khai's knife punctured her skin. Vrell released a ragged breath at the prick of pain. "You must give up this charade, boy. The Council's word is law, unfair as it may be. Esek is king and you are not. If you want to see this girl live, give yourself up. That's all it will take."

Khai's grip slipped suddenly. Vrell ripped free.

Khai groaned to a yell. "No!" He stumbled and dropped his knife on the moist dirt, limbs shaking, face twisted in fury.

Vrell darted forward and snatched it up.

Run, Sparrow! Achan's brow furrowed, eyes focused on Khai.

"You think you can control my mind?" Khai panted. "I may not have your strength there, but I have skills you do not."

He reached out a hand, palm facing the dark sky. *"Râbab reba-bah râbah yârad. Rûwach âphâr mayim êsh, machmâd pârar."*

Green light sparked in Khai's palm. Realization dumfounded Vrell. Khai was a black knight. All the time, on the journey to Mahanaim. What Jax had called his witchcraft?

Achan's gaze was so intense he looked pained. *Go!*

But she had tarried too long. Khai had triplicated himself. He and his apparitions drew their monstrously long swords. His apparitions advanced on Achan.

Vrell steeled herself, darted forward, and plunged the knife into the real Khai's back. She shrieked, horrified at what she had done.

The apparitions vanished.

Khai wheeled around and stabbed. His sword pierced her side. She felt it enter her flesh, gasped, but the pain didn't come until the Khai withdrew the weapon. Her knees buckled.

"No!" Achan rushed forward and arrived barely in time to catch her.

Khai fell to his knees, dropped his sword. Achan carried Vrell around the weasely man, past a long, dark tent. A cramp seized her side. She pressed her hand over it, holding her breath. Achan spoke, but she couldn't understand his muffled, slow voice. Her vision blurred, flashed, her senses reeled.

Arman, help me.

She smelled horses. Achan lifted her higher, pressing her against Dove's saddle. Her side screamed at her to fall, to rest, but she reached for the saddlehorn, amazed at the animal's girth.

Her cheek rubbed against the wooden saddle. She pulled. Her body rose like she weighed nothing. Achan hoisting her up, no doubt.

She wanted to speak, to beg him to ride with her, but her mind and mouth were not in harmony.

Dove tossed his head. Vrell dragged her right leg over so that she lay in the saddle, slumped against Dove's white mane. She hugged his neck and, without a word, he galloped away.

37

Good boy. Certain the animal wouldn't stop until the Mitspah gate, Achan released Dove's mind then sent word to Sir Gavin that Sparrow was coming.

"After her!"

Sir Kenton mounted his black destrier and gave chase. More of Esek's men had arrived. Sir Eagan and Shung now battled four New Kingsguards.

Achan found the mind of Sir Kenton's horse and asked its help. The animal was more than happy to assist Achan, who promised to feed him all the oats he wanted if he would carry his rider the opposite way. Hopefully Achan would have the chance to make good on his promise.

"What is he doing?" Esek cried out. "She went the other way, you fool!"

Achan stepped toward Khai. He should perhaps bind him before helping Sir Eagan and Shung. But Khai lay on the ground, chest barely moving. He wouldn't be alive for long.

"Fine! I will go after her, then." Esek strode toward the horses. "I can see I have no one else who will serve me."

Achan cut off his path. "You will let her go."

Esek withdrew Ôwr. "Stray, we must work all this out. If you agree to simply die, all will be well."

"Arman has spoken. I cannot refuse Him."

Esek snorted a laugh. "Arman, indeed. He is the reason I don't rule already. Lord Nathak fears his useless prophecies." Esek circled, Ôwr gleaming like a star in one hand.

Three of Esek's men approached, swords ready.

"No!" Esek said. "This time I will kill him and prove to you all he is not invincible."

Esek jabbed Ôwr forward. Achan barely jumped back in time to keep from being stabbed. Esek cleaved from high guard, inviting a horizontal parry from Achan's blade. Their swords clashed, jarring Achan's weary arms all the way to his teeth. Esek came on strong with a series of cuts: side guard, back guard, low guard. He'd been practicing since Achan fought him last. Achan could only parry . . . parry . . . parry.

"I have never seen proof that any god exists," Esek said, swinging for Achan's feet, "let alone one who protects strays."

Achan jumped back and yelled. He took a deep breath and swung his sword at Esek's neck.

Esek parried Achan's strike and thrust for Achan's heart.

Achan sidestepped, spun back and nicked Esek's shoulder.

Esek yelled and stumbled back, then swung for Achan's arm. Achan parried, but Esek dropped under Achan's parry and nicked Achan's side.

Achan winced and drew back to middle guard. Esek swung from side guard. Achan moved to parry, but Esek faked, pulled Ôwr back, and stabbed one armed, slipping his grip to reach farther.

Ôwr pierced Achan's left thigh. He roared and snapped his sword down from high guard over Esek's extended arm, wincing as his blade severed Esek's limb above the elbow.

Esek shrieked and stared at the bleeding stump.

Achan's trembling arm fell limp at his side. He dropped his sword, horrified. His leg throbbed, hot pain gripping every nerve. Esek collapsed in a heap of red wool. Fainted? Dead?

"No!" Chora rushed forward and removed his cape. He balled it up and held it to Esek's gushing stump.

Achan fell back onto his rear and clutched the underside of his thigh. Blood oozed from the dark center of the wound and stained his britches. Panting through his teeth, he reached up his chain shirt and tugged his rope belt free. He pulled it under his leg and tied it above his wound.

A burning sensation rose from Achan's chest.

TAKE YOUR SWORD AND GO.

Achan obeyed. He hefted himself onto his good leg, picked up Eagan's Elk, and limped toward the horses.

YOUR FATHER'S SWORD.

Achan wheeled around and reached for Ôwr. He had to kick Esek's gloved hand off the grip. His father's ring caught his eye, wide and gold against the black leather glove. He dropped both weapons and pulled it from Esek's finger.

Achan jammed the ring on his thumb, picked up the swords, and staggered back, glancing from the severed arm to Esek and Chora, to the circle of onlookers. "Give up this fight. You cannot resist Arman's will. I don't wish to harm anyone, but continue to attack me and you'll suffer the consequences, no matter how . . . v-vile. Sir Eagan, Shung, we ride."

Achan stepped over Khai's body and approached the horses. His wounded leg shook beyond his control and he tried to keep his weight on his good leg. He clipped both swords to the saddlebag on Esek's courser. Shung and Sir Eagan helped him mount the horse, who, compared to Dove, seemed small and bony. Achan spurred the horse away, east, toward Light.

Sir Gavin, has Sparrow arrived?

They are just opening the outer portcullis for her now.

She is wounded. We're on our way.

Shung and Sir Eagan slowed their horses alongside Achan. "How is your leg?" Sir Eagan asked.

"I've had worse." The light faded fast as they left the camp behind them. "No torch?"

Sir Eagan pushed a hand through his loose hair. "Didn't think to grab one."

"Should we be concerned?" Achan had cinched his belt so tightly his leg had numbed. He loosened the knot.

"I doubt anyone will follow. You defeated their leader."

Achan pulled the belt free and tied it around his waist, leg tingling with feeling now. "Think he's dead?"

"Depends on whether they have a healer nearby."

Achan closed his eyes, still shaken from the sight of Esek's bleeding arm. *I'm sorry, Arman.*

But was he? Esek had been trying to kill him, had taken Sparrow. It was the fool's own fault for never wearing armor. Still, Achan could have finished him rather than leave him to suffer such a death.

When he opened his eyes, the torchlight from Esek's camp had faded. Achan's horse tensed; Achan could feel the anxiety running through the animal. He rubbed the horse's neck, patting him down. In the woods on his left, something rustled. Achan's horse stutter-stepped and turned. Achan held the reins tight, hoping to keep the animal on the road.

The other horses neighed and stomped their feet. One set of hooves trampled away.

"Whoa!" Sir Eagan called out in the distance. The hoof beats slowed on the dirt.

What is it? Achan's horse rocked back on his haunches and whinnied.

Likely a wild animal, Sir Eagan said.

"Easy, boy." Achan patted the horse's neck and urged him on. "It's just some deer."

The rustling increased. The courser whinnied, trying to turn back. Achan held fast to the saddle horn and fought to keep his balance. His left leg proved useless to steady him. Maybe Esek had trained the animal and it knew it belonged elsewhere. Achan connected with the animal's mind. Fear overwhelmed him. He thought calming thoughts, hoping to somehow evoke Sir Eagan's gift of calming emotions.

But the horse continued to panic. Achan's heart thudded, unsure of what might spook a horse so.

The Darkness lifted suddenly to a dim twilight. Evenwall mist coated Achan's face. He had never been so relieved to enter this place. Shung rode just ahead on the right edge of the road, almost in the brush. Achan could see Sir Eagan stopped up ahead, looking back, his horse sideways on the road.

"You are well?"

"I'm fi—"

Something slammed into the side of his horse, knocking Achan into a pine tree. The sharp limbs snapped against his chain coat as he fell through branches to the fern-covered ground, landing on his back. Orange light flashed on the road. A terrible roar stifled the horses' whinnying. Achan scooted back on his elbows and right foot, dragging his sore leg.

Sir Eagan's panicked voice burst in Achan's mind. *Your Highness! Where are you?*

Achan paused under a patch of charcoal sky. He could see the dark shapes of Esek's half-downed, half-bucking horse and a massive animal. *I'm okay. I'm in the woods.* Another sudden burst of orange flame caused the horse to utter an unnatural scream and illuminated the beast. Achan lost his breath.

Arman help him. It was a cham bear, and his swords were with the horse.

Shung cannot connect with its mind.

Can you, Sir Eagan? Can you calm it? Achan asked.

A moment of silence passed. Achan squinted at the scene on the road. The cham roared again, ears flat, eyes flashing in its own orange fire. It seemed intimidated by the bucking horse, though Achan could see the large gash in the horse's side. It smelled oddly like roasted venison.

Sir Eagan finally answered. *Someone controls it.*

What? Who?

I know not, but its mind is shielded. An animal cannot do that.

Achan's shaking arms gave way, elbows bucking. He picked himself back up and stared at the road. The cham's dark eyes focused his way. Bile snaked its way up his throat. His movement had gained the cham's attention.

The beast crept toward him, illuminated in a flash of twilight between the trees. It was the size of a bull, shaggy, with matted, brown fur. Its paws looked as big as Achan's head.

He reached out, felt the shields around the cham's mind, and pushed past them.

Hello, Yer Majesty. Yer not the only one who can master an animal's mind, Atul said.

Achan withdrew, concerned Atul might be able to storm him. *Atul controls it. Should I run? Climb a tree?*

No! Shung's deep voice resounded. *Stay still. Curl into ball. Back facing the beast. We hunt it.*

Achan rolled to his side, wounded leg down, and tucked his head, thankful Shung, the cham hunter, was here. He held his breath, listening, praying the animal would bound past, into the woods, after a deer or fox, some more common meal, though he knew deep down that the cham would obey Atul.

He gagged at the smell of sweaty fur and dung. Hot breath wafted over his neck as teeth sank around his right shoulder. Multiple throbs pierced through the chain armor as the cham clenched down and dragged Achan's left side over roots and thorny bushes. His whole body burned from within, but he stayed still, hoping compliance would at least keep the cham from charring him with a burst of flame.

His chain coat snagged. The cham jerked its head. When Achan's body didn't budge, the cham tugged again. Achan's mind got lost in the blinding pain. A man screamed. Or had that been him?

Sir Gavin's voice came first. *Achan, what's happening?*

Be closing your mind, boy! Inko said.

Who are you?

You're hurting me. Please close your mind.

Dear one, a kind woman said, *you must shield yourself.*

Your Majesty, you must relax. Sir Eagan sent his calm and the pain faded some. *We are right behind it.*

Shield yourself, eh Pacey? Kurtz said.

The cham let go. A roar vibrated Achan's eardrums. Orange light flashed. Shung screamed. A sword entered flesh. Something thumped. Branches cracked. A man grunted.

Sir Eagan? What happened? Shung?

Somewhere behind Achan, Shung groaned.

The cham bit Achan's shoulder again. Achan's head swam with agony. Darkness closed around his vision.

Achan! Sir Gavin said. *Your guard is down and you're spilling out. You must focus. Tell me what's happening. What's wrong?*

If Achan was dying, he didn't want every bloodvoicer in Er'Rets privy to it. He drew up his shields and fixated on Sir Gavin's voice. *A cham. Sir Eagan and Shung are trying to fight it.*

Call on Arman, Sir Gavin said.

Achan's cheeks flushed at this obvious conclusion. He closed his eyes and recited the words Sir Gavin had taught him, knowing in his heart Arman *could* help him. But would He?

Arman hu elohim, Arman hu echâd, Arman hu shlosha be-echâd. Hatzileni, beshem Câan, ben Arman.

Achan had to act. For all he knew the cham had roasted Shung. He reached his trembling left hand to his chain armor and slipped the rings free from a root. The next time the cham tugged, Achan's body scraped easily over the forest floor.

He felt for the sheath that held his dagger. It took more patience than he liked to cajole his trembling fingers to the right place, but he managed to draw it. He clutched it to his chest, squeezing the ivory grip. He'd only get one try. If he missed, the bear would roast him.

Shung had suggested the way to kill a cham was an arrow to the side, behind the shoulder. The knife wouldn't go deep enough to reach any vital organs. He needed to cut its throat.

The bear pawed him, its massive claws clicking over the chain. It clamped down on Achan's torso, just under his arm. Its teeth seemed made to pierce chain armor. The pain made Achan so lightheaded he almost blacked out. He squeezed the handle of his knife and mumbled, *"Arman hu elohim, Arman hu echâd, Arman hu shlosha be-echâd,"* a half dozen times, waiting for his moment, praying he'd have the strength.

The bear released him. Achan rolled onto his back, onto a furry paw, brought the knife up over his opposite shoulder, and slashed back across the bear's neck, screaming as he did.

Hot blood spurted over Achan's face and chest. His breath hitched. He clamped his mouth shut. The bear groaned, thrashed in the brush, and loped away. Achan rolled the opposite direction until his body hit a tree trunk. He struggled to maneuver behind it, unable to see the bear. Off in the forest ferns rustled, twigs snapped, and a keening moan gave Achan hope.

Sir Eagan! Where are you? Shung?

A cool breeze filtered past the trees and Achan shivered. Saliva and blood matted his shirt to his shoulder and chest. His right arm hung limp. His shoulder and torso throbbed. His thigh still ached. Should he stay put? Esek's horse was likely dead. Should he climb a tree to get out of the bear's reach? What had Shung said about chams climbing trees?

Sir Gavin's panicked voice burst in Achan's head. *Achan! The cham?*

I dunno. I think I killed it.

A man groaned nearby.

Shung? Sir Eagan? Achan's voice came slow in his head.

Little Cham?

Shung! Are you hurt?

Shung will live. The cham burned Shung's arm.

What of Sir Eagan? He doesn't answer.

"Did I kill it?" Sir Eagan's voice sounded groggy.

The cham knocked Elk into a tree. Footsteps crunched and Shung's hairy shadow crouched before Achan.

"I'm fine," Achan said. "Check Sir Eagan."

"No need." Movement swished past Achan's boots. "A little dizzy, but I'll live."

With Shung and Sir Eagan's help, Achan staggered to his feet and limped to the road. He could see the dark shape of Esek's horse. Dead. Achan's limbs trembled, his body cold and sweaty.

Sir Eagan and Shung boosted Achan up to Sir Eagan's horse. His right side seized, and he held his breath to keep from crying out. He wanted to lie down. His body throbbed. The smells of saliva and blood sickened him.

Shung moved to the other side of the horse and tucked Achan's boot into the stirrup. "Where's the beast?"

Achan jerked his head to the side and his neck muscles cried out. "Back through . . . trees."

"Shung will come back tonight with men and light. Make frame to haul back."

Achan panted. "See if . . . you can find . . . m' knife."

Sir Eagan mounted up behind Achan. "And my sword."

A thrill seized Achan. "M' swords! On th' dead h'rse."

"Shung will get them."

Ôwr was finally his. "Yeh can have yer sword back now, S'r Eag'n. I've tak'n Ôwr."

"Thank you, Your Majesty."

Moments later the horses took off, galloping at top speed for Mitspah stronghold. Each hoofbeat jarred Achan's wounds so much that he lost consciousness.

38

Vrell awoke in her bed in Mitspah under a pile of blankets. A fire crackled in the hearth, warming her right side. She drew her hand along her middle and found she wore one of her boy's tunics. Strips of linen bound her waist.

A wave of heat passed over her. She'd left her undergarment in Esek's tent! Who had dressed her wounds?

Voices murmured nearby. She blinked and her room in Mitspah took shape. Men were speaking in Achan's room. The adjoining door stood open.

"Well, I'll be stormed, I will! What a relief, eh? I'd thought the lad was double—"

"Enough, Kurtz!" a man said. Sir Caleb. "Gavin, how long have you known?"

Sir Gavin drew a long breath through his nose. "Since the night we first defeated the black knights."

"I'm not liking it at all. It's being bad luck to be having a woman in camp."

"Does Achan know?" Sir Caleb asked.

Kurtz honked a loud laugh. "I'll say. If you'd seen wh—"

"Aye," Sir Gavin said. "But only since our first night in Mitspah."

"And you didn't bother to tell us?" Sir Caleb asked.

"Stingy lad wanted her all to himself, he did." Kurtz snorted. "Royalty, eh?"

"It was her decision to tell," Sir Gavin said. "It still is."

The memory of the day's events brought a gasp to her lips—or was this a new day now?—Khai had stabbed her. And she'd stabbed him back. Was he dead?

Achan!

She sat up. Fiery pain stabbed her side and she cried out.

A shadow shifted on the wall. Sir Eagan rose from a chair in the corner of her room and walked toward her. "Lay back, Vrell. You've been stabbed, though I suspect you remember."

"Achan is in trouble."

Sir Eagan stopped beside her bed. "Achan is here. He is wounded and moving slow, but he shall recover."

Vrell sighed. Praise Arman.

Kurtz stepped into the doorway and grinned. His lengthy stare made her uncomfortable. She pulled the blankets to her chin. She should lie down, but what if she could not sit up again? She wanted to go to Achan. He might need care.

"Kurtz, would you leave us a moment?" Sir Eagan asked.

Kurtz straightened. "Why would I do that, eh?"

"So I can check my patient's wounds."

Vrell stared at Sir Eagan with wide eyes. He did not smile but held her gaze.

"Bah," Kurtz said. "Nothing I haven't seen before, eh?"

Vrell's cheeks warmed.

"Stand guard outside," Sir Eagan said.

Kurtz growled and pulled the door closed behind him.

Sir Eagan sat on the edge of her bed. "Removing your gown was necessary to treat your wound. Forgive my invasion of your privacy. Sir Gavin insisted I not call a woman healer."

Vrell looked down at the bulges at the end of the blanket that were her feet.

Sir Eagan went on. "As I worked on your wound, I could not help but notice you do not bear this *mark of the stray* as Achan does. I have a theory, my lady, that might offend if I am mistaken. But if I am not . . . well . . . I must know. Might you be Lady Averella Amal of Carmine?"

Vrell's eyes swelled. "Sir Gavin told you?"

He grinned. "Nay, my lady. My strength has always been observing. Since the day we met, I knew you were not a man and most definitely not a stray."

"How?" Vrell thought of how Jax mi Katt had said, *You do not smell like a man.*

"You are elegant. Even when you try to be clumsy it is gracefully done. Your skin is fair, clearly not lived a lifetime of hard labor in the sun. You are petite, and I have never met a boy of fourteen who was not all arms and legs. You could not stomach being in the room where Achan was bathing. And though you sometimes try to doctor your speech, having lived my whole life as heir to my father's household, your highborn tongue is hard to hide.

"Of course, there is also the fact the duchess and I are . . . old friends. There are parts of you that look very much like her." He reached out and cupped the side of her face with his hand. "And parts of you that look . . ."

Tears flooded Vrell's eyes. It could not be as she had suspected. It could not.

He lowered his hand. "Have no fear, my lady. I mean you no ill will. Only, would you not be safer in your mother's household?"

Vrell released a shaky breath, thankful Sir Eagan had not voiced her fear. "Sir Gavin said we travel to Carmine next."

"And what of Achan? Does he know your real name?"

Vrell shook her head. "Please do not tell him. I never meant to deceive him so. Prince Gidon—Esek—he wanted to marry me, to control Carm. I would rather have died than marry him for any reason. Mother helped me hide in Walden's Watch with Lady Coraline."

"My aunt."

"Oh!" Vrell wrinkled her nose, mind spinning. "But . . . is she not younger than you?"

Sir Eagan nodded. "Life is funny that way sometimes."

"Yes." How could Vrell be so calm? Talk so easily to Sir Eagan? He was practically a stranger, yet—dare she think it?— maybe so much more. A peaceful calm compelled her to go on.

"The Kingsguards took me from Walden's Watch to train under Master Hadar. I was trapped until Achan came. I fled with him and the knights into Darkness. I knew he suspected something. My lies were becoming too complicated for him not to catch on. He is quite smart when he is using his head."

Sir Eagan raised his eyebrows.

Vrell pulled her hand to her lips. "Oh, I meant no disrespect. But Achan often gets so caught up in his plans, he becomes obsessed."

Sir Eagan nodded. "It is a trait his father had as well. Both blessing and curse."

Vrell studied the thick weave of her wool blanket. "Achan told Sir Gavin that I was hiding something. Sir Gavin cornered me the second night of our journey and demanded the truth or he would leave me behind."

Sir Eagan scowled. "Horrible brute."

Vrell cracked a smile. "He was only doing his duty. And once I confessed, Sir Gavin was a great help."

Sir Eagan chuckled and patted her hand. "It is hard to imagine Gavin as your only confidant. How awkward it must have been for you all these months."

"Yes. Yes, it was awkward, but . . ."

"You love Achan."

Sir Eagan's simple declaration brought a rush of heat to Vrell's head. An overwhelming ache seized her at the memory of his kiss, his intense eyes, the way he'll held her in his arms. "No, my lord. I . . . betrothed . . ." Her voice cracked. "Bran Rennan of Carmine." Tears swelled in her eyes. Bran did not love her, if he ever really had. Could anyone really? She was so plain and skinny, with a voice like a mule.

She continued trying to convince Sir Eagan, distract him from his train of thought. "Bran squires for your brother, you know. He and Sir Rigil are both working in Carmine."

"You do know Achan loves you?"

Vrell sniffled. "You are mistaken, my lord. He is like a brother to me." Achan was simply confused. Soon he would meet a beautiful woman like Tara or Gren. One the knights would approve of. Then he would forget about Vrell.

Sir Eagan offered a sympathetic smile. "When Achan returned, he limped outside your door, bleeding all over the floor, until the hops tea I forced him to drink bested him." Sir Eagan took her hand again. Calm stretched over her body like another blanket. "Will you not miss your *brother* when you are home and he moves on?"

"It matters not." Tears overflowed Vrell's eyes and coursed down her cheeks. "I will not let him think I betrayed him or did not trust him."

"Forgive me, my lady, but is that not what you have been doing all along? Why not confess?"

"Because I . . . I did not want to be one more liar in his life. I know it is deceitful. Please, I beg you. Let him know me as Vrell Sparrow, a stray girl who simply refused to be anyone's mistress. And let him meet Averella Amal in another life."

"If that is your wish, my lady, I promise to hold your secret safe. Though I have never found secrets make life easier."

"That is my burden to bear."

"Very well." He squeezed her hand and let go. "I will take you home myself. Tomorrow, if you are feeling up to the ride."

Tears flooded Vrell's eyes. "You would do that?"

"Yes. I would very much like to see your mother again. It has been far too long."

Vrell stared up at Sir Eagan. Could he also be suffering from a secret long kept? She wanted to ask if he was her father, but did she really want to know?

Regardless, the words would not come.

"Achan will shadow my mind, I suspect. I can do nothing to hide from him."

"There is a way, actually. I could teach you the trick, though it will not work forever. He is too strong. Eventually someone will teach him the way around our trick." He stood.

"Tomorrow, my lady, I shall teach you. For now, try to sleep. You must rest if we are to travel."

"Please do not tell Achan we are leaving."

"Sir Gavin will have to know."

Vrell nodded. "Thank you, Sir Eagan. Going home will bring me great comfort."

"I am happy to serve any way I—"

"I said, let me in!" Achan's muffled voice yelled from outside the door.

"Strike me as much as you like, Pacey," Kurtz answered in an overly loud voice. "Beat me, club me, flog me, torture me, eh? But my orders come from the master surgeon, they do."

Sir Eagan winced. "Our star dramatist hard at work. Shall we let our prince in to see you or shall I say you are sleeping? I may not be able to stop him either way."

Vrell swallowed. "It is all right. He may enter."

"Very well." Sir Eagan walked to the door. He opened it and patted Kurtz on the shoulder. "Kurtz, you and I are needed elsewhere."

Kurtz stepped aside with regal posture and bowed. His bottom lip had swollen as if he had been—Vrell's hand shot to her lips. Oh, Achan. Angry men could be so foolish.

Achan pushed past Kurtz, who winked at Vrell before closing the door. Achan stopped just inside as if he did not know where to go now that he had finally gained entry. He looked a mess. His hair frizzed out all over, bruises blackened his face and neck, scratches covered his face, dried blood caked around his left ear, and fresh blood soaked through his fresh white tunic in two places under his arm.

She shifted—her side ached—and clutched her blankets back up around her neck. "Are you hurt, Your Highness?"

"Barely," he mumbled. "You?"

"I am well."

He let out a long breath and limped forward three steps. His wince proved that every move pained him.

Stubborn as he was, she dared not point it out. "What happened at Esek's camp?"

"I believe you killed Khai."

Vrell clapped her hand to her mouth. "Oh, I did not mean to. I only wanted to help you."

Achan laughed silently, then crinkled his brow and stopped as if even silent laughter aggrieved his wounds. "You helped me fine."

"But I . . ." She had stabbed him only once. "I have never killed anyone."

Achan sighed. "It's not a pleasant feeling, is it? Even in regards to a man like Khai."

It did not seem real. "What else happened?"

Achan cast his blue eyes her way. He opened his mouth but did not speak. He limped the rest of the way to her bedside, seeming so much taller standing over her. He pursed his lips and, wincing, lowered himself to his right knee. Her pallet was so low to the ground his face was level with hers.

"I've learned a new trick. Open your mind." He reached out and slid his hand over the back of her hand, tucking his fingers between hers. He closed his eyes.

She tensed at the intimate way he held her hand, but her thoughts were interrupted by his. Flashes of activity flitted through her mind. His memories. Achan riding into Darkness on Dove, he and Shung fighting Khai, lifting Sparrow off Esek's bed, carrying her out of the pavilion, hearing her scream, watching her through Khai's apparitions, catching her as she fell from Khai's sword, carrying her to Dove.

Her chest swelled with the memory of his feelings and emotions, but it all moved so fast she could not stop to think about one thing in particular. Pain shot through her thigh when Esek's sword struck true. She was with him as he cut down Esek, took Ôwr and his father's ring.

Then Achan slumped on a horse. She experienced his agony and surprise at the cham bear's attack. Its teeth. Defeating it. Returning to Mitspah. Trying to see Vrell. Tiring. Sir Eagan looking over his wounds.

Vrell's mind became her own again. She opened her eyes to see Achan smiling. What reason could he have to smile? "Oh, Achan, a cham! How horrifying!"

His smile faded. "Aye, it wasn't pleasant. Glad I wore my chain armor."

She met his eyes. "Where did you learn to do that? Show me your memories?"

"Sir Eagan." Achan focused on their interlocked fingers and rubbed his thumb over the back of hers. "I may have killed Esek. I hadn't intended . . . he was in a bad position when I . . ."

Vrell stared at his pained face. From his memories, she knew exactly what he was thinking, reliving, regretting.

Achan licked his chapped lips. "Sparrow, I want to . . . I must speak with you about . . . . Sir Gavin tells me you intend to leave us soon."

She wanted to stop him from saying things they would both regret, but the intensity of his gaze kept her from protesting. "I do not belong here, Achan. You must understand that much."

"You belong with me. I need you."

"Whatever for? Sir Eagan has proven an excellent healer."

His blue eyes pierced her defenses, chipped away at the shield around her heart. He opened his mouth twice to speak, but said nothing. His tongue-tiedness set her pulse racing. "My heart does not beat for Sir Eagan."

She wilted. "No, Achan. None of that."

His brows furrowed. "Why do you fight it? I promised myself I would marry you no matter what anyone says."

She tried to pull her hands from his, but he held tight. "We are from different worlds, you and I. This can never be." Yet Lady Averella could certainly marry the prince. Would her lies never cease? How had everything gotten so twisted?

His eyes pleaded. "Don't say that, Sparrow, please don't. I want you here. I . . ."

She wanted to believe him, but how could it be true? "You wanted Tara a short time ago."

He puffed out a long breath. "I wanted Tara over a stranger, though she nearly was one."

"And Gren before that."

"But she . . . But you are different. You are my dearest friend."

Unlike Esek, and the other suitors over the years, Vrell knew Achan did not seek her inheritance, for he knew nothing about it. Still, Vrell pulled her hand from his grip. "You fall in love with every girl who crosses your path. I will not forget how you stared at Beska or Yumikak. Even Lady Lathia."

"Those silly girls are nothing like you."

She set her jaw. "Precisely. I will never be pretty enough for your arm." Even Bran had deserted Vrell for Gren—a peasant!— because she was prettier. "For three months we've known each other, you never once suspected me to be a woman—I mean, look at me." Tears gathered in Vrell's eyes, blurring Achan's face. "I am a shapeless, pale . . . twig! With hair like, uh . . . like tree lichen! I am as feminine as a broomstick. And a voice like a mule. I may as well be an adolescent boy."

He rose onto his knees, eyebrows puckered in sympathy. See? He agreed! He could see plainly that she was everything she knew she was.

But then he took the sides of her face in his hands and brushed away her tears with his thumbs. "No, Vrell."

He had never called her Vrell before.

"You were never a very good boy. There was always something bafflingly odd about you. I never cared for any of those other girls. You are so smart and tough. And you *are* beautiful."

She shook her head.

"Yes. You're a flower. You have the sweetest face. Your hair is like black corn silk." He pushed his fingers back through her hair. "You always smell like rosewater and have made me crave the smell. And what I love best about you—besides how soft you feel—is how your eyes pierce me every time you look my way, like I'm your target and your arrow struck true, bringing me to my knees. And the only way I can live is to look on those life-sustaining green eyes."

Her resistance dissolved at the tender honesty of his words. Joyous heart! He did care. Without a word, she brushed her lips against his.

His kiss was soft, hesitant this time. She felt their minds connect, sensed his caution, his exhilaration. His hands massaged her head, then one moved to her waist and he pulled her to the edge of the bed. His movement jarred her wounded side. He pulled back his face and gasped with her, feeling her pain.

Sorry.

He moved his hand back to her face, kissed her forehead, then hugged her head to his chest. She could hear his heart drumming. His thoughts spilled into her mind like water from a jug.

I never wanted to hurt Sparrow. Never. She means too much to me. Losing her was proof of that. But how can I keep her? What would Sir Caleb say? He recalled Sparrow's joke of a stray mistress. *Could she have meant that? Been hinting? Lots of noblemen took mistresses. Maybe my wife—from Sir Caleb's arranged marriage—could have her own space, and I could keep Sparrow with me, always.*

Fire coursed through Vrell's veins. She pushed away, closing her mind and sucking in a long breath to keep herself from crying. "I knew it! You are no different."

His wide eyes were unfathomable, as if he were innocent. "What'd I do?"

If Achan truly knew Arman, he would know that yoking himself to multiple women would ruin them all. "This matters more than any feelings we may have for one another. You do not love Arman. You only love yourself."

He pulled back, though not far enough to give her room to escape. "I-I love *you*. I told you so. I meant it."

"No, Achan. You think you can keep me in a room in your castle, to be your, your . . ." She blew out another furious breath. "Ladylove!" She seized her pillow and struck him with it, gasping at the pain stabbing her side. "Get out!" She struck him again and let her pillow fall to the floor. She panted, whispered, "Leave this chamber, now."

"I'm sorry!" He groaned to his feet, drew back a step. "I didn't mean those thoughts. They were for me alone. Just me. Just . . . thinking. W-we don't have to be together. No one even has to know you're a woman. Or you could be the prince's chosen sister. Wise female advisor. We could—"

"Achan, such a thing could not be done. It would be scandalous."

"I don't care. We could be the pair who changed their stations in life. W-we'll vow to abolish strays from all Er'Rets. Grant peasant rights to everyone." He stared at the floor. All was still, the crackling fireplace the only sound. "And if you grew to love me . . ."

She wished he would let go of his scheming. It took all her effort not to look at him, his eyes, his lips. Her throat burned. "Achan, I became a man to avoid marriage."

"To someone horrible. I'm not so bad, right?" He grinned, but it did not reach his eyes. "And I love you. So it won't be like marrying a man thrice your elder or one who only means to use you."

"It would be worse."

Achan pulled back farther as if she had slapped him. "You don't care, even a little?"

"Your own thoughts betrayed you, Achan. You must marry a noblewoman." And he would never know her real name. She decided that then and there. She should never have let down her guard. He could not be trusted.

Pain flashed through his pale eyes.

How could she make him understand? "For you, it can never be about love. A king is not free to love. Too many things distract. His realm must always come first."

"But a king can do what he wants."

"You sound like Esek, demanding your way."

He huffed, eyebrows sinking over his eyes. "I'll *not* lose you."

"You do not have me to lose."

"Tell me you don't love me."

Vrell had no idea where she got the courage to answer so calmly. "I do not love you. And I do not see how you can honestly love me. You have known I am a woman three days."

Achan set his jaw. Pouting.

She swallowed her threatening tears. "Achan, what you call love is your craving for love. And I do love you like a brother. But I will not be a convenience to any man's fears of loneliness. Let me go. Learn to be king. Take a real queen. Serve Arman and your kingdom. That is your purpose."

"A purpose I'll serve better with you at my side."

"It cannot be. Despite all the obvious reasons why we could not be together, I will not be a crutch for you to hide from Arman. He seeks your full heart, and you must face Him."

"You kissed me back."

She glanced down at her hands, squeezed them, and forced cold words past her swollen throat. "It was a mistake."

His jaw jutted out and his gaze seemed to burn into her. "I don't believe you."

"Believe what you must. I apologize if I misled you."

Achan's eyes glazed. He seemed to shrink. He limped toward the door, turned back, ran a hand over his head, and shuddered a sigh. "Forgive me, I—" Still limping, he fled from the room, the door swinging in his wake.

Vrell eased back down to her back and rolled on her side, finally allowing the tears to come.

• • •

Iron gauntlets squeezed Achan's chest. He limp-skipped out of the inner gate and across the lawn to the edge of the pool side of the moat, seeking a tree to destroy. A small cluster of pine trees stood between the curtain wall and the curve of the pool. His right arm hung slack at his side. At least the injury wouldn't hinder him as much, being left-handed.

He squeezed Ôwr's suede-wrapped grip in his left hand. A thin pine tree at the edge of the moat stream volunteered its service. Achan hacked into it. Ôwr, sharper than Eagan's Elk, peeled back a long swatch of bark, baring the white inner wood.

An image of Gren sitting under the allown tree flooded his mind, the day she'd watched him attack the wilted poplar with his waster. A great fury rose in his chest, and he sliced into the tree again and again, wanting to hurt it, wanting to make it look the way he felt. Broken, useless, vile, unlovable.

His blade cleaved deep into the trunk, and he screamed in frustration as he ripped it free. A sudden calm oozed over his fury. His arm fell to his side. Ôwr's tip swished through the grass. He stepped back, blinked at the mutilated tree, and recoiled.

"If it is firewood you seek, there are better ways."

Achan spun around to face Sir Eagan. Now he understood his sudden calm. He scowled, knowing Sir Eagan had used his bloodvoicing trick to pacify Achan's emotions. "Withdraw from my mind or I'll force you out."

Sir Eagan tipped his head to one side and smiled. "Only if you promise to let the tree go."

Achan choked up a knot of phlegm and spit it out. "This tree is helping me cope with my latest prison."

"It is not the tree that concerns me, Your Highness, but my sword. You shall dull the blade using it as an axe. I am certain we could find you an axe if you must chop, though I do not recommend such physical labor with your wounds."

"This isn't your sword. It's Ôwr. I took it from Esek after I cut off his arm. You may have Eagan's Elk back."

"Rhomphaia."

"Whatever." Achan lifted Ôwr in front of him and studied the gleaming crossguard. It was so beautiful, but had caused so much pain. Would it continue to kill at his direction? He tossed it onto the grass. A sudden ache seized his right shoulder and his body tensed against the pain. Gloom hung heavy on his body, like clothing drenched from rain.

Sir Eagan must have withdrawn his calming thoughts. Achan lowered himself to the wet grass, groaned, and leaned back on the mutilated tree. Spray from the waterfall misted him and he welcomed the coolness.

Sir Eagan slid his boot a step closer over the slick grass. "Care to talk about it?"

Achan's lips parted. "There's nothing to say."

"Maybe not. But confession is often like steam from a kettle. Without a place to release, it will explode."

Achan gestured at the tree. "That's why I chop."

"Are you certain I cannot help?"

Achan shook his head. "You wouldn't understand."

"No?" Sir Eagan sighed. "In your infinite wisdom of— what is it, fifteen years?"

"Sixteen."

"Beg your pardon, sixteen years. By your aged wisdom, you must have a detailed account of my life, is that correct, Your Highness?"

"No."

"Then do not assume you know me. I loved a woman in my youth. We were younger than you when we met. Known each other since our births, really, but it was not until I moved to Tsaftown to squire for Lord Livna that she captured my heart. Lady Nitsa Livna. Some know her today as—"

"The Duchess of Carm," Achan said. "I know. Sir Caleb told me."

"Aye. Then she was merely a lesser noblewoman from Tsaftown, and I was a lesser nobleman from Zerah Rock. I knew the gods had blessed me. We were perfect for each other. I spent the summer courting her with all my efforts. It worked quite well. She professed her love for me daily, and I her."

"But her father refused?"

"Her father did not care either way, until Duke Amal saw her at a banquet that fall. He saw her and wanted her. He was older, richer, and Duke of Carm. Nitsa's father gave his blessing that night. That night, my boy. Amal did not love her. He had never even spoken to her. But he snagged her from me and there was nothing I could do. I begged her to run away, of course, but she would not desert her family. They were married a month later.

"My father expected me to go on like nothing had changed. 'Pick another girl,' he told me over and over. But I did not want another girl. And I refused to go to court and pretend I did not see Nitsa by his side . . . then Averella."

"Averella? That's the lady Esek wishes to marry."

Sir Eagan met Achan's eyes. "What do you know of that story, for I have heard little?"

"Oh, I know little, as well. Esek wanted to marry her to gain control of Carm. So she went into hiding. She's betrothed to a friend of mine. Bran Rennan is your brother's squire."

"He is a nobleman?"

"The cousin of one, I think. Yet I fear Bran's feelings have changed." Achan frowned at the thought of Bran and Gren but forced himself to stay on topic. The conversation distracted his pain. "Both Esek and Lord Nathak have been trying to take Carm by marriage. Esek to the lady Averella and Lord Nathak to the duchess. He's been asking for her hand for the past few years. Before Duke Amal was in the ground, they say."

"Duke Amal is dead?" Eagan gripped Achan's wounded arm. "Are you certain?"

Achan cried out. "Careful!"

Sir Eagan released Achan's arm. "Forgive me. I forgot."

Achan cradled his arm until the throb lessened. "The duke died three or four years back. From a fever, I think."

Eagan exhaled. "Perhaps there is still hope."

"For what?"

"That after all this time, almost eighteen years . . . that Arman might reunite me with my family. This old man might find love yet."

Achan studied Sir Eagan's wistful expression. "Then you do understand."

"I do, my boy."

"But I've loved two women and both denied me."

"Two women and only sixteen years of age? My, you are wise to protect your heart so."

"You mock me?"

"I seek only to lighten your melancholy. You are a prince. You cannot marry just anyone, nor should you pledge your heart or body to anyone until you do marry. And frankly, Your Highness, I do not recommend taking multiple wives and mistresses. It is not how Arman designed it. I know kings have different views on such things, but—"

"I would never." Sparrow's horror had been enough to strike that idea from his mind. What might Gren say about such a thing? Would she agree with Sparrow?

Sir Eagan patted Achan's shoulder. "An admirable declaration now, but when the desire comes into your heart and you have the power to have anything you want . . . Temptation is a cruel thing. I urge you to understand: love is much more than what you feel. That, Your Highness, is the desire of a man for a woman. You would be wise to discern the difference before those feelings best you."

"Then what is love?"

"For you to love Vrell? Love is sacrifice, letting her go because it is her choice and the right thing to do."

But Achan had done that for Gren. He had arranged her marriage to Riga to keep her safe from Esek. And what good had come of it? Riga was dead. Gren with child. And Achan was still alone. "How can you say your sacrifice was right when your lady didn't wish to marry the duke?"

"Because I have lived through my pain to see the other side. Duty calls men and women to all kinds of sacrifice. But when the lusts of our hearts blinds us, we sacrifice goodness to get what we want. In anger I turned away from my birthright, I gave it up to wallow in my pity of losing Nitsa. Now I discover my father's second son has pledged his service to you. So who will rule Zerah Rock when my father dies? He has no other heir. Some minor noble will likely take the stronghold. Maybe he will be true to the Barak heritage, maybe he will not.

"And Zerah Rock is but a small city in a distant corner of *your* kingdom." Sir Eagan poked Achan lightly in the chest. "It means little in the scheme of things. But consequences are often more far-reaching than any man realizes. Should you forsake your birthright to chase after the love of your heart, what will become of Er'Rets? Who will rule in *your* stead? Esek? Lord Nathak? Who will protect your people? Each faction will attack the other. They will take the land in small bites until all is devoured by Darkness. Innocent men, women, and children will die."

Achan stared at Ôwr, partially hidden by the short grass.

Sir Eagan went on. "Whether you like it or not, Arman has chosen you. This is the highest calling a man can receive. So ask yourself, my prince, what price is the love of your heart worth? The death of your father and mother? Lord Livna? Fifteen men in battle yesterday? How many would you allow to die for nothing so you and the love of your heart can be together? You may not like the meal you have been served, but will you at least show yourself worthy of it? Many have given their lives to see you to this place. Would you forsake their sacrifice for your own?"

"Why can't I have both?"

"You will, someday, find what you seek. Arman will give you the desire of your heart when His timing is right."

Achan searched his memory for his least-favorable match on Sir Caleb's list. "Lady Halona of Nesos? She's twelve."

"She will grow. Girls do, you know, grow into women."

"But she's not my choice."

"No. And for that, I *am* sorry, and I do understand. You need only say the word 'sacrifice' to me and I shall spirit you and Ôwr away to the nearest forest and you shall attack whatever trees you see fit, if that will help you with the pain. But I assure you, my prince, from a man who understands your pain, destroying trees will not help. Only Arman can."

Achan lay in bed that night staring at the low tinder ceiling and listening to the waterfall pound on the roof like rain, the perfect cadence for his mood. Sir Eagan's words rang true in his heart.

But how could he let Sparrow walk away? What if he never saw her again? He couldn't lose another friend. He didn't have many, considering the scores of people who now surrounded him on a daily basis.

Shung. He did have Shung.

He'd go to Sparrow tomorrow and beg her forgiveness. He'd do his duty and let her go, but not before finding out where she lived. If she'd fled from a horrible place, it might not be safe for her to go back. Perhaps he could find her a better place to live.

A place where he could visit from time to time.

He'd revoke the declarations of his heart, even if that was a lie and against his nature. But he would not give up his friend.

PART 5

PARTINGS

39

Achan thrashed through the night, his right arm sore, his mind active with memories of Esek, the cham, and Sparrow.

The next morning, he and Shung found the great hall crowded for breakfast. The high table, however, was empty. Achan limped up the steps to the high table, ignoring the stares of those eating below. He and Shung must look half dead. Both had arms in slings, Achan's from the cham's teeth. Shung's from the cham's fire.

Shung stood against the wall behind Achan's chair, refusing to sit. Achan picked at his food, pondering what words might convince Sparrow to remain friends. He couldn't let anything inappropriate sneak into his confession and scare her away.

Sir Gavin and Sir Caleb approached the high table. Sir Gavin sat to Achan's left. Sir Caleb stepped over the bench on Achan's other side.

"Your Highness, did you really accost that poor girl? Kurtz won't stop talking about it." Sir Caleb pulled his other leg over the bench and reached for the pitcher of water.

"It was but one kiss." Achan straightened. "Two, actually. No doubt Kurtz has stretched whatever he saw."

Sir Caleb humphed and bowed his head.

Achan waited for Sir Caleb to finish his thanks. "I do hope someone has informed Kurtz that Sparrow is a woman. I hate to think what the man might be thinking otherwise."

Sir Caleb raised an eyebrow. "Kurtz is so informed."

Achan picked up a slice of bread and tapped the crust on the tabletop, feeling the need to explain further. "I liked Sparrow the boy a great deal. When I discovered the little fox was a woman . . . it stabbed. She lied to me. But even as a woman, Sparrow was Sparrow. I couldn't help but think how perfect everything would be if she and I could . . ." He drew in a heavy sigh. "I know, I know. I'm the biggest fool in Er'Rets."

"Not the biggest." Sir Gavin sipped from his mug. "I'm sure if I searched very hard I could find a bigger one."

"Trust you to be honest. I only felt . . . when she said she might be leaving . . ." Achan stirred his porridge, groping for the right words. "I don't want to lose her friendship."

Sir Gavin inhaled over his mug of tea. "She will always be your friend, lad."

Achan hoped that was true. He'd sensed deception in her when she'd claimed she didn't love him. Why would she lie? Did she think him insincere? He wished he hadn't thought about the mistress thing. That had been daft.

Sir Caleb propped his elbow on the table and stared at Achan. "What's the point for you, Your Highness? Of all this. Raising an army. Fighting Esek?"

"Arman called me to be king. You said it has to be me."

"Go back further. Before you heard Arman. What did you live for?"

"Not much. The hope of Gren, I suppose. Though I always knew her father would never allow it."

"So you lived every day, hoping for what you couldn't have. And when it was lost, what did you live for then?"

What could be the point of such questions? Didn't Sir Caleb already know all this? "To keep Gren safe. Esek threatened to harm her if I tried to leave his service."

"You sacrificed your freedom for her safety. That gave your life purpose. Every man must live for something, Your Highness. Serve a matchless cause beyond himself. Many live for the goal of riches, some for the love of a good woman, others for the affections of many. Some men live for their children or for the number of enemy soldiers they've killed in battle."

Sir Caleb paused to take a sip from his goblet. "Having lived longer than you, I'll tell you what I've learned. Though these causes are worthwhile and good, none will bring true, lasting satisfaction." Sir Caleb glanced at Sir Gavin.

The Great Whitewolf turned his mismatched eyes to Achan. "Only one cause has spurred my life, and it's the only one that follows a man into the Veil. I know Caleb serves the same cause."

Achan turned back to Sir Caleb. "Live for Arman, Your Highness. Serve Him. He created you for a purpose. He's proud of who you are. He deserves your respect, your sacrifice, your service. Only He can bring you satisfaction and meaning in this life. No woman can do that—even if your every hope were granted. Live for Arman alone, and He'll give you the desires of your heart."

Achan tried to comprehend the idea of loving Arman more than anyone. Sparrow seemed to think he didn't follow Arman at all. "But He seems so far away. Like that temple." Achan pointed to the ceiling, toward the temple above the stronghold he still hadn't found time to visit.

"Aye, the stairs are high, and slippery," Sir Gavin said, "for I almost broke my neck climbing them this morning. But before I knew it, I'd reached the top. And what a view. Arman is always worth the climb, lad."

"But I never know when He'll answer me. I feel like I'm bothering Him, like He's too busy."

"He hears every word you say, every thought you think. And He always answers, though sometimes His answer is 'no' or 'wait.' Live for Him, Achan. Give Him your trust."

"I will." Achan stood. "But first I'm going to speak with Sparrow and apologize for my recklessness. I hope she'll agree to remain friends."

Sir Gavin and Sir Caleb rose and bowed. Protocol for treating Achan like royalty in public. He still wasn't used to it.

Sir Gavin kept his head down, his curtain of white hair flanking his beard. "I fear Vrell has already gone, lad."

A savage rage swept over Achan. "What do you mean?"

"She left this morning. Sir Eagan agreed to escort her wherever she wanted to go."

Sir Eagan had betrayed him? "Why didn't you tell me?"

"She asked me not to."

"How is Sparrow going off with Sir Eagan alone following protocol?"

"Sir Eagan is trustworthy," Sir Caleb added.

Achan scowled at Sir Caleb. "And I'm not? Tell me where they went."

Sir Gavin frowned. "I cannot, for they didn't tell me."

"You lie."

"I never lie."

"You lied to me about Sparrow. Tell me what you know about her. You've always known more than anyone else."

"Achan. Calm yourself," Sir Caleb said. "You're acting irrationally. Moments ago you said you were going to revoke your proposal. All has worked out."

Achan gritted his teeth and reached out for Sparrow. *Sparrow, what is this? You just leave?*

He waited, wringing his hands. When she didn't answer, he tried to look into her mind. He felt her shields, strong and impenetrable as always. How did she do that? *Sparrow!*

Achan called to Sir Eagan next and received no answer. He lunged for Sir Gavin, slid his hands around Sir Gavin's neck, cradling the man's hairy cheeks with his thumbs. He stared into Sir Gavin's eyes. "You will tell me what I want to know." He tore into Sir Gavin's mind, seeking a conversation with Sir Eagan and Sparrow, but the knight seemed to know how to defend against such an attack, for Achan could find no shred of Sparrow in his thoughts. "Tell me!" He yelled so loud his throat seemed to rip.

"Achan." Sir Gavin gasped a breath of air. "This isn't what Arman would have for you."

"Your Highness!" Sir Caleb grabbed Achan's arm and pulled. "Please. He's an old man. This could kill him."

Do it, a boiling voice said. *This man has betrayed you and deserves to die.*

Achan withdrew instantly. Sir Gavin staggered back and fell onto the bench. His eyelids fluttered, his face pale and sweaty. Achan jerked free from Sir Caleb's grip and backed away, repulsed with his own temper, horrified to have again heard Hadad's voice, unable to use Darkness as an excuse this time.

"I'm sorry." He limped out of the great hall as fast as he could, clutching a hand to his arm to ease the ache. *Sparrow, please don't do this. Just talk to me. Tell me where you are.*

He climbed the tower stairs slowly, Shung, wisely silent, at his heels. Achan's temper rose the higher the stairs took him. Why did Sparrow not answer? Was she punishing him?

He limped to her chamber and fell on his knees beside her pallet, panting from fatigue. He placed his hand on the dent in her pillow. A jar sat in the middle of her bed, a red twine bow tied around the edge of the lid. A small scrap of parchment held three words in flowery script.

For your fleas.

Sparrow could write? Better than him? He lifted the lid on the jar and sniffed. It smelled of pine. He sat back on his heels, set his forehead on the edge of her bed. Sparrow gone? Forever? It couldn't be.

Picturing her face, he reached for her again, trying to push past her walls. Unfortunately, the fortress of Sparrow's mind was made of steel.

"Aargh!" Achan pulled himself up and limped back to the tower stairs, Shung shadowing him as usual. Moisture from the waterfall misted him as he stepped onto the lookout tower. He scanned the bailey and what little of the rolling road he could see before it twisted out of sight. No sign of Sparrow and Sir Eagan.

Achan turned and found the narrow stone steps off the right of the tower, just where Lord Yarden had said they'd be. He followed them up.

"Little Cham? Where are you going?"

"I must speak with Arman."

The stairs, cut from the mountain itself, tunneled through the moss-covered rock. Achan soon lost all light. Not having thought to bring a torch, he stumbled in the dark, his side, shoulder, back, face, and leg aching now. After a tediously steep hike, he exited into a green forest on the banks of the Betsar before the second major waterfall. Trees hung heavy with leaves and moss.

The white stone walls of Arman's temple appeared through the tangled greenery at the top of the first waterfall. The Evenwall misted most of it from view, but Achan could see the three circles etched onto the pediment of the temple roof. Despite his fatigue, he slogged up the mossy stone staircase that zigzagged up the rock wall. By the time he stood on the porch to the temple, his shirt was damp with sweat.

He stepped inside a square room built of stone with a cobblestone floor. A long polished altar covered in golden cups and flowers stretched across the far end of the room. No pillars. No gilded statue. Its beauty came from four long and narrow windows of colored glass, one on each wall. A fifth window with the design of three interlocking circles arched above the long window directly behind the altar. The sun shone brilliantly through the colored glass.

Achan had no patience to appreciate beauty at the moment. "I've done what You asked of me!"

A man at the altar jumped to his feet. One of Lord Yarden's advisors. Achan hadn't seen him, or he wouldn't have spoken aloud. The man bowed, then strode toward Achan.

"Forgive me, Your Highness. I'll come another time."

The man bowed again and breezed past. Achan felt a pang of guilt. These people treated him as if he were someone special. "But I'm not special!" he yelled after the man, who bounded past Shung on the porch.

Achan turned back to the altar. Why no statue? He wanted to look on Arman's face.

"I trusted You!" he yelled to the tall window. "I listened to Sir Gavin. I listened to Sir Caleb. I've done what everyone said. I'm trying to do what You want for Er'Rets. I serve despite my own desires. So why do You betray me?"

The room remained still. Achan shivered. No heat meant no voice of Arman was coming to give him answers. Why did Arman say so little?

"I'll wait all day if I must! No wars will be fought until I hear from You. Nor will I marry any twelve-year-old girls."

Still nothing.

"You use me, make me act the puppet. Well, I need Your advice, o great puppet master. What shall I do about my Sparrow? She has flown and I'm . . ." Achan knelt at the altar, placing his forehead against the smooth wood.

"What would You have me do? Why is it everyone else may do as they please, yet I am bound so?" A thought of Lady Tara entered his mind. He wasn't the only one who couldn't do what he wanted. It only frustrated him more. "I *am* trying. I thought You wanted me to be king. Then why don't You do something about Sparrow? How am I supposed to fix this?"

A bird's song caused him to raise his head. A tiny bird fluttered near the roof, then settled on a rafter of the hammer beam roof. Achan sat back on his heels and stared at the little black, grey, and white bird. A sparrow.

"Why do You toy with me? I'm not poetic enough to translate such symbolism. I demand to speak with You." He jumped to his feet. "I demand to see Your face!"

The floor trembled under Achan's feet. Heat swept through the room as though a fire burned on the air. The gold cups on the altar rattled on the wood surface, trembling until each fell off the edge and clattered to the floor. The window with the three gold circles exploded inward.

Achan cowered on the floor, throwing his arms over his head. Heat coiled in his heart and spread through him until it reached the tips of his fingers. Wedges of glass crashed against the stone floor around him, breaking into even smaller shards. The sting of their sharp edges bit into the back of Achan's neck and arms.

His skin grew clammy from the heat. He sucked hot air into his lungs, fearing each breath might burn him alive. The floor stopped trembling, the room stilled, unnaturally quiet, but the heat remained.

"Arise, Gidon Hadar, son of Axel." A deep voice reverberated in the temple.

Achan peeked out from his arms and over the altar.

A warrior dressed in antique armor stood before the broken window, His presence so bright Achan could hardly look. Achan rose on shaky knees, keeping his eyes focused on the altar. The heat and light from the warrior's presence still smote Achan's eyes until they watered.

Achan forced himself to look the warrior in the eye. Brown eyes. This young man couldn't be Arman. The brightness and heat stung and he looked away. "Where is Arman? Why won't He answer?"

"Because no one comes to the Father except through Me."

A familiar phrase, one Achan had heard before. "You quote from the Book of Life."

The warrior raised his eyebrows. "I am the author."

Really? "You are Arman?"

"I am His Son, Câan."

His Son. Figures. Câan had His Father's burning heat in common. Achan squeezed his hands into fists and dared eye contact once more. Câan's face was scarred, but His eyes were peaceful, despite the heat. "Why won't Arman answer me?"

Câan's gaze seared Achan's eyes. "It is also written: 'Do not put Arman to the test.'"

Achan squeezed his eyes shut, his eyelids cool against the burning. "But He's answered me before."

"Your thoughts are not His thoughts, nor are your ways His ways."

Why so confusing? "But if Arman has chosen me above all others—"

"Do not think of yourself more highly than you ought, son of Axel. You have been invited, but you have not accepted the invitation. For many are invited, but few accept."

Had not accepted? Achan glared at Câan, then dropped his gaze to the wooden surface of the altar. "But I have. I've been trying to do my duty as Crown Prince."

"If you acknowledge Arman in everything, He will make your path clear and straight."

Frustration oozed from Achan's pores. He felt foolish for not understanding Câan's words. "What more do You want? This is a difficult role. Why must I do it alone? I lose everyone I care for. Why does Arman allow this?"

"Arman forces no man against his will, nor should you."

"But . . . Gren was taken against her will."

"Gren obeyed her father."

"But she didn't want to marry Riga."

"Yet she chose to, in order to obey her father."

Obey her . . . what? "And you would say the same for Tara?"

"She obeyed her father as well. Both women's respect for their parents pleases Me. They sacrifice to show love for Me. I will bless them greatly in time."

What kind of an answer was that? Câan was twisting things around, just like His Father. Achan's knees pinched against the hard floor. He shifted them on the bumpy cobblestone. "But if their fathers loved them, they wouldn't force such a life on their daughters."

"You know these men personally?"

"I—It's not fair!" Achan recoiled as his voice resonated in the temple. A spoiled child having a tantrum.

"You are free to make your own opinions and choices."

Achan gripped the far edge of the altar, resting his forearms on the smooth surface. "But what I choose never works out. No one agrees with me."

"And you blame Arman for that? You think He should force people to obey you?"

Achan frowned. That wasn't what he meant. "No."

"But you suggest He should make people choose *your* will." Câan's powerful voice softened. "You do not know Me at all. Until you choose Me fully, you will understand nothing."

Achan forced his head up and stared into Câan's face.

The man had tears in his eyes. "You have honored Me with your lips, son of Axel, but your heart is far from Me."

"My heart?"

"I am the tree. My Father is the gardener. He cuts off every branch in Me that bears no fruit. No branch can bear fruit unless attached to the tree. Neither can you bear fruit unless you are connected to Me. For I am the way and the truth and the life. No one comes to the Father except through Me."

"You said that, but I don't understand."

"Because you do not know Me. No one can serve two masters. Either he will hate the one and love the other, or he will be devoted to the one and despise the other. You cannot serve both Arman and yourself. Commit to Arman whatever you do and your plans will succeed."

Achan floundered to pinpoint what plan Câan referred to. "My plans to find Sparrow?"

"*Your* plans are your own, but if you are truly committed to Arman, your plans will be His plans. You must commit yourself to Arman so the people may know Him. For I died to ransom all. To ransom you."

The words struck Achan like a fist to the face. He sat back on his heels and churned the words in his mind. Love Câan.

Achan thought back to the Teshuwah service in Melas. Trajen Yorbride had said Câan had come to Er'Rets so Light would shine in Darkness. But Darkness had not understood.

Achan had not understood because there was Darkness in his heart.

Yet he was called to bring Light back to Er'Rets. But how could he push back Darkness if there was no Light in him?

Câan is Light. Achan needed Câan's light to banish the Darkness in his heart. Fear. Selfishness. Anger. Hate. Insecurity. Loneliness. These things were not Light. And Achan clung to them.

Achan's heart was far from Arman's, clinging to Dark things. He had never discovered Arman's will for his life because he spent all his time consumed by his circumstances. He had carelessly guessed his role and tried to align that with his own desires for happiness.

Comprehension dawned, overwhelming Achan in grief. He needed to believe. To trust Arman's plan, even when that plan was unclear. "I'm sorry. I didn't understand."

"Your faith has ransomed you, son of Axel. Go in peace."

While the last word still echoed in the chamber, Câan vanished, taking the heat and light and sorrow with Him.

Achan gasped in a few deep breaths to get his composure and broke into a cold sweat. It took a while for his eyes to readjust to the sunlight streaming through the broken windows. Lord Yarden wouldn't be pleased with the state of his temple.

The sunlight vanished as if a storm cloud blocked the sun. Achan pushed himself up and turned to face the door.

Shung stood in the doorframe, staring at Achan with wide eyes. "Rare the man whose prayers move the earth."

Achan stopped before his Shield. "What did you see?"

Shung gestured his good arm at the altar. "The little cham knelt at the altar and the earth shook."

"You didn't see Câan?"

Shung shook his head, brown eyes wide.

The diminished light distracted Achan from Shung. He stepped over the shards of glass, past Shung, out the door, and onto the temple porch. The wide, fair valley stretched out below, sunny and bright, yet mist coated his arms. He descended the porch steps and turned to look back.

A thick fog hovered around three sides of Temple Arman.

JILL WILLIAMSON

"The Evenwall." Achan stumbled back, heart stampeding in his chest. Darkness was growing, as Sir Gavin had predicted. At this rate, it would reach the back of the Mitspah stronghold by morning.

Achan rubbed more rue juice over his arms, inhaling the thick piney scent, pondering Câan's words. He missed Sparrow. He didn't understand why she ignored his messages. But a peace had settled over his heart. Arman was in control, so Achan needn't fear.

He had been ransomed.

The door opened and Shung entered. He reached into his pocket and held up a sliver of bone on a leather cord, grinning, exposing his yellow teeth. "A symbol of your victory and the one to come."

Shung placed the charm in Achan's hand. Closer now, he saw, not a bone shard, but a claw the length of his index finger. He shuddered and rolled his sore shoulder. "Is this from . . . ?"

"Aye. There are more, but Shung thought the little cham too modest to wear them like Koyukuk."

Achan laughed, dryly. More like he'd have nightmares with a clutch of cham claws round his neck day in and day out. He supposed he could manage one, though the sight of it chilled him. He accepted the necklace and bowed his head, keeping eye contact with Shung. "Thank you, Shung. You honor me with this gift."

"Shung will not finish cape for many weeks. Little Cham needs symbol of victory now."

"You're making a cape?"

"The hide is tanning. Then Shung will trim and shape it."

"Thank you, Shung. You're a good friend."

Shung returned to his post outside the door. Achan inspected the claw. It was shaped like a long, curving beak, wide at the paw end and tapering to a sharp point. Shung had bored a hole through the wide end and strung it onto a braided leather cord. Achan reached over the jar of rue juice Sparrow had made him and picked up the length of red twine from the tabletop. He held one end at the knot of the leather cord on Shung's necklace, and drew the twine along, measuring its length. He smiled. It was long enough.

Achan spent the next hour unbraiding Shung's leather cord and adding Sparrow's length of red twine. This way, she'd be with him always.

"Are you certain it is working?" Vrell had eaten more karpos fruit that she had ever cared to and duplicated herself as sentries in her mind. Sir Eagan had promised this would help keep Achan from seeing her thoughts. "I can still hear every word he says to me."

"As can I." Sir Eagan chuckled. "Does the prince even know how to knock? Or does he always charge his way into any mind he wants?"

Vrell stroked her horse's neck and smiled to herself. "I tried to teach him."

"Well, my lady, until he learns the way into your mind, he will continue to message. I cannot mute him. The karpos will give you extra strength, but I doubt it will stop him once he is taught. And from what Sir Gavin told me, he plans to have your mother teach him."

Surely Mother would not help Achan break into Vrell's mind. Thankfully, Vrell would be able to discuss this with Mother before she had a chance to teach Achan anything.

The journey with Sir Eagan should have been awkward, but Vrell found herself unnaturally calm until Carmine appeared on the horizon and excitement brought her to tears.

She was home!

She rode with Sir Eagan to the front door of Granton Castle. Anillo stood waiting on the steps. A stable boy took their horses.

Vrell ran to greet Anillo, overcome with joy, but he held up a hand. "If you both will follow me."

Vrell sobered. Mother did not want to make a scene of her return. Could Lord Nathak still have spies lurking?

Anillo led them to Mother's study. Mother stood at the window overlooking the northern fields, her back to them. She wore a lavender and black gown. Her hair was down, curling in auburn ringlets to the center of her back. As soon as the door shut she turned. Her tear-filled eyes studied Vrell, flashed to Sir Eagan, then back to Vrell.

She lifted her skirts and ran across the room. "Averella, my darling!" She grabbed Vrell in a tight hug.

"Gently, Nitsa, she is wounded."

Sir Eagan's voice softened Mother's grip. She took Vrell's hand in her gloved one, gently kissed her forehead, and turned to face to Sir Eagan. Her bottom lip trembled. "Oh, Eagan. Time has aged you well."

Sir Eagan stared at Mother like a man in a dream. "'Tis kind of you to say so, my lady, though from my eyes, not a day has passed. You are as lovely as ever."

Mother inched closer to Sir Eagan, her lavender skirt swaying like a bell with each step. "You brought her back to me."

He reached out his hand. "I did."

Mother set her gloved one in his. The three of them stood in a line, holding hands. Vrell swallowed, tears streaming down her cheeks. She watched her mother and Sir Eagan stare at each other, wondering, wondering.

Vrell sucked in a short breath. She had always despised corsets. Having lived as a boy for nearly a year, this one felt horribly tight. It especially aggravated the wound in her side, though her maidservant, Syrah, had taken care not to lace the corset as tight as was proper. Vrell did feel pretty for the first time in ages. Syrah had aired out a green velvet gown with peach accents and had twisted Vrell's hair up on her head and secured it with a gold-beaded caul net.

Vrell stood at the window of Mother's study overlooking the inner bailey. Beyond, she could see the outer bailey and the road leading north from Carmine, edged on both sides by grape vines. It had been three days since Vrell left Mitspah. Captain Tristan Loam's soldiers milled about, anxious, no doubt, for the prince's arrival. Captain Loam had dressed his men in Old Kingsguard capes as a sign of Carmine's support.

Achan and his contingent of volunteer fighters were due to arrive in Carmine today. According to Anillo, the men could hardly wait to swear fealty to Achan and go to war. These were

Mother's soldiers, of course, who knew all too well of Lord Nathak's persecution over the years. It would be more difficult to persuade all of Carm to go to war on Achan's behalf.

Vrell had remained hidden since her arrival. Besides her mother and Sir Eagan, only Anillo and Syrah were aware of her return. She had chosen Mother's study to hide in because the secret passages that led out from it took her all over the stronghold. She might spy on Achan's welcome banquet but would not attend. If she were to meet Achan as Lady Averella, more time would have to pass. Preferably enough time for him to marry and forget her. The thought made her teary-eyed again. She had been crying since she arrived home. She was sick to death of tears.

A knock sounded on the door and Anillo poked his head in. "My lady? The duchess asked that Master Bran Rennan be brought to this room."

Vrell tensed and closed her eyes. The duchess. Anillo's use of Mother's title was a signal of a request not to be argued with. Vrell had put off her reunion with Bran Rennan, despite all Mother's urging to speak with him right away. Apparently Mother's patience had run out. Vrell had waited so long for this moment. Now that it had finally arrived, she dreaded it.

She nodded. Anillo opened the door fully. Bran stepped inside, looking strange in the red Old Kingsguard cape. The color matched his sunburned face and made him look red all over. She shook off the critical thought and forced a smile.

Bran looked her up and down, clearly uncertain of her identity. "Averella?"

She nodded.

He crossed the room at a run and swept her into a hug, twirling her in a circle.

Vrell cried out at the pain in her side. "Bran, please. Put me down. I am injured."

He set her down and, holding her shoulders, stepped back and peered into her eyes. He seemed shorter than she remembered him. Or maybe Achan was taller.

"Where?"

"My side. It is a long story."

"We have all the time in the world, my lady." He led her to the sofa and helped her sit. "You're so thin. Are you hungry? I could have Anillo bring a tray." Bran jumped up but Vrell snagged his hand.

"No, Bran. I have eaten. Please sit. You are making me nervous."

He slid beside her on the sofa. He took her hands again, brought them to his nose, and sniffed. "I want to breathe you in. How I've missed you. Is it true, what Prince Oren told Sir Rigil? Were you traveling with the prince?"

"I was."

"Is it true the prince can bloodvoice?"

"He can."

"And Sir Gavin?"

"Yes. He can bloodvoice as well. As can I."

"You, Averella? Why didn't you say so?"

"I only discovered it just before I left."

Bran's smile faltered. "Why couldn't you or Sir Gavin send word that you were well? For so long I didn't know. I begged Sir Rigil to ask Prince Oren, and I heard some rumors, but . . . Averella, how could you leave me wondering? When all this time you could have sent word to your mother yourself, you had no message for me?"

Vrell saw the hurt in his eyes. She did not know why she had not thought to ask her mother to pass along a message to Bran. "F-forgive me, Bran. These past many months . . . I have not been myself. I have lived in constant fear of discovery. My life has been threatened time and again. I have no other excuse."

"You were hiding from Esek and your mother sent you to Walden's Watch. That story your mother eventually confided to me. But then Esek issued a warrant for your arrest, claiming you'd run off with the prince. But others claimed no woman traveled with the prince. Only the Kingsguard knights and his—" Bran's nose wrinkled—"squire?"

"Mother did not tell you I had taken on the guise of a stray boy to aid in my shelter?"

Bran shook his head, and Vrell launched into her story. Bran's expression hardened when she told of how she had spoken to him in the Mahanaim dungeon, then how later, they all stood together in the Council chambers. But Vrell plunged on, anxious to get the whole ordeal over and done with before the fight, for she knew there would be one.

She left out Achan's latest declarations. They would do Bran no good to hear, and they were simply in Achan's mind. It was not possible he felt so strongly about her. Give him a few weeks and she would be as Tara was.

A silly, sad smile and a laugh at his folly.

She finished her story with, "Sir Eagan offered to bring me here, and so I am finally home. All is well."

Bran folded his arms and leaned against the opposite end of the sofa. "So the prince does not know you're Lady Averella Amal? He thinks you're a stray trying to avoid life as someone's mistress?"

Vrell nodded.

Bran's eyes widened. "You *lied* to the future king?"

She stared at her hands in her lap. "Long before I knew he was the future king. To tell him the truth now would hurt him. I figured bide my time as Vrell until I could slip away."

"You love him."

Her cheeks tingled. She turned her head, staring at Bran. "Who?"

He released a breath. "Who indeed? I've waited all my life for you to look at me like that."

"Like what?"

"The way you look at one of your hybrid plants."

"Do not speak riddles, Bran. There is no one in this room but you."

Bran fiddled with the hem of his Kingsguard cloak. "You must tell him who you are."

Vrell sighed. "We have been over this already. Why does it matter?"

"Because he can't very well marry a stray, my lady. Sir Rigil tells me he's being pressured to marry. Had he known your true identity, he might have asked."

Vrell huffed a cynical laugh. Achan's plea, fresh in her mind, brought a stab of sorrow. "Why would you think such a thing?"

"Because you're a jewel. Kind, smart, hardworking. I'm sure that even in trousers you would win any man's heart."

"Bran. Be serious."

"Your mother could make the offer. It's easily done. Let the prince decide. All you have to do—"

"No." Vrell glared. "I will *not* be queen. I did not marry Esek because I did not want to be queen. That has not changed."

"As if not being queen was your reason for refusing Esek. Achan is not Esek. Esek is a snake, my lady. Even his followers attest to that. I like the prince. He's a good man. I can tell."

"I know he is a good man."

"Sir Rigil said he attacked Sir Gavin when he discovered his *squire* had gone. At first I thought him mad, but now I imagine he was simply *madly* in love."

Vrell's eyes went wide. "Achan attacked Sir Gavin?"

Bran smirked as if he had caught Vrell in a lie. "Make the offer, my lady."

"Enough!" Vrell scooted to the edge of the sofa and straightened her skirts. "For many months, I have been desperate to get home, to Mother and to you, Bran. To put this wretched experience behind me. I am betrothed to you. I would not pledge my heart to another."

"With all due respect, my lady. I can see you no longer love me."

"Do not be ridiculous. Of course I love you. Mother said she would speak to me after the banquet about our engagement. I am sure she will give her consent."

Bran scooted to Vrell's side, set a hand on her shoulder, and kissed her. She stiffened. His lips were soft and familiar, but she felt awkward, disappointed, and wished he would stop. Was it because they had been parted for so long? Tears welled at her lack of emotion.

He broke away and his brown eyes studied hers. He released a shaky breath and swallowed. "Averella. I would never break my vow to marry you if that's your heart's desire. But I beg you be honest with yourself and me. I don't wish to see either of us married to someone we don't truly love. I'd hate to know you'd forced yourself to keep your vow to me, and I'd hate to have a wife who'd settled for me. Please. Think on it."

She inhaled a shaky breath. "I will consult Mother on the matter."

Bran stifled a laugh and shook his head.

"What?"

"Be honest. If you truly don't know, say so. If you no longer love me, say so. But don't use your mother like a crutch."

"It is wise to seek the council of one's elders."

"Aye, but that's not what you do, Averella. You only seek your mother's council when you don't want to face your own problems. When you don't like her answer, you do as you please. And if you can't have your own way or are too craven to deal with your own problems, you run back to your mother and beg she fix it. That's not seeking her wise council. That's seeking a method to get your own way time and again. You're a spoiled child."

Vrell gasped. "How dare you."

"Yes, yes. How dare I speak truth? The vicious barbarian, Bran Rennan. The man who recklessly tells women what they refuse to hear. Well, hang me if you must, my dear, but at least take a moment to consider what I've said. I fear you will see I'm quite right.

"You secretly love our king to be. I can see it plain as the Evenwall approaching. And the only reason you've stayed a stray-nobody in his eyes was so he could meet you on your own terms." Bran raised his thick eyebrows. "But what now, my dear? Your ploy has failed. Now he catches you in your lie or you never meet him again. My, what a tangled web a spider weaves."

Vrell stood. "You dare call me a spider? What of you and the widow Gren Fenny? Now who is weaving a spider's web?

She clearly loves you, but you will not sink to consider a mere peasant when you could marry a noblewoman. Wait and see if things work out with the duchesses' heir first. If not, there is always the widow Hoff."

Bran paled so much he didn't look at all sunburned. "I don't know what the servants have been saying, Averella, but I ignore Gren's affection because of my promise to you. It has nothing to do with my social status or hers. Don't twist this around. You're angry because I'm right. You and I are not meant to be. And it pains me I'm not more grieved. But that's wide of the point. I forgive you, Averella, for loving another. But don't punish me over your lies to the prince. And don't punish him, either."

Vrell pressed her hand to her heart, trying to control her breathing and the threatening tears.

Bran paused at the doorway. "Be warned, he still seeks you, my lady. He has men in the area."

Her eyes widened and she looked out the window, scanning the inner bailey. "Achan is here? Already?"

Bran chuckled. "No, my lady. *King* Esek. It was rumored you'd come home. His men have been seen nearby."

"Oh." Vrell fell back on the sofa. Surely this rumor had been before Achan had crippled him? If Esek were still alive, would he be a broken man or as much of a tyrant as ever? Would he give up his claim to the throne, or, after all her hiding, would he find her in her own home and take her away?

"Marry Achan, Averella. Be our queen. For you would be a marvelous one."

Vrell glared at Bran. What had she even seen in such a rude individual? "Please go."

"Very well." Bran bowed. "Farewell, my lady."

40

Achan sat atop Dove, his right arm in a sling to keep the pressure off his shoulder. Shung rode on his left, Cole on his right, riding Scout. The procession to Carmine passed several families migrating from the encroaching Evenwall. People carried packs and baskets, led animals, drove wagons, or pulled carts, packed with all their possessions.

Achan now understood his purpose, more than to be king, was to bring Arman's love to the people. Being king was simply the role he needed to complete such a task. But he knew so little of Arman. He had so much to learn before he could proclaim *Arman hu elohim, Arman hu echâd, Arman hu shlosha be-echâd* with confidence.

Lord Yarden had been distressed by Esek's attack, apologetic, even, as if he were to blame for Atul being a traitor. Achan had allowed the man to blame himself a bit longer than necessary before explaining about the broken windows in the temple. For a moment he'd feared Lord Yarden might faint, but Shung had spoken, repeated the words he'd said to Achan when Câan had vanished.

"Rare the man whose prayers move the earth."

That had been enough to bring Lord Yarden back, nodding and beaming as if having his property destroyed were the greatest honor to be had in all Er'Rets. Perhaps now he would intentionally never repair it.

The city of Carmine could be seen from miles away in the center of a luscious green valley. Farms and vineyards stretched to the horizon in all directions. The cupola roof on a brownstone tower, as tall as the one on Ice Island, peeked out of a matching curtain wall.

They approached the grounds from the northwest. A simple, six-foot brownstone wall enclosed the vineyards of Granton Castle. There were no guards at the first gate. The procession raised a cloud of dust as it trampled the dirt road. Vines stretched on and on, heavy with bunches of plump red grapes. Achan's mouth watered. He hoped he'd get to try some.

At the end of the vineyard, Sir Gavin stopped before a single tower gate at another brownstone wall. A wide moat separated another dirt road—which appeared to circle the inner edges of the vineyard—and the three-level curtain wall. The narrow drawbridge was down, but the guard had to raise the portcullis to let them enter.

A group of soldiers clustered on the sentry wall near the tower, looking down on their group. They pointed and chattered. Some cheered. A few guardsmen further down the wall ran toward the tower as if hoping to get a glimpse of the visitors.

Achan considered reaching out to hear what they were saying, but he had a guess. *Which one is he?*

He kept his head down and spurred Dove along. He, Shung, and Cole rode five pairs back from Sir Gavin. They crossed the drawbridge and entered an outer bailey ten times larger than the one at Sitna manor. Soldiers on horseback wore red Old Kingsguard capes like Sir Gavin's. Women bustled about with loads of fabric or laundry, boys carried wood or led animals, dogs and chickens ambled underfoot, children played games and laughed. The cool tones of a lute drifted on the air. As Achan's men neared, all went silent and stopped to stare.

The procession paused at yet another wall, this gate a double tower five levels high, like two rolls of stone parchment standing on end. More guards stared down from the wall.

Shung's voice pulled Achan away from the guards. "You are downcast, Little Cham?"

Achan glanced at his hairy friend. "I'm tired of traveling, and I know it won't stop until a war has killed many. I don't look forward to the coming months."

"But we do not fight tonight. Tonight we eat grapes and drink wine." Shung smiled. "Perhaps dance as well?"

"I don't want to dance."

"You are missing Little Vixen. Shung does not think she will be gone forever."

Achan hoped that were true.

The horses moved again, under the tall, double tower gate of the inner curtain wall. Inside, Granton Castle loomed, massive, like Mahanaim, only clean. It even smelled sweet. The building sat like two interlocking manors. The front, southwestern section was much smaller. Two narrow towers flanked a set of massive maroon doors, the front entrance to the castle.

The western tower stood eight levels high. The other stretched as high as the Pillar. Each had cupola roofs as if topped with gazebos.

The back, northeastern section of the castle stood like a gigantic brick, six levels high, with dozens of arrow loops on each level. Smaller towers supported the center and corners.

Hundreds of soldiers in red capes cheered and waved Armonguard's flag. Achan pushed the overwhelming sensation aside and searched every black-haired head for Sparrow's round face. He tried again to look through her eyes and failed.

Achan and the knights dismounted at the entrance. Cole scurried over and took Dove's reins.

"Thank you, Cole."

The boy beamed and led Dove and Scout away. Achan's body still ached. He limped after Sir Gavin and followed the knight inside one of the tall maroon doors.

A small foyer opened into a great hall. Bronze candelabras hung from a vaulted ceiling. Servants lined both sides of the aisle leading to the dais, which stretched the width of the hall. To Achan's right, a brownstone staircase fanned out into the foyer. Dozens of people stood along the railing, peering down. Achan kept his eyes on the back of Sir Gavin's head and trailed the knight to the foot of the stairs.

A woman descended, petite yet regally imposing. Her auburn hair was tucked under a gold circlet and gauze veil. She wore a maroon gown—the same color as the front doors—trimmed in ivory lace. The long skirt spilled over the steps behind her. Her bell sleeves trailed within inches of the floor.

A slender, white-haired man shadowed her like a bobcat, agile and aware. He wore a plain white tunic with a maroon vest and black trousers. A scar across his neck suggested he could cheat death. "I am Anillo, advisor to the duchess." His voice carried a slow authority, as if crossing him would be a poor, perhaps fatal, choice. "May I present her ladyship, Nitsa Amal, the Duchess of Carm?"

The woman flowed off the bottom step like a petal on a stream. She wove around the others and stopped before Achan. How did she know what he looked like? She probably owned the painting of his father.

So short, she looked up into his eyes. Achan felt like a giant. Her skin was like a porcelain vase. Not a blemish or wrinkle. She couldn't have lived more than thirty-five years. Hers eyes were green and bright, calculating yet kind.

No wonder Sir Eagan loved this woman still.

The duchess' silky and kind voice pulled Achan's attention to her lips. He knew this voice.

"Your Highness, I am honored to finally meet you. You are most welcome at Granton Castle. My home is yours." She curtsied then held out her hand.

A wave of heat rushed over him as he scrambled to remember what Sir Caleb had advised him to do and say. He took her hand and pressed it to his lips. Then a deep bow, keeping eye contact, while he released her hand. "It's I who am honored, my lady. I hear you have many concerns. I pray we're not a burden to you at this time."

"You are anything but. I have been praying to meet you ever since I first heard your bloodvoice."

Achan bowed his head again, comprehension dawning. He'd heard her so many times in his mind and hadn't known who she was. "I thank you for your kind words that day, my lady, for I feared I had lost my mind."

"My heart aches for what you have suffered at the hands of Esek." She glanced at his arm. "Are you badly wounded?"

"I am mending." He wanted to say something of Esek. "I hear Esek has plagued you as well. I'm troubled over the safety of your daughter, Lady Averella. Prince Oren informed me of her plight. Is there any way we might come to her aid?"

"Thank you, no. She is well and safe, though unable to greet you this visit."

Achan nodded, though his thoughts strayed. If the lady Averella ever made it home, how would she react when she discovered she'd lost her suitor to a peasant widow expecting a child? And if she were one of the candidates the knights thought might make for a good queen, he'd want to see if she looked like a horse or not. But he forced his mind back to business. "Has Lord Nathak caused any mischief for you recently?"

"We have not seen him in weeks. It is my hope he has moved on to Armonguard."

"There's much I have to share with you on that matter." Achan glanced at Sir Caleb. "Perhaps there will be a time later where we can talk privately with you and my men?"

The duchess smiled and curtsied again. "Of course, Your Highness. Are you hungry?"

"I'm sure my men could empty your kitchens in a day, my lady. We've brought provisions and don't wish to impose."

"Nonsense."

Offer your arm, Your Highness, Sir Caleb said.

Achan spun to her side and held out his left arm so that his sword and sling would be away from her.

She gripped his bicep with both hands and led him into the great hall. "How long do you plan to stay with us?"

"A week, to recruit men to our cause."

"You shall stay as long as you like. I offer Granton Castle as a base for you and your generals to plan your strategies."

Generals? "Thank you, my lady. You're most generous."

The duchess steered Achan up the center aisle toward the high table. They passed a host of servants and staff, including Sir Rigil, Bran, and Sir Eagan. Achan sensed each man's guilt and guessed the reasons. Sir Rigil, for failing to keep an eye on Bran and Gren. Bran, for his growing affection for Gren. Sir Eagan, for taking Sparrow away.

Bran could wait. But Achan stopped before Sir Eagan. "I must speak with you right away, Sir Eagan."

Sir Eagan bowed. "As you wish, Your Majesty."

"Forgive me, Duchess," Achan said, "I require a moment with my father's Shield."

Duchess Amal released his arm and curtsied. "Of course, Your Majesty."

Sir Caleb knocked, but Achan ignored it. He gripped Sir Eagan's arm and led him between two rough hewn tables, not bothering to lower his voice, though Sir Eagan's calm already poured into him. "Where did you take her?"

"As far as the front door." Sir Eagan's blue eyes looked pained, as if he missed Sparrow too.

Hope welled in Achan. "She is here, then? In Carmine?"

"She could be, yes. She did not confide her plans to me."

The crowd murmured. Achan sensed their curiosity. "Did she give any clue where she might go? Where she was from?"

"Only that she had been living in Walden's Watch."

"You think she plans to return there?"

"I cannot say, Your Majesty."

Achan wanted to harangue this man, despite his being so much older, but Arman had taken his anger. "I was prepared to heed your council, to let her go. I only wanted to say farewell."

Sir Eagan's sympathetic gaze needled Achan. "Sometimes it is easier this way. Farewells can be difficult. Dangerous."

"Perhaps, but I am not you, Sir Eagan."

After a hearty lunch with the duchess, Anillo ushered Achan to a bath and fitting. The duchess had insisted on providing Achan a new wardrobe. Maybe she doted on him because she was a woman with no sons, or maybe his clothing had been truly shabby for a king. He could hardly tell.

Dinner followed. Achan wore a fancy gold and maroon outfit that reminded him of Esek so much he loathed wearing it. He met the duchess' four younger daughters, ages twelve, ten, seven, and four, and danced with them more than any other, though he feared encouraging the eldest, for there were several twelve-year-olds on his list of possible brides.

Still, better to dance with twelve-year-old Gypsum Amal than the older, lesser nobles of Carmine who flaunted and flirted. He'd never seen a crowd of young women more bedecked, with the exception of Jaira Hamartano. Clearly these poor girls had been instructed to win his favor at any cost.

When Achan finally fell into his bed on the fourth floor, he couldn't sleep. This room was bigger than two full cottages from Sitna. The bed itself could have slept six comfortably. He lay on his back and spread his arms and legs wide, gently stretching his sore arm and leg. He liked the silky feel of the sheets and the way his body sank into the featherbed.

Shung's snore grumbled steadily from the pallet Sir Caleb had insisted be brought in. Achan felt safe. Peaceful. No fear of Esek or a traitor killing him in his sleep.

Had Esek died? If so, Achan doubted Lord Nathak would report it right away, if ever. Achan shook the horrifying image of Esek's severed arm from his head and turned onto his side, burrowing into the mattress again.

His stomach rumbled. It was truly no use. He supposed he could find sleep by shadowing one of the sleeping knights. Or maybe he could wander a bit, perhaps find the kitchens and a snack.

He climbed out of bed, put on an old tunic, and crept to the doors. Opening one a crack, he peeked out and sighed. Sure enough, three guards crouched at the end of the hall, next to the stairs, playing dice. More strangers willing to die for him because he was the Crown Prince. It still felt so awkward.

He peeked the other way. No guards to the left. Had the guards broken ranks to play dice? Clearly they were not concerned about Achan's safety. If he could sneak to the corner without being seen, he could go down that stairwell.

Achan slipped out of the room and pressed against the wall. Dice clattered over the wood floor and the guards erupted in a loud cheer. Achan sidestepped to the corner where a tower staircase stood. In Sitna, the kitchens were in the outer bailey. But this was a vast stronghold, similar to Mahanaim. The kitchens in Mahanaim had been in the basement.

Achan descended the stairs, his bare feet cool on the stone. A sudden thought made him wince. He should have dressed better, at least put on boots. If he was seen, Sir Caleb would berate him for not being properly dressed. Nothing could be done about it now. He was too far into his quest.

He reached the bottom without seeing a soul and found himself in the corner of a damp passageway that stretched out like an L. Concentrating on what he remembered from outside, Achan tried to rebuild the stronghold in his mind. Logically, the kitchens would be near the great hall.

He went right. At the next corner, the corridor turned left and led him past a laundry room, a bathhouse, a massive wine cellar, and a buttery.

The smell of yeast and smoke urged him on. The walls fell away into a vast open area. Achan gaped. The kitchens in Sitna had consisted of two small rooms. This place was the size of the great hall above.

Drum pillars rose to the ceiling every ten feet or so. Fat candelabras hung from thick iron chains. Baking ovens ran along the left wall, fireplaces along the right. Dozens of long tables filled the center, some covered with bowls, some empty, some stone with iron grills built into the surface. Achan saw no movement at the moment, but with the size of this castle, cooks and maids likely worked around the clock.

He veered toward the fireplaces on the right wall and lifted a bowl from a shelf as he passed. Only one fireplace still burned under a round, iron cauldron pot. Achan pulled his sleeve over his hand and lifted the lid on the pot. The smell of beefy, hot stew flooded his nostrils. He grinned and ladled his bowl to the brim, then carried it to a rack of fluffy rolls beside a drum pillar. He dunked a roll into the stew and bit down.

Shamayim.

Standing by the rack, he finished the first roll in three bites. He grabbed three more and walked toward a table surrounded by squat stools. Likely where the kitchen staff ate. He sat down and finished half his bowl when the sudden urge seized him to sit under the table. At Sitna Manor, when he hadn't wanted to be seen, he often sat under the tables.

A prince probably shouldn't sit under a table like a dog.

Despite the foolishness of the idea, he did it anyway. Crossing his legs, he pulled the stool in and set his bowl on top. He smiled as he ate, feeling at home for the first time in months. Silly, considering his comfort was due to a life of deceit and cruelty at the hands of Lord Nathak and Poril. Still, no amount of fancy clothes, featherbeds, or "Your Highnesses" could change his past. Being a stray was a part of him.

So engrossed in the stew, Achan didn't hear the light scuff of footsteps until it was too late. He sat motionless, hoping whoever it was would come and go quickly.

The rustle of fabric drew near until soft blue velour brushed his left hand. He jerked it into his lap, staring at the gold satin slippers that had stopped by his left knee. Slippers so fancy could only belong to a noblewoman. He held his breath. What noblewoman would walk in the kitchens at such an hour? The duchess' lady in waiting sent to fetch a snack, perhaps?

The layers of velvet rumpled as the woman crouched down, revealing inch by inch an immaculately embroidered robe and curling auburn hair cascading over her shoulders.

"Duchess Amal." Achan scrambled back and bumped into another stool. He pushed a stool to get out, but her hand on his arm stopped him.

"Why does the Crown Prince of Er'Rets sit under a table in my kitchen?"

Achan's cheeks flushed. "I . . . was hungry."

"Could you not call for a tray?"

"I wanted . . ." Achan cast his eyes to the bowl of stew on the stool. How could he explain without insulting this woman?

He swallowed but could not meet her eyes. "I could not sleep and thought a snack might help. Take no offense, my lady, but I'm not used to such gracious hospitality."

"But not just a snack, Your Highness. *Under* the table? Why?"

Achan's face burned. "As a boy, I spent many a night under the bread tables in the Sitna kitchens. Despite his best efforts, Sir Caleb has not been able to train the slave boy out of me entirely. I'm afraid I am still most comfortable in a kitchen. I know it must sound mad, but it . . . feels like home."

To his great relief, the duchess smiled. Her green eyes flitted over his face, hair, cramped body, and bare feet. Sweat moistened his brow at her scrutiny. Something tickled his wrist. He glanced down to see a tiny black bug. He jumped, dropped his roll, swatted the bug away. Every muscle tense. He'd used Sparrow's pine juice. The fleas had been gone. He scratched his wrist, arm, shoulder, neck. They couldn't be back.

The duchess chuckled. "It's only a few ants, Your Highness. I would think one so seasoned to eating on the floor would be used to them by now."

Achan ran both hands through his hair, which was loose and not tied back. Oh, horror. Again he couldn't look at the duchess. What would she think? "I thought they were fleas." His breath hitched. Why had he said that? Fleas? Blazes!

The lady raised a sculpted brow. "Did you enjoy your time with the soldiers?"

He studied his father's ring. "Except for the fleas."

"You'll go to war, then? And fight alongside your men?"

"Should there be one, yes."

"And your wife?"

Achan blinked and met the lady's green eyes. "I have no wife, my lady."

"But you will soon."

Could this conversation become any more awkward? He picked up the roll and dropped it in the remainder of his stew. "I suppose I might."

"And what will she do while you are at war?"

Achan shrugged. "Whatever pleases her. If she's good with a sword, I'd welcome the company."

The duchess smiled. "Ah, you are droll. But what if she is with child? When this war comes."

Achan's lips parted, his cheeks filled with heat. He would not come to this kitchen again. He didn't appreciate Duchess Amal's midnight interrogation. She'd clearly thought more about his bride than he had.

She pressed on. "I mean no disrespect, but these are things a man must consider when taking a bride. Many say you traveled with a woman. What will your wife think of her?"

Achan sucked in a sharp breath. "Please. It wasn't like that, my lady, I promise you. Sparrow wasn't who she claimed to be. We all thought her a boy. Have you seen her? Did she pass through Carmine? Do you know where she lives?"

"Why do you ask, Your Highness? I would think you better off without her presence tainting your reign."

"Vrell could never taint anything. She's sweet and good and lovely—"

"You care for her, then?"

Achan thudded his head back against the table leg. "My feelings don't matter. She refused me, and Sir Gavin berated me for my recklessness and Sir Caleb for my carelessness and I for my foolishness and Câan for my selfishness. I'm a wretched prince. Far too impulsive. But I'll do my duty and marry whom they choose, and I'll love her as best I can. Does that satisfy your curiosity, my lady?"

She smiled. "It does."

Finally something had. "You know, I was freer as a stray."

"I understand that feeling. I hadn't wanted to marry the duke. It was the loneliest time in my life. At first."

Achan recalled Sir Eagan's tale of their past and decided she did understand. "Your intuition is right on target, my lady. I haven't once considered the inner workings of my future marriage past the identity of my bride. If it were my choice I'd marry Sparrow and live in a cottage in the mountains. I'd hunt and she'd keep a garden of herbs. We wouldn't be rich, but we'd have our freedom and each other."

He sighed and met Duchess Amal's green eyes. "Alas, my life isn't mine to live. I've now given it freely to Arman. He appeared to me, you know. Fairly destroyed His own temple. He's my master now and I trust His plan, even if I can't understand it. I only wish my obedience didn't come so bitterly. I fear if He could, Arman would give me a sound flogging for my demeanor of servitude."

Duchess Amal's eyes widened. "I think you misunderstand how Arman loves His people. He does not punish them."

Such a statement didn't align with what Achan knew of masters. "I only mean that I've never been a very contrite servant. Ask Lord Nathak." Achan chuckled softly, then bowed his head low. "Forgive me, my lady. I must beg leave of your gracious company. I'm very tired and if I continue to prattle on, you'll think me drunk."

"Of course." Duchess Amal stood, allowing Achan to crawl out from under the table. "Please do not go out alone again,

Your Highness. You are welcome to sit under the table, but we recently had a traitor in our kitchens, and I would feel better knowing you were not wandering alone. At least bring your Shield under the table with you next time."

"As you wish." He scraped the contents of his bowl into the slop pail, rinsed the bowl, and set it on the drying rack. He bowed to the duchess again. "Good evening, my lady. You have a magnificent kitchen."

"Thank you, Your Highness. Good night."

41

Vrell perched on a stool in the dark corridor and stared through the peephole. The five Old Kingsguard knights sat around an oval table in Achan's bedchamber. Achan had dragged his chair down to the fireplace at the end of the room, where he sat alone, staring into the flames.

Sir Caleb held a parchment open on the table. "First we have Lady Tova Sigul of Hamonah, age fourteen. I still object to this offer. Hamonah worships Thalassa. We cannot consider anyone who does not follow Arman."

"But Hamonah is being at war with Jaelport," Inko said. "They're being extremely rich and would be bringing an immense dowry. The diamonds alone would be buying weapons and armor to be fitting a thousand soldiers. Surely Achan could be teaching the girl about the Way."

"Achan barely understands the Way himself." Sir Gavin said. "Don't burden him with an unbelieving spouse."

"Arman forbids it," Sir Caleb said. "In the Book of Life."

"Besides, 'tis too far away and unstable," Sir Gavin said. "And I trust Lord Sigul as much as I trust Queen Hamartano."

"Agreed," Sir Caleb said. "What say you, Eagan?"

Sir Eagan shrugged. "I say let him pick his own bride."

"Thank you," Achan said.

Sir Eagan continued, "But I would not marry him to any enemy, and I agree with Sir Caleb. He must wed a believer."

"But it would make for an interesting relationship, it would," Kurtz said. "Lots of sparks, eh?"

Vrell blanched. Could Kurtz think of nothing else?

"Is there a noblewoman at Zerah Rock?" Sir Caleb asked.

"None I know of," Sir Eagan said, "but it has been many years."

"A second cousin to Sir Rigil." Sir Gavin sniffed a short breath. "Were Achan a younger prince in a house of princes, he could marry whomever he wishes. We need a noblewoman of vast connections."

"And wealth," Inko said.

Achan groaned by the hearth. No one paid him any mind.

"Ladies Mandzee and Jaira are out," Sir Gavin said.

"Praise Arman for that," Achan mumbled.

Vrell smiled. A blessing indeed.

"I also recommend we reject Ladies Jacqueline and Marietta Levy of Mahanaim," Sir Caleb said.

Sir Gavin tapped his fingers on the table. "Agreed."

"You're throwing out all the options that are being the strongest," Inko said.

"Remind me your concern there?" Sir Eagan asked.

"They're Lord Levy's daughters," Sir Caleb said. "He voted for Esek as king."

"Ah." Sir Eagan nodded. "Wise to cut them, then."

Sir Caleb lifted the list again. "This leaves us with three options: Lady Gali Orson of Berland, age twenty-six—"

"Bah!" Kurtz wrinkled his nose and shook his head. "Berland women are rough. Trust me, I know."

Sir Caleb continued, "Lady Halona Pitney of Nesos, age twelve—"

Kurtz blew a raspberry. "Oh, come on! The lad won't even be able to—"

"Kurtz," Sir Eagan said, "silence your useless comments."

"I'm just pointing out what none of you are bold enough to say. How many of you would wish to marry a child, eh?"

Sir Caleb sighed. "And finally, Lady Glassea Hadar of Armonguard, age fourteen."

"Prince Oren's daughter?" Achan's forehead wrinkled. "Isn't she my cousin?"

"Aye," Sir Gavin said.

"It would be making a strong blood match," Inko said. "A Hadar and a Hadar."

Achan's eyes bulged like he had swallowed a fly.

"Let us talk this out," Sir Eagan said. "The ladies from Nesos, Armonguard, and Berland are all heirs to duchies?"

"All but Glassea," Sir Caleb said. "Achan will rule that duchy."

"So marrying Glassea gets him nothing," Sir Eagan said. "He already has Prince Oren's support and rule of Arman Duchy. There is no bonus in this match. Cross her off."

"Thank you," Achan said.

"That leaves us Nesos and Berland," Sir Caleb said.

"Both of which voted for Achan as king," Sir Gavin said.

"Is one stronger than the other?" Sir Eagan asked.

"I see them as equal," Sir Caleb said. "Both have decent control over their duchy. Neither are the strongest. Nahar has Nesos, Xulon, and Walden's Watch. They're also in a civil war with the Ebens. That could divide their service. Therion has Berland, Meribah Corner—which we now know is useless—Zamar, and Har Sha'ar."

"A bunch of nothing, eh?" Kurtz said.

"True," Sir Caleb said. "Berland is strong, but Darkness has weakened Therion, I fear."

"Well, Pacey? What do you think, eh?" Kurtz asked. "Aged twelve or twenty-six? Personally, I'd go with the twenty-six-year-old. At least she'll look like a woman, she will."

"You'd be surprised," Achan said. "She's quite . . . brusque. Six feet tall and built like you. Tough as nails and a little scary. Nice, though. I vote against her because Shung dotes on her."

"Achan, Shung would never be permitted to marry her," Sir Caleb said. "He's a peasant."

"Not if I knight him."

Vrell smiled. Achan would make an excellent king. He cared about all people, down to the peasants and strays.

"Oh, lad," Kurtz said. "You're just a bleeding heart, you are. We can't let that get out."

Achan stood and approached the table. "Shung is a good man and a great warrior. Why shouldn't I knight him?"

Kurtz reached across the table and grabbed a handful of grapes. "Knight him if you want. Marry the child. I don't care, eh? Just don't come weeping to me when all falls to dung."

Achan sighed. "Is there truly no one else?"

"None we deem safe, Your Highness," Sir Caleb said.

"What of Lady Averella?" Sir Eagan asked.

The room fell silent.

Vrell stiffened. A chill flashed over her arms. What was Sir Eagan doing?

Sir Caleb shrugged. "I don't believe she is an option."

"She's not," Sir Gavin said. "She's betrothed already."

"Bran Rennan," Achan said. "though he has proved himself unworthy of such devotion, in my opinion."

An ache passed over Vrell at the rawness of these words, and from Achan of all people.

"Well now, none of that matters any, eh, Eagan?" Kurtz said. "A prince beats a local lord any day, it does."

Vrell stifled a gasp. Kurtz deserved a slap. What a horrible thing to say in light of Sir Eagan and her mother's past.

Yet Sir Eagan did not seem bothered by Kurtz's audacity. "I will speak to the duchess about it. It is my understanding the engagement has been broken."

Vrell could not bear it. Bring her home to Carmine, then betray her? What was Sir Eagan's game?

"Carm is being the strongest duchy in all Er'Rets. Both Therion and Nesos would be siding with Carm," Inko said.

"That's true," Sir Caleb said. "But what of Sitna?"

"Many would side with Achan given the chance," Sir Gavin said. "There's little love for Esek or Lord Nathak there."

"Plus they're traveling," Inko said. "Who's ruling in their absence?"

"Likely Lord Nathak's steward," Sir Gavin said.

"If she were an option, I'd vote for Lady Averella," Sir Caleb said.

"Agreed," Inko said. "Esek was having that plan, after all."

"As would I," Sir Gavin tugged his braid, "yet I don't think that's the case."

"How old is Lady Averella?" Achan asked.

"Now you're thinking along the right lines," Kurtz said.

"Uh . . . seventeen, I think," Sir Gavin said.

"Eighteen next month," Sir Eagan said.

Heat swelled in Vrell. Sir Eagan knew her day of birth?

"Oh, that's much better." Achan took a long breath and sighed. "Okay. I vote for her too. To ask, anyway."

"Then you must give her a token," Sir Caleb said. "If the wedding is not to take place until after the war, you must offer something that will assure the young lady you're serious."

Vrell slid the peephole shut and laid her forehead against the wall. She would have to talk to Mother right away to stop this discussion from going any further.

Unfortunately, when Vrell sought out Mother, the duchess was in a meeting of her own. And when Vrell returned before dinner, Mother was already meeting with Sir Eagan.

Vrell stormed through the inner walls of Granton Castle, keeping to passages where she would not be seen. The peephole overlooking the great hall was low since it looked out of the second story of the hall. Vrell never liked this location. She had to sit on the floor and stomach rats and spiders that might scurry past. But if she wanted to look on the great hall, this was her only option.

She set her candle a few feet from her skirt and peeked through the slot in the wall. No celebration tonight. Achan sat alone at the high table, looking forlorn. Shung stood against the wall behind him. Shung should sit. Achan needed company.

"Still shadowing the prince?"

Vrell cowered. "Mother! You scared me." She clapped her hand over her heart and felt its rapid beat through her gown. "What are you doing here?"

Mother set her lantern beside Vrell's candle. "I would ask you the same question."

Vrell turned back to the peephole. "Well, I asked first."

"Seeking out my reclusive daughter. Shadowing the Crown Prince could be considered treason should the wrong person find out. Dearest, why not confess and end all this?"

"Mother! I am trying to save him a broken heart."

"I can attest it is far too late for that, Averella. I sense great sorrow in him."

"Which is why I will not parade out there in my finest dress and give him false hope."

Mother stepped up to the wall and looked down on Vrell, blocking the light. "Master Rennan came to visit me yesterday."

Vrell winced.

"He said you are no longer interested in his proposal."

Vrell looked up. "I never said that! Bran *told* me I was not interested. What kind of thing is that to say to a lady?"

"A very noble thing, I should think. Dearest, he is willing to give you up to see you happy. He knows, as well as I, that you care for our young prince."

"Do not try to make Bran look noble. He has fallen in love with a peasant and changed his mind about me."

Mother folded her arms. "Do you know, I found His Highness in the kitchens last night. He was sitting under a table, barefoot, eating a bowl of stew."

Vrell looked up to Mother's shadowed face. "Was he? Why?"

"He confessed he is trying but cannot erase his past. To him, sitting under the kitchen table feels like home."

Vrell found Achan's face in the peephole again. Two maidens walked by his table and giggled. He simply stared straight ahead, as if seeing nothing but his own thoughts.

"He is an interesting and honest young man," Mother said. "I know you do not wish to be queen, but if you are no longer interested in Master Rennan, I have no reason to deny the prince's offer of marriage."

"Mother! He believed me a stray when he said those things. It was not a true offer."

"That is not the instance I am referring to. This afternoon I received an official offer for you, Lady Averella Amal."

Vrell sighed. "Nor is that his proposal. That comes from his Kingsguards—from *your* Sir Eagan—for I heard the vote."

"Regardless, my dear, the offer is excellent and would provide a way to unite this duchy. If you can think of no better refusal than having to admit your falsehoods, I shall have to accept."

"Be reasonable, Mother! Achan pledges his heart to everyone *but* Arman. If I married him, it would not be long before he found a prettier wife to replace me. He admitted his temptation to give his heart to every pretty woman he sees."

"And yet look at him, Averella." She smiled sadly. "Your fear has you imagining a different man, I think."

Vrell got to her feet. "Perhaps. But as you say, I do not want to be queen. I have studied what happens to kings in Er'Rets. With power comes control and overindulgence. I do not wish to spend my life fending off those who would twist my husband's ear for their own gain or women who would throw themselves at my husband to steal his heart from me."

"If he has strong advisors, that responsibility would not fall to you alone."

"Regardless, I do not want that life."

"Won't you at least consider it? He's a dear young man. He says he has had a recent encounter with Arman."

"He does? What did he say?"

"Nothing much. But I sense Arman has his attention. Perhaps your leaving has made him look upward. At any rate, I trust Arman to sharpen his integrity, not weaken it." Mother took Vrell's hand. "This token accompanied the offer." She slid a small metal object into Vrell's palm.

Vrell crouched, held her hand to the candlelight. A ruby on the king's signet ring gleamed in the pale light, stealing her breath. "Mother." Vrell's voice cracked. She cleared her throat. "Do you know how Achan came to possess this . . . token?"

"It is the Hadar ring, passed down from King Echâd himself."

"Yes, but Esek had it, and Achan took it from his finger after having cut off his arm." Vrell shuddered. "Mother, this token is a symbol of violence." *To help rescue me,* she thought before she could stop herself.

"That ring is over six hundred years old. It has seen much violence on the hands of kings," Mother said. "It has also seen much joy. Achan is barely a man. His time with this ring has barely started. If he is successful, and Light can be brought back to Er'Rets, I have no doubt this ring will see much joy and happiness on his finger."

Vrell twisted back to the peephole. Achan still stared forward. What could leave him so blank? She gently reached for his thoughts.

Achan bolted to his feet, jostling the table and spilling his soup. "Sparrow?"

Vrell's breath caught and she closed her mind. He must have left his mind open to her, in case she initiated contact.

Achan scanned the room and ran down the dais steps to the men sitting at the nearest table. "Pardon me, do you know Vrell Sparrow?"

The men shook their heads.

Achan asked the same of the next three tables. He returned to the dais and looked up the wall beneath where Vrell hid. He put his good hand on it, his other arm still in its sling. "Sparrow?"

Vrell doubled her efforts to close her mind. Achan appeared to be staring right up through the peephole. Impossible. Still, she slid back out of sight and stood.

"Oh, Averella." Mother took her arm. "No more of that."

Vrell could still hear Achan calling. "Sparrow? Sparrow!"

She wrinkled her nose, his pleading tone bringing tears to her eyes. "I'm sorry. That was foolish."

They retrieved their candle and lantern and followed the corridor back to one of the secret rooms on the other side of Mother's study.

The room held a table and chairs and a cold hearth. Vrell sank into one of the chairs, folded her arms on the table, and laid down her head. Tears burned her eyes.

She felt Mother's hand on her back. "Do you love him?"

Vrell lifted her head and blinked away the tears. "I fear I do not know what love is. When I think of Achan, I have very strong feelings. But I once felt the same of Bran and that went away in time. Can love be so easily set aside?"

Mother claimed the chair beside Vrell's and took her hands. "Sometimes, wanting to be loved is half the passion. You convince yourself it is real because it is new and exciting. And maybe it is true. But that is why young women should not run off with men in the vineyards or traipse across Darkness. When you give your heart to a man who does not or cannot keep it, you lose a part of it and have less to give the next man who comes along. That is how Arman intended it. He designed a whole heart for one man. But alas, it cannot always be."

Vrell's throat burned at the idea of Achan marrying Lady Halona Pitney. "I confess I allowed Achan to capture my heart—"

Her eyes widened. That one statement of truth shocked her so much, it opened a flood of tears. She cupped her hands over her nose and mouth and let them come. Somehow her mother's presence made it worse. There was now a witness to the truth. Someone to hold her accountable.

It was some time before she managed to speak again. "I never intended to, Mother, I swear. And I will not consider him until he pledges his life to Arman. His heart must go to Arman first. That is what you taught me." She sniffled. "So what shall I do?"

"Pray, dearest child."

42

Anillo approached Achan and Shung as they were leaving the great hall. A full breakfast weighed down Achan's belly. Perhaps he would gorge himself daily and become a fat swine king. Why not?

"The duchess has prepared a private room for your gathering this morning. If you will follow me."

Anillo led them into the duchess' study on the third floor of the entrance hall. A small, carved desk with a shiny jade surface and matching throne-like chair sat before a wide, brownstone fireplace that stretched to the ceiling. A polished redwood floor matched redwood wainscoting carved in scrolls and flowers. Gilded ivory paneling, murals, and the occasional niche covered the top half of the room. The murals were of vineyards or people making wine, and each niche held a vase or small sculpture of a figure. A floor-to-ceiling tapestry divided each wall into thirds.

Anillo approached the wall on the east end of the study and touched the chair rail. A click sent an arched niche swinging outward. "For your safety, the duchess has granted you access to her secret meeting rooms and tunnels."

Anillo steadied the vase on the niche and motioned for Achan and Shung to enter.

Shung entered first, then nodded for Achan to enter. Achan ducked sideways through the opening into a dark, narrow corridor, careful not to bump his slinged arm on the doorframe. Anillo followed, holding a pottery lamp. Its single flame gave off plenty of light once Anillo pulled the secret door closed.

"Are these passageways all over the castle?" Achan asked.

"Yes, but please, Your Majesty. Do not go exploring alone. The last man who tried got lost and had nearly starved when he stumbled out into the barracks ten days later. I would be happy to give you a quick tour if the duchess agrees."

"Thank you." Did Armonguard have secret passageways too? Had Sitna?

Anillo barely moved before knocking on the wall opposite Duchess Amal's study.

The door swung in, spilling a stripe of yellow light across the dark corridor. This doorway was short and wide. Achan ducked inside after Shung, into small meeting room.

Sir Gavin and the other knights were seated in high-backed chairs around a long table that held two bright oil lamps, a tray filled with grapes, apples, and tarts, a sweating jug, and a stack of stone cups. A fireplace blazed in the corner.

A sudden bout of nerves seized Achan's gut at the sight of the empty chair at the head of the table. He poured himself a mug of water and approached the chair, knowing he needed to take charge. The knights continued to proclaim him Crown Prince and tell him what to do. Achan needed to step forward. Either he was the future king or he was not. It was time to decide, time to act.

He gripped the cham's claw at his neck and squeezed. He'd killed the bear. He could do this.

Achan pulled out his chair and settled into it. No one spoke to him. They continued their private conversations. Sir Gavin and Inko were arguing whether Esek still lived, and if so, whether he would try another attack. Sir Eagan and Sir Caleb were pouring over a scroll and a scrap of burgundy fabric. Kurtz held a stack of tarts in one hand and popped one into his mouth whole.

Shung stood beside the secret entrance as if someone might come bursting in at any moment and try to kill Achan.

Anything was possible in Achan's life, after all.

Clearly Achan needed to do something to take charge. Speak perhaps? A wave of heat crept up the back of his neck, yet the fire in the hearth seemed no bigger than before.

COMMIT TO ME WHATEVER YOU DO, AND YOUR PLANS WILL SUCCEED.

Achan smiled, relieved. *Of course. Thank You for the direction, Arman.*

He took one last gulp of water, scooted back his chair— which scraped loudly over the rough wooden floor—and stood. All eyes turned to him.

"Achan," Sir Caleb said. "We've received an acceptance for—"

"A moment, please, Sir Caleb," Achan said. "I feel we should first commit this meeting to Arman, so He may bless our endeavors."

Suddenly he had the knights' full attention. They watched Achan silently.

"Quite so, Your Majesty." Sir Caleb smiled and started to stand.

Achan held up his left hand. "Thank you, Sir Caleb, but . . . I'll do it."

Sir Caleb lowered himself back into his seat and stared at Achan, bushy blond eyebrows raised.

Achan bowed his head as he would before any great leader. "Arman, we come together this morning to discuss our plans to obey Your call. You've set me apart as king, so I ask You to come, hear our plans, and speak, should You like to. We'll be listening for Your voice in all we discuss. Thank You for Duchess Amal's support. She's everything I could have hoped for in a new comrade. So may it be as You say."

"So be it," the knights said.

Achan took a deep breath. "Now that you've all had your say, it's my turn. Here's what I plan to do. I'd like your opinions as to whether my choices be wise."

Achan fought to keep the tremor in his joints out of his voice. "First, I appoint Sir Gavin Lukos as commander over all the armies. Each duke or duchess loyal to me may suggest generals to Sir Gavin and me. Each general, once appointed, may determine his own captains and ranks as he sees fit. Yet Sir Gavin will be over them all to instruct and lead.

"Those in service to Prince Oren Hadar will return to him. I no longer fear for Gren's life. If Esek is still alive, he will soon be far too busy to harass my loved ones. Therefore Jax mi Katt, Sir Rigil Barak, and Bran Rennan will seek out their next order from Prince Oren. I'll ask my uncle to command the southern troops and Mârad and that he and Sir Gavin be in constant communication with each other and me so that, in time, we can coordinate our efforts.

"I appoint Sir Caleb Agros, Sir Eagan Elk, and Inko son of Mopti as my royal advisors. Kurtz Chazir, you're a fighting man. My inclination is to put you to Sir Gavin, but what is your will?"

Eyes wide, Kurtz swallowed whatever bit of food he had in his mouth. "What are my choices, Pac—Your Highness?"

"I've given you three: service to Sir Gavin, Prince Oren, or myself. Unless you have a fourth idea?"

Kurtz frowned. "No, Your Highness. If it's all the same to you, I'd like to stay with Gavin, I would."

"Very well. I had thought to appoint Trajen Yorbride as my priest, though his children are so young and he has such a strong flock in Melas, I hate to filch their leader. Ideas?"

"I am sure Duchess Amal would have a suggestion," Sir Eagan said.

"Could you ask her?"

"I will."

"Good." He paused, waiting to see what the men had to say of his ideas so far. When no one spoke, he continued.

"War is upon us, gentlemen. Esek commands the New Kingsguard and several powerful duchies, including most of what lies in Darkness. He fields an army whose size and location we must determine. Sir Gavin, please see to this.

"The task before us, as I see it, is to unite all of Er'Rets under my rule, so that Arman's rule may extend through it and thus eradicate Darkness. Our first task must be to raise a bigger army than we have now. Then, once Sir Gavin's scouts have located Esek's army, we must make our way to Armonguard. It is the prize, I feel. One Esek would already possess if he hadn't been so obsessed with destroying me."

"A fine plan, Your Majesty," Sir Gavin said, beaming.

"Have you tried to see into Esek's mind?" Sir Eagan asked.

Achan had never even considered it and suddenly felt foolish. "I haven't. An excellent suggestion, Sir Eagan, thank you. I shall do so directly following our time here." Achan paused and took a quick drink. He expected someone to jump in and contribute, but the men simply stared. He set his cup down with a trembling hand.

"We need to determine the agenda of this New Council the Duchess Amal spoke of. We should also consider what other forces might come against us—apart from Esek. There are the black knights—led by the shadow sorcerer, Hadad, perhaps? We must discover this man's identity."

The sooner the better, for Achan hadn't told anyone about hearing Hadad's voice again since Barth.

"Jaelport also seems to have plans of their own. Lord Nathak. We now know he has a motive apart from Esek's. I cannot say whether Esek will join him or strike out on his own, or if he's dead. Add Lord Levy and Macoun Hadar to the list of opposition. Then there are the Poroo and Eben forces. They likely support one of the factions mentioned."

"Yes, but which is it being?" Inko asked.

"I'd guess Poroo fights alongside Barth, eh? And the Ebens have partnered with Jaelport," Kurtz said.

"We cannot guess," Sir Eagan said. "We must know."

"I've never been knowing an Eben to associate with a Jaelportian," Inko said.

"You think the Ebens are with Barth, then?" Kurtz asked.

"The Eben we were slaying was giving us Lord Falkson's name," Inko said. "He is being is Lord of Barth. But is Lord

Falkson to be serving Esek or Hadad? And who is Jaelport to be serving?"

"I believe Jaelport serves Jaelport," Sir Caleb said.

Achan lowered himself into his chair. The men had gone off debating, but he'd said what he'd planned to. No one had disagreed. Did that mean they agreed? He shifted his sling arm and reached for a tart. He'd done enough for today. He'd taken the floor and made his appointments. It was a start.

"Lord Levy paid Eben mercenaries to keep Prince Oren's Mârad from traveling into Mahanaim," Sir Caleb said.

"You're suggesting Lord Levy was sending the Ebens after us in Darkness?" Inko asked. "And not Lord Falkson?"

"If he had a business relationship with them already, maybe he paid them to get Achan back to Mahanaim. Maybe Lord Levy and Lord Falkson work for Hadad."

"According to Vrell, skilled archers aided the Poroo who attacked Esek's procession," Sir Eagan said. "Who may have wanted to kill Esek?"

Achan tensed at the mention of Sparrow. "Anyone who has met him."

The men laughed and continued their debate. Achan couldn't help but think of Sparrow. She had opened her mind to him yesterday. Why? Did she want to speak? Did she wonder where he was? Was she nearby? And why open her mind only to close it again so quickly? What was the matter with her?

The men talked until the food tray was empty and their stomachs growled for lunch. Achan decided to conclude for today. Sir Caleb would work on recruiting new men. Sir Gavin would send out scouts. And Sir Eagan would speak with Duchess Amal about a suitable priest.

Anillo arrived to see whether they would like lunch brought in, but Sir Caleb jumped to his feet. "Your Highness, I almost forgot you've not yet heard our good news. Sir Eagan, please, you tell him."

Sir Eagan reached for the scroll wrapped around a swatch of burgundy satin. He turned his piercing blue eyes to Achan. "Duchess Amal has accepted our offer."

"Which offer?" Achan could hardly keep up with all the tasks to be done.

"Your offer to wed her eldest daughter, Lady Averella."

A chill ran over Achan's arms. "Oh."

Sir Eagan held up the scroll and passed it to Sir Caleb, who passed it to Sir Gavin, who handed it to Achan. Achan unrolled it, hands shaking, and set the fabric aside. He anchored the top of the scroll with his cup and held the bottom with his fingertips. The neat and curvy writing took him longer to read than he would have liked with everyone watching.

> Your Royal Highness, Prince Gidon Hadar, otherwise known as Achan Cham,
>
> It is with great honor that I received your request for my daughter's hand in marriage. I must confess she had long ago pledged her hand to another. Time and recent events have changed that matter, however, and I assure you her relationship with her previous suitor has desisted peaceably with no harm to her virtue.
>
> I vouchsafe to you my eldest daughter and heir, Lady Averella Amal, to wed once Armonguard has passed into your hands. As a token of this agreement, I have enclosed a sleeve from one of Averella's gowns. I chose one of the colors of Carmine so that when you

wear this token wherever you go, people will know of our alliance.

Though this wedding be delayed, I pray Arman give you patience to endure until the day you kiss your bride. Until then, allow me to think of you as my son.

Lady Nitsa Amal, Duchess of Carm

Achan leaned back and released the scroll. It sprang into a tight coil against his mug. Well, that settled it. A lightheaded spell gripped Achan. He hooked a finger around the cord at his neck. Farewell then, Vrell Sparrow.

The knights burst into laughter. Laughter!

Achan looked up, eyes wide, heat warming his face. "Does anyone know what she looks like?"

Another bout of laughter.

"She's a very comely young woman, Achan," Sir Gavin said.

"As pretty as her mother," Sir Eagan added.

Well, that was comforting. He reached one trembling hand for the silky burgundy fabric and lifted it up. It was, indeed, a woman's dress sleeve. Made of thick satin, the sleeve was narrow around the arm but tapered into a pointed bell at the end. A single golden cord ran down the sleeve's edge. The scent of rose water made him think of Sparrow.

He supposed all women liked rose water.

He stared at it for a long time, then found his voice. "I'm to wear this?"

The men sniggered. Achan dropped the sleeve, refilled his cup, and downed the water in one long gulp.

Sir Eagan came to his aid. The knight walked to Achan's side and snagged the sleeve from the table. "You have never seen a knight wear a lady's token at tournament?"

Achan nodded. "I've seen them tuck handkerchiefs into their helm or tie them 'round their arm."

"That is what you will do with this sleeve." Sir Eagan threaded the fabric behind Achan's right arm, around his sling.

"He's naturally left-handed," Sir Gavin said. "It should go on his sword arm."

"Is he?" Sir Eagan asked. "I should have guessed."

He gently tugged the sleeve from Achan's sore arm and, within moments, had tied it around Achan's left bicep. It hung bright against his light blue tunic, tied snugly so it wouldn't fall, a constant reminder of yet another yoke on his life.

Again he thought of Sparrow.

He met Sir Eagan's eyes. The knight smiled. "You look as though we have asked you to walk the castle in naught but your skin. 'Tis not so bad, Your Highness." He stepped behind Achan and rubbed his shoulders. Head bent down, he spoke softly in Achan's left ear. "Now, you are not only a hero to this land, you are a hero to one woman, which will tug at the heartstrings of every woman in Er'Rets, who will beg their men to go out and support you. For people are easily caught up in a great love story and are often eager to do their part in making it succeed."

And if the groom wasn't eager to be caught up in his own great love story, what of that?

Achan stood and handed the scroll to Sir Eagan. "Let us go eat, then, and tug at some heartstrings."

• • •

"How dare you!"

"I gave you opportunity to give me good reason."

Hot rage flashed through Vrell's body. "A day? One day? Mother! How could you do this to me? You have no right."

"I have every right. Averella, I have coddled you far too long. Not only can I see you love that boy, I know he cares for you a great deal. He respects you, dearest, enough to sacrifice his honor for a girl he thinks is a stray. I understand you are embarrassed, but I am convinced this is Arman's will. It is also the best possible match for uniting the people of this duchy and Er'Rets. It is far better than an arranged marriage, this—"

"—*is* an arranged marriage. Mother, you promised."

"Promised what?"

"That I could choose whom I would marry."

"No. I promised to consider your own choice for a husband. And I did consider allowing you to marry Master Rennan. But now that you both have relinquished your desires, and now that the perfect offer has come along, one from a good man, a man you love and who loves you—and happens to be our future king—so that you *are* marrying and choosing whom to marry, because you are too stubborn to admit your love, I am taking charge."

Vrell steeled her emotions. "I will not do it."

"You will leave your king standing at the altar? The man you love? You will disgrace him publicly in front of the whole kingdom? He already wears your sleeve. Averella, stop ranting about and act your age."

"*My* age?" Vrell could not stand it. She had been home less than a week and felt more trapped and suffocated than she ever had inside that disguise. She dug deep into a place she did not want to go, to concerns and questions she did not want answers to. "This is a nonissue if I am not your heir."

"Do not be absurd, dearest. You are the eldest. You are my heir."

"But if I am not the daughter of Duke Amal, I am not heir to Carm." She paused, watching her mother's porcelain skin pink, her sculpted eyebrows crumple.

"I do not understand you, Averella. What are you hedging about?"

Vrell stood tall. "I do not think Duke Amal is my father. My heart tells me you have deceived me in this matter. My heart tells me Sir Eagan Barak is my father. Do you deny it?"

Mother lowered herself to the sofa, put a hand to her cheek, and released a shaky breath. "What in all Er'Rets led you to believe such a thing?"

"Besides the fact that he and I have the same face?"

Mother stared at Vrell a moment then clutched her ashen face in her hands. Jagged sobs erupted from her, bringing tears to Vrell's eyes as well.

"I knew it." Vrell started to cry. "Mother, how could you allow yourself to . . . ?"

A silence passed where both women wept. Mother caught hold of her composure first.

"I did not want to marry Duke Amal. My heart was broken and I was weak. I felt Arman had abandoned me. In my sorrow I turned from Arman and clung to the one my heart loved. And it only made me love Eagan more, which made everything harder. But I obeyed my father and married the duke. Months passed before I discovered I was with child. I had no way of knowing who . . ."

Mother shook off her tears and lifted her chin. "But when you were older it was plain to my eyes. And when Eagan saw you, he knew at once. He promised not to claim you. He promised he would let me live in peace. But I could not. I had planned to tell the duke the truth, but King Axel died and Eagan went to Ice Island. I lost all hope and figured the truth would do no good then."

"And now?" Vrell sniffled. "Sir Eagan still does not wish to claim me?"

"He begged I tell you the truth but promised not to publicly claim you, not to upset your life."

"Whether all Er'Rets knows or not, my life is already upset. Mother, how can I live as I have? How can I pretend to be your heir? It is a lie."

"No," Mother said. "You are my eldest. I choose my heir."

"That is not how it is done. Carm should go to the Amal bloodline."

"No one need know."

"But *I* know." Vrell wandered to Mother's desk, trembling with a myriad of emotions. "I cannot live a lie any longer. It is all I have done these past months, and it has nearly destroyed my sanity. I will not be a fraud. I abandon my birthright to Gypsum. Let her accept this proposal."

"Averella!"

Vrell darted behind Mother's changing screen, behind the tapestry, and into the dark corridor.

Up, up, up the steps she ran, to the top of Ryson Tower. She hugged one of the stone posts that held the tower roof and gazed out over the vineyards that stretched to the horizon on all sides of Carmine. The sun hid behind a fluffy white cloud.

A cool breeze blew against her face and tightened her skin as it dried her tears.

For so long she had ached for home. But now that she was here, it no longer felt like a home. Where did she belong? Queen of Er'Rets? Heir to Carm? An illegitimate daughter did not deserve either. She could stay here and serve Gypsum, ready her for her calling as duchess. But if Vrell refused to marry Achan, did that mean Gypsum would have to?

Vrell wept. She could not bear to witness such a thing.

She stared at the signet ring in her palm. The ruby stone shone in the sun. Achan had agreed to marry a stranger. It might not have been his plan, but he had not fought it. Barely a week had passed since his declarations in Mitspah. He had given her up much more easily that even she expected. Was it because he was respectful of her choice to be apart from him or because he did not care?

Mother had said he still cared about Vrell Sparrow.

She *should* confess the truth and accept his proposal. But the proposal was breeched now that her lineage was confirmed.

"Ahh!" Vrell screamed out her frustration and sank to her knees. Three birds fluttered out from their perch in the roof's rafters, startled by Vrell's cry. She watched them fly away, wishing she could fly too, like a real sparrow. Wishing she could start over fresh, honest.

She hugged her knees to her chest. True, she did not want to be queen. Such a life would be so difficult, so demanding. But what else could she be? She was a decent healer. Perhaps she could serve in the coming war, use the gifts Arman had given her to help Achan's cause.

A thought sprang up at the back of her mind. It seemed insane, wild, scary, and completely reckless.

She sought the face of Jax mi Katt and sent a knock.

Vrell! It's good to hear from you. How can I be of service?

Are you still in Carmine?

How did you know I was in—

Never mind. Could the Mârad use another healer? A healer who is a woman?

A long silence. *War is coming. We can always use healers. But you must be able to defend yourself. I cannot watch over you.*

I do not need a nursemaid. When you are ready to ride south, I shall join you.

Vrell broke the connection. She would ride south, join the Mârad rebels as the stray healer girl Vrell Sparrow, a name that now fit her in every way, since her father would not publicly claim her. She *would* serve her king.

But she would do it her way.

NOT THE END

This is the end of book 2 of the Blood of Kings trilogy. Book 3 continues the adventures of Achan and Vrell as they fight for Light to overcome Darkness. Sign up for newsletters from Marcher Lord Press or Jill Williamson's website to get updates on the status of *From Darkness Won* (Blood of Kings, Book 3).

A Note from the Author

Thanks for reading *To Darkness Fled*, the second installment in the Blood of Kings series.

I'd love to hear from you. E-mail me with your thoughts on the book, join my Facebook page, or sign up for my free newsletter to get updates on the next book and my upcoming events.

If you'd like to help make this book a success, tell people about it, loan your copy to a friend, and ask your library or bookstore to order it. Also, posting a review on Amazon.com or BarnesandNoble.com is very helpful.

My email is: info@jillwilliamson.com.

If you'd like to download discussion questions or explore Er'Rets a bit more with my interactive map, check out my website: www.jillwilliamson.com.

Acknowledgments

Thanks to God for getting me through this last year. It has been an amazing journey. God is good to me, all the time.

Big thanks to Brad, Luke, and Kaitlyn for their patience and support.

Thanks to Jeff Gerke, a brilliant editor. He points out the best things, like magically appearing freckles and chairs. I have learned so much from him.

To the members of the Christian Young Adult Writers and Readers critique groups—Ann, Bridgett, Carman, Christopher, Crystal, Claire, Deb, Diana, Durga, Gretchen, Jacob, Kasey, Katie, Kathleen, Laura, Lynn, Maria, Mary H, Mary W, Nicole, Patrick, Shanti, Shelley, Stephanie, and Vernona—for your wisdom, support, prayers, and encouragement. You all are the best!

Thanks to my local readers: Philena English, Rachel Bentz, and Kylie Emery. I appreciate you taking the time to help me.

Laura Schuff, thank you! You are a brilliant young woman. What an amazing help you were.

Thanks to Cheryl Secomb and her friends JoAnna and Tamar for helping me with my Hebrew translations.

Hugs to all my readers. Thanks for reading about Achan and Vrell. One more book to go!

CPSIA information can be obtained at www.ICGtesting.com
Printed in the USA
LVOW101924130712

290002LV00001B/61/P